AEON CHAMPION

FRANK MORIN

ISBN: 978-1-946910-11-0
A Whipsaw Press Original
Book Design by Kate Staker
(https://katestaker.com/)
Edited by Joshua Essoe
(http://www.joshuaessoe.com/)
Cover art by Christian Bentulan
(https://coversbychristian.com/)
First Whipsaw printing Dec 2020

Created with Vellum

OTHER WORKS BY FRANK MORIN

Find all books on www.frankmorin.org

The Petralist Series

Set in Stone, Book One

A Stone's Throw, Book Two

No Stone Unturned, Book Three

Affinity for War, Book Four

The Queen's Quarry, Book Five

The King's Craft. Book Six

Blood of the Tallan, Book Seven

When Torcs Fly, A Petralist Origins novella: Tomas and Cameron

Game of Garlands, A Petralist Origins novella: Anika

Builder of Intrigue, A Petralist Origins novella: Ailsa

The Facetakers Series

Saving Face, Book One

Memory Hunter, Book Two

Rune Warrior, Book Three

Aeon Champion, Book Four (release in September 2020)

Short Stories

"Odin's Eye," included in *A Game of Horns: A Red Unicorn Anthology*

"The Essence," included in the *Dragon Writers: An Anthology*

"Only Logical," a purple unicorn story

"The Seventh Strike," included in *Cursed Collectibles: An Anthology*

ACKNOWLEDGMENTS

I love this epic book!

And I'm still the king of rewrites.

The first draft was great, but based on feedback, and some awesome new ideas, I heavily rewrote this novel in the second draft. When you read about Vlad, you'll thank me.

Thanks to my family, who continue to believe.

Thanks also to Eve Ledesma, Joe Morris, and James Morin for great beta reads and excellent comments. And thanks to my fantastic editor, Joshua Essoe. You never pulled any punches, but you were always fair, and the story shines because of it.

And finally, thanks to Christian Bentulan for a fantastic cover. You nailed it.

RUNES

Rune Warrior Rune

Healing Rune

1

THE HEART-WRENCHING CRY of a child in pain greeted Sarah as soon as she stepped through the door of the field hospital. The entry room felt cramped, with its sloping, white walls and registration desks overloaded with documentation. It smelled of sterilizer, like every modern hospital she had ever visited. She hated the soft, but pungent scent of despair that hung heavy over everything.

Fresh moans echoed into the room from the treatment buildings, connected by short hallways. Although all of the children were receiving the maximum dosages of painkillers, some injuries refused to be quieted.

A harried-looking nurse said something in Italian that Sarah had learned meant, "I'll be right with you."

Sarah knew better. They didn't have time for non-emergencies. This nurse was focused on a grieving mother begging for something more, anything more for her child.

The nurse couldn't do anything more for that woman's child, or for any of the other terribly injured children packing the hundred-bed medical unit.

Sarah could. The urgency of their need drove her like a physical presence, prodding her from behind. The danger she faced daring to implement her plan paled against the near-certain death creeping inexorably over those poor kids.

She waved her ID badge and hurried across the room toward the treatment areas. They were packed with staff trying to treat children injured during the recent fiery showdown with Paul. Sarah may have died that day, but her suffering had been blissfully short by comparison.

Hundreds of people had been killed, and ten times that number wounded. The flood of injured had overwhelmed Rome's medical services and damaged infrastructure. She appreciated the international aid that had swarmed in. The multiple clusters of low-slung, portable medical centers that packed the empty ruins of the Circus Maximus were part of that aid.

She had seen the Circus in its heyday. It had never been put to better use.

If only that outpouring of assistance could have helped the kids assigned beds in this, the most remote units. They were the ones too broken to fix, but not yet dead. Sarah had discovered that unit two days ago.

Some had suffered massive internal damage from being crushed under collapsing buildings. Worse were the second and third degree burns from fires that had raged through the city. The sight of all that suffering had broken her heart and driven her to act.

"Can I help you, miss?" a tired-looking doctor asked as Sarah stepped into the dining area squeezed between treatment wards.

He spoke with an American accent, most likely one of the physicians on loan from overseas. The few people sitting at the folding, white plastic tables looked exhausted. Some slumped over crossed arms, while others poked without enthusiasm at their bland meals.

Sarah gave the doctor a warm smile. People usually assumed she was a teen-ager. Her body was, so it was an easy mistake to make.

"I'm just checking that all the posters are in place."

He nodded toward the wall next to the door and made a vague salute. "The Sword of the Deliverer is the last hope in here. We've got her posted everywhere."

She was counting on that, but still had to conceal a grimace. The title the world had bestowed upon her for martyring herself to stop Paul still seemed ostentatious. If people knew she'd actually survived, things might get awkward.

"Have to check anyway," she said as she moved to the poster.

It showed the greatest moment of her first life, when she had transformed into a liquid-metal warrior. The poster showed her leaping at Paul in the shattered remains of the square, her arms changed into glittering blades.

Under the guise of smoothing the poster, Sarah peeled back one corner and quickly traced a complex symbol with her finger. She left softly glowing silver lines on the paper. She had memorized the cipher, had already drawn it on over a dozen posters, so only needed a couple of seconds to mark it.

Sarah moved through the complex, from one cramped building to the next, forcing herself to look at each agonized face as she passed. Their pain tore at her and gave her the courage to take the chance to help. In each building, at every poster, she paused and marked the same symbol.

When she stepped outside into the refreshing, cool air of early evening, she took a steadying breath. A sense of despair had permeated the facility as families struggled with the reality that death walked the halls among them.

Time to create a new reality.

Sarah moved around the building to one of the generators providing power. After making sure she was alone, she removed a small access panel from the back of one generator and marked the same symbol she had on the posters.

Then she added three additional marks to connect all the other marks into a cipher matrix. She concentrated over it, drawing upon the well of her rounon gift that allowed her to tap the strength of her soul to power her ciphers.

A rush of strength flowed out of her, leaving her feeling drained. The individual ciphers were not too complicated, but together, the dozens of them she had placed around the complex formed the most advanced matrix she had yet attempted.

Sarah leaned against the cool metal of the purring generator while invisible tendrils of energy flowed from her soul. Like whispers of light, they flashed across the city and connected with other ciphers she had placed in seven different remote locations.

A second later, a flood of energy roared back. The ciphers activated.

"It's working!" she squealed, barely remembering to keep her voice hushed.

That invisible energy poured through the key cipher on the generator panel and flowed out to the ciphers marked on the backs of all the posters. Those ciphers activated, transforming the invisible energy into healing power that settled over the complex like a gentle blanket of hope. It would lift spirits, vitalize souls, and could turn the tide for those children.

Sarah's own healing rune, marked into the skin of her side, fostered miraculous healing. She could recover from all but a mortal wound with incredible swiftness.

She didn't dare mark similar runes onto each of the children in the hospital ward. So young and so hurt, many of them probably wouldn't be able to bond a rune. The attempt might push some of them over the edge. So she'd come up with the next best thing.

The sounds of crying that had echoed from the building began to fade. Sarah felt a rush of joy so intense, she had to brush new-formed tears from her eyes. She wanted to shout. It was really working.

"Sarah! What are you doing over there?"

Surprised, Sarah turned as Tomas and Alter approached. She dropped the generator panel and rushed to embrace Tomas. She was so happy, she kissed him soundly and hugged him so hard only his enhancements saved him from suffering cracked ribs.

"I'm glad to see you too," he laughed at her enthusiasm.

"I'm having a good day," she said, then kissed him again.

"But why outside?" Alter asked, stepping past them, eyes averted, a frown playing across his lips. He rounded the generator and gasped. "What is this?"

Sarah ran over before he could interrupt the cipher. "Leave that alone."

Alter snatched up the panel and studied the cipher. His face paled and he rounded on her. "Sarah, taking the force of other souls is forbidden. This is abomination!"

"What are you talking about?" Tomas asked, his smile fading.

Sarah pried the panel away from Alter and faced him, refusing to be cowed by his anger. "The abomination is leaving those children to die." She gestured at the nearby medical tents.

"What did you do?" Tomas asked.

"I created a matrix to foster healing in there," Sarah explained.

"You can't," Alter interrupted. "It's—"

"Don't you dare preach to me until you go in there and look at those poor kids."

"Good intentions aren't enough to justify this evil. If my family knew . . ."

He trailed off and Sarah felt a pang of sympathy for him. Killing Alter would still be his family's first priority.

Then they'd kill Sarah.

Well, they'd try.

Sarah placed a comforting hand on his arm, but that time not even her touch turned his anger.

"Alter, this is not evil. It's all I can do for them, and I'm going to do it, no matter what you say."

Tomas looked torn. "Sarah, whose life force are you using?"

"Not the Tenth," she assured him.

In the last week, they had begun marking the soldiers of Tomas' secret fighting company with temporary runes. Sarah could draw strength from them in case of emergency. The principle was similar, but more restricted than what she had built for the children.

Alter said, "Using the soldiers is bad enough, but this time you're not even pretending to justify your abuse of power."

Alter had argued strenuously against the idea of tapping the life force of the soldiers of the Tenth, even though to a man they had taken oaths to give Sarah whatever she needed. She wouldn't ever take much, and felt the weight of responsibility for even that.

Every single member of the Tenth had offered the full measure of their souls, if needed. Only the threat of Paul's terrifying mother had persuaded Alter that the combined might of all those souls might be needed. Sarah couldn't imagine a time she'd actually consider sacrificing those brave men, though.

"It's not abuse if people agree to it," Sarah said.

"Then who?" Tomas asked.

"Pilgrims of the Deliverer," Sarah explained.

"They haven't agreed to this!" Alter cried.

"Sure they have," Sarah said, but under the level stares from both men, she added, "Well, they would if I asked."

"How can you justify that?" Tomas asked, looking like he was starting to side with Alter.

"Those shrines are dedicated to me, aren't they?"

"To your memory." Alter's frown deepened. It was amazing that the handsome young hunter could look so stern. "Everyone thinks you're martyred."

"How many times have you heard those people declaring they wished they could do something more to help?"

"Stealing their souls isn't what they intended," Alter objected.

"I'm only borrowing one percent. If we went over and asked people if jogging in place for five minutes would help save a child's life, how many of them would refuse to help?"

"That's not the point."

"It is," Sarah insisted. "I'm taking even less than that. They won't even feel it, and we're doing so much good."

"I cannot allow it," Alter said, reaching for the panel.

Sarah pulled it behind her back and gestured toward the hospital buildings where exclamations of joy were replacing the previous agonized cries. "Then you go in there and tell those families that you're going to kill their children in the name of your honor."

"You twist everything!" Alter shouted, then glanced at Tomas. "And what of you, Captain? Will you support Sarah in this abomination when you'd kill anyone else in a heartbeat for doing the same thing?"

Tomas looked torn. "Sarah, he has a point."

She pounded a hand on his well-muscled chest. "No, he doesn't! When have you ever tracked down a heka cell or a cui dashi because they were healing children?"

"What happens when you decide to justify stealing more?" Alter asked softly, his gaze intent. "What if one percent's not enough? Will you take five, or ten, or fifty?"

"You always assume people will abuse their power. You're not the only one with self-discipline."

"And you're the one who has stepped into darkness and taken the first step toward destruction," Alter retorted.

Sarah hated breaking with Alter. He was an expert runesmith, her main teacher in rune lore. She was so new to her powers, she depended on his knowledge. In the desperate fight against Paul, she'd ignored some of his warnings, and she'd lost her first body as a result.

It tore at her to fight him over this point. She didn't want to become a monster, to destroy the souls of innocents. Alter knew much, but he didn't know everything. In her heart, she felt absolutely justified in using her powers to heal those who would find relief no other way.

What if she was wrong, though?

No. She would take the risk for those kids. If she didn't, she'd be the worse monster for it. "I won't allow you to convince me to let those children die."

"Death is preferable to slavery."

"I'm not enslaving anyone! I'm healing. If we had stopped Paul sooner, those kids wouldn't be dying. Don't you feel any responsibility to help?"

"Not by embracing evil," Alter said. He gestured at the hospital tents. "What if you could save every one of those children, but had to steal fifty percent of the life force of other souls? Or a hundred percent of a few?"

"But I don't have to." She wanted to strangle him for refusing to see the truth.

"You've taken the first step. You have to ask yourself the hard questions, Sarah. What line will you not cross?"

"I don't have the luxury of making arbitrary lines. Ever since we faced Mai Luan, I've been hunted and attacked more times than I can remember. I died once fighting that evil, and if we're going to finish this, I'm willing to do whatever it takes."

"So is our enemy," Alter said.

Tomas stepped between them. "This kind of discussion cannot be settled when we're angry. There's too much emotion to think clearly."

"I'm not allowing you to disable this," Sarah promised Alter. "I'll argue all night if I have to."

Alter looked ready to do the same, but Tomas grimaced. "We don't have all night. We have to finish this discussion tomorrow."

When Alter started to protest, Tomas held up a placating hand. "No one is getting hurt by this matrix, and a lot of people are getting helped. No harm comes by taking our time in making a decision and defining those lines you were talking about, does it?"

Alter hesitated and Tomas added, "Remember why we came looking for Sarah in the first place. We've got a solid lead on that heka cell. The longer we argue, the more likely Harriett will make the hit without us."

"Where?" Sarah asked, moving to replace the generator panel. When Alter didn't block her, she allowed a flicker of hope. The argument might not be over, but by delaying the final decision, Tomas had at least offered those children a chance at life. One night of healing might be enough to drag them back from the brink where most of them hovered.

"Another Egyptian museum. Come on. The team is already staging," Tomas said.

Sarah headed for the distant road with him, and after a moment's hesitation, Alter ran to catch up.

"It's not over, Sarah," he promised.

"If it was, I'd be disappointed in you."

2

"YOU'RE sure this is the same group that hit the Vatican Egyptian Museum last night?" Sarah asked, peering through her advanced thermal imaging binoculars.

"I can't imagine anyone else bothering to break into this place." Tomas crouched beside her at the edge of the roof of the adjacent Accademia Belgica. They had donned body armor and tactical vests, heavy with their assault gear.

He was right. The building that the group of suspected heka terrorists had broken into less than ten minutes ago was completely unremarkable. With so many world-famous landmarks nearby in Rome, the Egyptian Fine Arts Museum, or Accademia d'Egitto di Bella Arti, seemed an odd choice for a hit.

Alter dropped to a crouch on her opposite side, so close his shoulder touched hers. He glanced at her and his eyes lingered on her face instead of focusing on their target. The prospect of taking down a rogue heka cell was enough to replace his previous simmering anger with coiled enthusiasm.

"What do you see?" he asked, leaning even closer.

"Take a look," she said, nodding toward the binoculars he held in his hands. She adjusted the tiny video recorder attached to her tactical helmet before turning back to her own binoculars.

Despite his unyielding sense of honor, Alter was a dear friend and one of her teachers in combat and rune lore, but he still hadn't accepted the fact that she was dating Tomas. He'd backed off a little when she had died. She had hoped the shock of losing the body that had first attracted him would help resolve his infatuation.

He seemed to be getting used to her new form, though. Sarah had inhabited more bodies than all but the most ancient of the facetakers, but always those transfers had been temporary.

Her young new body was barely eighteen, lithe, and very fit. She was a little shorter than she had been, and her hair was straight and black instead of gently curling brown. Tomas had assured her he cared for her soul more than which body she wore, and quickly added that her new body was very attractive. All things considered, she felt grateful to be alive, and was confident she would grow to enjoy her second life.

She wasn't sure what to do about Alter's ongoing attention. Crouching on a roof at midnight, overlooking a group of deadly heka fighters was not the time to deal with it.

Harriett, the last of the reconnaissance party, joined them. She had also died fighting the insanely powerful cui dashi, Paul, but as a facetaker, she had lived so many lives already that starting a new one was as easy as buying a new apron.

"Either this is the stupidest heka cell we've ever tracked, or that ugly building's got a secret recipe," Harriett said, frowning across the narrow street at the museum.

The building was situated across the Tiber River from the Vatican, northeast of the Piazza del Popolo, near the edge of the extensive, landscaped gardens of the Villa Borghese.

"Still no report of alarms?" Sarah asked.

Tomas shook his head, not looking away from his study of the three-story museum. "They disabled the security."

"Good," Alter murmured. "Enough police have died."

The world was still grappling with the reality of superhuman enhancements so explosively demonstrated during the running battle through the streets of Rome. Regular police officers would still be unprepared to apprehend heka fighters.

"Let's take them," Harriett growled, leaning forward as if impatient to leap across the street and into battle.

As the commander of the Yurak International mercenary forces, she was a legendary heka fighter. None of her troops were along for the night's raid, but she didn't seem to mind. She had thrown herself into the effort to destroy the remnants of Paul's scattered forces in the weeks since the battle. She showed little mercy for the men and women who had supported the monster who had murdered her elder brother. Poor Bastien had not survived to begin a new life.

Tomas said, "My enforcers are in position around the building. We'll take them when they emerge so we don't damage the museum."

"It's barely a museum," Harriett grumbled.

He shrugged, and Sarah caught herself staring at his muscular form. Spartacus had stolen Tomas' home body in the crazy days leading up to the final confrontation with Paul. Tomas was still wearing a replacement that he had captured from some of Alter's relatives the day the hunters assaulted Quentin's mansion and nearly killed him. She tried to see the world like Tomas did, tried to see his soul instead of his body, but it was hard. That temporary suit was becoming Tomas, and she didn't like that. They really needed to track down Spartacus and get Tomas' other body back.

One thing at a time.

"I know," Tomas was saying. "I visited this place a few years back when they had an excellent reproduction of the Tutankhamen artifacts, but that exhibit's been gone for a while."

"I wonder what they're after?" Sarah peered across at the shadowy figures she glimpsed through the museum windows. The heka were methodically searching the Egyptian exhibit, spread out through the first and second floors.

Alter said, "They hunt something. They seem motivated."

Harriet gestured with an oddly blocky pair of binoculars. "I've got indication of half a dozen soulmasks in there."

"Not good. With that many, they could make a lot of trouble," Tomas said with a frown.

"Are they after a new rune?" Sarah asked.

Tomas said, "I'd be surprised if they found anything useful. We have people scan every archaeological find before they get displayed."

"Every one?" Sarah asked, incredulous.

He nodded. "Standard procedure."

"Do you insert people into active digs, like that new one in Egypt getting so much media buzz?"

"Usually we review any finds once they hit museums. Unless there are indications we should take a closer look. Most artifacts don't contain runes. We might have overlooked something in Cairo or Paris, but this museum's got mostly replicas, and nothing I'd consider of major importance."

"What else would they be planning to do with so many soulmasks but initiate a new rune web?" Alter asked.

"Paul's group works from a whole different cookbook," Harriett said with a frown.

Thinking of Paul made Sarah want to hit something. They had killed or captured several highly-skilled heka enchanters from his cell. She easily believed there might be another with plans to unleash some kind of plague or other devilry on Rome in vengeance for their recent defeat.

"We can't wait," she said.

"Agreed." Tomas nodded, then spoke into his throat mic. "All units, prepare to move in. This cell includes a potential enchanter. Initiate plan Tango with extreme prejudice." After a pause, he added calmly. "Now."

On the ground level, the mighty enforcers from the Tenth legion smashed through doors and swarmed into the building. These men, following millennia of tradition, were among the toughest fighters in the world.

As their captain, Tomas always led from the front. He backed up a few feet to get a running start, then leaped from the top of the Belgian Academy roof. He soared across the narrow street and exploded through the wide windows of the museum's third floor.

Sarah, Alter, and Harriett followed a split second behind. Sarah loved how far she could jump with her enhanced legs, although the distance paled against what she could manage in the memoryscape. She plunged through the same hole Tomas had made, stuck the landing in the darkened hall, but slid on broken glass.

Tomas caught her, sweeping her off her feet and giving her a quick kiss as she regained her balance.

"Thanks," Sarah grinned to hide her nerves. A bunch of enhanced heka might represent laughable threats compared to Paul, but they could still be deadly.

As the group trotted toward the stairs, Alter and Tomas picked up the pace, jogging side by side.

Alter glanced at Tomas. "I'll win tonight."

Tomas shook his head. "Hasn't happened yet. Tonight won't be any different."

Alter glanced back at Sarah, then added, "Then how about the winner gets a kiss from Sarah."

Tomas hesitated and Sarah said, "Hey, leave me out of it."

Sarah didn't mind that the two always bet on who could capture the most prisoners. She hoped it was a sign they were learning to work together, despite Alter's unabashed interest in her. Only together had they managed to save her life in St. Peter's square, so she knew they could do it, but the new bet was a bad idea. If that was Alter's attempt at smoothing things over after the last argument, it wasn't working.

Tomas shrugged. "He doesn't really have much chance."

"You two are so juvenile," Harriett said with a shake of her head.

"The bet makes it fun," Alter replied, grinning that Tomas seemed willing to accept the new terms.

"I'm not here to have fun," she growled, her eyes igniting like purple LED screens as she activated her nevra core, the fuel source of her soul power. The purple flames of her nevron began rippling along her fingers. She didn't bother with a gun.

She didn't need one.

Sarah hoped the heka were wise enough to surrender, or lucky enough to fall to the non-lethal capture strategies employed by the Tenth. Ever since Bastien's death, Harriett did not take prisoners.

Gripping her stubby KSG shotgun, Sarah trotted after them. She didn't blame Harriett for her rage, but they needed intelligence from the captured heka. Those fighters weren't the threat. Paul's mother was.

As the group reached the open stairs leading down to the second level, shouting and the sound of gunfire erupted from below. The Tenth had made contact.

Sarah's pulse accelerated as she slipped down the stairs with the others, reviewing the battle ciphers she had been working on in recent weeks. She'd studied hard since her ciphers offered unique options when fighting enhanced enemies. Still, she felt a flash of joy to know that not all of her ciphers had to be used for destruction. If there was an enchanter in the museum, she would be ready to block and intercept any dangerous runes he tried to employ.

Just as they reached the second level, a group of three dark figures rushed out of a nearby display room and skittered to a halt in the corridor, barely twenty feet away. One of them dove back into the display room while the other two snapped up rifles.

Tomas and Alter fired at the same time, striking the two enemy fighters in the faces with electro-shock rounds. The jolts of electricity locked up every muscle and dropped them convulsing to the ground. They'd be unable to move for several seconds. More than long enough for the men to bind them.

Harriett led the charge toward the fallen men and their cowardly companion, her burning hands raised.

That last heka threw something into the corridor in front of her.

It was a soulmask.

The translucent, full-face mask of a dispossessed human soul seemed to tumble in slow motion, cushioned by the rainbow smoke trailing below it.

Sarah caught sight of a black rune marked onto the cheek. She couldn't tell exactly what the symbol meant, but she'd never known a heka fighter to mark happy runes onto soulmasks before sacrificing them.

"Look out!" Alter cried, yanking Harriett back behind him.

Sarah lifted a hand to trigger one of her protective ciphers. The problem was, the other three were between her and the soulmask.

It exploded.

3

Man, know yourself in each life and you shalt know the Gods.

~ANCIENT EGYPTIAN PROVERB

SARAH WAS ALREADY SLASHING one finger through the air in front of her, trailing a glowing line of silver light. Using that symbol to focus her rune warrior energy, she linked it to the shielding cipher already blazing in perfect detail in her mind.

Her strength rushed out to fuel the cipher, but Sarah barely noticed. The explosion catapulted the others back down the hallway. They tumbled past Sarah just as her shield began to form. The shockwave slammed into her with fire and superheated air, driving her off her feet.

The warding shield, invisible to anyone else, appeared in the air where she had made that mark, and cut off the blast. The angled barrier deflected the majority of the explosion up and away, sparing Sarah the brunt of the hit.

Sarah crashed to the floor, her face scorched, her eyes watering from the heat and smoke. The other three tumbled farther. Alter's tactical vest had caught fire, and he continued rolling to put it out. Sarah's aches were already fading as her special healing rune kicked in. The other three would recover just as quickly. They each had bonded several enhancements and would heal from all but the most critical wounds.

Getting caught by an explosion in the face would just tick them off.

The explosion continued to build, filling the corridor with billowing flame that sucked away all the oxygen. It shredded and melted the nearby exhibits, blasting out windows and spraying shattered glass across the street beyond.

Soulmasks were a potent, concentrated energy source, but most heka could not drain the full measure of a soul in one explosive blast. It looked like they'd found their enchanter.

Sarah focused on her barrier, which was shuddering under the force of the still-growing explosion. She marked several additional symbols in the air, forming a secondary cipher to reinforce the first, surrounding her tiny group with protective energy so they would not be consumed.

The blast grew too much for the confined space, despite flames pouring out the broken windows. The building shook, timbers screaming and stones cracking with reports like gunfire. The center of the roof melted, then exploded outward, in a geyser of debris.

"That'll probably draw some attention," Tomas grunted, glancing up at the column of fire spearing up into the night sky.

Sarah was relieved to see him on his feet again. He jogged up to her and gave her a quick hug. His face was blackened and his eyebrows singed, but his voice was calm. "Thanks for keeping us from getting broiled."

"Let's not give that guy a chance to try again," she said, then turned to check on the others.

Harriett was rising, her purple eyes glowing fiercer than ever. Alter, who had taken the brunt of the explosion, was still lying on the floor, although his clothing had stopped burning. Sarah rushed over to check on him, just as he sat up.

"I'm okay," Alter said, although he looked far too pleased that she had gone to check on him.

Sarah gave him a relieved smile, then turned back toward the explosion that was finally fading. The soulmask was consumed, along with the disabled heka fighters. The rest of the third floor was completely destroyed. The roof was gone, the windows shattered, all of the exhibits simply gone. Even the walls had caught fire or started to melt.

"Is the area stable?" Tomas asked.

Sarah nodded. "I think so. As long as the floor doesn't collapse."

She swiped her hand in the air to dismiss the shielding cipher, then followed Tomas, who dashed toward the room where the enchanter had fled. Harriett joined her, looking like she would prefer removing the enchanter's soulmask before allowing Tomas to simply disable the man. Sarah hoped they could stop the enchanter fast. With half a dozen soulmasks, the man could destroy the entire structure with a couple more supercharged soul grenades. She prepared another cipher, just in case.

Tomas leaped into the doorway, rifle at the ready, but muttered a curse and slipped into the room.

"What do you see?" Sarah asked as she reached the doorway.

Harriett proceeded her into the room, where Tomas was standing over a hole in the floor.

"He's dropped down to the second level," Tomas said.

The sounds of gunfire and fighting echoed from down below, where the fighters of the Tenth were still working to subdue the rest of the enchanter's cell.

Tomas added, "That enchanter's too dangerous to leave active."

Harriett jumped past him, through the hole. "Then what are you waiting for?"

Tomas followed, and Sarah dropped through after them. Alter jumped down behind her. On the second level of the museum, the exhibit hallways were lined with dark wood, subdued lighting, and recessed alcoves, which made it far too easy for heka to lurk unseen. Sarah's enhancements improved her eyesight, but the shadows and the flickering lights still made her a bit nervous.

She brought up her KSG shotgun and flicked on the powerful tactical light mounted under the barrel, sweeping it up the hall. At first she didn't see anything, but Tomas snapped his rifle up and fired off a pair of shots.

A man, who had been crouched behind an Egyptian statue with a dog-like head, staggered from behind his cover, convulsing under the electric shock rounds. Harriett reached him a second later, her hands already burning with her active nevron. She grabbed him by the chin, drove her burning fingers into his flesh, and ripped out his soulmask.

Usually facetakers needed several seconds to remove a soulmask from its host body. This time, Harriett yanked it free in one convulsive heave, ripping it from the underlying bone structure of the skull, and tearing it through the flesh of the face before it could slough free like it normally would.

The glittering, translucent soulmask, with the tendrils of rainbow smoke coiling underneath it, flattened a little as the eyes drew in the dangling nerve clusters. The body collapsed to the floor, the skin of the face flowing together, shaking like Jell-O as it formed an unbroken sheet, with only a single, narrow slit where the nose should be.

Sarah shuddered, even though she had witnessed the process several times. The sight still sent shivers up her arms. With the soulmask removed, the bone structure of the skull became flatter, and the blank face looked like an unfinished department store mannequin. The body without the soulmask would descend into a hibernation-like state while it waited for another soul to take possession.

"That's not the enchanter," Tomas said.

"Where did he go?" Alter asked, scanning the hallway, rifle at the ready. "I don't see anyone else on this level."

"He may have gone down to the first floor to rally his men and try to break free," Tomas said, moving back toward the stairs to descend to the first level.

Harriett moved after him, but Alter paused to look around. He shared a look with Sarah and she said, "He probably did go down."

Alter nodded. "But there's a chance he didn't. An enchanter that skilled should not be underestimated." He glanced at the stairs where Tomas was already descending with Harriett, and his expression was easy to read. He wanted to leap into the ongoing fight downstairs, eager to win that kiss from Sarah.

She offered, "I'll scan this area. I have a cipher that should be able to pinpoint his location, wherever he's hiding. In fact, I'll try to iden-tify how many of them are left, or how many have active runes."

"Can you do that?" Alter asked.

"I think so. I've been working on a variant of a scrying rune, and I think I can adapt it to lock onto active enhancements and dispos-sessed souls."

Shouting and rattling gunfire from downstairs drew their atten-tion. Alter gripped his gun and gave Sarah an encouraging smile. "Call me if you need any help."

"Go ahead. If you see him down there, notify me. He may have more explosives, and I don't want to leave the group unprotected."

Alter nodded and rushed down the stairs. Sarah paused to studying the spooky, dim hall again, then crouched to draw a cipher onto the smooth stone of the floor with her finger. The glowing, silver marks she made would linger for a time before fading if she didn't activate them.

Unlike the single, slashing mark she had used to activate the last cipher, which she had already held clearly in her mind, this time she was building a new symbol, so needed to draw it out in its entirety. The more accurate the cipher, the more powerful its effects.

It took only a few seconds to complete. Sarah was getting very adept at drawing the complex symbols that made up the foundational elements in her battle ciphers. Those symbols were most often taken from ancient Egyptian or Chinese, although there were some powerful ones she liked from other cultures.

In general, any symbol that was widely recognized to have a particular meaning could produce adequate power. The better ones were imbued with meaning over many generations. Joan of Arc, the rune warrior from the Middle Ages who Sarah had visited several times to study with, had often use the fleur-de-lis from her nation's flag as the heart of many of her runes. With her patriotic fervor, that symbol had proved exceptionally powerful for her.

Sarah leaned over the completed cipher, held her hand above it, and focused. The well of her rounon strength, like a fire in her soul, fueled her ciphers and her enhancements. Both the hunters and the heka possessed similar, if less extensive rounon powers. She could activate a far broader range of ciphers, with fewer restrictions.

The cipher she was using now did not drain much of her energy. Its purpose was strictly limited to that building, its intent straight forward, searching for souls that matched the parameters she had added as modifier marks. A small fraction of her strength flowed out of her rounon well to fuel the cipher, and it began to glow brighter on the floor.

"Such an elaborate rune is not required," a cultured voice spoke from behind her.

Sarah spun, hating the start of fear the unexpected voice triggered. Why did creeps always manage to step out of the shadows behind her?

The enchanter stood in the center of the hallway, looking confident and at ease. He was a broad-shouldered Chinese man with a hint of a goatee, and long, black hair tied in an actual topknot, with a jade pin stuck through. He wore a dark gray, traditional Chinese jacket, complete with mandarin collar and frog buttons up the front.

Many of Paul's henchmen had been Chinese like Paul and his mother. Few of them had embraced the role so thoroughly, though. The enchanter wore a round Egyptian golden pendant on a gold chain around his neck, and it glittered in the light of her shotgun's flashlight.

Sarah wondered if he had acquired the pendant that evening in the museum. It made a great spot to aim at, either way.

"Get on your knees and put your hands behind your head," Sarah ordered.

"I'm on my way, Sarah!" Tomas cried, his voice loud in her earpiece.

The enchanter only smiled, a condescending look similar to the ones Paul had often used.

So Sarah shot him in the face.

At a dozen feet, the hot-loaded buckshot rounds struck in a tight group. In any normal situation, she would have blown his face off.

Dealing with heka was never normal.

The buckshot rounds ricocheted away and he smiled again, drawing a thick-bladed Chinese sword from a sheath on his back. He gestured with the single-edge weapon. "I think you are familiar with this type of sword, yes?"

Sure, Paul had terrified her with a similar sword and stabbed her several times. The enchanter was playing his hand too strong, trying to step into shoes he could never fill. The sight of the weapon in his hands did not fill her with dread like he clearly hoped.

It enraged her.

Sarah dropped her shotgun on its tactical sling to hang from her shoulders. "Bad idea tapping that memory, pal."

She rushed the enchanter, who was stupid enough to raise his sword to strike. The gold pendant he wore glittered. A symbol was engraved on its face, but she couldn't make out the details. She'd investigate in a minute.

As she leaped across the distance to the enchanter, she threw out her right hand, slashing a glowing finger through the air just as he struck with the sword.

This was a cipher already memorized and blazing in her mind. It required only a basic mark as a focal point to activate. She'd planned it to deal with Paul's mother if they ran into her during the raid, and it drained a huge percentage of her rounon well.

She stumbled right in front of the enchanter, her feet feeling like they were packed in lead. The cipher unleashed a blistering wave of pure energy that struck the enchanter like an invisible battering ram. It smashed the sword out of his hand and catapulted him away. He tumbled down the hall and smashed right through the exterior wall.

Sarah whistled softly. She hadn't intended quite that much force.

Maybe the sight of that sword had affected her more than she had realized. She scooped up the fallen sword and rushed to the end of the hallway to look out the broken wall. That end of the building overlooked a manicured lawn, ringed by a patch of trees and bushes that separated it from a nearby street. She expected to see the broken corpse of the enchanter lying on the lawn, but there was no sign of him.

She muttered a Maori curse she had recently learned from Anaru.

Tomas arrived, with Harriett close on his heels. "Where did he go?"

Sarah gestured at the jagged hole in the wall. "I sort of blew him out through here."

He gave her a fierce grin and lifted a fist for her to bump. "Where's the body?"

"I don't see him. He had activated a protective web, but that blast should have shredded it."

"He might have other protections."

"He must have. He's gone."

"We need that guy." Tomas jumped out and landed lightly on the lawn two stories below.

Harriett frowned at the empty lawn. "You two find him. I'll go help mop up the rest of that rabble downstairs."

Before Sarah could follow Tomas, Harriett leaned closer and added, "Alter threw himself into the fight down there. You shouldn't have agreed to that kiss."

"I never actually said I agreed," she protested.

"He'll pressure you if he wins. You might have to beat that dough back down before it rises too high."

"I'll deal with him," she promised, then leaped out the gaping hole after Tomas, who had already headed into the trees. She hoped they'd find the enchanter, broken and bleeding, trying to hide in the bushes, but in her heart, she suspected he was already long gone.

She hated being right so often.

4

Love is all we have, the only way that each can help the other until they get this rune.

~EURIPIDES

THE NEXT MORNING, far too early for Sarah's taste, she followed Tomas through an open set of double doors into a training room of the Gruppo di Intervento Speciale. The GIS were an elite special-forces unit of the Italian Carabinieri military police dedicated to tactical response and counter-terrorism.

They had lost over twenty men in the recent showdown with Paul. No doubt they would be upset if they ever learned they'd been left out of the latest hunt.

Sarah slipped to Tomas' right to get a better view of the high-ceilinged, cavernous room where the dozen GIS soldiers waited. An extensive weight-training complex filled the left side, while mats on the right suggested it was used for group exercises, martial arts train-ing, and sparring. It smelled like every weight room she'd ever visited. Sweat and male body odor, with a hint of cleaning solutions that never managed to clear the air.

Tomas was dressed in his enforcer uniform. He bore no official military rank, but his black tactical pants and form-fitting, khaki polo shirt gave him a military air. That hunter's body really did look good on him.

Tomas didn't seem worried about the fact that it was only a temporary suit, but it bothered Sarah. They still had no idea when they'd get his real body back from Spartacus. Some aspects of living in the shadowy world of facetakers and soul powers were still unsettling.

Sarah hoped she wouldn't need to change forms again for a long time. She still struggled with nightmares about dying. She liked her young, athletic new body, but she'd need some time to really feel at home.

Two senior officers of the GIS, trailed by eight uniformed aids, led them across the training floor to the waiting commandos. Although the floor looked like hardwood, it gave a little under foot. The composite material probably helped reduce bruising.

The soldiers saluted, led by their sergeant, a thick-chested man with classic Italian features. Black hair and eyes, a handsome face, olive skin. He looked fit and very tough.

The sergeant shook Tomas' hand and smiled, revealing even, white teeth. "Welcome, signore Tomas. It is a great honor to see you again."

His voice was deep, his accent not too thick as he spoke in that singsong way most Italians spoke English. He was one of the soldiers they'd gotten to know in the previous weeks as they coordinated relief efforts and the hunt for escaped heka operatives. His name was Sergente Maggiore Carlo Salvatici. He was well-respected by his battle-hardened commandos.

"Happy to be here, Sergeant," Tomas said with a smile.

The captain who had led them to the training room spoke. "You men won the bid to learn about runes first. If approved, this unit will apply runes, test their effectiveness, and identify potential tactical applications."

Tomas nodded. "Everyone's clamoring for demonstrations, but you were there in the trenches with us, so you deserve first dibs."

The soldiers grinned, drawing a little closer, eager to hear more.

The day's visit was part of a delicate balancing act forced upon the facetaker council, known to the world as the Suntara Group, after the explosive confrontation with Paul. In order to defeat the cui dashi, they'd been forced to reveal publicly many of their special powers and enhancements.

Too many people had seen Tomas' enforcers and the fighters from Yurak International display superhuman strength as they fought to hold back Spartacus' rune-protected forces. International television had captured their heroic acts, miraculous healings, and unique weapons systems. Now governments were desperate to gain access to those secrets.

Gregorios and his council had so far managed the fallout with masterful tact, developed over thousands of years of maneuvering through the halls of power as they secretly affected world history. They were working with several governments to secure contracts to provide prototypes of their specialty weapons systems, and they were scheduling demonstrations of rune enhancements with many more.

Of course, not everyone wanted that information made public. More than a few countries already knew about rune enhancements and had been secretly building enhanced special-forces units.

Sarah hadn't paid too much attention to the political wrangling, but she'd absorbed enough from Tomas to understand the stakes were high, and likely to grow higher. The facetakers had thrived through the centuries only by keeping their existence secret. When people had learned about them, they'd invariably rioted, denouncing them as everything from heretics, to witches, to devil worshipers, or even vampires. So far the truth of the facetakers hadn't come out, and Gregorios and Eirene had kept a low profile, maintaining the focus on runes and special weapons.

This visit was part of that outreach effort. The Suntara Group was located in Rome, but despite long-standing relationships with local authorities and Vatican leaders, they'd wasted precious time gaining authorization to bring their full might to bear against Paul. Part of the reason she and Tomas came here instead of flying to visit the eager armies of more powerful nations was to secure an even tighter partnership with the local Italian forces.

An international conference on enhancements and their relation to the growing world terrorist threat was scheduled in Cairo in a few days. This Italian commando force had been invited to attend. Given their many interactions with Tomas' enforcers and the soldiers from Yurak, they were seen as experts. No doubt their captain was eager to learn enough to reinforce that image.

Tomas launched into his presentation, explaining the basics of rune enhancements and how the special symbols, cut into the skin like a form of tattoo, bonded to the force of the person's soul. If they possessed the strength of soul and enough force of will, they could bond the rune and unlock the amazing enhancements the soldiers had seen during the battle at the Vatican.

Sarah's own first rune had been a custom symbol that she had designed, resulting in unparalleled increase in strength and agility. She had not yet marked it onto her new body, and wouldn't until she felt truly connected with her second life. The body had three runes already marked on it when she took possession. They enhanced strength, agility, healing, and vitality, and they had all bonded without issue.

The details of how the runes worked and how they were powered was what a lot of people struggled to accept. These men were probably all Roman Catholic, so they'd believe in the existence of souls. However, rune powers had so often been associated with devil worship that most people felt reluctant to embrace them. Worse, in the scientific world, most so-called educated people scoffed at the idea of such intangible powers.

Sure enough, the sergeant-major raised a hand. "You cannot be serious, signore. You want us to use this . . . magic to fight?"

Several of his men looked equally hesitant, and a couple fingered their rosaries.

Tomas said, "These concepts can seem strange at first, but I'm being straight with you. This is the key to our enhancements. You were there. You saw what we can do, what the enemy can do. If you want to step into this world, this is the way."

The ranking official in the room, a colonel, spoke for the first time. "We're trying to keep an open mind, but this is highly unusual." He spoke with a cultured, British accent. "Can you guarantee the application of these rune enhancements won't compromise the religious integrity of our men?"

"I can. We're in contact with Vatican representatives to produce an official statement from the Church. It'll probably be classified, but you'll get access to it." He didn't mention that one of the Suntara Group council members, who had died only a few weeks ago, had spent one life as a cardinal centuries before.

The sergeant-major said, "If the church approves, we will try this. Will you demonstrate?"

Tomas pulled off his shirt and pointed out the three runes he wore on his torso. The symbols looked like they'd been drawn in black ink. The body he wore had runes of healing, strength, and a complex rune that included elements of speed, balance, and discipline.

The runes were of exceptional quality. The hunters tended to customize their runes more than the enforcers of Tomas' company. It was easier for them, since many of them possessed the rounon gift to inscribe their own runes. The Tenth relied on the services of several rounon-gifted people they'd recruited over the years.

Most non-hunter people with rounon gifts eventually fell in with various heka cells or cults and began developing runes to draw power from the souls of others. That was strictly forbidden by the hunters and the enforcers, and the response to such soul stealers was always violent and fatal. When the enforcers discovered rounon-gifted who had not made that fateful choice, they sometimes managed to bring them into the fold to work for the Suntara Group as resident rounon experts.

Tomas pointed to his runes and explained briefly what purposes they served. "Not everyone can bond a rune. Fewer can bond two or more."

Many soldiers wore tattoos, so they weren't terribly impressed by Tomas' runes until he drew a knife and dragged it across his forearm.

"What are you doing!" the sergeant cried.

Sarah hated seeing Tomas bleed, even though the body was temporary and the cut was not severe. The move made his point dramatically though, so she handed him a bandage that she'd brought along.

"You wanted a demonstration," Tomas said as he applied pressure to the wound.

"Proving that you bleed like the rest of us isn't what I had in mind."

"Bleeding isn't the lesson," Tomas said, removing the bandage with a flourish.

His arm had already scabbed over. As they watched, the scab darkened and faded. It took only seconds to heal. In less than a minute, only a thin scar remained. It would entirely disappear within the hour.

"This is the lesson. Runes of healing are generally the recommended first rune. Even soldiers with no added strength or fighting enhancements become far deadlier when they can shake off debilitating wounds, or fight longer without getting exhausted."

He had their attention now.

"So what do you say, Sergeant-Major?" Tomas asked with a smile, gesturing toward the open sparring floor. "You want a demonstration?"

The sergeant grinned. "As you say. We should put this to the test."

Carlo's men clamored their support, and the senior officers nodded approval.

The sergeant moved onto the sparring floor. "What formal military training do you have, signore, in addition to your runes?"

Tomas shook his head. "Don't worry about me, Sergeant."

He pointed to Sarah. "You get to fight my assistant."

5

It is a wretched thing to injure a poor man stuck in a single life.

~PTAH-HOTEP, EGYPTIAN VIZIER TO PHARAOH
DJEDKARE ISESI IN THE FIFTH DYNASTY, 25TH
CENTURY B.C.

"YOU MUST BE JOKING, SIGNORE," the sergeant said as he studied Sarah's petite frame.

Sarah concealed a smile as she moved onto the sparring floor. It wasn't his fault he didn't know that the power of one's rune mattered far more than their size. "Are you afraid of me, Sergeant?"

That elicited a round of laughter from the men. Had they not been in the presence of senior officers, she was sure she would have earned a few catcalls too. As a top model in her first life, she had learned to deal with such outbursts, but that didn't mean she liked it. She was relieved her relationship with those soldiers wasn't tarnished by such an opening volley.

"Not at all, signorina," protested the sergeant. "I have a daughter about your age. I don't want to hurt you."

Tomas chuckled. "Don't worry about Sarah. If you can land a single punch, drinks are on me."

As his men called out encouragement, the sergeant shrugged, as if to tell Sarah he had warned her, and the consequences were on her shoulders.

It was sweet, really.

When she gave him a warm smile, Sergeant-Major Carlo regarded her closely, then snapped his fingers. "Of course. That's why you look so familiar. He called you Sarah. Your face, signorina, it reminds me of the blessed Sword of the Deliverer."

Sarah hid her dismay. Most people weren't attentive enough to catch the similarities. Of course she looked like the famous Sarah that the world had witnessed die on the broken expanse of St. Peter's square. She might be wearing a new body, but her face would always be her own.

When transferring to a new host, a person's soulmask maintained much of their facial structure. This body was shorter, more petite, and the head was a little smaller. Francesca had done a remarkable job mating her soulmask to the underlying bone structure. Her features had transformed a little, but she would always look fundamentally the same, no matter which host she inhabited. Most people couldn't see past the different size and shape of her body, the different length and style of her hair.

She gave the sergeant a warm smile. "Thank you for the compliment, signore."

"But you look so much like her," he insisted. Some of his men started muttering about the similarity too.

"Yeah, I get that a lot. Wish I could add it to my resume." Before he could get too distracted, she settled into a fighting stance. "Now, if you've finished stalling, let me show you what rune enhancements can really do."

The sergeant grimaced. After a final glance at his superior officers, he advanced, fists up. "As you say, signorina."

"Don't worry," Sarah assured him. "I'll try not to hurt you."

He laughed.

Sarah vaulted over him.

His laughter trailed off into a gasp of astonishment as she soared close enough to the twenty-five foot ceiling to brush one hand against a heavy steel beam. It was dirty, and the stale air that high smelled of greasy ducts. Sarah landed lightly on enhanced legs and rushed the still-gaping sergeant. Despite his surprise, he reacted with the honed reflexes of an elite fighter, fists flashing out to strike her down.

To Sarah's enhanced reflexes, he moved with the sluggishness of someone trying to fight underwater. She'd been training hard with Tomas and Alter over the past couple of weeks, pushing her new body to the limits.

Even though she hadn't yet added the aggressive runes she'd worn on her first body, she was already impressed with this young battle suit's performance. It had come to her pre-loaded with useful muscle memories. Francesca, who had owned the body before her, had trained extensively in advanced martial arts and acrobatics, and Sarah had picked up those moves with the ease of sliding into a pair of comfortable jeans.

Her lithe young frame possessed wonderful balance and speed, and excellent muscle tone. She couldn't beat Tomas yet if he really wanted to win, but she could hold her own even against him most days.

Sergente-Maggiore Carlo Salvatici had less of a chance beating her than a mouse dropped into a kennel of hungry cats.

Sarah decided to start easy on him. She slipped around his fists and struck him with an open palm to the center of the chest. Air exploded out of his lungs, and the burly sergeant flew fifteen feet and rolled all the way to the far wall.

"Guarda!" cried several of the soldiers.

Others exclaimed, "Non e possible."

While some of the soldiers ran across the room to help the sergeant back to his feet, Tomas joined Sarah.

"I thought you were going to take it easy," he whispered.

Sarah grimaced. "Sorry. I did. I'm not used to fighting little people."

Tomas barked a laugh. "All right, Gulliver. Don't damage him too badly."

"Don't worry, I've got this." She kissed his cheek. Seeing it would help keep the soldiers off balance. Besides, she wanted to. She was still figuring out who she was, and Tomas was the rock upon which she was trying to build her second life. If anyone had a problem with that, she'd send them tumbling after their leader.

"Are you all right?" she asked the sergeant when he rejoined her.

"Bravo, signorina," he said, rubbing his chest. "This time I won't hold back."

"That's the spirit." She gestured him on. "Come hit me."

He tried.

The sergeant lunged and drove his fist with all his strength at her face.

Sarah caught it.

The weight and force of the blow should have thrown her from her feet, but her enhanced strength and balance more than compensated. His surprised look mirrored the whispered exclamations rippling through the gathered company.

Sarah could have unloaded a battery of punches against him, could have broken every major bone before he could manage to hit the floor. But that wasn't the point. So she grabbed his foot and threw him into the air.

He somersaulted backward and managed to land on his feet, eliciting encouraging cheers from his men. Before he could launch another attack, Sarah rushed past, throwing out an arm to clothesline him across the chest, blasting him off his feet.

While he soared backward, she caught him, flipped him back upright, then set him gently on his feet. When he snapped his arms up to a ready position, she caught them, letting him lift her off the floor so she could kiss his cheek.

Then she pushed away and retreated a step, grinning. "Very good try, Sergeant."

He laughed and threw his arms out wide. "I surrender!"

Then he grabbed her slender shoulders and pulled her close, kissing both cheeks. "Bravo, Sarah. Bravo."

His men gathered around, grinning and chattering in Italian, pounding their sergeant on the back and lining up to kiss Sarah's hand. Even though most of them towered over her, they seemed stunned by the demonstration.

Tomas pulled a sheaf of papers from a leather satchel. "Here's some more data about the basic rune enhancements and what type of performance increase you might see from them. Study hard, and we'll see you soon. If you're interested in pursuing runes for your troops, pick someone to act as a test subject, and we'll demonstrate how it works."

The colonel accepted the papers and pumped Tomas' hand. "Thank you, Tomas. Very impressive display."

Outside of the Carabinieri training facility, Tomas hugged her. "Good work in there."

"I like Carlo."

"Me too. I think we'll be able to work with his team."

He didn't need to add that they might need that connection soon. The hunt for heka operatives was still ongoing, as was the much more dangerous mission of tracking down the mysterious cui dashi woman they knew only as Paul's mother. Sarah hoped they wouldn't see pitched battle in the streets of Rome ever again.

They might not have a choice.

"Are we heading back to the mansion?" Sarah asked as they climbed into the little Italian Fiat.

"We have to stop at Suntara first," Tomas said with a wink. That intrigued Sarah. She loved surprises.

Well, she loved the good ones.

6

At the touch of love everyone becomes a poet. If only they had the runes to be good poets.

~PLATO

AS TOMAS FOCUSED on traversing the confusing maze of Rome's streets, Sarah marveled that so much of the city seemed normal. They crossed the Tiber River at the Ponte del Risorgimento, north of the devastated area of St. Peter's.

The trip south toward the Vatican became increasingly clogged with traffic. Tourists, construction workers, and religious pilgrims vied for space on the tight roads, but the congested area lacked the shouting and cursing Sarah would have expected.

They passed one piazza with a giant screen displaying real-time footage from the shattered St. Peter's square. Dozens of similar sites had been set up around the city to keep citizens and visitors alike updated on progress in a vain attempt to curb the masses trying to reach the famous site.

Religious pilgrims had thronged the disaster area ever since the battle ended. They hailed the fiery confrontation with Paul as the attempted uprising of the antichrist, but the dense crowds hampered the clean-up effort. Many sought to catch a glimpse of Pope Andrew Paul I. The aged pontiff was wildly famous, celebrated for his bravery in the face of diabolical evil. So few understood the forces unleashed upon the city that their only reference was obscure prophecy from religious texts.

Others left gifts and prayed at the shrine to the Sword of the Deliverer, which had instantly become one of the most popular destinations in the world. So popular that Rome had dedicated a dozen other sites as shrines to help with the overcrowding. Supporters of the slain heroine were lobbying for Sarah to be made a saint.

Sarah found it all very embarrassing. Most saints were dead and buried a long time before being canonized. She wasn't sure how her fanatical fans would react if they found out she'd survived and started a new life. Returning from the dead wouldn't be half so bizarre as some of the wild theories proclaimed by conspiracy nuts, or as devastating as the impending doom prophesied by Armageddon prognosticators.

Still, those throngs of devotees were the ones she was tapping to help heal the children. So their pilgrimage was doing good, after all. Interest in the heroine who had demonstrated such startling powers had reached a fever pitch. Enough people had recognized her from her days at Alterego that eager news media had dug up everything they could on her connection to the company.

No one could explain how a body model had become the living embodiment of the power of god and the papal-declared Sword of the Deliverer, and hypotheses had flooded the internet. Some of the claims were quite funny, like the one that suggested she was really Mother Teresa in disguise.

Some of the wilder ideas were downright insulting, and she refused to think about them. Thankfully most of those were ridiculed to silence by the general public.

Every old lady who had rented her body became persons of interest. They might have lost their access to the fountain of youth, but several of them seemed rejuvenated by public appearances on popular talk shows. Sarah caught several video clips featuring Marilyn, the elderly lady who had tried purchasing her body and ended up in one very similar. She still thought she owned Sarah's original form, and the fact that she had purchased it generated all kinds of additional interest. Some people revered her as a sister of the Deliverer, while others sent her death threats.

Instead of apologizing for hampering the clean-up efforts, some people lobbied the Vatican to leave the devastated area of the battlefield untouched to preserve the marks of martyrdom. That posed all sorts of issues since St. Peter's was already a famous iconic location. The Church was working with the Italian government and dozens of international relief agencies who all demanded participation in the effort, trying to find a solution to the quandary.

Sarah was glad they had agreed to fix the basic infrastructure. Simple necessity required it. Too many people came to the area to do otherwise. She hoped they chose to repair the devastated area. Better to move on with life.

With the Vatican so heavily impacted, and with so much local and international attention focused there, the Suntara Group had moved most of their operations from their headquarters. The building was too close to the battleground, situated near the Sistine Chapel.

Gregorios, Eirene, and their children had moved to Quentin's mansion, joining Sarah, Tomas, and Alter, who were already staying there. Sarah loved the company, and felt comforted to know her closest friends were all nearby. Despite the influx of so many new people, and even with repairs from the recent hunter assault still underway, the sprawling mansion had plenty of room.

"So why do we need to swing by Suntara?" Sarah asked. The enforcers had relocated to a secondary base of operations in the city where Tomas spent most of his time coordinating the hunt for heka operatives and the cui dashi.

"We need to pick up a new piece of equipment."

"I thought Quentin had moved everything to his home workshop."

Quentin was the dapper, middle-aged man who oversaw Suntara's weapons and armament division. Some of his amazing inventions rivaled the best that the Bond movies had ever produced.

"Just about," Tomas said, but didn't explain further.

"Fine, keep your secrets. You owe me dinner tonight."

"What? We went out last night."

"You getting tired of me already?" she teased.

"Never gonna happen," he said, taking her hand. He added with a sly smile, "Besides, if the day ever comes, a quick trip to Francesca would set you right."

Sarah smiled to hide her shudder. She appreciated Tomas' attempts at levity, but this one didn't work. He'd been sensitive to the subject in the first few days, but he was starting to slip.

He might have lived enough lives not to pay that much attention to what suit he wore any more, but Sarah's body was still a foundational element of her identity. She didn't want to think about changing any time soon, even if slipping into something different might finally seduce him into relenting on his obstinate decision to wait for intimacy.

When they reached Suntara, Tomas pulled into the underground parking garage. He led her down to the basement level where Quentin's shop was located, but instead of heading for the darkened workroom, he headed in the opposite direction. They passed through a security door where he entered a code on the keypad. Sarah's curiosity grew more when they took another elevator down deeper into the earth. She'd never visited this part of the building, hadn't suspected it existed.

"Will you finally tell me where we're going?" she demanded, bursting with curiosity.

"Almost there," was all he would say.

The elevator beeped, flashing "S7." Sub-level seven. That was as deep as the vault where they kept the memory-jumping machines.

Tomas led her down a short hall of whitewashed walls and white tile, lit by bright, fluorescent bulbs. He pushed through a solid, iron door and led her into a room sheathed in glimmering stainless steel. It looked like a hospital room, with several white sheet-draped beds, and medical equipment lining the walls. It smelled of antiseptic.

Francesca, one of Gregorios' and Eirene's children born with the active nevra core of a facetaker, was waiting for them. Sarah smiled. She was one of Sarah's favorite people. Although she grieved for her dead brother, she hadn't let that grief overwhelm her as much as Harriett.

She swept forward and gave Sarah a hug and proclaimed grandly, "Welcome to the body bank."

7

Do a good deed and throw it to Anuket wrapped in her rune.

~ANCIENT EGYPTIAN PROVERB

"WHAT DID YOU CALL THIS PLACE?" Sarah asked.

"It's the body bank," Francesca repeated. "Where do you think we keep the extra suits?"

"I hadn't thought about it," she admitted.

Alterego had kept spare bodies in their vault, a huge underground expanse containing long stacks that held soul coffins instead of safety deposit boxes. She didn't want to believe that Suntara kept souls prisoner the same way.

Tomas took her hand and led her toward a set of double doors on the far side of the room. Her face must have reflected her concern because he said, "Don't worry, Sarah. We don't keep dispossessed like the heka do. These are for our use only."

Behind the doors was another much larger room lined with clear cases, like vertical coffins, containing faceless bodies, naked but for briefs.

Sarah paused in the doorway, staring at all the dormant bodies. She'd been swept into the world of facetakers, heka and cui dashi. Sometimes it had felt like drowning as she struggled to come to grips with the reality of the world that most people would never know about. Her own newfound rune warrior gift had been a source of both inspiration and terror, but she had thought she'd mastered any hesitation about the world.

Now she wasn't so sure.

"Who did these belong to?" she asked.

"Does it matter?" Francesca asked.

She looked more mature in her new lovely, twenty-something form. She was a little taller than Sarah, with a fuller figure and soft, brown hair. It still felt weird sometimes to spend time with Francesca. Sarah liked the lively facetaker, but Francesca had worn the body Sarah now called home. The fact made them closer than sisters, but still felt odd sometimes.

"Of course it matters. Someone used to live in all of these."

"It matters," Tomas agreed. "But we didn't steal them like Alterego did."

Francesca nodded. "We don't steal them, but sometimes we buy them."

"What happens to the owners?" Sarah asked, trying to hide her revulsion. She wasn't naive. She knew that bad things happened in the world and that part of the reality of the facetakers was trafficking in human bodies. That Gregorios worked to keep innocents from becoming collateral damage helped a lot.

Tomas said, "These are high performance suits, Sarah. They're the hardest type to come by. Some we win like I got this one." He tapped his chest. "Enemies we defeat are sometimes granted second chances in a lesser form."

"You take their bodies and give them crappy replacements?"

"It's better than killing them."

She couldn't argue with that, but it still left her feeling a little dirty.

Francesca said, "Others we buy outright. People make stupid decisions and get stuck in debt all the time. We pay them substantial sums to buy these suits. They're most often traded for convicted criminals who are scheduled for execution."

Sarah made a slow turn, scanning the room. It held at least a hundred male bodies of all sizes. Most looked to be in top condition, although a few were overweight. She wondered if those were used when enforcers needed to work undercover like Tomas had recently done at Alterego.

After a moment she said, "All right. Why are we here?"

Tomas tapped his chest again. "I need to ship this suit back to the hunters, so I need a replacement."

"What about getting yours back from Spartacus?"

He grimaced. "Not likely. Gregorios is working on it, but Spartacus has those special forbidden runes inscribed, and that's making things difficult."

"Plus, he's becoming pretty famous," Sarah admitted.

"Right. We can't just go kidnap him and try to pull his face off."

He stood in a room full of empty bodies. It was a good sign that he could still discuss holding to a moral code. Many people would become insensitive to the inherent right of people to own their natural bodies. The code might seem bizarre to the rest of the world, but it fit their reality, so she tried to accept it.

She hated the thought of Spartacus keeping Tomas' beautiful body. She'd started making some specific life plans that had included that suit.

"What's Gregorios going to do about Spartacus?" she asked.

Tomas shrugged. "Not sure. He's a special case."

"That's an understatement," Francesca said with a grin.

She was right. The famous Thracian gladiator was unlike anyone Sarah knew or had heard about. His long, forced exile, while dispossessed, bronzed, and incorporated into a statue above the Arch of Constantine might have had something to do with that. His undying hatred for Eirene and Gregorios had faded and he'd turned to reflection and philosophy.

After Paul's fiery defeat, he'd fled Rome and taken Hollywood by storm, quickly becoming a hot ticket. He apparently wanted to become an actor as a way to win influence, similar to how he had sought victory in the ancient arenas. His message was that the world had grown soft, that people needed to stand strong and learn to live with honor, and that they could make more of their lives. He was gaining quite a following.

He was even starting a chain of academies called Thank Spartacus to better prepare children for the real world. The curriculum included financial management and principles of honor and self-defense. They sounded pretty fun, actually.

Francesca took Sarah's hands. "Life moves on, dear. We all wish some things had turned out differently."

A momentary grief dragged her normal smile down. No doubt she was thinking of her brother, Bastien. Sarah had really liked him, and missed him a lot.

The moment passed and Francesca's smile re-ignited. "But life is what it is. Let's celebrate every lifetime."

"I'll try."

"Good!" Francesca squeezed her hands. "Merry Christmas. This time you get to pick your present."

Sarah allowed the vivacious facetaker to lead her around the room to browse for Tomas' new body. Francesca pointed out the different models with bubbly enthusiasm. Most of them already sported three basic runes.

"Those are all blondes," Francesca waved at the left-hand wall. "Not your type."

"Hey, don't I get a say in this? It's my suit after all," Tomas said.

Francesca shook her head. "You've had plenty. This one's for Sarah."

"Fair enough." He winked at Sarah. "Be kind."

They ended up at the back wall, which was stacked with a long row of excellent subjects. They were all brunettes, from light brown to black hair, all cut military short.

"Let's start with the height," Francesca said. "We've got anything from five-foot-five to six-foot-seven."

"I prefer to be six-one," Tomas said.

"Hush," Francesca chided.

"No, he's right," Sarah said. "Keep him about the same."

Francesca shrugged. "It's up to you, but why not try something a little different?"

"I don't think I could date a guy shorter than me. But if he's much taller, it's too hard to kiss him."

"Good point," Francesca agreed.

She led them to the center of the wall and pointed out half a dozen possible selections. "Take your time. Check out shoulder width, head size, hand size." She gave Sarah a wicked grin. "We can even remove the briefs so you can make sure you like what's under the hood."

"Francesca," Tomas protested, actually flushing. "That's none of your business."

She laughed. "You're so old-fashioned. Still the prude of the eighteenth century. You love this girl, don't you?"

"Of course."

"Then you've got to think ahead."

Sarah couldn't imagine this conversation making sense in any other context. That Francesca was chiding Tomas for being old-fashioned made her smile. Francesca was far older, but she embraced the modern day with unreserved enthusiasm.

Sarah said, "It's all right. I'm sure they all function properly."

She shared some of Tomas' hesitation about discussing that upcoming aspect of their relationship.

Tomas had hesitated due to the strict moral code he'd been raised with. She'd respected him for that, despite initially feeling irritated. Then he'd lost his body and she hadn't wanted to become intimate while he wore a temporary suit. To think they were choosing a body that he'd wear throughout the life they were trying to build together was so alien to normal life, it was hard to wrap her mind around it.

Ever since plunging into the world of the facetakers, she'd been caught up in one desperate struggle after another and still felt like an outsider half the time. Add to that her newfound rune warrior powers, and she needed time to reach a stable place in her life. Only then could she move into that next stage of commitment with any confidence.

Sarah had developed the ability to live in the moment and not get derailed by the many mind-blowing revelations about herself, Tomas, the facetakers, and world history in general. She struggled to maintain that calm now. This wasn't something she could put off. She had to consider it. The decision they made here would affect their lives.

Then again, who else got to choose the perfect body for their perfect man?

Sarah walked the long row of potential bodies and focused on that benefit. Together they could make him whatever they wanted.

Struck by a sudden thought, she asked, "Is there a female body bank?"

"Of course," Francesca said.

She hesitated before asking softly, "Tomas, do you want to visit that one after this?"

He took her hand. "I can't see why."

Francesca looked hurt. "Sarah dear, are you tired of that form already?"

"Of course not. I love it."

She really did. It was different, but she was getting used to it, and as she'd proven in the recent sparring match against the sergeant, this lithe young form possessed many great qualities. She loved its boundless energy and athleticism, but did Tomas?

"Then why think of changing?"

Before she could answer, Tomas cupped her face in his hand, similar to the way Gregorios and Eirene often did. "Sarah, I love you."

"But . . ."

He shook his head. "You'll look different in every life. It doesn't matter. I've been around long enough to realize that the external form is just a shell. What's beautiful is what's inside, and you're the most attractive, beautiful, and amazing woman I've ever known."

Francesca wiped at her eyes. "You're lucky I'm such a sap. Harriett would probably throw you out and order you to find a room."

Relieved by his assurance, Sarah squeezed Tomas' hand. "All right, then. Let's get you dressed."

They eventually settled on a muscular suit very similar to the one Spartacus had stolen from him. Sarah had been tempted to go for something different, but this was the ideal form for Tomas, and finding one so closely matched made it easier for her to commit to it.

"Are you sure about this?" Tomas asked.

"Yes," she said, making the commitment in her heart. "I'll take you in this one."

"You bet you will," Francesca said. "Good choice. This one's a prime pick, and the structure will match his soulmask very well."

She grinned at Tomas. "Time to pull your face off."

8

FRANCESCA PRESSED a green button in a small, recessed panel next to the selected body. A yellow light began to flash, and a sonorous woman's voice declared, "Stand clear."

The bottom of the transparent case holding the body slid out from the wall, and telescoping legs capped with wheels extended from underneath, turning the vertical case into a wheeled cart. Francesca picked up a small remote control recessed into the outer edge of the case and headed for the steel-clad outer room. The case wheeled after her.

Sarah and Tomas followed her, and Tomas stripped to his boxers, then lay down on one of the available gurneys. The body he was about to vacate was in excellent condition, and Sarah caught herself admiring it. She chided herself for being foolish. This wasn't going to be Tomas any more, so she had to distance herself from it, even though those arms had held her often in the past weeks.

Life around facetakers was so weird.

Francesca positioned the wheeled case with Tomas' new body next to the gurney and pressed a button on the remote. The rounded front of the case split down the middle and the halves slid into recesses on the sides of the case.

Sarah slid her hand into that of the empty suit. It fit well. She gave it a squeeze.

"No second thoughts?" Francesca asked.

"None. Do it."

Francesca stood at the head of Tomas' gurney and cupped his face with her hands. Her fingers slid to his jawline and she closed her eyes for a second, taking a slow breath. When she opened her eyes, they blazed with purple light, like LED screens. Purple fire rippled along her fingers, and she pressed them against Tomas' skin. He didn't even flinch.

Sarah had endured more soul transfers than Tomas, but she still felt a flicker of unease when she witnessed a facetaker activate their nevra core. That purple fire didn't leave scorch marks, but it hurt to have one's soul removed.

Francesca's fingers sank through the skin along Tomas' jawline. She curled them around the edges of his soulmask and started to pull. Flesh sloughed off of his jaw and around his mouth as his soulmask began to separate from the underlying bone structure. Sarah cringed at the sickening sucking sound the soulmask made as it lifted free.

Francesca raised it high, a little smile all the emotion she betrayed. Many facetakers openly embraced the feeling of ecstasy they felt when taking the soul of another, but Gregorios, Eirene, and their children displayed far more control. It made it a lot easier for Sarah to participate in soul transfers without them gloating over her soul like some forbidden fruit.

Tomas' soulmask was a shimmering, translucent mask with tendrils of rainbow smoke curling below it. His eyes flattened to half-spheres and his lips curled into a smile. The flesh on the recently-vacated body flowed back together, and the body began to descend into that coma-like state that could sustain it for long periods while it waited for another soul.

Francesca stepped to the new body and pressed Tomas' soulmask into place. Skin flowed over the soulmask as it sank onto the skull, bonding to the underlying bone structure. The newly-forming face shook before solidifying into Tomas' familiar features.

Instead of removing her hands immediately, Francesca ran her burning fingers along Tomas' jawline. The fit of his face to the skull was quite good, but she took an extra minute to smooth the transition areas, perfectly melding his soul with the new host.

Sarah appreciated the extra care. It cost Francesca more energy, but hopefully Tomas would remain in this form for many years, and she knew that the tiny signs of misalignment would nag at her.

"Hold him down," Francesca said as she withdrew her hands.

Sarah reached for Tomas' legs to brace them against the inevitable shaking that resulted when a soul bonded to a new body. He'd only been dispossessed for a few seconds, which would reduce the shock for him, but she had no idea how long the body had lain dormant without a host.

On a sudden whim, she jumped onto the gurney and embraced Tomas in a full body hug just as his limbs began to shake. Every muscle of his new body quivered and flexed as nerves and limbs bonded to Tomas' soul. She held on tight as he shook and rattled under her.

The quaking subsided after only a few seconds. As he took his first deep breath, he wrapped his arms around her and held her tight.

"That's a technique I don't think I've used," Francesca laughed.

"I approve though," said Tomas. He found her lips with his and kissed her tenderly.

He might now inhabit a new body, and new skin might cover his lips, but they were still his. She kissed him back, then snuggled against his chest. "Welcome home."

They enjoyed the embrace for half a minute, then Tomas helped her stand. While he slipped into his pants, she admired his new form. It was a beauty and she looked forward to getting to know it. His clothes were a little tight now, but Sarah didn't mind.

"You're an artist, Francesca," Tomas said as he checked his reflection in the mirror. "The alignment is perfect."

"I'd say I did it for you, but sisters have to stick together, right Sarah?"

Sarah gave her a hug. She could never explain how much she appreciated Francesca's thoughtfulness. "You're a marvel." Then she added to Tomas, "Hey, leave your shirt off for a minute."

"You're awful friendly," Francesca teased. "Want me to leave you two alone for a while?"

Sarah rolled her eyes. "Stop it. I haven't even dated him in this body yet. I need to give him a rune."

Tomas sat on the gurney. "I've got a couple of the basics already covered. Should bond soon."

The body did have basic runes for strength, stamina, and health. Sarah poked the standard health rune on his side. It was a little higher than she preferred, but it would do. "This one needs enhancing."

Francesca produced a scalpel.

Sarah could trigger ciphers and inscribe temporary runes with nothing but her finger. Markers formed better runes on bodies, but permanent runes needed a knife. She took it and turned to Tomas. "Just a couple of marks."

"Go for it," Tomas said without hesitation. "You know I love your work."

Sarah had him lie back on the gurney, then cut several additional marks into his skin, adding complexity and power to the basic healing rune. She included enhancements to boost other runes he might bond to later.

The marks were based on the first rune she had ever formed, the one she had cut into his side when Mai Luan had stabbed him and nearly killed him. She hadn't known she was a rune warrior then, and the rune she now marked into Tomas had become a signature symbol for her.

She wore the same rune on her side. As soon as she completed the marks, the rune began to glow with a soft silver light. She felt the slight drain of her strength as the force of her soul flowed out to power it and facilitate the bonding between the rune and Tomas' soul.

"Now you're ready," she said.

"I bet you write your name on all your toys," Francesca said.

Tomas stood and wrapped Sarah's slender frame in his strong arms. She leaned into him, looking forward to enjoying this embrace many times.

"No more changing for a while," she said.

"Not if I can help it."

9

Invincibility lies in the defense; the possibility of victory in the attack.

~SUN TZU

QUENTIN'S MANSION was a huge affair set on a sprawling estate in the hills outside of Rome, surrounded by several outbuildings. Most of the Mediterranean-Style mansion was finished in yellow stucco, but two imposing square towers, sheathed in rough-hewn granite, flanked the main entry. Ivy crept up one wall, adding a splash of green, and red brick tile led up the circular driveway and under the covered entrance.

The broken skeleton of the west wing dampened the effect, surrounded by its cast of scaffolding and small army of construction workers. The hunters had made a mess in their surprise assault on the estate a few weeks back, and it would be months before everything returned to normal. Despite the construction noise and influx of personnel from the Suntara headquarters, the interior of the mansion still felt like home to Sarah. The clean citrus scent of polished wood and flowers managed to win out against the smell of sawdust.

Quentin met them at the doors. Dressed impeccably as always in an expensive, tailored suit, he hugged Sarah. "Welcome back, and I believe congratulations are in order. I hear you humbled that sergeant without damaging his pride."

She wasn't surprised he'd already received reports on that. His staff was amazingly efficient. "Don't you have anything better to do than hang around the doors and play greeter?"

"I can always spare a few minutes for you, my dear," Quentin said as he offered his arm to lead her toward the east wing that had been converted into the operations hub.

Tomas came around the vehicle grinning. "Don't let him fool you. He gets updates from the gate guard. Plenty of time to get into position to play host."

Quentin gave Tomas a stern look. "You're a cheeky devil today. Perhaps I should reveal some of your little secrets in turn?"

"Just withhold the latest toy for a few days," Sarah suggested. The enforcers loved Quentin's inventions and were always begging for more.

"Now you're just being mean," Tomas exclaimed.

Quentin guided them upstairs to a set of rooms on the top floor with panoramic views of the distant city. The spacious suite had been converted into Gregorios' command center. Here he held board meetings, oversaw the complex operations of the Suntara Group, and met in person or via video conference with political leaders from around the world.

Eirene greeted them in the outer sitting room. She was dressed in a conservative business suit that flattered her young frame. Her mature face fit the athletic body well, making her look in her mid-twenties. Sarah hoped she could look a fraction as good when she was three thousand years old.

Eirene must have participated in one of those recent meetings because those were the only times she dressed in suits. She preferred tactical clothing and heka hunting to meetings with long-winded politicians.

One time she had sighed and confessed to Sarah, "Sometimes I miss the days political torture involved pliers and sharp blades instead of only barbed conversations. I miss the honesty."

Sarah gave Eirene a hug. "How are things going today?"

"The schedule's getting cramped. Greg is recording a statement for one of the subcommittees of the UN special task force on rune enhancements and their effects on global warming."

"How could they possibly link those two?" Sarah asked.

Eirene shrugged. "Blaming something for normal climate fluctuations gives them the ability to leverage fear and control greater percentages of the world economy. It always boils down to power and money."

"You're such a beacon of good cheer after those meetings," Quentin said.

"I'll feel better after I blow something up."

He quickly said, "Oh, no. I haven't even tested the new model of the mini mortar yet."

"Come on," Eirene pleaded. "Just one shot."

"I cannot in good faith risk your health," Quentin said with impressive conviction. "I'm afraid my policy must stand unbroken."

Tomas said, "The benefit of running the magic shop. He gets to play with the new toys first."

"Well, I think Quentin is a perfect gentleman," Sarah said with a smile. "He loaned me his entire collection of twenty and thirty millimeter rotary cannons."

"It was hardly my entire collection," Quentin said with a twinkle in his eye.

"What are you planning with those?" Tomas asked.

"I'm working on some ciphers to add some punch if we ever get a chance to use them against Swamanaban."

"Have I told you yet today that I love you?" Tomas asked with a grin.

Quentin rolled his eyes. "Must you use that ridiculous name, my dear?"

Sarah shrugged. "I hate calling her Paul's mother. Spartacus referred to her as She Who Must Not Be Named."

"That's not a direct quote," Tomas said.

"Close enough." She gave Quentin a pleading smile. "Come on. It fits, doesn't it? Take the first letters of the words in that pompous title, add some vowels for pronounceability, and it works."

"It's not great," Eirene said with a chuckle in her voice. "Perhaps that will motivate us to find her real name sooner."

Alter entered the room from the hallway, already frowning. "Names are important, especially for the Chinese."

"Then I hope she squirms every time we say it," Sarah retorted.

Alter noticed Tomas' new form and glared. "Whose life did you steal today?"

"You're just jealous I've bagged more heka this month than you," Tomas said.

"But not last night," Alter pointed out, his gaze flickering to Sarah.

She groaned to herself. He was going to insist on claiming that kiss.

"I think he looks grand," Eirene said, walking a slow circuit around Tomas. "That form will fit very well. Better than that loaner you've been running in."

"That one's off to the hunters," Tomas said.

"About time you sent my cousin's body home," Alter grumbled.

"It was his choice that put him in a place to lose it," Tomas retorted.

The two looked ready to launch again into that favorite argument. Their relationship had been strained in the stressful days leading up to the showdown in St. Peter's. Alter's decision to briefly side with his brother during the assault on the mansion hadn't helped. Only Sarah's imminent death had forced them to work together.

Tomas had loaned Alter his body in order to save her life. Since that day, they had worked better together. They might never be close friends, but Sarah held onto hope that they might at least build a cordial relationship. Well, as long as Alter stopped pestering her to dump Tomas and choose him.

He couldn't seem to grasp the fact that she was committed to Tomas. The fact that she spent so much time with Alter, sparring and training in runes didn't help. Sarah liked Alter, and in honest moments she admitted she probably would have dated him if she'd met him first.

She did have Tomas though, so that changed everything. She needed to find a way to make Alter see. Too much depended on their ability to function as a team.

Sarah changed the subject before they could sink their teeth into the argument. "Are we ready for the next test?"

Alter said, "The sequencing is finished and the machines are checked and prepped, but we still need to resolve the question of your abuse of power, Sarah."

"What are you talking about?" Eirene asked.

Sarah spoke up before Alter could put his abomination spin on it. "I created a cipher matrix to help heal those children in the terminal injuries ward."

"Drawing energy from unsuspecting souls," Alter added with a frown.

"Only a little," Sarah protested.

Eirene glanced from her to Alter as the rest of the group drew closer. "This is serious business. I think you'd better explain yourself." When Alter opened his mouth, Eirene waved him to silence. "Sarah first."

Sarah launched into her explanation, focusing on the need to help those children and the sense of responsibility she felt for the destruction resulting in their showdown with Paul. She ended by explaining how she had distributed the ciphers throughout several of the shrines of the Deliverer, stressing the fact that she had only tapped one percent of the force of the souls caught in her matrix.

Alter looked ready to explode by the time she finished, and Eirene allowed him to speak next. He reiterated the evils of drawing power from the souls of others, particularly the unwitting who had not agreed to the sacrifice. He reminded them all that their organizations, despite their differences, always agreed that such abuses should be dealt with by extreme violence.

He finished by facing Sarah, his gaze intent, but his voice soft. "Sarah, please understand the dangers of this path. You're too important to . . ." His voice trailed off, and it was clear he was going to say, "to me." He recovered quickly, though. "to our mission to take such risks without sufficient justification."

Sarah felt moved by the depth of his commitment to preserving every soul, but he shouldn't have finished the way he did.

"I was justified," she insisted, then turned to Eirene. "I won't apologize for what I did, and I accept whatever consequences I have to face, but that matrix will stand."

"I applaud your commitment, dear," Eirene said, but didn't look convinced.

Quentin gave Sarah a salute, his expression approving. "It is always the right choice to save the children."

"Alter does have a point, though," Eirene interjected.

"That matrix is not doing any harm," Tomas offered, and Sarah gave him a little smile of thanks. His mission was to eradicate those who abused their power and stole the souls of others, so it meant a lot that he was willing to see what she had done was a special case.

"And what about the next time?" Alter demanded.

Eirene said, "That's a valid point. Sarah, the policy we follow, as do the hunters, is strict and unyielding for a reason. Taking the life force of another without their consent is forbidden. It always ends in disaster."

Sarah hated to think she'd crossed a line that neither the hunters nor the enforcers would accept. She understood that to take more from unsuspecting souls was too similar to what Paul had done. They'd risked everything to stop him. But saving those children was different. It had to be.

So she said, "It seems the problem is that I didn't give people the chance to agree to my plan. I still feel people would gladly sign up to help. So let's hold a press conference to explain our rune powers and ask the world for volunteers to help me."

Eirene shook her head, chuckling. "Oh, that would be something, wouldn't it? We'd all be too busy running from angry mobs to do anything else."

They discussed the conundrum for a few more minutes, arguing the merits and dangers of Sarah's course. Despite Alter's objections, they eventually decided to leave the healing matrix in place for the time being. However, Sarah agreed not to activate any new power-gathering cipher matrix without discussing them first with the group.

"It is abomination to even consider using such ciphers again," Alter reiterated.

Eirene nodded slowly. "Perhaps. Heka invariably use stolen life force for purposes we consider evil. I believe we must take into consideration the motivation before passing final judgment."

"Besides, heka have to directly mark runes on those they steal from," Sarah pointed out.

Alter shook his head. "That only makes the danger more severe. You enjoy a greater power, but you must discipline yourself with even greater caution."

"I didn't create that cipher without reason, and I have no intention of making more unless I feel the resulting good outweighs the cost."

"All of our decisions have to weigh such benefits and costs," Quentin interjected. "Whether in the form of life force drawn into your ciphers, or in blood of enforcers that must be spilt to intercept heka conspiracies."

"Exactly," Sarah said.

Alter didn't look convinced, but Sarah felt relieved that the rest of the group supported her.

"With that question settled," Quentin said, abruptly shifting topics. "I believe now is the right time to review what we've learned from last night's raid."

"Any sign of that enchanter?" Sarah asked as Quentin gestured a waiting tech to a bank of computer screens. The woman sat at the terminal and began to type.

Quentin shook his head. "He escaped. For now." The tech pulled up an image of the Chinese enchanter, taken from Sarah's helmet-mounted video recorder. "But you captured excellent footage. From it, and from initial interrogations of the prisoners taken during the raid, we have learned much."

"We haven't gotten a lot from previous prisoners," Tomas remarked as they studied the monitors.

Quentin said, "Perhaps we were asking the wrong questions. We have still gathered next to nothing about Paul's mother. Despite the use of truth drugs and special interrogation runes, none of the prisoners have spoken."

"It's like they're prevented from talking about her," Eirene muttered.

"Could there be a rune to silence them?" Sarah asked Alter.

The prospect of a deep lore rune question seemed to distract him from his lingering anger. "It may be possible, although I don't know one."

"It's worth investigating," Sarah said.

"What have you learned about the enchanter?" Eirene prodded.

"His name is Hongwu. Harald and his team are digging through the archives for references to him," Quentin explained. "From what we've already pieced together, he's been a player for some time, and we may have clashed with him without knowing it."

Tomas frowned at the photo. "I don't recognize him, but we rarely see heka dressed like they stepped out of the Ming dynasty."

"Which one's that?" Sarah asked. Her knowledge of Chinese history was limited.

"The second-to-last dynasty. The Qing were the last, and they lost power in the early nineteen hundreds," Tomas explained.

"How can we tell Hongwu's from the Ming Dynasty?" she asked.

Eirene gestured at the monitor. "The hair. Hair for the Chinese was considered sacred for much of its history, and people considered cutting it a terrible dishonor. The Qing changed that, forcing men to shave the front of their heads, but keep the back long and braided into a queue."

Sarah had seen men with queues in several movies, especially some martial arts films. She'd always thought the look weird.

"During the Ming dynasty, they preferred the top knot, like Hongwu's wearing," Tomas said.

Alter added, "One other thing. The name Hongwu is the era name for the first emperor of the Ming dynasty."

"Era name?" Sarah asked.

He nodded. "His real name was Zhu Yuanzhang. Every emperor is also given an era name, like a title. He was known as the Hongwu Emperor."

Tomas pursed his lips in thought. "Another emperor reference. That enchanter we defeated in Suntara when Mai Luan died referred to himself as Zhu. Now we've got a Hongwu."

"Are those actual names, or assumed names?" Eirene asked.

Alter chimed in. "For Chinese, the search for a name is an important endeavor. If they assumed these names, there would be a reason, and far more meaning than if any of us did the same."

Quentin said, "Interesting. I'll have the research team include those points in the data they're compiling. He pointed to the jade pin holding the bun in place. Sarah hadn't even noticed that the end was carved into an elaborate design. "And there we see the sign of the phoenix, signifying the empress."

"What does all of this tell us?" Sarah asked.

"Nothing conclusive yet," Quentin admitted.

"But it's clear he's making a statement," Eirene said.

"And our teams of researchers will figure it out," Tomas promised.

"What about those symbols?" Sarah asked, leaning closer to a second screen where the tech had brought up a zoomed-in view of the Egyptian gold pendant Hongwu had worn.

She had wondered if it might hold some new rune, but she didn't see anything special. Engraved on the surface were some symbols, including the Eye of Ra, which looked like an eye, with an eyebrow and a couple lines extending beneath.

It usually represented protection. It was bisected by the Ankh, the Egyptian symbol of life, which was cradled by the Ka, the Egyptian symbol for soul, which looked like a pair of crab arms. All of those symbols could be incorporated into runes and greater ciphers, and may have played a part in his defensive web, but that combination was nothing unique and wouldn't justify the break-in at the museum.

Alter leaned close to her, then frowned. "He wouldn't have been hunting that."

"Unless there's more on the other side," Tomas pointed out.

Quentin shrugged. "We don't know yet. He might not have found what he was looking for, or could have pocketed something. For all we know, that pendant might be a favorite accessory."

Sarah frowned. "You said he was making a statement with how he dressed. The pendant has to be a key to the whole thing. It's too obvious not to be."

"We'll keep looking," Quentin promised, "Digging into Hongwu may be the key to learning more about Paul's elusive mother."

"How so?" Eirene asked.

"The prisoners will not speak of her, but from what they've already told us about him, it is clear he stands near the head of their organization and wields tremendous influence. Learning of him might be the key to cracking the barrier blocking information about her."

Eirene gave him an approving smile. "Keep at it. Good work."

"I think you should reach out to my father," Alter said, surprising Sarah. "If Hongwu has indeed been operating for a long time, it is likely my family has clashed with him before."

"And perhaps working together against Hongwu will open better communication channels," Eirene agreed, giving Alter a compassionate smile. She was eager to help resolve the issue of the hunters' oath to slay Alter. She was his great-grandmother after all.

Sarah shifted closer to Tomas and leaned against him. He wrapped an arm around her shoulders and she sighed, drawing comfort from his touch. She spoke softly to him as the others discussed further details of Hongwu's appearance. "I wish we could focus more on doing positive things."

"We are."

"Stopping heka is positive, but we're always fighting and destroying the enemy. I wish we could explore other aspects of our powers." She drew his gaze. "We can do so much to build and make life better."

She'd managed to slip in a few good memories in recent weeks, including many visits to historical rune warriors to train. She'd met the famous Hannibal, Khalid ibn AlWaleed, and David the Builder, all rune warriors. She'd learned from each of them. Khalid had been particularly skilled in cipher shields and she'd advanced tremendously in those skills.

But she had felt most drawn to David. She'd loved the fact that he'd not only used his ciphers to strengthen his armies and win seemingly impossible battles. He'd also worked ciphers into the walls of his famous Gelati Academy to foster learning. His extensive cipher matrix had inspired her to develop her much simpler one for the children.

Tomas said, "Defeating Paul's mother makes life better. We have to find her and remove her before she can recover and regroup from Paul's defeat."

She suppressed a sense of irritation that so much of their time and effort was consumed by the difficult duty that they alone could fulfill. "I know, but I can still wish, can't I?"

"We'll get some quiet time soon. For now, let's focus on finding her."

Eirene overheard the last comment. "Since we haven't found her in the real world yet, I think it's time we hunt for her again in the memoryscape."

Sarah would never argue returning to the memoryscape, and she thought of that treasure hunt at Ksiaz Castle they'd recently enjoyed as a rare diversion. Still, their chances of surviving an initial encounter with the deadly cui dashi were greater there.

So she said, "My ciphers are ready, and the Tenth are on-line with their runes to help with the drain."

"Then let's hunt," Eirene said, her eyes glittering with anticipation.

"Is Gregorios joining us today?" Sarah asked.

"He should be finishing a call in a few minutes. He's planning on being there," Eirene said.

Sarah grinned. Having Gregorios along would bolster her confidence. Eirene was deadly and devious, but she couldn't quite match Gregorios for sheer bull-headedness. "Good. We should be able to run the full spread today."

Quentin said, "I'll inform operations. All stations will be ready."

Sarah squeezed Tomas one last time. "Let's hope they have a reason to be."

"We'll make it work this time," Tomas assured her. "Let's go hunting."

10

THE JUMP ROOM was located in one of five separate basements scattered underneath the sprawling mansion estate. Unlike the stainless-steel clad vault where they had kept the machines in the Suntara basements, this room had been a spare armory. The stacks of heavy weapons cases and boxed ammunition felt right to Sarah. The machines were their greatest weapon against the cui dashi.

The three machines stood in the center of the long, columned room, illuminated by powerful standing lights that had been brought in for that purpose. Six reclining chairs ringed the machines, and heavy helmets rested on each seat. Thick clusters of wires connected the helmets to the machines, but it was their faceplates that always drew Sarah's gaze.

They looked roughly like an optometrist phoropter, with myriad knobs, dials, and lenses. Unlike the benign devices used to check prescriptions, the inner edge of those faceplates included a series of protrusions that dug into the face around the eyes and along the jawline. Those were soul points, and helped link the wearers of the helmet to the memoryscape.

Only the facetakers' unique nevra cores could power the

machines, coupled with a whole bunch of unique runes. Another facetaker had to don the primary helmet. Their memories would form the memoryscape within which the rest of the team would be drawn.

The main bodies of the machines were squat, square boxes encased in shining steel, with small monitors and keyboards attached to one side. Alter had led the effort to modify the machines since the final battle with Paul. He had devised additional runes to grant greater control to the primary traveler and to add multiple redundant escape solutions.

Sarah approached the first one, which she still thought of as the Franken-machine, despite a new casing. It had been rebuilt after an explosion in the Suntara council chamber, and the helmets still bore scorch marks.

"They're daisy-chained together finally?"

"The connection looks strong," Alter said, moving to the second, shinier machine, stenciled with the name *Sotrun*. He typed a series of commands.

"What will that really do?" Tomas asked. He'd spent most of his time in recent weeks overseeing the hunt for heka operatives, or helping work the public relations effort.

Sarah said, "We don't know much about Swamanaban, but we know she's exceptionally powerful."

Alter frowned. "I still don't understand why she didn't appear in the square and help Paul. That would've probably tipped the balance in his favor."

"We'll ask her about it when we track her down," Sarah promised.

Tomas grinned. "Let's hope we get a shot at her today."

Eirene spoke up. "We've swept the last two thousand years, and I've felt another mind several times, but they've been subtle. Whatever Swamanaban is searching for in there, she doesn't want us knowing about it."

Alter's frown deepened. "I don't know how she's managed to block us from joining her memories. Let's see how my latest rune sequencing can lock onto even non-shared memories."

The door opened and Gregorios entered, dressed in a custom pinstripe suit, with his coat thrown over one shoulder. He looked a bit haggard. Sarah wasn't surprised. He'd been working long hours, deflecting public scrutiny from the details of the facetakers while pretending to cooperate wholeheartedly with dozens of international inquiries.

"Tell me how that works," he said to Alter after sharing a kiss with Eirene.

Alter hesitated, and Sarah wondered what he thought of his great-grandmother kissing the most hated facetaker demon. He finally said, "Before I get into that, can you tell me if my brother's body will be returned to my father along with those of the other hunters?"

"I'm keeping that suit for now," Gregorios said.

"It's not yours to keep," Alter protested with a glare.

Gregorios met his gaze, unfazed. "I haven't decided yet. I gave it back to your family once, and look what happened. I plan to discuss it with Melek soon."

Hopefully he and Melek could work out their differences. The hunters' meddling had nearly ruined efforts to stop Paul. If relations between the groups could be salvaged, then maybe Gregorios or Eirene could finally help intervene in Alter's behalf.

Sarah hoped Alter learned to think beyond his family's some-times-ridiculous prejudices. Sure, he was cui dashi, but he'd played a key role in defeating Paul and in saving Sarah's life. That should be enough for his family to get past the whole purification through martyrdom response.

"Tell them about how you figured all this out," Sarah told Alter, gesturing at the nearest helmet. The rest of the group wouldn't appreciate the subtle artistry that Alter leveraged in his rune work. She might possess a more powerful rune gift, but he was a master in his sphere. "Just the high-level overview."

Alter's love for runes and the challenge of working on the machines had helped him stay focused. He pointed to the third machine, the one they had captured from Spartacus. "Based on unique runes we found there, we've developed a sequence that should lock onto any active nevron in the memoryscape and link our memory stream to it. So even if you don't share the memory, you should now be able to merge your historical thread into theirs."

"Won't that leave us at a disadvantage?" Eirene asked.

"Probably. At least for the first few seconds. Once your memory stream syncs, you should be able to influence it like any other histor-ical moment."

"Swamanaban will still hold the advantage," Gregorios warned, and Sarah grinned when he used the nickname she'd come up with. "I've never seen anyone move like that woman. She's old, she's strong, and I guarantee she's siphoned many souls."

The nevra siphon was a unique ability the cui dashi enjoyed over all other types of soul powers. When they removed another's soul-mask, they siphoned a fraction of the force from that soul into their own, growing permanently stronger. Eirene had been working with Alter to strengthen his fledgling powers.

Alter replied, "We've factored that disparity into our calculations. That's why we've chained the machines together. Previously, they worked independently, and Paul held the advantage. Now the active nevron of all of us who participate in the memory, including those powering the machines, will link together. Whoever takes the driver seat in the first machine will wield that combined force."

"That sounds like fun," Gregorios said eagerly.

"I'll tell you all about it afterward," Eirene assured him with a grin as she snatched up the primary helmet on the first machine.

Gregorios made a gracious bow. "Ladies first."

Sarah appreciated their levity about what could become a deadly encounter. "If we do find her in there, we'll need to move fast to lock her down."

"I wish I was going in with you," Tomas said.

"No blowing up priceless artifacts for you," Sarah teased. "If we can keep her pinned in the memory, I'll activate a cipher that should provide a pingback loop to her physical location."

She tapped his bicep where she'd inscribed two other temporary runes with a marker prior to leaving the body bank. "It's linked to you. You'll feel the direction. Your strike team can take her out while she's sleeping."

"How accurate is that directional impulse?" Quentin asked.

Tomas flexed for Sarah and said, "We tested it during the last memory journey. I followed the prompting and it led me to the exact pillar she'd marked downtown."

"If we can hold her, you destroy her," Sarah told him.

"We'll bring the big guns," Tomas assured her.

"I wish I was done with those new ciphers on the Vulcan," Sarah said.

"Next time."

"What if she wakes up first?" Eirene asked, going right for one of the worst-case scenarios.

"I'll break the link." Sarah gripped Tomas' hands. "If you feel the direction fade off, no matter how close you are, run."

From Gregorios' accounts of the woman's superhuman speed, she could destroy even Tomas' enhanced strike team before they could bring her down. That was why they were hunting her aggressively through memories instead of in the modern day. With the runes they brought to bear, they might gain an advantage in the memoryscape they lacked in real life.

"You're ignoring the fact that she could just kill you all," Tomas protested.

"We should be able to hold our own in there," Sarah insisted.

"Plus, we've built in a triple redundant escape sequence," Alter added. "Even if she wrests control over the memory, we should be able to escape."

Gregorios grunted. "I'm not planning on escaping. We need to finish this. That's why Sarah marked the enforcers with her ciphers."

"I can draw up to twenty percent of their strength," Sarah confirmed.

She had added a series of marks to the company tattoos that all of the enforcers already wore, linking them into custom rune webs she could incorporate into her battle ciphers. She could draw upon all the enforcers at once, or select only specific companies.

She'd tested the sequencing with half of the enforcers at only five percent power, and the influx of strength had been a wild rush. That had helped give her the idea of using just one percent from more people to help those children.

The strength she could borrow from the enforcers might pale against the awesome power she'd unleashed through the master runes, but it was enough to temporarily triple her already-enhanced strength. In the memoryscape she'd easily lifted a tank off the ground and thrown it through a reinforced-concrete wall.

Sarah wasn't a fool, though. She didn't know if the cui dashi had access to other master runes, or if she had another expansive rune web at her disposal like the one Tomas' team had disabled on Palatine Hill.

While placing the ciphers to help the children, Sarah had secretly spread additional ciphers around the city. She'd placed some in major tourist destinations, including the Sistine Chapel, and had placed more at the various shrines to the Sword of the Deliverer.

She had linked all of those force-gathering runes into a cipher that acted like a remote charging station. She'd tested it and fine-tuned it until it seemed stable.

Like a huge, rechargeable battery, it pulled just a fraction of one percent of the soul force of people passing the various runes. Such a tiny drain wouldn't be noticed by any but the most self-aware, and once people passed out of range, their individual force would begin to slowly drain out of the pool.

The cipher was still increasing in overall power, but she suspected it would max out at some point and then remain roughly stable unless she added additional charging locations.

One of the reasons she had activated the cipher to help heal those children was to test the team's reaction. She hadn't expected them to find out about it so quickly, but had planned to reveal the secret to them after word began to spread of miraculous healings. With how strenuously they had all objected, she hadn't mentioned her broader power-charging cipher, and she wouldn't until after they defeated Swamanaban.

She would do whatever it took to survive and make sure her friends survived the encounter with that cui dashi, although she hoped she wouldn't need that cipher battery. Uneasiness plagued her after the confrontation about her web helping the children.

Was she making a mistake? Were her actions evil? Could she indeed slip like Paul had?

She didn't think so, and she was still willing to take the risk to ensure no more of her friends died. She would deactivate the ciphers after they won. No one needed to know about them unless things went horribly wrong. At that point, anything they decided to do to her would be better than the alternative they'd get from the cui dashi.

She hated keeping secrets, but she didn't feel like she had a choice. They couldn't afford to leave Paul's mother unchallenged. If they failed, the world would never be able to stop her from gaining enough master runes to rise as a false god like Paul had nearly done.

"Can you tap any of those master runes?" Tomas asked.

Sarah shook her head. "I've tried incorporating pieces of each of them into ciphers, but they wouldn't activate."

"I've been thinking of that," Alter said. "It's possible those master runes are still tied up in the greater cipher you formed in the square. Recreating that cipher might shift control from your . . ."

He trailed off, clearly hesitant to talk about her melted body.

"I can't risk it," Sarah said with a shudder. That cipher was too powerful. Dying once had been bad enough. She didn't want to go through that again.

Eirene gave Sarah an encouraging smile. "Stick to the training and we'll win the day. Sarah, you've developed the best control over shielding and containment ciphers I've ever seen. That should slow her enough for us to have a chance."

Gregorios clapped his hands together once. "All right. Let's get to it. Eirene's in the lead chair with Alter. I've got the second with Sarah."

Harriett and Francesca entered. Since Harriett's previous body had been killed fighting Paul, the sisters had both taken new bodies. They preferred to start new lives at the same time. Harriett looked determined, but tired. She'd taken the reins of Yurak International after Bastien's death, and the strain was showing.

She still brought along a tray of fresh-baked muffins and moved through the room, offering her famous goodies to everyone. If anything, she cooked better in her new life.

"I've got the third chair," Francesca said, waving to Sarah.

Eirene said, "I'm sorry, dear. We're short one nevra core. The rest of the council is all busy on assignment, and I need you and your sister powering the machines."

"Besides, you don't have a passenger," Gregorios added.

"Oh, I could give Quentin a ride," Francesca said, slipping an arm through his. "You've got the stamina for it, don't you old man?"

"Best offer I've had all day," he said, ice-blue eyes twinkling.

"More like the best offer you've had in years," she teased.

"As always, you make me feel forty again. I look forward to accompanying you on a future venture," he said, making a gallant bow over her hand.

"Stay focused," Gregorios said. "We don't even know if this will work."

The group settled into the chairs and Francesca helped Sarah position her helmet.

"Be careful in there," Francesca said, her tone serious again.

"It'll be all right," Sarah assured her. Then she called to Eirene. "Let's go visit Joan of Arc again."

Eirene nodded. "That's a great idea. I haven't seen her in ages."

"I hate the hundred years war," Gregorios muttered.

The machines activated and the faceplate heated against Sarah's skin as Francesca's nevron pulsed through the cold steel. The heat intensified and Sarah tried to breathe slowly against the uncomfortable faceplate.

Then her mind was swept away.

She awoke in bright sunlight. With her first glance, she realized they weren't in medieval France.

They were in China.

11

I don't need a friend who changes when I change, who nods when I nod, and who begins their next life on the same day; my shadow does that much better.

~PLUTARCH

"YOU MISSED, DEARHEART," Gregorios chuckled.

"I've never been here before," Eirene said as they stared out at an ancient Chinese city from the top of a tall tower.

"What is this place?" Sarah asked softly. She loved memory walking, although the feeling of wonder she usually enjoyed when visiting a new place was tempered by uneasiness to know this was not Eirene's memory.

The platform where they stood was about fifty feet in diameter, with a central pole extending higher, capped with a huge golden pineapple. Two dozen Chinese men, dressed in ancient robes were clustered nearby, looking out over a nearby river.

Sarah's eye was drawn to the one in the center, who towered over the others, a solid seven feet tall. She had always thought Chinese were short, but this guy's parents hadn't gotten the message. None of them appeared to notice the memory hunters, so they weren't memory walkers.

"I believe Alter's new runes worked," Gregorios said, looking satisfied.

Sarah glanced over the side of the building, and the sight took her breath away. They stood on a beautiful pagoda tower, nine stories tall, with each story flaring with the distinctive Chinese curved eaves.

It was made of gleaming, white porcelain bricks, but glazes and stoneware formed patterns of green and yellow. She glimpsed animals, flowers, and wide landscape designs. The entire structure sparkled in the bright morning light, standing in the center of a square courtyard.

"This is the famous Porcelain Tower of Nanjing," Alter exclaimed, pacing around the edge, his expression one of wonder. He pointed toward the towering fellow at the front of the cluster of Chinese officials and added, "That's Zheng He."

"How do you know?" Sarah asked.

"Because I did a thesis paper on the ancient Chinese treasure . . ." His voice faded off as he followed the gaze of the nearby Chinese. "I don't believe it."

Sarah looked out over the city. The high pagoda where they stood towered over all nearby structures, although rolling hills did block some of the views to the south and east. A river ran past, about a quarter mile to the north, and emptied into a much larger river that flowed northeast

She would have loved drinking in the view of the cute little Chinese homes and the junks plying the river, but her gaze was drawn to a cluster of the biggest sailing ships she'd ever seen.

"When did Chinese build ships like that?" she asked as they all moved to the western edge of the tower, not far from the Chinese officials.

Dozens of gigantic ships were moored along the shore or inside a long series of shipyard docks that consumed more than a mile of riverbank. Even though the huge sails on each of their nine staggered masts were all furled, the ships towered over the shore.

"That is part of the Chinese treasure fleet," Alter said excitedly.

Even Gregorios looked impressed. "I've heard of them. Sailed around half the world several decades before Columbus."

"Maybe farther," Alter said. "They were built in 1405. The fleet was made up of hundreds of ships and made seven voyages that ranged all across Asia and as far as Africa. Some people claim they might have reached the Americas."

That boggled the mind. Sarah asked, "Why haven't I heard of them? If the Chinese had that much naval force, how did the British become the world power?"

"Because of what we're witnessing today," Alter said, pointing.

The farthest ship, locked into the dockyard, burst into raging fire. It happened so fast, they had to have used gunpowder or some other type of accelerant. Within seconds, every other ship in the dockyards burst into flames in turn.

"What are they doing?" Sarah asked, shocked by the sight of those beautiful ships getting torched.

"They're destroying the fleet," Alter said, his expression solemn. "The Yongle Emperor, Zhu Di, had supported the fleet, but his son, the Xuande Emperor was swayed by court officials to oppose the fleet. He ordered it destroyed."

"Why would they do that?" Sarah couldn't tear her eyes away from the sight of the fast-burning ships. She wished Tomas was with them. She wanted to hold his hand. This didn't make any sense.

Alter scowled and muttered, "Politics. As usual."

He gestured toward Zheng He, who watched the burning ships with stoic calm. "Zheng He was a eunuch. In the days of the Yongle Emperor, the eunuchs wielded tremendous influence. But their primary political opponents were the Confucius scholar-bureaucrats, and they gained the ear of the Xuande Emperor. They were vested in established order, and Zheng He didn't fit with their vision. He was more a Napoleon-type admiral. So they burned the fleet and sidelined him."

Gregorios turned away from the sight of the fast-burning ships toward Alter. "That's all fascinating, but where's Swamanaban?"

Eirene added, "This is her memory. She has to be here somewhere."

Alter shrugged. "This was a major event. This marked the shift of Chinese foreign policy to pull back from world exploration and international affairs. They turned inward, banned most foreign trade, and focused on becoming self-sufficient and walling off the rest of the world."

"Maybe it gives us a clue into the identity of our mystery woman," Eirene said thoughtfully.

Gregorios said, "Let's find her first. Once she's secure, you can interrogate her while Tomas closes in for the kill."

"Fair enough."

Sarah closed her eyes and pressed her hand against the low wall at the outer edge of the platform. She could feel the flow of history against her fingers, stronger than ever before. Ever since she'd started her second life, she'd felt whispers of history like a gentle breeze against her skin when they journeyed through time. She hadn't figured out yet how it worked, but she wasn't complaining. At that moment it was more like a solid wind.

"What is it?" Eirene asked.

"This memory is strong. It's important."

Sarah willed a brush and inkwell into her hands, grateful that writing materials were handy in ancient China. She didn't want to start breaking with the integrity of the moment yet. Dealing with the nightmares that slipped through the cracks was a nuisance, but the ripple effects might warn the cui dashi they'd arrived. With quick, sure movements, she marked a cipher on her arms.

"The pingback is active. As soon as we get a lock on Swamanaban, I'll add the last component to start the trace."

"Any ideas where to look?"

"Actually, yes."

Sarah pointed at the largest of the ships, riding at anchor in the gentle current in the center of the mighty river. It was about four hundred and fifty feet long, and had not yet joined the conflagration. "She's on the command ship."

The runes she had just engraved granted her sensitivity to any active nevra core nearby. Gregorios', Eirene's, and Alter's pulsed like strong heartbeats, and she could feel the distant pulsing of the women in the real world running the machines, whose nevron kept the dream stable.

One other active nevra core called to her from the distant ship, like a drumbeat of a distant army. It was at the outer range of her senses, but now that she'd identified it, she wouldn't lose it again.

She marked an additional cipher onto her arm and activated it, linking it to that powerful nevron. The pingback was now locked on.

Gregorios grinned, but his eyes turned hard, his expression predatory. "Let's go pay her a visit."

12

Jie is overthrown and my dynasty rises from the ashes of his inferior runes. I will rule through endless lives. To honor this, my first life, I will order my people to reverence their ancestors. In this, they will reverence me, the first and permanent ancestor of this dynasty.

~TANG OF SHANG, FACETAKER, FIRST RULER OF THE
SHANG DYNASTY, 1600 B.C.

TOMAS TAPPED his tactical mic to activate it. His voice rang with excitement as he rushed from the jump room, leaving Sarah and the others in their softly glowing helmets.

"Command, this is Enforcer One. We have an alpha-level event. Priority scramble."

"Roger, Enforcer One." It was his second in command, the giant Maori enforcer Anaru who took the call in the command central. "Scrambling all units with Quentin's new toys."

"Bring it all," Tomas ordered as he sprinted for the mansion's northern exit and the helicopter pad. "I've got a rough fix southwest of here."

"So it could be anywhere in the city," Anaru said.

"We'll know soon enough. I'll meet you at the chopper."

As units scattered all around the city responded to the order, Tomas prayed they could reach the cui dashi lair in time.

Despite Sarah's warning, he didn't plan to retreat.

❋

"How many steps are in this place?" Sarah asked as they rushed down the long, winding central stair of the Porcelain Tower.

"One hundred and eighty-four," Alter answered immediately, still sounding thrilled that they'd landed in that memory.

"This isn't vacation," Gregorios cautioned. "We're here, but we don't know if she's sensed us and is laying a trap. Even if we catch her by surprise, she's dangerous."

"We can take her." Alter sounded cocky again, something Sarah had hoped he'd outgrown.

"Tell us about the ship she's on," Eirene said.

Alter was happy to talk about it. "Looked like the command ship. As long as four and a half soccer fields. Built with thirteen watertight sections in the hold to help prevent sinking."

"Armaments?" Gregorios asked as they exited the tower and followed the road toward the distant river.

"Shouldn't we just head for the roofs?" Sarah asked. She loved leaping across the rooftops in memoryscapes. It was one of her favorite parts of the experience.

Gregorios shook his head. "Take your time. She isn't running yet, so give Tomas time to get his forces into position."

Eirene added, "I haven't felt her fighting for control, although I haven't tried to change anything yet."

"Don't," Gregorios advised. "If this is an important memory for her, she might have let herself get caught up in the moment."

"We might have to get creative to reach that ship," Alter said.

"That's why we're taking our time now," Gregorios said.

Alter added, "Those ships carried thousands of sailors, passengers, and soldiers."

"She doesn't need local muscle," Gregorios said.

Eirene said, "Doesn't hurt to be ready to clear the decks. Enough of them can still slow us down."

"The ships carried bronze cannons, but they were considered trading ships more than warships," Alter added.

"Gunpowder might come in handy," Gregorios said with a smile.

"And we won't need to break the integrity of the memory to get it," Eirene agreed.

Gregorios glanced at Sarah. "All right. Let's discuss the plan."

"If we can get close enough, I just need you to keep her distracted for a few seconds." She felt a growing sense of nervous excitement as they approached their first confrontation with the cui dashi.

"A few seconds around that woman can be painful," Gregorios said with a grimace.

Eirene offered, "Try talking with her. You know, bluff. You're good at that."

Sarah summoned a cloth satchel like ones she saw locals carrying. She filled the inside with wooden disks, eight inches in diameter. With her brush and ink, she began drawing runes she would incorporate into activated battle ciphers once they reached the ship.

Her nervousness grew as fast as her excitement. They'd planned for this moment and she was confident in her runes, but this was a cui dashi they were facing. Each time she'd thought she'd outsmarted Paul, he had turned the tables on her. That had cost her a lot of pain, since his preferred response was stabbing her in the stomach with that infernal Chinese sword.

Hopefully they wouldn't get introduced to this new cui dashi's favorite torture.

"All units, this is Enforcer One." Tomas spoke into the integrated headset in the helicopter's copilot seat as they sped across open countryside northwest of Rome. "Get on the Four-Ninety-Three. The target is located outside of the city."

A chorus of acknowledgments confirmed his men were en route. A lair outside of the city was a mixed blessing. They'd probably have more opportunity to destroy the cui dashi without police or military intervention, and bystanders would be easier to protect. Depending on where the rune took them, any enemy scouts would likely spot them sooner, though.

Following the rune was a strange experience. It had gone cool against his skin, like an attached ice pack. The cold had shifted, pooling in the direction he needed to travel. It wasn't exactly a GPS, but all he needed was a location.

His team, armed with heavy weapons and Quentin's latest inventions, would take down the threat. He'd led these men into battle through several lifetimes and he trusted the current corps as much as he had any of their forefathers.

A few minutes later, he cursed softly as he gazed out at the wide, blue expanse of Lago di Bracciano, the eighth largest lake in Italy. On the southwest shore stood the iconic structure of the Castello Odescalchi. Built in the fifteenth century, the well-preserved castle was a popular tourist attraction.

Tomas ordered the pilot to circle the castle at a distance of five miles. His initial hope that its location on their path was coincidence faded as they got closer.

Finally, he grimaced. "That's it. She's somewhere in the castle."

"That's not good, sir," the pilot said. "We can't wreck another historical site."

They'd skated around the facts of their recent battle atop the Palatine Hill. The destruction of St. Peter's Square had trumped all other concerns. Attacking another major historical and tourist site would never get overlooked again.

Some days, saving the world from hidden evil was a miserable job.

But it was his job. So he ordered the pilot, "Set down south of the village. We'll approach by truck and figure out exactly where they're hiding."

This was going to get ugly.

Sarah stood with the others on a dock on the banks of the wide Yangtze River. Huge ships burned all down the length of the extensive shipyards to their left. From what she'd gathered, the Chinese planned to move more ships into the basins of the shipyard as soon as the first wave of ships finished burning.

Despite the lack of modern technology, the local engineers had managed to drain much of the water out of the basins, ensuring the ships would burn down to the keel line. Destroying the huge fleet would take days.

They were planning to steal an ornate rowboat when Eirene grabbed Gregorios' shoulder. "I think she knows we're here. I just felt a tug on the memoryscape."

He rubbed his hands together. "Time to take off the silk gloves."

"But what if Tomas isn't in position yet?" Sarah asked nervously.

"All the more reason. If this woman escapes now, Tomas might end up walking into a massacre."

"You want me to add a motor to that rowboat?" Eirene asked.

"Nothing so quaint," Gregorios said with a grin. "Let's make a splash."

He jumped off the end of the pier.

He didn't actually splash.

The water bowed under his weight, but he didn't break the surface. Instead, he started running across the surface of the river.

"I should have thought of that," Eirene said with a smile, then jumped after him.

"Wait for me," Alter shouted and leaped to follow.

He must have counted on Eirene to manage the water for him, because he hit with a splash and disappeared under the surface. He came up sputtering, but the water rippled around him and lifted him to his feet. With a glare toward Gregorios' rapidly receding figure, he took off running.

Sarah was about to leap after them when she got a better idea. She ripped a rough plank off the dock and jumped down onto the water with it. A second of concentration added a mast and sail.

The minor tweaks with the memory stream barely stirred the fabric of the memoryscape, allowing only a belligerent spider the size of a terrier into the world. Sarah hated spiders and squashed it with her board.

The wind was already blowing, but a little focused tweaking intensified it and shifted it in the right direction. She twisted the sail into the correct angle and shot across the glassy surface, quickly accelerating to more than twenty knots.

She shot past Alter a moment later and he called, "What, no dune buggy?"

"Are you kidding? That would be crazy." He had no sense of style.

When she caught up with Eirene, the facetaker leaped onto the back of the board and balanced there, grinning. They caught up with Gregorios about fifty yards from the huge ship.

"We've got a welcoming committee." He stopped running, but continued sliding along the surface next to them. Sarah wasn't sure how he managed it, but didn't feel any adverse effects on the integrity of the memory. Showoff.

A tall, slender Chinese woman stood amidships of the giant treasure ship, wearing an elegant, red silk dress of traditional Chinese cut. She surveyed the conflagration with a regal tilt to her chin and a slightly disapproving frown. She looked like a queen overseeing an onerous exhibition, and although both the forecastle and aftcastle of the ship loomed to either side of her, she radiated such an aura of power, she seemed to stand above the massive ship.

Swamanaban was every bit as intimidating as Sarah had expected. She felt ripples of power emanating from the slender figure, and icy fear slithered up her spine.

Gregorios confirmed her fears. "That's her. No baby this time."

Sarah took a deep breath to steady her nerves. "Keep her distracted. I need to get on that ship."

"Your intrusion is most unwelcome." The cui dashi didn't shout, but her voice rang across the waves like she'd used a bullhorn.

She flicked a hand, and twelve hinged doors crashed open along the near side of the ship. They concealed gun ports that held the wide muzzles of cast bronze cannons.

Gregorios called, "That's a bit preemptive. We're supposed to threaten and insult each other for a while first."

The cannons roared, belching fire and heavy iron balls big enough to rip a person in half. The sound thundered across the waves, and black smoke billowed out of the holes in a concealing cloud. The huge vessel barely rocked under the recoil of the big guns.

Sarah leaned far over, turning her sailboard sharply to take her out of the trajectory of the guns. Two of the projectiles passed close enough that she felt them tear through the air near her head.

Eirene vaulted off the sailboard, flying right over the incoming cannonballs. She hit the water in a graceful glide, and an ornately carved Chinese hand cannon appeared in her hands. The long tube of copper and wood was carved into the shape of a crouching dragon, and she fired at the cui dashi.

Gregorios continued sliding across the top of the water, but a giant baseball bat appeared in his hands. He swung it and connected with two incoming cannonballs. It sounded like a hundred wooden bats hitting home runs at the same time.

Instead of shattering his bat, he knocked the cannonballs back at the ship. They struck the wooden hull and cracked the outer beams.

Eirene's shot looked good, but if the bullet struck Swamanaban, the woman gave no indication of it. Eirene's voice drifted across the waves to Sarah as the echoes of the cannon blasts faded. "How did you do that, Greg? That broke at least a couple laws of physics."

Sarah glanced back as Gregorios shrugged. "You know I love messing with your dreams."

Then he called up to the cui dashi, who Sarah decided to call Red instead of the ridiculously pompous Swamanaban. "Give me one good reason why I shouldn't burn this ship to the waterline. Oh, wait, you're already planning to do that."

Red sounded a bit put out as she replied, "I had not yet chosen a time to wrest away your nevra core, but perhaps today is appropriate."

Alter slid to a halt behind Gregorios, and a heavy bronze cannon erupted out of the waters at his feet, the wick somehow already burning.

"Permission to come aboard and remove your head," Alter cried.

The cannon fired, and the dark cloud of its smoke obscured Alter. The ball barely missed Red, but struck one of the central masts, cracking it. It toppled into the next mast amid a squeal of grinding timbers and snapping lines.

Sarah lost sight of them as she circled the massive bow that towered like a four-story building above her. She leaped off her sailboard and soared fifty feet into the air, planning to land on the polished wood decking.

Her fear returned in a burst as she soared over the polished wooden rail and gained a panoramic view of the immense, open deck.

Red hadn't been distracted. She was already leaping up to the high aftcastle deck toward Sarah, a short-bladed Chinese sword in her hand.

13

He who overcomes others is strong; he who overcomes himself is mighty.

~LAOZI

SARAH RAISED a clenched fist as she fell toward the waiting, deadly cui dashi. The move triggered a cipher that unleashed a concentrated, invisible blow, like a dozen sledgehammers wielded by the mighty Anaru. The blow struck Red in the sternum and drove her back a couple of steps.

She might regenerate instantly, have nearly impenetrable skin, and move with blinding speed, but she was still a slightly-built woman, and physics still applied. Some of the time.

That much pressure, designed to push more than to penetrate, could not be ignored. Sarah had developed the cipher and practiced hundreds of times over the past couple of weeks until she could trigger it without even having to think about it. All she needed was to raise that clenching fist.

Red looked immensely annoyed. Hopefully she was about to get really frustrated by what came next.

Sarah barely cleared the rail and landed on the deck, already activating her next cipher. She threw the cipher block she'd engraved it on just as Red resumed her charge. The binding rune flared with the blue-white light.

Red tried to slice it out of the air.

Bad move.

As soon as her blade touched the block, the cipher blazed even brighter, intense white light pouring over the surprised cui dashi like a living waterfall.

Sarah quickly retreated from the deadly woman. Red tried to chase her, but moved as if walking through molasses. It was chilling to see that she could move at all. That rune had been designed to stop a charging elephant.

The rest of the team leaped aboard and Sarah cried, "Eirene, take control!"

She felt the memoryscape lurch as Eirene launched a mental assault against Red's control. Reinforced by the daisy-chained nevra cores of all of the involved facetakers, hopefully she possessed the strength to win.

Sarah didn't wait to find out. She grabbed three more rune blocks from her satchel and activated them. She slid two of them across the deck to either side of the slowly advancing cui dashi. She placed the third on the deck in front of her to complete a cipher triangle.

Their gazes locked, and Red's look of absolute confidence, mingled with a hint of annoyance, terrified Sarah, but also angered her. She'd seen far too much of that arrogant self-confidence in Paul.

As the cipher came to life, it drained a lot of energy from the well of strength in Sarah's soul. Enough remained that she could activate several more ciphers, if she needed them.

"I'm through running from your psycho family," Sarah declared.

Amber lights like lasers snapped into place between the blocks, then rose in glimmering walls eight feet high. Red reached the laser wall, already moving faster than she had a second before. She tried driving her blade through, and a sunburst of sparks erupted at the point of contact. The seemingly fragile wall held. For now.

Sarah felt a rush of satisfaction. Her training with historical rune warriors, coupled with intense practice were paying off. She could snap a defensive wall into place with a thought, a single flick of a finger, and a minute amount of her rounon strength.

Alter leaped up a nearby mast and perched on the crossbeam. A three-barreled heavy machine gun appeared in his hand, connected to a large ammo box by a chain of glittering ammo.

"Get back, Sarah," he shouted.

Sarah retreated as he opened fire. The Gatling-style gun, known as the Gecal 50, fired a blistering stream of fifty-caliber rounds through the open top of Red's prison. The bullets shredded the woman's clothes as armor piercing, incendiary, and explosive rounds shook the walls of the prison with waves of fire and lead.

Gregorios had mentioned that standard rifle rounds had only bounced off the deadly woman the time she had disabled his entire strike force in about a second. Sarah had expected the force of dozens of rounds per second would prove effective, but if that barrage broke her smooth, olive skin before Red healed herself, Sarah couldn't see it.

Either she was that enhanced, or she had support staff reinforcing her sleeping body with the power of additional souls.

The bullets did enrage her, and she shrieked with fury, slashing at the restraining wall.

The recoil from the weapon drove Alter back against the mast, but he kept the spinning barrels on target. Sarah had used a similar weapon in a memoryscape against Paul with fantastic effect, and wielding that heavy weapon from the hip had been a unique rush. Unfortunately, Red seemed to be taking less damage.

Alter was holding her in place, though. That was the most important thing. It hopefully granted Eirene greater leverage over the memoryscape too.

Sarah turned to check if Gregorios was ready to fire with the far more powerful .950 caliber rifle. It used a shell only a bit smaller than a twenty millimeter cannon.

He was not.

Gregorios had dropped to one knee beside Eirene, his head bowed in concentration. Eirene was leaning against a mast, her face ashen, fear in her eyes. A slimy, rotten-brown tentacle, as thick around as Sarah's waist was creeping up over the side of the ship and slithering across the deck toward the two facetakers.

The more they broke with the integrity of the memory, the bigger the nightmares that crept in through the cracks.

A Roman gladius sword appeared in Gregorios' hand and, as the tentacle snatched for Eirene, he slashed it in half, growling, "Do you mind?"

At his momentary distraction, which must have reduced the amount of nevron he was sharing with his wife, she groaned again. The ethereal flow of the memory stream trickling past Sarah's skin shuddered, then stopped, like a paused movie.

Sarah's nervous excitement faded under a wave of simple fear.

They were losing.

Time for containment measures. She reached for another rune

block to seal the prison and enhance its barrier. The best she could hope for now was to hold the deadly woman long enough for Tomas to find and destroy her.

Could they manage even that much? The woman was so strong! Containing her might not be enough. They needed . . .

Sarah paused, her glowing finger poised over the block, suddenly realizing what more she could do. Hope flared bright again. All she needed was three seconds.

Red didn't wait. Apparently bored with the torrential rain of fiery destruction beating uselessly against her, she leaped up, right through the blizzard of lead and out of the prison.

She blurred across the deck, snatched Gregorios in one hand, and threw him at Alter. Gregorios struck true, knocking both men off the crossbeam.

Before Sarah could activate her new cipher, Red leaped across to her and grabbed her by the throat in a crushing grip that allowed only a whisper of air into her lungs. Sarah beat against her hands, but it was like hitting living steel.

The cui dashi stood a little taller than Sarah, and her eyes blazed with a deeper shade of purple than any other active nevron Sarah had ever seen. "You've grown strong, warrior."

Red now spoke with no Chinese accent at all. She sounded like an English queen. "You proved the strength of your soul against my son, but I am disappointed by your interruption today."

Sarah tried to curse at her, but only inarticulate gurgles escaped her nearly-sealed throat. Panic raged through her, making it hard to focus as she tried to form a cipher in her mind.

"What do you call yourself now?" Red asked, loosening her hold enough for a delicious trickle of air to pass and for Sarah to whisper.

"I'm Sarah." The question made no sense, but it gave her a chance to breathe, so she was happy to talk.

Red looked disgusted by the answer, so Sarah asked, "And what should we call you?"

The woman made a dismissive gesture, then continued as if they were speaking at a social gathering and not standing upon a giant, ancient Chinese ship, with her grip a fraction away from crushing Sarah's life. "And what truths have you learned about history?"

That one was easy. "The books are wrong."

Red looked disappointed. "You still don't understand. Pity."

"Don't understand what?"

Red shook her hard enough to set her limbs dancing wildly. "You are a foolish, ignorant girl. You associate with descendants of a corrupt regime, and your unprovoked attack has interrupted a memory that could have become cherished. Your ill-mannered warmongering must be punished.

The shaking rattled Sarah and terrified her. With a flick of her wrist, Red could rip her head off, but why torture her with that browbeating?

She finalized a new cipher. Making a tiny mark in the air under Red's arm, in a place the cui dashi wouldn't see, her finger left a flicker of silver light, just enough to activate her powers.

Sarah yanked against Red's grip, digging her fingers into her own throat to get a grip against Red's thumb, and hauled against it with all her strength.

It moved. Just a fraction, but that much was a victory.

Well, maybe not.

Red frowned at her with those blazing eyes, and that vicelike grip began to close slowly, inexorably. She leaned closer and said, "Know your weakness, then, foolish child."

Sarah gagged as her airway was blocked and the crushing grip continued to increase. She couldn't stop it. Red was going to squeeze her life out and rip her head off. A crazy image popped into her mind of her helmet-covered head just toppling off of her sleeping body in Quentin's mansion.

Then a torrent of strength poured into Sarah as her recently-activated cipher drew the full measure of twenty percent of strength and health from every enforcer. She shivered under the magnitude of it and jabbed a finger into Red's eye.

It felt like jabbing a brick wall, but powered by all those enforcers, she drove her finger into the glowing orb and felt it give just a little.

Red yelped and threw Sarah away.

That was all the opening Sarah needed. She landed on the deck and marked the escape rune with a glowing finger. They couldn't defeat Red today. Their initial assault had faltered, and now the cui dashi held the advantage. Better to fight another day.

As the memory faded, Red's voice chased Sarah back to reality.

"You've desecrated this moment. I will repay in like measure."

Tomas stepped out of the black SUV in the castle parking lot. The tinted windows concealed the heavily armed members of the Tenth waiting inside. Seven black panel vans had pulled up behind the SUV, all holding more enforcers and heavy weapons. If he gave the order, they could turn the Castello Odescalchi into a battlefield.

The only problem was, he didn't know who to shoot yet. The directional rune was drawing him toward the main gate. He had left his tactical gear behind and donned a windbreaker to scout the area alone before calling in the rest of the men.

It left him exposed, but delayed the inevitable panic and frantic calls to the police. He still wasn't sure how they were going to pull off this assault without all ending up in jail for decades, but he had a mission and he would do it, regardless of the cost.

He paid the entrance fee and moved into the museum. The rune drew him through the medieval displays toward the restricted, employee-only access parts of the castle. He wasn't surprised. Why hadn't the cui dashi chosen a nice hilltop mansion they could mortar from down the street?

After scanning the area, he determined which access point he'd insert through. A quick recon of the area should pinpoint the location. Then they'd bring down the castle if they had to.

In that moment, the rune faded, its directional chill draining away like frost before the sun.

"Oh, that can't be good," he muttered.

He'd sworn to take down this cui dashi, no matter the cost, but he still had half a castle to explore.

His earpiece crackled and Sarah's worried voice tumbled over the encrypted network in a fearful rush. "Tomas, she was too strong. Get your team out of there before she kills you all!"

14

It is possible to provide security against other ills, but as far as death is concerned, men live in a city without walls unless they gain the favor of Gregorios.

~EPICURUS

"WELL THAT COULD HAVE GONE BETTER," Gregorios said as he surveyed the team gathered around the long conference table in his command suite at the mansion. Most of them looked frustrated with the failure, but it didn't look like fear of that woman's incredible power was affecting them. The entire group who had participated in the memory hunt were present, along with Tomas, Anaru, and Quentin.

Alter rounded on Sarah. "Why'd you pull us out? We could have taken her."

"No we couldn't. The containment failed and she owned the memoryscape. She would have destroyed us."

"Sarah's right," Eirene said. "Even with all our nevron united and magnified by the new rune sequence, she blocked me out."

Gregorios added, "I knew she was strong, but we should have gained more traction. I'm wondering if she was sucking juice from another rune web."

"It's likely," Harriett said around a large double-chocolate cookie.

She had brought four dozen into the room, and most of them had already been consumed. She must have baked them that morning before the memory hunt because they still had that first-day perfect cookie feel to them.

It rankled that he had only managed to snag two. No one seemed motivated to pass the plates all the way to the head of the table.

"She has a history of using advanced rune webs," Francesca agreed around a mouthful. "From what we've gathered from the captured heka, she uses them a lot."

"Any leads on where she's getting all the dispossessed souls?" Gregorios asked.

"Your suggestion that we assault that island vault is the best guess so far," Eirene said.

He hated that they hadn't had time to make that happen. "We need to follow up on that."

Tomas nodded. "I'll bump it up on the priority queue. If we can cut off her supply of soulmasks, it might give us the break we need."

"I'm just glad you didn't run into her after she woke up. That final threat has me freaked out," Sarah said.

Gregorios grunted. "That's probably going to turn out to be something drastic and unpleasant. Keep the alert level elevated."

"Already done," Tomas said.

Quentin leaned forward to grab one of the last triple-chocolate cookies. Gregorios had been eying that one. "We do have some new tech that should help slow her down. I want each of you who witnessed her capabilities in the memory to debrief thoroughly. Any detail can help us fine-tune our tactics to stop her when we do track her down."

Tomas frowned. "The problem will be getting the heavier weapons in place. She's so fast, we need to be portable."

Alter nodded agreement. "We need to hit harder. I poured fire from the Gecal into her for nearly three full seconds. That many fifty-cal rounds should have done some kind of damage."

Quentin pursed his lips, considering the challenge, but it was Sarah who spoke first. "I think I can help with that."

"You've got our attention," Gregorios said, snagging the very last cookie as everyone turned to her.

"I think I figured out how to hurt her." Sarah's expression turned downright vicious, and Gregorios winked at Eirene. That girl was turning out all right. "And I've got an idea about how to add ciphers to some of those big Vulcans, the thirty millimeters, to make them lighter."

Tomas grinned. "That's a good start."

"And maybe even transfer that brutal recoil into energy to replenish your enhancements," Sarah added.

That got everyone's attention. Quentin let out a low whistle as the men leaned in. Alter was nodding, and he still hadn't figured out how to conceal how much he still wanted her. Gregorios needed to have Eirene find a way to talk to him.

"I haven't finalized the ciphers yet," she said quickly before the warriors got too excited. "I need to review a few things with Alter, but I think it'll work."

"We'll get right on it," Alter promised.

Sarah added, "I think I can enhance the rounds. If we can hit her with something hard enough to break the skin."

"The thirty millimeters ought to do," Quentin promised. "Even she can't be immune to that kind of firepower."

Gregorios hoped he was right. Those cannons could pierce armored vehicles.

"Assuming they do and I can add ciphers to some of the shells we fire into her, I think I can drain some of her strength and turn it against her." Sarah flashed another fierce grin. "I'm thinking of converting it into fire."

Tomas laughed, and Anaru grinned wider than Gregorios had ever seen. "That's brilliant! Cook her with her own power."

Alter muttered, "Such a rune would be . . ."

"What? Abomination?" Sarah demanded.

He shook his head. "Amazing."

She gave him a happy smile. "We'll make it work."

Gregorios liked the way they were thinking. "Anything you need, it's yours. Let's cook up that cui dashi barbecue cipher ASAP."

"Then we track her down and ignite the grill," Tomas said.

"The question is," Eirene interrupted the gloating mood. "Is she going to ground, or does she have bigger plans?"

"That whole life desecration threat sounds like big plans," Francesca pointed out.

Sarah's expression turned worried again. "I got the sense she had a plan. The things she said while she was choking me didn't make much sense, but might offer some clues."

"She confirmed that she's Paul's mother," Gregorios said.

Quentin shuddered. "Like rats breeding in the basement. A family of cui dashi! It shouldn't be possible."

"She's figured something out that we haven't," Eirene said.

Gregorios raised the remnants of his cookie in salute. "Here's hoping that secret dies with her soon."

"If she's still holed up in that castle," Sarah said.

"I've got teams monitoring that entire sector," Tomas said. "They're keeping a very low profile, but the sensors should pick up a cui dashi that powerful."

That was good. Gregorios said, "I hate having to deal with another historical site, but I hope we've found her lair. In the meantime, what can we learn about her from the clues in that memory we interrupted? Why China? Why the burning of the treasure fleet?"

Alter piped right up. "She wasn't happy we barged in. It seemed like she lived that moment, which would mean she's at least five hundred years old."

"She may even be older," Gregorios said with a grimace. "That also tells us something. Most cui dashi don't live that long."

Eirene nodded. "So she was a clever kid too, or we would've noticed her and eradicated her a long time ago."

Sarah leaned forward, her expression thoughtful. "Something doesn't make sense, though. She told me we interrupted a memory that could have been important to her. What's that supposed to mean?"

"It's an odd way to phrase it," Gregorios agreed. He wasn't surprised the cui dashi didn't make sense. Despite the millennia he had lived, even he couldn't understand normal mortal women, let alone a cui dashi.

"And the other stuff she was spouting," Sarah said with a frown. "She was chastising *us* for warmongering and unprovoked attacks."

Francesca chuckled. "Nothing like an evil psychopath feeling like they're the hero of their own story."

"She seemed to think she was justified in whatever she's doing. It was weird," Sarah said, rubbing at her arm, as if chilled. Gregorios didn't blame her.

"Weird is the least of the problems when dealing with cui dashi," Gregorios said. He wished they knew more about the woman's plans. Maybe that would explain her odd behavior. "Do we have any concrete leads from that conversation?"

Quentin spoke up. "Harald's historians are combing the archives. They'll pull up everything we've got on the time period."

"I doubt we have much," Gregorios said with a frown. "We never made much headway into China."

"Not since old Tian Fei visited Rome," Eirene agreed.

"Who?" Several people asked in unison.

Gregorios explained. "One scary lady. A powerful facetaker. Led an expedition to Rome in the early days of the empire, all the way from China."

"I thought there was no interaction between those empires," Alter said.

"Not after that," Gregorios said with a chuckle. "The initial meeting didn't go well. She killed one of Shahrokh's most powerful allies and threatened unending warfare against any facetaker that set foot upon Chinese soil. She scared a couple lives off him, I think. He never pursued China after that."

Eirene added, "We did try a few times to get into China eventually, but every mission failed. Lost some good people. We lost track of Tian Fei, but she eventually started her own goddess legend."

Gregorios remembered. That woman had style to spare. "In one of her lives in the tenth century, she was known as Lin Moniang. She was worshiped for a long time along the Chinese coast as Mazo, or Tian Fei, patron goddess of seafarers."

Alter snapped his fingers. "That's right. Zheng He, the eunuch admiral of the treasure fleet, worshiped her."

"Might be some connection," Harriett offered.

Gregorios was happy to hear her engage in the conversation. She'd taken her brother's death hard and had lost herself in the operations of Yurak. If not for her close bond with Francesca, he would have worried about her long-term health.

He mourned his son, but they couldn't afford to lose focus. The fate of too many hung in the balance.

"Is she still alive?" Sarah asked.

Gregorios shook his head. "Marco Polo swept China for reports of heka and facetaker activity during his travels there in the thirteenth century. He found surprisingly little, and nothing about old Tian Fei."

"I wonder if Red's related somehow," Sarah said, then noticed everyone's quizzical looks. "I decided that's a better name than Swamanaban."

"Agreed," Gregorios said. "I'll have Harald's team look into it. I didn't recognize our girl on the ship, but Tian Fei did like to wear red. There might be some clues buried in the histories somewhere."

They were moving forward on multiple fronts. Gregorios decided it would be enough. He scanned the room. "I'll call our first attempt against the cui dashi a qualified success."

"We didn't kill her," Alter protested.

"And she didn't kill any of us," Gregorios retorted. "Against her, I consider that a win."

He turned to Quentin. "Anything you can add to your tech, do it. You've got a blank check."

"That's music to my ears," Quentin said, rubbing his hands together. He turned to Sarah and added, "I'll send up a sampling of some of the thirty millimeter cannons to your suite to make your work easier."

Sarah beamed at him. "You're a rare gentleman, Quentin. And you send the best gifts."

Gregorios appreciated the humor. It helped keep the group grounded. "Francesca, Harriett, Eirene, go visit the prisoners and encourage them to spill a few more secrets now that we've got some new questions to ask. See if they respond better to the name Tian Fei. We need to know who this woman is."

"What about you?" Eirene asked.

He frowned, not hiding his annoyance. "I've got to fly to New York. The UN committee debating the wisdom of regulating rune enhancements across international armed forces is holding a series of hearings. I need to participate."

Eirene grimaced. "Be careful, or those politicians will suck out your soul."

15

The great library of Alexandria burns! The fool Romans have no caution. All they want is plunder and conquest and new runes, but they burn when they should study. Only the strange foreigners offer any hope to salvage our treasures. We will assist them in saving all we can, for even the flames obey their leader and his burning eyes.

~PANEHESY, CURATOR OF THE LIBRARY OF
ALEXANDRIA, 48 B.C.

SARAH SNAGGED a kiss from Tomas before he could rush off to join his troops and oversee the delicate operation of establishing surveillance of Red's lair. She still deeply relieved they'd escaped before Red discovered them lurking.

She trusted they knew how to stay out of sight. The unexpected location of the cui dashi's lair posed major challenges for the next strike, but now they had time to prepare and plan an effective strike.

Sarah decided to think of Red as Tian Fei. The name fit that regal Chinese woman who had so easily flipped their well-planned assault back against them. She'd left Sarah feeling like a child battling a trained warrior. Paul hadn't scared her so completely until he had tapped the power of three master runes.

Despite Tian Fei's strength, the new ciphers Sarah was planning filled her with a renewed hope. If she could make them work, could actually turn Tian Fei's own strength against her, they'd have a real chance.

With the last cui dashi gone, maybe Sarah could get a chance to live a normal life. Well, as normal as any life could be among facetakers and superhuman soul powers.

Sarah chewed on the problem as she left the council room. She felt a burning drive to make progress, convinced that every minute counted. She didn't doubt for a second that Tian Fei would make good on her promise to wreck their lives.

"Sarah, hold on a minute," Alter interrupted her thoughts, catching up with her in the hallway.

She smiled. "I'm glad you're here. There are a few runes I still need to figure out to finalize the sequence on these new ciphers."

Together they headed for the second-floor library they'd converted into their rune workshop. When they entered, Sarah clicked on the wall-mounted television and paused to watch when the screen showed a news report on location in a desert setting.

"Hey, that's the archaeological team digging in Egypt."

Alter frowned at the tv. "They're crazy. Every other expert insists there can't be any artifacts wherever their 'secret dig site' is actually located."

"Listen," she urged as the video shifted to the lead archaeologist, a Chinese-American man named Charles Wang, who spoke with a Boston accent.

The reporter was asking, "Doctor Wang, are you saying you've made a discovery?"

"Indeed we have," he answered with a happy smile. "It's too early to discuss the find in detail, but I can say with assurance that it appears to be uniquely preserved, and rich with artifacts that may shed new lights on ancient Egyptian history."

Alter grunted. "That's surprising. I bet the government's furious they didn't help fund that dig."

Whoever the privately-funded dig's sponsors were, they must be thrilled. Sarah silently applauded their audacity to dare the dig. The exact location of the project had been closely guarded, but she loved that they had found something.

If only there was time to visit a site like that, where unadulterated history was being uncovered. She loved walking through history with Eirene and Gregorios, but it still frustrated her sometimes how much history had been twisted. An important archaeological find felt pure and undefiled in comparison.

The news report shifted back to the talking heads in the studio, so

Sarah clicked off the television. She joined Alter at the long table covered with runes, symbols of power from the ancient Chinese oracle bone-script, and books on Egyptian hieroglyphs.

The nearby window was open, with a view over the inner court and the pool. The debris from the mortar strike had been cleared away and the muddy water drained. She hoped the workers would complete repairs soon. An empty pool always seemed depressing.

"Sarah, I've been thinking a lot since that memory hunt today."

"Me too. We totally underestimated her. We got lucky no one was badly hurt."

"You almost were. I was worried about you." Alter faced her, his handsome face worried.

"You're the one that got knocked off the mast by a flying Gregorios," Sarah said with a smile, trying to keep the mood light. Sometimes Alter could be a bit too intense.

"She nearly killed you," Alter said. As she had feared, his gaze became intent, and when he took her hands, his skin felt hot.

Sarah tried to back away, but Alter gripped her hands tighter. Sarah knew what was coming, but wished he wouldn't. She'd let him kiss her twice a few weeks ago. Big mistake.

They'd all been going through difficult times. Her justifications had been complicated, and she'd been confused about a lot of things. Alter was handsome, enthusiastic, skilled with knowledge she needed, and had a good heart. She cared for him deeply.

The problem was, she didn't love him romantically.

Instead of declaring his undying love, which he clearly wanted to, he instead said, "Sarah, don't you realize your safety is all that matters?"

"Don't get all sappy on me," Sarah said, taking the chance to bleed off some of the emotion with a joke.

Alter wasn't capable of masking his emotions, and she easily read the depth of his feelings. She'd punch him if he tried to claim that kiss from the bet he and Tomas made during the heka raid. She'd feel bad about it, but she'd do it.

"You know how I feel," Alter said, his voice calmer than she expected. "But you're committed to another. I get it, Sarah. I really do. I think it's the wrong choice, but you'll come around eventually. Until then, I promise not to burden you with my feelings."

"I appreciate that," she said, surprised by his unexpected attempt at self-restraint. He'd eventually see his hope of her dumping Tomas wasn't going to happen.

"But it's not my feelings for you that dictate that I'm prepared to sacrifice whatever it takes to keep you safe."

"You're getting sappy again," she warned.

Alter dropped her hands and retreated a step. "Don't make everything emotional. Every single person on the team understands the truth. It may make you uncomfortable, but you have to face it. Without you, we don't stand a chance against Red."

"We're calling her Tian Fei now," Sarah reminded him.

"Don't try to change the subject," he said with that frown he assumed when teaching her. While sparring, it always made her want to hit him harder.

He must have realized she was tempted to punch him because he quickly added, "Your safety is our paramount concern." He leaned just a bit closer, his gaze growing intense again. "I swear on my honor to keep you safe, whatever it takes."

His sincerity moved her. "Thank you. Really, I appreciate it, but don't over-dramatize things."

Of course, with Alter, that was nearly impossible.

"Do you think it was easy for me to share bodies with Tomas?" Alter asked, surprising her by the question. "It wasn't, but we both did it for you, Sarah."

This time, she stepped closer and gripped his hands. She knew that act had been a huge sacrifice for both of them. "I've said it before, Alter, but I can never say it enough. Thank you for that."

She'd kiss his cheek if it wouldn't send the wrong message. "You're one of my best friends, my rune teacher." The emotion was getting a bit too thick again, so she added with a wry smile, "And my practice dummy."

"Instructor," he corrected, but actually cracked a bit of a smile.

"Are we okay?" she asked, amazed that he seemed willing to accept a situation not to his liking.

He hesitated a moment before nodding. She gave him a warm smile, but then he added, "But Sarah, you have to be more careful with those ciphers. Some of what you're planning could get you into trouble."

Sarah felt relieved the conversation had shifted back to comfortable, solid ground where they had already established a firm working relationship. "Then let's work on them together. Come on, I'll show you what I'm thinking about with those thirty millimeters."

As they started crafting promising ciphers, Sarah dared hope that Alter had turned an important corner. He was dear to her, but she had feared his infatuation would end up alienating him. His family had turned against him, and she knew he was suffering, although he tried to hide it.

Alter needed the team, the mission, and his friendship with her as much as they needed him. He might claim she was critical to their ultimate success, but so was he. They couldn't defeat Tian Fei without him, their only cui dashi hunter.

She allowed herself to feel a bit of hope. They only needed a little time, and they'd be ready to take the fight to Tian Fei.

16

Friendship is a single soul dwelling in two bodies.

~ARISTOTLE

SARAH RECLINED in one of the padded chairs next to the machines in the jump room. Eirene and Francesca took chairs to either side.

"What if Tian Fei tracks you down in there?" Harriett asked. The others had all agreed with Sarah to assign the name to Red until they knew her real name. Harriett would run the single machine for this last-minute memory jump.

"She's never bothered us before," Eirene said. She had taken the primary seat and would run the memory.

"And if she does, we leave," Sarah promised.

Tian Fei had promised to desecrate their lives, and that threat had carried with it a feeling that she intended to make their waking hours miserable, not just haunt their dreams. Even so, Sarah was ready with the escape runes. She wouldn't take foolish risks where Tian Fei was concerned.

"So where do we want to go on our girl's day out?" Francesca asked.

Sarah said, "Anywhere. I need to work through a few things."

"Big air time then," Francesca said with a grin.

"Yeah, that would work." Sarah loved the sense of near-flight she achieved in the memoryscape where they could bend physical rules to the breaking point.

"I know just the thing," Eirene said, securing her faceplate. "Harriett, you're on."

"Have a fun trip. Keep your hands and feet inside the vehicle at all times," Harriett quipped as the faceplate heated against Sarah's skin. "I'll have peanuts waiting for you after you've landed."

A flash of heat, then darkness covered Sarah's mind as the machine dragged her into the memoryscape. A moment later, a steady breeze, laden with sea brine blew the darkness away, revealing bright sunlight.

Sarah blinked and looked around. Blue skies and a bluer ocean mixed to the west. To the east, the water changed to emerald green around the shores of a tropical island. The sun was bright and warm, and the salty air carried a hint of underlying sweetness that Sarah couldn't place. She stood on the deck of a trim, two-masted sloop. Four other ships were floating on the gentle swell nearby, their sails all furled.

Eirene rounded the mast, wearing a white cotton blouse and black vest. Sarah glanced down at herself and found she was wearing similar garb.

Francesca dropped off a spar to the deck beside her, laughing. She sported a cutlass and a flintlock pistol on her wide leather belt. "I haven't been on one of your ships in years, mother."

Eirene said, "I like to come here when I need to think. This what you were thinking?"

"Absolutely." Sarah paced down the deck. Sailors moved around them on their unending tasks of maintaining a sailing ship, but none paid the ladies any mind.

"What's got your skirt in tatters?" Francesca asked as she drew her pistol and checked the powder.

"These ciphers. They're very complex, and if I screw up, people could get killed."

"If you get them right, the plan is to kill someone," Eirene pointed out.

"Are you sure Alter's not causing trouble?" Francesca asked.

Sarah shook her head. "Actually, I think we're all right. Can you believe he actually said he accepts the fact that I'm dating Tomas?"

Francesca frowned. "He's besotted with you, girl."

"It's a good sign that he's at least admitting Tomas has a claim," Eirene pointed out. "He's a lot like his ancestor. When Ronen got an idea into his head, he pursued it forever."

"It's not like you ran that hard," Francesca teased.

"No, I didn't. It was a good life," Eirene said with a smile.

Sarah still found it odd how Eirene and Gregorios viewed each lifetime as separate, but linked. They'd been together for nearly two thousand years. Most lives they recommitted to each other and then remained faithful until their next life.

Once in a while they started new lives and did not renew those vows, knowing their assignments would prevent them from honoring them. Eirene had given one lifetime to Ronen, Alter's great-grandfather. She was Alter's great-grandmother, Elizabeth. Everyone seemed okay with that.

Maybe once Sarah had lived for centuries she could see the world that way, but she just couldn't yet.

"We talked it out today," Sarah insisted.

"You didn't kiss him again?" Francesca asked, edging closer.

"Of course not. I never should have kissed him at all."

Francesca spun her pistol with practiced flair, then holstered it. "Oh, I don't know about that. Tomas was dawdling and Alter's got very kissable lips."

"That's not helping," Sarah said. She was tempted to mention that Alter was a terrible kisser, but she didn't want to give Francesca any more ideas.

"Well, it got Tomas motivated, didn't it? A little jealousy goes a long way sometimes," Francesca said with a wicked grin.

"Tomas is fine," Sarah insisted. He might be a slow mover, but she was willing to wait.

Eirene pursed her lips in thought. "If Alter can't come to terms with your relationship, he might do something rash."

Francesca laughed. "That's about all Alter ever does, but don't worry about Alter." She patted Sarah on the shoulder. "I've got a few ideas about helping him refocus his energies."

Eirene gave her daughter a stern look. "Be careful. Relations with the hunters are already strained."

Francesca grinned that wicked smile again. "That's all I'm after, better relations with that hunter."

Sarah hoped Francesca knew what she was doing. Only around facetakers could anyone even consider the idea of a woman dating her great-nephew who was several hundred years younger.

Francesca didn't seem to worry about it, and Eirene hadn't protested that point. Thinking about their family tree gave Sarah a headache. Eirene had worn different bodies, lived extremely different lives as mother of those two, so in some ways, it made Sarah wonder how related Francesca really was to the young hunter.

"Enough talk," Eirene said crisply. "We came her for some action."

She ran for the mainmast and jumped straight up, leaping all the way to the crow's nest in a single vertical leap.

Sarah joined her. The fresh air whipping through her hair felt great, and she exulted in the feeling of strength that allowed her to soar dozens of feet. They'd tested the limits of how far they could bend nature's laws and found they could push things pretty far without interrupting the integrity of the memoryscape.

Today she decided to push it even more.

"Ship-to-ship," Francesca called as she landed beside them. Without waiting for a response, she vaulted again, sailing sixty feet to the nearest ship. She landed on the deck and waved them on.

Eirene grinned. "One of my favorite games. Come on, Sarah. Last one to the little clipper over there buys dinner."

"You're on," Sarah said, loving the idea of the challenge.

Eirene vaulted after Francesca, who was already ascending to the top of the next ship's mainmast.

Sarah didn't take the same course. She was already behind, and she wanted to push the limits today. Eirene and Francesca would have to jump to two other ships before reaching the clipper that floated farther out than the rest of the convoy.

If she really wanted to, Sarah could break the law of gravity and fly across, but that would violate the unspoken rules of the game. It would also rip a large enough hole in the integrity of the memoryscape to allow a pretty big nightmare through. If only broken dreams could be positive instead. She'd love shredding a memory if she could get a purple unicorn as a reward.

She didn't have to break any physical laws, though. She just needed to bend them creatively.

Sarah oriented on a two-masted ship about a hundred yards away. It would be the third ship Eirene and Francesca would jump to. With a bit of focus and a deep breath, Sarah marked a pair of ciphers on her thighs with a finger, leaving faintly glowing silver lines on her skin. Then she threw herself into the air in a mighty leap toward the distant ship.

Open water flashed by far below and a gust of wind propelled her forward. She spread her hands out wide, and a parachute-sized chunk of sailcloth appeared in them. The wind caught the sail and it snapped outward with a sharp report.

"Hey, no fair!" Francesca shouted from the top of the mast where she perched. She vaulted to the next ship, moving with frantic speed.

Driven by her conjured wind, Sarah crossed the wide gap to the distant ship. She could have hardened the air under her feet and run along the wind to speed up her journey, but that would have shaken the integrity of the memory too. She'd used only materials readily available in that setting, so hadn't ripped any holes in the memoryscape.

She snatched the cutlass from a sailor when she landed lightly on the ship. Rushing forward, she swung it with all of her enhanced strength, chopping through half of the shorter foremast. Then she slammed her shoulder into the mast, toppling it with a snapping of timber toward the other ladies, who were in mid-jump from a nearby ship. The mast swatted them out of the air, splashing them into the ocean.

Sarah laughed as the sailor approached, looking angry. "Here now, what are ye thinking, breaking the ship?"

The more they broke with the integrity of the memory, and the more they made a nuisance of themselves, the more the dream characters noticed them. Usually that led to conflict, riots, and eventually to a complete degradation of the memoryscape.

"Sorry about that," Sarah said, returning his sword. Then she leaped to the top of the mainmast, leaving the gaping sailor behind.

She reached the final clipper ship twenty seconds in front of the other ladies.

"I like ribs with my pasta," Sarah said when Eirene landed last on the ship.

"We need to talk about your sense of etiquette," Eirene said, wringing water out of her blouse.

Just then, Sarah felt a strange twinge in her back. She held up a hand to forestall Francesca's comment.

"We need to get out of here. One of my heka sensors just went off in the real world."

17

Of course you can have them. Take all the children you can afford. The price for each is the same, paid in grain, for the city starves. Every child you take is one less child we must sacrifice to keep Carthage alive.

~BOSTAR, MUNICIPAL OFFICIAL TO AN UNNAMED
CONTACT, CARTHAGE, 300 B.C.

ALTER WORKED across the empty expanse of smooth sand in the practice yard of the Tenth in the Suntara building in a series of brutal, Krav Maga martial arts moves. He'd left the mansion after working ciphers with Sarah, feeling a deep sense of frustration that needed venting.

Sarah had needed to hear that he accepted her choice, that Tomas was a fitting partner for her, but speaking those words had been one of the hardest things he'd ever done. Maybe his father was right. Maybe he'd spent too much time with Sarah. Life had gotten too complicated, simple truths twisted almost beyond recognition.

He couldn't help it. He yearned to kiss Sarah again, but he couldn't risk pushing her away. He would find a way to prove he was a better choice. Somehow.

Alter sparred across the sand, taking his frustrations out on imaginary foes that all wore Tomas' face. Reuben had been wrong to attack the facetakers, but the ugly part of Alter's mind wished he hadn't spared Tomas that day. Had his integrity destroyed his best chance at winning Sarah?

He was tempted to pack up and leave. But where would he go?

He couldn't return to Jerusalem. His family would kill him to purge his soul from his cursed cui dashi powers. Before he'd come to Rome, he would have been first in line to volunteer to execute such a dishonored clan member.

Now he knew the world wasn't such a simple place, but his expanded understanding called into question too many of the strict precepts of his people. That doubt was like a cancer, creating questions and confusion where he needed purity of soul and strength of purpose. Even if the clan allowed him back without sentencing him to death, he was starting to worry he could never truly fit in again.

That left him feeling homeless and lost. If not part of the hunters, what was he? Where was home? If it could be with Sarah, he'd be happy anywhere, but without her, where did that leave him? Could he remain with the facetakers, perhaps become an enforcer? The idea felt wrong, but what other choice did he have?

He crushed the insidious worries and pushed his body to the limits, seeking for clarity through exhaustion. He kept up the brutal pace for a half hour before pausing to rest. Sweat drenched his face and shirt, but he wasn't breathing hard. His custom enhancement runes allowed him to perform at fighting peak for extended periods.

He had left his shirt with his jacket and his pistol by the door. When he turned in that direction, he realized he wasn't alone.

Tian Fei.

Alter gaped, momentarily stunned, frozen by the unfamiliar grip of icy terror.

Tian Fei wore a form-fitting, single-piece, Chinese qipao dress of red silk with gold trim. She carried a pair of black heels in her left hand.

She nodded to him and said, "You are graceful and beautiful. Now you will serve me."

"Abomination," Alter spat. He had trained his whole life to defeat evil creatures like this, but his gun lay at her feet.

Tian Fei shot across the arena floor, kicking up rooster tails of sand behind her blurring feet. Alter tried to dodge, hoping she'd overshoot so he could go for his gun.

No luck. She shifted course and shot past, snatching him off the floor before he could land a single punch. The abrupt acceleration strained the muscles of his neck and back.

He struggled in her hands, punching at her face, her ears, her throat, but only managed to bruise his hands. Hitting her was like striking living steel.

She circled the arena and dropped him next to his clothing. "Get dressed, my newest son. We have much to do."

Alter snatched up his pistol and emptied the magazine into her face and throat at point-blank range. The bullets ricocheted off her skin.

When the slide locked back on the empty chamber, she cocked her head to one side. "Are you finished?"

"I'm going to get some napalm," he said, turning toward the exit.

"Don't test my patience," Tian Fei said, sounding bored. "If you do not obey my command, I will rip out the souls of every living mortal in this building."

Fighting her with fists and normal weapons was useless, but he was a hunter, sworn to destroy spawns of darkness like this woman with every weapon at his disposal. Even those that tainted his own soul with evil.

Alter embraced his nevra core, tapping the active center of his soul and igniting its power. His vision shifted to prism-like hues, and purple fire flickered out of every pore on his hands. The rush of it filled him with strength and exultant joy, a feeling only matched by those two brief moments when he'd kissed Sarah.

He lunged with burning hands for Tian Fei's face.

She made no move to stop him.

Her arrogance thrilled him. He would destroy her and prove his worth to Sarah.

His fingers found the soul points along her jawline, those invisible contact points that locked the soulmask into the host body. Alter drove his nevron against the soul points of Tian Fei's jaw, planning to sever them.

He found no purchase. Every other soul he had attempted to take, even those of Eirene and her children, had felt like putty under his fingers. He'd driven his nevron through, slicing the invisible anchor points and freeing the soulmask.

Tian Fei's soul points were like reinforced concrete. He beat against them with his nevron to no avail.

She watched him, her black eyes like mysterious pools. For the first time, he noticed that she wore a gentle fragrance of lotus flowers. It seemed incongruous. Shouldn't a vile creature like this smell like brimstone and ash?

"What are you?" Alter asked, refusing to drop his burning hands, despite his utter failure.

"Your new master, granting your first lesson."

She grabbed his jaw with fingers like iron and drove them through his flesh. The force of her nevron was like a freight train, overwhelming and unstoppable. She shattered his concentration, dispersed his nevron, and broke his soul points in a fraction of a second.

Alter tried to strike at her, but she severed his control over his body. His senses contracted until he felt nothing but the skin of his face sloughing away as Tian Fei ripped his soulmask from his skull.

He lost his sense of smell and touch. His vision faded to rainbow hues and everything took on a two-dimensional flatness. His hearing sharpened tenfold and he heard his empty body collapse.

The loss of senses only served to magnify the feeling of absolute terror that consumed him.

18

Youth is the best time to be rich, and the best time to be poor, as long as Shahrokh is your friend.

~EURIPIDES

"GIVE ME A TARGET," Quentin ordered as soon as Sarah rushed into the command center.

The room was packed with technicians and enforcers, all clustered around the huge screen mounted on one wall. It was currently displaying eighteen different security feeds from around the mansion and the city.

"My cipher was tripped at Suntara," Sarah said.

"Get me eyes," Quentin ordered his staff. As their fingers began dancing over their keyboards he added, "Bugger it all. We've got almost no assets left there."

"Then why hit us there?" asked Tomas, who had just entered the room with Eirene. He was already kitted up in level three armor.

Sarah suggested, "Maybe they don't realize it's mostly vacant. Someone triggered a sensor near the east entrance."

One tech reported, "Main desk is responding. No sign of hostile forces. But I haven't been able to raise the east entrance security office."

"Show it," Quentin ordered.

One section of the screen shifted to a blurry display of the guard-room at the east entrance of the Suntara building. The camera looked cracked, but still functioned enough to display a devastated room of upended furniture and broken doors. Two bodies lay unmoving at the edge of the screen.

Quentin muttered a curse. "We added new defensive measures since the last assault, but whoever hit the building broke through before they could even trigger the alarm."

That confirmed Sarah's initial suspicion. "Quentin, get everyone out of there before Tian Fei kills them all."

Tomas tapped his earpiece. "All units, target acquired at Suntara. Converge at rally point echo and prep the rainmaker."

"I haven't seen that one yet," Sarah said.

She'd heard good things about Quentin's latest cui dashi stopper, and she tried to focus on that instead of the terror that chilled her insides.

Tomas growled, "I hate using it against our own building. They haven't even finished repairs from the last explosion."

"Sweep every level," Quentin ordered the techs, his voice clipped and tense. "Sound the priority urgent evacuation, and find the intruders."

Tomas moved toward the door, but Sarah held him back. "Wait till we see her."

"Got her," a tech announced.

They all turned to stare at the monitor. Tian Fei walked toward the camera, dressed in a red silk Chinese dress. Over her shoulder, she carried a limp body. In her other hand she carried a pair of black heels and a dispossessed soulmask.

Sarah recognized the soulmask and gasped, "That's Alter!"

"What's he doing there?" Tomas asked.

Sarah whispered, "Oh, no. I can't believe it."

Eirene joined Sarah by the monitor. "She said she was coming after us, but I hadn't expected this."

Sarah fought back a wave of terror at seeing Alter helpless in the hands of that demon. "I need something solid. A block of wood, a binder, anything."

Quentin handed her a clipboard while one of the techs relayed identifying information to the enforcer teams.

"Can you slow her down until my teams get into position?" Tomas asked.

"I don't think so." Sarah snatched a marker from a nearby desk and began inscribing a rune onto the clipboard. "What exit is she taking?"

Quentin said, "East exit again. She'll reach the outside in thirty seconds."

"Nearest enforcer team is four minutes out," one tech reported.

Tomas clenched a fist in frustration. "Not enough time."

Sarah said, "Tell them to stay back. No one engages until we've got everything ready or she'll slaughter them."

"We can't let her walk away with Alter," Quentin protested.

"Actually, that's exactly what we're going to do," Sarah said, terrified by the decision, but seeing no alternative. She rushed to complete her new cipher and focused over it. The black marks began to glow silver against the clipboard.

"What are you planning?" Tomas asked, shifting to look at her work. His jaw was clenching in suppressed frustration, but otherwise he looked calm.

Sarah said, "I've triggered Alter's tracking rune. It'll be reinforced by a charging rune located at the east entrance. I can track him, as long as he doesn't get more than ten miles away."

Eirene placed a hand on her shoulder and said, "Good idea. We track her until she goes to ground."

"Then we destroy her," Tomas added, his expression fierce.

"What about Alter?" Sarah asked, voicing her terrible fear.

The best plan for destroying Tian Fei was to firebomb whatever location they could trap her in. Fire was one of the best weapons for delivering permanent, catastrophic damage even to someone as enhanced as Tian Fei.

Sarah's new ciphers for the cannons weren't complete, but if she could confine the cui dashi in place with binding runes, that would give the fire teams even more time to wear down Tian Fei's regeneration ability. With enough time, even her soul force would run dry and she'd become just as mortal as anyone else.

Alter would never survive such an onslaught.

Eirene squeezed her shoulder and said, "We'll figure it out. Tomas, call up everyone."

"Already mobilizing," he reported.

"Quentin, bring all your tech. Let's end this today." Eirene turned as Harriett rushed into the room, adjusting her leather gloves. "Dear, do we have any Yurak forces close enough to help?"

Her daughter grimaced. "I doubt it. I've got teams in eight different countries right now, giving demonstrations with our new weapons systems. Most of the other forces were withdrawn to Switzerland for post-op conditioning and fleet maintenance. We figured we had till next week to get strike teams back here."

Eirene sighed. "We thought wrong. Have your commanders prepare contingencies for deploying quick-response teams back here."

As they ran for the car garage, Sarah asked, "What if she returns to that castle?"

"I'm on it," Tomas said. He tapped his throat mic again. "Operations, patch me through to Master-Sergeant Carlo Salvatici."

19

The death of a person is the result of the body losing the animating qi, and once the qi is separated from the body, the body decays. All will admit to this. Thus recent rumors of Tian Fei walking the shores and cursing people with ghostly burning runes must be false.

~WANG CHONG, ANCIENT CHINESE PHILOSOPHER

"ABSOLUTELY NOT," Master-Sergeant Carlo Salvatici exclaimed. "We cannot destroy another historical landmark."

Sarah felt relieved that Tomas faced the angry Italian calmly. He said, "Just consider it. It's the safest way to contain the threat."

The master sergeant started sputtering a string of Italian curses, his face flushed as he pounded on the table for emphasis.

Sarah interjected before the argument could get really rolling. "Cut it out. We can't destroy the castle, Tomas."

"They wouldn't let us destroy Sant'Angelo either," he muttered with a scowl.

"Of course not," Carlo sputtered.

Sarah said, "If we could be sure it was only Tian Fei in there, destroying the castle might be worth it. But she's got Alter, and we'd never clear out civilians without her realizing what's going on."

The three stood in a second-floor private dining room of a restaurant in the town below the Castello Odescalchi. Carlo had recommended the location for its excellent views of the towering castle, but Sarah wondered if he'd had ulterior motives. The restaurant offered an impressive array of wines, and she'd noticed him scanning the list several times.

Carlo made a little bow to Sarah. "Bravo, signorina. It is a relief that at least one of you can see reason."

Tomas said, "You're the one who doesn't see. You thought Paul was bad. The woman we're hunting is worse."

"No woman is worse than that monster. He assaulted the Pope!"

Sarah interjected again. "What reports are you getting from the advance team?"

The men already in position doing surveillance had spotted a Town Car with tinted windows pulling up to a side entrance of the castle. They had captured images of Tian Fei entering, followed by a man whose face was blocked by Alter's body, carried draped over one shoulder.

By his size, it might have been Hongwu. That entrance was closed to the public, but they had swept through, as if expected.

Some of Tomas' team, along with four of Carlo's soldiers, had begun a walking reconnaissance of the castle. They'd purchased tourist clothing from a local retailer and begun their reconnoiter half an hour ago.

The rest of the company was still arriving and gathering in a nearby warehouse. To reduce the chance of getting spotted by any watchers Tian Fei had positioned in the castle towers, the arrivals were spaced out.

"I'll check." Tomas had been eager to join his men, and only reluctantly left them to the dangerous mission of reconnaissance as he helped plan the assault.

After a moment of listening he said, "There's a lot of activity at the castle. Lots of civilians. Sounds like they're prepping for a big wedding tomorrow."

Carlo exclaimed, "Grazie a Dio, we cannot attack tomorrow. I heard of this wedding. A rich American and his Italian bride. There will be hundreds of guests."

"Sounds like quite a party. Maybe we should hang around," Sarah said, trying in vain to lighten the tense mood. Carlo started to protest again, but she added, "After dealing with today's problem, of course."

Tomas frowned as he studied the distant castle. "Well, if we can't blow the place up, maybe we can lure her out into the open where we can trap her and hit her with the big guns."

"How much room would you need?" Carlo asked. He and his men

had brought some explosives and had access to additional military fire support if he deemed it necessary.

"The rainmaker would probably level a square block. That would be our best bet at stopping her, or at least slowing her down enough to finish her off with incendiary mortars."

Carlo blinked. "You're serious?"

Tomas gave him an exasperated look. "Haven't you been listening? This woman is not human. You've seen basic enhancements. Think of her as having thousands of them. She would slaughter us if we tried to face her without serious fire support. As it is, this is a very high-risk operation."

"I could call for more troops," Carlo suggested, but he was starting to look a little sick.

Sarah said, "No. That much troop movement would just alert her, and lots of people would die." She paced to the window and studied the imposing castle. "Tomas, if we lured her out, how sure are you that we could direct her to wherever we could set our trap?"

"Twenty percent," he said after a moment's thought.

He joined her by the window and wrapped her in his arms, leaving Carlo to examine the wine list again.

She leaned against Tomas. "This is going to get ugly, isn't it?"

"If she gets out, I don't know how we'd stop her in these little streets," Tomas admitted.

The town below the castle was a warren of narrow lanes, a quaint medieval holdover. Under other circumstances, it would be exactly the kind of place Sarah would love to visit.

The thought of a running battle through those narrow lanes, surrounded by innocent bystanders, made her shudder. If she could prepare a battlefield with her ciphers, she might slow down the cui dashi enough, but they had to find a better way.

Eirene entered the room. "Where are we with planning this assault?"

Tomas admitted, "Not far. Too many restrictions." He cast a sour look at Carlo. "Too many civilians, and not enough room to bring in the heavy explosives."

"I was afraid of that. Contingencies?"

"Just starting to work through them."

Eirene moved to the table and shed her body armor. "Good. Send for some wine and let's get to work."

Carlo eagerly recommended several local vintages. Tomas called for Anaru and his unit commanders, and when they arrived, the group spent the next hour working through possible entry scenarios. The scout teams passed regular reports and managed to enter the outer castle courtyard without being challenged. They identified two likely heka sentries, but did not engage.

Sarah barely listened as the group worked on a plan. She had brought along her half-formed ciphers from the mansion and spent the time working on them. In particular, she focused on the cipher to hurt Tian Fei, drain energy from her, and convert it into fire. It offered their best chance for stopping the monster.

"There are just too many unknowns," Tomas finally said with abundant frustration. "This is too complicated, and if anything goes wrong, a lot of people are going to die."

Eirene leaned back in her chair and said, "Our other option is to walk away. No one dies in the fight, but we'd likely lose Alter."

Sarah didn't like that idea. "His tracking rune will expire in a couple more hours. We'd lose Tian Fei."

She felt a growing sense of guilt that she was the one who had urged the others to let Tian Fei leave with Alter. They might not have had much choice, but she'd made the call. His death would be on her hands.

"Or we catch her when she exits," Tomas added.

He seemed to have already accepted the possibility of losing Alter. Sarah doubted he would have agreed to consider walking away from any of his other men. That fact angered her, but she couldn't afford to turn the planning session into a fight.

She pointed out, "If she slips through, then the next time we see her would probably be when she ambushed another one of us."

Eirene said, "Then we agree. We need to hit her now while we know where she's hiding and it appears she doesn't anticipate our assault."

"I can't condone this plan," Tomas said, gesturing at the pages of maps and notes spread across the table. "We can't hurt her enough to justify risking so many lives."

"Maybe we can," Sarah said as she completed the new cipher.

She stared at the graceful lines that combined in deadly harmony on the page, and shuddered. That symbol scared her. It was perhaps the most dangerous cipher she had ever designed, and she wished Alter was there to review it and to complain about how she'd again pushed the limits too far.

"What have you got for us?" Eirene asked as everyone looked to her with so much hope that it only increased her nervousness.

Sarah held up the cipher. "If we can get her out of the castle and hit her with the thirty millimeter cannon, I think this will hurt her. It might tip the balance in our favor."

Tomas gave her an approving smile. "We've got a Russian GSH six-barreled cannon in the trucks."

Anaru, the gigantic Maori enforcer, grinned where he stood at the end of the table. None of the chairs were solid enough to support his mass. "I get dibs as gunner."

Tomas nodded. "Done. Take a squad to help carry the ammo. That'll make the entire package light enough to move fast and shift positions if needed."

Carlo frowned. "But signore, that cannon is truck-mounted." He pointed at the map of the town. "We discussed this. The streets are too small for fast movements."

Anaru grunted. "I don't need a truck. A little gun like that, I just run with it."

The master-sergeant blinked a couple of times, at a loss for words. Sarah gave him an understanding smile. "He's right. I've seen Anaru throw trucks."

Even for most of the other enforcers, the three-hundred pound rotary cannon would prove difficult to wield, but Sarah didn't doubt the massive Maori could sling it around like a rifle. With other men to lug the five hundred pounds of ammo the gun could rip through in a matter of seconds, they would act as a highly mobile unit, capable of doing fantastic amounts of damage.

Tomas considered the plans on the table and nodded. "I think we can make it work. How long do you need to mark your ciphers?"

She glanced down at the complex, deadly cipher. "I'll probably need about a minute for each shell."

"Can you manage thirty of them?" he asked.

She nodded. "With that many, I'll have to tap some strength from the Tenth, but probably no more than five percent."

Tomas glanced at his captains, who all nodded. "That'll work. Start with teams eight and eleven. They're fire support, so they'll be away from the direct fighting."

"I'll fetch the shells for you," Anaru said, heading for the door with an eager spring in his step. Sarah would mark every fiftieth shell. That way, if Anaru missed with his first burst, he might get a second chance to make it work.

Tomas turned to his commanders. "Relay the orders and prepare your teams." He pointed at the map of the castle. "No unnecessary heroics. We hit hard, startle her into the open, and let Anaru cause some pain. Hopefully that will slow her enough to bring the rain. This one will be tricky, but this is what we train for. We'll win the day."

As everyone rose, Sarah gave him a kiss. "Good luck."

Then she turned to Carlo. "Ready to be my date?"

20

Know how to listen and you will profit even from those who talk badly.

~PLUTARCH

SARAH ENTERED the Castello Odescalchi beside Master-Sergeant Carlo Salvatici, dressed in a flower-print dress and light jacket. She'd picked up the bright clothing at a local shop.

If she'd realized they were going to pose as tourists, she could have easily packed another day bag. The dress looked good on her, but she missed her ballistic vest.

She had been injured facing cui dashi more than once. This wasn't a memoryscape where one could heal themselves with a thought, or summon additional weapons and gear.

She carried a pair of forty-five caliber pistols in shoulder holsters concealed under her jacket, with several spare magazines in her large purse. She also concealed one of Quentin's customized Tasers. Tomas called it the Super Juicer because it delivered up to one-hundred-thousand volts of electricity with a one-hundred amp current.

Sarah hadn't understood the danger of the Super Juicer until Tomas explained that a standard Taser might deliver fifty thousand volts, but only about six mili-amperes of current. The weapon in her bag was guaranteed to fry any mortal to a crisp. It would probably kill even enhanced enforcers or heka, and it might rattle a facetaker long enough for their body to die and drag their soul down too.

She hoped it would delay Tian Fei long enough to slap a dozen binding ciphers onto her.

Even with the Super Juicer's promised electro-shock power, she wished she could think of a credible accessory that would allow her to conceal her M4 rifle with its attached M203 grenade launcher. The giant shotgun-type rounds were a personal favorite. They wouldn't kill Tian Fei, but Sarah would feel more confident with it.

Instead, she had included a clipboard, paper, and markers. The runes she could combine into battle ciphers were her most powerful weapon, and would play a key role in the success or failure of the mission.

She really should focus on planning her ciphers, but the beautiful interior of the castle kept intruding into her thoughts. The central bulk of the castle was locked within high walls, complete with turrets and crenelated battlements, forming a roughly triangular shape. The eastern wall broke the symmetry, bulging out in an additional blocky keep.

She and Carlo passed through the open, central courtyard into the long, southwest wing. Unlike the looming, blank stone walls of the central courtyard, the interior was made up of a series of long galleries and huge, vaulted rooms. Sarah paused in front of magnificently preserved frescoes of women performing their daily activities. Carlo seemed far more interested in a display of medieval weapons nearby.

"This is amazing," she commented.

Carlo stopped beside her and draped an arm over her shoulder. He was taking the undercover role of date a little farther than she had anticipated, but punching him through the next wall might give her away.

"Si, signorina, this is a favorite wedding destination." Despite his casual stance, his voice was all business, his eyes moving constantly as he scanned the area.

A steady stream of tourists flowed through the gates into the various levels and rooms of the castle. A small army of caterers moved through the tourists who thronged the central court. They were also preparing the nearby duomo for the upcoming ceremony, and the north lawn with its panoramic views of nearby Lake Bracciano.

Tomas and Eirene were infiltrating the castle through the east entrance, posing as caterers. Other team members would follow in small groups. Only four enforcers on the assault teams were women, so they would pose as tourists with dates like Sarah and Carlo. All together, they planned to slip forty team members into the castle for the initial strike.

If they had to engage Tian Fei, Sarah would try to slow her down with ciphers while they drew her out the north exit. Anaru was already positioned near there with his squad. They would act as the back-up assault team when the fighting started and stealth was no longer important.

Fewer civilians clustered near that north entrance. More importantly, the castle was built upon the top of a steep slope overlooking the lake. So the rainmaker was being positioned at the base of that slope.

It would be targeted in minutes. That flat north lawn would be a perfect location to trap Tian Fei and bring the rain. It was narrow enough to pen her in and concentrate the firepower. The assault would likely shatter the north face of the castle, but the rest might survive.

Carlo had objected to that option, but had finally relented. There was simply no better place to engage the deadly cui dashi without huge numbers of potential casualties, or without destroying the entire castle.

A woman dressed as a museum tour guide paused beside Sarah and spoke in fluent English. "Do you or your father have any questions?"

While Carlo tried not to look offended by the suggestion about his age, Sarah played up the wide-eyed teen-ager angle. "This place is gorgeous! We want to see it all. We're going to start upstairs, but I heard there are real dungeons in the basement. Can we see those too?"

The guide gave her an apologetic smile. "I'm sorry, miss. Lower levels of the castle are off-limits to visitors right now."

"Why? Is someone getting tortured down there?"

The guide laughed, "Such things don't happen any more, miss."

Sarah didn't share her mirth. Alter could very well be getting tortured. She gave the guide another happy smile. "Maybe next time. Thanks." She grabbed Carlo's hand. "Come on, Dad! I'll race you upstairs."

They returned to the brick-paved central courtyard and Sarah slowed to let the fuming Carlo catch up. "She was so nice, wasn't she, Dad?"

Carlo gave her a disgusted look. "Enough, please. I don't look so very old, no?"

Sarah gave him a charming smile. "Not hardly, but I look young."

"You aren't though, are you?"

"Haven't you heard it's rude to ask a woman her age?"

"Si, but you are a mystery, Sarah. You look so much like our beloved Sword of the Deliverer, and you share her name. You wear runes that make you stronger than any of my men, and even Suntara leaders like Tomas and Eirene grant you respect. So you tell me, Signorina Sarah, should I not be curious?"

"You know what curiosity did to the cat," Sarah said, trying not to show him how much his words rattled her. She had assumed no one would put the pieces together, but perhaps her false identity wasn't as rock solid as she had assumed.

Carlo frowned. "No. What does your cat have to do with this?"

"I'll tell you later. We need to get to the basement."

"The dungeons that are closed to the public, yes?"

"Yes. Our target wouldn't hide in public places. Besides, Alter is below us somewhere."

"Another mystery," Carlo commented as he followed her through a wooden door with a sign that said, "Limitato," which Carlo confirmed meant restricted. It led them into a chilly hallway of simple, stone walls. "How do you know this?"

"I told you, we're tracking him."

When he tried to ask another question, she shushed him. "I need to call this in."

She affixed her throat mic after making sure they were alone in the hall. "Tomas, we're in. Alter's in the basement levels. We're heading for the stairs in the restricted access area."

"Roger. We'll meet you there. All teams, converge on the stairs to the lower levels. Unit three, run interference with any staff in that vicinity."

Sarah moved along the stone corridor as it cut deeper into the castle, her tension snapping to a much higher level. This area, shadowed and cold, lacked the museum pieces along the walls. They had left the concealing camouflage of the tourist sections. Anyone they encountered here might be an enhanced heka.

She doubted they'd run into Tian Fei on this level, but it was possible, and the thought set her heart racing. She longed to draw one of her pistols, but instead she drew the clipboard and a marker out of her shoulder bag.

Carlo had unzipped his light jacket and walked with his hand on his pistol. His expression had hardened and his eyes scanned the hall. His entire manner had changed, his movements now predatory. He felt the same tension she did. In any other situation, his tough, military presence would have bolstered her confidence.

Today, he was a liability. If they encountered even a Charlie, the lowest form of heka, who wore enhancements applied by another, she'd have to worry about protecting Carlo as much as dealing with the threat.

"What are you going to do with that?" Carlo asked, gesturing toward her clipboard. "Give them a ticket?"

"Very funny." He'd seen the cipher she drew during the meeting, and he had looked like he wanted to ask more questions about it, but the meeting had moved along too fast. She didn't want to reveal too much. The fewer who knew what she could do, the better. But she couldn't let him get in the way. "It's all part of the disguise. Stay a little behind me. If we run into any hostiles, I'll engage. Don't shoot unless there's no alternative. Gunshots would give us away."

"But it is my responsibility to protect you," he protested.

Sarah raised an eyebrow. "Have you forgotten already what happened in the gym?"

"It is a matter of honor."

"Fine, then how about I knock them down and you deal with any that try to get up again?"

He looked torn, but agreed. "I can shoot then, yes?"

"If you have to, but remember if they're enhanced you might need to pour in a lot of lead before they stop."

She took the next corner and led half a step ahead toward the distant stone staircase. They met Tomas and Eirene, who appeared from the opposite end of the hallway, and the four of them descended.

Units four through ten would assemble and follow as a backup force. One of the units had smuggled some heavier weapons into the castle inside a box that was supposed to hold a dozen crystal vases. They'd have the benefit of three flamethrowers and a couple grenade launchers with those room-clearing buckshot rounds.

"Where?" Eirene asked as they ghosted down the stone stairs into the murky depths of the castle.

Sarah whispered, "Close. Off to the right."

With every step, Sarah's nerves tightened another notch. She focused on keeping her breathing even, and shook out her writing hand a couple of times.

The wide staircase smelled of ancient stones, with a hint of mold. The air became chillier as they descended, a welcome relief from the heat.

No lights shone in the hallway at the bottom of the stairs, so Tomas donned a pair of night vision goggles and peered down the right-hand hallway.

"There's one sentry stationed beside a closed door," he reported softly, drawing his double-barreled dart pistol. "Eighty yards."

"What caliber is that?" Carlo asked.

"Custom."

Tomas braced his arm against the corner of the stone wall and sighted for several seconds. Sarah held her breath.

That was a long shot for a pistol, but Tomas was a brilliant shot. He'd been training with just about every type of firearm known to man, and a few that weren't, for a couple hundred years.

The gun spat twin projectiles, and Tomas leaped around the corner and sped after the bullets.

The rest of the team gave chase. With their enhancements, they left Carlo far behind and covered the distance in seconds. The sentry was still staggering under the effects of the electric shock dart.

Tomas caught him and lowered him to the floor as the fast-acting drugs turned off his brain. Sarah shackled him with steel mesh zip-ties.

Eirene pressed a listening device to the thick, oak door and concentrated for several seconds while they waited for Carlo to catch up. She reported, "Two voices. One is Alter. The other I can't make out, but it's not Tian Fei."

"This is our chance," Tomas said, holstering his double-barreled pistol and drawing from under his jacket an M203 grenade launcher. The stubby weapon was a standalone version of the launcher mounted under Sarah's favorite carbine.

"Hey, why didn't I get one of those?" she asked.

"As if it would fit under that little jacket." Tomas extracted a bright purple round and loaded it.

"What round is that?"

"Insurance. Carlo, the door."

Sarah drew her Super Juicer and they gathered around the door. Carlo flung it open and followed it inside and to the right to stay out of the line of fire.

The room was a large, low-ceilinged chamber, lit by four standing floodlights positioned in each corner. It was mostly bare, with boxes stacked along the walls, and a single table in the center of the room. Alter was strapped to the table, his soulmask once again bonded to his body.

His eyes met Sarah's, and he looked afraid.

"Sarah, look out! It's . . ."

His voice faded away, and a second later Alter and the entire table flickered, then vanished.

21

Wisdom begins in wonder. It progresses in runes.

~SOCRATES

SARAH RUSHED INTO THE ROOM, scanning for Alter. "Where'd he go?"

"I have no idea," Tomas said, eyes sweeping everywhere. "But people don't just vanish."

Sarah had to wonder if there might be a rune that could make that happen.

"Our presence is most likely compromised," Eirene cautioned as she entered the room.

"We can't just give up," Sarah insisted. She spotted an arched doorway to the right. The light penetrated only far enough to illuminate the top step of another set of stone stairs descending into blackness.

Eirene joined her and said thoughtfully, "If that wasn't really Alter, then we were seeing some kind of projection."

"Or illusion," Tomas said with a growl.

Carlo joined Sarah and touched her arm. "Signorina, we must be cautious, yes? This room may be a trap."

Sarah turned back to ask Tomas a question, but he and Eirene were gone, vanished as completed as Alter had a moment ago.

"Carlo!" Sarah cried in alarm.

He turned and muttered an Italian curse as he and Sarah scanned the empty room. Sarah felt a flash of terror to think someone was splitting the team, striking them down, snatching them away to who knew where?

Was it Tian Fei? How could she have taken both of them with no noise and no sign of struggle?

"Where'd they go?" she breathed.

Carlo's expression was worried. "I have no idea, but I think we should leave before we fall too."

Sarah tapped her earpiece. "All units, this is Sarah. We've lost contact with Tomas and Eirene."

"Did you make contact with Tian Fei?" Anaru asked.

"Negative."

"Backup teams are on route," he said.

"*Sarah*." A soft call echoed up from the stairs beyond the arched doorway, too faint to identify.

It came a second time and she turned toward it. "Someone's down there. It has to be one of them."

Carlo eyed the dark archway dubiously. "Perhaps we should wait for the back up."

"They'll catch up. I'm not waiting." Sarah felt freaked out by the strange vision of Alter, and rattled by the disappearances of Tomas and Eirene. She felt convinced that if they tried to run, something would strike them down from behind. She refused to give their mysterious enemy the chance. She'd face them and destroy them.

The Italian commando gestured her forward. "Then I follow."

Sarah trotted to the top of the stairs. Digging a high-powered flashlight out of her handbag, she flicked it on, then followed the bright beam down. Carlo trailed her, moving like a ghost in the shadows.

The stairs were narrow and descended in a slow spiral, making it impossible to see more than a dozen feet. The heavy stone walls on either side were made of large, rough blocks that seemed ancient and immovable, flecked with moss, but not damp. The air grew chillier, a dry cold that stabbed through her light clothing and made her shiver.

Again the soft voice called her name, and it sounded like Alter. If she could find him, maybe he could explain what was going on. She just hoped they didn't run into Tian Fei first. She prepared a protective cipher, just in case.

The stairs seemed to spiral forever, and her pulse pounded with every turn. Carlo seemed to sense her nerves. He leaned close and whispered, barely louder than the distant voice calling her name.

"Calm, signorina. We will deal with any threat we see, yes? So do not waste your strength fighting those you only imagine."

Sarah forced herself to relax. Carlo might not have any enhancements, but he had a warrior's heart, and he was right. Feeling a little more settled, Sarah reached the bottom of the stair and led the way down an arched corridor of tight, black stone that seemed to press in on either side.

After a moment creeping down that hall, they reached the entrance to a chamber. The ceiling rose to a dozen feet, and the room opened wide. Sarah stopped and stared.

A little boy stood about twenty feet away, barefoot and clothed only in tattered cotton trousers. He looked maybe six years old. His skin was streaked with dirt, and his tousled, dirty-blond hair obscured most of his face.

As soon as her flashlight illuminated him, the boy started toward them, little hands lifted pleadingly. He made no noise, not even the soft slap of bare feet on the cold stone.

"Oh, are you all right?" Sarah asked, lowering her pistol. "How did you end up down here in the dark? Where's your family?"

The little boy made no response, but kept coming, and a flicker of unease dampened her initial burst of concern.

Carlo stepped in front of her. "Get back, signorina! This is not right." He raised his pistol toward the little boy.

As soon as he did, the boy hissed a sharp, piercing cry and leaped off the floor, moving with superhuman speed. His body elongated into the lean form of a man, with wiry muscles and unusually long fingers. His hair seemed to dissolve, revealing a skeletal face with glowing, white eyes and sharpened teeth.

"Whoa!" Sarah shouted, stumbling back in surprise.

Carlo opened fire. He got off two rapid shots before the thing smashed into him, knocking him from his feet. Even as he fell, Carlo continued to fire, the bullets tearing into the creature's torso, but drawing no blood.

The two crashed to the ground, their sprawling legs knocking Sarah back another step. The creature's wounds were already closing as it batted Carlo's gun aside, then punched him twice in the torso. Its frail-looking hands beat the Italian with brutal force. Sarah distinctly heard the sound of snapping ribs.

As Carlo doubled over, the manlike beast lunged. Instead of going for the throat, it tore into Carlo's jaw with those jagged teeth, right at one of his soul points. Carlo screamed, and the pale, glowing rainbow mist of his soul began seeping out of the wound. It looked just like it would if a facetaker was extracting his soulmask.

The creature sucked at those wispy tendrils of Carlo's soul and let out a guttural sigh.

That was disgusting. Sarah had no idea what the thing was, but she'd seen enough to know it had to die. So she kicked it with all her enhanced strength.

Its ribs felt like bands of iron and the impact bruised her leg. The blow knocked the beast flying, but it rolled and grabbed the smooth floor with clawed hands and feet. Its long nails dragged deep marks across the stone, and the shrieking sound tore at her ears.

The beast snarled at Sarah, its eyes now glittering with the rainbow shades of the bit of soul it had sucked from Carlo. Her initial surprise gone, Sarah glared back. She'd descended into the dark dungeon worried about Tian Fei. Whatever that creature was, it was no cui dashi.

It launched itself toward her, so Sarah drew her second pistol, raised them both, and opened fire. The bullets tore into the thing's chest, but it ignored the wounds and leaped the last dozen feet, clawed hands reaching for her.

Sarah dropped her right-hand pistol and slashed a finger through the air, activating the defensive cipher she had prepared moments before. The creature collided with the invisible wall that she summoned, and bounced off like a cat.

"Carlo, are you all right?" Sarah cried, not taking her eyes off the thing, which had paused in a crouch to study her with those freakish eyes.

How intelligent was it? It moved with deadly speed, and it had attacked Carlo's soul. Tomas had only dropped hints about real-life monsters, but she had dealt with enough imaginary ones in the memoryscape to understand she only needed to discover its weakness to destroy it.

Carlo grunted, "I think so. What is . . . look out!"

The beast scuttled to the right, and Sarah spun with it, modifying her defensive wall to keep it between them.

It leaped at her again, and when it bounced off the wall a second time, it shrieked, a high-pitched keening, full of bloodlust and frustration.

"I'll give you a reason to scream," Sarah growled, wishing she was in the memoryscape so she could summon a bigger weapon. She began preparing another cipher, one that would take the fight to the beast.

Suddenly it opened its mouth wider than that human skull should have allowed. A howling wind erupted out of that maw, struck her shield wall, and rolled across it. The noise intensified like a dozen damned souls screaming from the abyss. A smell like rotting compost filled the dark room.

Shapes formed within the wind as it expanded across her shield wall and fastened to the edges. Glimpses of ethereal faces, like shadows of soulmasks, flickered in the wind, mouths open in endless screams. She recoiled in horror, struggling to retain the calm she needed to wield her ciphers.

The creature threw its hands to the side, as if ripping away a curtain. The wind mimicked the move, yanking aside Sarah's shield wall. Before she could restore it, the creature leaped at her. The new cipher wasn't ready, her guns were useless against it.

So Sarah punched it.

Drawing upon the weeks of intense training with Tomas and Alter, Sarah smashed it in the sternum with her best punch. The impact jarred her all the way to the shoulder.

That much enhanced force would have shattered any unenhanced person, broken most stone walls, and seriously dented the steel side of a truck. It only knocked the creature back, hissing and baring its teeth at her.

Carlo shot it.

The Italian commando had managed to sit up and retrieve his pistol. Despite obvious pain, his arm remained rock solid, and the first bullet struck the beast in the eye. The monster flinched and spun under the next shot, then leaped upon Carlo. With a single blow, it broke his forearm and snatched the pistol away.

As Carlo fell back to the floor with a curse, clutching at his broken arm, the beast turned the gun on him and opened fire. Bullets tore into Carlo's chest and stomach, and he screamed as blood erupted from the wounds.

Sarah charged the monster, shouting a challenge, horrified by the terrible damage it was doing to poor Carlo.

It spun to meet her and made a throwing gesture. That same invisible wind that had wrenched at her defensive wall grasped her limbs, encircling her with restraining force, like invisible bands.

Sarah shrieked with fear as she fought the restraints. Those ethereal, howling faces pressed against her limbs, their teeth biting at her skin.

The creature leaped upon Sarah in that moment of distraction, knocking her from her feet and pinning her arms with feet that grasped at her like hands. It grabbed her face and ripped with those horrible fangs at the soul points along her jaw.

Sarah screamed and writhed in its grasp as its fangs tore into her chin, ripping through skin, then deep into the bone. Worse than the physical pain was the agony that seared her soul. Her enhancements dimmed and the well of her rounon strength bled away as the monster somehow drained her vitality.

She needed to break its hold, had to activate another cipher, but her thoughts scattered under the horror of its assault and the pain as it fed on the force of her soul. She screamed again.

Then its weight disappeared as it tumbled away, grappling with another person. For a second, Sarah thought somehow Carlo had managed to shake off those brutal injuries and come to her aid. It wasn't Carlo.

It was Tomas.

He and the creature tumbled over each other, and he maintained a secure hold on its throat with his left hand, even though it was punching and raking with those deadly claws. All the while he slashed it with deadly precision, using a short, curved knife.

Instead of stabbing for arteries in the bloodless creature, he struck joints. The blade drove into wrists, elbows, and shoulders, parting tendon and slashing cartilage.

In seconds, the creature's struggles lessoned, its limbs quivering but not able to move. It couldn't seem to recover as quickly from the devastating damage Tomas had delivered. With it momentarily disabled, Tomas changed tactics and drove the blade for one of its glittering eyes.

The creature howled right in his face, the force of its howling tornado breath catapulting him across the floor. The sight of him being driven by that awful, creepy wind helped Sarah shake off the paralyzing effects of its recent attack and focus her thoughts. She would burn that monster to ashes.

"Tomas, to me," she cried as a cipher snapped into focus in her mind. He rolled to his feet and ran in her direction, but that wind of half-formed, screaming faces assaulted him again, driving him back.

"Whatever you're going to do, do it now!" he shouted.

It took an agonizing second to draw enough soul strength to activate the cipher.

"Hurry!" Tomas shouted through the deadly wind.

Sarah raised her hand to make the focus mark and release her cipher, but the creature dissolved into thin air.

"Bloody hell," Tomas growled as the wind died away, his voice slipping into his native British accent. "Illusion!"

Hands like iron bars grasped Sarah from behind and wrenched her around so those horrible fangs could strike at her face again.

Not this time.

Sarah slashed a glowing finger across the beast's face. The cipher already blazing in her mind activated and drained most of her remaining rounon strength. It was worth it. That cipher transformed pure energy into a wave of white-hot fire that engulfed the monster.

Sarah sagged against the floor, momentarily exhausted. She retained enough focus to drive the flames around the creature in a raging firestorm. The monster staggered back, shrieking that awful cry, and somehow its howling breath drove back the flames.

"How does it do that?" Sarah shouted.

That ugly beast was really ticking her off. She felt a deep exhaustion as she tried to make the flames hotter. She was tapping too much too soon after that thing had fed on her vitality.

"They really are annoying," Eirene said in a conversational tone as she strode past Sarah, her eyes glowing with her activated nevron. "Quench those flames, will you, dear?"

Sarah did so. The flames winked out, and the creature turned toward Eirene. That disgusting wind of half-formed, screaming faces blasted her.

The purplish glow of her active nevron became visible around Eirene, like a soft halo, and it parted that wind like the prow of a ship cutting through a wave. She lunged at the beast.

It leaped away, moving incredibly fast.

Tomas was ready. Somehow he anticipated both Eirene's approach and the creature's flight and was already diving on an intercept course. He dragged the monster to the ground. Eirene leaped upon it and grabbed its face with fingers already burning with her active power.

She drove her fingers through the skin of its face, and it screamed, far louder than a single throat should be able to. The sound echoed through the chamber in a painful crescendo.

The beast thrashed in wild panic, but Eirene and Tomas held on. The scream suddenly dropped in volume, and Sarah glimpsed one of those half-formed faces peel away and tear across the room. Its scream softened to a sigh before it splattered into a scorch mark against the stone wall.

In quick succession, more ghostly faces broke away, and with each one, the sound of the monster's scream faded. Its body began to shake, its skin wrinkling and peeling, as if aging decades in seconds.

With a final heave, Eirene extracted the creature's soulmask. Its body collapsed, breaking into a dusty pile that looked nothing like a human corpse. The soulmask looked cankered and diseased, lacking the usual tendrils of glowing, rainbow smoke.

"Your suffering is at an end," Eirene said, a hint of pity in her voice as she handed the soulmask to Tomas.

He smashed it under his boot. It shattered like glass, spraying glittering shards in every direction. They melted as soon as they touched the stone floor.

"Are you all right?" Eirene asked Tomas.

"Time to get another vampire rune, I guess."

"Vampire?" Sarah asked, rubbing her arms against a sudden chill.

Tomas moved to her side and crouched beside her. "Are you okay?"

She shivered. "That thing was gross."

"You can say that again." He gingerly touched her chin where the creature had bitten her.

Sarah's eyes widened in horror. "I've been bitten. Does that mean . . . ?"

Tomas shook his head. "Vampires are real, but as usual, reality is stranger than fiction. It takes more than a bite to turn someone into one of those creatures."

She breathed a sigh of relief. "Gregorios mentioned vampires once, but I never thought . . ."

"We haven't seen one in decades. They're hard to make, and it's always a bad idea." He glanced at the dusty pile of the creature's corpse. "If that thing had escaped alive, it could have posed a lingering threat to you, but now you should be fine."

Eirene joined them. "When you and Carlo disappeared, we realized what we must be facing."

"Carlo!" Sarah spun to the fallen commando. He was still alive, but barely. Sarah counted seven bullet wounds, plus the broken arm and ribs. Then there was the damage to his soul from the vampire bite. She still felt shaky herself, and her rounon well felt shallow.

Carlo blinked open his eyes at Sarah's touch and gave her a weak grin. "Tutto benne?"

She forced a laugh. "Me? Worry about yourself."

"And the mostro?"

"Dead."

"Grazie Dio. Tell my men I helped," he breathed.

"You tell them."

Tomas handed her his curved knife before she even had to ask for it. It was beautifully balanced and sharp as a scalpel.

Tomas knelt beside her as she ripped open Carlo's shirt and began marking her signature healing rune on his side. Tomas cut chunks of the shirt to use as bandages and pressed them over the ugly wounds.

"I should have gotten here sooner," he muttered.

Not slowing her work, Sarah asked him, "What happened to you? When you disappeared, we followed what we thought was Alter calling us."

"That was the vampire. We didn't go anywhere. It must have hit you with the illusion of us being gone at the same time it struck us with the distraction of Alter lying dead on the opposite side of the room. By the time we investigated, you were already gone."

"It can do all that?"

"Depends on how potent they are. Their abilities vary dramatically. This one was more than a baby, but not really that powerful."

"You've got to be kidding," Sarah exclaimed, pausing for a second to glance at him. "That thing was terrifying."

"Only because you've never dealt with them. You were lucky you distracted it enough that it couldn't mask the sound of the gunfire."

"Vampires," Sarah muttered in disgust. She wondered what a powerful vampire might be capable of as she completed the healing rune. Then she focused over it, willing it to life, willing Carlo to have the strength of soul to bond to it.

It flared blinding blue-white, and she breathed a sigh of relief.

"He's family now," Tomas commented, looking solemn, and pleased.

"One of the guides thought he was my father."

"Better that than an old creep with a young girlfriend."

Thankfully Carlo passed out. He had to be in excruciating pain. As Tomas worked to bind the wounds until the healing rune could stabilize him, Sarah added a second rune on Carlo's bicep. It enhanced his strength and vitality. She added secondary marks to allow her to track him like she could the enforcers.

"You plan to add that rune to everyone?" Tomas asked.

"It never hurts to know where to find friends."

When Sarah moved to Carlo's bloody stomach and prepared to mark a third rune, Tomas gently took her hand.

"Just one more," Sarah insisted.

"You've done everything you can."

"But . . ."

"Sarah." He cupped her face in his hands. "You can't mark three new runes on an untested soul. You're going to overwhelm him and block him from bonding any of them. Especially after the trauma of that vampire bite."

She closed her eyes and sagged against him, hating that she couldn't do anything more.

Eirene crouched beside them, looking grave. "Have either of you noticed that our comms aren't working?"

They shared a glance and Tomas spoke into his throat mic. "Anaru, report? Can anyone hear me?"

Nothing.

Then the cultured voice of Tian Fei spoke from the doorway. "Now that you've finished playing with my pet, perhaps it is time for proper introductions."

22

SARAH ROSE to face Tian Fei, fighting to control a rush of fear. Tomas and Eirene stood beside her. Eirene's eyes began to glow with her active nevron, and Tomas' hand was already inside his jacket, probably gripping the stubby grenade launcher, but neither of them attacked.

Sarah wondered if they were thinking the same thing she was. Tian Fei could have killed them all while they were distracted. Why hadn't she?

The slender Chinese woman wore her long, black hair loose down her back, and had changed into black slacks and a pink, silk coat. It struck Sarah as incongruous that such a deadly woman would bother with such a feminine look. Spiked leather and burning chains would have fit better.

The cui dashi turned her imperious gaze on Tomas. "You are known to me, Captain. You have eclipsed the auspicious circumstances of your first life and gained much honor. Will you facilitate introductions?"

Tomas withdrew his hand from his jacket and made a formal bow. He spoke in his British accent. "It would be my pleasure." Then gesturing toward Eirene, but not looking away from Tian Fei he said,

"It is my great honor to introduce the Lady Eirene, second in command at Suntara."

Eirene gave Tian Fei a slight bow, which the woman accepted with an even smaller nod and said, "Such a simple name to encompass such a vibrant soul."

She spoke softly, but with intensity. Sarah wasn't sure what that meant, but she wondered at the overly polite exchange. Was it just the prelude to murder?

"You seem to know much about us," Eirene said, studying Tian Fei, her expression curious.

"Indeed. You and your husband have gained unprecedented mastery over your nevra cores and grounded well the ascendants of your souls. I applaud your recent elevation to rule the might of Suntara."

Eirene managed the strange interview with remarkable grace. She said, "I confess surprise since your daughter, Mai Luan, was responsible for the vacancies in the council."

Tian Fei made a dismissive gesture. "The service she rendered you requires no thanks. The previous council was long past due for removal. Their ages-long corruption resulted in much suffering throughout the world."

"I wasn't a fan of their policies at the last," Eirene allowed, her expression unreadable.

"Which is why I arranged this convocation. I had hoped your rule with your husband might offer a unique opportunity to leverage the strength of your organization to foster a better future."

"I suppose that depends on what you believe makes the future better."

Sarah was struggling to figure out what Tian Fei was playing at. The old council had been a bunch of corrupt old fossils, and she totally agreed that Gregorios and Eirene would do a better job. But what did Tian Fei want out of all that?

The cui dashi continued, "However, after your most inconsiderate interruption of that newly-cherished memory at Nanjing, I realized that your aggressive traits are too deeply ingrained."

"As I recall, you're the one who greeted us with a full broadside," Eirene pointed out.

"The only appropriate response to such belligerence," Tian Fei said in a reprimanding tone. "Don't try to pretend your intentions were anything but combative."

"Given the history of our interactions with your family, it seemed only prudent," Eirene said.

Sarah was amazed that she could speak with such outward calm with the terrifying woman.

"So I should hunt down all of your descendants and murder them simply because you and I don't agree?" Tian Fei asked, one fine eyebrow raised.

"That's not what I was saying, and you know it," Eirene responded, her tone sharper.

"I know enough," Tian Fei said, still outwardly calm. "And I have taken steps to address your arrogant, militant ways. Perhaps then you will be willing to learn and we can explore an accord to build a better future."

Eirene replied, "That depends on what steps you refer to, and what you consider a better future."

Sarah couldn't hold her peace any longer and interrupted before Tian Fei could respond. "You're such a hypocrite! You dare call Eirene belligerent, when your own children have killed thousands, wrecked Rome, and continually threatened our lives."

Tian Fei gave her a disapproving look. "Given your lack of proper education, Rune Warrior, I will forgive your breach of etiquette for interrupting our parlance, particularly when you have not even been introduced yet."

Tomas smoothly interceded before Sarah could shout the curse that came to mind. "Then let's rectify that lapse, shall we? I am deeply pleased to present Sarah, Rune Warrior, and Sword of the Deliverer."

Tian Fei gave him a tiny nod of appreciation, but her eyes did not leave Sarah's. Despite her anger, Sarah struggled to meet that stare. A tiny, lavender spark glowed in the center of Tian Fei's eyes, and her stare held as much weight as Gregorios'.

"When you took my son's head, you destroyed a beautiful thing."

"Your son was disgusting," Sarah retorted, having to suppress a shudder as she thought about Paul and his deviant advances.

"He was impetuous, and perhaps overly zealous to prove himself and earn his new name," Tian Fei admitted. "But together, we could have molded him into a better man. In a century or two, he could have developed into an unrivaled ruler."

Sarah shook her head. "One of us would have died in the first week."

Tian Fei pursed her lips, her expression turning sad. "I sometimes forget how rash and short-sighted first-life mortals are, despite the strength of their souls. What matters your petty personal concerns when compared to the good you could have done for the world at my son's side?"

The suggestion flabbergasted Sarah. "Your son was broken. He would never have made a good ruler."

"And Sarah can choose who she wants," Tomas said, his voice hard with anger.

"Your infatuation is clouding your judgment, Captain," Tian Fei said.

Tomas responded formally, "And yet it's you who has interrupted introductions with insults and derogatory comments. You have yet to introduce yourself."

Part of Sarah wanted to claw the woman's eyes out, but she also very much wanted to know more about the terrifying woman. Tomas' choice to change the conversation was probably a good idea.

"What you call me matters little. You westerners understand little of the weight of a proper name."

Tomas bowed his head slightly to acknowledge the point. "We may not grasp the full import of your name, but we would prefer knowing how to address you, nonetheless."

"Very well. You may address me as Empress Xiao."

The pompous title didn't surprise Sarah. The woman spoke the name with a distinct Chinese accent, making it sound like 'shee-ow'. The name meant nothing to Sarah, but she hoped Eirene was gleaning something useful from the strange conversation. Sarah's nerves were stretched taught. She expected any second that the facade of polite conversation would get stomped by the return of preemptive violence.

So she said, "Well, Empress Xiao, I demand the return of Alter, or I guarantee we'll keep interrupting you the same way we did your son."

"The hunter lives," Xiao said, her voice still calm. "He is now in my service, and his fate is no longer your concern."

"Like hell it isn't!" Sarah cried, raising a hand as a new, deadly rune popped into her mind.

Tian Fei actually made a tisking sound and shook her head, her expression warning. "Don't tempt my patience, girl. Are you incapable of speaking rationally without resorting to violence?"

"But it's you who kidnapped Alter," Eirene pointed out.

"I require the hunter's service," Xiao said, as if that was enough.

"Whether he enjoys comfortable lodging or endures endless torture is entirely up to you."

"What do you mean?" Sarah asked, worry for Alter snuffing out her anger.

"Show self-restraint, and he will be fine. Interfere again, and he suffers. Your next interference will guarantee that at the end of his service to me, instead of enjoying the rewards of my gratitude, he will suffer the demands of my justice." Xiao's eyes shone with the unique lavender light of her nevron and her voice became deadly hard. "Choose wisely. You will not be given a second chance."

Fury and horror boiled through Sarah. Where was Anaru with the rotary cannon and those cipher-marked shells? Without him, they couldn't hope to stop Xiao, and that feeling of hopelessness fueled her anger.

Xiao smiled at her hesitation. "Perhaps you can be taught."

Sarah warned, "If you harm Alter, I promise to take your head next."

"We don't have to be enemies," Xiao said, speaking to her like she was a child. "Much that you wish to know I alone can teach, but you must demonstrate the respect every student owes their teacher before such grace can be imparted." Then her voice hardened and her eyes lit again with her powers. "But if you choose the road of conflict, you alone will bear responsibility for the consequences."

The woman was actually offering her . . . what? An apprenticeship? The idea was ludicrous. Sarah wanted to strike the woman down, and a cipher came to mind, burning with deadly clarity in her thoughts. She might not be able to kill Xiao, but she could hurt her.

Eirene must have sensed her intention, because she placed a gently restraining hand on Sarah's arm. Sarah forced calm on herself, and the moment of rage passed. Eirene was probably right to hold back, but she really wanted to wreck Xiao's face.

Xiao's lips twitched in the hint of a smile. "You have much to learn, warrior. When you understand the truth, only then will the path to action and enlightenment become clear."

And now Xiao was actually giving her advice? The incongruity of it nearly made Sarah laugh.

Eirene asked, "What truth are you hunting, Xiao?"

"My search is no concern of yours." Xiao seemed irritated that she asked.

"Then there's no way for us to know if our actions might interfere, is there?" Tomas asked.

"You'll know when your men begin to die."

Eirene said, "Return Alter to us, and we can meet again to speak at greater length."

"The matter of the hunter is resolved. Learn well the lessons I have arranged to be taught, and I will contact you again soon." She glanced at Sarah. "Look beyond the limits concealing your vision, warrior. You may yet prove a productive servant."

"You really don't get it, do you?" Sarah asked, astounded by the woman's audacity.

Xiao turned to Tomas, "Recall your men, Captain, and do not interfere with my departure. Should I glimpse any surveillance or encounter any resistance, I will kill every last man of them and dump their bodies at your feet."

Tomas' calm cracked, and his hand slowly closed into a fist, but his voice remained calm. "Until we meet again then, Empress."

Xiao glanced from him to Eirene, then to Sarah, her gaze clearly communicating that she considered them at best potential servants. Then she turned and walked into the darkness of the hallway.

Sarah watched her go, trying to decipher the bizarre meeting, barely believing they'd escaped pitched battle. She glanced at Tomas, who gave her a helpless shrug.

"That woman is one messed up piece of work," Sarah breathed.

Eirene looked after Xiao, her expression thoughtful. "She is not what we expected, but is she more or less than we feared?"

23

THE LID of Alter's dungeon flipped open. Blessed light entered for the first time since Tian Fei had locked him in the horrible soul coffin. Even the black, felt-lined sides of the coffin looked amazing in his two-dimensional vision.

Alter had learned that there were limits to how long he could scream angry curses in his helium-high, dispossessed voice. It wasn't like he had a voice to scream himself hoarse. Shouting had helped hold the terror at bay for a while, but all that effort had taken a toll on the force of his soul. That realization silenced him. Did a soul regain its strength without a body to provide new nourishment?

Now the enchanter Hongwu reached in with a careless hand and scooped up Alter's soulmask. That was a foolish mistake, but Alter would never complain about getting a perfect chance to escape.

He had been taught since childhood never to take up a dispossessed soulmask. It might belong to one of the demon facetakers for fear that their evil powers might overwhelm the purity of his soul. The enchanter should have known better, but his arrogance would prove his downfall.

Alter's powers might represent the blackest form of evil to his family, but he would use every weapon at his disposal to fight Tian Fei and her minions. Alter unleashed the full force of his nevron.

Purple fire erupted from his soulmask, boiling up Hongwu's arm. Alter sought to overwhelm the evil soul, take command of the man's soul points, and own that body.

As Hongwu lifted his soulmask from the soul coffin, Alter's nevron reached the man's elbow, but then rebounded back from an invisible barrier, like water glancing off a mirror. Alter wanted to scream with frustration. He struck again, but with the same effect.

"I love when a soul retains a sense of optimism," Hongwu said, giving Alter a condescending smile. "It helps preserve the full measure of your strength until it is harvested."

"I will destroy you!" Alter raged, but the threat sounded childish in his high-pitched whisper voice.

Hongwu's smile only widened as he strode into a stone-lined hall-way. Alter didn't recognize the location, but he was distracted, trying to puzzle out the mystery of how Hongwu had so easily defeated his attack. He had never heard of a rune that could block a facetaker nevron, let alone a cui dashi one. Hongwu was far more dangerous than Alter had supposed.

Dangling in Hongwu's grasp, Alter could do nothing but imagine the many forms his vengeance would take when he was restored to his body. His dark thoughts were interrupted when the enchanter entered a long, stone-sheathed room with a low ceiling supported by thick, stone columns.

In the center of the room stood one of the machines, gleaming in a bright floodlight.

Hongwu placed Alter's soulmask on a nearby table next to a wire harness. Mai Luan had used similar ones to connect soulmasks to power their machines. His anger chilled to growing fear. Tian Fei planned to sacrifice him to fuel her next memory journey.

He tried to focus on rage at the thought that the force of his soul would be spent facilitating her search for more master runes to use against Sarah and his grandmother. He couldn't hold back the fear wen Hongwu attached wire leads to his soulmask.

He had failed. He was the mightiest of all hunters, but she had defeated him with terrifying ease. She would insult the purpose of his entire life by destroying him this way.

"Wait!" Alter cried.

Hongwu paused to glance down at him and he added, "Restore me to a body, any body, and allow me to die in honorable combat."

"Your purpose is set," Hongwu said, looking completely uninterested in Alter's predicament.

"Not like this!" Alter shouted, hating his impotence, racking his brain for some way to turn the situation back against the cursed enchanter.

He came up with nothing.

Outside of the angle of his vision, he heard someone else enter the room. They sat in the nearby chair and donned the heavy helmet in preparation for entering the memoryscape.

"Release me! Grant me the chance to face you again, demon!"

Hongwu thumped a heavy finger onto his soulmask, without bothering to look down at him. The threat was clear. Settle down, or the enchanter would smash his soulmask.

Alter started shouting curses. Let the cursed enchanter shatter his soulmask. At least that way, the demon wouldn't gain any value from the destruction of his soul. The thought of dying in such a helpless way terrified him, but he would not allow them to desecrate what little honor he had left.

"You really are annoying," Hongwu muttered as he thumped his soulmask again.

"And your mother was a facetaker slave," Alter shouted.

Hongwu glared down at him, and Alter braced for the killing blow. Instead, Hongwu flipped a nearby cloth over him. It blocked his view and muffled his continued shouting. Alter railed against the insulting treatment, but Hongwu ignored him as he locked him into the web that would leech away the force of his soul and kill him.

Alter knew the rune sequences of every part of the machines better than anyone. He had rebuilt one from scratch, had updated the rune sequencing on the others to modify their functionality. He stopped shouting and tried to concentrate.

He could beat this. Somehow. If he could withstand the drain, perhaps with his active nevron he could disrupt the web or even turn it from its regular purpose. Without fingers to draw runes, he lacked the normal means for focusing his nevron, but there had to be a way.

Sarah could activate her battle ciphers with no more than a single glowing mark. She had explained that the key was to hold the cipher clear in her mind. That single mark was but the focal point.

Alter was no rune warrior, could not activate the same advanced ciphers, but he was a master runesmith. He was in tune with the force of his soul, had far more experience, and he had the strength of the cui dashi to draw upon.

Gregorios and Eirene could focus the power of their nevra cores without the use of runes. He would find a way to do the same thing, to turn the elegant execution Tian Fei planned for him on its head, and strike at her unprotected soul.

As the first flickers of power rippled down the web to him, Alter steeled himself for the challenge. If he had teeth, he would have bared them in defiance.

The machine activated, and a wave of energy rippled across his soulmask. Instead of sucking at his strength, he was surprised to feel the familiar blackness encircling his mind as he was drawn into the memoryscape.

His final thought before darkness sucked him under was that something was very wrong.

24

Can it be true that one can cheat Anubis and step from this life into a second? None of the runes any of the priests have studied can do such a thing, but I hear rumors of one who walks with the gods and wields the power of souls.

~PHARAOH TUTANKHAMUN, ABOUT 1300 B.C.

BLINDING sunlight snapped on like a light switch, and Alter blinked against the piercing brilliance. Then he laughed as he realized he was clothed in his own body.

He took a moment just to stand on stone-paved ground and exult in the movement of every muscle. He might only be standing in a dream sequence, but it felt real, and that bolstered his confidence.

Tian Fei was a fool to draw him into the memory. Now that he was again restored, he could fight her. He looked around, hands clenching into fists, but then paused to gape when he recognized the memoryscape in which he stood.

Egypt.

Alter had never set foot in ancient Egypt, but the location was easy to recognize. A huge wall of Nubian sandstone reared nearby, split down the middle by a massive gap. Bright hieroglyphs covered everything. Alter recognized it as the entrance pylon to an ancient Egyptian temple.

Two slender stone obelisks, also covered in hieroglyphs, reared eighty feet into the air. The stone-paved avenue where Alter stood passed between those obelisks and through the entrance.

The size and grandeur of the architecture awed Alter. Two enormous, seated statues of a pharaoh guarded the entrance, with pairs of statues standing to either side. The entry pylon reared a solid seventy-five feet into the air, and stretched nearly two hundred feet in both directions from the central entry gate.

It took three seconds of awed staring to realize where he stood.

Luxor.

The ruins of the ancient temple were a major tourist attraction. If people could see the majesty of the temple in all its ancient splendor, they'd swarm the site by the millions.

Other people moved along the paved avenue around Alter. Egyptian men in white, kilt-like loincloths mingled with women in simple linen dresses. As usual in a memoryscape, everyone ignored Alter.

He saw no sign of Tian Fei, but let his gaze linger on the long avenue of human-headed sphinxes that stretched into the distance toward another massive temple structure. If he remembered correctly, that would be the famous Karnak complex.

The air was hot, a bit humid, and it smelled like dust and smoke from the cook fires of the surrounding city. Alter longed for a chance to study the hieroglyphs, but he couldn't let himself get distracted. He had to find Tian Fei, had to learn her purpose in dragging him into that distant memory.

In fact, how did she get them so far into the past? Not even Gregorios was that old. Alter refused to believe she had lived so long. Either the facetakers or his family would have discovered and destroyed them. Besides, every indication suggested that Tian Fei was Chinese. How could she have a memory dating back to ancient Egypt?

The puzzle wouldn't solve itself, so he jogged through the temple entrance and into the cool shadows between the massive pylon gate towers. The long entrance emptied into a wide, paved court, flanked by rows of huge papyrus columns. He couldn't imagine Tian Fei returning to such an iconic location without seeking something inside.

Paul and Mai Luan had hunted through history for pivotal moments where master runes could be discovered, but nothing unusual appeared to be happening. The temple was crowded with priests, government officials, and worshippers, but their activity lacked the intensity he would expect if the pharaoh was scheduled to arrive.

He had studied Egyptian hieroglyphs, but not enough of Egyptian history. He had no idea which moments might be tied to master runes. If not seeking a master rune, why would Tian Fei have gone there?

The mystery of it only grew as he jogged deeper into the temple complex. He passed through a covered colonnade. Tall papyrus-carved columns flanked the colonnade in pairs, each over fifty feet tall. It took seven of those giant pairs to support the long ceiling.

The vibrant colors of the hieroglyphs took his breath away. He picked out many of them. The culture was such a gold mine of power runes. He wondered how many runes he could rediscover if he only had time for a little study. So many had been lost to time.

Perhaps later. First he had to find Tian Fei and figure out what she was up to.

That proved harder than he expected. He ranged through open courts and enclosed shrines, dedicated to gods and pharaohs. The high-ceilinged chambers were cooler than he'd feared, and they smelled faintly of incense. Finally, in the inner sanctuary of Amun, he heard her familiar voice.

Feeling a rush of adrenaline, Alter crept closer. He wondered if Tian Fei even realized she had drawn him into the memoryscape with her. The standard power-draining web would have been designed to work with a non-enhanced soul. Had his cui dashi nevra core produced an unexpected side-effect? If so, he might be able to take her by surprise.

Slipping between some smaller columns in the intimate sanctuary, Alter finally caught a glimpse of Tian Fei. She was dressed in a standard Egyptian white shift, with a black headdress. The attempt to look Egyptian would have worked better if she'd done something to conceal her telltale Chinese features. She stood over the sleeping form of a man, who was reclining on a divan, positioned near the alter to Amun.

Even though the man was clearly sleeping, he spoke in a slow, tired voice. "As I have foreseen, one who is my equal will manifest herself to me, with the promise of salvation from the dark days of my prophesy in her grasp."

Tian Fei looked pleased. "Good. You already recognize that failure waits at the doors to take your soul and destroy your life's work. I am more than your equal, Sutekh, and I hold the power to change your future. But you must prove yourself worthy, and demonstrate you are capable of accepting me as the mistress of your soul."

Alter edged closer. The name Sutekh was not familiar, but the situation was intriguing. What was she up to? The talk of changing the future of one long dead seemed ridiculous. Why would she lie to him, and would he actually believe such a thing could be possible?"

"I am master of the occult and the secret right hand of the pharaoh himself," Sutekh said in a sleepy, offended tone.

"Do you know of the ascendants?" she asked.

Alter slipped to the closest column, wishing he had arrived sooner. Why would the demon have traveled so far back in history only to speak with a shade of the past? If this was her memory, wouldn't she know everything Sutekh could tell her? If not her memory, then was there some other memory walker there with them that he had not yet discovered?

"I alone know their secrets," Sutekh said proudly. "It is this sacred knowledge that granted me the vision of the unthinkable calamities that are to come. Such horrors I cannot share even with the pharaoh, for he would never believe the slaves could actually succeed, or that their powers might somehow exceed those of all the gods of Egypt."

"Your future is known to me," Tian Fei said, dropping to one knee beside him.

"How can you guarantee success that even I cannot obtain?"

"Prove yourself to me. Conditions are not yet right, but events are in motion to prepare them. Some can be influenced by you. Others depend upon the actions of mighty souls."

She turned and glanced directly at Alter, where he leaned around the nearest column. She did not look surprised to see him.

Since she knew he was there, he marched across the smooth floor toward her. The element of surprise might be lost, but he would discover her purpose.

"I know your ultimate doom," Tian Fei told Sutekh. "But that future perhaps can be altered."

"What must I do to prove my worth to you, oh great mistress of time?" Sutekh asked.

Alter frowned. For one so full of himself, he was accepting the possibility of her dominance with remarkable ease. Apparently he really did believe he was doomed, but still Alter felt he was missing something.

"I seek a name worthy of the future I will build," Tian Fei said, her voice soft, but intense. "I seek pivotal moments in deep history to reveal the final components of my name. You will introduce me to those moments."

"Oh no, you won't," Alter declared, slipping into a fighting stance and activating his nevra core.

His fingers started to burn, although the force of his nevron seemed partially shuttered. Perhaps the matrix that the enchanter had strapped him into was interfering.

Tian Fei frowned at him. "Don't make me chastise you for interrupting."

The force of her gaze rattled him, but he refused to let her see fear. "I will not allow you to seek more master runes. Your son made a huge mess with three of them."

"Hush," Tian Fei said, turning back to Sutekh, then adding in an off-hand way. "Those three were nothing. I've visited dozens of pivotal moments."

"Really?" Alter let his hands drop and stared at her back in astonishment

If she had acquired so many master runes, they were doomed. So why hunt deeper into history, and how was she managing to access such ancient days? He would wait to strike until he investigated the mystery.

Tian Fei ignored him, but again leaned over Sutekh's sleeping form. "Tell me of the past. I must see the pivotal moments spiraling back into the ages obscured from the world."

Sutekh tilted his sleeping head, brows furrowed. "What truths can the past offer that the future fails to overshadow?"

"Perhaps the key to everything." She placed a hand over his eyes in a surprisingly gentle movement and leaned close, whispering, "Sleep, Sutekh. We will speak again soon."

Then she rose to face Alter. "What do you think of Egypt, young hunter?"

"I don't think you look Egyptian. Whose memory is this?"

"One who is no longer living," she said as she swept past, gesturing him to follow. She headed across the inner sanctum toward the distant exit.

He was tempted to kick her in the head to prove he didn't have to obey her commands, but getting beat up again by the vile woman wouldn't answer his questions. So he fell into step beside her. "Impossible."

"And yet here we are," she said with the hint of a smile.

Paul had seemed to be searching for a way to reach moments beyond his memory where the master runes he sought could be found. Those moments had existed within the same time frame as the actual memories of the dreamers. Alter couldn't imagine how Tian Fei had managed to drive beyond the farthest reaches of living memory. The idea intrigued him far more than he would ever admit.

He asked, "Why am I here? You're not using my soul to power this memory, are you?"

"I need your help," she said simply.

Alter barked a laugh. "You want my help? After kidnapping and imprisoning me?"

"You would not have listened to reason any other way."

"If that's reason, I want nothing to do with it." If only he could imagine even a whisper of hope of defeating her, he'd attack without hesitation.

"You will come to understand your purpose," she said, as if explaining something to a child.

"My purpose is to destroy you." It was foolish to goad her, but he couldn't help it.

"You are a child who must learn to become a man," she said, unruffled. When he opened his mouth to argue again, she cut him off. "Listen before you speak and avoid making a fool of yourself."

"You speak only lies," he growled, turning away. He might be trapped in the memoryscape, but that didn't mean he had to wait around and listen to her poisoned words.

"Hear me out," she snapped, and suddenly she stood in front of him, barring his path. She had moved so fast, she might as well have teleported.

"Speak then," he said with a sullen frown.

"You will learn manners," she said softly, her eyes glowing with the unique lavender glow of her nevron. "Or I will not spare the rune warrior you love so dearly, even though she has spurned you at every turn."

"How do you . . ." He bit his tongue, hating to validate her words.

Tian Fei gave him a compassionate look, which only infuriated him. She said, "Truth is apparent to those who know how to see. I brought you here to begin unshackling your mind. There is much more possible than you have been led to believe, and you can accomplish far more than the limits of your heritage allow."

"My heritage is dear to me," Alter growled.

"It shackles your soul," she replied in a dismissive tone. "You will see. But before you allow your childish anger to overrule your sense, consider the welfare of Sarah. I spared her life just hours ago when I could have destroyed her."

"You lie," Alter said.

Her chin raised and her eyes glowed again with her power. Her voice, though still calm, became as hard as steel. "I never lie, young hunter. If you impugn my honor again, I will chastise you."

She made no threatening move, but Alter could feel the heat of her active nevron like a distant furnace. He managed not to retreat a step from her anger, but swallowed the retort he had been planning.

When he hesitated, she continued calmly. "I allow Sarah and your great-grandmother to live as a show of good faith to you. Whether or not they continue in good health is up to you."

"What do you want from me?" he asked, hating that he felt driven to speak the words. He would never help her, but he couldn't risk the lives of Sarah and Eirene out of hand either.

"I want you to willingly walk these ancient memories with me," she said, gesturing at the temple around them.

"Why?" That made no more sense than that odd conversation with the sleeping Sutekh had.

"Perhaps I prefer your company."

"What did you mean when you said you were hunting master runes to fashion a new name?"

"Names carry more power than most realize. The search for a true name is of paramount import, particularly for those like us who will do great things."

Alter had learned a little about the Chinese fixation on names. They sought not only a meaning that resonated with their life, but ideally one that connected with their ancestors, or well-known moments in history. In addition, the symbols used to write the name had to mesh well, not be linked to other, conflicting meanings, and the sounds needed to flow well together.

Finding a good Chinese name could take years for an average person, so he could understand someone like Tian Fei needing to hunt farther afield for a properly amazing name. Hunting for symbols within the unique and powerful master runes took the concept to ridiculous levels, though. That was assuming she was even telling the truth. It was an unexpected and clever way to justify gathering master runes.

Could she really be looking for nothing more than a name from those deadly runes? He couldn't believe it. "Once you find your name, what do you plan to do with those master runes you've acquired?"

"My plans will require time for you to understand. I will explain them to you as well as to your friends. They too have a part to play in the future we will build together."

"I can't imagine building anything together." She had to be crazy, but if she really was planning to meet with the facetakers and Sarah again, perhaps together they could take her.

Walking memories with the terrifying demon might offer her the chance to find more master runes, and he hated that thought. But if she really did already have as many as she boasted, he could never hope to stop her alone. Defying her wouldn't stop her, but it would place Sarah at risk.

"Swear that what we'll be doing won't harm Sarah or Eirene," he said, watching her carefully.

Her expression remained unreadable. "Nothing we do involves them. Their fates depend wholly upon their choices."

Alter hated speaking the words, but forced himself to say, "I'll accompany you, but only if you restore my body in the waking world." The words were like offal on his tongue, but he couldn't do anything if he remained locked away in that soul coffin.

She considered him for a moment, then nodded and gave him a motherly smile. "Very well. All of my servants come to learn that to please me brings great benefits."

"I'm not your servant," Alter snarled.

Her smile faded, her expression turning hard. "And to displease me will return you to that soul coffin and guarantee the destruction of all you love."

Alter fought down a flash of rage. He couldn't fight her. Not yet. But he would find a way.

25

Those who live today will die tomorrow, those who die tomorrow will be born again; those who love MAAT will not die.

~ANCIENT EGYPTIAN PROVERB

GREGORIOS SAT in the front row of one of the larger UN committee chambers, facing a long, circular table that in turn was positioned around a central conference table. Ambassadors, dignitaries, and lesser officials packed the tables and the seats around Gregorios.

Unlike many of the mind-numbing political meetings Gregorios had endured through the centuries, this one had promised to turn lively. The meeting of "The States Parties to the Convention on Regulating or Restricting the Introduction of Certain Enhancement Markings into the General Military Population" had drawn lots of global attention.

It hadn't gotten lively yet. Gregorios stifled a yawn as the officiating secretary called for a short recess. He rose to look for some food. Politicians were as good at stuffing their faces as they were at stuffing their pockets with other people's money.

He never made it to the buffet, didn't even reach the exit. Far too many people were eager to speak with him. He tried to remain pleasant as he worked through the crowd, deflecting questions about Suntara, enhancements, and his involvement in the events in Rome.

He got bogged down by the representative of Tunisia, who was desperate to secure an agreement for a contingent from the Tenth to visit Tunis and being training their army. The man was persistent, and Gregorios finally sighed and directed him to contact Suntara and ask for Harald to schedule something.

Unfortunately, that encouraged representatives from other smaller nations to press their cases. They were all frothing at the mouth to gain access to the secrets of enhancements. Although they didn't understand all of the possibilities, even basic enhancements would help enormously. Many of them were dealing with terrorism and internal strife.

Some of them were terrorists. That posed a whole different set of challenges that the world would have to deal with.

None of the players from the larger nations made any move in his direction, even though he already knew them all. The Americans refused to even look at him. They were taking the sulking act to extremes. Not even the Brits or the Russians were acting so childish.

Those major powers had reason to look nervous. Despite the stalling tactics they had employed masterfully, the committee was planning to plunge directly into specifics about rune enhancements. Those first-world nations were about to lose the edge they had held with their secret, enhanced special-forces teams.

He had to wonder what they would do to obtain a new advantage. Was that why the Americans were acting so aloof?

He enjoyed a long history with the young country, all the way back to several of the founding fathers. Did their behavior mean they planned to distance themselves from existing agreements, to push the limits on more powerful enhancements, or maybe dabble in rune webs? Generations of secret treaties supposedly prevented such acts, but desperation could make people do stupid things.

Breaking contracts with him would definitely be a stupid thing.

He finally excused himself from the throng, making vague promises to speak again after the next recess. He needed to find the Yurak International representatives to discuss their upcoming testimony. He also wanted to get a few minutes with the delegation from Thailand. With Paul gone, it was time to normalize relations with them and finalize the penalties they would pay for having attacked Eirene during her last visit.

Their continuing belligerent tone against China needed to be explained too. Paul had been pressing them to escalate international tensions. What didn't make sense was the fact they hadn't changed course.

Before he could find them, the room seemed to grow chill in a way Gregorios hadn't felt in more than a century. He slowly turned, scanning the room. His gaze settled on a man about thirty feet away, who was moving in his direction. At first glance, the fellow looked unremarkable, just another staffer in a dark business suit, but he was the source of that prickling feeling of chill danger.

The tie gave him away.

Red was a popular color, but that tie was such a vibrant, blood-red shade, it looked like it must be dripping blood into his jacket. No dye could produce such a look.

Gregorios embraced his nevra core, and as a rush of nevron filled him, the illusion protecting the approaching man rippled and parted. Feeling a rare start of shock, Gregorios recognized him.

Vlad the Impaler.

He was the last person Gregorios had expected to see. After Tian Fei, Vlad was perhaps the deadliest predator in the world. All vampires were dangerous, but Vlad was the eldest, and by far the worst.

The illusion Vlad was projecting looked exceptional, but Gregorios' nevron-fueled gaze penetrated the façade. He calculated how many people might survive if Vlad attacked.

Not many.

As Vlad slipped through the crowd, people shifted away from him without being aware that they did so. More than a few rubbed at their arms, as if against a sudden chill. Their conscious senses might be shuttered to the danger stalking through their midst, but their souls knew at a primal level that danger prowled nearby.

If Vlad had planned to fight, he wouldn't have given Gregorios so much time to recognize the danger and prepare. Vlad had never actually made a social call, so Gregorios wasn't sure what he intended. If it came to a fight, he would need to unleash every ounce of his power in the first strike.

He would get no second chance.

"I was thinking I'd have to search the blackest crypts, buried in the deepest swamps to track you down again," Gregorios said in a conversational tone as Vlad dew close. "You're making the hunt far too easy this time."

Vlad smiled, a twitch of his pale lips that did not extend to his eyes, which remained fixed on Gregorios with a terrible hunger. If his illusion hadn't been shuttering the power of his stare, it would freeze most mortals with insurmountable terror. The strongest of them might summon the courage to flee in screaming panic.

That would just draw his attention. The result would be grisly.

When he spoke, Vlad's voice was low, but intense, like a slender blade, poised to slip between a couple of ribs. "You are no longer the hunter, Gregorios."

Gregorios grunted. "Let's step out of this crowd and find out."

He would prefer facing Vlad with a full company of Tomas' finest at his back. Then again, he already stood close enough to the mighty undead to perhaps reach him. Once he locked his hands onto Vlad's face, not even the incredible powers the vampire could unleash could save him.

He was tempted to try, despite the mess that would make of the hall. He hadn't gotten such a good shot at ending Vlad's trail of destruction in over a century, but he hesitated.

Partly he was curious about what would goad Vlad into the light to risk a face-to-face meeting. Besides, he doubted he'd manage to lay a hand on the creature that easily.

Vlad leaned his pinched face a bit closer, his colorless eyes blazing with bloodlust. The illusion rippled out to include Gregorios, concealing the truth of their interaction from mortal eyes, and Gregorios braced himself for a fight.

A light wind rippled around them, full of the faint, hopeless keening of souls shackled to the vampire's will. It pulsed against Gregorios, but recoiled from his active nevron. He didn't bother to look, but still caught glimpses of those tortured souls, like flickering shadows at the corners of his eyes. Ethereal mouths gaped open in endless screams that no one else in the room could hear.

Vlad said, "We have sparred many times, but today the tide turns against you."

"That's easy to say, but every other time we've met, you're the one who ran." Gregorios lifted a hand to scratch his chin, and he was satisfied to see Vlad flinch. "I was impressed last time that you managed to run with so much of your body destroyed."

Vlad let out a hiss that would make any snake proud, but then his humorless smile returned. "I consumed a dozen souls in order to recover. You'll be pleased to know your action forced me to sacrifice an entire family to my need."

Gregorios suppressed a flash of anger, his mind conjuring up images of brutal horror those poor mortals must have suffered.

"One more nail in the coffin," Gregorios said, his eyes igniting like purple LED screens with the force of his nevra core. Vlad recoiled, looking like he was torn between the desire to flee and the lust to join in battle.

"You're broken, Vlad," Gregorios said softly, although any pity he felt for the fallen rune warrior had faded centuries before. "And it's past time to end your suffering."

"Worry about your own suffering," Vlad snarled, but took another step back. Whatever had driven him to crawl into the light and reveal himself wasn't quite enough for him to make his move. Yet.

Good thing. Gregorios wasn't ready for that fight either. Vlad didn't have to know that, though. So he growled, "I find those kind of empty threats really annoying. Back it up, or get out of my face."

Vlad retreated, but did not turn away. He might be powerful enough to rip apart the UN building in a fit of rage, but he was no fool. The bubble of illusion retreated with Vlad, and Gregorios shuttered his nevra core before anyone noticed his glowing eyes.

He watched Vlad pass through the crowd, wondering at the exchange. Tracking down the vampire had been on his to-do list for far too long. He'd planned to start the hunt after they had resolved the cui dashi threat.

Vampires had no sense of timing.

After Vlad left the committee room, Gregorios pushed through the crowd, ignoring requests to talk. The meeting would convene again soon, but he couldn't wait to initiate a response. The folks from Yurak needed to know Vlad was active. They could help spread the word. With luck, one of their teams or the surveillance assets from the Tenth could pick up the vampire's trail when he left.

Why choose that venue to make an appearance? It had to be more than the fact that crowds of innocents pressed in all around, that Gregorios was not armed, and that the Tenth were not close at hand.

Was Vlad making a statement about the current political discussion? Most nations were desperately seeking for any individuals with channeler or enchanter-level powers.

Ramifications of those efforts extended far beyond their attempts to begin forming their own enhanced armies. Hunters and enforcers were already monitoring for confirmed heka, although their efforts at elimination would prove trickier than in the past.

No doubt Vlad was just as interested. Knowledge of the locations of soul-powered individuals around the world would facilitate his hunting.

Gregorios found the Yurak officials in the buffet line and pulled them aside to a quiet corner. They were all direct descendants of his, and he wished he could spend some time catching up and asking about their families. Eirene was better at keeping in touch, but he also enjoyed connecting with his descendants. They were the living fruit of his centuries-long love affair with the most amazing woman the world had ever known.

Family reunions would have to wait. As soon as they were out of earshot of anyone nearby, he said, "I just ran into Vlad, not five minutes ago."

Their good humor faded, and several of the younger men glanced around nervously. Tomas was the best vampire hunter in the world after Gregorios and Eirene. He had trained a special team within the Tenth to take on the monsters, but Harriett made sure Yurak forces knew how to deal with them too.

The eldest of his descendants, a full legion commander, grimaced. "We're not equipped to fight him here."

Gregorios frowned as he thought back on the strange conversation. "I don't think he came to fight, but I want you to take precautions. Send out a security alert to your assets in the city, and forward it to my people."

"Immediately," the commander said, gesturing to one of his aides. "Maybe we'll pick him up when he leaves."

"My thoughts exactly," Gregorios said, pleased that his many-times-removed son was thinking along the same lines.

Before they could make specific plans for tracking and disposing of Vlad, a United States under-secretary joined them. The aging gentleman was a long-time acquaintance who had worked for Eleanor Roosevelt before she slipped away from the world view and started her second life as a UN-funded activist in Africa. His name was Frederick Thomason, and he'd been working for decades to stash enough funds to schedule his own transfer.

Gregorios greeted him warmly, happy that at least one American seemed willing to speak with him. "How are things on the home front, Freddie?"

Frederick was usually a jovial man, but today his expression remained serious, almost frightened. "I don't know what's going on, Mr. Gregorios, but you're about to be thrown under the bus."

"What do you know?" Gregorios *had* been thrown under a bus once. It was an ugly memory that had prematurely ended what had been a pretty good life.

"The ambassador just received orders to blow the lid on your organization to the world."

Gregorios tried not to show the shock he felt. No doubt they were under surveillance and he didn't want to tip off any watchers. His descendants from Yurak were professional, but they couldn't quite hide their reactions. They hadn't been betrayed as often as he had.

He tried to think past the initial rush of indignation and focus on why the Americans would make such a disastrous move. Why now? With the kind of global scrutiny the committee was already getting, any information leaked about facetakers would spread around the world like the wildfires of the apocalypse.

Had Vlad somehow known about the impending revelation? Was that what he had been hinting at, why he had risked a daylight meeting? If that was the case, it suggested some kind of agreement between Vlad and the Americans, although Gregorios struggled to believe the Americans would make such a titanic mistake.

He said, "There's too much vested in keeping this secret, particularly by the current administration."

"I know, but it's happening. The ambassador's scheduled to speak in half an hour, so you don't have much time to make yourself invisible."

Gregorios growled low in his throat. He needed to coordinate the effort to chase Vlad, but Frederick's warning trumped even that effort. He needed to protect his people first.

Then he would see to dealing out retribution.

Gregorios squeezed Frederick's hand. "You've just earned your spot, my friend. On me."

Frederick gaped, looking like he might faint. A joyous grin spread across his face, despite his efforts to retain a calm expression. His hand quivered in Gregorios', and he looked ready to start dancing in place.

Gregorios smiled. "After this blows over. First, make sure you stay alive."

"And you," Frederick urged, squeezing his hand in thanks, then hurrying away.

Gregorios watched him, thoughts racing. Someone was about to make a direct move against his family.

They would regret it.

He turned to his children. "You heard the man. Get out of here. Do you have contingencies in place?"

The commander nodded. "Several. We'll send the coded warning to all our assets. But what about the vampire?"

Gregorios gripped his shoulder. "I got the feeling Vlad will be paying attention. Initiate the Bram Protocol, but your prime objective is to weather this new storm.

Take every precaution. This is going to go bad and a lot of people are going to get hurt." That was a promise he planned to keep, and it wasn't his people who needed to be most worried.

The commander asked, "What about you? Yurak's connection with Suntara is buried deep enough we should be able to claim an independent contractor relationship, but you'll be the main target."

"I never travel without backup plans. Begin distancing the company from Suntara immediately. If you can get some kind of press release out before the American makes his announcement, that would be even better. I think we're going to need you soon. Good luck, my sons."

He left them and headed for an elevator, careful to not look like he was in a hurry. No doubt plans were already moving to snatch Gregorios and hold him prisoner.

Only epic idiots would dare declare war on the facetakers without careful planning. If they could take him out in the opening salvo, they'd start the war in a decidedly superior position.

Killing whatever security detail they assigned to take him would be too public, though. He didn't want to give them even more fuel to stoke the bonfires of world bias against him.

Gregorios studied the milling diplomats and spotted three separate tails. Whoever had set the trap seemed interested only in keeping him under surveillance. If only he had time, he'd interview those trailing operatives, but he doubted they'd know anything useful.

He jumped into one of the many elevators just before it closed.

"Third floor," he told the attractive brunette standing near the buttons. As the elevator started to descend, he did not doubt his pursuers were calling for back-up and moving to intercept.

He hadn't had this much fun at a UN meeting in decades.

Softly, Gregorios started to whistle his favorite battle tune.

26

I am sorry to report we arrived too late to reach the villa before Vesuvius erupted. You were right, the mountain destroyed Pompeii entirely, and the villa is buried under a mountain of ash. I'm afraid the scrolls must be destroyed.

~YEHUDI, HUNTER TEAM LEADER, OUTSIDE OF HERCULANEUM, 79 A.D.

SARAH WAITED ANXIOUSLY while Tomas spoke on the phone. She shouldn't be surprised that the soldier from Carlo's unit had called him instead of her, but it still rankled. Tomas kept an infuriatingly straight face as he listened to the report on Carlo's condition.

She exchanged glances with Francesca and Harriett, who sat with her at a conference table in the small sitting room of a converted suite in Quentin's mansion.

When Tomas hung up, she grabbed his hand. "Well?"

"Carlo is stable. It sounds like both runes bonded."

She sagged with relief. "I'm glad he'll be all right."

Tomas squeezed her hand. "He sounded strong. Promised to visit after he gets back from that summit in Cairo."

"He's still planning on going?"

Tomas chuckled. "More than that. He claims he was touched by an angel. The conference is about the effects of enhancements on regular forces. He'll probably be a keynote speaker now."

"That man has a lot of vitality for a first-lifer," Francesca said with a twinkle in her eye.

Sarah rolled her eyes. "Oh, stop it. He's old enough to be your . . ." She trailed off as she realized how ridiculous that statement was about to be.

Harriett laughed. "Her great-grandson several times removed."

Francesca shrugged. "What can I say? I like younger men."

The door opened and Eirene entered. Sarah blinked, startled by her dramatic new appearance. Eirene had changed bodies, and she'd opted for a very different model.

Her last body had been that of a fit woman with a slender frame and athletic build. Now she wore a striking model that only lacked a leather battle outfit to look every inch the amazon. She stood six feet tall with bronzed skin and a powerful frame. Her face fit the skull well, and Sarah spotted no telltale misalignments along the jawline. Her long black hair was pulled back into a simple braid.

Tomas rose and gave Eirene a little bow. "I haven't seen the Battle Mistress suit since Waterloo."

"It has aged well," Eirene said with a smile.

Sarah rounded the table and gave Eirene a hug. "You look fantastic, but why?"

"Thank you, my dear." Eirene's voice was richer than before, and a little deeper. "Next time we track down Xiao, I'll be better prepared."

She pulled up her form-fitting, royal blue athletic top to reveal several runes along her stomach. "This battle suit was custom-built for times like these. I've got eighteen runes bonded."

Sarah gaped. No one bonded that many. She had bonded to several runes in her first life, and already wore three permanent runes on her current form. Eighteen was a whole different level of amazing.

Eirene's choice to change to a more powerful battle suit made sense, but seeing her switch to another body rattled Sarah more than she'd expected. She was surprised to feel a flash of jealousy. Eirene could return to her previous form whenever she finished with that new suit, but Sarah could never go back.

Then she chided herself for being foolish. Eirene's last body hadn't been her original form either. She'd experienced hundreds of lives, and she'd learned to make each one important. Sarah needed to let go of the past and embrace her current life without the lingering regrets.

"How are you managing the drain?" Tomas asked.

"With careful balance," Eirene said with a smile.

Harriett saluted with a cookie she'd produced from somewhere. "She's an animal. Not even Frannie and I could manage so many. Mom's a true gourmet chef with her nevra core."

Eirene said, "Even so, this suit won't stop Xiao. I'm hopeful it will help me better focus my nevron to stand against her in the memoryscape, though. Tomas, any word on Alter, or sightings of Xiao?"

"Negative. We pulled all our assets out from around the castle. I couldn't risk her hunting them down."

When Eirene turned to her, Sarah shook her head. "None of the tracking ciphers I left around the town were triggered. If she left, she somehow avoided them all."

She felt a fresh wave of self-recrimination. She had failed Alter, had failed the team. She added softly, "It's my fault he's in danger."

Tomas tipped her chin up so she could look him in the eye. "It's Xiao's fault, Sarah."

Eirene said, "We'll track them down. From what Xiao said, her plans do not include killing Alter yet."

Sarah tried to not focus on that last word. How long before Xiao got what she wanted from Alter? He must be terrified. No, she realized as she thought about it. He must be furious that he hadn't managed to defeat her. He'd keep fighting to the last breath. The thought helped, until she realized that fighting Xiao would only guarantee Alter got hurt more.

Tomas squared his shoulders and said in a businesslike tone, "The incursion into the castle didn't go as planned, but the strange interview with Xiao offered the first real clues about who we're dealing with."

Sarah said, "I still can't believe she started browbeating us like that. It's like she thinks we're in the wrong, not her."

"She revealed some interesting hints about her personality," Eirene agreed.

"Like she's whacked," Sarah said.

"Look deeper, dear," Eirene said as they all settled back around the table. "She chastised you for killing her son, but she didn't fly into a rage."

"It's like she didn't really care about him at all," Sarah agreed. That thought was disturbing. What mother didn't care about their son?

Tomas said, "I got the sense she was sad, but wouldn't allow herself to get sidetracked."

"From what?" Sarah asked.

Eirene sat, and even that movement looked predatory while she wore that intimidating body. "She offered some clues. When she spoke of building a better future, it sounded like she has plans to change things."

"Paul had a plan too," Sarah said with a shudder.

Tomas squeezed her hand and gave her a reassuring smile. "But he wanted to dominate. He attempted to take power through force and intimidation. I'm not sure Xiao sees things the same way. Remember, she suggested that over time she could bring Paul around to a better approach."

Sarah grimaced. "I'm glad we didn't give him the time. How many thousands, or millions even, would have died while we waited for him to get bored with killing?"

Eirene turned to Francesca. "You and I need to review every word of that conversation. I wrote everything down as soon as we left the castle. I'd like to see if we can develop a profile on her."

"Good idea," Francesca said. She'd trained under investigators during the Spanish Inquisition. She knew how to read people better than anyone.

Tomas said, "I left the alert level elevated. Those threats she made about beating down our arrogance suggest an imminent attack."

"Agreed," Eirene nodded.

"Anaru's team is ready to roll with that Gatling gun with the ciphered rounds," Tomas added. "If she shows up personally, I'm hoping they can get a chance to test the weapon on her."

Sarah had considered marking ciphers on smaller rounds, but they would just bounce off of her or get so deformed, the cipher would get wrecked. She was starting work on ideas for adding defensive ciphers into helmets and tactical vests for the enforcers instead.

The potential for saving lives was huge, but she would need to broach the subject of how to power all those ciphers. She couldn't tie them to her rounon strength alone or she wouldn't have power to fight Xiao. She worried that the team might not approve using a wider matrix, like the one she had activated to help the children in the hospital.

No one had spoken about that healing matrix again, which was still running. She had checked in at the hospital when they returned to Rome and found young patients, their families, and staff alike all celebrating the miraculous healings.

Seeing some good come of her cipher gift reassured her they were doing the right thing. She'd felt very emotional as she headed for Quentin's mansion. Once they resolved the threat posed by Xiao, she vowed to dedicate more time to exploring other positive aspects of her powers. Rune warriors were supposed to affect change, and she felt a deep-rooted drive to make the change a good one.

"What have we pieced together about Xiao's identity?" Eirene asked, dragging Sarah back to the present.

Harriett tapped the computer on the table in front of her. "Research teams are combing through your initial transcript, and we already got a hit on her name."

"Empress Xiao," Sarah said.

Harriett nodded. "There are actually several references to the name Xiao throughout Chinese history, and even more than one Empress Xiao."

"That's frustrating," Sarah mumbled.

Tomas shrugged. "There were eleven King Edwards. It's pretty common for rulers to re-use names."

"And in China, rulers took on titles in addition to their birth names," Francesca added, leaning over Harriett's shoulder to view the screen. "Xiao means filial piety. It's a title more than an actual name, with references to relationships between family members, between people and their ancestors, and between the common classes and their rulers."

"Do you mind?" Harriett asked.

Francesca planted a kiss on her sister's head, then mussed her hair before returning to her seat. Harriett blew hair out of her eyes and continued. "Xiao has something to do with connecting the past with the present, and from there into the future."

"That's interesting, given how much her entire family is focusing on the memoryscape," Tomas said.

Eirene nodded, her thoughtful expression odd on that powerful face. "She seemed fixated on names. I'm not sure she was conscious of the clues that offered. There's something about names that holds particular meaning to her."

Francesca said, "That's a Chinese thing."

"Alter mentioned something about that once," Sarah agreed.

Francesca grinned. "Who do you think I got that tidbit from?" She sighed. "I had to work so hard to get that boy's tongue moving, but it was always worth it."

"He said Mai Luan didn't work as a Chinese name," Sarah added, ignoring Francesca's inferences. The facetaker loved to tease Alter, but he'd always kept his distance.

"And Paul is a ridiculous name for a Chinese man trying to take over the world," Tomas added.

"So is Xiao even her name?" Eirene asked.

Harriett shrugged. "Maybe not, but it's the best we've got so far. One interesting match is Empress Dowager Xiaozhuang from the seventeenth century."

"Too young," Tomas said.

"Here's a direct match," Harriett said, scanning her list. "Empress Xiao, who lived from about the year 566 to the year 648."

Tomas let out a low whistle. "Could she really be that old?"

"Perhaps. If she remained in China, it might have been possible," Eirene said thoughtfully.

"Another possibility is Xiao Gang Kuang," Harriett continued. "She was the mother of the last emperor of the Ming Dynasty."

Sarah asked, "That was the last dynasty, right? The one with the hair styles like what Hongwu was wearing?"

"Correct," Harriett said.

"Interesting," Eirene said.

Tomas shook his head. "But too young. We tracked her to the burning of the treasure fleet. That happened in the fifteenth century."

"The connections are interesting all the same," Eirene said.

"Do you really think she could be one of those historical figures?" Sarah asked.

Francesca asked, "That's the question, isn't it? If she is, why would she tell us?"

"And what is her goal?" Tomas added. "She didn't elaborate on what she meant by a better future."

Eirene said, "There's no doubt she wants something and she's got a plan to get it. Unfortunately, until we know more, we have no idea how to intercept her, rescue Alter, and bring her down."

Sarah leaned back, fighting a sense of growing frustration. Despite the in-person conversation, they still knew little. They needed to know, and soon. Those threats she had made sounded all too real, and her inference that she planned to somehow use them in her plots worried Sarah.

The conference phone on the table rang. When Sarah hit the button, an operator said, "I have Mr. Gregorios on the phone."

"Put him through."

As soon as he came on the line Eirene said, "Hey honey, you won't believe what kind of day we've had."

"Can't wait to hear about it, but we've got other problems. Turn on the TV and find the open broadcast station from the UN commission. This one you've got to see."

27

Time passes, day by day. The greatness of this country lies in the inexorable journey it has taken through time.

~YO YO, GHOST TIDE

"THE MEETING YOU'RE ATTENDING?" Sarah asked as Tomas moved to the wall-mounted television and picked up the remote.

"Not any more," Gregorios said. The phone suddenly crackled with the unmistakable sound of gunfire, followed by a series of grunts and a scream.

"You haven't resorted to killing politicians, have you?" Eirene asked, and Sarah couldn't tell if that bothered Eirene or not.

"Sorry about that. I hit speaker instead of mute."

"What happened?" Sarah asked.

"And do you need me to scramble back-up units?" Tomas asked. He was leaning forward, left fist clenched, the muscles of his arm standing out sharply against his shirt.

Gregorios responded, sounding far too calm for a guy in the middle of a fight. "They wouldn't arrive in time to help. I should be fine. I usually wish these meetings were more interesting, but this one's . . ."

The line switched to hold music.

Sarah glanced around the table. The others seemed content to wait for Gregorios to come back. Even Tomas, after his initial tense reaction, seemed to have calmed down.

She asked, "Aren't any of you worried?"

Eirene said, "Not really, dear. Greg's considerate like that."

Gregorios came back on the line. "You've got to give it to the Americans. They do train some excellent fighters."

Tomas said, "I've recruited quite a few over the years."

"Why are you fighting Americans?" Sarah exclaimed, worried to bursting.

Gregorios said, "There was a particularly clever team of Russians too. I'll have a scar, I believe."

"Why are you fighting at all?" Sarah demanded.

"And can you reach safety soon?" Eirene asked.

"I'm clear of the UN building. Certain parties had stationed teams to prevent my exit. I'm now heading for the safe house in Brooklyn."

"What happened?" Sarah asked.

"You'll see. Is the TV on yet?"

"Got it," Tomas found the right channel, showing a packed council chamber.

"That's the US ambassador," Eirene said with a frown.

The ambassador had a voice as smooth and polished as his hair, and he was pointing toward a large display screen. "I share the council's stated goal to understand and regulate the newly revealed pictogram-based enhancement protocol."

"More like he hopes to convince other countries not to explore runes," Eirene muttered. "The US has one of the best enhanced companies. They've clashed with the hunters a couple of times over their use of runes."

The ambassador continued. "However, I feel it my duty to point out a more pressing and sinister danger facing the world. That danger is known as the facetakers."

"He didn't!" Eirene gasped.

The screen behind the ambassador showed a video of the assault of the Castel Sant'Angelo. Unlike most other videos of the incident, instead of focusing on the special weapons and tactics Harriett and her Yurak forces had employed, this one focused on Gregorios.

Sounding abundantly annoyed, Gregorios said, "He is. Old Freddie tipped me off."

"He's earned his next life for that," Eirene said.

"My thoughts exactly."

"They're showing your assault against the heka on the wall," Eirene explained to him.

"Makes sense," Gregorios said, sounding far calmer than Sarah believed possible. "Be right back."

The hold music returned while the television showed Gregorios leading his strike team against the entrenched heka who were distracted by Harriett's force. A rain of bullets and blinding flares temporarily obscured the heka from view. The image zoomed in on Gregorios, who was in the process of removing a heka's soulmask, and tracked him working down the heka lines.

Gregorios came back on, breathing a bit heavier. "I'm in an armored vehicle now. Should make better time."

"They got you on film at the Castel. Sloppy," Eirene said.

"Did you see what we were dealing with? I was kind of busy."

"I hear you, but managing the battlefield is so important, dear."

"I was improvising."

"Well, that improv routine is getting witnessed around the world," Francesca added, her voice solemn.

"I need a cookie," said Harriett, digging into her purse.

The ambassador was speaking again. "That man Gregorios, who has participated in these very discussions as the leader of Suntara, is a facetaker. They are a secret society who possess diabolical powers of extracting living souls!"

Many voices clamored for explanation or demanded the ambassador refrain from religious references, but he spoke over them. "They have been known by many names. Sometimes they call themselves Vitans, or Naftara Specialists."

"That one's always been my favorite," Eirene muttered.

Francesca grimaced. "Not any more. We're all going to need new business cards."

"Does he have any idea how hard it is to come up with a good name?" Harriett asked.

The ambassador continued. "In earlier centuries, they were known as demons, maggi, or vampires."

Sarah leaned closer to the television. "Hey, I know what vampires are now. That's so wrong."

"They have lived in the shadows, wearing many faces, but always bringing disaster and grief," the ambassador continued. "I have evidence that shows they were involved in some of the worst atrocities in history, including the holocaust and apartheid."

More angry voices rose into a tumult and the secretary pounded his gavel for order.

"We had nothing to do with apartheid," Eirene said with a frown.

Francesca said, "But they're eating it up. Do you really think we'll get a fair trial?"

Sarah started to understand their fear of public discovery. What would the world do to them now that this information was being revealed? What rumors would it start? What other crimes would be thrown at their feet? Every facetaker and everyone who associated with them were now in grave danger.

The ambassador switched the screen to a poor-quality video feed of St. Peter's Square, just as the transformed Sarah was slicing Paul in half. The critical moment commanded enough respect that the other voices of complaint faded.

"Behold, their ultimate crime!" the ambassador declared in ringing tones.

The video focused on Sarah as she collapsed, her quicksilver limbs melting away. She had seen the footage several times, and it still gave her goosebumps to witness her own death. The angle of this feed was slightly different, and the smoke that obscured other videos from seeing her final moment did not entirely block out this one.

The quality was poor, but she recognized Alter crouching over her, burning hands grasping her face as he pulled her soulmask from her dying body. The billowing smoke concealed the scene long enough for Alter to disappear, but the damage was done.

"These criminals desecrated the body of one of the world's greatest heroes," the ambassador declared. "The Sword of the Deliverer. And I am calling for them to be brought to justice."

For the moment, those offended by the ambassador's words were drowned out by a united clamor for action. It became clear that the committee, which normally moved at a glacial pace, would actually decide to pass a resolution calling for the incarceration of all facetakers and seizure of their assets.

Eirene sighed. "Turn it off. We've seen more than enough."

As Sarah scanned the shocked expressions around the table, Harriett said, "I don't understand. We have so many ties with the Americans."

Gregorios' voice sounded grim on the phone. "Something has changed. Someone's got leverage strong enough to trump all our safety protocols."

"Xiao," Eirene said. "She promised to beat us down, and I can't think of a more effective way to do it. I just can't imagine how she pulled it off."

Sarah said, "We were so worried about Alter, but that was just the beginning."

"Did you free him?" Gregorios asked.

"No," Eirene said. "No casualties, but the mission was a failure."

"We actually spoke with Xiao in person, right after dispatching a little vampire," Tomas added.

Eirene gave him a quick summary of their conversation with Xiao. "We were just discussing it when you called."

"You're lucky no one got killed," Gregorios said.

"I switched to the Amazon," Eirene informed him.

"I love that one." He sounded enthusiastic, didn't seem bothered at all that his wife would look dramatically different the next time he saw her.

"We need to initiate counter measures," Eirene said.

"Before you do, you need to know that Vlad's active again," Gregorios said.

That seemed to shock everyone as much as the ambassador's announcement. Sarah glanced around the table. "Vlad the rune warrior?"

"Where?" Eirene asked, leaning closer to the phone, her expression grave.

"In the committee chamber, during the last recess. Walked right up to me and made a few empty threats."

"Wish I'd been there," Tomas muttered, his expression fierce. "We should have finished him last time."

Sarah demanded, "What are you talking about? Why would you be trying to finish off Vlad? He was a good guy, wasn't he?" When they all looked at her she added, "Well, you know, before his cipher failed."

Eirene said, "He wasn't an enemy until the sultan's forces captured him and tried to turn him into a zombie."

"What?" Sarah exclaimed.

Francesca muttered, "Fools. Only unenhanced mortals make zombies."

Tomas explained. "That cipher matrix Vlad attempted broke something in him, turning him into that monster the world knows as the impaler."

Francesca added. "But it was the sultan's forces that created the real monster."

Tomas grunted in agreement. "The fools had more power than brains. They thought they were creating a mindless zombie the sultan could parade in front of the world, mocking a once-great enemy. They ended up creating the worst vampire the world's ever known."

"How? And why didn't you tell me?" Sarah demanded.

Eirene shrugged. "Vlad's ultimate fate wasn't important while we faced Paul. You needed to focus on becoming a rune warrior."

Sarah rubbed at her chin where the vampire had bitten her. "Another vampire. What are they, really?"

Tomas explained, "Vampires are created by facetakers bonding the soulmask of an enhanced person to a recently-dead body. It can only be managed by simultaneously activating a complex rune sequence."

"Which is a closely-guarded secret," Harriett chimed in.

Eirene added, "In Vlad's case, we've gathered that he also activated some kind of cipher at the same time. The result was very, very bad."

"So Vlad Dracula was really a vampire after all?" Sarah asked.

Tomas nodded. "He was, but the whispers of rumor that Bram Stoker discovered were so far from the truth, we never bothered blocking that novel."

"He's deadly," Gregorios said over the phone. "And we've attempted many times through the years to put him down, but he's a slippery devil."

"And he chose today to appear?" Eirene asked.

"The way he spoke, it sounded like he knew what the Americans were planning," Gregorios said.

"That's disturbing," Eirene said as Tomas began cursing under his breath.

"Perhaps worse than that. I think you're right. I think somehow Xiao has turned the tables on us, but it seems she may have also found a way to recruit Vlad to her cause," Gregorios said.

"What could she possibly offer him?" Harriett asked around the final bite of an enormous cookie she had devoured while they talked.

"Gregorios, probably," Eirene said. At Sarah's questioning look she added, "He's got a particular hatred for Greg."

Sarah wasn't surprised. It seemed like a lot of people held particular grudges against him.

Gregorios said, "We'll have to analyze these facts once the dust clears a bit. Can you initiate the response from there, love?"

"Of course," Eirene said, then turned to her daughters. "Girls, go.

Get the word out. This is a level-one Pyrrhic event. Scramble all assets and initiate cloaking strategy Pitchfork-Seven."

"Pitchfork?" Sarah asked.

"Greg's idea," Eirene said with a roll of her eyes.

Gregorios chuckled. "Every time the world finds out about us, they respond with torches and pitchforks. So with that name, everyone knows exactly what we're dealing with."

Sarah had to admit, it made a lot of sense.

"Ooh," Harriett whistled, looking up from her laptop. "My commanders are already positioning Yurak. They're off to a good start. Looks like today we filed a lawsuit against Suntara for defaulting on several million dollars in payments for services rendered.

Eirene nodded approval. "It's a good strategy. People will be more willing to believe Yurak is separate if they see us fighting over money."

"Just make sure to drop that lawsuit after this blows over," Gregorios said.

"We'll see," Harriett said with a wicked grin. "I'm off to help my teams."

As she left, Eirene said, "Tomas, send for Harald. He can start the political wheels moving and prepare Suntara's public rejection of the ambassador's claims."

"The rest of you need to pack," Gregorios said.

"What do you have planned?" Eirene asked.

"We need to move fast before the international community mobilizes against us. I get the feeling our normal delaying tactics aren't going to work this time. Xiao has the upper hand, but we need to take it away from her. We need intel, and there's only one person I can think who might be able to help."

"Who?" Sarah voiced the question in everyone's eyes.

"Spartacus."

28

One knows a wise one because of his wisdom. An official is at his good deed: his heart is in balance with his tongue, his runes insist upon truth, and his lips are accurate when he speaks.

~PTAH-HOTEP, EGYPTIAN VIZIER TO PHARAOH
DJEDKARE ISESI IN THE FIFTH DYNASTY, 25TH
CENTURY B.C.

THE NEXT COUPLE hours passed quickly as everyone scrambled to respond to the looming threat of a world suddenly made aware of the true nature of the facetakers. Even though Sarah was a newcomer to their world, she shared everyone's concern.

She loved these people. Yes, their soul powers challenged the recognized truths of the world, and many people would react out of fear. But could they really overlook the heroic actions of the recent conflict with Paul?

No doubt some would. Xiao would surely try to twist the truth, as would others seeking gain from the crisis. She refused to believe the world at large would follow the lead of those few. Surely they would see the truth.

Still, she helped prepare for the worst-case scenario. Sarah saw Tomas only briefly before he left with a long convoy of enforcers repositioning weapons and equipment away from the well-known mansion. Apparently the Suntara Group owned a lot of property around the city and the world through numerous independent subsidiary companies that would be hard to connect to them. Since night had fallen, it was a good time to move.

Eirene, who looked far too calm for someone with a worldwide death threat now looming over her, explained, "We've had to go into hiding before. We know what to do."

Sarah packed a suitcase for the trip to Hollywood where they'd meet Gregorios and visit Spartacus. She appreciated getting a little alone time to prepare for that meeting. He had been an enemy, and he wore Tomas' body. She wasn't sure what to expect.

She packed her guns and handed them off to an enforcer who would include them in another shipment away from the mansion. She hated that she couldn't bring them on the trip to the States, but Eirene had assured her they'd stock up at a safe house in L.A. Sarah didn't plan to meet Spartacus unarmed, despite his current acting career.

"I don't see how we can trust him," she said to Eirene as they met for a late dinner. "He worked for Paul."

"Spartacus is a unique individual. He went through a lot of effort to position himself outside of the conflict. I think he's telling the truth about wanting to lead a movement to empower people through non-violent means."

"But you fought him for centuries," Sarah protested.

"He was a different man back then. His long dispossession changed him. We'll approach the meeting with caution, but I agree with Greg. His involvement with Paul, and the comments he made about Xiao at the castel suggest he may know more about her."

"What about Tomas' body?" Sarah asked.

"I don't know," Eirene admitted. "The forbidden runes he possesses complicate efforts to extract him."

"But we can't just let him keep it."

"We might have to."

Sarah wished she could maintain the same calm Eirene projected, even though the facetakers were the ones facing the prospect of being hunted again by a superstitious world. Quentin joined them a few minutes later, dressed in charcoal slacks with perfect creases, despite the late hour. He had shed his customary jacket and had rolled up the sleeves of his white shirt.

"How are you going to get everything out of here?" Sarah asked.

"Not to fear, my dear," Quentin said with his normal good humor. "We have several well-stocked armories concealed around the city, with others in virtually every country. Some of the latest creations are being transported now, but I promise you we won't run out of bullets."

They talked about the mobilization effort, the plan to shift enforcer units to the network of safe houses, and to clean out the Suntara headquarters.

Quentin explained, "We'll use the tunnels to move most of the Suntara equipment, including the suits in the body bank. Those tunnels lead to a series of secret cellars below the Sistine Chapel that the world has long forgotten."

Sarah wanted to ask him more about that, but a white-coated servant entered the room. "Excuse me, sir, but the gate guard requests guidance in dealing with a visitor."

"What's the problem?" Quentin asked.

"A man named Melek seeks a meeting with you and with the lady Eirene."

Eirene nearly choked on a meatball. "Melek? You've got to be kidding."

Quentin considered the news for a moment. "Raise the alert level. Keep it low-key, but I want everyone ready. The last time hunters visited, they made a mess."

"I don't think he'd announce himself if he planned to fight," Eirene said.

Quentin rose. "Better to be safe." He told the servant, "Inform the guard to escort Melek to the main entrance. Check him carefully for weapons."

"We'll join you," Eirene said.

"Very well. I'll meet you at the door after I find my jacket."

Sarah had no doubt he'd have at least two guns concealed under that jacket too. She followed Eirene to the main entrance, curious to meet Alter's father.

Despite the strained relations of late, she appreciated the information the hunters had shared with them. She couldn't have progressed in her rune studies nearly so well without that assistance. Then again, she had some words to say to Melek regarding his treatment of Alter, and the clan's stubborn insistence that he had to die to purge the evil taint of his cui dashi powers.

Melek entered the mansion slowly, leaning heavily on a wooden cane. Two muscle-bound hunters flanked him. The two young men bore strong resemblances to Alter, and they looked nervous.

Quentin took Melek's hand in a firm greeting. "Welcome to my home."

"Thank you for seeing me." Melek's voice was deep, with the same hint of an accent as Alter. He was a sturdy-looking man with salt-and-pepper hair cut military short. Despite his cane, he still radiated strength.

Quentin said, "I must confess surprise to find you at my door. The last time your family visited here, we exchanged harsh words."

Melek grunted, his lips turning into a wry smile. "And not a few bullets. I again apologize for that rash action."

Quentin nodded graciously. "Please come in and sit."

"Thank you." Melek nodded to the two hunters following him. "This is Heber and Nabil."

The two looked remarkably alike and dressed in similar hunter garb, so it was kind of hard to tell them apart. Heber did have a slightly crooked nose, as if it had been broken and not quite reset properly, while Nabil's eyebrows were a bit bushier and his face a little wider.

Quentin greeted the two hunters, then asked Melek, "Is that a new injury?"

Melek walked slowly with Quentin toward a nearby salon. "No. I'm still recovering from the attack on our home."

Sarah exchanged a surprised look with Eirene. Melek had to possess multiple enhancement runes like Alter did. He should have healed long since.

Eirene took his arm, and his young assistants tensed. Sarah drew closer, prepared to take them apart if they made any threatening moves.

Melek thanked Eirene for her assistance, then looked again. His face paled. "You're Eirene."

"Mistress of Darkness in the flesh," she said with a warm smile. "At least, that's what Alter said you call me."

"You've changed since our last photograph."

"I've probably changed several times." She took a step back, lifting her arms to show off her striking figure. "What do you think of my latest makeover?"

"I don't think I need to tell you what I believe," Melek said, his expression hard.

Heber moved toward Eirene, as if to step between her and Melek.

Sarah stepped into his path. "Hello. I'm Sarah."

He gasped, "Sword of the Deliverer."

"That was a past life," Sarah said, extending a hand.

Heber took it, a look of awe on his face. Hunters weren't Catholic, so she was a little surprised by the reaction.

Melek extended his hand to her. "I had hoped to meet you here, young lady. We all greatly admired your work." Melek's grip was firm but not overbearing.

"Alter taught me most of what I know."

"Where is he?" Melek asked, his expression pained.

"If you're planning to hurt him, you'd better think again," Sarah warned.

"No, I must speak with him." Melek settled into an overstuffed chair. "Will you send for him?"

"Alter's not here," Eirene said, her expression neutral.

"When will he return?"

Eirene sat on a nearby couch. "We don't know. He was taken by Paul's mother."

Melek did an amazing job of controlling his shock. His grip tightened on the head of his cane and he hissed in a breath. "What happened?"

Eirene explained briefly about their recent attempts to track Xiao in the memoryscape, the confrontation in ancient China, Alter's subsequent kidnapping, and the failed attempt to free him.

"She claims the title Empress Xiao?" Melek asked.

Eirene nodded. "Indeed. We're studying possible meanings.

"My archivists will join that effort," Melek promised, glancing toward Nabil, who produced a phone and stepped to one side to make a call.

Melek leaned back in the chair, his face anguished. "I should have listened to my son."

"Yes, you should have," Sarah said, not bothering to soften the words. She appreciated his obvious grief, and hopefully when they recovered Alter the two could be reconciled. "The threat's real and getting worse."

"How can it get worse?" Melek asked.

"Did you see the news today?"

"No."

Sarah told him about the surprise announcement at the UN.

"That will complicate things," Melek agreed. He looked concerned, although Heber, who hovered nearby couldn't quite mask his excitement. From his perspective, the thought of wiping out the long-hated demons had to be welcome news.

Quentin said, "That is an understatement. Given the rather busy schedule ahead of us, I have to ask your intentions, sir."

"My intentions are to help you find my son."

"And your family?" Quentin pressed. "We all know your position regarding the facetakers and the Suntara Group. Will you help us in good faith, or will your family join the witch hunt?"

"It's no secret we don't agree on a lot of things, but I can promise you my assistance until we find my son and remove these cui dashi from the world. You have my word."

Sarah nearly gave the man a hug. They'd need the rune expertise of the hunters in their upcoming confrontation with Xiao, especially now that Alter was missing. Besides, they had enough enemies lining up against them. If Melek was speaking truthfully, the hunters' help could prove critical.

Eirene gave Melek a warm smile. "Then don't get too comfortable there. We've got a plane to catch."

29

He created the dream to show the way to the dreamer in his blindness.

~P. INSINGER

LOS ANGELES WAS warmer than Rome in the fall, and Sarah gazed longingly at the shopping centers they passed on the highway. With this new body, she still needed to replace most of her wardrobe.

She'd acquired a good selection of tactical wear, workout suits, and a couple of tasteful evening gowns, but she longed for a quiet day with no heka assassins or cui dashi plots so she could simply shop.

She wasn't going to get it.

Tomas was driving the Suburban they had rented after landing in LAX. Flying by chartered private jet was even better than first class on a commercial plane, and Sarah had managed to sleep in the comfortable cabin during the overnight flight.

She was glad she had. Although Melek had slept most of the flight, at least one of the two young hunters had remained awake, trading wary glances with Tomas and Quentin, who likewise kept watch. The uneasy truce became really boring after a while.

Sarah was grateful, but a little surprised they'd accepted Melek so easily into the group. They needed the information the hunters could share, and it was better having them as allies than enemies. If the hunters betrayed them, a lot of people would get hurt.

Heber sat in the front passenger seat of the Suburban, while Nabil shared the cramped rear seat with Quentin. Melek sat in the middle, between Sarah and Eirene.

"This is my first visit to Los Angeles," he admitted. "I am finding it more enjoyable than I expected."

Quentin chuckled. "Indeed, you have the best seat of all, between the two beautiful ladies."

Nabil muttered about insults to the family honor, but Melek didn't argue the point.

"We'll have to come back when we're not so busy," Eirene said, patting his hand. "It's a wonderful place to visit."

Melek said, "Perhaps. Where are we headed now?"

Tomas spoke without taking his eyes off the road. "Pasadena. Spartacus is renting a property north of town, near the Angeles National Forest. Apparently he's an avid hiker."

Eirene said, "I'm not surprised. He was always very active, and after his long imprisonment, he must love moving again."

Sarah still hated to think Spartacus might get to keep Tomas' old body without a fight. She had to admit the issue was complicated, but there had to be a way.

"I wouldn't expect to accomplish much today," Melek said, reiterating his concern about visiting a well-known kashaph.

"Except maybe assassinating him," Heber muttered from the front seat.

"No killing," Eirene said, slapping him on the back of the head. Heber looked horrified that she touched him. "It's that very association with Paul and Xiao that we hope to exploit."

"But how can you trust him?" Melek asked.

"We're trusting you," Tomas said.

"Point taken," Melek admitted.

Eirene added, "He's changed. I fought him for centuries, and this Spartacus is a different man."

"He sure wrecked the image I had of him," Sarah muttered.

Her initial thrill at meeting the famous gladiator had dimmed when she'd learned the truth about him. He'd wrecked any lingering fan-girl feeling when he stole Tomas' body and helped Paul attempt to become the new-risen ruler of the world.

When they arrived at the spacious, two-story wooden home in the hills above Pasadena, a dark blue Ford sedan was already parked in the driveway beside a bright red Hummer.

Tomas shook his head as he considered the big Hummer. "Figures he'd go for one of those. The Ford matches the one Gregorios rented."

Gregorios met them at the door and swept Eirene into a fierce embrace. In her Amazon form, she stood as tall as he did, but they adapted to the height change without issue.

He cupped her face briefly. "Good to see you, love." Then he grinned and showed his left hand, where he wore a steel wedding band. "In honor of your new suit, I picked up this little beauty from the Pennsylvania armory."

Sarah leaned closer, noting a beautiful Damascus pattern in the steel. That had to be more than a simple ornament. Sure enough, Gregorios flicked a finger against it and a short, curved blade popped up.

Eirene grinned. "You haven't worn a ring knife wedding band since Valley Forge." She touched the little blade, and Sarah noted a series of tiny runes marked along its length. "When did you get these inscribed?"

Gregorios flicked the blade closed. "After Stalingrad. It's been in storage for a while." He turned to Melek and shook the old hunter's hand. "I'm surprised to find you here, Melek."

"Our goals are the same. Find my son, stop the cui dashi."

Gregorios' expression turned serious. "Before this is over, you and I have some things to discuss."

Melek managed to meet his gaze without flinching. "For now, you have my word we'll work together."

Gregorios grunted and gave him a nod of approval. "Your word's usually worth something. You have a deal."

He glanced at the young hunters, who regarded him with unconcealed hostility. "Don't do anything stupid, boys. The last hunter who did is hanging on your wall at home."

They bristled, looking ready to fight right there.

Gregorios turned his back on them and led the group into the house. He paused in the entryway. "Spartacus, where'd you disappear to?"

"I had to flip the burgers," Spartacus called as he hurried into sight.

He was wearing khaki pants and a tight-fitting t-shirt. It was Tomas' body all right, and Sarah felt a powerful urge to rush across the room, but she wasn't sure if she'd hug him or slap him. She glanced at Tomas, but he watched Spartacus with a neutral expression, revealing nothing of what he might be thinking.

Spartacus grinned, and he did look very handsome in that body. It fit him well and he bubbled with enthusiasm. "I love hamburgers! It's my favorite new food next to ice cream."

Gregorios replied, "Your taste is improving. You used to love crucifying Romans most."

Spartacus slapped Gregorios' shoulder. "I live in the now, my friend.

He turned to Eirene and saluted in the Roman way, fist to heart. "You look stunning, most honored adversary."

"I call this one the Amazon," Eirene said, returning the salute, then stepping forward to take Spartacus' hand in an ancient hand-to-forearm grip.

Spartacus beamed. "Of course. The Amazon have taken much glory in today's world. They are mistresses of the internet and invisible commerce." Then he gestured to everyone, "Come in, all of you. Lunch is almost ready." He rushed out of the room.

Sarah asked, "What was he talking about?"

"Amazon," Gregorios said with a smile, then led the way inside.

The only hint Sarah caught from Tomas that he might not be as calm as he projected was the slow clenching of one fist. She found it comforting to see it did bother him to witness Spartacus wearing his old body. No one should take their body too seriously, but neither should they discard it without a second thought.

They ate around a long picnic table in the back yard. Spartacus had grilled fifty hamburgers and insisted his recently-developed barbecue sauce was the best in the world. He planned to create his own brand and sell it online.

He added piles of grilled shrimp and sausages to the feast, along with large bowls of olives and pears. He produced eight different wines, several cheeses, and a huge platter of corn on the cob. The feast could have fed ten times as many people, but he insisted repeatedly that he could fetch more if they needed it.

The young hunters quickly dropped their initial suspicion as they dug into the feast. Melek ate a little, but studied their host, his expression thoughtful. "You survived a long dispossession. What kept your mind intact?"

"Curiosity and commitment," Spartacus said. He pointed with a half-eaten hamburger. "I knew many of your forefathers, Lord of the

Hunters. They were men of great honor. When you are recovered, perhaps we will meet in single combat to celebrate their memories."

"Thank you. I would enjoy that," Melek said sincerely.

"Non-lethal, of course," Spartacus added with a laugh. "One of the odd quirks of the new world."

He turned to Sarah and saluted with his wine. "You do my house great honor, Lady Sarah."

"I'm glad we haven't had to try killing each other today," Sarah said, surprised that she actually meant it. Spartacus' good humor was infectious, and although she had much reason to dislike him, she found herself hoping they didn't have to be enemies.

"Indeed," Spartacus agreed, taking a long drink. "You won much honor defeating Paul. I wonder why you haven't risen to claim it in front of the world."

"It wasn't the right time."

She had looked forward to a quiet second life, although with the recent revelation that she had survived, she wondered if that would be possible. Spartacus might be hungry for adoring crowds, but she longed for quiet days to get her new life in order and spend quality time with Tomas.

Spartacus declared, "The time will come. When it does, I will champion your name and challenge any who dare defame it."

Sarah glanced at Tomas. "Are you taking notes?"

He speared a pear with his knife. "You really want me to talk like that?"

"Sometimes," she said with a smile. "But mostly I just like hearing the support."

Gregorios said, "Let's not get distracted. Spartacus, we need your help tracking down Paul's mother. She's calling herself Empress Xiao."

"She has used that title in my presence," Spartacus nodded.

"What other names has she used?" Eirene asked.

Spartacus shrugged. "None hold meaning. She tries on different names like some might try hats or shoes."

He turned to Sarah. "Have you considered recently the wonder of telephones?"

"I don't often think about it," she admitted, surprised by the abrupt turn of the conversation.

He laughed and slapped the table. "Phones! Communication even the gods never enjoyed. Such is the everyday boon to even the poorest of mortals. These days are an endless wonder!"

"Not if Xiao has anything to say about it," Gregorios said.

Spartacus waved a dismissive hand. "Always there are those who seek dominion. As I warned you in Rome, I am beyond such things. In fact, just today I refused her envoy, who sought my oath of allegiance to her cause."

"Whoa!" Sarah exclaimed. "Xiao tried to recruit you?"

The ancient Thracian grew solemn for the first time. "Indeed, but her minions lacked respect and when challenged to prove the worth of their cause in single combat, fled like cowards."

"I'm assuming you have no plans to join her then?" Gregorios asked carefully as everyone paused eating to listen.

"Correct," Spartacus boomed, then fixed Gregorios with a serious gaze. "I fear she will attempt to wrest the world from you. You will stand against her to defend your own. The world has ever moved such."

"What if she calls on you again?" Eirene asked.

Spartacus shook his head. "I fulfilled my debt to Paul. That his conquest failed is not a burden I carry. I care not for her plans to change the history of the world."

"What?" Melek asked, leaning forward, his expression intense. "What about history?"

Spartacus shrugged. "Eat, man. How do you expect to heal when you barely eat?"

"Later. Explain that comment."

"It is of no moment. A passing phrase, repeating promises I heard her make at various and sundry times."

"What exactly did she say? This is important," Melek asked again.

Spartacus considered the old hunter for a moment. "I wished to forswear this conflict, and as such would be honor-bound not to answer your question or risk falling from the neutral state I wished to maintain."

"Wished to?" Gregorios prodded.

"Indeed, my most ancient rival. The envoy of Empress Xiao swore the oath of an enemy, promising unending interference in my new life for refusing his mistress. Thus am I forced, against my avowed intent, to join in brotherhood of arms with you to ensure such disturbance is rendered impossible."

Sarah glanced at Tomas to see if she was understanding him correctly.

"Why didn't you just say so?" Gregorios demanded, looking a bit flustered.

"Such matters are not appropriate to discuss before the feast is concluded," Spartacus said, gesturing across the table. "Behold, the conversation has already slackened the intent of your party to vanquish this mighty feast."

Sarah asked, "Why do you sound disappointed that you have to help us stop her? You saw all the destruction Paul caused."

"Indeed. Ever has war brought suffering." He sighed and glanced down at his wine as he swished it in his cup. Then he looked up and his somber mood bled away. "I have arisen from centuries of prison, Lady of Steel, with my mission clear before me. I must win honor so the world will listen. I will teach them to become strong again and live as men fit for glory."

"You can't do that if the world is enslaved," Eirene said.

Spartacus fixed her with an intent stare. "Are they not enslaved now? Such riches and wondrous technology available to all, and yet most of the world wallows in squalor. They need but a strong voice to guide them, and all could rise to greatness."

"Don't think trying to make changes like that won't result in blood-shed too," Gregorios said.

"It may, but I will empower the many, not support the few."

Sarah was surprised to realize she believed that he spoke in earnest. He really had changed during those long centuries bronzed to a statue on the Arch of Constantine. He seemed honestly interested in helping the world, but for the first time he wasn't planning to pursue military conquest. Such a fundamental shift was impressive, all the more because he was the one making it.

Eirene saluted with her wine. "But if Xiao wins in whatever she's planning, how do you know they won't shut down Hollywood and banish movies?"

Spartacus sighed. "Such fears have whispered their counsel to my ears also. Thus have I decided to join ranks with you, most honored adversary, and your husband. My assistant, Rita, shall take command of my affairs while I embark upon the campaign with you."

Sarah expected Gregorios to turn him down, to insist they only wanted a little information, but instead he extended a hand, which Spartacus clasped hand-to-wrist in the ancient Roman way.

"We are honored to accept your sword into our company," Gregorios said solemnly.

Sarah glanced at Eirene, who rose from the table to face Spartacus, her expression unreadable.

As Spartacus rose to face her, he drew from under the table an actual Roman gladius.

Both Heber and Nabil shouted warnings and leaped up, knocking aside benches as they produced automatic pistols. Sarah rose with them, feeling a spike of fear at the sight of the sword.

Even as Gregorios growled, "Stand down," the two hunters opened fire, unleashing a barrage of deadly, hollow-point bullets at Spartacus' face and chest.

"No!" Sarah shouted, but her cry was drowned out by the rolling thunder of gunfire. Within three seconds, the hunters had emptied their magazines.

None of the bullets so much as scratched Spartacus. As each projectile reached him, it stopped, its energy drained away. He caught them as they fell from the air.

"Excellent!" Spartacus boomed, grinning widely as the echoes faded away. "You wield your chosen weapons with skill to make your ancestors proud."

He flung the pile of spent bullets into a nearby trash can.

"Are you finished?" Gregorios asked the hunters, who looked unsure how to react. "If you'd waited a minute, I could have told you he bonded both of the forbidden runes he acquired at St. Peters. He's basically impervious."

"Indeed," Spartacus said, then gestured the hunters back to their seats. "The runes were the key to my intent to remain aloof from ongoing conflict and focus all of my energies on gaining the ear of the world. They grant me freedom to stand apart."

Sarah wished she could get a glimpse of those runes. To snatch away all kinetic energy like that was amazing. She could imagine so many uses for it.

Spartacus turned back to Eirene, raised his gladius in salute, then tossed it across the table. Eirene snatched it out of the air and saluted in turn. Then she drove the point into the table. The sharp steel sank several inches into the hard wood and quivered in place when she released it.

Only then did Eirene smile. She rounded the table and embraced Spartacus. They kissed each other's cheeks with ritual formality.

"Thus do animosities of old surrender ground to newfound alliance of mutual defense," Eirene grinned.

Spartacus gripped her shoulders, his laugh booming across the yard. "You stood athwart my purpose for too long, Queen of Conflict. Today we unite in purpose to win glory and honor!"

"Glory and honor," Eirene repeated softly, looking moved.

Sarah looked from one to the other. They were all insane. How long had they faced each other as bitter enemies? And yet, now they stood together as allies against a greater evil. Accepting Melek into their company had seemed a bold move, but to accept Spartacus too?

Spartacus turned to Melek as everyone again sat around the table. "To answer your question, then. I overheard Xiao mention the goal of changing history, or conquering it. I assumed she was talking about writing herself into the annals of time like other conquerors always yearn to do."

"What were her exact words?" Melek asked. Color had drained from his face.

"Several times, Paul spoke of wresting the power of history. On occasion, I heard Xiao state they must gather master runes to form the greater whole. Only then could they master the scroll of time."

Eirene asked, "Can you tell us anything else about her? We're tracking her connection to ancient China."

"The Chinese connection is valid." Spartacus selected another hamburger and spoke around an enormous bite. "Her ancestry is written large in her features, and in private she sometimes slipped into mannerisms that Paul said dated from old China."

"How old?" Gregorios asked.

Spartacus shrugged. "He revealed little, but let slip that she was of imperial stock, an empress in her own right. That made him royalty, a fact he thought would impress me more than his character had."

Eirene said, "That confirms some of what we guessed. We never gained much access in China." She turned to Melek. "What about your clan?"

He had been staring at his plate, a bit distracted. "What was that?"

"China. Did the hunters have much history there?"

Melek shook his head. "Very little. We tried several times, but those teams always disappeared."

Gregorios swallowed a bite of his fourth hamburger. "Interesting. I'm starting to wonder if we've had a blind spot."

Nabil spoke up. "There was the one team sent to deal with a rogue facetaker in Japan. When was that?"

Heber said, "It was the mid-seventeenth century."

"We had no one sanctioned to work Japan back then," Gregorios said.

Melek nodded. "I remember the case. There were reports of a facetaker and a high-level enchanter working the fledgling Yakuza gang."

"The big crime organization?" Sarah asked.

Melek said, "It was still little more than loosely affiliated gangs back then. A strike team was dispatched to investigate. As far as we know, they eliminated the threat."

"As far as you know?" Sarah asked. That didn't sound good.

"The strike team never returned," Melek said.

"Another team was sent a couple years later, when it became clear they weren't coming back," Nabil offered between bites of his seventh hamburger. "They found no traces of the demon or the kashaph, but did recover the bodies of half of the hunter team from a group grave."

"That's an interesting story," Gregorios said.

"What are you suggesting?" Melek asked.

"Nothing yet. But a pattern is starting to emerge. Someone went to a lot of effort to keep us all out of that part of the world, and they managed it in such a way that never seriously aroused suspicion. That's very hard to do."

"You think maybe it was Xiao?" Sarah asked.

"It's a possibility we can't ignore. It suggests she's been a player far longer than any of us imagined possible."

"Ideas and conjecture," Spartacus said, sounding disinterested. "They accomplish nothing but distract from the mission at hand. Eat, my friends!"

As the rest of them returned to the feast, Melek rose from the table. "I must excuse myself."

"But we haven't even brought out the ice cream and the desserts," Spartacus exclaimed.

"Enjoy your feast. I will wait in the car," Melek said.

He waved away his helpers and insisted they remain at the feast, which they seemed happy to do. Sarah watched him leave. When he reached out to support himself on the door, his hand shook.

Spartacus waved at the piles of food. "Enough of such talk, my friends. Come, together we will vanquish this feast!"

While they ate dessert, Spartacus told them about the acting roles he was practicing for. Filming would start soon on a movie depicting recent events at the basilica. In the meantime, he was starring in a romantic comedy set in ancient Rome. Gregorios seemed delighted to hear about it.

Sarah ate slowly, wanting to follow Melek and ask him what he wasn't telling them. Tomas leaned close and said softly, "He's not going anywhere, Sarah. Don't make a big deal of it. Not yet."

30

Do not hate a man to his face when you know nothing of his soul.

~THE INSTRUCTION OF ANKHSHESHONQ, FROM THE
PTOLEMAIC PERIOD

THEY DIDN'T RETURN to the waiting jet until after dark. After Spartacus spoke at length with his assistant on the phone, he loaded the Hummer with a couple of large duffel bags. Eirene claimed shotgun in the Hummer, and Sarah got to ride in the front beside Tomas in the suburban. The rest of the men piled in the back.

Even though Eirene had seemed eager to talk with Spartacus and learn more about the extent of his changed outlook on life, Sarah wondered at the wisdom of them sharing a ride. After so many centuries as bitter enemies, could they really maintain a truce?

Gregorios didn't seem worried, however, and he only laughed, "I just can't wait to see him in that film."

"Do you think he's got useful information?" Sarah asked as they slowed in heavy traffic, despite the hour. She still felt frustrated that no one had addressed the question of body ownership.

Tomas placed a hand over hers. "Every little bit of information helps. He confirmed that she's from Chinese imperial heritage."

"And as bizarre as it feels to have Spartacus on our side, it's still far better than having him as an enemy again," Gregorios pointed out.

Sarah was turned in her seat, looking back at the others, and she noted the two hunters didn't look so sure. Calling Spartacus an ally must have rankled. They'd find it a lot harder to justify assassinating him, and actually working with such an infamous kashaph must offend every ounce of their finely-honed family honor. At least Melek hadn't seemed outwardly upset about their unusual new ally. In fact, he'd seemed distracted the entire trip.

She longed to ask him about that, but held her tongue. Tomas had seen Melek's strange reaction. She'd trust his instincts on when to broach the subject. For a while, anyway.

After driving in silence for a few minutes, Gregorios said, "The question is, was Xiao really born into an imperial family, or did she assume the identity of one of them?"

"Hopefully our research teams can unearth some clues," Quentin said.

The conversation faded out until they reached the airport and their waiting jet. Everyone piled in, and Quentin took a seat at the rear of the plane, behind the hunters. The position made the young men a little nervous, and they kept turning to check on him every minute or so. He pretended to ignore them.

After the plane reached cruising altitude, and after Spartacus gushed about the wonders of flight, Gregorios swiveled his chair around and said, "All right, Melek, I think it's time you told us what you realized today."

"It is a suspicion, no more," Melek said after a brief hesitation.

"What suspicion?" Gregorios insisted.

"You cannot force him to talk," Heber declared, rising.

Melek waved the young man down. "It is all right. Gregorios is correct. There are things we must discuss." He scanned the group, his gaze lingering on Spartacus and a tiny frown tugging at his lips. "This situation places me in a difficult position."

Sarah admired the understatement. Melek was the head of an organization sworn to eradicate cui dashi when his own son was one. His other son Reuben was dispossessed, his soulmask on a wall in the hunter compound, having been removed by his own brother. Spartacus was perhaps the most infamous of all kashaph, while Gregorios and Eirene were long-hated enemies. Now they had to work together. It made for interesting times and light sleeping.

Gregorios made a shooing gesture. "Just spit it out. We all know the score."

"Not this one."

Melek waved to Nabil, who produced a steel attaché case with a complex, eight-wheeled lock. Sarah leaned closer, extremely curious as Melek spun the dials, popped the case, and extract a second, smaller locked case with a thumbprint reader and a key slot. He extracted an oddly square key that hung on a leather cord around his neck.

"I admit you've got me curious," Gregorios said as they all watched in hushed anticipation.

The lock popped with a loud click. Melek hesitated before opening the case. Inside rested a waterproof tube.

"Really?" Gregorios asked, sounding impatient, although Sarah only felt her excitement growing. She doubted anything but another of those hunter secrets would be so carefully protected.

Melek opened the tube and gently extracted an actual rolled scroll with an ornately carved handle.

"Haven't you heard of transcribing to new media?" Eirene asked, looking amused.

Melek hefted the scroll, his expression reverent. "Some things are worth preserving through time. This vellum is made of the hide of a Passover lamb from the time of the Maccabees."

"They ruled Israel for a while, right?" Sarah asked, trying to remember her long-unused primary lessons.

"Correct. The information on this scroll dates back to the time of Moses."

He stood. "It contains my family's most treasured secrets."

Sarah smiled to herself. She knew it. And she really wanted to read that secret.

Eirene raised a hesitant finger to touch the wooden scroll. Melek didn't pull it away, but he looked like he wanted to. Heber muttered under his breath, "Sacrilege."

"All those years, and I never knew," Eirene said softly.

"You couldn't have," Melek said, carrying the scroll slowly to the table at the rear of the cabin. The rest of the group followed. As he carefully unrolled the scroll, assisted by the two other hunters, he added, "Few of my own family even known of this scroll's existence. It has never been revealed to outsiders."

"I'm not as much of an outsider as you assume, and you should stop keeping secrets from your wives."

"What are you talking about?"

Eirene sighed. "Since we're sharing secrets today, I think you deserve to know the truth about me."

"What truth?" Melek asked slowly, looking wary.

Sarah clutched Tomas' hand, barely able to contain her nerves. This needed to happen, but how would Melek react?

"Your grandmother Elizabeth didn't die in that assassination attempt so long ago."

"What are you saying?"

"It was the kashaph assassin sent to murder Ronen who died that night. I left in her body."

Melek recoiled and dropped into a nearby seat. The young hunters scrambled to catch the forgotten scroll. "Impossible!"

Eirene kept her gaze fixed on Melek and asked softly, "Why do you think her face was crushed? It was the only way I could leave that life without hurting him."

"You . . . Demon! How dare you defile her memory?" Melek surged to his feet and swung a fist. His leg might be injured, but he still struck with power.

Eirene caught his fist and held it. While he struggled to free it, she patted his hand. "I've kept an eye on your family ever since. You've always made me proud."

Nabil moved to assist Melek, but Quentin stepped in his way. "Let it play out, son."

Melek looked from his hand to Eirene, his expression torn. "You can't. It's . . ."

She sighed. "Unexpected, yes. I've wanted to have this discussion with you for so long, Melek. I know how hard this is to accept, but it's true."

Sarah squeezed Tomas hand harder and he whispered, "You're cutting off my circulation."

"This is so exciting."

"I don't believe you," Melek declared, his jaw set in a stubborn line.

"I'd be surprised if you did, but I can prove it."

"How?" he asked reluctantly.

"Show me your grandmother's locket."

Melek clutched at his shirt, glaring. Then he slowly drew a locket from under his shirt where it hung on a silver chain.

Shaped like a Star of David, it looked old and valuable. At her urging, he pried it open, revealing an aged, black-and-white photograph of a woman. Sarah leaned closer to get a look. The face did look strikingly similar to Eirene's.

"This proves nothing," Melek said, but his voice trembled.

"May I?" Eirene asked, extending a finger.

"Do not damage it," Melek warned.

Her finger burst into purple fire.

Melek cried out in alarm and snatched the locket away, clutching at the precious heirloom. "I warned you. This has been in my family—"

Eirene gave him an annoyed look. "I know exactly how long it's been in the family. Stop acting like a baby and look."

He glanced at the locket, then exclaimed in surprise and sank into the seat again. The photograph had peeled back from the inner edge of the locket, revealing Hebrew letters that glowed softly with purple light.

"What does it say?" Sarah asked.

"It says, *'I am Eirene and I love you'*," Eirene said softly, kneeling beside Melek's seat.

Sarah felt like bursting with joy. Eirene was so clever to leave a way to declare the truth to her stubborn descendants.

Melek looked from the locket to Eirene, clearly torn.

"As you said yourself, that's an heirloom," Eirene said. "It's always been in your care, just as you received it from your father and your grandfather before him. I could not have tampered with it."

"Why would you do this to me now?" Melek asked, snapping the locket closed, his expression turning angry. "First you steal my sons, now you desecrate the memory of my grandmother."

Eirene, her expression calm, said, "It's difficult, but face the truth like the man dear Ronen raised you to be."

"That's why Alter is cui dashi," Melek said. "You corrupted our bloodstream."

At least Melek was accepting the truth. Sarah wished he was taking it better, but at least this was a start.

"Oh, posh. Do you really think the nevron is what makes a person evil?"

Melek snapped, "Don't try to justify yourself. You've undermined the purity of our family."

"Our family is important to me too," Eirene said, gripping his hand. "And I've never met anyone as pure as your son. It's for Alter that I'm sharing this truth with you. He needs us, and we need him to restore order."

"I don't . . ." Melek muttered.

Gregorios spoke gently from where he stood a few feet away. "Give it time. It'll make sense eventually."

Melek turned to him. "Why would you do this to us? You corrupted us, destroyed my grandfather, took the life of my Reuben again, and now look what you've done to poor Alter."

Gregorios said, "Reuben made his own choices, and Alter's the best hunter you've ever produced. Nothing was done to hurt you. In fact, Eirene's original mission was to kill Ronen and weaken your family. She chose a different path that saved him."

"She's destroyed everything," Melek cried.

Gregorios asked, "How does it change this situation, really? We still have a job to do."

"I refuse to hear this," Melek exclaimed, snatching his hand away from Eirene. "There is no truth in your words."

Sarah knelt beside the other arm of Melek's chair. "Please, Melek. I know things are crazy, but don't push us away."

"You don't understand," Melek said, his tone anguished. "You're too new to this world. My son was right to try to save you."

She took Melek's hand. "Your son is a good man and a close friend, but it's because I'm so new that you should listen to me. My world was turned upside down, every anchor point cut free. I had to learn to make decisions on facts as they exist now, not based on old biases. And the truth is that these people are the best hope for the world."

"You haven't seen their history," Melek protested.

"I've learned much of it," Sarah countered. "There are bad things there, things I wished hadn't happened. But at the same time, your family is not without its mistakes."

Melek snapped, "Don't compare us with these demons. There are truths they don't even know."

"Then share what you know with us, and give them a chance to prove to you who they are today." She waited, barely allowing herself to breathe, hoping Melek possessed the same strength of spirit and resilience that Alter had shown.

After a moment, Melek blew out a breath. "You are indeed a rune warrior. You bend all to your will, without realizing your power."

He rose and faced Eirene. "I will consider your words."

"Take all the time you need. I look forward to speaking with you at length." She gave him a warm smile.

Gregorios said, "For now, we're all stuck together for several hours. Why don't you tell us some of what we don't know?"

Melek accepted the ancient vellum scroll from the younger hunters. "Fathers, forgive me if I choose wrong."

Still he hesitated, looking from Gregorios to Eirene, then to Sarah. With a deep breath, he returned to the table and unrolled part of the scroll. Fine writing covered it, beautiful letters in both Hebrew and Greek.

"This is the record from Alter, our first father, who journeyed with Moses and taught his children to hunt the kashaph and stand ever-watchful against them. We have held his charge for over forty generations."

Sarah studied the ancient text, awed by the weight of history she felt radiating from it. This text provided a link back through the generations to the days before Christ. She slipped her arm around Tomas' waist, feeling suddenly small.

Melek continued. "When our compound was attacked, the intruders obtained our master rune book, but failed to discover the hiding place of this greater treasure."

"Do you think they were after it?" Eirene asked, leaning forward to scan the long page. She had lived since the days of the Roman Republic. She knew Greek. She'd spent a life with the hunters. She had to know Hebrew too.

Melek refused to look at Eirene as he spoke. "With what we learned today, I suspect this was part of what they sought, yes."

"What's this all about?" Gregorios asked.

"History."

31

Cycle follows cycle, living life and dying death. Only the great River rolls on, unending with a few special souls astride its waters.

~YO YO, GHOST TIDE

MELEK TRACED his finger down the page and pointed to a line of text that looked like gibberish to Sarah. "Our first father warned of difficult times to come. The most critical charge he laid upon his descendants was to protect and preserve the fabric of history."

"How do you do that?" Sarah asked.

"By hunting the kashaph and removing cui dashi as soon as they arise. Their rounon powers pose a direct threat to the integrity of the scroll of history."

Gregorios leaned a little closer over the table and asked, "How is that possible? History is the flow of time. You talk of it like it's a tangible thing."

Melek glanced up and held his gaze. "Perhaps it is. Not tangible to mortals or even to you under normal circumstances. However, you must realize the rune sequencing Mai Luan and Paul used on their machines created a link to the past far stronger than even your memories should have allowed."

"This is tied to the master runes, isn't it?" Sarah asked. She'd felt the flow of history sliding past in the memoryscape. Some of what Melek was saying sounded like a science fiction story, but there was truth buried in there somewhere. It resonated with her.

Melek nodded. "It is. Those master runes are tangible links back to pivotal moments in history, but they are not the only link through time. They are not the most powerful either."

Gregorios touched the vellum, despite an angry look from Heber. "So what does this scroll have to do with that?"

Melek looked like he longed to punch Gregorios for touching the scroll, but after another steadying breath he continued. "Know that I share what I do only because of what the great Alter prophesied."

"You know prophesies are dangerous business," Gregorios said. "I've lived long enough to see some come to pass, so there's power there. But they're hard to interpret."

"This one is fairly clear." Melek unrolled more of the scroll and pointed.

"Incredible," Eirene breathed, leaning closer, eyes scanning the ancient text.

Melek frowned at her, but did not push her away. "In his writing, our first father told us that at a time of ultimate importance, a hunter bearing his name would arise. He would draw together allies that we must confide in, despite overwhelming justification not to."

"That's a tough one," Gregorios agreed.

"Indeed. It is my belief that we are in this time. That is the only reason I am sharing this with you now. My son must be found, for he will play a critical role in defeating these cursed cui dashi."

Gregorios chuckled. "I'd hoped you were about to tell me something I don't know. Did your ancestor tell us where to find him?"

"It's not that specific."

"So why is Xiao after this record?" Sarah asked. She was fascinated by the discussion and really wanted to ask for a full, English translation of that text to study.

Melek unrolled more of the scroll, revealing a long list of runes. "You will recognize some of the runes that Xiao and her offspring are using to link their machines to your minds to access history." Sarah nodded as she studied the symbols. "Others had been lost for centuries and are beyond forbidden. Until Alter shared those symbols with me, I would have sworn no one in the world but us knew about them."

Gregorios frowned. "You recognized the threat so far back?"

"A secret so long kept is not easily shared. We provided what guidance we felt appropriate, and we watched to see if further intervention might be warranted."

"Like shelling my house?" Quentin asked, sounding annoyed.

"Reuben is aware of this scroll and this most-sacred charge," Melek admitted. "His actions were rash, but he felt not only did he need to maintain the purity of the family honor, but he needed to remove knowledge of these secret runes."

Eirene, who looked thrilled to be having any conversation with her grandson said, "Trying to kill us was the wrong choice. I'm glad you think a little deeper than your son."

"Are there more?" Sarah asked, fighting the urge to help Melek unroll the scroll further.

There was clearly more to it, and she sensed the greatest secrets remained concealed. She had felt in recent memory jumps that there was more she should be able to do, stronger ties to the flowing moments of history. Perhaps the rest of the scroll he hadn't showed her yet included the runes she sensed must exist.

"Before we discuss additional runes, you need to understand the danger. Master runes are indeed powerful. However, they are but pieces of a larger whole, individual symbols within a grander mosaic."

"You're saying there are greater master runes?" Sarah asked. The thought was both exciting and terrifying. She'd died trying to manage the power of three master runes. Could Xiao wield something even greater?

Melek nodded. "That is an apt description. We refer to them as the Kyriarchos, or Ascendants."

"And what exactly are these ascendants?" Gregorios asked, looking honestly intrigued by the discussion.

"Sources of unrivaled power."

"You're backsliding on me. We're trying to get more specific, not less," Gregorios said with a frown.

"If they're greater than master runes, I don't see how anyone could hope to control one," Sarah said.

Melek leaned over the table and the ancient vellum. "Most of the time they are a secret so secure, barely a handful of people in the world know it. My family has held this secret, and yet we've never actually experienced an ascendant rune. This Xiao however." He glanced from Gregorios to Eirene. "I fear she may be poised to do so."

"Do we know what she could do with one if she did learn how to reach it and actually managed to control it?" Sarah asked. The hunters were right to conceal this information, and yet she wanted to know more.

"Only guesses at this point," Melek admitted.

"That's all we seem to have these days," Eirene said softly.

"That has to change," Gregorios said. He gripped Melek's shoulder and gave him an approving smile. "Thank you for trusting us enough to begin sharing these truths. This information is vital."

He gestured to Sarah. "We've got a few hours before landing. If you work together, can you develop a new cipher before we land?"

"What kind of cipher?" Sarah asked, a little nervous. She wouldn't inscribe the rune sequence that might reconnect with the master runes that had already killed her once.

"One that will find Xiao. If she's still hiding anywhere around Rome, I want to know it."

"The last assault didn't go all that well," Sarah pointed out.

Gregorios didn't look worried about that. "Find her and we'll do better. She's made this personal, tried to turn the world against us. It's time to remind her why the world learned to leave us alone."

32

I am not afraid of an army of lions led by a sheep; I am afraid of an army of sheep led by a lion.

~ALEXANDER THE GREAT, 325 B.C.

MOST OF THE rest of the company returned to their seats. Eirene and Spartacus started an animated discussion about the pros and cons of issuing formal duels in a world where mortal combat was frowned upon.

Sarah sat at the little table beside Melek. She was eager to get to know Alter's father better, but also a bit apprehensive. Alter approached runes with a brilliant, artistic flair and he had taught her much, but he had always spoken of his father as the true master. What would Melek think when he realized just how new she was to rune-smithing?

"My son spoke very highly of you," Melek told her as he accepted a pad of paper and a couple of pens from Nabil. "I think we should begin with some of the ciphers you have developed so I can get a sense of your style and aptitude."

That sounded reasonable, so Sarah sketched out some of the ciphers she had designed for the recent memoryscape confrontation with Xiao. Melek studied the barrier cipher with a thoughtful nod. He traced with a thick finger her most recent creation, the deadly cipher she had applied to those thirty millimeter shells.

"This cipher," Melek said softly, glancing up at her. "It is beautiful and very deadly."

"I was hoping it would help slow Xiao down long enough to hit her with the big guns."

"I suspect it could have done so, and I am impressed by how much you have grown into your powers in so short a time." He tapped the cipher. "Under any other circumstance, such a cipher would be . . ."

His voice trailed away and Sarah finished the thought for him. "It would be horrific."

She shuddered to think of the devastation such a cipher could cause. Of course, for unenhanced mortals, getting shot with a thirty millimeter cannon would be brutally fatal anyway. The added horror of that cipher was overkill.

"I am glad to hear you say that," Melek said with an approving smile. "In the unending war against evil, we must sometimes do terrible things. The risk is always there that we could become unfeeling, or worse, come to enjoy the power we wield."

"I'd rather build ciphers to help people." Sarah nearly mentioned her healing cipher, but bit her tongue. No doubt Melek would object to what she had done even more strenuously than Alter had.

Melek pointed to her barrier cipher. "Your gift is impressive, as I would expect from a rune warrior. However, your education has been so rushed, you lack some refinements that could strengthen these ciphers."

"What refinements?" Sarah asked eagerly. She'd been proud of that barrier. She'd used information from David the Builder, who was a genius at barriers. It had slowed Xiao to a crawl in the memoryscape. Well, until it had failed.

Melek added four small marks to the cipher, modifiers that Sarah was familiar with already. Many symbols used in her ciphers, as well as in more basic runes, could hold multiple meanings. The modifiers helped complete the sequences, tie the various symbols together, and clarify meaning.

"Why apply those like that?" Sarah asked, studying the modified cipher. He had linked those add-on marks to key parts of the cipher, but she didn't understand how those changes improved it.

Melek pointed to one modifier he had linked to the triquetra, a common triangular shape marking the intersection of three circles. "It is clear in this cipher that you wish to use this symbol to reinforce the defensive and protective components of your wall."

"That's right." That symbol was critical.

Melek explained, "With this additional modifier, we can isolate that meaning. This symbol has been used widely by many different cultures and religions, so is therefore a potent rune symbol. However, some of its alternate meanings can serve to weaken the overall effect, particularly when combined with the other symbols you chose."

"But I thought those other symbols helped reinforce my intent," Sarah protested. "And that by combining them, I was actually increasing the resulting effect."

"If you maintain your purpose fixed in your mind, perhaps you managed to do so," Melek conceded. "As a rune warrior, much of the effect depends on your clarity of purpose. However, it is still preferable to design the symbol to reinforce your intent further."

He took a few minutes to review in detail the possible modifiers, many of which she already knew. He delved deeper into their meaning and the effects they produced. He explained the rather complex concepts with a simplicity that made so much sense, she couldn't believe she hadn't seen it before. As she reviewed the cipher with him, she quickly understood his point, and grinned.

"Amazing. If I'd understood this, I might have held Xiao a few seconds longer."

Melek shrugged. "Don't waste energy focusing on what might have been. Let us instead apply the lessons we can take from that past to reinforce the success of the future."

They spent a little while reviewing other symbols she already knew, and he explained the underlying reasons why they worked and how they meshed. She sketched more of her ciphers, growing more excited the deeper the discussion progressed. Studying with Melek was turning out to be a singular opportunity, and she wished the plane would slow down to give her more time.

When she showed him her custom rune, the same rune Eirene had developed when she had lived with the hunters as Elizabeth, Melek's expression clouded. He touched the rune softly and Sarah caught a glimpse of his anguish. He still hadn't reconciled his grandmother's memory with the reality of Eirene's revelation.

She placed her hand over his. "I was inspired to create this rune. I feel it binds me to both Eirene and to you."

"You could not have started on your path with a more meaningful rune. You are the first rune warrior in a long time, and I believe you are here now for a reason. You defeated one of the greatest threats the world has known in generations."

She smiled warmly. When he wasn't threatening to kill her or Alter, he was quite charming. "Thank you, but I didn't do it alone. Only the united efforts of the facetakers and the hunters succeeded."

Melek nodded, but she caught his lingering worry. It must be incredibly hard for him to rise above the biases he'd embraced his entire life. "That is why we're here. Our differences are great, but for the time being, our enemies are greater."

"Let's hope those differences can be mended."

"Perhaps." He squeezed her hand. "This much I can swear to you Sarah. My clan will stand with you without reservation and for all time."

Sarah felt moved by the simple but sincere declaration. She cared for Alter and in that moment felt optimistic about getting to know Melek and his clan.

"Thank you for teaching me today."

"You take to it like a hunter to the chase. Alter was right, you're an exceptionally apt student."

"What are your plans for him, really?" Sarah hated to risk breaking the fragile connection they had made, but she had to know.

Melek's expression fell and he leaned back from the table. "Alter's condition produces some difficulty."

"It's not a condition. It's what he is and it doesn't make him a bad man."

"There is much you still do not understand."

"I understand enough. Without Alter, I would have died and Paul would have succeeded. Facetakers, hunters, and a *cui dashi*, your son, won that victory. Alter's *condition* played a critical role and you should be thanking him, not trying to kill him."

"I need to speak with my son," Melek said, his gaze steady, clear of doubt. "Much will be decided then."

Sarah leaned forward. "Don't you dare hurt him, Melek. You've seen what I can do when I get upset."

Melek surprised her by grinning. "One of my favorite video clips of all times, my dear."

"I'm serious," she insisted.

"I know. Your loyalty to my son is heart warming. It is good to see his devotion to you is not unanswered."

"We're good friends," Sarah said, feeling uncomfortable with his choice of words. She glanced to the left where Tomas was sleeping in a nearby seat. "And I stick by my friends."

"As you should." Tapping the rune-covered papers they'd been working on, Melek added, "Back to work. We've covered the basics. Now let's build this new cipher."

Sarah allowed him to change the subject and together they immersed themselves in the runes. She hadn't planned to reveal to Melek the rune she had devised in her first life to identify nearby nevron, but he surprised her by drawing it out for her.

"Alter shared this compound rune with me. Very impressive and very creative."

"Thank you." She wasn't sure how she felt about the hunters possessing it. They might not be able to trigger it without her, but what if they found a way? If relations between them and the facetakers took another negative turn, this rune could prove dangerous.

Melek added, "Your instinctive mastery over complex runes is unparalleled. This rune makes sense now that I see it, but the construction is foreign to how we think. We never would have devised it."

"How is that possible? You know so much more about runes than I do."

"I know all the existing runes and how they connect. My knowledge is like a dictionary." He tapped her rune. "This is art, the application of principles in a unique way."

That surprised her. "You've developed compound runes. How is this different?"

"How is a painting of Picasso or da Vinci different than that of most other painters? They all know the principles of applying paint. Anyone in the world could conceivably produce the same masterpieces, but they don't. Why not?"

Sarah shook her head. "That's not a good comparison. Those are masters who spent years developing their art."

"Indeed, but they all possessed a natural gift that others lack. In a similar way, you possess a rounon gift that elevates your ability to a level we simply cannot achieve. Within you lies a greatness that, once you learn to tap it, will allow you to make history."

"I don't want to make history."

In a way, that promise sounded too much like what Xiao wanted to do. She loved working with runes and building ciphers, and longed for quiet times to devise positive ones. If the world found out what she could do, she'd have to deal with all the people who would try to leverage her abilities for their personal gain.

"That's why I am confident you will." Melek pointed at the rune. "You provided the core of what we need. I can help you refine it."

Over the next hour, that's exactly what he did. With his guidance, Sarah developed a beautifully sophisticated cipher, more subtly powerful than anything she had yet attempted. She felt confident it would allow her to sweep the entire city for active nevrons and pinpoint them.

The next difficulty came with the question of how to power it. This level of cipher required a significant power supply, although Melek taught her how to apply modifiers to better focus the cipher and reduce the power requirements. Even so, she would drain more of her strength than she felt wise to attempt.

She dared not share with Melek how she had placed charging runes around the city to pilfer small amounts of energy from passing souls. Their newly forged friendship lacked the strength to support such a break with his tenets. So she explained how she had developed the ability to siphon a little power from all of the enforcers and the workers within the Suntara Group headquarters.

Even that gave Melek pause. "You are skirting along a dangerous line," he warned in a voice so similar to Alter's that she could imagine the earnest young hunter sitting beside her whispering, "Abomination."

"I know, but these are people who willingly agreed to share their strength."

He finally relented, but she sensed that if he had been able to think of another way to power the cipher, he would have insisted they do that instead. She secretly hoped he would figure out a better way.

Although she still felt justified in siphoning the tiny bits of energy from people to help sick children, she would love a better way. She didn't like having to resort to what was essentially theft of the very vitality of so many souls. No one was permanently harmed by what she did, few would even recognize the tiny temporary drain on their energy, but did that make it right?

Forcing her concerns aside, she focused on the upcoming hunt. She'd track Xiao and, with the hunters' assistance, they would take her apart.

As they prepared to deplane, Gregorios received a phone call. After listening for a moment, he lowered it with a scowl.

"We may have less time than we thought."

33

I hate cui dashi more than ever. Only those vile creatures could twist the world so far. In quiet moments I yearn for simpler days when I could shoot heka and facetakers alike.

~HEBER

SARAH SHARED a questioning look with Tomas as the group drew closer to Gregorios.

"What's going on?" Eirene asked.

"I just got off the phone with Francesca. We've got a crowd of protesters gathering outside of Suntara. Several hundred and growing. She said they seem to be working themselves up for a riot."

"That's too fast," Eirene said with a frown.

"It's not unexpected that the world might react like this. The masses always respond with fear," Melek said.

Eirene shook her head. "Not like this. The UN announcement came just a couple days ago. As much as they think they're the center of the universe, most common people don't pay that much attention to them."

Quentin said, "I just spoke with my staff. New reports have spread around the world and been featured here in Rome. The media have latched onto this story with unusual intensity."

Eirene said, "There has to be a reason for that. We had plenty of goodwill and positive press. It should take longer for public sentiment to sway."

"Usually I'd agree, but not this time," Gregorios said.

Eirene met his gaze. "Too fast. Someone's playing a very strong hand."

"I'll give you one guess as to who," Tomas said. He muttered an oath. "We only need a little quiet to track her down again."

Eirene nodded. "No doubt she senses that. She wishes to maintain the upper hand."

Gregorios frowned. "Not going to happen. Quentin, what's the status of the evacuation?"

The dapper Englishman said, "On track. The body bank and most of the important equipment has already been moved."

"Good. I've instructed Francesca to move the machines and order the staff out."

"Won't the protesters try interfering?" Sarah asked, worried that something might happen to the precious machines.

Gregorios shook his head. "Not at this point. There's a process of escalation that crowds go through from protest to mob."

"It can be accelerated," Melek warned.

"You'd know. Your clan has incited enough riots against us over the years." Gregorios pointed out, but without rancor.

"Indeed," Spartacus declared with a grin. "The hunters are unrivaled foes. I have suffered the effects of their manipulations of the public mind many times."

"Let's hope Xiao's group isn't quite as organized," Eirene said.

Gregorios said, "Don't count on it. We'll head to the mansion and implement our plan from there."

That made sense, but Sarah protested, "I need to stay in the city. The cipher will work best if it's located centrally."

"You just want an excuse to visit the Colosseum again," Tomas teased.

"That's a good idea," Sarah said with a straight face.

"I'll take you," Tomas offered.

"I too will unite with this effort most bold," Spartacus declared.

"It doesn't bother you to return to the place where you were held prisoner so long?" Sarah asked.

The gladiator shrugged. "I overcame that herculean challenge, Mistress of Symbols. Once defeated, a foe maintains no longer any sense of lingering threat. To visit the site of trial engenders nothing but renewed confirmation of the honor won by the victory."

"That's a really good way of looking at it," Sarah admitted. She wasn't sure she could turn such a harrowing ordeal into a fount of continuous enthusiasm like Spartacus did, but she definitely saw the advantages of his attitude.

"My sons and I will accompany you too," Melek said.

Sarah glanced again at the two young hunters hovering behind him. They did look a lot like Alter, but she hadn't realized they were all brothers.

Melek noticed her glance and explained, "An expression. I consider all hunters my sons."

Gregorios nodded. "Assign a full support team to back you up. This is our best bet, so take no chances."

"I'll make it happen," Tomas promised.

While the rest of the company headed for the mansion, Sarah's group piled into one of the waiting SUVs, with Tomas in the passenger seat. Their driver was Domenico, the Italian enforcer who loved to laugh. While Tomas called for backup, Domenico regaled them with stories of some of the ridiculous things pilgrims had done in the name of devotion to the Sword of the Deliverer.

"You can't be serious," Sarah laughed after he told them of one woman who had become a popular sensation at the shrine to the deliverer. She coated her arms in liquid-metal gallium to replicate Sarah's quicksilver limbs, and sliced apart dummies made to look like Paul. She sold the resulting mutilated forms for hundreds of dollars.

Tomas grinned. "You're big business. Now that the world's realizing you might not be permanently dead, maybe you can get a royalty cut from those sales."

Sarah stuck out her tongue at him. "You're not funny."

They found a parking spot not far from the Colosseum and Sarah was tempted to head inside. She loved this place.

She'd visited the famous amphitheater with Eirene during one of their memory jumps and seen it in all its glory. The ruined structure that had survived to modern day was but a shade of what it had been, but she felt the weight of history around it.

She always marveled that it had stood for so long. Then again, with Spartacus in tow, they might end up fighting a duel to honor the slain gladiators of old. So she remained in the vehicle and engraved the new cipher onto a block of wood that Domenico had brought along for that purpose.

"I need two companies at ten percent to fuel this. Which ones should I tap?" she asked Tomas.

"Fourth and sixth," he said after a moment's thought.

"Let them know they might feel a bit tired," she cautioned as she applied the modifiers to draw upon the souls of those squads. At ten percent, the drain would be manageable, about as bad as a mid-afternoon slump.

She focused over the finalized cipher and the inscribed lines began to glow silver against the dark wood. She felt an incorporeal connection with the rune as some of her soul strength flowed out to give it life. She closed her eyes in concentration and an image appeared in her mind of the nearby area. The Colosseum shone in her mind's eye like a shimmering, silver shadow filled with the softer shadows of moving mortals.

The image shrank, her perspective changing as if she were floating into the air. Her view expanded to include the nearby Palatine Hill, then the Circus Maximus. Tens of thousands of souls passed under her gaze, shadows of the lives surrounding her.

If she focused on any of them, she could bring them into sharper focus, but it would cost a lot of energy so she didn't bother. In the center of her view, the souls of the hunters and Spartacus, with their rounon gifts, glowed with gentle yellow halos. Her own glittered like gold.

The image in her mind began to shift, scrolling away to other parts of the city. She floated across the expanse of Rome, past the Tiber, and on to the Vatican. Her gaze was drawn to two bright blue souls as she drew closer. The image rushed toward her as she descended over the Suntara Group headquarters. Inside, she found Francesca and Harald.

Of more interest were the yellow halos surrounding five of the souls mingled with the crowd chanting for justice outside the building. She ghosted over them and recognize one of them.

The enchanter, Hongwu.

His soul glowed brightest of all the heka. Two others glowed in her cipher vision about as brightly as the hunters, so they were probably channelers. The others were much weaker, either occans or charlies. Eirene had been right. This was no ordinary crowd, and Xiao was definitely behind the event.

She had to wonder if Xiao meant to assault Suntara and steal the machines, or if she was just trying to distract them from hunting her? Sarah felt a flicker of fear for Francesca and the others in the Suntara building and was tempted to return to the SUV to raise the warning.

She decided not to. It would waste precious time and energy.

There were enough enforcers still in the Suntara headquarters to fight off any attempt to storm the building, and if Hongwu was foolish enough to challenge Francesca, she'd own him.

Driven by a renewed sense of urgency, Sarah swept back into the sky over the city and continued sweeping the area with her mind. When she reached the end of one pass, she drifted into the nearby hills and confirmed Gregorios and Eirene had returned to the mansion. She didn't draw close, but returned to the city for another pass.

She exulted in the feeling of flying her consciousness across Rome, untethered to the physical world. It was an unrivaled experience, and she felt deeply grateful that Melek had taught her so much. Without his deft guidance, she never would have created such a fine-tuned cipher.

After an hour of fruitless searching however, her strength began fading. She was just about to return to the vehicle when she spotted a new glow at the outer limits of her vision to the north.

She swept in that direction, closing on a large estate in the countryside just north of the circunvalacione settentrionale, the highway encircling the city. Inside the large central building on the estate glowed two bright crimson souls, although one blazed far brighter than the other.

Sarah cautiously drew closer, approaching the weaker of the two. The soul felt familiar and as she reached the house, she recognized it.

Alter.

Her soul touched down on the rooftop.

An electric jolt crashed through her mind with searing pain, scattering her thoughts. The shock of the unexpected blow knocked her right out of the cipher-induced vision. She rocked back against the headrest, her limbs quivering with agony. As her eyes popped open, she realized she was screaming.

Tomas nearly ripped the doors off the vehicle in his haste to rush around to her side. The others all drew weapons and scanned for threats.

Tomas grabbed her shaking hands. "Sarah, what's wrong?"

She slumped in her seat, feeling a tear dripping down one cheek. She felt exhausted and her muscles ached like she'd sparred full speed with Tomas for an hour. She closed her eyes and breathed deep, trying to center her thoughts.

Tomas cupped her face. His grip was gentle, but she could feel a quiver through his fingers. "Talk to me, Sarah."

She opened her eyes. "I'm all right, I think."

He breathed a sigh of relief. "What happened?"

"I made a mistake. I know where Xiao is hiding, but she had defenses in place."

"Did she hurt you?"

"Nothing permanent."

"My son?" Melek asked eagerly.

"There too. Melek, I've never experienced anything like that. As soon as I touched the building, I triggered something like a Taser strike."

Melek nodded gravely. "There are ways to guard against souls. Such a rune sequence is quite advanced."

"She has talented help," Tomas said angrily.

Spartacus said, "Indeed. Her minions are often formidable."

"There's more." Sarah told them about the heka embedded in the crowd outside Suntara.

"Not good." Tomas' frown deepened. "I'll notify Francesca. They'll have to accelerate evacuation. We can't move against Hongwu and his supporters in that crowd. That would incite the very riot they're hoping for."

Melek's expression turned grave, "We must move quickly. I can imagine a few ways Xiao might have constructed her defensive runes and in every case she would have included triggers to notify her of the breach."

"She'll bolt," Tomas growled. He returned to his seat. "Domenico, go! Get us to the mansion."

While the SUV tore through the city, Tomas called Gregorios and informed him that they had a fix on Xiao. "We're en route now. Mobilize everything and get the rainmaker prepped. I'll notify the Italians for a coordinated strike."

Sarah's phone rang. When she answered it, she was surprised to hear the familiar voice of Carlo Salvatici. She had expected the sergeant major to still be in the hospital.

She exclaimed, "Carlo, I'm glad you called. We were just about to dial your company."

"Signorina Sarah, it took much effort to find your cell number."

His tone was serious, and her happy smile faded. "What's wrong? I heard you were healing well."

"I am fine, grazie, but I must warn you of danger."

Sarah's heart sank, and she felt a flash of frustration. They didn't need more danger right now. "What danger? We've located Xiao. We can stop her this time."

"Impossible, I am afraid. My superiors will not authorize another joint strike."

"Why not? We can do it this time, I promise."

Carlo said, "You must listen to me. You don't have time. The army is coming. You must flee."

"What?" Sarah breathed, floored by the news. Her confident enthusiasm about the upcoming assault against Xiao faltered.

"Signorina, you saved my life. I believe you and signore Tomas. That is why I call now. Orders are already given. Forces are en route to Suntara and to the mansion on the hill. They will arrest everyone and confiscate all assets."

"Why would they do that? They know us, they know what sacrifices were made to fight Paul."

"It is no matter. Orders come from very high. You must go. Go now."

"Oh, Carlo. This is terrible timing," Sarah exclaimed.

"I am sure you will abandon your phones. When you can, call me from a secure line and I will share any new information I have. Good luck."

The line went dead.

Sarah swore softly, but with feeling. When she looked up, Tomas was watching her with concern. When she explained, he pounded the dash and took a moment to swear in several different languages.

"We're going to lose Xiao," Sarah said, full of bitter disappointment.

"We have no choice, not if you believe Carlo."

"He was telling the truth."

Melek muttered something under his breath that sounded like a Hebrew curse. "You cannot take the risk that he was lying. You are fortunate you make such a powerful impression on those around you, Sarah."

Tomas was already on the phone. He relayed the situation to Gregorios, who ordered them to stay away from the mansion. He and Eirene would initiate the evacuation. When Tomas told him about the heka embedded in the crowd, Sarah heard his curse.

Tomas nodded while he listened. "I know. She's outmaneuvered us again. I'll call Francesca." He listened for a moment before saying, "Roger. Good idea."

When he hung up, Sarah asked, "What did he say?"

Xiao isn't the only one with defensive measures. He turned to Domenico. "The city is now considered hostile territory. Get us to the nearest armory."

Melek nodded. "Indeed. I think we're going to need a lot of guns."

Spartacus started humming a battle tune, his expression joyous.

34

Hemiunu assures me the great pyramid is almost complete. It seems impossible after twenty-three years of construction that my great monument will finally be ready. My priests are prepared to fill it with the runes to guarantee my reign forever. My only fear is that no facetaker exists in my kingdom to officiate at the life sacrifice.

~PHARAOH CHEOPS, FAMOUS FOR BUILDING THE
GREAT PYRAMID AT GIZA

THE MEMORYSCAPE FORMED GENTLY around Alter. The impenetrable darkness faded to the soft light of a single oil lamp set on a low table made of brass. The lamp was nothing more than a linen wick floating in oil in an ornate jar.

They had returned to ancient Egypt, but the vaulted, stone-walled room that formed around them was a bedchamber, not a temple. Alter glanced around with interest at the bright hieroglyphs painted on the walls.

The room was rather bare, dominated by the sleeping form of Sutekh. His bed was made of wood, with legs carved like cat paws. The foot of the bed was a bit lower, and his head rested on a curved, wooden headrest instead of a pillow.

A few large pottery jars stood in one corner, and a long, ornately-carved wooden chest stood opposite, its closed lid inlaid with ivory. The only other furniture were a pair of low stools flanking the table, and a very ornate wooden chair, with cat feet to match the bed.

Xiao moved one of the stools close beside the bed and seated herself gracefully upon it. For this visit, she had appeared in full Chinese regalia. She wore a silk gown of petal pink with long, draping sleeves. Her silky black hair was wound atop her head, and she wore a simple circlet of gold, adorned with pearls.

Alter drew closer as Xiao stroked a hand across Sutekh's forehead. "Awake and speak with me again," she whispered, her expression intent.

Sutekh was tall for an Egyptian, and appeared to be in excellent shape. For sleep, he had removed his priest's robe and wore only a common, white-linen kilt. Three beautiful enhancement runes showed black against his pale skin.

He had shaved all of his body hair. His head was shorn, including his eyebrows. He'd even shaved his arms and legs. He seemed strangely naked, even with the loincloth, and his sleeping face looked younger, although Alter suspected he was probably in his forties.

Alter held his tongue, content to listen for the moment. He didn't trust what Xiao had told him, but perhaps this conversation might offer additional clues.

Xiao's eyes glowed with the unique lavender shade of her activated nevron, She tapped a glowing finger on Sutekh's brow and spoke again with more authority. "Release your mind."

Sutekh shuddered and his eyes opened. They glowed with active nevron. He blinked up at Xiao and frowned. "You visited my dreams before."

She nodded as he sat up in the bed. "Indeed. I am come from the distant future to seek knowledge you alone possess."

Sutekh glanced around, noting Alter but then ignoring him. "This space is not my home, although the resemblance is nigh reality."

"We term this place the memoryscape. Think of it as the gateway to the ascendants."

Alter frowned, edging closer. She had mentioned that word the last time she had visited Sutekh, but he did not know it. The way they were speaking, it was almost as if she had somehow connected with the Egyptian through the reaches of time. But that was impossible, wasn't it?

Sutekh regarded Xiao with interest. "I salute your power, woman. I have foreseen the return spiral of the ascendant, but did not expect the truth to materialize in this way. I do not recognize your dress, and I will know your name."

"You may call me Xiao, but my search has yet to reveal the deepest name that will define my eternity."

Alter listened intently. He'd suspected Xiao was but a temporary label, and hoped she'd reveal other names. Such information might prove vital.

Sutekh sagged where he sat. "The search for vital moments and the symbols you call master runes can be a long road, but I grow weary. This audience tasks my soul."

"It is difficult as yet to penetrate the ages. I seek those pivotal moments in the history you know, but which have been lost to time."

Alter bit back a question he wanted to ask. So far, she seemed to confirm what she had told him, but he wanted to know how she managed the visit at all. It broke everything he knew about history.

"Knowledge is power." Sutekh's expression turned calculating. "I have foreseen one rising to stand athwart the aeon, but can you prove you are the one? Only then could I swear allegiance to you."

Xiao extracted from her pocket a gold pendant. Alter recognized it as the simple item her enchanter, Hongwu, had worn the night they had interrupted his heka cell looting the Egyptian museum.

It still looked unremarkable, and he wondered what it meant. She marked a rune on the back of the pendant with a feather quill that appeared in her hand. Alter leaned closer and recognized the simple rune of revealing. The rune glowed, then faded away, taking with it the gold veneer of the pendant, revealing a crimson layer underneath. Marked in white was a complex rune, made up of several Egyptian symbols.

"Behold, I have recovered your symbol," Xiao said, holding out the pendant to Sutekh.

He smiled. "Indeed, this rune was concealed from the world."

"Not from me. I have trod the ascendant, and you will help me."

Alter did not like the way the conversation was going, and he definitely didn't like that rune. The scarab beetle on it represented resurrection or transformation, and was often used as a symbol of protection. But in Sutekh's rune, it carried the *Was* Scepter, with its slanted top and two-pronged end, which represented dominion.

Facing that symbol was the unique head of Set, the Egyptian god of the storms and violence, among other things. He was a powerful god, whose story was full of conflict, and he eventually became known as the god of evil, chaos, and war. The unique Set animal head looked like the snout of an aardvark, with tall, rectangular ears. Integrated with that symbol was the Uraeus, the rearing cobra, a symbol used on pharaoh headdresses, an emblem of power and the right to rule.

The resulting rune filled Alter with unease. It suggested that Sutekh was one who sought dominion and power, and his connection with Set was disturbing. Hunters rarely used the symbols associated with that god, for they always drew upon the elements of rage and chaos. Any man who used that symbol as a key component in his signature rune was a man Alter distrusted.

"The truth of your words is thus established," Sutekh told Xiao. "I will share the memories you seek, but you must in turn open the way to salvation for my future."

"I have seen the unfortunate fate that awaits you at the hands of Moses."

"Moses?" Alter blurted out, unable to hold his peace any longer. Had they really traveled so far back in time?

"Hush," Xiao said, without turning to him. "Your place in this has not yet come."

He was tempted to summon a tank to remind her what his place was in the world, but he resisted the urge. Her time would come, and her overconfidence would offer him the chance he needed to destroy her.

She focused again on Sutekh. "As I said before, the path to salvation is forming in your future, but is not yet laid before you."

"I cannot help you until the assurance is given," Sutekh said.

Xiao shook her head. "Your refusal will seal your fate. Grant your memories to me and accept my rule, and the chance of salvation will increase."

Sutekh glowered at her, but she seemed content to wait. Alter wasn't sure what kind of salvation she intended for Sutekh, but he planned to find out. Then he'd make sure she failed. He could already tell Sutekh was not the kind of man to set free in any time period.

Sutekh raised a hand that burst into purple fire, matching the glow in his eyes. Xiao clasped it, her active nevron burning with lavender intensity. They held the grip for several seconds, eyes locked together.

Alter tensed to strike. In that moment of distraction, Xiao might be vulnerable, but what could he hit her with powerful enough to do lasting harm?

Before he figured out an answer, Xiao broke the grip and rose smoothly to her feet. She glanced at Alter and raised one fine eyebrow, as if wondering why he wasn't already holding a rifle.

"Now the hunt begins," she said as Sutekh fell back onto his bed, already asleep.

Alter stood his ground. "I agreed to walk with you while you sought a name. I never promised to help you change the history of this man."

"We will discuss your choice in his future later. For now, we will search the ascendant for the moments he shared with me." She seemed honestly excited by the prospect.

"What truth are you looking for in those moments? Most master runes are from times of conflict, and your children sought the worst truths of conquest and destruction from them."

Xiao shook her head. "We cannot fashion a better world using those truths, dear Alter. That is why your presence is so important. Together we can draw out only the most honorable truths."

"We're not friends," Alter said, furious that she would dare assume to call him dear.

"We should be." She actually smiled and extended a hand to him. "Come. Join me in ferreting out the most honorable master runes the world has ever known."

He wasn't ready to fight her yet, but he hated allowing her to take his hand. As the memoryscape faded around them, Alter swore to learn the secrets of how she moved so far back in time. He would learn the truth about the man Sutekh, and above all, he would find a way to strike back.

35

What I hate is ignorance, smallness of imagination, the eye that sees no farther than its own lashes. All things are possible. . . . Who you are is limited only by who you think you are and which runes you can bond.

~EGYPTIAN *BOOK OF THE DEAD*

EIRENE SAT in a command chair in the tiny communications room of one of the many safe houses Suntara owned around Rome. She monitored the positions of their forces from her console. Everything had been going smoothly until just moments ago when the light representing a safe house across town had gone dark.

She had hoped it was a communications glitch until a second light blinked out, then a third.

"All units," she said into the microphone headset she wore. "Be advised Suntara safe houses twenty-one, five, and fourteen appear to be compromised. Repeat, safe house locations may be non-secure. Move to alternate plan Delta-Six."

As the acknowledgments rolled in, she suppressed a growing anger. It galled to think Xiao had outmaneuvered them so completely.

The fallen safe houses were not critical assets, and any unauthorized entry would automatically fry all electronic components, so no communications or intelligence data would be compromised. Still, she hated to think their operations had been so thoroughly compromised.

Gregorios' voice spoke into her headphones. "Quentin and I are away finally."

"How did it go?"

The two of them were the last to flee Quentin's mansion prior to the arrival of the Italian government forces. They had deployed some nonlethal defensive measures around the mansion before leaving.

"We bruised their egos and they'll waste some time digging out of that mess."

"Did you hear my last broadcast?"

"I did. Are you on the move?"

"Shortly. The team is pulling all the supplies we can carry."

"Don't waste time on non-essentials. With an assault this well orchestrated, the strike teams hitting the safe houses will no doubt be armed and ready to subdue anyone they catch."

She was starting to hope she'd run into one of those strike teams. Xiao had attacked her family, and a feeling of battle lust was thrumming through her system. All she said was, "I'll be careful. Have you heard from the children?"

"Harriett's gone to ground at Yurak headquarters, and Francesca's overseeing redeployment of the heavy weapons depot."

A fourth safe house light went dark. Eirene muttered a favorite curse from fourteenth century Hungary. "They got number eight."

Gregorios chuckled. "A lot of spam in that one. They're welcome to it."

"This isn't funny," Eirene said through a smile. She hated spam. "How did those assets get compromised?"

Gregorios didn't respond for a moment, then said, "Love, those are all Suntara locations. Who knows what Shahrokh and those idiots let Mai Luan access while she had their ears? Have you seen any of our personal assets compromised?"

She should have spotted that. "No. Good point. It'll be good to know we can count on something at least."

A beeping in her headphones announced another call. She linked it to the open conversation and found Francesca on the other line. "How are you, dear?"

"Haven't seen this much excitement since the days of playing tag with the blitzkrieg," she said, her voice cheery. She always loved danger. "We barely got the last personnel out of Suntara before government forces overran the building."

Eirene hated retreating, but sometimes it was necessary. "All the useful information's been purged, and the body bank is safely concealed under the Vatican."

Francesca said, "The interesting thing about the incursion was that the carabinieri weren't in charge. I monitored their entrance through some remaining video feeds. Looked like Hongwu was in command."

"Xiao's playing her hand pretty strong," Eirene commented.

Gregorios muttered, "I'm starting to hate that woman."

He could say that again. She asked, "Where's Sarah and Tomas? We need to gather everyone at our personally-owned safe locations and regroup. Xiao's got us running like rabbits."

Gregorios' voice turned grim. "Notify everyone, we move operations to Titano."

He was right, but Eirene muttered, "I hate abandoning Rome. We haven't ceded control of the city to hostile forces in over a thousand years."

"We'll get it back, but right now we need a place of strength."

"You're probably right. Meet me at the honeymoon house."

"I love it when you mix business and pleasure," he said with a grin in his voice. "See you there."

Francesca groaned. "You two are incorrigible. I'll relay the new orders to my teams."

"Be safe," Eirene said, then cut the connection. She called Tomas next.

"How are you all doing?" she asked.

"Secure. We picked up a second truck and loaded it with gear and weapons. I let the hunters take that one."

"Are you sure that's wise?" Eirene didn't really think Melek would turn on them, but leaving three hunters unchaperoned with a truckload of weapons in close proximity to her people still made her nervous.

"They're eager for a chance to hit Xiao. Melek realizes their best shot at her is to stick close to us. He can't do too much damage to us right now. Besides, I've got Spartacus with me."

She heard the gladiator's voice clear enough that he must have leaned close to Tomas' earpiece. "Tell Tomas to let me drive."

Tomas replied before Eirene could. "This is my vehicle, so I decide who drives." His voice held a hint of irritation, as if they'd argued the point more than once already.

"I've been practicing," Spartacus insisted.

"Where's your license?" Tomas asked, and Eirene read his amusement.

Spartacus cursed, and she heard Sarah arguing with him about the merits of submitting to the decision of the DMV about his readiness to drive. He complained loudly that they had refused to accept a challenge to duel when he objected to their ruling the last time.

"Sounds like you're all doing fine," Eirene said through a smile. "Meet us in Orvieto."

"I've been meaning to take Sarah there for a visit anyway. We can eat dinner near the Duomo."

Eirene appreciated his attempt to find something positive in the dire situation. He was right. Sarah would love the beautiful hilltop town. Every time Eirene visited, it reminded her of a very happy life she had spent in Tuscany.

"Then we head for San Marino."

36

He who conquers himself is the mightiest warrior.

~CONFUCIUS

"SARAH, WAKE UP."

She rubbed sleep from her eyes and straightened in the passenger seat of the big SUV that Tomas was driving. She had dozed off after they passed the city of Rimini, right on the Adriatic. As she blinked away the effects of sleep, she shivered, feeling an unexpected chill, as if ice water had trickled into her veins.

"Are we there yet?" she asked, slipping into her jacket, which had fallen to her lap while she slept.

"Almost. Take a look."

The view out the windshield was like they'd traveled back to the Middle Ages. They drove through rolling, rocky hills and lush, green valleys, dotted with beautiful little Italian villages. But her eyes were drawn to a squat mountain rearing ahead of them, dominating the early morning landscape.

"That's beautiful," Sarah breathed. A village of red-roofed houses clustered at the base of the mountain, while a gorgeous little castle commanded the peak above. "That's San Marino?"

Tomas nodded. "The view is best from this side. We'll circle Mount Titano and head into the upper town from the opposite side."

When Tomas had told her they were heading for San Marino, she hadn't realized they'd be hiding out in such a beautiful place. "You said this isn't really part of Italy?"

He nodded. "It's an independent country. One of the smallest in the world at about twenty-four square miles. Its official name is the Serenissima Repubblica di San Marino."

"The what?"

"The Most Serene Republic of San Marino," Eirene said from the middle seat.

Spartacus sat beside her, craning forward to peer out the windshield between Sarah and Tomas. Gregorios had scored the cramped seat in the back and lay sprawled sideways across it, head pillowed in a jacket, not bothering with a seatbelt.

"When I knew this land, it was barely settled," Spartacus said.

"It's been quite a while," Eirene pointed out softly.

"These old settlements remind me of those days of glory when we oft joined in battle."

"I usually try to convince myself that these days are better," Eirene said.

"Well, when we're not getting chased by half the world," Gregorios grumbled.

Spartacus turned to look at him. "Never fear. If attempts at flight and concealment fail, we can meet our foes in single combat."

"Let's hope it doesn't come to that," Eirene said.

"Such honest contest of arms is at least familiar," Spartacus said, turning to stare out the window again. "Most of the rest of the world is unrecognizable."

The gladiator had adjusted remarkably well to the modern world after his centuries-long imprisonment on that statue in Rome. Sarah wondered how she would handle such a shocking transition. His penchant for dramatic declarations and honor duels didn't seem so exceptional when she thought about it that way.

"I'm glad this area feels more like home," she said.

Spartacus shrugged, then his ready smile returned. "Such a tiny nation would perhaps lack a standing army."

Gregorios barked a laugh, but Eirene shook her head. "I'd have an issue with you laying siege to our little country."

"Your country?" Sarah asked.

Eirene nodded, the gesture very stately in her imposing Amazon figure. "We do technically own it. We have since it was founded back in the year 301."

Why didn't that idea surprise Sarah?

"Not that most of the population here have any clue," Gregorios said, heaving himself upright in the back seat. "The truth about our ownership is secret from all but the senior leadership."

Eirene nodded. "No use owning hidden bases if everyone knows you own them. And speaking of shared secrets, are Quentin and the hunters still on our tail?"

Tomas nodded. "The rest of the convoy is spreading out. We don't want to show up in force and draw everyone's attention."

They stopped for breakfast at a little cafe with a great view of the mountain. It was chilly, but they ate outside anyway. Sarah enjoyed the clean, crisp air while she watched the local traffic of bicycles, mopeds, and tiny delivery trucks, sprinkled with the little cars common in Italy.

Sarah wanted to get one when she got home to the States. Some of them were so small, they seemed more like toys than real cars, but they fit the narrow, winding streets much better than the big SUV Tomas was driving.

Eirene pointed toward the castle rearing high above, which she said was named the Guaita Tower, the tallest of three fortress towers of San Marino. "Disney World is bigger than this whole country. Disney is about forty square miles."

"How would you know that off the top of your head?" Sarah asked. She loved Disney.

"We've invested heavily in amusement parks."

"I don't think I want to know." She didn't want to imagine Walt Disney as a facetaker or a secret heka. Some truths were better left unknown. "What made you decide to buy your own country?"

Tomas swallowed a gulp of coffee and said, "Makes sense. Who would ever hunt for us here?"

Despite driving through the night, he looked alert. They'd spent a lovely afternoon in the mountain town of Orvieto. Sarah had enjoyed visiting the beautiful duomo cathedral there, with its towering front facade covered in beautiful artwork, and the unique, striped stone interior. They'd left late and taken their time traveling the Italian highways, careful to watch for pursuit.

"I hate abandoning Rome," Eirene muttered.

"Drop it, love," Gregorios said around a large bite of croissant. "We haven't visited San Marino since that honeymoon in 1912."

She shook her head. "You might not have, but I've popped in here a few times since then."

Over their cappuccino and pastries, Eirene explained more about the tiny country. With only about thirty-five thousand citizens, it was one of the tiniest in the world. Much of its economy was now based on tourism, mostly from neighboring Italy, and it claimed to be the oldest republic in the world.

"So what made you choose San Marino?" Sarah was fascinated by everything about the little country.

"Back in those days, Italy was made up mostly of independent city-states," Eirene explained. "We wanted to keep an eye on some ruling families who were recruiting heka mercenaries to their armies, so we sponsored old Marinus to start the community."

Gregorios interjected, "*Saint* Marinus. They canonized him, remember?"

"Asoka thought he was so funny with that one," Eirene said with a smile.

"Was that during the life he spent as a Catholic Cardinal?" Sarah asked.

"You got it," Gregorios said.

Eirene added, "He secured our properties in the Vatican, but that life started wearing on him so he began looking for ways to entertain himself."

After breakfast, and once the scouts reported to Tomas that they saw no signs of pursuit, they drove around the mountain. Instead of immediately climbing the hill through the upper town like Sarah expected, they left the road and took a narrow, winding track toward a sprawling estate perched atop a prominent hill a couple miles to the west.

The three-story structure of adobe, with red-tiled roof, looked like it had to be a couple hundred years old, but it was in excellent condition. They followed a narrow lane around the back of the mansion, past the manicured lawn and rock-lined pond, and through an actual olive orchard.

The lane emptied into a hidden valley on the back side of the hill and ended in a cluster of stone buildings. Some looked like residences for staff, others looked like sheds or garages. One big barn with its huge double doors open had an enormous stone vat on the paved floor.

"What's that?" Sarah asked as they passed.

Tomas said, "A vintage wine press. There's a very productive vine-yard on the far side of the property."

"You're kidding. That's awesome."

They pulled into a long, hangar-like building set behind the others, big enough to conceal the entire convoy. Sarah asked, "What is this place?"

"This is the staging area," Gregorios said as they exited the SUV and stretched. "The underground complex up on Titano is quite extensive, but it's hard to get the big equipment in there, so we stage it all out of here."

"We've also got barracks for three hundred enforcers concealed under the houses," Eirene said, gesturing at the nearby cluster of stone buildings.

"Sometimes it's so much fun traveling with you guys," Sarah breathed.

So much of the secret world of facetakers, heka, and cui dashi was dangerous, lurking along the shadowed edges of society. She loved seeing the other aspects of their long, prosperous lives which somehow got overlooked so much of the time.

While Gregorios and Eirene headed for the mansion at the top of the hill to speak with the caretakers of the property, Sarah and Tomas entered a quaint stone cottage. They passed a comfortable living room, then entered a state-of-the-art communications room, staffed with a pair of female techs and three enforcers, who all greeted Tomas enthusiastically.

"How's the world?" he asked.

The woman in charge grimaced. "Despite the delaying tactics Harald's team has been deploying from South Africa, there's way too much information about Suntara out there. The world seems to have forgotten how much we did to stop Paul, and sentiment is turning ugly."

"About what we figured." He gave her an encouraging smile. "Don't worry, we'll weather this storm like we have everything else."

"Yes sir," she said, but didn't sound convinced.

So Sarah asked, "Is there any good news anywhere?"

The woman chuckled and said, "That archaeological dig in Egypt is celebrating another big win. They've started releasing some artifacts from their secret dig site."

The young tech seated next to her grunted. "Didn't seem to help much. I'm seeing reports claiming those artifacts only proved the dig is false. Some of the items included symbols tied to major religions that didn't appear until centuries later."

The woman shrugged. "Only seems to confirm the dig is real to me. Lots of modern symbols were used prior to their current meanings, isn't that right, Captain?"

Tomas nodded, looking thoughtful. "Do we have any assets in that dig?"

The woman shook her head. "Surprisingly, no. This one was set up way under the radar. But our people in the Cairo museum should get a chance to study those artifacts soon."

"Good. Send them a note to forward a copy of their analysis directly to me."

"Will do," she said, and turned to a different keyboard and started typing.

"What are you thinking?" Sarah asked.

"It's probably nothing, but with so much crazy stuff going on, I don't like the idea of ancient artifacts with surprising symbols showing up right now."

He had a point. Sarah would love to visit an actual archaeological dig and see unbiased history. "Maybe we should go pay them a visit."

"If the artifacts are unusual, we will," Tomas promised. Then he turned back to the techs and started checking the status of the other enforcer squads scattered around Italy and the world.

Over the next hour, while he did that, Sarah caught up on the news and email. Most of the world thought her dead, but Francesca had set up a feed for her that collected articles from her home town, and regular updates about her parents, siblings, and their families. She hadn't explained how she collected that information, and Sarah hadn't asked.

Sarah groaned when she spotted an article from the local news channel. It was an interview with her parents. Her mother had tried to say positive things about Sarah's bravery in Rome. She still couldn't help criticizing the fact that Sarah had done so much to support a false church. Her father didn't show such restraint. He shared his fury about reports that Sarah had sold her body to heathens at Alterego.

She didn't bother reading the rest. Her parents had never understood her, and even a world-famous martyrdom hadn't broken through their small-minded view of the world. How they could be related to some of the amazing historical figures, like Joan of Arc, who she had met, boggled the mind.

At least her brothers and their young families seemed to be doing better. She reminded herself to find a way to send them some more money once the current crisis blew over. Surely Francesca would know a way to make that happen without angering her parents.

While she caught up on non-facetaker events, the other vehicles of their convoy arrived, one every few minutes. About half were troop transports and disgorged enforcers, who headed for underground barracks. The other large trucks were packed full of weapons, equipment, and the precious memory-walking machines. When Anaru arrived, Tomas left him to oversee the settling of the men while he and a few other enforcers strapped one of the precious machines to the back of a tiny delivery truck.

As they carefully wrapped it with padding and moving blankets, Sarah asked, "Where are we taking that?"

"Up to the complex hidden under the fortress. We have to bring them up one at a time. Gregorios wasn't kidding when he said it's tricky getting the larger equipment up there."

Sarah was really looking forward to seeing the concealed base under the ancient city. She wanted to tour San Marino too. She couldn't see the fortress from the hidden valley behind the mansion, and that's probably why the spot had been selected. No one could easily spy on them there.

Sarah squeezed into the tiny cab of the truck with Tomas. They drove into town, followed by Gregorios and Eirene, who each drove local cars. Quentin, Melek, Spartacus, and the two young hunters squeezed in with them.

As they climbed through the upper town of San Marino, Sarah soaked in the views. The road zig-zagged up increasingly steep, narrow roads toward the fortress and the walled old town. Like most Italian towns, cars weren't allowed in the old quarter at the center.

Instead of taking one of the public parking lots, Tomas turned into a tiny drive, barely wide enough for the little truck. He drove under a stone archway and parked in a private lot behind an ancient brick building. The other cars edged in beside them, so close they could barely squeeze out the doors.

"What now?" Sarah asked.

Tomas took her hand. "Now the others will take care of getting the machine downstairs while I show you around."

Gregorios started to protest, but Eirene shushed him. "Let the kids have some fun. Sarah's never been here."

He sighed and gave Sarah a wink. "Fine, but get me some gnocci to go." Then he turned to Heber and Nabil. "No, you don't get to wander off. You help me bring this thing down."

Sarah followed Tomas eagerly. Once they passed the open gate in the ancient outer wall, they entered the medieval old town. Much of the original architecture appeared to be still intact. These days the streets were lined with souvenir shops, jewelry stores, and ristorantes with their outside tables draped in red cloth.

The narrow, stone-paved streets wound up and down and around the steep hill in hairpin switchbacks. Three-story stone and brick buildings with orange-tiled roofs crowded close on both sides. Tomas led Sarah through the mazelike streets to a long, open piazza with breathtaking views out over the city.

"This is the Piazza della Liberta." He gestured at the narrow, stone building across the piazza, with a tall clock tower rearing over the square. "That's the Palazzo Publico, the government building." A couple of sentries in distinctive green jackets and red pants stood guard at the entry.

Just about every Italian town Sarah had visited sported a central piazza, usually with a grand palazzo and a magnificent cathedral. San Marino lacked the space, but Sarah found the much smaller scale of things charming.

"I love this town," Sarah beamed, pulling out her new phone to snap photos. From the piazza, they could look out over the tiny kingdom.

A couple of trattorias were situated on the square, and she decided that would be the perfect place to watch the sunset. The center of the square was dominated by a statue with a crown made up of the three towers of Mount Titano.

Tomas seemed to relax as they paused to enjoy the view. "I haven't been here in years. Almost feels like a vacation."

They spent another hour walking up and down the steep, narrow streets, peering into souvenir shops and smelling the delicious aromas of the many eateries. They ordered Gregorios his gnocci, which looked like squat little pasta chunks, but Tomas explained it was made mostly from potatoes.

"I've never heard of it." Sarah stole a bite, and the chewy piece was almost like a mini dumpling. The sauce was delicious and she said, "I'm getting one too."

They ordered Eirene's favorite local lasagna from a different ristorante, then wandered the town some more while they waited for the orders. Sarah enjoyed the chance to spend some quiet time together. It seemed their lives had become one hectic blur of memory battles, intrigue, and hunting rogue heka.

The situation with Xiao was dire. The threat to the facetakers from the world was more severe than ever. But for a few minutes, Sarah could relax and just enjoy exploring the ancient little city with the man she loved.

After visiting the beautiful little cathedral one winding street up from the main piazza, Sarah was struck by an unexpected wave of exhaustion. She swayed and leaned against the nearby shop window.

"What's wrong?" Tomas asked.

She frowned. "I don't know. I'm suddenly so exhausted I could sleep on the cobblestones."

Tomas slipped an arm around her waist to offer support. She leaned against him, happy with the contact, but worried. "My enhancements shouldn't allow me to feel like this."

Tomas tried not to look worried. "It's unusual, but you haven't had much rest since getting hit with that psychic Taser jolt. It might have hurt you more than you thought, and there's only so much your enhancements can do." He gave her a tender smile. "You do tend to push the limits."

"Maybe. I definitely don't feel well."

She squashed fears that maybe she'd somehow drained too much of her rounon well. She was tempted to tap some of that vast power building through her remote charging ciphers. A fraction of that power would restore her to full fighting trim, but she resisted the urge. If she used it, she'd have to explain where she'd drawn the power from, and she wasn't ready to do that yet.

"We'll visit the tower museums later," Tomas said, leading her to a high curb so she could sit down. "Rest a minute, while I pick up the food orders."

She nodded, and while he sped off on the errand, she closed her eyes and focused on her rounon well. She hadn't felt so weak since before she'd bonded her first rune. She was surprised to feel that her rounon strength felt shallow.

Maybe Tomas was right. She really had pushed herself too hard. That triggered another round of worries. She couldn't afford to lose touch with her own strength, to run low on reserves at a time when she might need them to fight Xiao or her minions. Maybe she should tap that remote power after all.

Tomas returned before she could convince herself it was worth the risk. He was carrying the bags of their take-out orders. "How are you feeling?"

"Only a little better. I think I do need a rest."

"First, let's get a bottle of wine."

"Don't you like the label from the mansion outside of town?"

"Absolutely, but you've got to see this."

He led her down one street, then into one of the shops that sold wines and cheeses. He nodded to the smiling woman tending the store, then led Sarah through a narrow wooden door labeled privato.

They crossed a narrow hallway, made even smaller by piles of wine crates stacked along one wall. Then they descended a set of narrow stone steps to a lower level filled entirely with racks of bottled wine. Not stopping there, Tomas took a second, even narrower staircase down three more levels.

Instead of exiting on a different street, which Sarah had learned was common in the hill towns of Italy, they continued down again. Eventually the emerged in a long, low room lined with massive wooden barrels, with an arched ceiling supported by stone buttresses. It felt ancient, and the air in the dim room was cool and probably didn't vary, despite the weather high above.

Tomas gestured at the barrels that towered over them as he led Sarah down the center row. "They make wine in these. Ten thousand liters each."

That was impressive, but Sarah asked, "What are we really doing here? You just walked past thousands of bottles of wine, and not even Spartacus could make a dent in ten thousand liters."

"Look."

Tomas stopped at one huge barrel and turned the tap on the front. No wine gushed out, and he kept turning, spinning the tap a total of seven times before turning it back the other way for five rotations.

"This is more fun than going all the way back down to the cars," he told her with a grin.

With a soft click, a concealed door set into the front of the wine barrel swung open. Tomas led the way inside and down yet another set of dimly-lit stairs. After the secret door swung closed behind them, brighter lights turned on, illuminating the long stairway of ancient stone that seemed to stretch forever down into the mountain.

"You're enjoying the mystery, aren't you?" Sarah didn't tell him it was working. She couldn't wait to see their final destination. She just wished she didn't feel so weak.

He took her hand. "I love this place. Built in a time when people took the effort to build things right."

"I prefer the days when they built escalators."

They descended for a full ten minutes, passing deep into the mountain. The stairs finally emptied into a well-lit cavern, at least two hundred feet across and over sixty feet tall at its peaked center. A huge chandelier hung there, casting a soft glow from a hundred candle-like lights.

Sarah slowed to take in the unexpected grandeur. Ivory-colored tiles paved the floor, reflecting the light and giving the room a cheery feel. Five arched exits, spaced around the cavern, led deeper into the complex. Ancient artifacts lined the walls, including coats of arms of old noble houses, huge tapestries depicting the famous San Marino towers, medieval weapons, and delicate pottery.

The entire upper half of the cavern was covered in frescoes. Some were scenes of ancient battle, while others depicted beautiful scenery or castles. She paused to look closer when she noticed many of them includes portraits of Eirene and Gregorios. Sometimes they were dressed as lords and ladies holding court, while in others they led armed forces. A few even showed them with eyes and hands burning with their active nevron powers.

A man stood at attention near the foot of the stairs, and his appearance made Sarah wonder if she'd wandered into a reenactment event. The man wore a medieval costume including a teal jacket, complete with puffed sleeves, and a little round hat. His right hand rested on an enormous crossbow, resting point-down on the floor. It was cocked and loaded with a thick bolt that looked like it could punch right through a knight.

The man saluted and said in a typical sing-song Italian accent, "Welcome, Captain." He turned to Sarah and added, "Mirco Gennari at your service, signorina."

"At ease, Mirco," Tomas said, descending to the floor to shake hands with the fellow. "How have you been?"

Mirco's formal pose fell away and he grinned. "Bene, signore. Molto bene." He patted his crossbow. "The latest bolts, they are fantastico."

"They'd better be, after all the work we put into them." Quentin entered the cavern from the nearest entryway.

While Sarah moved to greet Quentin, Tomas asked Mirco, "What's the staffing level in the complex today?"

"I alone. I could call up some of the others, but we hadn't been expecting visitors."

Quentin said, "Don't bother. They'll find out soon enough. We may be here a while."

Gregorios led the rest of their group from the same hallway that Quentin had used. "Good timing, Tomas. Take the hunter boys and go get the other machines."

Tomas gave Sarah an apologetic look as he handed the bags of food to Eirene, but she smiled. "Don't worry. Looks like I have some exploring to do."

Gregorios added to Tomas, "Bring the other item we discussed."

"Are you sure?" Tomas looked surprised.

"Am I ever wrong?"

Eirene laughed. "Don't answer that."

"He doesn't have to," Gregorios said with a knowing look. "We all know the answer."

"Let it go, dear," Eirene said with a shake of her head. She handed him his food. "And eat your gnocci while it's hot."

"Do you really use a crossbow?" Sarah asked Mirco.

He bowed. "To be a member of the San Marino Crossbow Corps has been a matter of pride in San Marino for centuries."

She had once tried using a small crossbow while walking a memory at the Colosseum. It had been trickier than she'd expected. "I hope you don't ever have to face someone with an automatic weapon while you're trying to reload."

"Indeed. For this we are much pleased with signore Quentin's latest bolts."

"Explosive?" Sarah asked, impressed that Quentin would worry about something as minor as the archaic armament of the men stationed in this remote facility.

"Among others."

"You'll have to show me."

Mirco grinned. "My pleasure, signorina. But first I must alter plans for lunch." He glanced to where Gregorios was already eating. Eirene seemed content to wait for a table and utensils. Mirco headed out of the cavern down one of the other arched exits, the crossbow resting over his shoulder.

Gregorios and Melek moved off down another exit, speaking intently. Eirene and Spartacus fell in with Sarah and Quentin. "We'll join you on the tour while the boys get things set up. Then I think we'll give the memory machines a run. I don't like leaving the memoryscape alone to Xiao for too long. But for now, where would you like to start?"

She was going to suggest a nap, but was surprised to find her exhaustion had faded away under the unexpected grandeur of their hidden base, replaced with renewed enthusiasm to explore.

"Do you have any creepy torture chambers?" she had to ask.

Spartacus, who had been trying to convince Eirene that he should carry the food, perked up at that, but Eirene shook her head. "No, those were taken out during the remodeling of 1687 to make room for the jacuzzi."

"I think I'm going to like it here," Sarah said with a smile.

37

He who does not fail in the requirements of his position continues long; he who dies yet is not forgotten has longevity.

~LAOZI

SARAH BLINKED against a flood of bright sunlight as the memoryscape formed around her. She found herself in a beautiful garden of manicured lawns and trimmed shrubbery, lined by tall, slender cypress trees. She caught glimpses of an adobe-colored mansion in the distance.

Melek appeared beside her, handsome in a strong, young body that must have resembled what he'd looked like in his prime. The similarity to Alter was more pronounced than ever. That only heightened her anxiety to track down Xiao and rescue him.

Eirene appeared nearby, wearing a beautiful young body. Her light brown hair was worked into a long, intricate braid. A tall, broad-shouldered man appeared beside her, looking so much like Melek the two could have been brothers. He was holding Eirene's hand.

"Grandfather Ronen?" Melek asked in an awed tone.

Sarah wondered if Eirene's choice to bring Melek to that particular memory was really such a good idea. She wasn't sure he was ready to see the truth about her identity in living color, so to speak.

Ronen ignored Melek and Sarah, just as other memory-spawned people always did until they started breaking things. Eirene whispered something in his ear.

"I'll see you later, love," Ronen said. He kissed Eirene on the lips and headed down the garden path, whistling.

Sarah nearly cringed. She knew Eirene and Gregorios had chosen to separate for that particular life, but their moral code still seemed weird to her. Could she leave Tomas for a life with another, only to return to Tomas for the next life as if nothing strange had happened? She didn't think so.

Melek glared at Eirene. "Why did you bring me here?"

"You know the truth, but you're still not dealing with it."

He definitely didn't look happy. "You defiled his life. Does it grant you so much pleasure to celebrate that lie again?"

"Open your mind," Eirene said the same tone she used to scold Alter. "We can't work together effectively until you accept who I am and who I was."

"We'll work together, but that doesn't mean I'll celebrate the tainted blood you mixed with my family," Melek declared.

"For a smart man, you can be incredibly dense," Eirene said with a frown.

Melek faced her angrily. "You posed as a mortal, made a mockery of my grandfather, and defiled the blood of our family. That act has defiled my son. I accept that." He folded his arms. "Now take us somewhere else."

Sarah appreciated what Eirene was trying to do, but wished she'd chosen a different time to do it. They'd agreed to enter the memoryscape together to practice with new runes Melek had agreed to share. They also hoped to catch a hint of Xiao.

They didn't want to confront her yet, but hoped to gain some clue as to what her intentions were in the memoryscape. Was she looking for more master runes like Paul had done, or was there something else she sought?

"The men of your family are always so hard-headed," Eirene said, but her tone was warm, and her lips curved up in the hint of a smile.

The memoryscape shimmered around them, then re-formed into a familiar location. Sarah and Melek stood in the steel-clad vault in the sub-basement of the Suntara headquarters. The original machine stood nearby, with Gregorios under the jagged faceplate. Sarah and Quentin were connected as well, seated together on a little couch. All three of them were bloody and battered from the terrible wounds they'd suffered in the final confrontation with Mai Luan. Those wounds had trickled through to their sleeping forms.

Sarah shivered to see the memory from that angle. They had all nearly died in that fight, and she'd been more terrified than perhaps any other moment in her life. She was surprised that the sight of her original body didn't trigger intense feelings of longing. That life was over, and she was learning to be content in her new form.

Memory-Eirene crouched on one knee behind Gregorios, powering the machine, exhaustion lining her face. Alter knelt beside her, head bowed, sweat pouring down his young face. His right hand held her throat, his arm trembling under the strain. He'd cut a rune across his hand and onto her collarbone, binding them together. It burned with an unusual blue purity.

Memory-Eirene leaned her forehead against his and whispered to him, "Hold on, dear boy. You can do it."

Sarah had not understood her rune warrior powers at the time, hadn't known how she'd become insubstantial, barely grasped the basic concepts of how they'd fought Mai Luan in Berlin.

Eirene suddenly appeared beside Melek and pointed down at the memory version of herself still crouched beside Alter. "Perhaps this memory will help you see the importance of really accepting each other, Melek."

Sarah blinked between Eirene and her memory persona. "Wait a minute. How are we all here, but also there in the memory?"

Eirene winked. "I wasn't entirely sure it would work. Maintaining both aspects separate is very tricky, and it's giving me a splitting headache. I bet poor Greg is having to deal with a significant drain trying to power all this."

"But if it hadn't worked, you could have hurt yourself," Sarah protested.

"It was worth the risk. This needs to be seen and understood."

Melek dropped to one knee beside Alter, placed one hand on his son's quivering frame. "Oh, my son. The trials you endured alone."

Eirene said softly, "He wasn't alone. He assumed the bulk of the drain in my place, but only together could we hold the connection and bring the others out alive."

Melek frowned up at her and gestured at the bright, glowing rune Alter had activated. "That is not what an active rune should look like. By forcing him to assume such a desperate burden, I believe you triggered the rise of his cui dashi curse."

"Without it, we would have all died."

Melek rose angrily. "If you hadn't forced that upon him, he might never have triggered that curse."

"Alter is who he has always been," Eirene said, unperturbed. "His actions and his powers played a key role in defeating Mai Luan. That's what hunters do."

"Not like this!" Melek shouted.

The outburst did not faze Eirene. "Have you not taught your children to fight the heka with every weapon, to the bitter end if need be?"

"This is different," Melek insisted, but some of his belligerence faded.

Sarah dropped to one knee beside Alter and touched his cheek. He wasn't real, but seeing him helped ease her constant worry for him.

"Alter was strong, Melek. He saved us that day, and he saved me again after I defeated Paul. If he had refused to keep fighting, we would have died twice, and by now everyone you know would probably be dead or enslaved."

That made him pause, and Eirene added, "Power is not inherently evil, Melek. You hunters and the kashaph share the same power, yet you do not embrace the same evil they do."

Melek gestured at his son again, his expression agonized. "How can you expect me to accept this? Every single cui dashi has fallen to that power and turned evil."

"Not any more," Eirene said, her voice ringing with conviction.

Sarah rose and gripped Melek's strong hand. "I trust Alter with any power, Melek. He's the most unwaveringly honorable man I've ever met. Do you really think he would turn evil?"

She held his gaze, saw the conflict in his eyes, and silently wished him to accept the truth, despite a lifetime of rigorous bias.

After a moment, he blew out a breath and gave her a weak grin. "You're right. Alter is not the enemy."

Sarah grinned and gave him a fierce hug, nearly overwhelmed by a rush of hope. With Melek finally opening his mind, she had to believe they'd rescue Alter.

Melek gently pushed Sarah away and turned to Eirene, a tear glistening in his eye. "My son is perhaps a wiser man than I."

"Only rarely, but you get there eventually," Eirene said with a smile, gripping his shoulder.

"Usually he's so zealous and inflexible I have to punch him to make him listen," Sarah added.

Melek took Eirene's hand in his, then cast another glance at his son. "I can't say I forgive you for what you've done, but I will accept the truth as my son did before me." He bowed over her hand, and his voice quavered. "Grandmother Elizabeth."

Eirene swept him into a hug, her voice choking with emotion. "I'm so happy to hear you say that."

"We have a lot to discuss," Melek said, still looking a bit shocked by the magnitude of what he'd just accepted.

Sarah wiped at her eyes. If only they could simply take some time to celebrate this long-overdue family reunion. Time wouldn't wait, and she was even more eager to learn more runes. "First we have work to do. You've got some runes to share with me, right?"

Melek nodded, looking relieved to focus on something else. "Yes, let's get to work."

The memoryscape blurred around them again, re-forming into a wide field, ringed with oaks, maples, and fir trees.

"Where is this?" Sarah asked.

"A quiet place to work," Eirene said.

"Fewer distractions is good." Melek crouched, and the grass at his feet faded to bare ground. "I could get used to this."

He drew a rune in the dirt and Sarah breathed out a soft gasp of wonder. She felt its power radiating up from the ground like heat from a bed of coals. This rune possessed a latent energy even greater than the Chinese Oracle Script ciphers Alter had taught her. No wonder Melek had kept it secret.

"What is this?" she asked, tracing the lines with her finger, committing them to memory.

The symbol was constructed as a flower of life, similar and yet somehow different from patterns Alter had taught her. The geometric pattern of overlapping circles formed a sixfold symmetry, like a hexagon. Sarah had always loved the resulting flower-like pattern.

"The flower of life," Eirene muttered, crouching beside Sarah to study it. "This symbol has been found as far back as ancient Egypt."

Melek said, "Indeed. It is one of the most sacred of the old symbols, and was found in ancient China too. It's tied to the concept of the sacred geometry, the seed of life, the Fibonacci numbers, and fundamental forms of space and time."

"That seems appropriate," Sarah said, then turned her attention to some other symbols Melek had worked into the leaves of the various flower segments. She recognized some ancient Egyptian and Chinese symbols, as well as two Celtic ones. The resulting rune was very complex, but the innermost circle was devoid of any additional symbols, and that nagged at her mind. Something belonged there.

Melek said, "This symbol is one of the keys you will need in order to remove the veil from your senses. This rune begins to bridge the gap between you and the nearest ascendant rune."

Sarah wanted to squeal with delight at learning these deeper runes. They filled her soul in a way other runes couldn't. "And what exactly is an ascendant? On the plane you only said they're somehow tied to history, and they're some kind of greater master rune."

"Indeed. There is much we don't know about ascendants. No hunter has possessed the strength of soul to dare activate this rune."

"Alter could do it," Sarah said.

"Perhaps. Xiao certainly is powerful enough, if she has this rune. And you, Sarah. As a rune warrior, you should be able to activate this."

"What will it do?" she asked, still studying the beautiful rune. She felt eager to try it, but also felt a shiver of fear. Alter had warned her so many times about tempting powers she wasn't ready to control. Melting her first body had finally taught her a bit of caution.

"As I understand it, this rune, once activated and attuned to your soul, should allow you to see the ascendants."

Sarah frowned. "We don't have to go to a specific moment in history like the master runes?"

"No. Master runes are the embodiment of truths evident in those pivotal moments, powered by the souls focused there."

He paused and Eirene said, "Don't hold back now, Melek. I know these secrets are dear to you, but we need to know."

Melek took a long, slow breath, then nodded. "You're right on both counts. Ascendants are more than master runes. They are . . ." He trailed off again as he struggled to find the words.

"How sure are you about this information?" Eirene asked.

"The information is sure. It's just, you lack some foundational information that I do not have time to impart. Without it, under-standing is difficult."

"Well, if we need that information to understand, we have to take the time to learn it," Sarah said, although she yearned to know now.

"As I mentioned before, the ascendants are tied to history."

When both Sarah and Eirene nodded, he added, "And history, on some plane not accessible to mortals, is not just the intangible passage of time."

"What do you mean?" Sarah asked. That sounded confusing, and fascinating.

"We see only the current moment." Melek snapped his fingers for emphasis. "Then that moment becomes the past, and is gone forever. We have a new *now*, but the future has yet to arrive. We have developed tools to measure the passage of time, but we are all locked into the same now as everyone else."

Sarah nodded. "I've heard there are theories about space and time being somehow linked, but that kind of talk usually gives me a headache."

Eirene said, "The space-time continuum. I've always thought talk of a fourth dimension was pretty radical."

"For us who live in a three-dimensional world, it is," Melek said. "I am not a mathematician either, but the concept of time existing in some dimension as a tangible thing is helpful for this discussion."

After a moment to gather his thoughts, he continued. "In the space-time continuum theory any particular object, if it could be viewed in that fourth dimension, would have a twisting, spaghetti-like structure. Think of it like a DNA helix, representing its location throughout its entire existence in space and in time. Taking a slice of any part of it would show its location in that instant in time."

"That sort of makes sense," Sarah admitted, trying to wrap her brain around the concepts, and wondering if those foundational elements Melek had mentioned she should know included a PhD in theoretical physics. "But what does that have to do with ascendants?"

"Think of history not as a fleeting moment in time, but as an eternal spiral." Melek raised his hand off the ground in a spiraling motion. "Think of ascendants as fibers woven into that spiral."

Sarah frowned, trying to envision what he suggested. "So you're saying ascendants are like a sliver of eternity?"

He nodded, smiling. "In a manner of speaking. Understand that I have not experienced an ascendant, and I'm not sure any living being has, but in theory it's possible."

Eirene was slowly nodding. "And you fear that Xiao might have learned how to access an ascendant."

"Perhaps."

Sarah paced away, considering his words. "So a master rune is . . ."

"They are each a single key point on the spiral of an ascendant. All of the ascendants, woven together like strands in a twisting rope, make up the scroll of history," Melek said.

That seemed hard to believe. "But they're so powerful. If an ascendant is so much more, how could Xiao ever hope to control it?"

"Perhaps not control it so much as unleash it," Eirene suggested.

Sarah shuddered. Would that break history somehow? "I don't understand enough to even guess what that might mean."

"That is why we're here," Melek said, gesturing at the rune on the ground. "This rune, if you can activate it, may allow you to sense that fourth dimension and gain a sense of an ascendant."

Sarah crouched beside the beautiful rune again, tracing it with her finger. It called to her even more powerfully than bone script runes. She closed her eyes and traced it in the air from memory. The image flowed through her mind, as clear as if she were still staring at it with open eyes.

All of a sudden, she understood what was missing at the center.

"This rune is incomplete," she said, pointing at the innermost circle. "It needs the rune warrior mark here." She touched the small of her back where the rune warrior cipher was marked.

"Are you sure?" Eirene asked.

Sarah crouched over the bare earth and added the rune warrior mark into the center. Its distinctive yin-yang symbol seemed to caress the central point, while the other components of it fit perfectly between the flowered petals of that inner circle. The completed rune became a layered construct that magnified the strength of the underlying symbols many times. It took her breath away. It felt so right and so familiar, she had to test it.

"Mark it," she told Melek. "Quick."

He studied the rune for another minute, tracing the design, his face expressionless.

"What? Is there a problem?" Sarah asked, her heart racing with fear that she'd somehow broken it, even though deep inside she knew she hadn't.

"No, Sarah." Melek looked up from the rune, emotion in his eyes. "This addition is perfect. I was just enjoying it."

Eirene said, "You're sweet, but we've been in here long enough. We don't have all day."

Melek moved around behind Sarah, and an ornate carving knife like those in the runesmith kit Alter had gifted to Sarah appeared in his hand. He wielded it with medical precision as he marked the complex rune across her lower back. The razor sharp blade barely stung as it parted the outer layer of her skin.

As soon as he completed the last line, the rune glowed brilliant blue, filling the glade with gentle light. Its warmth radiated through Sarah and for a moment she felt a bit light-headed.

The feeling passed, replaced by one of health so profound she could scarce describe it. Exulting, she glanced around the clearing, but then frowned. Everything looked subtly wrong in a way she hadn't felt before.

"What is it?" Eirene asked.

"Something . . ." Sarah took a step, one hand outstretched, and reached *through* the air, like parting a gossamer curtain, to touch an invisible barrier.

It felt slippery, like glass coated with liquid soap, and it flowed very slowly past her hand. Not quite a wall, it was more a vast column that rose in a graceful arc above her, and extended back into the ground at her feet.

"Can you feel this?" she asked, filled with wonder.

Eirene and Melek approached, passed their hands through the area several times, but felt nothing.

When she described it, Melek grinned. "It's working! You're actually touching an ascendant rune."

"How is that possible?" Sarah breathed. The master runes had all burned in the air, searing themselves into her memory and shaking her with the power of the souls linked to those points in time. Power radiated under her fingers, and she sensed it filled the ascendant, but she was touching such a tiny part of it, the power was far less concentrated than in a master rune. "I thought you said these were more powerful."

"Which is more powerful, a flashlight right in front of your eyes, or the sun?" Melek asked.

"This is so weird," Sarah whispered, sliding her hand across the slightly curved wall of the ascendant. She couldn't quite see it, but she could feel its slippery edge. "Time's not supposed to be tangible."

Melek shrugged. "On certain planes, it must be. Otherwise our runes could not affect it or draw us back along its curve."

Sarah closed her eyes and spread her hands wide, trying to gain a sense of the ethereal construct. She did not reach any edges and sensed it extending far to either side. Above her, the slowly flowing column extended in a slight curve. She concentrated on that and her mind rose along it, as if her closed eyes had been given wings.

That column wasn't just a simple curve. It flowed into complex forms as it rose. She looked down and could somehow see through the ground, as if they had been walking on a thin crust over an eternal drop.

The mighty curve of the ascendant arced and looped down into the emptiness of the past, and a greater shape began to filter into her mind. The spiraled loops and turns were so huge they must cover entire countries. Embedded within the wider construct were brightly glowing nodes that drew her mind's eye like lightning bugs.

Sarah gasped, stunned by the magnitude of what she was sensing.

"What?" Eirene asked, her voice tense, but somehow distant.

Without opening her eyes, Sarah said, "Master runes. I can sense them connected to the ascendant."

She couldn't hope to describe the magnitude of what she was sensing, and she felt nearly overwhelmed with awe. She refused to focus on those distant master runes, sensing that if she did, they might come into focus in her mind. She wasn't sure she could handle that much raw power linking to her soul while she was touching the ascendant.

As she tried to comprehend the enormity of the ascendant, she struggled to understand how it worked. It wasn't a rune in the same sense as any other. She didn't understand its symbol to engrave it on her skin. She doubted it was even possible to see it in its entirety. So what was its purpose, and how could one hope to draw upon its power?

She did sense pieces of its shape in her mind, like fleeting glimpses of distant peaks through roiling clouds. Those pieces she glimpsed felt familiar somehow, but were too vague. They suggested a greater pattern, but she couldn't fit it together in her mind.

As she tried to figure it out, she let her thoughts trace the edges of the great arc of the ascendant. Its vast size defeated her though, and she slid her thoughts back down along the slippery arc. As the ground solidified to her mind view, cutting off the vast loops of the ascendant, she was surprised to feel a strand of the ascendant connect to a single point nearby.

That point was located in the center of Eirene's nevra core.

Sarah started in surprise, lost concentration, and her connection with the invisible construct faded. She glanced at Eirene, who was watching her eagerly.

"You don't feel it?" Sarah asked.

"What?"

Then Eirene frowned and clutched at her head. "We have to get out of here. I think Xiao just realized we're in here and she's not happy about it."

Eirene groaned and swayed where she stood. Sarah caught her before she could fall, but the ground began to shake, and the trees surrounding the clearing burst into fire. An icy wind began howling around them, somehow smelling like burned toast.

"Get us out of here, Love," Eirene shouted, and the memoryscape faded to burning darkness.

38

TOMAS HELPED Sarah remove the jagged faceplate and heavy helmet. "How'd it go in there?"

"It was a close call," Sarah said, shivering.

Eirene sat up, looking a bit haggard. "Xiao discovered us and was trying to yank us into another memory. If I hadn't been wearing the Amazon, I wouldn't have been able to hold her off long enough to escape."

Melek sat up and jumped to his feet. "You felt it, Sarah. You—" He doubled over in a vigorous coughing fit, nearly falling.

Heber leaped to assist him. When it finally passed, Melek looked exhausted, his color pale, his hand trembling. Heber helped him from the padded chair to a more comfortable couch. His limp looked worse.

"Melek, what's wrong with you? Why can't you heal?" Sarah asked.

"That's not important," he said, waving away the question. "We need to discuss what you experienced."

"It is important," Eirene insisted, dropping to one knee beside him so she could look him in the eye. With her Amazon figure, she had to crouch pretty low. "You're a key member of the team. We can't have you collapsing in a critical moment."

"Leave him alone," Heber said, clenching his fists as if preparing to fight them all.

Melek placed a hand on Heber's arm. "Easy, son. They have a right." He leaned against the back of the couch. "My health is broken. I lost the bond to my runes and have not been able to restore the link."

"Why not?" Sarah sat beside him, despite a glare from Heber. She took his hand in hers. "I've never heard of anyone losing their bonds."

Gregorios drew closer, his expression concerned. "It happens if the soul suffers severe trauma."

Sarah thought about Melek's situation. He was the hunter's leader, the man his people looked to for direction and protection. Yet the compound had been raided, hunters killed, their greatest treasures stolen. Paul had corrupted his eldest son, who would have committed mass murder if not dispossessed by his own brother, who just happened to be cui dashi. Alter's situation would be the greatest dishonor for his bloodline, despite what he'd learned about Eirene. No wonder he'd lost his bond.

Melek sighed, looking tired. "Indeed. I was hoping to stabilize after meeting with Alter, but . . ." He spread his hands in a helpless gesture.

Sarah promised, "We're going to save him. Surely knowing that will help you reconnect."

Melek shook his head. "When so many links, held so long, are severed, chances are slim I'll ever bond to those runes again."

"We can draw you new ones," Sarah offered.

"Thank you, my dear, but I'm afraid this body cannot support any more."

"But you're not bonded to the others," Sarah protested with a frown.

"Even so, I have reached my limit. I cannot undo the past."

"But you can change your future," Gregorios said softly.

"What do you mean?"

"We need you, and you need your health. You suggested the solution yourself," Gregorios said.

"What solution?" His tone turned suspicious.

Sarah sucked in a sharp breath as she realized where Gregorios was headed with the conversation.

"You need to start a new life," Gregorios declared.

Melek looked shocked, Nabil horrified, and Heber enraged. The young hunter snatched for his sidearm, but Gregorios lunged with remarkable speed and grabbed his hand.

"I'll kill you before I allow you to corrupt him," Heber snarled.

"Stand down," Melek ordered, regaining his composure. When

Heber relaxed, still glaring, Melek said, "I appreciate the offer, Gregorios. There is some merit to what you suggest."

"You can't," Heber cried.

Melek waved him to silence. "However, I could not accept a body of another, assume a stranger's life. It breaks every tenet of our creed."

"I figured you'd say that," Gregorios said, not looking surprised. He waved to Tomas, who left the large conference room they had turned into their memory lab.

Tomas returned a moment later, pushing a gurney holding a body covered in a sheet.

"I told you I—"

"I know," Gregorios said, holding up a hand to forestall Melek's protest. "And again, you suggested the solution yourself."

"What solution?"

Eirene helped Melek to his feet as Tomas pushed the gurney to a halt in front of him. At Gregorios' signal, Tomas pulled off the sheet, revealing a powerful body dressed in a pair of boxers.

Melek gasped, eyes wide, and leaned against the gurney for support.

Reuben.

"My son," Melek whispered, touching the motionless hand.

Gregorios looked pleased with himself. "Like I said, you need a new form, but not that of a stranger."

"Demon," Heber cried, again reaching for his sidearm.

Eirene wrapped an arm around him, pinning his arm and giving him a warm smile. He looked like he wanted to fight, but wasn't sure what to do against the non-threatening move.

Gregorios said simply, "I can think of no better solution, and I am sure your son would be honored to serve you in this capacity."

Melek stared down at Reuben's body, emotions flickering across his face. Surprise shifted to anger, then faded to deep sorrow. He bowed his head over the body, as if praying.

Sarah held her breath, barely restraining herself from rushing over to encourage him to make the right choice. He'd made important progress in the memoryscape, and she silently urged him to embrace the elegant solution that Gregorios had offered.

After a long moment, he spoke without opening his eyes, his voice agonized. "I cannot do this, Gregorios."

Sarah wanted to shriek at him, but bit her lip to keep silent.

"Melek—" Gregorios started.

He opened his eyes and rose to face Gregorios. "No. What you ask is forbidden. Too many generations of my family have fallen because of your manipulations."

"You need this," Gregorios insisted, not hiding his frustration. "Stop with the demon blather. This is reality we're dealing with."

Melek's expression did not waver. "I said no."

Gregorios waved Tomas to take the gurney away. "The day will come when you'll change your mind."

"And you'll be ready to gloat?" Melek asked.

"No," Gregorios said, rolling his eyes. He gripped Melek's shoulders and shook him softly. "How many times do I have to tell you I'm not your enemy? I'll be there to help."

Sarah silently applauded Gregorios. He was making such a significant offer, she hated to see Melek throw it back in his face.

"To corrupt him, you mean," Heber said, taking Melek's arm to offer support and pull him away from Gregorios.

Gregorios paced away muttering, "I hate working with close-minded mortals." He took a deep breath, then turned. "If we're not going to fix your issues, let's discuss what happened in that memory."

"First, Melek has more to explain," Sarah said. She wanted to slap Melek a few times until he saw reason, but forced an expression of calm.

Eirene, who did not conceal her sorrow at Melek's choice suggested, "Let's head over to the lounge then. It's a lot more comfortable for talking."

The lounge was a long, low-ceilinged room, situated at the junction of three hallways. One half was set up as a comfortable living room, with several couches and padded chairs arranged near a huge television and a cold fireplace. The other half of the room held a pool table, a foosball table, a full bar, and a well-stocked little kitchen.

"What do you need to know?" Melek asked as they settled onto the couches.

Sarah recounted for those who hadn't witnessed it how she had bonded with the new rune in the memoryscape, then tried to explain her experience touching the expanse of the ascendant rune. The memory filled her with wonder, but she couldn't hope to really make the experience clear to them.

"Can you draw it?" Tomas asked.

She shook her head. "I don't have a sense for the entire thing yet. Even if I do, I'm not sure I could draw it."

Melek agreed. "It's a living thing, ever-growing. I doubt a single rune could ever capture it all."

Sarah added, "It's more than that. Can you tell me why the ascendant rune I felt was anchored on Eirene?"

"Say that again, dear," Eirene said, looking as surprised as anyone.

Melek rose painfully and began to pace between the couches and the fireplace, his expression troubled. "You sensed more than I expected."

"More secrets, Melek?" Gregorios asked, sounding exasperated. "I thought you said you were sharing."

"He shared more than he should have," Heber snapped.

Melek silenced him with a look. "I shared what you needed to know at the time."

"I need to know more. Spill it," Sarah said, squashing her annoyance at his reticence.

Melek sighed. "The ascendant rune you felt was indeed anchored on Eirene. Or to be more precise, it is anchored to her nevra core."

"Explain," Eirene said, looking troubled.

Melek hesitated and glanced at Heber and Nabil, who sat alone on a couch slightly apart from the others, closer to the door. They both shook their heads, and Sarah nearly went over there to punch them both.

Melek sighed. "We cannot go back now."

"No you can't," Eirene urged gently.

The young hunters looked frustrated, and Sarah hoped they didn't start trouble. The alliance was all too fragile already. It wouldn't take much for Melek to refuse to share more.

"Ascendant runes are inseparably linked to nevra cores," Melek explained after a moment. "Each and every ascendant rune is thus linked. More than that, it is the ascendant runes that spawn, support, and sustain each active nevra core."

While Sarah digested that information, Eirene leaned forward, looking amazed. "Ascendant runes power our nevrons?"

"Indeed."

"Why haven't I ever heard of this before?" Gregorios asked. He looked deeply troubled.

"And how do you know?" Sarah asked.

Melek said softly, "It is a secret never before shared. The truth was discovered alone by the great Alter."

"And shouldn't be shared with them," Heber muttered.

"How? And to what purpose?" Eirene asked, once again composed.

"Again we return to the course of history, and the motivation why I share these things." He turned to Spartacus. "You heard Xiao claim a desire to stand astride history and shape the future."

"Indeed," Spartacus said. He looked fascinated by the discussion. Sarah was really impressed he hadn't interrupted more often with declarations of honor and glory, and offers to fight a duel for dibs on dessert.

Melek said, "I fear her declaration was more than a simple boast. The runes we've glimpsed that she possesses are too closely tied to the secret rune I shared with you. Together with the machines, the attempt to gain master runes, and the attack on our family compound, it all suggests they've learned something of the true nature of history."

"And what truth is that?" Eirene asked.

"The ascendant runes. They are a power not understood by any, but we know pieces of what they do. Each ascendant rune spawns an active nevra core and embeds it into an otherwise mortal soul. The soul powers you enjoy are a byproduct of the ascendant's true purpose."

Sarah listened in fascination to every word, eager to understand.

"Through that active nevra core, you secure the ascendant rune to a particular place and time. The act of living your lives grants access for the ascendant rune to record history and create a transcription of time."

While the rest of them considered those words, and the two young hunters scowled at Melek for sharing the secret, Gregorios said. "You're saying ascendant runes are some kind of giant, eternal transcription service?"

"In a manner of speaking, yes. It records all of history, like a giant database."

"That's why I felt master runes embedded within it," Sarah said, struggling to understand these bizarre concepts.

"Exactly. Master runes are points where many souls are focused on a single moment in history. Something about the process of recording history links the power of the affected souls to those moments in time. It's as if mortal souls power the process and keep it alive."

"Is that why most master runes seem to be tied to moments of conflict?" Sarah asked. "Because only when enough souls die to power the moment can it form a master rune?"

Melek considered that for a moment. "Perhaps, although the focus of so many other souls on those moments seems to impact the magnitude of the master runes too."

Tomas leaned forward and said, "Hold on. Sarah bonded to three master runes and that was enough power to melt her into a puddle. You're saying ascendant runes hold all of history?"

"Partially correct. Each ascendant rune spawns a nevra core. So there are many ascendant runes, and each of them records separate parts."

"That's why when we die, our nevra core passes to another," Eirene said softly.

Melek nodded. "I believe so, although we've never been able to determine why a particular soul is chosen."

Sarah frowned with a sudden thought. "But if you understood all of this, then you know that nevra cores are necessary. Why do you view facetakers as demons?"

Nabil broke his angry silence, glaring at Gregorios. "The nevra core is necessary, but what facetakers do with them is not. You corrupt it by dominating the souls of others."

Sarah responded, "But Alter doesn't. Yet you consider him tainted and plan to kill him."

Both young hunters nodded slightly, but Melek looked uncomfortable by the turn of the conversation. "There is more that fuels our concern about facetakers and particularly cui dashi, but now's not the time to digress into that philosophical discussion."

Eirene was looking thoughtful. "Perhaps, but we need to find time for that discussion at some point, regardless."

"Perhaps," Melek agreed.

"So you want us to possess a tool and not use it?" Gregorios asked, sounding incredulous.

"I possess a gun," Heber interjected, his hand hovering over the butt of the holstered weapon. "Using your logic, I should feel justified using it now."

Gregorios chuckled. "Nice try, kid. Don't make me put you in time out."

Melek gestured Heber to settle down. "The tool may be valid, but the use of the tool causes problems. We may never agree on this point, but this is deep truth that you must understand. If Xiao somehow gains access to her own ascendant, she may be able to access the entire scroll of time recorded by it."

"I don't see how that allows her to reshape the future," Sarah said.

Melek spread his hands in a helpless gesture. "That is a mystery I cannot yet solve, and that is why we must stop her."

Tomas asked, "Is that why she has Alter? So she can gain access to his ascendant rune too?"

"Perhaps," Melek said, although by his expression, Sarah suspected he worried about other reasons. She did too.

Eirene added, "That's what Xiao was talking about when she mentioned harvesting our nevra cores. She's found a way to hold onto that link and transfer it."

Gregorios grunted sourly. "We're going to have to think about this. You just dumped a boatload of information on us, Melek."

"We needed to understand," Sarah said, smiling her thanks. "If we're going to have any chance at blocking her, we need to know everything that you know."

Melek glanced behind Sarah and his eyes widened in surprise. He shouted, "Look out!"

Sarah spun. A man stood in the nearest doorway, completely encased in advanced body armor, a flamethrower in his hands. Tongues of fire trickled out the nozzle as he lifted it and depressed the trigger.

39

Seek to perform your duties to your highest ability, this way your actions will be blameless and you may earn a new rune.

~ANCIENT EGYPTIAN PROVERB

SARAH DOVE OVER THE COUCH. The surprise attacker was blocking the nearest exit, and she didn't have a gun. She'd left it near the memory machine. She'd felt safe in this underground complex.

As most of the others mimicked her move, Tomas drew his pistol and opened fire. Heber followed a split second later, getting off half a dozen shots before the first gout of flame sizzled out of the flamethrower and engulfed him.

Heber tumbled over the couch he'd been sitting on just a moment ago, screaming as he burned. Eirene snatched a blanket from the nearby couch and dove, sliding along the floor to him to try smothering the flames.

Nabil joined Tomas with his handgun, but their shooting was an act of futility. Their small caliber bullets could not penetrate the attacker's armor, and another gout of fire sent them diving for the dubious cover of the couches, which lit up like torches.

Sarah slashed one finger through the air, activating a barrier rune, already berating herself for not moving faster. The initial sprays of deadly flame had turned the air blistering hot. It stank of burning fabric, charred hair, and cooked flesh. The attacker turned his deadly weapon toward Sarah.

Too late.

Sarah's barrier rose between the group and the attacker, invisible to the others, but looking like a shimmering, golden wall to her. Flames erupted again from the nozzle of the flamethrower, but rebounded from the invisible wall, engulfing the attacker instead.

He staggered back, releasing the trigger, and Sarah felt a rush of satisfaction. His suit might be too much for the group's pistols, but it couldn't withstand a concerted blast from his own flamethrower.

Tomas shouted, "I've got nothing to stop this guy. Cipher him!"

"Working on it."

The attacker backed into the hallway, and Sarah wondered if he planned to try another doorway to hit them from the other side. Then she realized with a rush of horror what his secondary objective must be.

The machines.

She'd cipher-squash him before he got ten steps.

Even as a new cipher came to mind, the attacker suddenly dropped to his knees, then pitched forward onto his face. A crossbow bolt stood out from his back.

Mirco entered the room, giant crossbow over his shoulder. "Sorry I'm late. Lunch is ready."

Sarah canceled her shield wall, then wished she hadn't as another rush of blistering air and smoke rolled over them. Through a fit of coughing, she ran to Mirco and threw her arms around him, kissing him on the cheek. "I'll never question your crossbow again."

He patted the weapon. "Grazie, signorina. Quentin's bolt worked molto bene."

Quentin joined them, clapping Mirco on the shoulder. "How'd that bloke slip past you?"

"I do not yet know." Mirco's smile faded to a worried frown. "No alarms were triggered."

Spartacus suddenly leaped into view in the doorway, a massive, ancient battle-ax held high overhead. Sarah had never noticed him leave the room. He paused above the attacker, then glanced at Mirco and nodded approval. "You have the skill of Sagittarius! And you do your service great honor today."

"Gracie." Mirco stood a little taller.

Eirene had lifted the horribly burned Heber into her Amazon arms. She rushed past, calling to Mirco, "Medical bay. Burn trauma. STAT!"

Mirco dropped his crossbow and rushed down the hall after her.

Tomas, who had already run from the room, returned with fire extinguishers. He tossed a couple to Nabil and Gregorios, and the three of them attacked the burning couches.

"Do you think Heber will be all right?" Sarah surveyed the mess while breathing shallow, one sleeve pressed over her mouth and nose.

Quentin grimaced. "If not for his advanced healing rune, he'd already be dead. Burns are a bloody mess, even for enhancements."

He and Sarah joined Spartacus over the fallen intruder. Quentin crouched and switched off the flame thrower. He pointed at the crossbow bolt.

"Normal bolts, even from Mirco's crossbow, wouldn't have done much through this armor. Good thing I sent him the new batch last month."

"What did it do?" Sarah asked, grateful to have something besides poor Heber's fate to think about.

"Tip is titanium, but hollow. It would've had the force to pierce the armor but not penetrate. So the core is packed with an explosive charge that detonates at impact, firing three spring-loaded blades up through the tip." He held up his hand and spread his fingers wide. "Those blades sweep open like a tripod, slicing out through the torso. Eight inches total spread."

Sarah grimaced. The simple bolt had filled the attacker with deadly steel.

Quentin tugged at the bolt, shaking the body. "Blades lock in place. Impossible to remove. So even advanced healing runes wouldn't help much. He'd need a level-one trauma unit with surgeons willing to open him up to try to cut the steel out of his guts."

Sarah started to feel sick. She loved training with Quentin and his marvelous weapons, but this clinical description of an archaic weapon turned into a high-tech tool of death was a little too much at the moment. Sometimes it was a little scary to see how good he was at his work.

Spartacus clapped Quentin on the shoulder, nearly pitching him to the floor. "I salute your clever mind, Master of Death."

Quentin plucked another of the eighteen-inch, wooden bolts from the four still clipped into individual sheaths on the stock of the crossbow. He handed the bolt to Sarah.

"What do you want me to do with this?"

"Keep it. I want you to consider this lesson as you plan how best to build your battle ciphers. Today it was a simple crossbow that took down an enemy which Tomas' modern handgun, loaded with the best ammunition available in the world, could not harm."

Gregorios and Melek joined them, leaving Tomas and Nabil to finish mopping up the last of the flames. Gregorios pulled off the fallen attacker's helmet.

He was actually a woman. Whoever had applied her soulmask to the large body she'd worn to attack them had done slipshod work. The woman's delicate Chinese features fit the skull poorly, and the skin was stretched and scarred all along the jawline.

"Quentin, get me something bigger than a handgun," Gregorios said, then raised his voice to Tomas and Nabil. "When you two are done, kit up and come join us. We'll sweep the compound and verify the security status."

Sarah planned to follow as they all left, but she was struck by another wave of unexpected weariness. She sagged to the floor and leaned against the doorway.

"Are you well?" Spartacus asked.

"Just tired. The last few days have taken a lot out of me, I guess."

"I must see to Heber," Melek said, his eyes sad. He headed in the direction Eirene and Mirco had gone.

Sarah closed her eyes, wanting nothing more than to sleep.

Spartacus said, "I will fetch some wine to rejuvenate your spirits."

She was starting to drift away into blessed sleep when that strange chill she'd felt just after waking in the SUV returned. It grew rapidly until her limbs shook with cold, and her teeth chattered.

Something was very wrong.

Sarah blinked open her eyes, but they felt like lead weights, and she found it hard to focus her thoughts. The hallway seemed to grow dim, and she was struck by an overwhelming sense of terror. Before she could call out to Spartacus for help, a vicelike grip grabbed her face, covering her mouth.

As if materializing out of thin air, a man appeared, crouched close beside her. Sarah's terror quadrupled as she stared into colorless, dead eyes. She recognized the pinched face and impressive mustache. All hope seemed to burn to ashes in her heart.

Vlad the Impaler, deadliest of all vampires.

40

As for the ignorant man who does not listen, he accomplishes nothing. He equates knowledge with ignorance, the useless rune with the harmful. He does everything which is detestable, so people get angry with him each day. Such a one can bond nothing.

~THE LIVING WISDOM OF ANCIENT EGYPT
TRANSLATION

EIRENE MOVED to the head of the gurney where Heber lay in an inner room of the hospital wing. The white tile, stainless-steel machinery, and antiseptic hospital smell offered no comfort. Heber was too far gone to heal, and his soul wouldn't linger long.

"Hurry," she urged as Mirco pushed a second rolling gurney into the room. The empty host body it held was a solid specimen that would serve perfectly.

The frosted glass outer doors of the hospital wing slid aside and Melek limped through.

When he saw what she was about to do, his eyes widened and he shouted, "Stop!"

Eirene wished he'd waited just a few seconds more. He might have been angered by her action, but it would have been too late to prevent her from saving Heber's life.

"We've only got seconds before he slips away. I can save him." The heart monitor Mirco had connected to Heber beeped slowly, its rhythm erratic.

"No," Melek said, approaching the gurney with his limping stride. "There must be another way."

"Melek, I know your family better than anyone else," Eirene told him, not hiding her impatience. "I understand the dilemma, but this man will die if I don't remove his soulmask."

"If you do, you'll condemn him to a worse fate."

By all the forgotten gods, she hated idiots. "You'd rather let him die than take another body? Think about what you're saying."

Melek was not moved by her outburst. He faced her with stupid, unyielding conviction. "I am, but it is you who don't understand. You keep meddling in my family, thinking you're helping, but instead you keep corrupting generation after generation of the purest among us. I cannot allow you to do it again."

She glared at him, wanting to turn him over her knee and spank him. She had thought he had turned an important corner, but in the stressful moment, he was reverting to his long-held bias. She didn't bother shuttering the nevron burning in her eyes. She needed to act now.

Mirco cried out, "Per amor del cielo, be quick signora. He dies!"

Eirene turned toward Heber, but Melek grabbed her arm. "Let him go. This way he faces eternity with a clear conscience."

"You're the biggest fool I've ever known," Eirene cried, grabbing Melek by the collar, lifting him off the floor and pulling him close to snarl, "Heber's blood is on your hands!"

Melek did not flinch from her wrath. "I am the leader of my clan. Their safety, body and soul, is in my care. Heber dies a martyr, an honorable man."

"You're going to regret this choice," Eirene growled, dropping him to the floor. He stumbled on his injured knee, but she squashed the impulse to reach out and offer support. Instead she left the small room, followed by a shocked Mirco.

She heard Melek speak softly. "Join the fathers with honor, my son."

Then the heart monitor's slow beep turned into a single, flat tone.

Eirene clenched her fists in frustrated fury. She'd teach Melek what it meant to waste life.

Before she could unleash her fury on him, Quentin's voice echoed through the hospital wing. "Answer if you're there, Eirene. We have a serious problem."

Eirene rushed to the intercom and pressed the answer button. "What is it now?"

"Sensors just picked up a vampire in the complex."

"Where?" Eirene growled, happy for a new target for her anger. She didn't care how a vampire had found the base. They would regret it.

"The lounge."

Her anger evaporated under a chill of fear. "Sarah!"

"Go!" Quentin urged. "Tomas and Gregorios are already en route."

41

Jupiter was very large and bright. There was a small reddish star appended to its side in an alliance. Only my unique rune of sight grants me the vision to see such details. There must be a way to share the glories of the heavens with others, but I do not know how else to unlock the secret.

~GAN DE, CHINESE ASTRONOMER, OBSERVATION IN
SUMMER OF 365 B.C

VLAD THE VAMPIRE lifted Sarah easily off the floor, letting her dangle in his grip by the chin like a fish on the line. She tried to punch him, to struggle, to scream, but her body didn't seem to work. It was racked by terror and impenetrable cold. She couldn't look away, her gaze stuck to Vlad's like a mouse frozen in fear before a deadly viper.

"Unhand her, villain!" Spartacus' voice boomed across the charred lounge, and Vlad turned toward the gladiator.

As soon as he broke eye contact, Sarah blinked and her thoughts began working again. She glimpsed Spartacus stalking across the lounge, his battle-ax raised high. She also realized that Vlad was wearing a lot of cologne. She must be really messed up to focus on that. She tried to bring her thoughts into clarity, to figure out how to fight back.

"I will stand to defend the great lady," Spartacus declared, looking far too happy about the prospect of fighting a duel. "And you will—"

His words choked off into a surprised gasp as he staggered to a stop, clutching at his throat. Sarah couldn't see anything there, but he pawed at his own skin, shoulders heaving in silent tension, mouth open, but not speaking.

With a shock of horror, Sarah realized he was trying to breathe, but couldn't.

Hongwu the enchanter entered the room from the nearest door, a triumphant smile on his lips. He wore the same Ming Dynasty outfit and hair style as he had the last time Sarah saw him. The big, golden pendant again hung around his neck, and he had even acquired another Chinese sword.

"Ah, the mighty Spartacus," Hongwu said as he approached the silently gasping gladiator. "You spurned my queen, disrespected her envoys, and thought to avoid consequences?" Spartacus dropped to one knee and Hongwu's smile widened. "The runes you wear are indeed powerful. They offer unrivaled protection."

To punctuate his words, he slashed Spartacus across the chest, but his sword skipped off the gasping gladiator without effect. "But what if an attack is no attack? You walked of your own free will into this vacuum, no?"

Paralyzing cold and fear still gripped Sarah with icy hands, but without Vlad's gaze reinforcing it, she managed to focus enough to move one arm. She lashed out with a fist, striking Vlad's inner elbow, hoping to break his hold and free herself. Vlad didn't even flinch.

He turned back to her, and Sarah clenched her eyes shut to avoid that dead gaze. It was the only act of defiance left to her. The paralyzing cold deepened anyway and Vlad pulled her closer.

A soft but insistent wind began tugging at Sarah's clothes and skin, and a low keening grew in her ears. It sounded like the hopeless wails of the souls imprisoned to the vampire that had bitten her in the basement of Castello Odescalchi.

The sound draped around her, and when she peeked out for a second, she caught glimpses of those doomed souls at the periphery of her vision, like ethereal faces, crying out in hopeless torment. Her skin prickled in disgust as they pulsed against her, ghostly teeth only half-felt gnawing at her.

Vlad's low voice whispered into her ear. "You will join the family soon enough, dear Sarah. They are eager to welcome one so strong into their midst."

When she had met him in the memoryscape with Bastien weeks prior, seeking training for her new-found rune warrior gift, he had seemed a bit creepy, but now he was absolutely terrifying.

Vlad leaned in so close that she felt her breath bouncing off his face. He wasn't breathing. Was the disgusting creature going to kiss her or something? She couldn't help it. She opened her eyes.

He was indeed scant inches away. That close, the noxious smell of his cologne failed to conceal the underlying scent of decay that clung to him, as if he had only recently climbed out of a rotting coffin.

"Allow me to introduce myself," he said with the briefest of smiles on his bloodless lips. "I am Vlad the Third, Lord of Wallachia. Most people know me as Vlad Dracula." He paused and added, "I'm rather famous these days."

Sarah managed to whisper, "The movie was better."

A look of surprise flicked across his features, followed by one of rage. He opened his mouth, revealing sharp teeth.

Sarah raised one clenched fist to his chest.

She barely had to concentrate to activate the well-practiced cipher. The focused, invisible blast that exploded through that simple, glowing mark broke his grip and tumbled him away. He somersaulted right over the nearest charred couch.

Hongwu turned at the sound, and Sarah slashed a glowing finger through the air to point at him. "You're next, pal."

Behind Hongwu, Spartacus dropped to one knee, his face turning purple from lack of air. He drew a tiny knife from his boot and began marking his chest.

Sarah couldn't tell what rune he was trying to activate because Vlad launched himself at her from behind the couch, flying through the air with superhuman speed, arms extended toward her, leading with long fingernails like blackened claws.

Perfect.

The barrier rune she'd activated while distracting Hongwu rose in front of her, and Vlad bounced off the invisible barrier like a freight train crashing into a mountain. The barrier shook under the onslaught. The drain on her rounon well doubled, but it held. Vlad tumbled back into that same couch he'd just sailed over, snapping it in half.

"Home run," Sarah grinned.

Vlad leaped into a crouch atop the broken furniture and howled, a blood-curdling wail, as if a hundred dogs were getting eviscerated by white-hot irons. His mouth opened wide enough to swallow her entire head, and a mighty wind full of ash and cinders blasted forth.

It struck her shield and tore at it. Some of the wind rolled right over and around the shield and struck at her, ripping at skin and hair.

After what had happened with the first vampire, she'd thought about ways she could have handled the situation better, so she wasn't surprised. She still shrieked with disgust as the wind tore at her, ethereal faces emerging from the murk to snap and bite at her.

The air held the foul odor of burning tar. Sarah closed her eyes against the biting wind, concentrating on a more complete cipher, and activated it with a single swipe of her hand.

The wind died away as her shield expanded into a dome that settled around her, sealing her off from the rest of the room. She opened her eyes and allowed a satisfied smile.

Vlad's angry breath still howled around the dome, obscuring her view with swirling murk. The souls chained to Vlad's will bit and tore at the shield, the contact triggering cascading showers of orange sparks. They were somehow weakening it, as if their spirit forms could actually bite into the invisible barrier.

Sarah reinforced it, pouring in more energy. The shield was small enough that she could keep up that level of intensity for hours if she had to. She doubted Tomas and the others would take that long to respond to Vlad's incursion.

The raging vampire wasn't going to wait that long. He crashed into the shield directly in front of her, but bounced off again with a howl of rage.

"Hit it again," Sarah called, happy to keep him distracted. The longer he kept at that futile effort, the more likely she'd get back-up to destroy him.

Vlad obliged, but somehow he struck the shield from two directions at the same time. Half a second later, he struck again, but in three places. Then again, from four. Then five.

What the freak? The shield wobbled under the concentrated onslaught and Sarah only barely kept it from collapsing. The drain increased exponentially until she began to sweat from the effort.

She couldn't imagine how he was doing that. The barrage continued to intensify. It was as if he had cloned himself a dozen times, and every one of those clones was ramming her shield like a charging elephant. After each clone struck her shield, they dissolved into dark, billowing mist that magnified that howling torment of Vlad's soul-wind. Soon that billowing, wailing murk concealed most of her view, and she caught only glimpses of Vlad as he slammed again and again into her shield.

Then one of the clones leaped upon the shield and stuck there for half a second before dissolving. The hideous creature glared at her. Its hair was gone, and its bald head glowed white in the murk. Its fangs had elongated, stretching below its lips, and its eyes glowed like yellow lamps.

"You're one of those guys who gets ugly when you're mad, aren't you?" Sarah teased, but she wondered what was taking Tomas so long. She wouldn't be able to hold the shield much longer without tapping extra strength from the enforcers.

Another crashing body startled her as it erupted out of the billowing murk and collided with her dome right in front of her face. This one too had changed shape, becoming a massive, apelike creature with enormous arms and fists as big as frying pans. It pounded against the shield with incredible force.

Then the attacks stopped, leaving Sarah huddling alone and afraid under her shield as the murky, howling wind of tormented souls tried to eat its way through to her.

Vlad's voice reached her softly. "Sarah, you really understand nothing, do you?"

"I understand you're going to die soon," she shot back.

His soft laugh swirled around her dome, as if caught in the billowing murk and unable to escape. "I can take whatever form I need. And I know your fears."

"I'm not afraid of you," Sarah promised.

Another laugh. "Such pride in your ignorance. I love it. Do you fear this?"

At his words, the murk parted and instead of Vlad, she saw Paul striding toward her, Chinese sword in hand, that infuriatingly smug look on his face as he beckoned to her. "Come, beloved, and I will father a nation of rulers through you."

"Eww," Sarah grimaced. "Try again, pal. I killed that fear already."

The murk swirled the vision of Paul away, then parted again. She caught sight of Tomas rushing into the room with a fifty-caliber machine gun at his shoulder, already firing.

Sarah grinned. Vlad's mind games were about to come to an abrupt end.

But the gun was yanked from Tomas' grip, while souls chained to Vlad's will seized Tomas' limbs and lifted him aloft, spread-eagled and helpless. Vlad stepped from the gloom, a sickle-shaped blade in his hand. He slashed down, ripping open Tomas' stomach, spilling his guts to the floor.

Tomas screamed and met Sarah's horrified gaze, agony in his eyes. "Sarah. Help."

"I'll kill you!" Sarah shrieked and was just about to drop her shields to call forth another, far deadlier cipher.

Vampires were masters of illusion.

The thought made her hesitate. Was it really Tomas suffering there, needing her help, or was Vlad baiting her? She couldn't tell, and the agony of indecision tore at her.

The swirling murk blocked away the image and she heard another long, agonized scream from Tomas before it was cut abruptly short. She stared at the billowing darkness, horrified, barely able to breathe. Had her hesitation just killed the man she loved?

Vlad's laughter echoed around her again. "You have strength as well as heart. Well done. But deep inside, you still lack confidence."

The murk cleared again. All signs of torture were gone. Instead, Tomas stood looking at her with an expression of disappointment on his face. "I'm sorry, Sarah. You're just not good enough, and I'm tired of pretending you're that interesting."

He turned away, and the murk closed over him again.

Sarah laughed.

The swirling whirlwind seemed to pause, as if surprised. Sarah said, "You really think I'd fall for that one?"

Vlad appeared in his normal form, standing in front of her shield. Then a dozen identical clones appeared, ringing her dome. It was an intimidating sight as Sarah turned a slow circle, all of those deadly vampires standing motionless and silent, just staring.

They all spoke together. "You fear losing him. You fear failure and rejection."

Sarah shrugged. "Don't we all? Life moves on, and it's time this little chat does too. You've got nothing but a bunch of empty lies."

All of the surrounding Vlads laughed in unison. "On the contrary, Sarah. I'm full of your vitality. How do you think I found you in this secret lair?"

That gave her pause, and the many cloned vampires smiled together. "When my slave bit you, he did not take your strength for himself, but for me."

Sarah touched her jaw where the vampire had bitten her, remembering the agony and terror of that moment. Could he be telling the truth?

"I feel your heartbeat in my ears, Sarah," Vlad crooned, leaning casually against the dome. "I can follow you anywhere."

As she considered that he continued. "You must be familiar with the saying 'Once bitten, twice shy'. It means that once a slave of mine has tasted your soul, I own you."

The clones threw out their hands, fingertips touching in an unbroken ring around her.

Sarah frowned. "That's the stupidest alternate explanation I've ever heard."

His veneer of calm evaporated into howls of rage as the clones erupted into furious pounding against her shield. Some of them began tearing at the floor, as if planning to dig under it to reach her.

"Tantrums? Really?" Sarah taunted. "I am so done with this."

She slashed her left hand through the air, leaving a glowing mark that allowed her to focus and activate a second cipher that she'd been preparing. The drain doubled and she nearly dropped to her knees as strength flooded out of her, but she held her focus with grim determination.

A second domed shield settled over the first, big enough to seal all of the cloned, raging vampires in the space between.

"Have you ever heard the saying, 'If you play with fire, you get burned'?"

She didn't wait for an answer, but drew a glowing cipher in the air, adding modifiers to take a full ten percent of every enforcer squad. With deadly intent, she completed the last mark and unleashed the cipher.

Fire erupted into the space between her two domed barriers, tearing through the howling, murky wind, and enveloping all the vampire clones.

As flames blocked her view of the nasty creatures, already writhing in agony under the power of her assault, Sarah said, "One of you is real, so you all die together."

She caught glimpses of the vampires vainly trying to escape the flames, to beat through the barriers, or to protect themselves with the wind of their chained souls, all to no avail. Their undead bodies burned under the intense heat, their flesh melting, and they howled like condemned souls.

The sight was gruesome, but Sarah felt only satisfaction. She was destroying a vile creature that had evaded even Tomas and Gregorios for centuries. That was a pretty good day's work.

"You know, you really are amazing." Vlad spoke in a conversational tone.

Sarah spun. He stood inside of the shield dome, right beside her.

42

Wit is educated insolence. In other words, Gregorios.

~ARISTOTLE

A HUNDRED QUESTIONS boiled into Sarah's mind. What . . . How . . . ?

Before Sarah could react to the shock of seeing Vlad somehow inside her protective dome, he snatched her off her feet. His merciless fingers grasped her face, tilting her head up and to the side. He lunged with inhuman speed, sank his sharpened teeth into her jaw and bit deep into the bone.

He didn't bother gloating, or anything, but just bit savagely into her face.

Sarah screamed, prying at his arms, but she lacked the strength to pull free. Her body convulsed with searing pain, then she screamed again as he sucked at her soul.

He drew deep from her rounon. Her soul seemed to freeze, her remaining strength become unresponsive. It felt like all the love and hope she'd ever felt withered and died.

The two dome walls crumbled, and the flames that had been boiling between them fizzled, leaving only smoke floating heavy in the air.

Vlad raised his bloody mouth from her jaw and laughed, a throaty chuckle of satisfaction. Sarah yearned to strike him down, but nothing worked. She had defeated him, hadn't she? And yet, she was the one trembling with agony, unable to move or fight.

Vlad turned her head to the side, and she was powerless to resist. He licked a tear from her cheek, his tongue rough and rasping, leaving a trail of icy corruption on her skin. The wailing sound of souls chained to his will grew louder in her ears, and she could now make out a few individual words.

Torture.

Endless torment.

Hopeless.

That wasn't helping at all. This freaky spawn of hell made Paul seem like a gentleman. Sarah refused to listen, trying to ground herself again. She had to fight, had to do something. The thought of waiting for her doom, helpless before that monster as he chained her soul to his stoked a growing rage.

Vlad sighed with pleasure, caressing Sarah's trembling face. "Ah, the taste of a mighty rune warrior soul is an exquisite treat. For one so strong to have remained almost entirely undefiled is like the aging of a perfect wine."

He released her and she collapsed to the floor.

"Your soul now belongs to me," he told her. His lips had taken on the color of her blood. He grinned down at her.

"I'm going to rip out your heart," Sarah whispered, despite the agony still rattling her to the core. Her innards felt on fire, and her rounon well, usually the solid source of her inner strength, felt terrifyingly weak and brittle.

"It is rare to find one so young already so powerful, but how can you be so unlearned and so lacking in understanding?"

He leaned closer. "I don't have a heart, Sarah. I'm a vampire, remember?" That seemed to strike him as incredibly funny and he threw his head back to laugh.

The sharp clashing of steel drew her gaze. Even though her muscles remained frozen, she could move her eyes a little. Spartacus' rune must have worked to break free of that web Hongwu had caught him in because he and Hongwu were dueling on the far side of the room, sword against ax.

The gladiator looked exultant. He was singing loudly as he steadily beat Hongwu back around the foosball table, although the words didn't register. Sarah's ears were ringing with the slow thumping of her own heartbeat.

She glanced up at the still-chuckling Vlad, hating the feeling of helplessness. What was he?

Vlad glanced down. "What am I?"

At her look of surprise, he nodded. "I own you now, Sarah. I can rip from your mind any thought, any memory, any truth I desire. I command your soul and can strip it bare."

His voice rang with power and he clenched a fist over her. She screamed again, writhing on the ground as the pain intensified to unbearable levels. Her already-weakened soul drained of strength until she nearly fainted.

Part of her yearned for the sweet comfort of unconsciousness, but she desperately fought against it. If she passed out, would she awaken as one of those tormented souls chained to him?

Vlad crooned over her as the pain subsided enough for her to breathe again. "All in good time, Sarah." Then he snatched her off the floor and yanked her close, shouting into her face. "I am Dracula!"

She lacked the strength to scream, wished for nothing more than her favorite carbine with the attached grenade launcher. She'd shove it down his throat and see how loud he could shout with a giant shotgun round ripping out his innards.

Vlad composed himself and continued in a calm, conversational tone. "The movies were quite entertaining, really. But they failed to capture the scope of my nobility, don't you think?"

Sarah felt completely exhausted, bereft of emotion and strength, barely conscious of the pain as she hung in his grip.

Vlad said, "Once negotiations fail, I'll come for you, have no fear. Your soul added to the chorus of my slaves will make me invincible!"

Gregorios' voice was like a lifeline dragging Sarah from the depths of growing despair. "You're so full of yourself, Vladdy boy."

He stepped into the nearest door, eyes already glowing with his active nevron. The sight of him was like a beacon, and Sarah's fears faded as hope blossomed anew in her heart. Tomas stepped into the next doorway, farther down the wall, hefting a fifty-caliber machine gun almost exactly like the one the fake Tomas had carried before getting eviscerated. This Tomas was no projection, though. He wouldn't let Vlad escape.

Nabil flanked Tomas, a huge-bore hunting rifle held at the ready. It looked big enough to knock a hole in a tank. Eirene stepped into the far door, her eyes also glowing with active nevron.

Vlad twisted so Sarah hung between him and the armed men. "It took you long enough. I nearly devoured my new little pet out of boredom."

With a shout of victory, Spartacus slashed his ax across Hongwu's throat. The heavy blade struck the chain of the pendant Hongwu wore, and a cascade of brilliant blue sparks exploded from the contact.

The impact knocked Hongwu sprawling. He looked dazed, but unhurt. That ax should have sheared right through that slender chain and cleaved his head off.

It had broken the chain. Spartacus scooped the pendant off the floor with a shout of triumph, and Hongwu leaped to his feet, eyes on the lost artifact, his expression horrified.

"Leave the gladiator and see to your duty," Vlad barked.

Hongwu looked like he wanted to lunge at Spartacus. His gaze lingered on the pendant for another moment before he snarled something in Chinese and retreated toward Vlad. Spartacus followed, ax held at the ready.

Nabil shifted his aim to the enchanter and Tomas ordered in a deadly, cold voice, "Stop right there."

Vlad laughed. "You can't hurt us. Any aggression on your part will kill this pretty thing." He shook Sarah to emphasize his words.

She decided she'd cut off those fingers before taking his head. As soon as she could dredge up the strength to activate a cipher.

Hongwu didn't look concerned about the hunter's huge gun. "Now that you are arrived, my mistress requires that you attend her in the memoryscape."

Gregorios chuckled. "I was going to ask if you had any last words, but that'll work."

"Sarah is mine now," Vlad said and tossed her across the room at him.

Gregorios caught her, cradling her close to his chest.

"Shoot him already," Sarah begged, fighting back tears of relief, knowing she was safe with him.

She twisted her head, expecting to see Tomas rip Vlad apart with that machine gun. Although his finger was on the trigger and his furious expression made it clear he wanted nothing more than to squeeze it, he did not.

"It's not that simple," Vlad said. She wasn't sure if he had read her thoughts again, or if his hearing was really that good. "Your soul is linked to mine. Any damage they cause will only get transferred to my slaves. In this case, of course I'll use your soul first."

"Is that true?" Sarah asked.

Gregorios, expression grim, nodded. "It is until I remove his soulmask."

In the center of the lounge, Vlad threw out his arms. "One step, old man. Take one step, and I snap the living spark that keeps her soul in that body. You might kill me, but I guarantee you will lose her forever."

"Give her to me." Melek said softly. He had slipped into the room behind Gregorios and now gestured for him to set Sarah down.

As Gregorios did so, Tomas took a step into the room, drawing Vlad's attention. "What do you want?"

"What Hongwu said." Vlad looked disgusted by the message. He continued, rolling his eyes and speaking quickly, like a child reciting a required line before they could go play. "Sarah lives as long as you enter the memoryscape and attend Xiao."

"She's gone through a lot of hassle to arrange this meeting," Eirene said from the other side of the room. She had joined Spartacus, one restraining hand on his arm. Her words drew the attention of both Vlad and Hongwu.

"What are you doing?" Gregorios breathed as Melek turned Sarah, pushed her hair out of the way, and began cutting into the back of her neck with a pinky-sized runesmith knife.

She really hated feeling so completely useless. She wanted to scream with fury, but the exhaustion Vlad's bite had wrought on her left her so weak she couldn't lift her head off the floor.

"I'll tell you when to move," Melek whispered back. "Keep them talking."

Sarah hoped he knew what he was doing, but tried not to think about the secret rune he was working into the back of her neck. If Vlad really could read her thoughts from across the room, she didn't want to give him any warning. It was all too easy to think only about all the different ways she was going to kill him when she got her strength back.

Hongwu said in a sneering tone to Eirene, "My mistress grants you more honor than you deserve."

Spartacus declared, "And you deserve less than you've received, cur. Upon my honor, we will complete our duel, and I will take your head."

"In time," the enchanter said, but he didn't seem entirely eager.

Sarah didn't blame him. Even at full strength, fighting the mighty gladiator would be daunting, especially now that he was protected by those forbidden runes.

"Defy her and I get Sarah," Vlad crooned. Then he shrugged. "I'll get her eventually anyway, but this way's more fun."

Melek must have completed his work because he pressed a hand to the back of Sarah's neck and she felt the pulse of his rounon against her skin.

"What are you doing?" Vlad hissed, twisting back to face Gregorios.

The pain faded away and Sarah's stricken soul recovered a bit of its strength. The icy grip of Vlad's influence had been somehow severed, or at least weakened.

Melek cried in triumph, "Done. Take them!"

"Tomas!" Gregorios shouted, leaping into a sprint toward Vlad.

Tomas instantly opened fire with the machine gun, followed a split second later by Nabil with the hunting rifle. Eirene and Spartacus were already charging from the other side.

The bullets sparked and ricocheted away from a shimmering veil of ethereal, howling faces that became visible, surrounding Vlad and Hongwu.

Vlad shrieked, and a torrent of black-winged bats erupted from his mouth. The disgusting little creatures filled the room in a living whirl-wind. They tore at the shooting men, although they parted around the facetakers. The psycho-vampire-bats snatched up furniture, flinging pieces in every direction.

Melek dropped over Sarah, protecting her from the onslaught.

The firing stopped, and a few seconds later, the howling bat-wind faded to echoing laughter. Melek heaved himself upright with a grimace of pain, and Sarah looked around. The room was destroyed, with broken furniture impaling the walls or lying in shattered piles in the corners. Even the heavy pool table had flipped over.

The fear was gone, though, and Sarah's strength started to return as her icy limbs warmed. She managed to sit up with Melek's help.

Vlad was gone.

Gregorios and Eirene stood where Sarah had last seen the vampire. The storm of bats had tossed Spartacus against the wall. Tomas rushed into the room, followed again by Nabil. Apparently the storm had thrown them right out into the hall.

Tomas cursed. "He runs faster every time we see him."

"Took Hongwu with him," Gregorios added.

"I must fetch my sword," Spartacus declared, dropping the ax to the floor. "The coward will not escape me again."

Tomas ran to Sarah and dropped to his knees beside her. "Are you all right?"

"No," she admitted, letting him wrap her in his powerful arms, but forcing back the sobs that threatened to completely overwhelm her. She let him hold her for a moment, then pushed back and met his worried gaze. "We have to kill that thing, Tomas."

"We will," he promised.

Then Vlad's voice echoed in Sarah's ears, as if from a great distance. "*You belong to me.*"

She jumped and turned to Melek, fear shaking her voice. "I can hear him in my head."

Melek grimaced. "He is the strongest of the undead. The protective rune I marked on you would seal out most others. To keep such a mighty vampire at bay, I need more strength than either you or I have available."

"Show me the mark," Sarah told him. "I can draw from the tenth, at least for a while."

It was a testament to how worried the situation made him that Melek didn't even pause to remind her how much he disapproved of taking strength even from willing souls. He produced a small piece of paper and drew out the symbol.

"That's a lot like the vampire rune I usually wear," Tomas said.

"Where do you think you enforcers learned the symbol?" Melek asked with a wry smile. "The rune that you know helps cut through vampire illusion and defend against the assaults of their chained souls. This is a higher form of that rune, with the defensive properties magnified to shield an already-infected soul from further degradation."

"Infected? I thought a vampire bite wasn't contagious." Sarah asked with another shudder.

Melek shook his head. "The bite does not transform you into a vampire like the movies suggest, but it does deteriorate the defenses of the soul. Eventually one becomes helpless, easy prey for even weak vampires to chain to their will."

"How long can we hold him off?" Tomas asked.

Melek considered that, then peered more closely at the bite marks along Sarah's jaw. "He bit deep, and she had been bitten once before. Most souls would have succumbed already."

"That's not very encouraging," Sarah said, studying the rune again to stave off her terror. She couldn't believe that despite all her powers, she faced such a horrific fate.

The outer ring of the rune was made by a twisting rope symbol of protection, surrounding the Helm of Awe, a mighty, ancient Norse symbol, also of protection. It looked like eight spiked tridents radiating out from a common core. Between each pair of those tridents were supporting symbols from ancient Egyptian and Chinese scripts. The whole produced a sense of tremendous protection, deflection of evil, and reinforcing energy to the soul.

"I'll activate this and we'll hunt down that thing and remove its head. Then I'm free, right?"

Tomas nodded, then added, "Sarah, I'm so sorry. I never imagined he might have been involved, that the other vampire might have been bound to him. I could have . . ."

She placed a finger over his lips to quiet him, touched by the anguish in his voice. "I know. We'll make it right."

"This needs to be marked on my inner, left forearm, right?" Sarah asked.

Melek nodded.

She borrowed his little knife and started marking it into her arm. After the agony of what she had suffered at Vlad's hand, the ache from the scalpel-sharp knife parting her skin was easy to ignore.

"Do you have the strength for it?" Tomas asked.

Sarah paused before adding the modifiers to draw strength from the Tenth. She hated weakening those brave men. Who knew what they would be called upon to do soon?

"I think so, but if I start drawing from the Tenth, I won't be able to release them until we kill Vlad. That might make them vulnerable, and I still won't have enough to face Xiao again any time soon."

Tomas grimaced. "That's what worries me. This attack was designed to take you out of the equation."

"Then I need to get back in." Sarah made a decision and turned to Melek. "I need more power, and I have a source of power outside of the Tenth. I think the situation merits tapping it, but you're not going to like it."

Melek sat back, expression turning hard. "You can't mean to draw upon the master runes again!"

"I could, but that's not what I'm talking about." Using the master runes was actually a good idea, but she wasn't sure she could handle that much power.

The master runes had stopped Paul, but they'd killed her too. She chided herself for her lingering fear to tap them again, but the fear was there and it was real.

"What, then?" Melek asked uneasily.

Sarah glanced to Tomas, hoping he'd support her. Then she told Melek about the matrix she had set up to heal those terminally-ill children in Rome. As she expected, Melek's expression darkened more and more until he barely waited for her to finish.

He exclaimed, "I can't believe it! You know better than to use your power for such evil."

"I healed those who would have died if I hadn't stepped in," Sarah explained. She was a little surprised by a look of anguish that flashed across Melek's face when she said that.

Then she realized she hadn't seen Heber. "Oh, Melek," she said, feeling a heavy sadness. "I'm so sorry. I hadn't realized that poor Heber . . ." She trailed off, not sure what to say, and placed a hand on his arm.

Melek met her gaze, not hiding his sorrow. "He is an honored martyr. I can only hope I meet my fate with as much honor when my time comes."

Sarah hated how much recent events were torturing the powerful old hunter, but she couldn't afford to limit herself to his world view. "I know you don't approve of what I did, but those children will live because of a tiny sacrifice from people who don't even realize they've helped. That cipher has stood long enough, though. I'm going to transfer that power to me. It should be enough to strengthen me against Xiao."

Melek looked torn. He rose and paced away, fists clenched at his side. After a moment he turned back. "I cannot give you my blessing, but I will not oppose you in this."

That was better than she had hoped.

"Thank you. For everything."

"These monsters must be destroyed," Melek growled.

Tomas nodded. "After that, we'll have all the time we need to argue through the ethical questions."

Sarah marked a new cipher in the air, including the modifiers she needed to deactivate the healing cipher and transfer some of the power of those souls passing through the shrines of the deliverer to her instead.

The remainder she left building, like a pool of energy ready for her to tap. She felt confident the children would all recover. They'd enjoyed that healing strength for days.

A moment after she activated the cipher, strength thundered into her, and she gasped. It wasn't the mighty torrent she'd felt when connecting with the master runes, but that fraction of the power she tapped was enough to wipe away her lingering exhaustion and begin refilling her nearly-empty rounon well.

"Oh, that's so much better," she breathed.

Vlad's laughter sounded in her mind. *'I know the feel of captured souls, Sarah. I had not expected you to tempt the wrath of the enforcers and the hunters.'* His tone turned approving. *'Make the hunt interesting, Sarah.'*

"Will you get out of my head?" she snapped as she completed the vampire protection rune, drawing only from her strength, which was reinforced from that remote cipher. She focused over the completed cipher. It glowed against her skin immediately, and she felt enveloped in calm, like donning a warm jacket on a cool day.

Sarah breathed a sigh of relief, then stood and faced Melek. "I think it's working."

Tomas hugged her, looking immensely relieved. "Let's hope it keeps him out until we put him in the grave for good."

"Now what?" Sarah asked as she gingerly touched her jaw where Vlad had bitten her. The pain had faded. Her healing rune would take care of it soon.

Tomas took her hand. "Let's get a cloth to clean your face. Then we'll find the others. We've got to prepare to face Xiao."

"I wonder what she wants." Sarah asked as they headed for the machine room. She felt terrified of entering the memoryscape, especially if Xiao had prepared the meeting.

"At this point, I'm not sure it matters. I'm sick and tired of running," Tomas said angrily. He was still fuming about losing Vlad, and by the way he held her hand, she could tell he was worried about her. That would make him even more eager for a fight.

"Me too," she told him.

The others joined them near the machines a little while later. Gregorios was the last to enter the room. He rubbed his hands together and considered them all.

"This should be interesting. I can't remember the last time I've attended a peace accord as the party expected to surrender."

"Surrender?" Sarah asked, not like the sound of that.

"He's right," Eirene said with a disgusted look. "Although the setup is more elaborate than most, she's clearly trying to position us so we feel obligated to accept her demands."

"So we show up with the big guns?" Tomas asked hopefully.

In the memoryscape, they could conjure up whatever they wanted. Well, they could if Xiao didn't interfere. Sarah wondered if she could pop into the memoryscape in a battleship.

She'd take a single gun turret. The sixteen-inch diameter cannons were over sixty feet long. Not even Xiao could take one of those to the face without breaking a few teeth.

Before Sarah could get too excited about the idea, Eirene shook her head. "I doubt she'll allow us that much control."

Gregorios added, "Besides, no use bloodying her nose before hearing her terms. This ought to be good."

"Then the big guns," Tomas said.

"Not for you, my boy," Gregorios said with a little shake of his head. "Sorry, but without the girls here, Eirene's got to run the machine. That allows only three seats. I have to go negotiate."

Sarah was tempted to suggest Eirene go instead. Gregorios' negotiating technique usually meant unrivaled violence or irritating whoever they were parleying with until negotiations broke down, bringing them back to violence. Usually she heartily approved of the tactic, but she wasn't sure it was the right approach against Xiao.

"That still leaves room for me," Tomas argued.

"I need Melek with me," Gregorios said with another shake of his head.

Melek looked as surprised by the choice as Sarah felt. Gregorios noted the look and added, "You know runes better than anyone, so maybe you can get a sense of what she's doing. Plus, having a unified facetaker and hunter presence might throw her off a bit."

"Unified?" Melek asked, one eyebrow raised.

Gregorios chuckled. "After all we've been through together, we'd better be. Besides, I figured you'd want to meet the woman responsible for kidnapping your son and ordering the hit that killed Heber."

"You're right. It's time to see the face of our enemy."

Tomas looked defeated. "And Sarah gets the third seat, of course."

"All in good time," Gregorios said, giving Sarah a wink. "First we play out the game. Then we flip it on her."

43

Experience will show you a master can only point the way. You must bond the rune.

~ANCIENT EGYPTIAN PROVERB

GREGORIOS APPEARED IN THE MEMORYSCAPE, dressed in modern tactical gear, carrying a Russian AA-12 automatic shotgun. He refused to face Xiao completely unarmed, but nothing short of an Apache helicopter or an Abrams tank would more than tickle her.

A young and fit Melek appeared beside him, his similar shotgun already held in a firing stance.

"Easy," Gregorios urged as he glanced around the room that coalesced around them. "Only when the time is right."

Xiao would assume their pitiful armaments were one more symptom of their ineffectual resistance to her. She couldn't see Quentin's specialty Curtain Call rounds in the drum magazines feeding both guns. Gregorios wasn't entirely sure what firing those rune-disrupting rounds at Xiao would accomplish, but he felt confident they'd distract her long enough for them to escape.

The two of them stood in an open, rectangular hall, decorated with Japanese paintings and pottery, with windows overlooking a hillside garden. Japanese and Chinese officials mingled nearby, dressed in formal state attire of the late nineteenth century. Gregorios spotted a couple of high-ranking soldiers from both America and Great Britain among them.

The room felt like a peace treaty, with false smiles failing to conceal underlying tension. He'd attended enough such meetings to pick up on the subtle vibes.

A simple, rectangular table dominated the center of the room. An earth-toned cloth bordered with ornate Japanese designs embroidered in gold draped the table, and four wooden chairs, padded with red-velvet cushions, lined each side.

Xiao materialized at the head of the table, already seated, her expression one of calm confidence. She wore a bright yellow silk dress, accented with black and gold scrollwork and the ornate phoenix images of an empress. Her long, black hair was tied up into a huge headpiece from the Qing dynasty, sporting long crimson tassels and dripping with gold, emeralds, and jade.

Gregorios grunted and approached the table. "And here I was expecting to show up in the Forbidden City, with you staring down from the imperial throne."

"A fitting venue perhaps," Xiao conceded, either not noting his sarcasm or choosing to ignore it. "But this location suits my purposes better."

"And what are those purposes?" Gregorios asked, pulling back a chair halfway down the table and dropping into it. "From the looks of things, I'd say we're at the signing of the Shimonoseki Treaty, back at the end of the nineteenth century."

"You are astute, as always," Xiao said with a tiny nod.

"Doesn't exactly make sense," Gregorios said, willing a large plate of Peking duck to appear on the table in front of him. It smelled delicious, and having another sharp knife on hand never hurt.

"Why not?" Xiao asked, looking displeased by his lack of manners.

He forked a big chunk of meat into his mouth and added as he chewed. "Aren't you a little out of character wearing a Chinese imperial gown at the table where the Qing dynasty submitted to Japan? I thought you were all pro-China."

Xiao glanced at the nearby Chinese officials with disdain and declared, "The Qing were corrupt and beyond rescue. They surrendered at my bidding. Imperial Japan was the rod I used to chastise my homeland."

That was very interesting and, if true, it meant she hadn't limited her early activity to China after all. The facetaker council had little to do with the First Sino-Japanese War, which Gregorios had always thought was a mistake. It would've been a great opportunity to try gaining a foothold in the east. Shahrokh had been preoccupied with playing the emerging European and American empires against each other.

"So, how'd that work out for you, supporting Japan and all?" he asked, wondering why she chose to appear in Chinese attire. The Chinese had been widely expected to win that war, but had been routed by the Japanese. If she was trying for a deeper meaning by the location, he wasn't getting it.

"Not as well as I had hoped," Xiao admitted, with a tiny downward turn of her crimson-painted lips. "The Japanese proved inconsistent rulers and overly cruel to the peoples they subjugated."

More and more interesting. He rarely heard anyone with nefarious plans show any concern for the ignorant masses they trampled.

"So why choose to meet here?"

Xiao ignored the question and glanced at Melek, who still stood behind another chair, glaring at her. "Sit, master hunter," she urged, gesturing at the seat. "I am interested in learning why you side with the facetakers after millennia of opposition."

Melek's glare didn't soften. "You owe me for the loss of one of my men, and I demand the return of my son."

"Funerary reparations for your fallen hunter may be agreed to as an appendix to our accord. Alter's service to me is not yet concluded. I need his memories. You will understand once you too prove your dedication to my service."

Melek looked on the verge of turning his shotgun on Xiao, who had ignored their weapons entirely. Gregorios gestured for him to sit, then pushed some of the duck across.

Still glaring, Melek settled into a chair, but ignored the food. Gregorios shrugged. His loss. Since Gregorios had summoned it, the meal was seasoned perfectly to his taste. No sense suffering unnecessarily through the boring parts before the fun began.

"That still begs the question," Gregorios said, lounging back in his chair as he chewed, projecting a bored expression. "Why did you ask to meet us here?"

"I didn't ask," Xiao snapped, her calm facade cracking for the first time. "I grant this audience as a show of respect. I could have arranged for you to arrive in chains."

A set of iron shackles dropped onto the table with a loud, clanking jangle.

Gregorios grinned and poked the shackles. "Excellent touch, but you went through a lot of trouble to arrange this little chat. It wasn't just so we could start shooting each other again, was it?"

"Even you must recognize that shooting me would accomplish nothing," Xiao said as she regained her composure. "I rule the memoryscape and your best recourse is to flee should your incessantly irritating manner provoke me."

He let his smile fade, then replied in a deadly serious tone. "I'm done running, Xiao. So stop dodging the question and get to the point. What do you want?"

"Your sworn fealty, of course."

He'd been expecting something along those lines, but her audacity still impressed him.

While Melek bit back an outraged response with great difficulty, Gregorios said, "Do you always try wooing potential employees by setting the world after them, attacking their families, and sending invitations by vampire courier? As a business practice, it's not really the most successful model."

"I attempted to open negotiations with your wife. She spurned my offer and chose the path of arrogance instead."

"In her defense, you had just kidnapped Alter," Gregorios pointed out. "We have a standing policy not to go into long-term relationships with business partners who treat our employees like that."

Xiao countered calmly, "Your policies are to shoot first, and then shoot again, just to be sure."

Gregorios shrugged. "It helps avoid misunderstandings, like the one with your son."

"He was an impetuous youth," Xiao admitted.

Melek snapped, "He was a monster. He caused the death of thousands."

"They would not have died had they obeyed," Xiao pointed out.

"Is that what you have in mind?" Gregorios asked. "Death or slavery?"

"Not at all." A delicate glass of red wine appeared in her hand and she sipped it. "I summoned you here to establish an accord to work together to bring to pass the first long-term dynasty capable of establishing real peace in a suffering world."

"Your son tried that," Gregorios reminded her.

"In time, he would have bowed to my counsel and become the ruler the world needed," she said, sounding a bit annoyed.

"I doubt it. His soul was damaged."

"But mine is not." Xiao leaned forward. "You have lived long upon the face of the world, Gregorios. You have seen empires and dynasties come and go. No matter how much promise they show at their founding, without exception, they all crumble."

"It's the way of the world. Kind of sad, really," Gregorios agreed.

"Worse than that," Xiao said, her voice impassioned. "How many millions suffer and die because the world cannot figure out how to govern itself?"

"Probably not as many as would die if you took over."

"You're not thinking clearly, Gregorios. The Suntara council amassed unrivaled wealth, but never leveraged their position to help the world improve."

Melek looked angry enough to start chewing on the table. "You speak of peace, yet your son and your daughter both killed at will."

"Change is never easy."

"So you want us to help you kill everyone who stands in your way?" Gregorios asked.

"I am offering you a chance to help create a better future," Xiao said, and she really sounded like she believed what she was saying.

"Think about it. Mighty Rome failed from within. The European nations bickered and squandered their might, despite gaining control over most of the world. Their cesspool of corruption and greed kept the world wallowing in warfare, famine, and poverty for centuries."

"I'm not hearing anything I don't already know," Gregorios said.

"And your Suntara council," Xiao said, contempt heavy in her voice. "You did nothing but play the sides against each other."

"The council couldn't take over. People don't react well to learning what we really are." She wasn't wrong, but what she was suggesting wouldn't have worked.

She glanced at Melek. "And your clan, despite your insufferable claims to honor, committed endless atrocities against anyone who did not fit your strict view of the world."

Melek looked undeterred by the accusation. "We fight corruption and evil at every level, demon."

"Your incessant fighting only serves to weaken the world."

"What's your point?" Gregorios asked, growing tired of her ranting. "You're better at blaming other people for problems than most, but I'm not seeing why the world would be better under your rule."

"I've seen many dynasties fall," she said, her expression turning sad. "Even the great American experiment, which started with such promise, is faltering."

"People aren't perfect," Gregorios offered.

"Exactly. Mortals are so weak, so easily beguiled by greed, selfishness, and ignorance. Surely you've seen the same truth."

"What truth?"

"Only one who is more than mortal can lead them."

"Most tyrants think they're better than everyone," Gregorios pointed out.

She shook her head. "You cannot deny that we have an advantage. Our many lives grant us a long-term view that simple mortals cannot hope to attain. I can succeed where all others have failed because I know what works and I have the experience to make changes that will endure."

Gregorios shook his head. "Won't work. Facetakers tried taking over way back in the early days. People never accept us once they learn we're different."

"They'll accept us now," Xiao said with a little smile. "Why do you think comic books, movies, and other arms of the entertainment industry have focused so much on super-human heroes?"

He chuckled. "Are you saying you've been prepping the world to accept you as over-queen for the past hundred years?"

"I have done what I could," she said with a nod.

"You can't be serious," Melek exclaimed.

Gregorios shared his surprise. They had invested heavily in entertainment, but he'd never looked that closely at the content, just at the returns.

She gave them both a disapproving look. "You both wield such mighty power, but you lack vision. We can accomplish so much more than you allow. Once peace is established, no longer will the few pillage their own people. The small-minded greed of first-life mortals blinds them to the fact that a prosperous population will enrich them far more than an impoverished one."

"That's probably true," Gregorios admitted. "But slavery doesn't usually produce prosperity for the slaves."

"Expand your thinking," Xiao snapped. "I'm not talking about enslaving people, but freeing them from their historical constraints. I will not reign as a tyrant, nor will I give in to the misguided attempts at generosity that so often result in a populace enslaved to the dole and incapable of working to contribute to the greater whole."

"I'll admit, you have a grander scheme of world conquest than most dictators I've met," Gregorios said.

Melek was frowning at Xiao, studying her as if trying to diagnose her mental disorder.

Xiao was warming up to the topic. "I will deny religious fanatics the ability to murder and wreak mayhem just because some people believe in a different god."

"You can't snuff out religion," Gregorios warned. For a moment, she'd almost sounded like she'd thought things out, but trying to stomp out religions was a guaranteed path to destruction, even to one as powerful as Xiao.

She made a dismissive wave. "Let people believe what they want. I don't care what faith people choose, but I will not allow religious wars or intolerance."

Gregorios clapped softly. "An amazing performance, Xiao. You've outlined just about every major world problem, and twisted every single one of them into justification for world warfare. I'm very impressed."

She glowered at him. "You are in no position to mock me. Your power base is gone. You are in hiding, with the world turning against you. I had hoped that your current circumstances would humble you sufficient to see reason and consider the merits of the future I propose."

"Well, if your future includes treating everyone else the way you've been treating us, I can't see how it's any kind of improvement."

Melek declared, "We will stand against you and snuff out your evil, just as we have every other cui dashi before you."

"Like your precious son?" Xiao asked, scorn in her voice. "It's not the power that makes evil, hunter, but the use of it."

Gregorios didn't like her basically quoting the same argument he had recently made. The cui dashi power in and of itself might not be evil, but it usually led to evil choices.

So he said, "You make great promises, Xiao. You promise peace and prosperity and equality to all the world. But in the same breath that you offer us a place in your new world order, you threaten everything we are."

Xiao gave him an imperious stare. "Don't spurn this offer. I can see to it that the world again sees you as heroes, or I can ensure you are hunted and destroyed. I've left most of your personal assets intact, but that can change."

Not good. He had hoped she only knew about the Suntara assets. Of course, she could well be lying, but she might also be telling the truth.

"I welcome your experience to my cause," she continued. "But I can just as easily harvest your nevron to create another obedient child, if I must."

"So we're moving to the threat and counter-threat part of the accord, are we?" Gregorios asked.

Xiao's calm cracked. Good. He glanced at Melek and winked. At the pre-arranged signal, the hunter placed his right hand over his left sleeve to activate the rune he'd already marked on the concealed skin.

"Think before you speak again," Xiao warned. "Vlad has taken your precious rune warrior, and he refrains from consuming the rest of her strength and chaining her soul to endless servitude only at my command. If you defy me, she will be the first of many casualties."

Summoned by Melek, Sarah appeared next to Gregorios, looking healthy and calm. "Vlad's day is coming soon enough, don't worry about that."

Xiao looked momentarily stunned by Sarah's unexpected arrival.

Gregorios rose to face her. "Maybe the situation isn't quite what you assumed, old girl."

Xiao leaped to her feet, her expression turning furious. "The world is on the brink of self-destruction anyway, you fools! Together, we can save the future."

"From you!" Sarah cried. "You're the one wrecking everything and stirring up war." Another shotgun appeared in her hands. "Without you, the world would be a lot more peaceful."

Xiao stood to her full height, shoulders back, and a disapproving, regal expression on her face. "Gregorios, you have elected war when I offered peace. War will come to you. I will strip everything away."

Her voice fell to a fierce whisper. "I will leave you alive to see the death of your beloved before I harvest your nevron too."

Gregorios didn't even have to think about it, activating his nevra core out of pure instinct as fury boiled through him. His hands burst into purple fire, and his eyes blazed with his rage. "Now you've gone and made it personal. Bad idea."

Xiao turned to Melek, who stepped from the table, raising his shotgun. "And war will come to you and yours, fool. Know that you have doomed your entire family."

Sarah raised her shotgun, but paused to ask, "You really thought we'd support you as the new world leader after working so hard to defeat your son?"

Xiao shook her head. "I never said I would rule. I plan to establish one who the world can unite behind."

That gave Gregorios pause, just as he was wrapping a finger around the trigger. Xiao was still ignoring the threat their shotguns offered, and he was eager to see what she thought once they fired.

"And who is that?" Sarah demanded.

Gregorios expected her to reveal the name of yet another crazy cui dashi child like Paul.

"Alter."

She faded from the memoryscape before Gregorios recovered from the shock of that declaration.

He threw the shotgun down onto the table in disgust. "I really wanted to shoot her in the face."

The memoryscape shuddered and turned black, and Gregorios felt his mind getting forcibly ejected. He hadn't known she could do that.

As soon as they removed the helmets, Gregorios met Melek's worried gaze. "No way she's turned your son yet."

"What are you talking about?" Eirene demanded.

"I'll explain on the road. War's on, love. Pack your things. Time to move."

44

It looks like they're planning to destroy the entire thing. I wouldn't have thought it possible. The city is so vast. I don't know how you knew this would happen, but we arrived in time to rescue several thousand families and over four thousand orphans. We collected as many artifacts as we can carry, as ordered. I hope you have a big place to store all of this, and a plan for all these kids when we reach Germany.

~EPHRAIM, EXPEDITION TEAM LEADER DURING THE
DESTRUCTION OF BENIN CITY IN AFRICA BY THE
BRITISH, 1897

"ARE YOU MOCKING ME?" Alter demanded.

He felt more astonished by what Xiao had just told than knowing they were somehow walking a memoryscape from the twelfth century B.C.

"I speak in earnest," she assured him, and he could detect no lie in her expression, voice, or manner. That just made her words all the more insane.

"You realize my entire purpose is to destroy you, right?" Alter asked. He was a hunter. He shouldn't have to remind a cui dashi of his primary mission.

"Of course it's not," Xiao said, giving him a reproving look.

She continued down the wide, paved avenue of Kadesh. She'd informed him the strategic trading city was part of the Hittite Empire, but was fiercely contested by Egypt too.

The sun was bright and hot in a clear, blue sky. Kadesh seemed to be a large, prosperous city, somewhere to the northeast of Egypt. He wasn't entirely sure. Crowds of people thronged the city around them, wearing summer-weight, woolen clothing. Most looked concerned, and there was a feeling of impending battle in the air.

As Alter grudgingly followed Xiao toward a distant city wall, she said, "You fall back on old habits when you're startled. I understand that. However, you must learn to see the big picture if you are to serve the world as the first leader in the history of all mankind to establish a lasting dynasty of real peace."

"How can you suggest I want to rule the world?" Alter demanded, still thunderstruck by her suggestion. How could her diabolical plan center on supporting *him* in rising to power?

"You recognize the world wallows under corruption, suffers under evil leadership, and endures unnecessary hardship because of war, famine, and hatred?"

"Of course. Those problems have always existed."

"But why?" she asked, pausing for a moment to hold him with a steady gaze.

Alter shrugged. "It's just the way things are."

That answer clearly did not satisfy her, and it sounded weak even to him. They resumed walking toward the wall, passing through a district of close-packed, stone buildings that appeared to house wealthy shops. He barely noticed as he considered the question.

Eventually he said, "It is the nature of mankind to be imperfect. Too many lust for power and riches, but fall to pride, selfishness, and greed."

"Indeed. Yet there have been successful dynasties and empires at various times. Why did they all fall?"

She spoke in a teaching voice and sounded a lot like his father. He found it immensely annoying, but like his father, she would probably grow cross if he did not pay attention to the lesson she sought to teach. He couldn't risk angering her yet.

So Alter thought about what he knew of history. The great empires of Egypt, Rome, the Ottomans, European powers, and finally America. He knew too little of Chinese or Egyptian history, but they had both enjoyed tremendous prosperity for centuries under some dynasties.

All but the most recent empires had all collapsed. Given time, no doubt the current world powers would also stumble and fall. It was kind of depressing when he thought about it.

Xiao seemed content to wait for his answer. They reached the high city wall and ascended a set of stone steps to the top. The parapet atop the wall was crowded with soldiers, but Xiao moved through them unseen. She aimed for a delegation of officers, flanking a man who had to be a king. He wore no crown, but his rich dress and the subservient manner of everyone else clearly declared it.

Xiao nodded toward the leader and said, "That would be King Muwatalli the Second of the Hittites."

She then pushed to the front ranks, where they got a great view of nearby lands between the city and a wide river. Thousands of troops massed near the city, standing in formation, despite a fierce battle raging half a mile away, on the nearest bank of the river. Another, smaller army, which looked Egyptian with their light chariots and sickle-shaped swords, were fighting with more Hittites.

The Hittites were losing, even though they outnumbered the Egyptians. Alter studied the battlefield, his pulse quickening at the sight of armed conflict. Then his gaze narrowed as he spotted the leader of the Egyptians and the man's guards. Tiny in the distance, he still clearly recognized that they were fighting with enhanced speed and strength.

He whispered, "Kashaph."

Xiao too was watching the battle with a critical eye. "Ramses did not possess enough rune-enhanced troops to gain a decisive victory, but he avoided the defeat due him this day. King Muwatalli lacked any enhanced troops, which is why he did not send in the reinforcements that would have otherwise secured his victory."

"Why are we here?" Alter asked.

"This was an important moment of the ancient world, one worth visiting until I can glean better moments from Sutekh. I hope to find a master rune, since this battle set the stage for all future interactions between these nations until the Hittites fell."

Alter clenched his hands in anger, tempted to strike, despite the futility of such open opposition. "I thought you had enough master runes."

"None have yet revealed my true name. Now stop stalling. You never answered my question about why great dynasties fall."

Still fuming at his impotence, Alter shrugged. "Some were conquered."

"Not the greatest. They might have been conquered at the last, but that was not what brought about their downfall."

"Internal strife and corruption, probably," he offered after another moment's thought, his eyes drawn back to the battle still raging along the river. They stood too far away to hear much but a distant rumbling of battle noise. He couldn't smell the blood or fear, but he could see enough.

She smiled approval. "Correct. Most of mankind don't live long enough to overcome the frailties of their condition or learn to control their baser lusts and self-destructive tendencies. Even the great dynasties cannot endure because rising generations that inherit power lack the vision of their forebears and succumb to all the common vices."

"So you think only one who can live many lives has a chance of establishing lasting rule."

"And lasting peace. I am gratified to see you understand. Even many powerful souls like yours fail to grasp deeper truths in their first life. You'll make a fine ruler."

That idea still shocked him. It also terrified him. "I don't want to rule the world. What gave you the idea that I would?"

She gave him an understanding look. "Duty is sometimes a hard burden. You possess a unique gift and a mighty soul. You have been schooled in discipline and honor, and you are not swayed by the base vices that claim so many. Would you condemn multitudes to suffering and death when you could spare them?"

She gestured at the struggling armies. "Would you entrust rule to lesser beings like those who fight for useless causes?"

"You're twisting things," he said, but in his heart he was struggling to maintain his hatred for her.

She had said nothing of the type of tyrannical rule that Paul had sought. She was right about the problems facing the world. He could agree to all of that. Her proposed solution was the problem. Conquering everyone seemed a poor way to begin her lauded peaceful reign.

"Of course you can't rule alone," Xiao continued, undeterred. "I believe Sarah would be the best partner for you."

"What?" he exclaimed, astonished again by her insight, and horrified by how the idea latched onto his mind. He loved Sarah with a passion that only seemed to grow hotter the more he tried to suppress it.

Xiao continued in that calm, rational tone. "She's the perfect choice. She is a mighty soul, and she'll easily sway much of the world to your favor with her simple charm and bravery. Perhaps the death of my son will serve a better purpose after all, since by falling to Sarah, he may have opened the pathway to your rise to power."

Alter was still distracted by images of himself with Sarah, and struggled to process Xiao's cold analysis of her son's demise. "You don't sound like a grieving mother to me."

"I mourn the loss of my son," Xiao assured him, showing a glimpse of sadness. "But I cannot allow personal loss to distract me from my purpose. Too many souls depend upon our success."

"You know how to bait people," Alter acknowledged. "But Sarah is not yours to give, and she already has a boyfriend."

"Everything I have learned about Tomas confirms that he is an honorable man, but duty for Sarah and for Tomas is just as unyielding as it is for you and for me. Sarah cares for you, and she will come to understand that it is a small sacrifice to make for the greater good."

"I doubt Tomas would agree."

Xiao shrugged. "He is a leader of men. He understands duty. If not, I will deal with him."

Alter shook himself, breaking free of the spell her words were weaving into his heart. He couldn't believe he was actually considering her insane proposal. He didn't want to conquer the world, didn't believe that was the best way to help people.

"I won't force Sarah to make such a choice," he declared, crushing the dark little part of his heart that was tempted to consider it.

Xiao considered him for a moment before responding. "I still believe she would make an ideal partner for you. However, she is not the only choice."

Alter couldn't help it. He ran through his mind all the women he knew who could match Sarah in any way. He didn't come up with any.

When he didn't speak, Xiao added. "I'm sure you've made the connection. I may not yet fill your heart with desire like Sarah does, but together we could become an unrivaled partnership, perfect for the duty we must embrace."

Alter gaped at her, momentarily at a loss for words. His first instinct was to summon a Gatling gun. That seemed like the wrong response to a woman who had just propositioned him, didn't it?

Noting his astonishment, Xiao gave him a warm smile and patted his arm. "You flatter me, Alter. I may be powerful, but I am no better than you. I honestly believe you must become the face of our dynasty for this to work. I will play the part of your adoring, supportive wife."

"I don't . . . I mean, how . . . ?" Alter stammered.

He had almost no experience with women. Despite a few crushes that had resulted in nothing but some awkward kisses, he had always been too busy training and hunting kashaph to fall in love. Then Sarah had stormed into his life and stolen his heart. He had absolutely no idea how to respond to Xiao.

She took his hand in hers. She might look slender and willowy, but her grip was like an inescapable, if pleasant, vise. "I'll take whatever form suits your interest, my dear. I guarantee I can please you beyond your wildest dreams. In early lives, I worked among the Yakuza and mastered the art of physical love." She actually winked.

Alter recoiled, disturbed more by her attempt to appear flirtatious than by her threats to rip out his soul. She allowed him to slip his hand free of hers.

"I appreciate the offer, really," he said, furious at himself to feel a flush of embarrassment creep into his cheeks. "But are you insane?"

Her smile faded, changing to a look of reproach. "Are you rejecting the singular destiny just revealed to you?"

He hated that he couldn't fight her, couldn't rip that condescending smile off her lips. Always in the past his strength had been sufficient to confront kashaph head on. These mind games and attempts to ferret out a weakness he could exploit against her exhausted and infuriated him.

"I don't believe that's the only way to find peace," he managed.

"Trust me."

Alter barked an incredulous laugh, but she continued. "I've studied this for centuries. I've supported one dynasty after another, but they've all failed!"

Her voice rose in intensity and he could read her honest frustration. "They cannot learn. They refuse to see reason or to understand! The only way to solve the world problems is to step out of the shadows and take over, to show them the way and discipline those who refuse to behave."

"Your way sounds like slavery," Alter retorted, regaining his composure. "Freedom has inherent risks, but it's better than safety in chains."

"The world will be free," Xiao insisted.

"I don't see it that way."

She regained her composure with some difficulty, and Alter filed that bit of information away. When the time came, perhaps he could goad her into rage and foolish mistakes by challenging her insane plan.

"We will speak of this more," she told him with forced calm. "You will come to see the truth."

"And if I don't?" he couldn't help but prod.

"Duty is unyielding," she declared, her expression turning stern. "It requires one to rule. If you refuse to see reason, I may be forced to take your nevra core and use it to bring forth one mighty enough to succeed."

There it was, the threat of deadly violence that always lurked under her grand claims of peace and freedom.

They had already suspected she'd discovered the secret to control the transfer of a nevra core to its next host. Of course, it would take years for a newborn to grow until they could fill their role. Would his sacrifice grant the world another decade or two of freedom from her rule?

What if she could somehow transfer his nevra core to another adult? He didn't think that was possible, but until she had started producing cui dashi at will, everyone would have insisted that was impossible too.

What if she could harvest his nevra core without killing him? He could be free of the curse that tainted his blood and dishonored his family. The thought was immensely tempting.

Then again, who would she bequeath his demon powers to? Would they accept her rule? Would they be evil like Paul? If so, the act of freeing himself from his curse would condemn the world to slavery under Xiao.

She studied him, her expression calm and unreadable, tiny points of lavender fire in the center of each eye. "Consider my offer. There is still a little time to decide. For now, let us enjoy the moment." She gestured toward the battle again.

The Egyptians had clearly defeated the Hittite forces committed to the battle, casting many of the enemy soldiers into the river to drown. Instead of advancing against the city in a hopeless suicide charge, the pharaoh led his troops away to the southwest, bloody sword raised in victory.

Then everything stopped. Everyone around them froze. All sound and movement ceased as absolute stillness settled over the memoryscape. Alter's eyes were drawn into the sky where an enormous rune blazed into golden light.

The master rune burned itself into Alter's soul, and he barely breathed as he drank it in. It consumed his senses and shook his soul to the roots. He sensed it was not the greatest of the master runes, but even a lesser master rune contained shocking amounts of power. It somehow triggered the warm scent of challah bread, the long-lost sound of his mother's cherished laughter, and the taste of Sarah's lips against his own.

Alter eagerly savored that sensation, focusing on the many memories of Sarah, whose beautiful face came easily to mind. Xiao interrupted him, turning abruptly away from the sight of the master rune, bumping his shoulder and knocking him out of his reverie.

She glanced at him, looking somehow disgusted instead of impressed by the vision they'd just witnessed. "Another waste. That one offers nothing of value to me." She glared at him. "Were you not focused on honor and truth?"

"I always focus on that."

She sighed, sounding exasperated. "This moment lacked those truths in sufficient abundance. It showed nothing but domination and intolerance."

"Isn't that what you're after, dominating the world?"

She actually stomped a foot in annoyance, cracking the stone underfoot. "Have you not listened to anything I've said? I seek to free the world."

"By dominating everyone," he pointed out.

She glared, and her eyes burst into fire. "I will end oppression and destruction. I will remove all obstacles to your rule so you can establish real lasting freedom, real justice, and lingering honor. Why is it that you refuse to help me create a better future?"

"I want a better future too!"

"Then help me."

"Destroying everything in order to start over isn't a solution," he retorted.

"Then tell me a better way," she said with infuriating calm, once more composed. "If you can illuminate my understanding, show me how to transform the world, I will join you."

That made him pause. Would she really abandon her designs? He really would love to help improve the world and remove the wickedness so prevalent. The problem was, he didn't have the answer. He doubted anyone did. The world was full of imperfect people.

Her words whispered into his mind, insisting that the world

included people mighty enough to make the changes no one else could. He turned away, hating how she twisted things beyond recognition, hating even more the fact that he could see her reasoning. Was he evil to want to fix the world, to be tempted to use his unique abilities to help billions of other people achieve better lives?

"I need some time to think," he told her.

"The first intelligent thing you've said today." She smiled and made a shooing gesture. "I will wait for you here. Take what time you need, my dear Alter. Visit any memory that will help you find truth."

He stomped away, resenting her more for being so accommodating. He leaped off the wall, then pushed roughly through the crowds below. They ignored him. Then he stopped in front of a tall, white-painted building that had the look of a temple, struck by a crazy idea.

He knew where he needed to go.

45

Am I vain and shallow because I worry about my body? Sure, I'm young and fit, but I'm different than I used to be. Am I foolish because I worry what people will think when they know?

~SARAH

ALTER STOOD on the roof of his family compound in Jerusalem, looking down on the most cherished place he knew. He hadn't consciously picked that particular memory, and the movement of his family below looked like any other day. The sight of them all made him deeply homesick.

He jumped off the roof. The four-story fall was easy to manage in the memoryscape. For a moment, he soaked in the feel of home and the sight of beloved family and friends who he had not seen in weeks. Some of them had died in the heka assault on the compound, and he felt a rush of tender emotion to see them looking so vibrant and happy.

He melded more deeply with the memory, living again that moment as he crossed the courtyard. Everyone greeted him warmly, but they were seeing a younger Alter, and the disconnect with reality only saddened him, so he drew back just a bit so he could watch the moment, but not live it.

If he returned home today, they would look upon him with horror, seeing not his purity of soul or his determination to stay true to the tenets of their cause. They would see one fallen to disgrace, defiled by demons, one worthy only of death.

He was tempted to return to a much older memory and see his mother again. If only he could really speak with her, ask her advice. Most of the compassion in his life had left with her, leaving him to focus on training and eradicating kashaph. It was all he'd known, and he was good at it.

As he wandered the halls, he considered the cui dashi he seemed to be serving, despite his resistance. He wished he knew how she planned to launch her assault on the world. That might give him an idea how to fight back or thwart her plans.

He needed Sarah and Eirene. He hated to admit it, but he needed Gregorios too, and Tomas and the mighty Tenth. He really needed his father and the strength of the hunters united, but he couldn't imagine how to make that happen.

Alone, he could not stop her, but he couldn't stop trying. If he relented even for a moment, she might persuade him through her twisted words to assist in her mad scheme.

Alter snarled and punched a stone wall of a nearby building. A large section shattered, but the pain in his hand didn't help clear his head. In that distracted state, he entered his father's comfortable study. On the wall above the fireplace, in a place of honor, hung the soulmask of his brother, Reuben.

That confirmed that he'd returned to a date prior to ever meeting Gregorios, a day before his life had gotten so completely turned upside down. Alter approached, considering the shimmering mask with its tendrils of rainbow smoke floating about it like a living halo.

"Brother, sometimes I envy you," he whispered, sliding a finger along Reuben's cheek. "At least you never had any doubts."

"Don't touch me," Reuben cried, his whisper-voice shrill. "You're defiled."

Alter snatched his hand back, filled with renewed frustration. Even in a memory he couldn't escape his fate. Would he never find acceptance anywhere?

He started to turn away, but paused. This was a memory from several years ago, but at that time, Reuben hadn't known about his tainted blood.

"Why did you call me that?" Alter asked, prodding Reuben's rigid forehead.

Reuben again shouted in his helium-high whisper voice, "I said don't touch me. You defiled us both by using your demon powers to unman me."

"I haven't done that yet."

"Of course you have. Just because we're both remembering doesn't mean it's not real."

"Whoa!" Alter leaned close, a flicker of hope lighting the darkness of his heart. "Are you saying you're memory walking my memory?"

"What else do I have to do?" Reuben asked, his whisper-voice filled with venom. "You returned me to the wall, so I can't spend time anywhere but in my head."

"Will you remember what we talk about when you wake up?" Alter asked.

"Get away from me. Let me remember in peace."

Alter flicked Reuben's cheek with a finger. "No. Listen to me, Reuben. This is important!"

"I said leave me alone. You wrecked my life. Don't torture me."

Even though those words tore at his heart, Alter refused to relent. The beginnings of a wild plan were forming in his mind. "It wasn't me. Don't you remember? Paul corrupted you with a rune, broke your will and sent you to kill our cousins."

Reuben started to laugh. "You're as insane as I, brother. You share my fever dreams."

"That wasn't the dream," Alter said, wanting to beat Reuben out of pure frustration. His one possible link to the real world was the broken mind of a dispossessed soul.

Reuben's laughter faded. "Life is but a dream. Memory, time, none of it is real."

"What if I told you I could restore your body?"

That broke through Reuben's delirium. "Do it." Desperation set his voice quivering.

"I will. I'll set you free, but first you have to help me escape."

"Wake up. It's simple, but I can't do that for you."

"Listen." Alter leaned close, his mind racing. "I'm being held captive by Paul's mother."

"Is she nice?"

"No! She's cui dashi like Paul, only worse."

"Destroy her, brother. It's what we do."

"She's too strong. I need help."

"You always were disappointing."

That wasn't helpful, but he decided to try another approach. "Together we can destroy her."

"How?" Reuben sounded interested again.

"I need you to wake up. Get father's attention in the real world and pass a message to him."

"Father's gone," Reuben said, closing his eyes. "He went looking for you."

"What? When?" Alter snatched Reuben's soulmask off the wall.

If his father showed up in Rome now and found him gone, what would he think? Would he blame Gregorios? The last thing they needed was renewed war between the facetakers and the hunters.

"Put me down, demon," Reuben demanded.

"Not until you agree." Alter didn't dare activate his nevra core while strapped to the machine. That would certainly draw Xiao's attention, but he was tempted.

"You promise to set me free."

"Yes. I swear. Together we can defeat her. Her name is Xiao."

"That's not a name, that's a title."

"I know, but it's all I've got so far. Get someone's attention. Tell them I'm trapped. Xiao is hunting history for master runes to use to build a new name."

"Abomination!" Reuben shouted, finally sounding like himself.

"She also has some kind of plan to set up a new world order."

"Typical."

"Not really. She seems to think she can establish a ruling dynasty to bring world peace and harmony."

"Her mind is broken. Trust me, I know about that. Destroy her, brother."

Alter suppressed a flash of annoyance. "If you'll get me some help, I plan to. I'll try learning more and see if I can pass information to you."

"Just kill her."

"Soon. When you're whole."

Alter returned Reuben's soulmask to the wall. "You'll do it, won't you?"

"What else have I got to do?"

"Thank you."

Alter left the room, loving the feeling of renewed hope. Trusting Reuben might be a long shot, but it was better than nothing. With help, he could find a way to defeat Xiao and prove to Sarah and his family that he was worthy of their respect.

If he couldn't get help, he worried Xiao might force him to do her bidding. If she forced Sarah upon him, he wasn't sure he could resist.

Would he even want to resist?

46

~EGYPTIAN PROVERB

SARAH DECIDED that owning a super yacht might be even better than owning a mansion. Well, it might be if life ever quieted down enough for her to pursue such frivolous things.

She stood on the aft pool deck on the seventh level of the most beautiful yacht she'd ever seen. Owned by the Swiss billionaire Leandro Blickensderfer, the sleek, silver and black vessel sported two pools, four gorgeous salons, two conference rooms, and over a dozen expansive guest suites.

She hadn't realized privately-owned boats could get so big. *Second Chances* stretched over six hundred feet long and more than eighty feet wide. It was like a younger sibling to a cruise ship, and she couldn't think of a classier way to slip away from Italy.

Tomas joined her outside. He had left his normal tactical wear in his cabin and sported a swim suit, sandals, and a t-shirt. She grinned and moved to meet him, giving him a lingering kiss.

"You look good," she said, loving the feel of his powerful arms around her.

"You're one to talk," he said, glancing down at the deep blue, tankini she wore. It really set off her toned young body. The fuchsia sarong she wore around her waist added a bright, tropical flair.

She felt a shiver of delight to see him so openly admiring her. Although he had never shown even a hint of regret that her gorgeous, top model first-life body had died, she still sometimes wondered if he ever found her new form less pleasing.

She didn't doubt any more.

Sarah kissed him again and he responded with abundant passion. After a moment, she sighed and leaned against him, tracing his muscular pecks through his shirt. It felt good to get a moment of peace.

She hadn't felt nearly enough of that lately, especially after Vlad's attack. The vampire had tried reasserting control over her several times since their flight from San Marino. She'd felt his voice, like chill whispers in her ears, but the words had been so faint, she could easily ignore his vile promises of endless, torturous servitude.

The protective rune she had developed with Melek seemed to be keeping Vlad at bay, and Sarah had reinforced it with a secondary rune to boost its power. The cipher that drew strength from pilgrims to her shrines in Rome was still functioning, so for the moment she felt safe, but she planned to discuss in detail with Tomas the best way to destroy the creature the next time they met.

"I love the sea," Tomas said softly, gazing out at the wide horizon beyond the stern of the boat.

"We'll have to borrow one of Gregorios' yachts and sail for a while." A nice, quiet vacation at sea sounded wonderful.

Tomas nodded, smiling. "He's got some nice ones, although Leandro's setup is pretty sweet."

"A little better than that," Sarah agreed.

Off the starboard side of the boat, she caught glimpses of the mountains above Sardinia sliding slowly past as the yacht powered south through the gently rolling waves of the Tyrrhenian Sea. Italy lay beyond the wide, blue horizon on the opposite side. She had never heard of the Tyrrhenian Sea, which hugged the west coast of Italy, but she loved it.

Their course would take them south, through the narrow strait between Carthage on the African side, and Palermo on the very tip of the Italian boot. There they'd enter the wider Mediterranean and head east. After the failed peace accord with Xiao, they'd decided to leave San Marino and Italy altogether.

Eirene had insisted Xiao had to be bluffing about knowing their personal assets, but they had decided not to risk heading for an airport or putting to sea in one of their own boats. They had still scheduled dozens of flights of Suntara-owned planes, along with a few of their own, and ordered several yachts to set sail. Hopefully all the activity would mask their real movements from any agents Xiao might have watching.

That left the question of how to make good their escape.

Gregorios came up with the answer and called Leandro, who owed them a favor. He'd been close enough to Italy on his super yacht to meet them off the coast of Livorno.

With how many things had been going badly, hitching that ride was a welcome dash of good luck. They'd sent Anaru and most of the Tenth north to slip into Switzerland and connect with other units in a secret staging area in the Alps. Then they had flown out to the yacht on Leandro's helicopter.

"So, why Malta?" Sarah asked after a few quiet minutes. The tiny island nation just south of Italy still played an important role in international shipping, as it had for centuries, but there had to be more.

"It won't be a primary search target on anyone's radar. But from there we can travel to a lot of places pretty easily. Plus, we have a lot of support in Malta."

"Gregorios and Eirene don't own another country, do they?" Sarah asked.

He nodded. "Most of the citizens there have no idea."

"Do you own any countries that I need to know about?" she teased.

"I haven't lived nearly long enough. After over two thousand years, I think it's a little surprising they only own a few of the smallest ones."

"Like which ones?"

"I haven't looked at the list in a while. I'll dig it up when we get a chance. I know they've looked into Liechtenstein, but that sale fell through. Obstinate bunch."

"That's the tiny country near Switzerland that the guy in *Knight's Tale* was supposed to be from, right?" She loved that movie.

Tomas nodded. "Beautiful, remote country, but it's right on the Rhine River, so it's got access all the way out to the North Sea. It would be a good spot to own. I wouldn't be surprised if they tried again some day to make a bid for it."

"You should get in on that deal, if they do," Sarah suggested. She'd planned to buy a nice mansion like Quentin's, but owning an entire country was a whole other level of amazingness.

The sliding glass door from the main salon opened and Leandro stepped out with his fiancé, a striking Greek beauty named Chrysa. The tall woman, with luxurious black hair, big sea-green eyes, and olive skin, smiled as much as he did. The two seemed deeply in love and ridiculously happy together.

"I see you've found the best spot on the boat," Leandro said with a cheery smile.

The billionaire looked good for an old guy, with a deep tan on his young, second-life skin and a constant sparkle in his eyes.

It felt good to see him happy. Sarah had arranged for him to swap his aged body with Walter, who had been stuck in a strong young body after the collapse of Alterego. Walter had longed to return to an older form that better matched his aging wife. Leandro had been all too happy to oblige, and the swap had benefited both of them. If only more body transfers could result in such win-win scenarios.

Sarah smiled and admitted, "I love it here. I could get used to living like this."

"You are my guests for as long as you like," Leandro said immediately.

Chrysa added in her warm voice, "After what you did for dear Leandro, we are forever in your debt."

"I'd say we're pretty even after this," Sarah said.

She had secretly worried that Chrysa would react badly to the truth about Leandro's age, but she'd handled it exceptionally well. The previous night, while the ladies were all soaking in one of the five jacuzzis, Chrysa had confided, "I thought there was more to him. He has the energy of a young man, but he knows how to treat a woman. Such skill is only acquired over a lifetime."

Sarah liked Chrysa immensely. Under her beautiful exterior, she possessed a sharp mind and compassionate soul. She served as the CEO of a major charitable organization and was distantly related to the Greek billionaire, John Paul Jones Dejoria.

It was nice to meet people outside of the shadowy world of facetakers who could accept Sarah and her companions for who they were. Most of the world was not so gracious when they learned the truth.

Somehow Xiao had made good her threat to take the war to Gregorios and his family. Reports were already pouring in about several nations that were moving with unprecedented speed to seize facetaker assets and to declare Suntara a terrorist organization. Eirene was working with every resource she could bring to bear, trying to figure out how Xiao was manipulating the world against them.

Francesca, who had met them in Livorno, stuck her head out the door and beckoned. "Dad wants you to see this."

"Another news flash," Sarah guessed, not eager to see more bad news.

"It's important to know what's going on," Tomas said as they all headed for the door into the main salon.

"I'm glad you have so many TVs," Sarah told Leandro.

"The world is a puzzle right now," he said, gesturing her through first. "I don't understand the hostility after all the good you've done."

"It's complicated," Gregorios said from the leather couch in the center of the salon where he sat facing four large, flat panel televisions that had been set up in a row. Each one was tuned to a different news agency.

"What's the latest?" Sarah asked as she settled onto the couch beside him.

"Nothing good."

"More assets gone?" Tomas asked, taking a padded chair near Sarah.

More and more of the Suntara assets were getting confiscated in various countries. Still, the council owned many subsidiaries and investments that dated back so far, they were nearly impossible to track. The group had already suffered hundreds of millions of dollars in losses. Despite Xiao's threats, at least the financial assault didn't seem to have extended to assets owned by Gregorios and Eirene.

Gregorios pointed at the TVs. "Worse. It's like every political leader in the world took a long drink of stupid potion this morning."

Chrysa laughed, but when no one else joined in, her smile faded and she said, "You're acting like that's possible."

"It's unlikely," Gregorios admitted. "Although Sarah could probably whip up a cipher-draught to do the trick if we really felt it necessary."

Sarah shrugged. "I can't see why. People are pretty dumb without needing a push from me."

It felt weird speaking openly about their abilities with non-enhanced people, but Leandro and Chrysa knew the truth. He had recognized Sarah immediately and had gushed over her heroism fighting Paul. Chrysa had treated her like a superstar at first. She'd gotten over it quickly, and the two of them were becoming good friends.

"The idea of a love potion could be fun." Francesca said from where she sat beside Spartacus on another couch.

The two had spent a lot of time together on the boat, discussing Xiao's enchanter, Hongwu. Spartacus was eager to track the man down and finish the duel. Francesca had pointed out that capturing such a high-level member of Xiao's organization might help lead them to her. Even if it didn't, removing him would surely deal Xiao a major blow.

"Probably not a good idea," Sarah said. She didn't want to encourage Francesca's flirtations.

The youthful facetaker grinned. "You never know. Of course, you'd have to test it out first, maybe see what it might do to encourage a hesitant someone to make a move, eh?" She gave Tomas a wicked grin.

He made a point of ignoring her, and asked Spartacus, "Speaking of Hongwu, do you have any idea why he was so upset when you took that pendant in San Marino?"

Sarah had been so distracted by Vlad that she'd forgotten all about that.

Spartacus pulled the gold pendant from a pocket and held it up. "I thought nothing more of this prize since that unfinished duel ended with untimely speed. I carry it as a trophy of war, but perchance he but lamented the loss of its protective runes."

Francesca took the pendant from Spartacus and examined it for a few seconds. She shrugged. "It's really nothing special."

Tomas insisted, "He definitely hated losing it. There's got to be more to it than we realize."

Spartacus took it back. "Methinks you speak truth, Captain of Honor. Hongwu and his allies have proven their cowardly reliance upon deceit and obscuring illusion. Perchance this too encourages obscurity of the senses."

He pulled a sharpie from his pocket and marked a rune across the pendant. Sarah leaned closer and recognized the mark as a rune of revealing. Alter had shown it to her, but she'd never actually used it.

Spartacus added a twin rune to his left forearm to power the runes from his rounon, and focused over it. The rune on his arm began to glow, followed a second later by the rune on the pendant.

Sarah rose and stepped closer, interested in watching the difference between how Spartacus fueled his runes and how she activated her ciphers. He was limited to the force of his own rounon, but the process of activating the runes seemed similar.

The silvery-blue light of the rune crept over the pendant, clinging to the surface. After several seconds, the glow faded, but the pendant didn't look any different.

Francesca patted Spartacus' thigh. "Good try, big guy."

He shrugged and turned over the pendant. His face lit with a smile and he pointed at a new rune, now visible, engraved into the gold pendant. "Thus does the force of my rounon dispel darkness and deceit."

Sarah leaned closer, studying the rune. It was a complex design, built around the three interconnecting loops of the triquetra. A seven-pointed star nestled within those loops, the points touching the edges. A crescent moon was set in the left-hand loop, the Dharma wheel filled the center of the star, and above that stood the Ophiuchus symbol, like a "U" with a tilde through the middle.

The entire construct was wrapped within the crab-like arms of the Egyptian ka symbol for the soul. It was complex and beautiful, and powerful.

Francesca whistled softly and gave Spartacus a kiss on the cheek. "Well done."

He grinned at her. "The kiss of a battle maiden of such grand renown is the greatest boon a warrior could hope to receive for such a simple act."

"Keep talking like that, and maybe I'll help you figure out how to get another one," she said with a wink.

"I don't know this one," Tomas said as the rest of them gathered around to study the rune. Sarah extracted her phone and took a photo so she could study it later.

She said, "I'm not sure, but it's powerful and ancient. I haven't seen anything quite like it."

"It is not used in battle runes that I have ever seen," Spartacus said.

"It has to be important, though," Gregorios said.

Sarah nodded. "I agree. It must be why Hongwu didn't want to lose this pendant. I'll review it with Melek and see what we can figure out."

"Good. Keep us informed. In the meantime, we have to deal with the insanity of the world's leaders," Gregorios said.

"What are the politicians doing now?" Tomas asked.

"Insanity," Eirene said, entering the salon from the lower deck and sitting on the other side of Gregorios. In that Amazon body, wearing a bikini, she looked like a goddess from legend.

Even though he'd lived so many lives with her, Gregorios paused to admire his wife and give her a roguish smile before pointing toward one TV, showing yet another press conference. Sarah was interested to note the official speaking looked Chinese.

Gregorios kept the sound muted. "Right now it's just a bunch of idiot journalist talking heads trying to analyze the insanity. The Chinese just denounced Thailand."

The screen changed, showing a picture of the current president of Thailand, then his recently-deceased father, followed by a photo of the new crown prince.

Eirene grimaced. "That's horrible timing."

"They figured it out," Sarah breathed, not sure what the ramifications might be, but suspecting they couldn't be good.

Leandro looked to Sarah. "Did you all give the king of Thailand a new life as his own grandson?"

Eirene said, "We were supposed to, but it got complicated."

Paul had attacked facetaker powers with an insidious forbidden rune that somehow turned their own nevra cores against them. While the group had reeled under the unprecedented assault, he had slipped into Thailand and completed the transfer, stealing the contract from Eirene and gaining leverage over the nation.

"I still don't get why Paul made them get all belligerent against China," Sarah said.

Gregorios said, "Xiao's pushing even harder. Their rhetoric has been heating up over the past couple of days, but now with this announcement, China is trying to flip the game."

Eirene grimaced. "With the witch hunt against facetakers, that gives them a huge stick to beat them back down."

"Hold on," Gregorios interrupted, unmuting another television. "What's going on here?"

The screen showed a UN meeting of the committee exploring rune enhancements. After the sensational news they'd revealed to the world about the facetakers, the committee was enjoying unprecedented coverage. The U.S. ambassador was again speaking.

Eirene scowled at the image of the man. "I'm fond of Americans in general, but that fellow is proving downright unpleasant."

The ambassador said, "One aspect of our research into the potential benefit of performance-enhancing runes not yet examined by this committee is the very real danger of abuse and misuse of this power. In fact, what I am about to show you confirms that some nations have been leveraging the evil potential of runes for some time."

He looked into the camera and declared, "In particular, China is guilty of mass murder to gather souls to feed a complex array of advanced rune webs designed and maintained to prop up the communist government and boost national output so they could compete with other world powers."

The council chamber erupted into shouted protests by the Chinese delegation and many of their closest allies, but the American ambassador spoke over them. "You are guilty, but today you will be held accountable. Your long history of human rights abuses served to cover up the systemic culling of your own population to gather souls to sacrifice to this dastardly evil!"

A large screen behind the ambassador flicked on, displaying images of a huge cavern. A mazelike framework of low scaffolding spread across the vast floor. Dozens of Chinese workers scurried across the scaffolding, while underneath glowed the unmistakable sight of the biggest rune web Sarah had ever seen.

Eirene whistled softly. "By all the broken gods, can it be true?"

Paul had leveraged huge rune webs, consisting of hundreds of souls, and Tomas had said those were some of the most complex he'd ever seen. The rune web on the screen looked to be several times bigger.

Spartacus rose and leaned closer to the television. "They have harvested enough souls to empty an arena, but I cannot read the full scope of the purpose."

Sarah couldn't either, but she felt sick just looking at it, thinking of the thousands of souls sacrificed to power that web. "We'll have to get Melek up here and review the recording. Is there any way to get an enlarged view?"

The ambassador pointed at the screen. "I will share additional images that prove China's guilt. They are trafficking in human souls and committing atrocities on an unprecedented scale."

After that, the meeting degenerated into shouting and name calling, culminating in the angry departure of the Chinese delegation.

Gregorios muted the television again, and Tomas said, "Those two announcements are like political nukes. It's going to shake up everything."

"We'll watch developments," Gregorios said, his expression grave. "Let's have Harald's team focus on analyzing the political fall-out."

Eirene nodded. "I bet you a small country that there'll be even more coming."

"What do you mean?" Sarah asked, distracted by the thought of which nation Eirene planned to bet.

Eirene looked grim. "Xiao warned you all that war was coming, and that the world was heading for self-destruction. This is too much of a coincidence. Maybe the Chinese just happened to figure out about the Thailand transfer, but there's no way the Americans would gain access to all that incriminating information about China's rune webs without inside help."

"You think Xiao is feeding both sides?" Sarah asked. How could Xiao control so many things? The thought reinforced the fact that they were operating so many moves behind the hated woman.

Gregorios said, "Makes sense. If she can keep stirring the pot, she could trigger global conflict."

"What better way to justify establishing a new regime than to knock the current world order into chaos?" Tomas asked, sounding far too calm. The idea of worldwide warfare made Sarah feel sick.

"You will stop her, won't you?" Chrysa asked, her eyes bigger than ever as she considered the dire news.

"We plan to," Eirene told her.

"What can we do to help?" she asked.

"Get us to Malta," Francesca said.

"And maybe dig up a few more of those little sandwiches we had earlier. Those were delicious," Gregorios added.

Eirene slapped him lightly on the back of the head, but she was smiling. "You're incorrigible."

Chrysa smiled. "I'll get the cook working on it immediately."

She left, followed by Leandro.

Sarah blew out a breath, scanning the somber group. "How are we going to stop Xiao? We don't know where to find her, and we don't know how she's pulling all the political strings."

They considered the question for a moment. Eirene spoke first. "We have the machines. As soon as we get them unpacked in Malta, it'll be time to hunt Xiao again. Maybe we can learn something about what she's searching for in the memoryscape."

"Or something about Alter," Sarah added.

Tomas said, "Or something, period. Anything would be better than what we have now."

"Agreed," Gregorios said, gesturing to a staff member who entered, carrying a huge tray piled high with little sandwiches. "But today we focus on regaining our strength."

47

MALTA TURNED out to be more densely populated than Sarah had expected. She surveyed the cityscape of Valletta, the Maltese capital, from the window of a spacious suite she'd been assigned in an upscale hotel.

It felt more like an older version of New York than an island paradise. Still, the views were fantastic. The fort of St. Elmo was a few blocks to the northeast, and she enjoyed an excellent view of St. Elmo Bay and Marsamxett Harbour.

She hoped to find time to explore the area with Tomas, but doubted it would be easy to slip away. The machines should be ready for their memory hunt soon, and who knew where that would lead them?

She fingered the crossbow bolt Quentin had gifted to her. His words had haunted her, and she'd taken to holding the bolt as she considered how best to breach Xiao's overwhelming strength.

She had begun teasing out a new rune along the bolt's length, but it was still only a half-formed sequence of symbols that she felt had to be included. Working on it helped settle her mind when she started worrying.

The bolt would have to wait, though. She dropped it on her bedside table, then headed for the penthouse suite that Gregorios and Eirene shared. The machines had been set up there, and their people occupied the entire top two floors of the high-rise hotel. Only those with special key cards could access those floors by elevator, and Tomas had posted additional guards and security measures in and around the building.

Then he'd explained, "The best security is keeping a low profile. No one knows we're here. As long as that continues, we'll be fine."

Tomas answered the door to the penthouse when Sarah knocked, and ushered her past the two enforcer guards. She gave him a kiss in the entry salon and lingered in his embrace for a minute.

"You know, I'm feeling pretty well established in this body," she said, giving him an inviting grin. "And I don't think you're ever going to get yours back from Spartacus, are you?"

He shook his head with a grimace. "I doubt it."

"How do you feel about that?"

Tomas shrugged, his expression hard to read. "I've lived in enough that I'm not bothered too much, but the important question is, how do you feel about that?"

She slid one hand across his well-muscled chest and down one firm bicep. She smiled to see the spark of desire grow in his eyes. "I think your current suit will do nicely."

She gave him another kiss, pressing against him to make sure he got the message. "But I might have to really check it out before telling for sure."

Tomas' face reddened, but before he could try stammering another excuse, she kissed him, quick and hard. "Relax, my love. Just teasing my slow-moving partner."

"When this is over, we'll have time to move faster."

She liked the sound of that. His strict, rather old-fashioned moral code had frustrated her when they first started dating. She did appreciate the space he'd allowed her to get comfortable in her new life. She'd been surprised to realize that by waiting for the physical intimacy, her love for Tomas was growing deeper, becoming something special and worth taking the time to nurture.

"So what's going on today?" she asked in a lighter tone, slipping under his arm to walk with him as he led the way into the main sitting room.

"Eirene's teams are still trying to sniff out how Xiao is influencing the various governments, particularly the Americans and the Brits. Gregorios has Francesca leading a team initiating economic sanctions against the U.S."

"How can they do that?"

"They've got extensive financial holdings worldwide. They could instigate a worldwide economic meltdown if they wanted to."

"Is that what they're planning?" Such a move would hurt millions of innocent people.

"We discussed it, but that would probably play into Xiao's plans for triggering world conflict. Francesca's team will cause some waves though. Just enough to give the world something else to worry about besides shaking the bushes hunting us, or rattling their sabers at each other."

"That's not going to stop her in the long run."

"No," Eirene said, entering the sitting room from the master bedroom. "But delaying tactics are welcome right now. Before we initiate the memory hunt, there's some news we need to review."

"What news?" Tomas asked as the two of them fell in behind Eirene, who led them down a short hall, past a second bedroom, to the conference room.

Gregorios, Melek, Quentin, and Francesca were already seated around the shiny, mahogany table, looking serious. Spartacus sat eating a giant hamburger, looking content.

"Bad news, of course," Gregorios said. "Xiao's pushing her agenda hard."

Eirene took one of the two remaining seats, and Sarah gestured Tomas to take the other, then settled onto his lap.

"Did she hit your other holdings?" Sarah asked as she leaned happily against Tomas' solid chest.

Gregorios shook his head. "Our personal assets haven't been touched, although all of those diversionary Suntara-owned flights and yachts we sent out have been intercepted."

"Terrorists attacked my family," Melek said, his expression grim.

Sarah leaned forward, filled with fresh fear. "Oh, no. Are they all right?" Paul's original strike against the hunters had left several dead and many injured, including Melek.

"They are safe for now. After the last assault, we upgraded our defenses."

"Xiao wasn't lying when she threatened to bring the war home," Gregorios said.

Francesca looked up from her tablet and said. "I just received an alert message. Harald's team was attacked on his ranch in South Africa. The facility there suffered major damage, but his status is still unknown."

"What happened to the enforcer units I ordered there yesterday to supplement his security?" Tomas asked, reaching for his phone. "The threat board was clear just five minutes ago."

"Looks like they got delayed," Francesca said, scanning the tablet. "They're arriving now. Tebogo is in command."

That seemed to ease Tomas' worry a little. "He's a good man. He'll get the situation sorted."

Gregorios didn't look satisfied. "Issue a network-wide alert. If she's hit two targets, she's probably planning more."

"But she hasn't hit our property yet," Eirene pointed out.

"So she was lying about knowing how to hurt you,". Sarah said. That was a relief, but they needed to track Xiao down and bring the war home to her too.

Spartacus said, "Xiao is not one to make idle threats. As one preparing to step into the light of open battle from her long sojourn in the shadows, she cannot but have a plan of assault against such worthy opponents."

"You're probably right," Francesca said, leaning back in her seat, regarding Spartacus approvingly. "She might be trying to lull us into making a mistake and revealing our current location."

"Classic cat-and-mouse game," Gregorios said, looking like he actually enjoyed the challenge. "If our gambit of jumping ship with Leandro caught her by surprise, she needs to find us as badly as we need to find her."

Spartacus rose and extended his hamburger, as if it was a sword. "We shall discover her secret lair, and together we shall meet in battle glorious to make the gods proud again."

"I like the way you're thinking," Eirene said.

"Then I must sally forth without delay," Spartacus declared.

"We're trying to keep a low profile here," Gregorios reminded him. "She's not on the island."

"It is to prepare for the conflict that I must embark upon a mission to restore to my hand the hilt of a treasured friend."

"You've got a sword stashed on Malta?" Eirene asked, sounding excited by the idea.

"Indeed, and I will employ the stealth and discretion of the frumentarii to remain innocuous in my hunt."

"Fruimen-who?" Sarah asked, having a hard time believing they'd just let Spartacus derail the entire discussion.

Eirene was smiling. "The secret service of the Roman Empire. We recruited a number of very good enforcers from their ranks over the years."

Sarah couldn't see Spartacus as a spy. He might be wearing tourist clothing, but she doubted anyone would mistake him for a common tourist. He carried himself like a warrior, and in that gorgeous body he'd stolen from Tomas, he'd get noticed no matter where he went.

Spartacus took another enormous bite of the burger, then said, "I resided upon these very shores over eighteen centuries ago. I confess I yearn to visit again the isle of previous lives. More importantly, Lady Francesca has employed her skills at divination across the realm of Google and unearthed the startling revelation that gives hope to my endeavor."

"What did you do?" Eirene asked.

Francesca assumed an innocent expression. "We did a little internet surfing. One of the famous caves on Malta is the Hal Saflieni Hypogeum."

Tomas leaned forward, his chin resting on Sarah's shoulder. "I've heard of the hypogeum. An extensive burial complex."

Francesca nodded. "Discovered in the early nineteen hundreds. Three levels were excavated pretty extensively."

Spartacus declared, "And yet, the deepest truths remain concealed from the grave robbers. For on the fifth level, I personally entombed an honored companion, slain under your very hand, Gregorios, and buried with a wealth of my best weapons and armor of the day, including my second-favorite gladius."

Well that made sense, considering Spartacus' avowed commitment to finish the duel with Hongwu. He'd need the right sword to do it properly.

Gregorios looked intrigued. "Where is this crypt? I don't want you wandering too far."

"Not far," Francesca said. "Just south of Valletta actually, near the Addolorata Cemetery."

"Who was your companion?" Gregorios asked.

"Marcus Nasus."

He laughed. "Old Marcus the Nose? That's where he ended up?"

"Do not mock his memory," Spartacus declared, looking ready to fight for the honor of his long-dead companion. "His valor was without peer."

"His nose was without peer," Gregorios chuckled, then raised a calming hand. "You're right, though. He leaped into battle with consummate courage and an absolute lack of caution or good sense."

Spartacus nodded. "Indeed. The traits of a great warrior."

"Don't start backsliding on us now," Gregorios warned.

"Don't worry, Dad," Francesca said, smiling at Spartacus. "I'll go with him. I'd like to see this famous Marcus and the secret cave."

"It will be my honor to escort you to the location and regale you with the account of Marcus' grand valor. One as lovely and mighty as you will appreciate his feats."

"Lead on, big guy," Francesca said, linking arms with him. "Sounds like fun."

Sarah looked after them with a smile as the two left the room. At least they were getting to see some of the island.

"I hope she's ready to intercede if he decides to launch a conquest of the island once he gets his sword back," Tomas said.

"More likely, if the weapons have been discovered, she'll need to prevent him from ransacking whatever museum has them on display," Eirene said, although she didn't look worried. "With Spartacus suitably armed, the only thing left is to find Xiao."

Gregorios grunted. "And soon. She's pushing ahead on the political front with no one to stop her."

"What's new?" Sarah asked.

"The US and UK are escalating the rhetoric against China, and tensions are skyrocketing," Eirene explained. "They're leveraging that rune web human rights angle to the fullest. Thailand seems to think the world is on their side, and they're rattling their tiny saber against China too. The two countries are on the verge of open war, and that spark could ignite everything."

"They can't be moving so fast," Sarah breathed, horrified by the thought of such widespread conflict.

Gregorios said, "That's just the opening act. Russia is backing

China, and North Korea is threatening to attack everyone they can reach once hostilities break out. That's got the entire region worried."

"And the Middle East is no better," Melek said with a grimace. "A news article leaked through Saudi Arabia suggests that Jerusalem has been experimenting with sacrificing captured Muslims to their own secret rune webs."

"Oh, they'll be frothing at the mouth," Tomas groaned.

That news made Gregorios look grim too. "Xiao's hitting the world hard, and somehow she's got enough of the political leaders under her thumb that they're going along with it."

Eirene shook her head slowly, looking disgusted. "If we can't figure out how to break her leverage, pretty soon the situation will escalate beyond our ability to turn it around."

Sarah rose. "So let's turn it around. Time to hunt."

She turned toward the door, planning to head for the memory machines, determined to find a way to locate Xiao, but Melek's voice stopped her.

"Not yet." He spoke softly, but firmly. "Before we enter the memoryscape again, there is something I must explain to you."

48

What if Melek is right? What if I'm becoming a monster like Paul? I'm stealing from people at such a fundamental level, isn't that evil? It's such a tiny bit, and I'm sure they'd agree to share if I just asked, but I haven't. Leaving the world to Xiao would be worse. I'm sure of that, but sometimes I stay awake at night wondering what I'll do when I reach that line I won't cross.

Is there a line? There had better be.

~SARAH

"DID you discover what that rune meant on Hongwu's amulet?" Eirene asked.

Melek shook his head. Sarah had shared the rune with him on the yacht, but he had hadn't recognized it either.

He'd explained the various meanings of the different components and how they reinforced each other in remarkably powerful ways, but the rune hadn't seemed to be used for anything specific.

Sarah had been drawn to the strange Ophiuchus symbol, the one that looked like a tall letter "U", with a squiggly line through the middle. It was associated with a constellation, which was considered by some the thirteenth zodiac symbol.

It was particularly popular in Japan, where it was known as "The Serpent Bearer". It was usually interpreted as a man grasping a mighty serpent. The symbol had often been associated with medicine and, historically, poison. Strangely, it was also seen as representing unity, its people seekers of knowledge.

Sarah had suspected the symbol might hold other meanings, particularly when combined with the other powerful symbols included in that rune, but hadn't been able to figure it out.

Melek said, "No. From what I can tell, that is a signature rune."

"Not a lot of people sign their names in rune," Tomas said.

Melek responded, "Symbols have meaning. Signatures have meaning. Some feel the need to reinforce their position at every level."

Sarah added, "Maybe this ties in with the weird name issues Xiao seems to have."

Melek considered that. "Perhaps, but I do not think this is her name. It belongs to another, but I do not know who."

Gregorios said, "I'm glad it's not used to melt our brains in the memoryscape. If you figure out anything else about it, let us know."

He gave Melek a slightly annoyed look and added, "If you weren't planning on talking about that, what do you need to tell us? You've been holding out on us again, haven't you?"

The hunter looked more preoccupied than apologetic. "You don't share all your secrets with me either."

"But your secrets are necessary for making all this work. So what's the latest tidbit you're planning to share with us?"

"Something Xiao revealed during our last meeting with her has been eating at my thoughts."

"What did she say?" Sarah asked, trying to remember the conversation. They had all said quite a bit.

"Xiao claimed that she needs Alter's memories."

Eirene said, "That part didn't make sense. He's too young."

"Exactly. And yet, perhaps that gives us a glimpse into her true purpose in abducting my son."

"You're enjoying this, aren't you? Just spit it out," Gregorios said.

"I want to make sure everyone understands the gravity of what I'm about to share with you."

"We will once you tell us what you're holding back," Tomas said. Sarah returned to the table and took Francesca's recently-vacated chair.

"Xiao would not want Alter for his personal memories, but for the memories possessed by the facetaker who last held connection to his ascendant rune."

Whoa. That was a lot to take in. Sarah looked from one to the other, wondering if she'd heard that right.

"You're saying she's found a way to walk memories of the person who shared Alter's same nevra core before Alter was born?" Eirene asked finally.

"That's exactly what I'm saying. Whoever owned that nevra core prior to Alter would have died at the same moment he was born. In that moment, the ascendant chose him and imbued his soul with that nevra core."

"But that's impossible," Eirene said, voicing Sarah's thoughts.

Gregorios added, "If you're dead, no one can get into your head. He poked himself in the side of the head.

Melek sighed, once again looking like he hated sharing so much sacred information with them. "This is a deeper truth. Ascendant runes power the nevra core and transfer that from one soul to another."

Gregorios interrupted. "It still doesn't add up."

Melek held up a hand. "Patience. This is not a simple topic. While connected to your soul via your nevra core, the ascendant rune records a fraction of the world's history in a never-ending spiral that maintains the integrity of that timeline."

"How does it do that?" Sarah asked, feeling out of her depth.

Melek shrugged. "I don't know, but I believe I am speaking the truth."

Eirene took a long slow breath and placed her hands flat on the table, as if bracing for more mind-twisting truths. "For now, let's assume you are. What's the catch?"

"When the soul bonded to that active nevron dies, it is absorbed into the ascendant rune."

"Whoa, like sucked in?" Tomas exclaimed.

Melek nodded. "In its entirety. Its connection to the fabric of history is too tight to be released. That soul, intact, with its entire life-time of memories, is absorbed into the ascendant rune, sealing the record of its life with the full force of its soul."

Eirene looked as shocked as Sarah felt, but Gregorios looked thoughtful. "That's why faith and nevron don't mix. There's no after-life for a facetaker."

Sarah leaped upon the chance to ask about that intriguing point, which he'd alluded to before. "Explain that to me. You've mentioned something about faith and nevra core not being compatible. Why not?"

"Later. Don't interrupt."

"But—"

"I promise. Maybe over dinner, since Tomas still hasn't taken you out," Gregorios added with a grin.

"Hey, we've been busy," Tomas protested.

"Excuses don't fly, my boy. A sincere man finds a way," Gregorios said.

"So you're saying we're going out tonight, dear?" Eirene asked in a soft voice that made Gregorios suddenly look nervous.

He recovered quickly, with reflexes honed by generations of being married to her. "Of course. I've got just the place."

Eirene winked at Sarah. Melek looked a bit annoyed that they'd lost track of his important truths.

He added, "The point is, I believe Xiao has chosen Alter as the tool she will use to slip back into history via the memories of a deceased facetaker."

"Why Alter? Because he's also cui dashi?" Tomas asked.

"Perhaps. I do not yet grasp the full extent of what she intends, but I fear the danger," Melek said.

"If she doesn't find what she wants, she'll kill him," Sarah said, her worry for Alter's safety spiking again.

"That is the least of our concerns," Melek said, surprising her. What could be worse than losing his son?

Melek explained. "To my knowledge, no one has ever managed to make a life jump like this. Before now, it was always considered a potential reality only because our first forefather, Alter the Elder, warned in the days of our ultimate challenge this threat would appear."

Gregorios said, "I wish I'd met that forefather of yours. His prophecies seem more accurate than most. When did he live?"

"Thirty-three centuries ago, during the time of Moses."

Gregorios grunted. "That's old, even for me."

"The soul that is bonded to the active nevra core at the present is known as the Nevra Prime," Melek explained.

"Sounds like a Transformer," Tomas chuckled.

Gregorios said, "Stop interrupting. Besides, those movies were terrible."

"The first one wasn't so bad," Tomas muttered.

"The soul who most recently held that bond prior to the nevra prime is known as the Nevra Prius," Melek said.

"As in the little car?" Sarah asked, sharing an amused look with Tomas.

Melek gave her a frustrated look. "No. It's Latin, referring to this as the former soul. And thus, making a successful transition from the nevra prime to the nevra prius is referred to as the Prius Commute."

Sarah couldn't shake the image of Xiao driving a little car, stuck in traffic on the L.A. highway.

"You can't be serious. That's a silly name," Tomas said, wiping his face to hide a grin.

Melek bristled. "This is one of the most sacred truths held by my family."

"It's still pretty bad," Gregorios pointed out.

"Don't mind them," Eirene said, patting Melek's arm. "In fact, to preserve the sacred nature of this truth, why don't we refer to it as a double jump?"

Melek scowled, but that sounded so much better to Sarah. "I agree. It's easier, and we won't offend you every time we say it."

"Very well," Melek said, still looking grumpy.

"You should have told us about this sooner. This is important," Sarah told him.

"You barely managed to accept the truth of the ascendant. You weren't ready for any more," Melek replied.

"So you're saying Xiao might be trying to do a double jump along Alter's ascendant rune," Gregorios repeated. "She can walk farther back in time, but how does that make what she's doing more dangerous?"

"Because of the runes involved. I haven't heard of anyone outside of my family possessing those runes in over thirty centuries."

"But you suspect she's got them, and that's bad," Eirene guessed.

"Terrible." He pointed to Sarah. "You've felt the power of master runes. Their power is so great because they tap into the force of the many souls focused on those events. Every soul involved leaves its mark on the ascendant rune, so such large numbers weave a node of extraordinary power into the fabric of its history, creating the master runes."

"Sure," Sarah said, shivering at the memory of the wild torrent of power she'd unleashed by taking ownership of those master runes.

Melek continued, voice filled with intensity. "Part of what makes those master runes so powerful is that they allow you to tap into the pure essence of history. If Xiao really does possess the secret runes that allow her to make the prius . . . the double jump, then her threat is uniquely dangerous. Those runes not only grant her access to higher spirals of the ascendant rune, but also grant her far greater access to the essence of history."

"How much access?" Eirene asked, looking concerned.

Melek shrugged. "It is unclear. No one's done this before."

"Worst case?" Gregorios asked.

Melek paused to take a slow breath. "Worst case is that she gains the ability to thrust her will into the flow of time and not only draw upon its power, but affect its course."

"You're saying she might be able to change history?" Eirene exclaimed, mirroring Sarah's horrified thoughts.

"That's exactly what I'm saying."

49

"WE HAVE TO TRY IT," Gregorios said.

That started a heated argument. Melek at first refused, claiming it was abomination. He'd only shared the secret with them so they understood the potential threat.

Gregorios argued just as hotly that they couldn't fight Xiao with suppositions and hypotheses from moldy old documents written on pigskins.

Sarah wasn't sure which side of the argument she favored. The knowledge gained by trying it would prove invaluable, but what did it mean to gain greater access to the pure essence of history? She'd seen how easy it was to commit suicide by history at the end of her first life, and didn't want to make another fatal mistake.

Melek slapped his hand on the table. "You don't understand what you're suggesting. There are dangers you don't even bother to ask about."

The two looked on the verge of coming to blows when Eirene stepped in. "Settle down, boys. Melek, you can't share this information and not expect us to want to learn more. You say there are dangers. Fine, explain them so we can make an informed decision."

Melek sat back, face flushed. He held Eirene's gaze for a moment before finally nodding curtly. "First there is the drain. You've experienced how severe the drain can be returning to shared memories and fighting another for control."

Gregorios settled back in his chair, nodding but looking unhappy about having to agree. "We've learned to deal with it."

Melek frowned at him. "I cannot know for certain, but I suspect the drain to do what you propose will be at least double the worst you've felt before."

Sarah cringed. That was definitely a danger. During the confrontations with Paul, the drain had grown severe. Even with Gregorios' and Eirene's three facetaker children powering the machines, they'd only managed the load due to Sarah's cipher that drew upon the strength of everyone in Suntara's headquarters. A drain as severe as Melek proposed would kill them all.

After a moment's thought, Gregorios said, "You shared your concerns with us, so you suspect she's really planning to try double jumps." When Melek nodded he added, "Then we must assume she can do it."

Tomas said, "She won't worry about the drain. We've already seen her employ some of the most advanced heka webs ever. She'll sacrifice as many souls as she must to power her machine."

Eirene nodded. "Agreed. But we cannot allow the risk to prevent us from making the attempt. If we don't figure out a way to power our own double jump, we cede all of ancient history to her without a fight."

Gregorios shook his head, expression resolute. "We can't do that. She's already got too much advantage."

Melek rose. "I absolutely refuse to take part in the sacrifice of dispossessed souls. No matter how important our mission, we cannot allow ourselves to adopt the ways of abomination espoused—"

"Oh, pipe, down," Gregorios said before Melek could really get on a roll. "We're not proposing that. It's too messy."

"What are you suggesting?" Melek asked cautiously, settling back into his chair.

"I can generate enough power," Sarah said softly. "I can siphon just a little from—"

"No!" Melek interrupted, coming to his feet again.

He lurched on his bad leg, lessening the dramatic effect, but shouted anyway. "I did not oppose what you did to protect yourself from Vlad, but I refuse to consider more uses of those unwilling souls. What you propose is strictly forbidden."

Quentin spoke for the first time. "A wise man will first understand what he faces before staking out his defensive position. Avoids embarrassing redeployments later."

"I doubt anything you can say will change my position," Melek stated with such confidence Sarah felt sorry for him. Almost.

She explained how they had linked all of the enforcers to her ciphers, how she could draw upon some or all of them, up to twenty percent of their strength, and that they volunteered to give the service. By the time she finished, his defiant scowl had faded to a thoughtful frown.

"I've never considered drawing upon the strength of allies like this."

"It's kind of like crowd funding at a soul level," Tomas said. At Sarah's surprised look he shrugged. "Hey, I'm old, but I'm connected."

Sarah decided not to mention to Melek that when she had redirected her cipher in Rome from those children, she had found it generated far too much energy. After topping off her rounon well and securing her defenses against Vlad, she hadn't needed it all. She had updated the cipher to add that captured energy to the remote, ever-charging, ethereal rune battery already building from souls in Rome.

She wasn't sure how long it could continue charging, but it was quickly becoming a mighty power source. It would easily do the job assisting with powering the machines, but she doubted Melek was ready to hear about that yet.

"It might work," he admitted finally, looking like he hated admitting it.

Gregorios stood and slapped his hands on the table, looking pleased. "Done. Eirene, you drive. We'll use my memories."

"Why yours?" Eirene asked.

"Because I've lived longer. I've always wanted to see what it looked like in 700 B.C."

"Why?" Eirene looked like she was preparing to argue for the right to take the driver's seat.

"Because Shahrokh was born in 625 BC, and he never let me forget that he completed his first life before I was born."

"That's probably as good as reason as any," Tomas said.

"No it's not. It's immature," Eirene protested.

Gregorios shrugged. "What would you do?"

"Oh, I don't know. Maybe I'd track you down in Athens and see what you were like as a boy."

"That's not fair."

Tomas laughed. "I like her idea."

Gregorios looked terribly offended by his change of sides and glanced to Quentin for support. Quentin shook his head. "Never ask me to stand against a lady. Especially not against this one."

Eirene chuckled. "I knew I liked you, Quentin."

"I've managed to pick up a few nuggets of wisdom. First and foremost is never oppose Eirene when she really wants something."

Gregorios threw up his hands in defeat, although his eyes were twinkling with mirth. "Fine. You try first. Once we work out the bugs, my turn."

"Unless Xiao and Alter are in there already. Then we'd just get sucked into their memory," Sarah reminded them.

That deflated Gregorios' good humor, and his expression turned fierce. "I'd prefer it if we don't run into them on this jump. But be ready. Our primary objective is still to find Xiao, so if the opportunity presents itself to track her down, we cannot afford to miss it."

Sarah tried to draw from his indomitable optimism to bolster her nerves. "I'm ready. I've got a plan to adapt the tracking beacon cipher I used in Nanjing to give us a starting point in the hunt for her in the real world."

"And if Xiao decides to fight?" Eirene asked.

Gregorios thought for a moment. "We'll pop the tires on her Prius and see how she likes being stranded on the timeway."

50

EVEN THOUGH MELEK still didn't like the idea of drawing strength from the willing enforcers, Sarah felt relieved that he was at least willing to try. The idea of making the double jump both thrilled and scared her.

They didn't know anything about the person who was linked to Eirene's nevra core before she'd been born. How long had they lived? What kind of memories might they stumble into? Many facetakers lacked Eirene's integrity, so Sarah could be jumping into some gruesome times.

While Eirene questioned Melek about what she might experience trying to direct a second-hand memory, Sarah prepared a new cipher on a block of wood. She included modifiers to allow it to draw upon her remote Roman battery rune if the drain proved greater than the fifteen percent max she included from the enforcers.

Melek popped the outer casing off the shiny Sotrun machine they preferred to use and inspected the runes engraved along its inner supports. After a few minutes he pointed to a spot where two of them intersected and supported the base of the wire harness.

"This spot is a crucial juncture, yet it's free of runes."

"Do you think they planned that?" Sarah asked.

"It is possible. If so, that suggests Xiao was preparing to use the same rune sequence I will be adding."

"So yours will fit?" Gregorios asked, crouching beside Melek to watch.

Melek frowned at him and motioned him back. "Only Sarah sees this rune."

"You swore to be open with us," Gregorios reminded him.

"You don't need to see this. This is the most sacred—"

Gregorios rose. "Yeah, I know. Just don't confuse who your friends are, Melek. We need each other to make this all work."

Thankfully, Melek didn't reply. Sarah crouched beside him, eager to see the rune. He drew it with a fine-tipped marker. It was small, yet intricate, including the Egyptian ankh symbol for life as well as a pair of Chinese symbols she didn't know.

Melek pointed to them. "These represent birth, death, and the link from ancestors to the present and on to future generations."

"Wait. That's very similar to what you said the title Xiao means."

"Exactly."

"Her name is a key component to the secret rune?" Sarah asked. Xiao had mentioned that names held power, but would she really include such dangerous marks in her name? What did that say about her?

"As we've discussed, her choice of that title was no accident. Other Chinese rulers might have lacked her understanding of runes, but the weight of its meaning has always tied present souls to the past."

When he completed the rune, Sarah spent a moment studying it, tracing her fingers along its intricate lines. It called to her, but not with the overwhelming rush of a master rune. There was power there, but of a unique, subtle flavor. Its gentle tug on her mind reminded her of the feel of the ascendant rune under her fingers in the fourth dimension.

After a moment, she nodded. "You nailed it. This rune is good."

"No. It is neither good nor evil."

"I meant it feels correct."

"Let us hope so. Perhaps our efforts may offset the evil Xiao intends."

Sarah pressed her hand over the rune and concentrated, activating it and linking it to the long line of runes already worked into the machine. They would all come to life under the power of Eirene's nevron when Gregorios cast her into her memories, but Sarah felt it important to ensure this rune was active. This way, she established a personal link to it too.

They took their places after she activated her strength cipher and slipped it into Gregorios' pocket.

His eyes widened as the rush of energy began pouring into him. He stood taller and winked at her. "Enjoy your trip."

He kept his tone light, but Sarah could read his tension. He clearly didn't like sending them into the unknown.

She suppressed her own concerns as she settled into one of the reclining chairs and allowed Quentin to press the faceplate into position. The machine hummed to life and the heat of Gregorios' nevron pulsed against her face. Then blackness drew her mind into the memoryscape.

The darkness usually dissipated in seconds. This time, she lingered in limbo a lot longer, feeling nothing, sensing nothing. She started to worry.

What if something went wrong? What if the load was too much for Gregorios, even with her cipher in place? If he died trying to power their double jump, would that leave her mind permanently stranded in limbo?

She should have asked more questions before agreeing to test the double jump.

Then the darkness condensed, becoming thicker. How was that possible? She already couldn't see or hear anything, but suddenly it felt like she was sitting in a closed room that began to shrink. The air pressure increased fast enough to pop her ears when she swallowed.

Then bright sunlight erupted around her. Sarah blinked against the unexpected brilliance as the memoryscape formed. It came more slowly than normal, almost like rendering video on a slow computer. The buildings constructed themselves over a period of half a minute while she stood in mute astonishment. The architecture was easily recognizable as ancient Greek, with lots of white stone, fluted columns, and massive temples.

Eirene had said she wanted to visit Gregorios, and it looked like she had pointed them in the right direction. Sarah still didn't understand how Eirene could influence which memory they found, since they weren't hers.

A steep, rocky hill grew above the city, topped with easily recognizable buildings. Sarah instantly recognized the Acropolis of ancient Athens. In particular, her gaze was drawn to the many-columned Parthenon.

People began to appear in the empty streets, popping into existence in mid-stride and mid-sentence. They wore white togas and sandals for the most part, exactly as Sarah had imagined. It was nice when something she supposed about history proved accurate.

Sarah took a deep breath. The air felt heavy against her skin. She closed her eyes and allowed herself to just feel it. She was startled to sense the ascendant rune close beside her. It felt more solid, more accessible, even though she hadn't reached out to touch it.

She parted the air in front of her and connected with the slippery slope of the ascendant rune's slowly flowing history. The construct shimmered in front of her, far more tangible than the last time she'd touched it. She craned her neck upward, gazing at the coiled spiral twisting up into eternity. She caught glimpses of the bright nodes of master runes.

The bottom end of the ascendant was secured to Eirene, who appeared beside Sarah, dressed in the ever-present sleeveless toga of ancient Greece. Hers was a bright blue, unlike the normal peasants in their unbleached wool.

"Wow," Eirene breathed. She was gazing up into the sky, at the spot where the ascendant began to flare.

"Wait, can you see it too?" Sarah asked.

"A little. Like glistening shadow."

"How?"

"I have no idea. Maybe because we're linked tighter to history through the double jump. We'll have to ask Melek when he arrives."

Tomas appeared beside them, and he looked amazing in a Greek toga.

Melek appeared last. He noticed the ascendant rune instantly and grinned like a little boy. "I can see it!"

"I think that rune you added to the machine does more than you thought it did," Sarah said.

"Don't mess with anything," Melek warned, his grin fading to a look of concern.

"We did it. It actually worked!" Sarah laughed.

"I'd expect nothing less from Melek," Eirene said, giving her grandson an approving smile.

Sarah wrapped Tomas in a fierce hug, and savored his return embrace.

Eirene finally looked around. "I don't want to leave Gregorios for long, but before we leave, come on. I've always wanted to see the inside of the Parthenon in its heyday." She took two steps toward the distant, famous structure, but paused and frowned.

"Do you feel that? Someone else is moving through the memoryscape, but the connection is faint.

"Can you lock in on them?" Sarah asked, her good humor fading to renewed worry. They had hoped to find Xiao, but now that she faced the prospect of actually confronting the deadly cui dashi, she wondered if they could handle it.

"Are you ready?" Tomas asked, his expression turning serious, his eyes scanning for threats, hands slowly clenching, as if yearning to summon a firearm.

"I am," Sarah said, forcing herself to believe it. "The new sequence will hit her hard."

During the long yacht ride she, Quentin, and Melek had worked out some new battle ciphers. She had also developed an improved tracking cipher, similar to the one they had tried in Nanjing, but connected in the real world to a spinning world globe. If it worked the way she hoped, it could help pinpoint Xiao's location just about anywhere. The trick would be keeping it active long enough without getting killed.

"Hold on," Eirene said, closing her eyes in concentration. "I'll try to sync with the memory of whoever's skulking around. It's almost as if they've figured out how to conceal their presence."

Sarah grabbed Tomas' hand as the memoryscape faded to black, then snapped abruptly into a new focus.

They stood in the broken ruins of Saint Peter's square in Rome, where they fought the fiery showdown against Paul. They had jumped from four or five hundred B.C. to the near-modern day. Crowds of tourists and faithful thronged the square. If Xiao succeeded in jamming peace down everyone's throats, how much more of the world would get similarly destroyed?

"Why here?" Sarah asked as the rest of the team spread out and scanned for any other memory walkers.

Eirene shrugged. "I just followed the tug of the memory."

"I don't see her," Melek said after a moment.

Sarah drew a cipher, forming burning silver lines in the air. When she activated it, she drew it to her face, looking through two looping symbols like the lenses of a pair of glasses.

She'd come up with the idea just the other day as a faster alternative to marking it onto her skin. Turning a slow circle, she scanned for any active nevron or shimmering residue from recent soul activity.

Nothing.

After making two complete circuits she broke the cipher and drew another. The others waited silently while she worked. This new cipher was more complex, its purpose more subtle, built around another of those sacred runes Melek had shared with her on the plane.

When the cipher activated, Sarah closed her eyes and reached through the air to touch the slippery column of Eirene's ascendant rune that trickled past as it recorded time through her sleeping soul. The new rune she had just drawn pulsed against her finger, sending a quivering sensation through to her other hand and into the ethereal ascendant rune.

A second later it pulsed gently back against her, and with that touch came a flood of energy. A cascade of joyous memories flickered through her mind, a thousand happy recollections that left her grinning. In her ears rang dozens of her favorite sounds, from Tomas' laughter, to the chirping of songbirds, to the wump of her grenade launcher. She was surprised to recognize Alter's voice calling her name.

Then she felt a tug on her mind, turning her from the ascendant rune and toward the distant Castel Sant Angelo. She started walking in that direction.

"What is it?" Tomas asked.

"I think I've got a lock on someone. This way."

Tomas fell into step beside her, a black bullpup rifle appearing in his eager hands.

51

He who works hard gets wealth; he who knows when he has enough is truly rich.

~LAOZI

WHILE SARAH LED the way down the via della Conciliazione, the rest of the team flanked her, scanning in every direction, looking tense and ready for battle.

"Can you activate the tracking beacon?" Eirene asked.

"Not yet. I need to get a visual on Xiao."

Tomas dropped his rifle, and it disappeared from view. A six-barreled minigun on a rolling base appeared in front of him. A large box of ammunition rested on the base, feeding the gun by a shining silvery belt.

He pushed it along, his expression turning eager. "Armor piercing and explosive rounds. Four thousand rounds a minute might make a dent."

The cobblestone street in front of them ripped asunder as a huge wolfhound with deep black fur tore its way to the surface. A half-second burst from Tomas' minigun tore it to a bloody pulp.

"See if you can hold her with that until I reach her," Melek said. Instead of summoning an assault rifle or other modern firearm, he hefted a heavy hammer engraved with many runes. The beautifully complex patterns flowed over the pointed head of the hammer and down the handle.

"What enhancement is that?" Sarah asked.

Melek, who stood tall in his youthful body, grinned at her like a Viking. "My own design. Took years to perfect. Get me an opening and this hammer will make a dent, I guarantee it."

"You should apply those runes to my bullets," Tomas said. "Then we'd have a winner."

"Stay focused," Eirene said. She had not drawn her sidearm yet, and strolled beside Sarah calmly, as if they were out for an afternoon walk. "I don't feel any minds tampering, but I do feel something. It's vague though, and I get no sense of direction."

"That cipher you used should identify active nevrons and give you an accurate position," Melek said to Sarah.

She shrugged. "It should, but all I'm getting is a subtle feeling that we need to head toward the Castel."

Eirene suggested, "She might be employing some kind of shielding. Stay sharp and keep walking. Maybe the feeling will tighten up."

Although the road was only half a mile long, straight, and unbroken between St. Peter's Basilica and the Castel Sant Angelo, memories saturated every step. Sarah kept seeing images of that titanic battle between Spartacus' rune-web-protected soldiers and the enforcers and Yurak mercenaries.

When the group reached the Castel, she pointed up. "Somewhere atop the tower, I think."

Tomas abandoned his rolling minigun with a great deal of grumbling, swapping it for a slightly smaller model he could lug in his arms. They carefully worked up through the spiraling ramp inside the Castel to the roof.

Sarah expected an ambush at every turn, but they met no one but tourists. Her nerves felt raw from anticipation, but she didn't dare let her guard down. She'd only get a split second to hit Xiao with a restraining cipher before the deadly cui dashi struck.

Finally they reached the top level and Tomas vaulted the last five steps to the roof, minigun at the ready, finger poised above the trigger, ready to engage. Sarah followed in a rush, but nearly collided with him when he abruptly stopped. She scanned the rooftop for the threat, then stared.

"Reuben?"

The hunter stood at the far end of the roof, staring down over the lower courtyard. He turned at the sound of her voice. He looked the same as he had the day of the battle for St. Peter's Square, right before Paul's runes broke his mind and sent him to commit murder.

Reuben rolled his eyes and threw up his hands. "Can't I get any peace?"

"What are you doing here?" Sarah asked.

Melek rushed past. "Son, you did it!"

"Oh, hey, Dad," Reuben said, giving his father an absent wave. "The other day was too depressing, so I came here for some quiet."

"How did you manage to do that?" Eirene asked, following Melek. Sarah trailed after, but Tomas shifted out to the side, keeping his gun trained on the hunter who had caused them so much grief.

"I figured out how," Reuben said, again turning to stare over the courtyard. "I've got nothing better to do on that wall anyway."

Sarah exchanged a confused look with Eirene. That didn't explain anything.

Melek said, "I've been working with him to free his mind and travel the memoryscape at will. It gives him respite from the torture of living a dispossessed life."

Sarah frowned. "But this doesn't feel like the day we fought Paul. It's not really your memory, is it?"

Melek shook his head. "We were testing a rune sequence to allow him to extend beyond his personal memories."

"How? We don't know any runes like that," Sarah asked. It was a really cool idea.

Melek looked a bit guilty. He should, after denouncing them all as evil demons of abomination for trying anything new. "Usually it wouldn't work, but since that traumatic day, perhaps because of the forbidden runes he used and Paul corrupted, Reuben began showing memory-walking abilities no one else has managed."

Reuben turned to his father. "I can do it because I'm pure. Oh yeah, since you're here, I can give you Alter's message."

"What message?" Melek asked, looking confused.

Reuben shook a finger at Eirene. "He promised. You give it back."

"What message?" Melek repeated gently.

Reuben continued glaring at Eirene. "He can't kill her alone. Your fault for corrupting him."

"Who?" Melek asked, gripping Reuben by the shoulder.

Sarah turned away. She hated to see the once-powerful hunter reduced to madness. Sure he had caused them a lot of grief, but he'd acted out of a twisted sense of honor. She'd still beat him to a pulp if he was sane, but she couldn't be angry with the broken mind that remained.

"Xiao," Reuben said, as if it should be clear.

Sarah spun back to the hunters and asked a surprised-looking Melek, "Did you tell him about Xiao?"

He shook his head. "When did you learn her name, Son?"

Reuben gave them an exasperated look. "I hate repeating myself. Alter said he needs your help to kill her."

"When did he tell you this?" Eirene asked softly, carefully, like she was talking with a child.

Reuben made a vague gesture to one side. "We ran into each other in a different memory. He's working for Xiao. Said he'll try to get more information about her."

Sarah exchanged surprised looks with Eirene. "Could this be real?"

Reuben barked a laugh. "Nothing's real. Time, history, life. It's all illusion." He pointed at Eirene. "Alter promised. Gregorios restores me."

"I'm sure he did," Eirene said, not appearing bothered by Reuben's abrupt changes. "But before he can, we have to defeat Xiao."

"That's what Alter said," Reuben muttered with a frown. "Said we could fight her together."

"Good idea," Sarah said, approaching him. "You walk the memoryscape a lot these days, don't you?"

"What else can I do?" Reuben shouted, advancing with a raised fist. "I'm hanging on a wall!"

"Easy, Son," Melek said, trying to hold the angry young man back.

"Why are you defending this demon?" Reuben rounded on his father. "I thought we were supposed to kill them."

"No. We're working together to defeat Xiao."

Reuben spat at his father's feet. "You're defiling yourself, Father. Working with them is abomination."

"Not today," Melek said calmly, although his expression looked pained.

"Reuben," Sarah said, drawing his attention. "We all want to defeat Xiao together, and with your help we can."

Reuben turned toward Eirene, a grin on his face, his expression expectant. "Give it back."

"Soon," Sarah said, stepping between them. "First you have to talk with Alter again."

The hunter turned away with a dismissive gesture. "I don't want to."

"You want to get your body back, right?" When he nodded Sarah added, "Then we need to set up a time to meet with Alter so we can make a plan."

"Will you do it for us, Son?" Melek asked.

Reuben shrugged. "I guess. If I see him again."

The conversation was so weird, but it wasn't the strangest thing they'd seen, so Sarah decided she believed the crazy young hunter. "Tell him we miss him, and we'll help."

"Yeah, whatever."

Reuben leaped away, vaulting over the low rail and off the edge of the tower. He disappeared before striking the ground.

"I have no idea how to read that guy," Sarah muttered. When she turned back toward the stairs, Tomas was approaching, a frown on his lips.

"Tell him we miss him?"

"He must be so scared and alone."

Tomas frowned. "Don't encourage him. He still wants you."

She leaned against him. "I know. I worry about him, though."

She turned to talk with Eirene and found Melek considering her, a thoughtful expression on his face. They really should have spoken more quietly.

Eirene had lingered, gazing over the wall where Reuben had disappeared. "Reuben might offer a unique opportunity that I doubt Xiao has considered. I know I hadn't."

"If we can believe anything he said," Tomas said, looking like he didn't.

Sarah did. She clung to that belief like a lifeline back to Alter. "I'm not sure he could have just made all that up. Particularly about Xiao's name."

Eirene said, "We'll explore the possibility that Reuben offers soon enough, but our visit here has distracted us from our primary mission of locating Xiao."

Sarah spread her hands. "I don't have any new ideas."

"Perhaps I do," Melek said.

"More secrets?" Eirene asked, one eyebrow raised.

"Not this time. Just simple caution."

"I don't like the sound of that," Sarah said.

"I might be able to help you gain the vision necessary to locate Xiao along the ascendant," Melek said.

"So what's the catch?" she asked hesitantly.

"The drain will grow more severe for Gregorios."

Well, if that was all, she'd take the risk. "With the cipher I left in place for him, he should be able to handle it. Is that the only danger?"

The old hunter shook his head. "To see more, you must step further into the fourth dimension. There are risks inherent in such an act that none of us can really anticipate."

"Do you know another way to find Xiao?" Eirene asked.

"Nothing that will find her as soon as we need to," he admitted.

They all looked to Sarah, and she shrugged, trying to ignore her growing nervousness.

"Let's do it."

52

How should a man be capable of grooming his own horse, or of furbishing his own spear and helmet, if he allows himself to become unaccustomed to tending even his own person, which is his most treasured belonging?

~ALEXANDER THE GREAT, 326, B.C.

THE MEMORYSCAPE FORMED AROUND SARAH, and she found herself in the modern-day Colosseum. It was a Saturday, and eager tourists packed the venue. They jostled her, the disruption worse because they barely noticed her.

Worse, a couple overweight tourists standing close to her in the crowded, warm afternoon sun had forgotten to use deodorant. She hadn't seriously broken a memory in weeks, but she was suddenly tempted to summon something destructive and make some room. She'd prefer the nightmares that crawled in through the resulting cracks to the stench.

"This seems an odd choice," Melek asked as he and Gregorios appeared nearby.

They had decided to exit the memoryscape to check on Gregorios before attempting Melek's new cipher. Although the drain had been severe, Gregorios reported that he'd managed just fine with the influx of strength through Sarah's cipher. Eirene had suggested that she run the machine for the second attempt.

Gregorios glanced around, looking annoyed. "It's busier than I remember. Come on."

He pushed through the crowd to the balcony overlooking the ruined lower levels and vaulted the rail. Pedestrians and guides exclaimed in surprise while security guards called for polizia.

Sarah jumped after him and no one voiced a single complaint. Sometimes walking in Gregorios' shadow could be a real downer.

She landed lightly on the hard ground after the twenty-foot fall and followed him through the passage between broken half-walls. She'd explored this area once in real life with Tomas while chasing a heka operative who'd had the gall to break one of the ancient walls on them.

Gregorios vaulted up to the wooden platform near the death gate on the far side. Tourists had to pay extra to access that area, and no tours seemed to be running at the moment, so they had it to themselves.

"I still don't understand why you chose this memory," Melek said as he easily vaulted the twenty feet up to join them.

Gregorios shrugged. "What better place to slip along the mystic timeline than from within this place that has stood silent witness to so many centuries?"

"Why Gregorios, you've got the soul of a poet," Sarah teased.

"I know," he said with a wink. "I keep him in a pocket and let him sing for his dinner once in a while."

She laughed. "You're incorrigible.

Melek gave Gregorios a guarded look, as if deciding whether to check his pockets for any dispossessed souls. Then he frowned and turned to Sarah. "I must mark this new rune onto your face."

She grimaced. "Is that necessary?" When he nodded, she sighed. She didn't like the idea of runes on her face, but it wouldn't be as embarrassing as the rune she'd needed Alter to mark onto her hip.

Melek used a black marker to inscribe a series of symbols around her eyes and forehead. She summoned a hand mirror to watch.

She grimaced. "I'm not making this one permanent, just so you know. I'd have to start wearing a mask."

"Masks have never been a good style choice," Gregorios agreed.

When he finished, Melek stepped back to survey his work. "It looks good. Activate it when you're ready."

She focused and felt a shimmering warmth spreading over her face.

"You look like a radioactive raccoon," Gregorios chuckled, holding up a camera that appeared in his hand. "Say cheese."

"Don't you dare."

He clicked the button anyway. "I'll show this to Eirene some time when we take a stroll down memory lane. He tossed the camera over his shoulder and it disappeared. "What do you do with your x-ray vision?"

She looked to Melek, a question in her gaze.

He said, "Grasp the ascendant. These runes will draw your sight deeper into the fourth dimension, which should enhance your view of the ascendant and anyone else attempting to reach it."

Hopefully it didn't draw more than her sight into the fourth dimension. Those unknown dangers he had warned them about still worried her, but what could she do about it? Taking a calming breath, Sarah reached through the air again, parting it like a curtain to slip her fingers into that hidden space-time dimension.

When her fingers brushed the slippery ascendant she said, "Got it."

Melek was right. As soon as her fingers made contact, more of the huge, spiraled expanse came into view. The tilted arc of this lowest coil stretched through the walls of the Colosseum and rose into the air at a steep angle. Above it, she caught glimpses of other spirals radiating out much farther.

"You should be able to slide your thoughts up the spiral," Melek said, leaning forward as if to catch a glimpse of what she was seeing. "Any other active souls that have recently crossed the spiral's timeline should leave some kind of mark."

"Like a tire track?"

"More or less. Some kind of thread or ripple to mark passage through that moment." Melek spread his hands in a helpless gesture. "That's all I know."

Mingled excitement and nervousness set her heart racing. "I'll see what I can find."

Sarah concentrated on exploring the ascendant rune, but it was harder than it sounded. She willed her mind to slide up it like that first time she had made contact.

After a long, breathless moment, her vision seemed to detach from her physical form and drift up along the spiral. It was a strange feeling, as if her eyes had grown gossamer wings and started to fly.

More of the ascendant became visible, stretching into the sky and across the city. It was massive and breathtaking, glowing softly with muted hues. She could sense high above her the glittering points of master runes, and wondered how long it would take to slip up the spiral of time to find them.

Then the construct vibrated, like a long harp string getting plucked by a distant finger. The vibration rippled through her, followed in quick succession by others, each more distant and fainter than the last.

Her view snapped back into her head and she blinked a few times as she reoriented herself, frowning as she concentrated over that weird, distant feeling. "Something's happening."

Melek stood close beside her, his expression intent. "What? Did you find them?"

Gregorios cracked his knuckles, then the shotgun he'd hoped to shoot Xiao in the face with the last time they saw her in the memoryscape appeared in his hands.

Sarah shook her head slowly. "No, it feels like someone is bouncing across the spiral, touching the ascendant across multiple times. They're moving back through time. Fast."

"How can you tell?" Gregorios asked, looking up into the sky, which to him would be empty but for a few high clouds.

She shrugged. "I can't see the whole thing. It's more like echoes of vibration down a string that I'm touching."

"Can you follow them?" Melek asked eagerly.

"How?"

"I don't know." He clenched his fists, showing his frustration. "I'm not the one experiencing this. You are."

"To us, you just look like a confused mime," Gregorios said with a grin.

"Not helping," she muttered, then concentrated on the ripples, but they faded. "I can't. I'm losing it."

She closed her eyes, reaching for the distant movement, but it was like trying to grab hold of ripples in a pond.

With a focused effort, she cast her gaze deeper into the fourth dimension, up along the spiral of the ascendant, hoping to gain a clearer view of what it looked like. The first grand, looping spirals grew more distinct, but higher up, they disappeared, as if into a fog.

Flashes of light, like lightning in the fog, gave her glimpses of what might lie above her. She realized with a start that there were other spiraling loops, twisting around the ascendant she was gliding up, but not quite touching.

"There are other ascendant runes out here," she exclaimed.

Melek said, "Of course there are. I told you there's one for every nevra core."

"But I haven't felt them before." She frowned, trying to understand what she was seeing with her cipher vision. The vast sizes were hard to comprehend, and the murky view made it harder.

More lightning leaped between the ascendants, and she caught a glimpse of distant movement. "If that really is Xiao, it's like she's shifted to another ascendant somehow. I'm losing the connection."

Melek bit his lip. "Do you trust me?"

"Ah, most conversations that start that way end badly," Gregorios cautioned.

Sarah couldn't spare the time to look at Melek, with her vision locked along the fat spiral of the ascendant, but he sounded nervous.

"Do you trust yourself?" she asked.

"Excellent question. I see what Alter likes about you."

Bad timing to bring that up. "Just answer me."

Melek hesitated for just a second before saying, "If I could do this myself, I would. I may know a way to give you a chance to find them."

"What's the catch?" Gregorios asked.

"Only Sarah goes. We stay behind. I link her to the distant memory journey and she jumps ship."

"Like a hitchhiker?" Sarah asked. That was not sounding like a wonderful plan.

"More like a stowaway," Melek said. "You would lack any control, so there is danger. But it might allow you to catch them unawares."

"How do I get out?" Sarah asked.

"Your normal escape rune should work." He didn't sound entirely convinced.

Gregorios said, "Bad idea. Throwing Sarah overboard won't help find Xiao."

"It might," Melek insisted. "I would do this. For my son."

"We're leaving. I'm going to have Eirene take us home."

They were out of time.

"Do it," Sarah said, gripping Melek's hand. Hers shook, but she bit back the urge to flee the memory. They needed information, and this might be their one chance to get it.

He produced a slender blade, stepped behind her and began cutting into her rune warrior mark.

"Don't," Gregorios said, grabbing for Melek's hand. "We're leaving. Love, get us out of here," he shouted.

The memoryscape began to fade to black as Eirene pulled them from the grip of the machine.

A searing heat blossomed across Sarah's back and an invisible force yanked her off her feet and dragged her through the air at a terrifying speed. She screamed as the Colosseum vanished, then all of Rome faded to black. As darkness enveloped her and deadened her senses, she heard Melek's voice echoing from a great distance.

"May the fathers forgive me."

$$53$$

If anything is worth doing, do it in this life and with all your heart.

~BUDDHA

THE UNBROKEN DARKNESS that had been smothering all of Sarah's senses vanished with a suddenness that left her gasping. She found herself kneeling on a wide, stone-paved street, surrounded by men and women with bronzed skin, wearing Greek togas. She was back in ancient Athens.

It wasn't the same street as the one she had walked with Eirene so recently, but she noticed the Parthenon up on the Acropolis, above the city.

"Well, I'm not dead yet," she muttered to herself as she slowly rose and looked around to get her bearings.

She felt relieved that at least she'd woken up somewhere and hadn't just gotten lost in the never-ending blackness of a memory cast-away. Hopefully she was still tethered to her body. Ancient Greece seemed pretty cool, but she didn't want to get stuck there forever.

As she scanned for danger, she realized she couldn't understand anyone. The babble of foreign voices echoed from the stone buildings, as if teasing her.

She shrugged and muttered, "It's all Greek to me."

In other memories when she'd been linked to Gregorios or Eirene, their knowledge of the language had somehow translated everything into English for her. She'd taken it for granted.

That meant Melek's rune had indeed severed her from Gregorios' memory. That was really scary, but she fought down the urge to activate her escape rune just to confirm she could get out. Nothing had hurt her yet.

Had Melek's rune linked her to the other unknown memory walker, or left her stranded, her mind floating disconnected along the historical timeline? The only way to know was to try leaving, but that would make the entire risk they've taken worthless. If it didn't work . . . well, she wasn't in a hurry to learn Melek had turned her into a ghost in history.

With no idea which way to go, Sarah decided to head for the distant Acropolis. Important landmarks seemed to attract memory walkers. The sun was bright, the air warm, and the population seemed friendly to each other. She was still tempted to summon a weapon, but decided to wait. Any break in the integrity of the memory might notify the other memory walkers of her presence.

Merchants, shoppers, and officials mingled through the busy streets. She caught sight of several groups of soldiers, all carrying spears and enormous bronze round shields. They looked like that memory of the Spartans at Thermopylae she'd fallen into with John.

The Greek soldiers wore bronze armor sporting excellent muscle detail. She chuckled to see vanity alive and well even so far back in the past. The only abs she'd seen that good in the flesh were on Tomas and Alter.

When she rounded the next corner, she entered a wide, paved square with a huge fountain sporting a gigantic statue of one of the ancient Greek goddesses. Her graceful arms held aloft some kind of pot. Sarah had no idea what that meant.

The view of the Acropolis standing proud above the city was fantastic, though. Seeing ancient Athens in all its glory took her breath away. The Parthenon with its many-columned exterior shone in the bright sunlight above the city. Its smooth stone walls looked so different from the pitted ruins that had stood for millennia.

"What am I doing here?" Sarah whispered to herself, scanning the crowd.

This was an ancient memory. From what Gregorios had told her about Athens, she was probably standing in the fourth or fifth century B.C., maybe even before Gregorios had been born.

Whoever she'd hitched a ride with had to be double jumping. Sarah moved to a white granite bench outside a towering temple and sat to scan the crowd. She must have tailed Xiao, but how to find her? She closed her eyes and felt for the flow of the ascendant rune.

It was very close, tethered right there in the square.

Sarah's pulse raced and she cringed back on her seat so a large woman sitting next to her would help conceal her from view. She scanned the crowd again, nervousness growing with every second. Was Xiao there, preparing to attack her?

Then through the shifting crowd, Sarah caught a glimpse of a familiar figure.

Alter, walking beside Xiao.

They were walking toward the far end of the square. Xiao dressed in a form-fitting, crimson Chinese dress with intricate gold embroidery. Alter walked beside her, half a step behind, dressed in his normal hunter garb. He looked healthy, although in the memoryscape he could dress himself in whatever body he chose.

Sarah rose and sidled to her right to better hide behind an overweight Athenian who was loudly munching on a bunch of grapes. With her quarry in sight, Sarah made a tiny, glowing mark in the air with one finger to activate the tracking cipher she'd prepared. Whatever happened next, at least she'd accomplished that much.

She should slip back into the crowd and hide for a few minutes to give her rune time to work, but Sarah was filled with curiosity. What was Xiao doing there? Was Alter really okay? Could she somehow find a way to catch Alter's attention?

If they could chat, even for just a few seconds, she could reassure him that they were hunting him, and that they'd gotten the message from Reuben. She couldn't bear to not make the attempt. He must be desperate for contact and support.

Sarah started across the square. She doubted she'd stay concealed from Xiao for long, but couldn't help it. She moved carefully through the crowd, trying to keep people between her and her quarry, but not lose sight of them. She reached the fountain just as Xiao and Alter were about to exit the square past a towering temple. Alter turned and looked right at her, his expression more frightened than she'd ever seen him.

"Run, Sarah!" he shouted before Xiao clamped a hand over his mouth.

She froze as the cui dashi met her gaze across the square and smiled, a cold flicker of her lips. Then Xiao turned and dragged a struggling Alter away.

Not good.

They had figured out she was there. It was a trap.

Sarah leaped high into the air and landed atop the big granite jar at the top of the fountain statue, trailing a glowing finger to focus her rune warrior power. An upgraded barrier cipher activated, creating a dense, invisible barrier that fit her like a full-body glove. Heart racing, she spun atop the statue, scanning the crowd of Athenians, who still ignored her. There had to be a threat somewhere.

Something struck her a hammer blow in the back. Her shield prevented the blow from damaging her, but the kinetic energy still catapulted her off the statue. She spun in the air and landed on her feet, spinning to face the threat.

Nothing.

A low voice echoed across the square, sending a chill down her spine. "Hello, Sarah."

Vlad.

Sarah marked three quick modifiers across the defensive barrier over her forearm. She'd prepared the suit-like barrier cipher with Vlad in mind. He'd managed to somehow slip inside her domed shield in San Marino, but she'd vowed never to give him the chance to do so again.

Now the barrier shifted again as her modifiers activated. It grew denser to ward off his biting wind breath and his deadly fangs. It grew thicker around the ears to block out his insidious voice, and grew opaque over her eyes, dimming her view. If she had included the correct symbols in the cipher she held firmly in her mind, it should counter the effects of his paralyzing eyes.

Vlad appeared right in front of her, stepping out of the concealing illusion that he wore like an invisibility cloak. He lunged with super-human speed, clearly attempting to snatch her like he had in San Marino and sink those deadly teeth into her jaw again.

Not this time. Sarah was ready, and this time she was in the memoryscape.

She leaped backward, soaring across the square and keeping just ahead of him. Her favorite carbine appeared in her hands, and she opened fire.

Bullets tore into Vlad's face, and his predatory grin faded under the withering fire. He might not bleed, and the wounds might close almost immediately, but they still hurt. The vampire shrieked in pain and rage, and his demon breath howled forth. It billowed over her, full of ghost-like faces that bit and tore at her shields, trying to drive her to the ground.

Safe in her protective barrier, Sarah landed on her feet. "You walked into the nightmare today, pal."

Vlad leaped at her again, clawed hands grasping, dead eyes glittering with blood lust.

Sarah slashed a finger to activate another cipher, then lunged to meet him. Vlad might be the deadliest vampire to ever walk the earth, but in the memoryscape, Sarah was the predator.

She deflected his raking claws with her forearms, then punched him hard enough to have shattered the fountain statue. The impact tumbled him twenty feet, and his demon breath faded to soft, painful whistling.

Vlad lunged to his feet, and suddenly he was dressed in a black tuxedo with blood-red bow tie. He bowed and grinned at her. "Ah, Sarah, my dear. You make the hunt such a joy."

His eyes began to glow like amber. She felt a shiver of fear, but not the paralyzing terror he'd inflicted upon her in San Marino.

"I'm glad you're enjoying yourself. You're going to love it when I rip out all of your teeth," she promised.

He sauntered forward, not showing any frustration he might have felt for failing to affect her more with his gaze. "Oh, Sarah, we can play together in here, but your soul belongs to me, and I will collect it in good time."

While he talked, a sinister whisper tried worming its way into her mind, but her defensive runes held it at bay. She caught only distant hints of the words, just enough to realize she didn't want to hear more.

She spat, "You're the rotting corpse of a man who was almost great. In life you failed, and in death you've been a disaster."

Vlad's veneer of calm evaporated and he opened his mouth wide enough to swallow her head. The wind of his soul-powered breath boiled forth to attack her again.

Perfect.

Those howling, tortured faces chained to his will triggered the last cipher she'd just activated. Barrier walls snapped into place around that wind, capturing it and sealing those enslaved souls away from their master. The prison cube shook the plaza when it fell to the stones nearby, and Sarah grinned at the dumbstruck vampire.

"How long can you be fully separated from the souls you enslave before you lose your connection to them?" she taunted.

Vlad transformed before her, changing from a gaunt man into a giant rock troll, right out of the *Lord of the Rings* movies. He hefted a huge club and bashed to the cobblestones for effect. Those had been great movies, and Sarah had to admit seeing a troll looming over her was frightening.

Well, it was scary until she summoned an M2 fifty-caliber machine gun, with a long belt of specialty ammunition. The Raufoss MK211 round was one of Quentin's favorites. Not only did it have an armor-piercing core, but also explosive and incendiary components. It was designed to drill through walls and vehicles.

She opened fire on the Vlad-troll.

Firing the M2 from the hip was a rush, and she rode the wave of exhilaration as she stitched a line of rounds up the troll, from knee to head. The explosive reports shattered the troll's thick hide, while the armor-piercing cores burst through its back, showering the square with gore.

The sound was a constant rolling thunder that echoed back from the tall stone buildings lining the square. The Athenians, who had mostly ignored her and Vlad, finally took notice and fled in terror.

After a couple of seconds, the smoke billowing around the creature obscured it from view, so Sarah paused firing until she could get a new target.

Then Vlad erupted out of the smoke, transformed into a mythic gryphon with the body of a lion, the beak of an eagle, and enormous wings, which he was beating furiously to gain altitude and escape.

"You're supposed to turn into a bat!" Sarah shouted. That was super lame. It was his tradition, after all.

She snapped the M2 up and opened fire, raking the creature and ripping it apart. With a final shriek of fury that tore painfully at her ears, despite the protection of her full body shield, Vlad disappeared.

"Ha!" Sarah shouted, pumping the air with her gun.

Then the weapon was snatched out of her grip by Xiao, who appeared so abruptly next to her, she seemed to have teleported. The cui dashi frowned as she grabbed Sarah by the throat and lifted her into the air. Her grip was so powerful, she compressed Sarah's protective shield, choking her with her own defense.

Xiao pulled Sarah close, her eyes glowing with her unique shade of nevron. "You're growing annoying. Good-bye, Sarah."

She threw Sarah across the square so hard she crashed right through the outer wall of a temple. The impact tore away her protective barrier and stunned her. Sarah lay on the cool stone inside, trying to regain her breath and to focus her mind to activate the escape rune. She had to get away before Xiao killed her.

The escape rune snapped into focus and she made a glowing mark to activate it.

Nothing.

Rising panic made it hard to focus. Was she really trapped in ancient Athens? What if Xiao killed her? How could she get back to herself? She drew the full rune in the air with glowing lines, double-checking to make sure she had it right.

Xiao's voice echoed into the building. "The memoryscape is mine, Sarah. Entering here is a death sentence for any I do not invite."

The building collapsed. Tons of stone rained down over Sarah with a thunderous roar that shook the world. She screamed, throwing all of her power into activating that last cipher.

A flash of agonizing pain.

Then nothing.

54

In every rune there is something of the divine. In all things of nature there is something of the marvelous.

~ARISTOTLE

THE TRANSITION from pain-filled nightmares to pain-filled wakefulness broke across Sarah's mind as gently as the coming of the dawn. She wasn't sure she had actually awakened until she blinked the haze from her eyes and recognized Tomas, who sat in a chair close to her bed, gripping her hand.

He smiled, looking relieved. "Welcome back to the land of the living."

"If this is living, it's overrated," she mumbled through dry lips.

She felt sore all over, with pain radiating deep into her chest and her left leg. "If they're waiting for my permission to give me pain killers, do it."

Tomas grimaced. "They've given you all you can take. You absorbed a lot of damage, so it'll take a bit for your runes to catch up."

"What happened?" She noticed for the first time that she was lying in a hospital bed, with beeping machines nearby. Several beautiful bouquets of flowers tried in vain to mask the scent of bleached bedclothes and industrial cleaners. The door was closed and they were alone.

Tomas leaned forward to shift her hair back, looking worried but trying to conceal it. "I was hoping you could tell me. You just started screaming. Then you started bleeding. Tomas rarely looked scared, but now he gripped her hand like he feared he might lose her.

"How bad?"

He hesitated before saying, "You're stable. I've seen lots of injuries, Sarah, but I've never seen bones break themselves. You had us all pretty freaked out."

It couldn't have been too bad, or Eirene would have removed her soulmask. Then again, maybe she had. "I'm still me, right?"

Sarah moved to sit up, but Tomas pressed her back down with a gentle hand. "You're you. I wanted Eirene to extract you, but then your body would have died. Only your runes kept you alive."

She sighed with relief. The pain was severe, but she would rather deal with pain over ending her second life so soon. She was just starting to get used to herself again.

"Where am I now?"

"Local hospital. We didn't have the kind of facilities needed to deal with your injuries. You're officially listed as a hit-and-run victim."

"I hope you got the license plate. That jerk should be in jail."

Tomas kissed her gently. Keeping his face close to hers he whispered, "I'm very glad you're back."

"Me too."

The door opened, and Gregorios and Eirene entered, followed by a young, handsome doctor. The facetakers greeted her warmly, but with unusual reserve while the doctor poked and prodded and asked Sarah questions about her condition.

Eventually he said, "You're a very lucky young woman."

She felt weak, her body broken in a way that scared her so much, she didn't want to think about it. "I don't remember much. Thanks for putting me back together."

The doctor frowned. "We had hoped you'd remember the accident."

She tried to shake her head, but grimaced at a flash of new pain. "Nothing."

"Rest. Maybe it will come to you."

After he left, the others gathered close. Eirene hugged her carefully, and Gregorios muttered, "Good thing you pulled through, or I would've sent Melek home to join Reuben on the wall."

"I'm not sure I would've shown so much restraint," Eirene said. Usually she treated her hunter descendants with remarkable patience, but in that moment, she seemed to be barely restraining a deadly fury.

Sarah said, "Don't blame him. He said it was a risk. It was worth it."

"More than you know," Tomas said, smiling for the first time.

"The tracker worked?" Sarah asked. She wanted to feel excited, but hurt too much.

He nodded. "Pretty slick, really."

Sarah breathed a sigh of relief. "I was worried I didn't last long enough before Xiao smashed me flat with that temple."

Tomas' fists clenched in anger, and Gregorios patted his shoulder. "We know she's in Beijing somewhere. We'll get our chance at payback soon enough."

"Beijing? So she's gone home to her roots," Sarah asked.

Eirene said, "Perhaps. Could be part of her plan to stir up the international conflict."

"Then again, she keeps talking about setting up an enduring dynasty," Tomas interjected. "A lot of people in China would jump right on the bandwagon if they felt they could take the top spot in the world from the U.S."

The scope of what Xiao was planning still boggled the mind. Sarah said, "She could recruit an awful lot of soldiers out of China. We need to find her."

Eirene nodded. "We're preparing transport as soon as you're ready to leave. Tell us what happened in there."

Sarah felt so weak and so tired, but she managed to tell them about her visit to Athens, spotting Alter and Xiao, and the trap. When she described her fight with Vlad, Gregorios laughed and gently fist-bumped her. "I wish I'd been there to see you spank him, Sarah."

"Next time, we hit him in real life," Tomas promised.

Eirene patted her shoulder. "Brilliant idea with that barrier. We need to explore other uses of that cipher."

Sarah felt pleased that Eirene approved. "I was thinking of that. Maybe linking it somehow to the enforcer armor, with some kind of on-demand activation sequence. That would reduce the drain, but could save some lives."

Tomas said, "I like the way you're thinking. And that was a great idea to try severing him from his chained souls. Not sure it'll work in real life, but we've never tried it."

"It's worth considering," Eirene agreed.

"Athens," Gregorios said softly, a distant look in his eyes. "Sounds like fourth or fifth century B.C. from what you described."

"So Xiao had to be double jumping," Tomas said.

Gregorios nodded. "Has to be. I haven't been that far back to Athens in a very long time."

"And you're the oldest man alive," Tomas said with a grin.

"Amazing," Sarah breathed. Gregorios had actually seen the world grow and develop from those ancient roots all the way to the modern day. The thought made her feel young and small.

"I was born when Athens was barely a city-state. Spent a lot of good years there," Gregorios said.

Eirene kissed his cheek, then said, "History lesson later. What happened after you wrecked Vlad?"

"Xiao threw me across the square and dropped a temple on me," Sarah said with a grimace. She related Xiao's final words.

"Queen of memoryscape now, is she?" Gregorios asked with a grimace.

"We'll have to incorporate additional defensive measures the next time we go in," Eirene said.

Tomas said, "I vote for a space-based impact weapon. That'd splatter even Xiao, if we could get a hit."

Sarah loved that idea, and wondered if they could figure out how to make it work. Adding such a huge technological leap would be a massive break in most memoryscape, but if they formed it all the way up in space, would it really generate monsters?

"I wish you'd gotten to speak with Alter," Gregorios said.

"Me too. He must feel so alone."

"I was thinking it would be nice to confirm Reuben can actually communicate with him."

"That too."

Eirene said, "As soon as you can travel, we'll get going. Leandro has made his yacht available to us again."

"Good. I can rest on the boat. Help me up," Sarah said.

Tomas shook his head. "Sarah, you're not going anywhere. You got broken up pretty bad."

Eirene said, "We could transfer you to another host. That would get you functional sooner."

Sarah hesitated. "But this one wouldn't heal without a soul attached, would it?"

"Not noticeably."

She couldn't just discard her body, not without trying to save it.

"I have a better idea."

It took a moment for Sarah to muster the focus to draw glowing runes on the sheet above her chest. She fashioned another healing rune, added modifiers to focus on bone sealing, limiting the effect to herself alone. Then she wrapped it all in an outer rune that drew power from her remote charging rune in Rome.

She limited the drain to five percent and activated the cipher. It blazed with blinding brilliance that filled the room with silver light. Everyone turned away, hands shielding their eyes.

"What did you do?" Eirene exclaimed.

Sarah couldn't answer as a torrent of energy thundered through her center like an invisible waterfall. She gasped, her body arcing off the bed, her mouth opened in a silent cry. She could not have guessed if the noise would have been of pain or of ecstasy.

Her limbs shook and the movement triggered waves of agony that were quickly snuffed out. Heat pounded her innards like a kiln.

Sweat poured down her skin as the fiery power of healing blasted through her. She wasn't sure if that white-hot power fused her bones, or just melted them and re-formed them. It also knit torn flesh, and restored her to health in several agonizingly blissful seconds.

She had called more power than she needed to heal, and the excess topped off her rounon well and filled her with so much energy that her muscles quivered with the need to move. She wanted to leap out of bed, but at the same time, the abrupt healing left her feeling spent. So she ended up sagging in bed, with every muscle quivering.

"Wow, that was a rush," she whispered, wondering if maybe she should have thought those modifiers through a little more carefully.

Tomas rushed to her, still blinking away the aftereffects of the blinding light. He wiped her brow and asked, "Are you all right? You've soaked your gown, as if you just had the world's most abrupt post-fever sweat."

"I'm fine. Get me some clothes."

Gregorios pressed her back down when she tried to sit up. "In a minute, young lady. You're not going to pull a parlor stunt like that without explaining how you did it. Not even your pretty soul has enough juice to heal those injuries in a matter of seconds."

"No, but I'm a rune warrior," Sarah said, loving his look of annoyance at the cryptic answer. "You can wait outside, old man."

"No respect," Gregorios muttered, but Sarah caught a hint of a smile as the door swung closed behind him.

"How did you do that, really?" Eirene asked while Tomas fished her clothes out of the room's little closet.

Sarah explained about how she'd modified that charging matrix in Rome to build like an invisible, giant battery.

Eirene whistled. "I've never heard of anyone using ciphers in quite that way. What happens if you let that soul force continue to build?"

"I'm not sure. It fades some each night. I think the strength absorbed from passing souls throughout the day does bleed off. But if I had a bigger target area, I could generate a lot more power."

"Let's not tell Melek about it for now. He's still adjusting to all the other concessions he's had to make to his creed this week."

"He'll come around. He's motivated right now," Sarah insisted.

"Let's hope it's enough to carry him through the critical times ahead," Eirene said with cautious hope in her voice.

55

My KA dwells in each body. Insult it not.

~PAPYRUS OF ANI, ELABORATED

SARAH HAD JUST CHANGED into her swimsuit in her comfortable cabin on Leandro's super-yacht when Tomas burst into her room. He barely paused to glance approvingly at her before beckoning. "Come on. You'll want to see this."

Sarah grabbed a sarong and joined him in the luxurious salon that was again acting as their central meeting room during the trip from Malta toward China. The others were already there, all clustered in front of several large-screen televisions. Eirene sat beside Quentin, who was working the remotes.

"What's up?" Sarah asked as she joined them and slipped an arm around Tomas' waist. He draped a hand over her shoulder. Together they watched the nearest television, which was showing a news report.

The camera was panning across an unremarkable stretch of brown desert, then zoomed in on a group of dust-coated men and women standing on a stage before a large audience. Sarah recognized the lead archaeologist from that secret dig in Egypt.

Another camera, positioned much closer to the group, took up the feed. The reporter reminded viewers that the group was a privately funded archaeological dig that had been working in a section of the Egyptian desert never before explored by archaeologists. They were gathered to announce an important find.

"What's so important about this?" Sarah asked, glancing at Gregorios, Francesca, and Spartacus, who stood clustered behind Eirene.

Eirene said absently, "Shush. Listen."

The same Chinese-American lead researcher began to speak, his Boston accent sounding strange in the Egyptian desert. He was grinning so wide, they must have found something amazing.

Sarah really wished they'd had time to visit the dig site. He said, "Many of our colleagues scoffed at digging in such a remote location. Most believed there was nothing of historical import so far from the Nile. They were wrong."

"What exactly did you find?" A reporter with a British accent asked.

"Only the most significant and perfectly preserved archaeological find of all times," the man declared.

That generated a buzz of excitement and cries of, "Prove it!" from the gathered reporters and intellectuals in the audience.

Sarah glanced at Tomas, who was watching with great interest. They'd heard that some of the early artifacts released for review by the dig were already generating a great deal of debate, but it sounded like they'd made an important new find.

The man said, "I plan to do just that." He gestured, and a woman wearing a large, white hat clicked on a projector. A large image appeared on a screen nearby, and the man said, "These are only a few of the images we've gathered. The actual artifacts will become available in the coming days."

The first image was of a stone sitting in a large cave. The stone was covered with bright Egyptian hieroglyphs in stunning detail. Sarah recognized many of the symbols from her rune study.

"We've dated this tablet back to approximately 1200 BC. Initial translation suggests it is a prophecy recorded by the high priest of Set during the reign of a mighty pharaoh, in a time of plagues and slave revolts."

"Are you saying this is an Egyptian record from the time of Moses?" One reporter called jokingly.

"Indeed, I am."

The screen flipped to another image. This was of a table with a dozen golden artifacts displayed. "Here you can see some of the artifacts included in the treasure vault. The staff of a pharaoh, gold coins from the day, records of daily life in the palace of the pharaoh, royal weapons, and many more."

"So this wasn't a tomb?" Asked an elderly man who wore an actual tweed jacket, despite the heat.

The lead researcher shook his head. "This was no tomb. This was instead a secret treasure vault containing royal artifacts and these exceptionally well preserved tablets dealing with the history of the times."

He gave the crowd a conspiratorial smile. "I'll share some tidbits with you. The tablet includes remarkable details of a distant future that describes the modern era, complete with depictions of railway, airplanes, and computers."

"Fraud," cried a voice from the crowd. "They wouldn't be able to describe those things."

The researcher did not look troubled by the outburst. "I wouldn't have believed it either. Not until I saw it for myself. They found a way. You will see. As we did with our earlier finds, we will make everything available for independent confirmation, but every indication is that this find is genuine, that these artifacts remained undisturbed for close to thirty-five centuries, and that the source of this information somehow foresaw the modern day."

"What else does it say?" A female reporter from the Middle East asked.

For the first time, the lead researcher hesitated. He added in a tone that suggested he expected people not to believe his words. "It declares that a new god will rise during a time of global conflict and bring peace to the world."

He wasn't disappointed. Many in the audience openly scoffed at the announcement, but Sarah felt a chill creep down her spine. The news report switched back to the studio, so Eirene muted the channel.

Melek began muttering Hebrew curses under his breath then added, "As we feared."

Francesca looked like she was struggling to believe what she'd just heard. "We hadn't feared this. Sure, we've discussed how Xiao was double jumping and seeking something in deep history. You suggested maybe she could draw close to the actual scroll of history, but really? Do you think she actually went into history to plant a fake prophecy about herself rising as a god?"

Eirene said, "It's troubling."

Tomas chuckled without humor. "It's more than troubling. Planting artifacts in history, then sending a team of archaeologists to find them is entire magnitudes of insane beyond what we thought we were dealing with."

Sarah said, "It's terrifying to think she could mess with things like that, but it's elegant, don't you think? She's orchestrated a world conflict and plans to rise with the promise of safety for everyone. Why not reinforce the illusion that she's the savior instead of the architect of the disaster by adding an ancient prophecy to reinforce her claim?"

Eirene grimaced. "We need to reach out to that team."

"I'll find contact information through our sources," Tomas promised. He extracted his phone from a pocket and started typing.

Quentin looked deeply worried. "If she can plant physical evidence, what's to prevent her from killing any one of us at some point in the past before we develop the strength or skills to become a threat to her?"

Melek shifted in his seat, extending his bad leg and rubbing it, as if it was paining him. "That may be her ultimate goal, but it is far harder to change the timeline of a soul than it is to reposition a few dead artifacts."

"But she could eventually get to that point?" Tomas asked, glancing up from his phone.

Melek paused before answering, and Sarah found it hard to breathe. To think someone could go back in time and kill their enemies as children was horrific. Or kill their parents before they were even born?

No one could ever threaten Xiao again. She could kill them at a time of her choosing and they would be powerless to defend themselves. Would that kill everyone whose lives depended on that person? The ramifications were so mind boggling, she couldn't wrap her head around it. Would such acts unravel the ascendants? Could Xiao break history?

Melek said, "It may be possible. If she continues on this path and gains sufficient power over the flow of history."

Gregorios muttered a curse. "That's why she attacked Sarah so brutally in the memoryscape. She wants to scare us out of history. We're the only ones who can challenge her dominance of the world."

Eirene nodded gravely. "If she controls history, and if she can push the current world powers into global warfare, she could take over and shape the future as she sees fit."

Spartacus declared, "Thus we understand the full scope of her fell purpose. On more than one occasion, she spoke of straddling the flow of time, of shaping the future, and such lofty talk that many despots are fond of. At the time I thought no particular import connected with such claims."

"I'm thinking she doesn't waste time making idle threats," Gregorios said.

Spartacus patted his belt, and when he turned, Sarah noticed for the first time an ancient gladius hanging at his hip. "We are embarked upon the great quest of our age, and together we will vanquish this enemy and preserve the world order."

Eirene smiled fondly at him. "Glory and honor will once again be ours."

Spartacus saluted her with fist to heart in the ancient Roman way. "Indeed, Queen of Mystery, we will celebrate our great victory with a feast to rival the legendary grandeur of ancient Rome. The glory of this combat will eclipse any honor we have enjoyed through our many years. Such a victory will secure my position and win the platform required to bequeath greatness once again upon this tired world."

Gregorios matched Spartacus' grin. "Let us join in honored combat for the glory alone reserved for fearless victors of the global ring."

Spartacus laughed. "My heart swells to hear you speak thus with the depth of honor your ancient wisdom demands."

Eirene slipped her arm around Gregorios' waist. "He's always full of surprises."

Gregorios surveyed the group. "I want all teams working on battle strategies. When we get a chance to close with Xiao, we have to take her out. Time is running short and we can't afford any more delays."

He focused on Sarah. "No more hesitation, Sarah. I want ciphers to beat her. Whatever it takes."

Sarah felt moved by their commitment to block Xiao's evil plot, her confidence buoyed by their optimism.

Melek frowned at Gregorios. "And yet we must exercise caution. I cannot endorse stepping into the realm of the kashaph."

Gregorios clapped Melek on the shoulder and gave him a fierce grin. "We're on the same side, but you have to decide how far you're prepared to go, Melek."

"I'll do what it takes," Melek promised him.

"Remember that," Gregorios said, fixing him with an intense stare. "You may face some difficult choices in the days ahead, Melek. I personally believe you're strong enough to make the right choices."

Melek inclined his head, accepting the compliment.

Gregorios added, "The right choice is not always the traditional one. Think on that, and be ready."

The group split up after that, and Melek pulled Sarah aside. "I feel it necessary to share some new runes with you."

Sarah eagerly followed him to a smaller salon. Studying runes was still one of her greatest passions, and she was eager to learn everything Melek was willing to share. "Do you have new ideas for fine-tuning our ciphers hunting Xiao?"

The old hunter shook his head and extracted a few sheets of paper from an inside pocket. The papers looked new, and they were covered with complex runes. As he spread them on a table, Sarah leaned in close, recognizing instantly that they were special.

She breathed, "What are these?"

"These runes are forbidden to any but the inner circle of hunter leadership. I believe you should know them too."

He passed the sheets to Sarah and she eagerly scanned them. The runes were elegant and old. They contained a mixture of ancient languages. She recognized ancient Chinese script, Egyptian hieroglyphs, and Celtic runes among them. She sensed great power in those runes, although some felt darker than others.

"Why share them with me now?" Sarah asked, forcing herself to glance up from the papers to meet Melek's serious gaze.

He sighed. "Because you need them. I risked your life, sending you unprepared to piggy-back on Xiao's double jump."

"I knew there were risks, and I accepted them."

He shook his head. "The fault was mine, and you nearly died. I'm grateful that you saw Alter, but I realized I need to trust you more."

Sarah smiled and placed one hand over his. "That's what we've been telling you for days. I'm glad you finally understand."

"Old secrets carry a weight that makes it difficult to share them, but you must be armed if you are to lead the fight against Xiao."

"So tell me about these," Sarah said, turning back to the pages of symbols.

"These were collected from David the Builder and from Hannibal."

"I know them. I've visited them several times in the memoryscape. David was a wizard at shielding."

"Indeed. As far as I know, these runes were never actually used, but rune warriors have a way of collecting the most powerful runes."

Melek turned the page and gestured at a beautiful, complex rune that Sarah immediately felt drawn to. It included a mixture of Egyptian symbols and others that looked more Native American. It was an unusual mix, but the symbols fit together perfectly.

He said, "I believe this one allows greater quantities of soul power to be channeled through your control without overwhelming you."

Sarah nodded slowly as she studied the rune. She saw that possibility, and it excited her. She also sensed others, linked to the strength of one's ancestors, coupled with concepts of purification and rebirth. Did Melek know about those too, or did he not understand all that rune could do? She was tempted to ask him, but didn't want to spook him into taking back the pages before she memorized the other runes.

She whispered, "If Vlad had access to these, his story might have turned out so very different."

"Perhaps. Or perhaps he would have risen to become a monster to rival Paul. We shall never know."

"He's monstrous enough. Thank you for sharing these."

"We must defeat Xiao. For my son, and for the welfare of the world. You will play the critical role in the upcoming confrontation, my dear. To become the champion able to face this unrivaled demon, you will need these."

Sarah met his gaze and said, "Then teach me everything you know about them."

56

ALTER FOLLOWED Xiao into a vaulted basement of rough-hewn stone, blackened with age. He had no idea where they were, only that they were no longer outside of Rome.

He'd been drugged prior to the journey, so had no reference to how long it had taken. Even though his enhancements would dispel most drugs in a matter of minutes, whatever had been pumped into his veins had knocked him out for quite a while.

The architecture of the large building he'd awakened inside was old, mostly stone, and had an oriental flavor. Some effort had been spent trying to mask that, but he still picked up on little details. Carvings on the wood-sheathed walls and the layout of the tile on the floor screamed Asian influence. Every window had been shuttered, so he could not see outside, but he sensed they had traveled to a foreign land.

This time, when Xiao summoned him to join her for another memory journey, she had not forced him to wear a hood. Every other time, she'd prevented him from seeing her machine.

Now he eagerly approached the shining steel machine standing in the center of the long room. It was the only one visible, but he suspected she had more.

Xiao made no move to prevent him from inspecting the machine, but instead made a gracious wave of one slender hand. "Examine it. You have earned the right to understand the full brilliance of its construction by your dedicated service to me."

If only she knew.

Alter scanned the tiny, precise runes marked along the inside edges of the helmet and jagged faceplate, traced them along the wire conduits, and even popped open the back panel on the machine. If Xiao was foolish enough to allow him such a close look, he'd push the limits.

He had worked on the machines they'd taken from Mai Luan, had rebuilt one from scratch, and knew every rune and where it belonged. He'd modified their machines to block some of the more onerous aspects of the memory journey, so he understood the construct better than anyone.

In seconds he identified the differences. This machine retained the markings that allowed Xiao as the passenger to control the memories of Alter as the primary dreamer. He had expected as much. What drew his gaze were four unknown runes. One was an intricate design placed at the junction between two primary supports where the cluster of wires originated. One of the markings within the rune was familiar.

"Your title is part of this rune," he exclaimed, glancing up at her in surprise.

"Indeed, it is the core of my destiny. Does it surprise you to find it is also a source of great power?" she asked calmly.

Alter memorized the design as he had the other three. "What do these other runes do?"

Xiao gave him a disapproving look. "Knowledge of such a sacred nature cannot be shared in such a base manner, cast like pearls before swine. You of all men must understand the importance of self-revelation."

For once, Alter wished he didn't. He'd tease out the true measure of these runes over time, but that was one thing he now lacked.

When he completed his inspection, he forced himself to thank her for the opportunity. He hated playing nice, but such access might prove critical to his eventual rebellion.

She smiled. "You are welcome, dear Alter. As you see, dedicated service brings great rewards."

They settled into padded couches while assistants prepared the helmets. The enchanter who had nearly blown them up in that museum in Rome entered the room and stood behind the techs, surveying the process. It irritated Alter to think he'd failed to destroy the kashaph when he'd had the chance.

"You have met my chief eunuch," Xiao said, noting Alter's gaze.

"Not by name. Only by reputation."

The enchanter stepped a bit closer and made a slight bow. "You know nothing of my reputation, boy hunter. I am Hongwu."

Alter refused to return the gesture, despite the risk of angering Xiao. He could pretend to serve her in meaningless tasks, but never grant respect to a polluted enemy. "You consider yourself a builder of great dynasties?"

"You have studied history," Hongwu said with a tiny nod of respect. "Indeed, I have chosen the title of Vastly Martial as my era name, just as the great Zhu Yuanzhang did after establishing the Ming dynasty in 1368."

"You disgrace his memory," Alter declared.

Hongwu chuckled. "He was an arrogant man, but he would be honored by my choice."

"You knew him?"

Xiao had been watching the conversation with unreadable calm. Now she said, "One of the benefits of service to me is longevity. Remember that, my young Alter."

He wanted to ask if Hongwu was castrated anew with every life, or if the reference to eunuch was a carryover from his first life. The Ming had used many eunuchs. Alter hoped Xiao had dropped the practice. He would never allow his pretend support for her to extend that far. The thought left him feeling a bit queasy.

Submitting to the faceplate would be harder knowing that Hongwu hovered nearby. What might the enchanter do while he lay helpless in the chair?

Xiao interrupted his worry by declaring, "I will take the primary seat as the memory walker today."

At his surprised look she said, "There is something you must see."

For a moment, Alter harbored the hope of gaining access over Xiao's memories. He was the passenger now, and the runes were designed to grant him control.

His hope died as Hongwu marked a series of runes across Xiao's helmet with a marker. Alter recognized them and fought to conceal a scowl. They would counter the runes granting him control. They were similar to ones he'd developed for Gregorios and Eirene, but more complete.

Alter hated granting the hated enchanter any respect, but he recognized master talent in that sequence. Xiao might allow him to see a memory, but she would not risk submitting to his control. So much for trusting him as her most beloved servant.

The memoryscape materialized quickly, more so than it had in the past couple of memory jumps. He had equated the lag with journeys back to deep in the past. He still didn't understand how Xiao managed to jump so far back with him as the memory walker, but it must have something to do with those new runes.

The great vista of the memoryscape materialized around them. He recognized the stone tower upon which they stood, as would most people in the modern world. Pictures of the Great Wall of China were available everywhere.

The famous wall stretched below him, down a steep slope and across a wide plain. It was manned by thousands of Chinese soldiers, who faced north toward Mongolia, fighting a desperate struggle to defend their lands.

An enormous army spread across the plain, with soldiers packing the ground at the foot of the wall, waiting for their chance to scramble up ladders and ropes to fight the Chinese. One section of wall had already been overrun and fighting was fierce. The sound of thousands of bows firing made a steady thrumming backdrop to the clash of weapons and the screaming of dying men.

Xiao stood beside him, staring out over the battle, hands clasped behind her back. Her expression remained unreadable, something she did often, which frustrated him to no end.

"Why did you bring me here?" he asked.

"We stand in the mid-seventeenth century. In those days, the Ming dynasty fell to the Qing out of Manchuria."

"Every dynasty falls," Alter said.

"Exactly." She turned to him, her eyes flashing with emotion. "This moment represents the futility of human existence. The Ming built this wall, stretching hundreds of miles, and yet they still fell."

Alter shrugged. "No wall is impervious. Sometimes they just get in the way."

Xiao said, "The Ming set many walls. Some were less tangible, and all equally weak. Their kingdom fell, as all mortal kingdoms have. Corruption. Intrigue. Selfishness." She spoke the words with open disgust. "All of these lesser traits crept into every dynasty and toppled it."

Her expression hardened into one of resolve. "Mine will be immune from such base conceits."

The intensity of her stare warned of her passion for her goal, but perhaps she might reveal something important in that moment of honest zeal. So he asked, "How can you prevent people from acting that way? Those temptations are the everlasting temptation of humankind. Every generation has to prove that it can stand strong, or it collapses under the weight of its own iniquity. Then the next generation gets a turn. No one can know until the moment of proving."

Xiao shook her head. "I'll know. That's why you're helping me."

"I don't understand what I'm doing, or how that is possible," Alter admitted.

She held to lofty goals, the same ones shared by founders of great dynasties and great religions. No matter their strength, their integrity, or the purity of their teachings, none of them could guarantee the integrity of future generations.

"That doesn't diminish the importance of your task."

"Then will you tell me what our last journey had to do with your mission?" he dared ask. On the wall below, the attacking Manchurians gained a foothold on another section of the wall and began pushing the Ming soldiers back. "All we did was set up that fake treasure chamber."

Xiao did not browbeat him, but said, "That work will play a critical role in our future plans. For now, look to your upcoming role. We will visit the fall of Constantinople soon. That pivotal moment will provide a master rune I hope will add a component to my new name. You will assist me again."

"Very well," Alter forced himself to say.

He hated the thought of her gaining yet another master rune, but he honestly believed her claim to have found dozens of them. If she really did plan to tap their power, she had more than enough. One more wouldn't make any difference.

He actually believed she was indeed seeking a special name, although building one from master runes was such an abominable intent, only his commitment to eventually destroying her kept him from refusing outright. He added, "First, allow me to walk the halls of my homeland again."

"To what end?" she asked.

"It helps remind me why I am doing this." Alter gestured toward the battle raging below them. "Just as this memory strengthens your resolve."

She considered him for a long moment, but he refused to reveal his nervousness. Finally she nodded once. "I grant you leave to go."

The memoryscape faded, and Alter found himself once again standing on the rooftop of his family's compound. Had he shifted his presence, or had she pushed him? He decided it didn't matter. She hadn't followed yet, but who knew how long she'd allow him alone?

Eager to find his dispossessed brother, he jumped off the roof.

57

O people of the earth, men and women born and made of the elements, but with the spirit of the Divine within you, rise from your sleep of ignorance! Be sober and thoughtful. Realize that your home is not on the earth but in the Light of each life. Why have you delivered yourselves unto death, having power to partake of immortality?

~MUATA ASHBY, ANCIENT EGYPTIAN PROVERBS

SARAH ENTERED the large living room of the spacious suite the team used as their meeting hub. Located in the Chaoyang District of Beijing, not far from the well-known shopping area of Sanlitun, the high-rise apartment building blended in with dozens of similar structures marching away in every direction.

Sarah felt small in Beijing. The city might officially claim to be the home of about twenty million people, but Quentin had informed her that the true number was probably at least twice that. There were people everywhere. Sarah considered herself a gregarious person, but she felt sometimes like she was suffocating in Beijing.

Probably the bad air. Beijing's infamous smog was even worse than she'd heard. She'd taken to wearing a mask over her nose and mouth when she ventured forth, a habit followed by most of the locals and many foreigners. They'd landed barely two days ago, and she was already eager to move on. Despite washing her face and neck every time she came indoors, she still felt gritty.

"How'd it go?" Eirene asked when Sarah dropped into a padded leather chair with a great view of a local six-lane highway. Traffic was super congested, like it always seemed to be here. It had surprised her to see so many Volkswagens on the roads. She'd expected smaller cars like in Italy.

They'd learned quickly to take the subway, or MRT. It served their purposes better anyway, despite every train car being packed to overflowing. Sarah was just glad winter was on the way. The stench of sweating bodies was bad enough now with cooler temperatures. In the summer, she'd have needed a thicker mask.

Sarah gave her a tired smile. "We covered another hundred stops at least." She couldn't remember what colored lines they'd taken. They all started blending together after a while.

Tomas entered the living room and took a seat on a nearby couch. He was probably tired too, but concealed it better. She was tempted to stick her tongue out at him.

Eirene rose and walked to a nearby table where a large map of the entire MRT system was spread out. "Don't forget to mark the locations."

Tomas said, "I tagged them on the GPS. I'll have Domenico update the database."

Eirene said, "Good. That covers most of the system. How are the runes holding up?"

"Better than I'd expected," Sarah admitted.

During the long cruise from Malta to Beijing, they had worked out a plan. With such an enormous city to canvas for Xiao, and with few local resources to muster, the task was daunting. So they divided to conquer.

Sarah and Tomas had spent the bulk of their time over the past couple of days riding the tightly-packed subway trains back and forth across the city. They stopped at every station for Sarah to inscribe a rune onto the stones.

Invisible to anyone else, the runes were similar to the ones she'd left in Rome to sweep for nearby rounon or cui dashi. She powered them with a one percent energy drain on passing souls, not even enough to slow a commuter's frantic rush to squeeze into the next train. Every station fed a common power source that she had set up through a broader cipher that linked the stations together in another remote battery.

It was going to be a big one.

Already the accumulated soul power had eclipsed the one she'd left in Rome. Unlike Rome, Beijing was a city that did not sleep, so the battery kept charging right through the night. The question of how much a constantly charging rune could handle before becoming overwhelmed was no longer a hypothetical one.

She needed to figure it out or face some of those dire consequences Alter always warned her about. The problem was, the person best qualified to help her determine how much load her runes could support was Melek. She hadn't dared broach the subject with him yet.

Gregorios and Spartacus had spent their time rooting out the gangs that filled the city's back alleys. They had already recruited two gangs as scouts and informants through hefty bribes and intimidation.

The night before, Spartacus explained how he had challenged one gang's champion to single combat, then beat the guy and his friends to submission.

The story left Eirene shaking her head. "I knew it was a bad idea to set you two loose on the city together."

Gregorios and Spartacus had shared a grin, and Sarah wondered what they planned to do once they cowed all the gangs into submission. She had felt immensely relieved that Gregorios had never shown interest in world-domination. She didn't doubt that if he really wanted it, he'd succeed. Especially if Eirene supported the plan.

Eirene's time had been spent coordinating their global intelligence network and economic machine. They'd scaled back the economic assault on the US and other major allies because it was only pushing the countries toward imminent hostilities faster.

They still hadn't figured out how Xiao was coercing the nations, but had determined she must have subverted the President of the United States as well as the British Prime Minister. The queen was due for another transfer soon, and it appeared Xiao had gotten the queen's ear also.

"I don't think it's blackmail," Eirene had said the night before. "This is too insane for that."

"Perhaps a binding rune," Melek had suggested.

"It's possible, but both countries know about rounon powers. Ever since Abraham Lincoln, they've had countermeasures in place as part of their standard defensive strategies. We're missing something, I know it," Eirene had grumbled.

"You'll find it, love," Gregorios had said. "You always do."

Quentin entered the room now, whistling, holding Sarah's crossbow bolt.

"That's where that ended up. I thought I'd lost it in customs," Sarah said when he handed it to her.

Quentin winked. "Nearly did. I managed to reacquire it for you."

"How?"

He shrugged. "That's not important. Let's focus on the fact that with the assistance of Gregorios' new ground troops, I've procured some excellent quality materials."

"You're setting up a lab here?" Sarah felt excited by the prospect of more of Quentin's inventions becoming available again.

Eirene had ordered an entire shipping container sent from Hong Kong with heavy equipment and weapons they could never slip through airport customs. Gregorios had promised they'd get the container safely through the nearest sea port with the help of the well-bribed gang members. He expected the crates to arrive by midnight. It would be nice to have a machine gun under her bed again.

Sarah leaned back in her chair, running her fingers across the shaft of the bolt, tracing out potential runes. An idea was forming for how best to use it. She just needed a little more time.

"Any hits?" Eirene asked.

"Nothing yet," Sarah said. She'd felt a couple of distant tremors, but they'd faded away too quickly. After today's work, she could pick up the passage of Xiao or one of her Rounon-enhanced henchmen along any of the major train lines.

Since they crisscrossed or paralleled many of the major roads, she should be able to intercept any of their moves throughout the city. The runes contained a tracking component that she'd be able to sense for at least half an hour. They'd have to move very quickly.

"It's like searching for a needle in a haystack," Tomas grumbled.

Sarah flashed him a smile. "Except we've got a magnet. We'll find her."

Gregorios entered the room, followed by Spartacus, who now wore a white Chinese linen shirt and black pants. If he was trying to fit in, he'd have to change more than his clothing. He stood out like a lion in the midst of a pack of jackals.

After kissing Eirene and getting their updates, Gregorios said, "We've reached baseline. Well done, everyone. To celebrate, we're going into the memoryscape."

Eirene cautioned, "If Xiao is in the city, the proximity will magnify the pull. We'll get sucked in."

Sarah added, "Especially with the runes we're adding. Should allow us to hitchhike even onto unfamiliar memories."

That rune sequence had been Melek's brain child. He shared Alter's flair and artistry with runes, coupled with vast experience and profound understanding. If the new runes worked, it'd be a huge win for them in hunting Xiao even across double jumping timelines.

Gregorios said, "Let's test it out. Better to work out any kinks now before it really matters."

"It'll matter if she's in there too," Tomas said.

Spartacus declared, "I will join you, my friends. I will declare to their faces my intent to spurn their hollow threatenings and to meet them in battle most glorious."

Quentin surprised Sarah by saying, "I'd like to join too. It's been a while, and I want to feel what this double jump process is like."

"Count me in," Tomas said immediately.

Gregorios shook his head. "Melek updated the configuration so we can link four helmets together now. That's the limit. Eirene or I will drive. Francesca will assist the other one of us with powering the machine. Sarah and Melek need to be there. That leaves only one seat. I don't think it matters which of you come, so you three figure it out."

"I challenge you to a duel," Spartacus said immediately. "Your choice of weapons. We fight to first blood."

Tomas looked tempted, but Quentin shook his head. "I prefer rock, paper, scissors."

Spartacus grinned. "Done! I have mastered the art of this mental warfare since my awakening."

Quentin matched his grin. "I haven't lost in years."

"Then your fall will bring even more glory."

While they argued about rules, Tomas pulled Sarah aside.

He started to speak, but she interrupted by wrapping her arms around his neck and kissing him soundly. He reacted quickly, wrapped his powerful arms around her slender waist, and lifted her off the floor. For a moment, she forgot all about the mission and lost herself in the kiss.

When he finally lowered her, he looked a bit flushed, and she wanted to fan her face from the heat of her passion. They really needed to get some alone time.

Back to business, he said, "Good news. My contact in the Smithsonian did better than get me the number for that lead archaeologist of that Egyptian dig. They got a full scan of a stone uncovered in the dig that seems to be the critical piece of the discovery. Check out this image I spotted on it."

He held up his phone, and Sarah gasped when she saw the image. "That's the same rune Spartacus found on Hongwu's amulet!"

"Yup. The lead archaeologist is a man named Charles Wang. Apparently he's on a tight deadline to get these images out to the rest of the world, so he leaped at the chance to get some collaboration in translating the images in time."

Sarah was thrilled by the find, but she frowned. "Isn't that odd? Don't they usually want to control the entire process so no one else tries to claim any credit on their find?"

"Usually, but if these artifacts were really planted by Xiao, it seems she's pushing the team to spread their false narrative to the rest of the world. The team determined that this mystery symbol is the signature of the high priest of Set, god of chaos. The high priest's name was Sutekh."

Sarah considered the image again. Anyone who used such a powerful symbol as their signature mark had to be someone important. "What do they know about him?"

"Quite a bit, actually. Apparently the stone includes remarkable detail of his life, including information that might allow researchers to confirm the date that Moses lived. And get this, it includes an amazingly detailed prophecy of a distant future."

Sarah groaned. "Really?"

"Pretty clever, really. Apparently Sutekh foresaw a terrible war, exactly like what we'll be facing if we can't turn around current events. And he foresaw the rise of a new leader who would bring peace and stability to the world."

"Like a Christ figure?" Sarah asked, disgusted to think Xiao would draw upon sacred religious texts to prop up her world domination scheme.

"I haven't studied it yet, but probably something like that. Apparently the researchers are becoming true believers. They're intent on sharing this information with everyone and trumpeting the impending arrival of a person who will save the world."

"Xiao has really planned everything, hasn't she?" Sarah asked in disgust. "Where's the rest of the stone? We need to study it."

Tomas shook his head and put his phone away. "I've ordered print-outs. We'll get them after the memory hunt."

"But . . ." She protested.

"Oh, no. If you get your hands on those runes, we won't see you for days. Shouldn't take long to beat Spartacus and Quentin both, despite their boasting. I'll join you for the hunt."

58

I enter the arena confident of victory, as all must who participate in the great trial. Only when the sands are cleaned of blood and peace clasps the world in her gentle embrace does the warrior face their greatest test of honor. Conquest without bloodshed is perhaps the only battle that yet remains to win.

~SPARTACUS

SARAH APPEARED beside Gregorios atop a high stone pyramid. The sun was just setting in the west, coloring the entire horizon brilliant crimson and gold. She glanced around in astonishment at the pyramids and stone structures all around.

They weren't in China, but stood in some other giant ancient city. She'd visited some ruins of the Aztec pyramids in Mexico, so she recognized the similarities.

The air was thick and warm, humid but not hot. It smelled of dense vegetation, flowers, and wood smoke. The location helped take her mind off her longing to get her hands on those images from Mr. Wang.

Melek, then Spartacus, appeared beside her. Spartacus was still grinning from his recent victory over Tomas and Quentin. Quentin in particular had been deeply offended by the loss and had left the room, muttering about leaving an incendiary under Spartacus' bed.

"South America?" Sarah asked Gregorios, who was looking east into the lengthening shadows.

"Tenochtitlan, 1519. The year Hernan Cortez destroyed every-thing," Gregorios explained.

"You were here?" Sarah shouldn't be surprised by that fact, but she was.

Gregorios shrugged. "I travel a lot. The new world was big news back then and the council wanted information about it. Also, the conquering European powers, particularly the Spanish, were fond of employing powerful heka to lead their expeditions. Cortez was one of the worst."

Melek, who was dressed again in his youthful form, was looking around with interest. "We heard of his exploits, but our hunters couldn't catch him before he returned to Spain and forsook the prac-tices of his youth."

Gregorios nodded. "He and I disagreed. He was brutal, but bril-liant at his job."

Spartacus said, "I'm surprised you didn't kill him. Ever was that your preferred method for dealing with those you disagreed with."

"I would have. Like I said, he was brilliant. He sent a squad of enhanced conquistadors to trap me in a mountain cave. I eventually escaped, but by then he'd already conquered the city." He shook his head in disgust. "Moctezuma was such an idiot."

"So why bring us here?" Sarah longed to descend the pyramid and explore the area. She'd always been fascinated by stories of the Aztecs.

"What do you feel? Any tug on the ascendant runes or anything?" Gregorios asked.

Sarah checked. Nothing.

"About what I figured. I'm not getting any tugs from other memory walkers either. This location is so foreign to Xiao it should minimize the pull long enough for us to abort before getting sucked into her dreams."

Melek nodded approval. "Good thinking. And here I thought Eirene was the clever one."

"Who says she didn't suggest it?" Gregorios asked with a smile. "We've got some time. Let's get to work."

They spent half an hour testing out new rune sequences and engagement tactics against Xiao. Gregorios summoned mannequin-like replicas of the cui dashi and sent them zipping around the cere-monial center where the team practiced.

Sarah and Melek fine-tuned the process of slowing, binding, and burning those test dummies, while Spartacus attacked with a wide array of summoned weapons. He might have lived in ancient Rome, but he was a quick study. He loved RPGs and M60 machine guns until Sarah introduced him to portable miniguns. He took to that weapon like a T-rex to the slaughter.

"I've created a monster," Sarah muttered as Spartacus vaulted off the top of a nearby temple and soared over a hundred feet, raining high explosive rounds into the windows of the Templo Mayor.

Smoke poured from the building and stone disintegrated under the barrage. The sound was like constant thunder that merged with the fierce buzzing of the minigun's astronomical rate of fire.

Spartacus landed and released the trigger. The echoes faded, but he remained motionless, watching the savaged temple. Just as silence returned to claim the area, the entire upper level of the magnificent structure collapsed with a thunderous roar, blasting a cloud of dust into the shadowy night.

Spartacus threw his hands up in victory, allowing the minigun to swing at his waist on its harness. "I am as one of the gods!"

Melek regarded Spartacus with distaste. "It pains me to fight monsters with monsters, but I can't see any way around it."

Sarah squeezed his hand. "Spartacus isn't all that bad, you know."

"How can you say that? He's a confessed heka with the blood of thousands on his hands. Just look at him." He gestured at the celebrating gladiator.

"He's different in this life. Give the guy a break, won't you? He's changing. That's hard to do."

Melek actually stopped to think about that one. She caught him glancing at Spartacus throughout the rest of the practice session, a thoughtful look on his face.

Good. She really liked Melek, but he needed to learn to be a little more flexible. If he could see new options with Spartacus, maybe there was hope for smoothing out his differences with Alter.

Gregorios called them to the center of the smoking ruin they'd made of the city center. Crowds of locals had begun gathering, looking increasingly hostile. "Our time's about up. Good work, everyone. Did we learn anything?"

Spartacus hoisted his heavy minigun into the air and declared, "This magnificent weapon shall be incorporated into my coat of arms."

Sarah smiled at his youthful enthusiasm. She didn't blame him. She loved firing the Gecal-50 from the hip. "I think we've got a real shot at stopping her this time. I can hold her longer and we can do some real damage. Tomas and his strike team will need to reach her in the real world fast, though. I'm worried she'll be hiding across town and he won't have time."

"We're working on that, but that's our biggest risk, for sure," Gregorios agreed. He cocked his head, as if listening, then added, "Hold on. I'm getting a flicker."

Before Sarah could ask what kind of flicker, the memoryscape blurred around them, then re-formed into the familiar tower of the Castel Sant Angelo. Reuben lounged nearby, leaning against the outer wall of the tower. Sarah breathed a sigh of relief and relaxed. She'd feared they'd show up next to Xiao and Vlad.

Gregorios headed for the dispossessed hunter. "I thought I'd find you here. Any word from your brother?"

Reuben stood, but his eyes fixed on Spartacus. "You bring a kashaph with you, father?"

Melek nodded. "He's an ally today, Son. The world's become a complicated place."

"No, father, you're allowing them to taint your purity." Reuben approached, poking his father in the chest. "I can see it. That's why you've lost your runes."

"How . . ." Melek looked pained.

Sarah wanted to club Reuben with a train car. He was going to undo everything she'd accomplished with Melek. She stepped between them.

"Your father's part of a great work, Reuben. You should've learned the lesson to listen to his wisdom. You wouldn't be in this mess if you had."

Reuben made an intricate bow. "You think to bring balance, but you can't do that without breaking what's in place. I don't think you have the courage."

Spartacus lunged past Sarah and delivered a mighty blow to Reuben's face, knocking the hunter twenty feet. He shouted, "Dishonor! I stand as champion for Lady Sarah to defend her virtue from your poisonous lies."

"Thank you, Spartacus, but I can stand for myself," Sarah said, placing a restraining hand on his shoulder.

She wasn't sure where that reaction of his had come from. It was gallant and chivalrous, but the thought of Spartacus standing as her champion was so bizarre, she couldn't quite wrap her head around it. He was still wearing Tomas' old body, after all.

Reuben leaped back to his feet, but Gregorios said, "Enough games. I'll make you boys an arena later if you want. What message from Alter?"

The young hunter glared at them and spat, "Only this. Xiao seeks the master rune from the fall of Constantinople tomorrow night. She seeks more pieces for her new name." He then pointed at Spartacus. "When I'm restored, I'll find you."

Spartacus grinned and saluted. "Indeed, youth of the noble heritage. We will meet in glorious combat, and I will instill into your flesh lessons on proper manners."

"No killing," Gregorios warned.

"I shall leave him lingering on the cusp of the great gate," Spartacus assured Gregorios. "Thus may he employ his time of recovery to reflection on the error of his ways."

Reuben turned to Melek. "Father, this path leads to destruction. Don't walk it blindly." Then he faded from the memory.

"That is one strange young man. What a waste of talent," Gregorios said.

Melek started to argue, but Gregorios interrupted. "Eirene. Take us home, love."

59

I'm terrified I won't be able to keep the people I love safe. The only good thing about all the danger we're in is that it's helped me see beyond my fixation on our physical forms. I think I'm getting the hang of looking at the heart more than the stature, muscles, or skin tone. You'd think I'd learn something deeper, but I'll take every little bit I can get.

~SARAH

SARAH APPEARED atop the highest tier of a massive stone fortification, dressed in fifteenth-century German gothic plate armor. It covered every inch of her except her left forearm.

She willed the helmet away too, replacing it with modern Kevlar. Her armor looked authentic to the time period, but was lined with more Kevlar to handle the rudimentary firearms of the day. All in all, it was a functional design, maximizing defense against whatever they might encounter in Constantinople without breaking the memory too much.

She hadn't trained much with a sword, so several knives of varying lengths hung from her belt. She was getting pretty good at throwing blades. When the situation deteriorated, she'd summon whatever weapons seemed most appropriate at the time.

She was going to need a lot of them.

Sarah gazed out over a scene of insanity. Dawn was breaking in the east, on the far side of a vast city. The shadows were creeping away from the wall upon which she stood, revealing desperate struggle.

Tens of thousands of Turkish troops were churning against the outer wall of the three-tiered defenses of the city. They clambered up ropes and ladders and broken stones like a dark tide of creeping, deadly insects. They broke upon the thin lines of defenders who looked pitifully few to stand against such an onslaught.

Heaps of bodies piled against the walls testified of the brutal struggle. The distant sounds of screaming and sporadic gunfire echoed above the din of shouting men and clashing steel. Even standing this high, the air carried a sharp tang of fresh-spilled blood and opened bodies. The grim horror of the pitched battle reinforced Sarah's nervousness.

There had been no question about responding to Reuben's message and challenging Xiao before she could win another master rune. Despite her lofty talk of initiating a new dynasty of world peace, she'd set the stage for a new world war that would kill millions. Finally they knew where to find her, and they'd planned to bring the fight to her.

The rest of the battle group materialized around Sarah, also dressed for combat. Gregorios wore a lighter suit of armor, while Melek wore a suit similar to Sarah's. Spartacus wore the traditional garb of a gladiator, which meant he wore little. Sandals, a leather kilt, and armor on his right arm and shoulder. He carried a gladius.

Gregorios glanced over the raging battle and grunted. "May thirtieth, 1453. An ugly day."

"This is what it really looked like?" Sarah asked, feeling a bit queasy. History books failed to convey the brutality of armed conflict.

"Pretty much. Eighty thousand Turks storming a city defended by a motley group of seven thousand men. This day was the culmination of years of planning and months of continuous combat. And the defenders almost made it."

Melek's expression was grim, his voice pitched low. "Definitely a pivotal moment. The fall of Constantinople marked a fundamental shift in the world powers and opened the doors for Turkish expansion into Africa and Europe."

Gregorios nodded. "Many claim this event marked the end of the Middle Ages. It sure marked the end of a lot of lives. Old Murad started a long trend of conquest after this."

Melek turned to him, frowning. "Hold on. The sultan was Mehmet II."

Gregorios shook his head. "He was Murad II, in his second life.

The old Turk was a brilliant strategist and as ambitious as he was devious. He paid the council enormous fees over centuries to continue his reign."

"How did we miss that one? Such an obvious target for your demonic services," Melek said, looking disgusted.

Gregorios winked. "You were busy in Europe. We always tried to hold a more global view, even back then. The first ten sultans of the Ottoman Empire are regarded as exceptional. They were all Murad, building upon previous successes. After he finally died of advanced soul fragmentation, his descendants never could live up to his legacy and the empire began its long decline."

Melek scowled, as if considering tracking down the sultan during the battle and ending his stolen second life. It wouldn't change things, but it might help him feel better.

"So this was his big day," Sarah said, glancing again at the terrible battle. What a mess.

Gregorios nodded. "This is a day of history. Today the Ottoman Empire began its long expansion, rising into a dominant world power. It was also the day the Eastern Roman Empire fell, ending the Roman rule that had lasted for fifteen centuries."

Spartacus declared, "Xiao has chosen a day most fitting. Taking this day's rune would add important undertones to her new name. This day saw the downfall of empires, and the building from the dust of their remains a new and glorious kingdom to cover the world."

"Not if we can help it," Sarah promised.

Spartacus grinned. "Indeed, Lady of Steel, we will snatch her victory and assume her glory as our own!"

"How's your connection?" Gregorios asked Sarah.

"Strong." She had already marked runes onto her forearm to activate the pingback to Tomas and to initiate a scan to alert her to any active nevron in the area. "No sign of Xiao yet, though."

"I'd be surprised if you could find anyone in that mess," Melek muttered, still staring out over the wall.

They remained atop the tower, watching the fighting while Sarah waited anxiously for anything from her rune. Hopefully she'd be able to pinpoint Alter as well as Xiao.

She'd love a chance to talk with him, reassure him that they were receiving his messages, and offer comfort and encouragement. He must be feeling so alone. He needed to know they were doing everything in their power to help.

As the minutes slipped away, she started to worry Xiao might somehow be blocking her. She considered other modifiers to add to the rune to circumvent any defenses she might have in place. The city would fall soon. Time was so fleeting.

Spartacus pointed toward the fighting. "The defenders are mighty men of valor to stand boldly in the face of such odds."

Gregorios said, "The city wouldn't have lasted half as long without some talented help from foreigners. Giovanni Giustiniani, a brilliant Genoese soldier, led seven hundred experienced men to the city's aid. He ended up taking charge of most of the city's defenses and personally led the fighters on the wall."

He gestured toward the heart of the raging battle. "He used his rounon gift much like you hunters, Melek. You would have liked him. The enhancements of his men played a critical role in holding back Murad's enhanced Janissaries. If he hadn't suffered a severe wound today, the assault might well have failed. If the Turks hadn't won this last assault, they were planning to abandon the invasion altogether."

"So close," Sarah breathed. To think so much destruction could have been avoided by such a tiny margin.

Melek also looked impressed as he studied the battle. "I was not aware of his rounon gift, but he'd been left to stand against an army more than ten times larger, better equipped, and with powerful enhancements. The Turks were led by a brilliant leader, but the defenders were left with virtually no help from the rest of Christendom. Their political squabbles were far too similar to today's world. Mehmet capitalized on those weaknesses with terrible success."

Gregorios added, "He had help. The council was involved in those politics, working to undermine support for Constantinople and delay assistance."

"Why? That's so mean," Sarah exclaimed. Sometimes she hated learning the truth about history. It was usually even more depressing than the tidbits that made it through to the history books.

"At the time it seemed appropriate. The Christian world had turned against our kind, driven by religious stupidity and hunter conspiracies. Several prominent facetakers had been killed. The Turks were more open to diversity of culture and religion. Plus, they were paying us more."

"So world history was changed so much because your council was holding grudges?" Sarah demanded.

"Sometimes the greatest events pivot on the smallest of choices," Gregorios said calmly.

"You mentioned the Turks were enhanced. What runes did they use?" Sarah asked.

She was dismayed by the conversation, but it was still better than watching men hack each other apart. Why didn't Xiao appear so they could go kill her once and for all? In her current frame of mind, she'd welcome a chance to take the fight to the terrifying woman.

Gregorios said, "Yes, the Janissaries were heavily enhanced, much like our enforcers today. In fact, we still use some of the rune placements they developed. They were the elite Turkish infantry and the sultan's bodyguards. On the Byzantine side, runes were frowned on, but Giovanni Giustiniani was a realist. His forces included a corps of channelers whose skill with rune webs helped support the walls despite the long, brutal bombardment from the Turkish cannon. Many of the Genoese were personally enhanced. That's why they were able to stand against such terrible odds for so long without cracking."

"Sometimes I hate knowing the truth about history," Sarah said, pacing away along the crenelated rooftop.

Gregorios shrugged. "Constantinople would have fallen. If not this day, then in the near future. We had already returned to Rome. The empire had decayed until this city that had once been the crown jewel of the greatest empire in the world had wasted to ruin, its wealth spent, its population shrinking. It already had one foot in the grave, as they say."

"Well you didn't have to push it over the edge," Sarah retorted.

A great shout below drew them back to the edge overlooking the battlefield. The defenders had broken and Turks streamed through the breach into the city. Sarah felt sick at the sight, guessing at the barbarous acts about to be committed on the helpless population.

"Where is she? The rune will appear any time now," Sarah hissed.

Gregorios didn't look affected by the carnage below. He'd seen a lot more battle than Sarah had. "I've been thinking about that. The fall of the outer wall was a major milestone, but the symbolic fall of Constantinople was when the great church, the Hagia Sophia, was breached."

"Where's that?" Spartacus asked.

"On the eastern side of the city, near the Golden Horn."

Melek said, "We'd best hurry then."

Spartacus declared, "Indeed, Master of Warriors, or we must needs carve our way through those thousands of marauders."

"Oh, I can think of a better way to get there." Gregorios grinned and leaped off the tower, soaring sixty feet across the open avenue running along the inner edge of the wall and landing atop a much shorter tower. He rolled with the landing and vaulted the next street onto another roof.

That was more like it. Sarah smiled as she backed up and took a running start to follow. She loved running the rooftops of memory cities. The rush of cool air helped clean her lungs from the stench of battle and center her thoughts. She stopped worrying about when Xiao would show up and focused on chasing Gregorios.

They raced across the city in leaping bounds that spanned the widest boulevards and quickly outpaced the attackers streaming down the streets. Sarah glimpsed many isolated battles as groups of defenders collided with attackers, or panicked citizens were caught outside their homes and cut down by merciless invaders.

She ran faster.

They reached a vast square that extended to a gigantic domed cathedral and Sarah slowed to stare. The enormous structure reared one hundred and eighty feet above the ground and was just a little longer than it was wide, about two hundred and fifty feet per side.

"That's a big church," she breathed.

Gregorios paused on the edge of the last roof beside her. "Wait till you see the inside. The central nave is a wonder, even compared to the best that Rome had to offer."

They dropped to the pavement and Sarah trotted toward the church, noting that the massive bronze doors were closed. Then she paused and looked up, drawn by a tug on her locating rune.

Two figures, tiny in the distance, stood atop the wall of the front facade. She pointed. "There. Looks like Xiao and Hongwu."

Spartacus cracked his knuckles. "Let us declare our intentions and close in battle without delay."

"I hate how much I've been agreeing with you lately," Gregorios said before breaking into a run toward the cathedral.

60

Curse all the gods and the priests who serve them! Sutekh has fallen, my facetaker is dead, and now I hear that Muwatalli is gone. I never thought my future lives would hang by such a thread. I can fill a tomb with gold, but without access to my next life, I am little more than a beggar on borrowed time.

~PHARAOH RAMESSES THE GREAT, THIRD KING OF THE
19TH EGYPTIAN DYNASTY, THIRD LIFE OF RAMESSES I

AS THEY CLOSED on the giant church, Sarah considered how best to reach Xiao. She couldn't usually jump a hundred feet straight up, but she could easily break handholds in the wall and make it in a couple jumps. This might be the right time to try summoning a jet pack again.

While they were still fifty yards away from the cathedral, Xiao's voice boomed across the square, magnified like she'd swallowed a loudspeaker. "Manipulating you fools has again proven too easy. I warned you, Sarah. To enter the memoryscape without my consent brings with it a death sentence."

Gregorios slowed at the head of the group, and Melek muttered, "Not good. She was expecting us."

"Worse than not good," Sarah said, suddenly terrified that all their plans and training was about to prove meaningless. She tried to focus on the ciphers that could slow Xiao and disable Hongwu, but her heart was racing so fast it was hard.

Hongwu raised his hands and a brilliant silver light shot down like a laser beam and struck the stones of the square. The light shattered into a thousand streamers that arced in every direction, rippling past Sarah's group and filling the square with tendrils of light that hung in the air like cobwebs.

Melek exclaimed, "A rune web! Sarah we have to—"

His words trailed off into a grunt of pain as he was hoisted off the ground and shaken like a kitten in Xiao's grasp. She had somehow descended the cathedral and appeared behind him. The terrifying woman had moved so fast it looked like she'd teleported. She threw Melek into the air and he disappeared with a flash of golden light.

Sarah stumbled away from Xiao's surprise appearance and bit back an ancient Greek curse that she'd picked up from Gregorios. She had no idea what Xiao had done to Melek, but it couldn't be good. This close, Xiao was far too deadly for them to fight, so Sarah leaped up and back, forming the image of a binding rune in her mind.

She never got the chance to use it.

Xiao jumped after her, moving at twice her speed. Wearing a slightly annoyed expression, Xiao back-handed Sarah in the ribs. The blow shattered her armor, cracked two of her ribs, drove the air from her lungs in an explosive blast, and hurled her across the square. Sarah smashed into the brass gates of the cathedral, cracking them, and fell in a heap onto the stone steps.

She lay dazed, trying to think through waves of agony. She couldn't catch her breath, and the effort of trying triggered fresh waves of pain. Voices echoed as if from a great distance through the roaring of her ears, but it took a moment to bring the words into focus. She tasted blood and smelled the heavy scent of fear oozing under the door from the packed citizens hiding inside the cathedral.

Her personal runes helped drain the edge off her pain, granting her the ability to think. Everything hurt, and she wasn't sure she could stand. This encounter had started out worse than she'd imagined. They'd been the ones surprised, not Xiao.

Where was the woman? Was she looming over Sarah already, prepared to rip her head off?

Sarah blinked away tears of pain and focused on the unmoving figures of Gregorios and Spartacus, who still stood fifty yards away. They seemed frozen in place. She saw no sign of Xiao. Not good.

In the square, Gregorios' eyes bulged as if he were trying to shout, but his mouth moved only a fraction of an inch. That's when Sarah realized that Hongwu's rune web must have trapped them. It must be an exceptionally powerful one if it could block Gregorios' ability to alter the memoryscape. She'd never seen him so completely subdued.

Time to change that. But when Sarah tried to slide her hand to mark a cipher, she found her muscles also frozen.

That's when she felt truly terrified.

At the same time, that feeling of helplessness enraged her, so she focused on that.

Hongwu landed gently on the cobblestones, his ancient blue ceremonial Chinese robes flapping. He looked like an extra in *Crouching Tiger*.

He approached Spartacus and made a little bow. "You who once was chosen for honor have fallen from grace. I accept your request for duel, but first I ensure a fair contest."

A scalpel appeared in his hand and he began cutting a rune into Spartacus' bare chest. The sight flamed Sarah's rage. This was wrong! They couldn't fail now, not when she'd learned so much.

She gritted her teeth, and that tiny movement felt like she was biting through frozen taffy. It was movement, though.

Her exultant feeling faded when she glanced past Gregorios and spotted a dark cloud boiling into the square behind him. It moved far too quickly to be smoke, and after a second she realized what she was looking at.

Bats. Hundreds of huge, black bats.

Oh, no. Vlad.

The bats swept past Gregorios without slowing, aimed directly at Sarah. Her fear escalated to full-blown panic, and she poured every ounce of willpower into moving.

One finger twitched.

It was like pushing through a wall, but she managed it. That little movement created a tiny, silver mark. That was enough to focus her rounon strength and call forth the shielding cipher that she held in her mind.

Strength roared out of her, and hope blossomed as a mighty shield appeared between her and the bats. Once they rebounded off of it, she'd alter its shape to collapse around them, forming a cage that she'd shrink until she squashed all of Vlad's little creatures to pulp.

But the bats shifted mid-flight from that formless, black mass into well-defined lines. In an instant, they used their bodies to create a huge counter rune.

As soon as they locked into the right pattern, they began to glow silver, and Sarah realized with a start that the huge rune was already active.

She didn't have time to wonder how Vlad was fueling that rune. It must have been prepared as part of the trap, with Hongwu or Xiao herself activating it ahead of time. The bat-rune drove into her shield wall and burst right through.

Sarah tried unsuccessfully to scream as the swarm of bats swept over her. The little creatures grabbed at her face, her hair, and her arms, nasty clawed legs latching on and heaving. In seconds they lifted Sarah thirty feet off the ground.

Sarah decided she hated bats. The flapping of their wings sent shivers of revulsion crawling down her spine. Their ugly mouselike faces seemed malevolent, and they smelled foul, as if they slept in their own droppings.

She tried to activate another cipher, but couldn't manage the concentrated focus required to even twitch her finger again. The touch of the little beasts chilled and sapped her strength, and weakened her will, as if they were imbued with that same unnerving influence that Vlad possessed over her.

Her fear still worked, and it escalated to panic levels. She couldn't let Vlad bite her again, not even in the memoryscape. Was that why Xiao left? She didn't need to destroy Sarah. All she had to do was let Vlad finish her off. If he bit her again, would she ever awaken from this nightmarescape, or would he simply suck out her soul and add it to his collection? Would her body just die lying in that chair?

Sarah glanced through the mass of fluttering bats, desperately seeking help, but seeing none. Gregorios was still standing frozen and forgotten. Hongwu was just completing his rune. It felt wrong, twisted, even when viewed at that distance. She was glad she couldn't make out the specific marks he was using. The rune began to burn into Spartacus' skin, smoldering and sending tendrils of black smoke drifting into the air. That was a dark rune, unlike anything she'd ever seen.

Spartacus' eyes widened, but he couldn't even scream. Then the rune faded away and Spartacus slumped to the cobblestones, his body racked with spasms.

Hongwu stood over him. "You are no longer worthy to wear the forbidden rune."

Spartacus coughed, leveraging himself to his knees. He looked confused, and that made Sarah feel even more afraid, if that was possible.

Spartacus clutched at his wounded chest and gasped, "How? It was immune to rune assault."

Hongwu gave him an arrogant smile. "Not when the counter rune is known and powered by sufficient souls. Did you really think you would be allowed ownership of such power if there was no way to undo it?"

Spartacus staggered to his feet, glaring. He rolled his shoulders and looked eager to fight. Somehow the binding rune web no longer restrained him. He declared, "Your life is forfeit."

Hongwu smiled, unfazed. "You hold much honor from days of old. I will claim it as my own and you will learn the humility of a disgraced servant."

That kind of challenge was exactly what Spartacus was used to, and seemed to help him regain his equilibrium. The ancient gladiator grinned, despite the still-smoking burn marks on his chest.

"Your empire is yet to rise. Come, prove you possess the strength to meet me in single combat. Glory to the winner." He drew his gladius with a flourish.

"Glory to me," Hongwu replied as a curved, single-edged Chinese sword appeared in his hand.

He bowed, and Spartacus saluted with his sword.

In unison, they lunged, their blades flashing in the morning light. The clashing of their weapons rang across the square. They fought with superhuman speed and grace, but neither scored a hit.

Sarah wanted to scream at Spartacus to help, but couldn't make any sound. She felt frozen twice over. She couldn't move, and a deep, deadly cold was seeping into her bones.

Then Vlad stepped through the mass of writhing bats, as if walking through an invisible door. The vampire stood in the air in front of Sarah, a smile on his pinched face. He wore his stupid crimson hat, with its wide strip of pearls above his brow, and a huge, golden star set over his brow. A black cape billowed behind his crimson waistcoat, and his black-eyed gaze seized Sarah's eyes and seemed to bore into her mind.

She tried to scream again, this time out of primal terror. The vampire had come for her, and she couldn't do anything to stop him.

Behind Vlad, down in the square, hordes of Turks began pouring out of nearby streets. They would reach the cathedral soon. The time for the master rune to appear was at hand, but Sarah doubted she'd live to see it.

Vlad leaned close and gently brushed her hair from her face, the gesture sickeningly intimate. Sarah struggled in vain to move, to recoil. Vlad's smile widened, as if he was again reading her thoughts.

He leaned close and crooned, "Sarah, my dear, Xiao offered you the chance to earn your glory, but you refused. She no longer has time for your games. She wished still to offer you a place in her empire, but I convinced her you could better serve her by serving me."

He kissed her gently on the cheek. Her skin crawled, and the touch of those thin, old-man lips sucked away her strength. He wasn't even biting her yet, but already she could feel him imposing his dominance. The thought disgusted her.

No way she'd surrender to that creep without a fight. Sarah couldn't move and couldn't draw a cipher, but she had to do something. So she changed her focus to simply summoning something to help. Vlad opened his mouth wide, long fangs extending. A wild look came into his eyes and he leaned in slowly toward her neck.

Sarah screamed and threw every ounce of willpower into summoning a weapon to save her soul from that horrible fate. Something in the restraining web gave way, and a giant bug zapper appeared in the air right next to Sarah.

Vlad's fangs contacted the charged cage and the souped-up zapper released a hundred thousand volts of electricity at a thousand times more current than normal. With an explosion of blue lightning and a high-pitched crackle, the shock blasted the vampire away screaming. Most of his teeth had shattered.

Yes! A bug zapper was perfect.

Sarah laughed with relief. She hadn't actually expected a bug zapper, but loved it. In that second, the rune web eased further and Sarah regained use of her arms. She yanked her hands forward, flinging bats into the giant zapper. The little creatures simply exploded when they touched the electrified cage, and others released her to flit away from danger.

She fell through the cloud and landed near the huge bronze gates. In the square, Gregorios was moving again, a shotgun in hand, firing at Vlad, who had landed not far away from him. So had she freed herself, or had he finally figured out how to circumvent the web?

Didn't matter. She was free, and she'd slam a cattle prod between Vlad's legs and see if vampires could ignore that kind of pain.

Vlad collapsed to the stone pavement under Gregorios' fresh barrage of buckshot and slugs, bloody and limp. Nearby the stones erupted and a huge beast shouldered its way up from below.

Sarah blinked in surprise. She expected monsters when anyone broke the integrity of the memoryscape, and that bug zapper was definitely a break. Still, who would expect a mammoth-sized ant-eater? The weird monster immediately began rampaging around the square, stomping soldiers flat and sucking bats up its long, flexible snout.

Sarah lost sight of Vlad for a moment as the ant-eater mammoth charged past him. After it passed, Vlad was gone.

"I hate vampires," she hissed.

The giant anteater turned toward Gregorios, aiming its long trunk at him like a spear. A grenade launcher appeared in his hands and he fired the grenade right up the monster's snout. It exploded into a huge cloud of blood and gore. Sarah grimaced. That one was juicy.

A large squad of Turkish soldiers abruptly turned on Gregorios and charged him, swords, axes, and spears raised. He leaped impossibly high, firing down on them. Sarah wasn't sure if Xiao was doing that for Vlad, or if he or Hongwu were somehow imposing their will on the memoryscape.

Gregorios could take care of the soldiers easily enough. She had to find Vlad before he recovered from that brutal electric shock. Other soldiers were rushing the cathedral, but didn't seem focused on Sarah. The swarm of bats descended around her again, blinding and confusing, chittering loudly and flapping into her eyes.

Vlad liked to strike from behind, so Sarah slashed a finger through the air and activated an attack cipher she'd planned. A wave of energy exploded out from her in every direction, scattering bats and squashing many of them against the cathedral.

The blast caught Vlad, who had indeed been sneaking up behind her, masked by the cloud of bats. He struck the huge bronze doors hard enough to dent the metal.

"Can't keep using the same old trick, Vladdy boy," Sarah said as she made another glowing mark and activated another cipher.

It connected to her remote-charging cipher in Beijing. A flood of strength poured into her, super-charging her healing runes and topping off her rounon well.

Vlad hissed like the world's ugliest tea kettle and launched at her, his teeth extending, clawed hands reaching to seize her. Sarah leaped back and away, already marking yet another cipher, focusing a binding rune through the glowing mark.

He moved faster, but she stayed ahead just long enough for the new cipher to activate. The invisible binding seized Vlad like a full-body straight jacket when his grasping claws were but inches from her face and slammed him to the ground. That look of impotent fury that flickered across his face filled Sarah with renewed hope. She was going to destroy this monster once and for all.

Then soldiers crowded around them, and for a second Sarah thought Xiao had summoned more memoryscape minions to fight her. The soldiers ignored her, however, and began battering against the gates of the church.

Sarah seized Vlad by the hair and dragged him back down the stairs to the square. Gregorios was trotting in their direction, shotgun over his shoulder. Could he remove Vlad's soulmask in the memoryscape?

If not, she bet he could figure out how to destroy the vampire. Spartacus and Hongwu were still dueling. Hongwu no longer looked so smug as Spartacus drove him back.

Idiot. Dueling was what Spartacus lived for.

Even though he was bound, Vlad's voice still echoed in Sarah's mind. *"The world order will collapse. You cannot stop it. Your resistance has only guaranteed the suffering of all who you've ever loved."*

Sarah dropped the immobile vampire and summoned a silver stake. She drove it down through his heart with enough force that it pierced the stones underneath. She doubted stakes through the heart really worked, but she hoped it hurt a lot.

She said, "You can read my thoughts, so here's what I plan to do with you." She focused on the worst tortures she could imagine, and in that moment she would eagerly inflict them all on him.

Vlad's voice laughed in her mind. *"You can't kill me here, Sarah, and your torment will be exquisite when I take your soul."*

Sarah turned away in disgust and waved Gregorios to move faster. "Let's kill this thing already."

Farther away, Hongwu fell from a heavy blow, blood spurting from a terrible gash across his chest. Glaring at Spartacus, who retreated a pace to allow him to stand and face his ultimate defeat, Hongwu yanked a dispossessed soulmask out of a deep pocket and marked a rune onto it. Sarah hadn't realized it was possible to carry dispossessed souls in the memoryscape.

"You defile the contest of arms," Spartacus growled, raising his gladius to strike.

Hongwu marked something on the soulmask and most of the square exploded. The blast knocked Spartacus flying, sent Gregorios tumbling away, and even threw Sarah from her feet. She lost sight of Vlad in the billowing smoke and cursed. No way she'd let him get away again.

Before she could pursue him, all sound, all movement stopped.

Sarah silently raged as her eyes were drawn upward by a force impossible to resist. She hadn't even noticed the invaders break into the cathedral. She'd only needed a little more time. It was annoying that even in the memoryscape they kept running out of time.

The master rune blazed in the sky and seared itself into her soul. Like the others she'd seen, it rattled her to the core and overwhelmed her senses.

The sound of war drums rang in her ears, coupled with the screams of dying soldiers. She smelled both ash and flowers, and tasted a dozen fruits. The master rune carried with it a sense of lingering sadness at the passing of this once-great empire, but that was somehow mingled with a feeling of exultant celebration at the birth of a new one that would grow to rival the might of the old.

Sarah shuddered under the raw power of this master rune. It contained within it the power to topple nations, to change the course of history, and to give rise to new dynasties. This rune in Xiao's hands could accomplish great and terrible things.

After a long moment, she managed to blink away the sight of it and forced her eyes back to the square. Vlad was gone, and she no longer felt him contained within her binding cipher. She still saw no sign of Xiao, but didn't doubt Xiao had still seen that master rune.

Hongwu had dropped to his knees. The annoying enchanter was marking a complex rune into the cobblestones. Even though he was still nearly a hundred feet away across the blasted, rubble-strewn square, she recognized the master rune at its heart.

Crap. The idiot couldn't even wait a minute after getting the master rune to try desecrating it. Sarah charged.

As she shot across the square, leaping forty feet over a blast crater in the center, she got a better view of his rune. It also incorporated some of the secret runes Melek had shared with her. Really not good.

Those secret runes might allow him to bind that master rune to one of the ascendants. Sarah didn't have time to study the rune and understand his purpose, but she could read enough to know she couldn't allow Hongwu to activate his rune.

The buzzing roar of a minigun broke the stillness that still lingered over the square. Spartacus hadn't bothered charging like Sarah, but had summoned his favorite modern weapon and advanced on Hongwu, gun blazing.

A concrete barrier appeared between the men, deflecting the bullets away amid showers of exploding stone. That was annoying. Sarah scanned for Xiao as she ran, but still saw no sign of the cui dashi.

Gregorios too had recovered, and he closed on Hongwu from the opposite side, firing his shotgun from the hip. Somehow, none of the rounds seemed to make it to Hongwu.

Sarah summoned a Japanese katana to hand as she lunged the last thirty feet in a flying leap. Spartacus' barrage had distracted Hongwu for a precious second. The enchanter caught sight of Sarah as she soared over his barrier, but rose to intercept her a second too late.

She had planned to remove his head, but her aim was off. She landed in a slide at his feet. Leading with her katana, she drove its tip through the nearly-completed rune, scraping a new mark on the stones and altering its purpose. Unfortunately, she slid farther than she'd intended and severed the heart of the rune, linking the new line with the secret, ascendant rune.

Hongwu paled and shouted, "You fool!"

She could fix it. All she had to do was—

The ground shook, the cobblestones cracked, and darkness swept over the square in a black tidal wave. Wind tore into Sarah, knocking her away from the rune. Rain and hail lashed her face like the claws of an invisible demon, and she lost sight of everyone and everything. It was as if black chaos had swallowed the world.

Then the sky directly overhead whipped into a funnel cloud that descended over her like the grasping hand of hell. The wind smelled like molten sand, it howled like a thousand freight trains, and it snatched her off the ground, helpless as a child in a flood.

Sarah screamed as the air yanked her violently upward. Invisible debris crashed into her from every side. She couldn't see, couldn't tell which way was up, couldn't focus enough to activate a new cipher. All she could do was curl into a ball and scream.

Then she erupted up through the funnel cloud into bright

sunlight. But up suddenly became down and she crashed onto unyielding stone, battered, soaked, disoriented.

At least she was alive. The storm disappeared and she lay in the sunlight, and just breathed for a few seconds.

Chattering voices drew her attention and she forced her eyes open. "What the . . ."

She lay sprawled on the cobblestones of a huge square. Unlike the massive open space beneath Hagia Sophia, this square was lined with red-painted walls twenty feet tall. The position of the sun suggested it was mid-afternoon.

On the east and west sides of the square, wide ramps led to ornate buildings with distinctive Chinese rooflines. Larger Chinese buildings towered over the square to the north and south. Several gates tunneled through the high wall to the south, while multiple stairs with elaborately handrails rose to the building on the north. A canal meandered through the square, not far from where Sarah lay, spanned by five white stone bridges.

She knew this place. It was the famous Forbidden City, the heart of Beijing where emperors had ruled for centuries. The rest of the city she'd explored in recent days had lacked the sense of pervasive history of Rome, despite how many millennia the Chinese had lived there. This place was different, though. Here she could imagine scenes from ancient dynasties.

Tourists flocked the square, a mixture of Chinese and foreigners. The nearest people had backed away from her sudden appearance, phones raised to record her on social media.

Gregorios and Spartacus lay nearby, and they too sat up, looking battered, but whole. Sarah saw no sign of Xiao or Vlad, but Hongwu stood about a dozen feet away, one hand driven into one of those annoying deep pockets, probably grasping a soulmask to power his runes.

Gregorios groaned. "What happened? Are we really back in today?"

"Is that possible?" It sure felt like they had somehow gotten spat out of the memoryscape and returned to real life. Or whatever she'd done to that nasty rune of Hongwu's had just broken their minds.

In that case, would they all suffer the same delusion? They were still dressed like they had been in the memory. She still wore the battered remains of her plate armor. Spartacus looked like a beaten-down gladiator. Gregorios stood, looking surprisingly whole after the recent ordeal.

He turned a slow circle and said in a matter-of-fact tone, "Well, I suppose we should deal with the dragons first."

That's when the screaming started.

61

MELEK BLINKED his eyes and groaned against a pounding headache. He sat up and looked around. He was no longer in Constantinople.

It took a moment to remember what had happened, then he leaped to his feet and settled into a fighting crouch. Xiao had grabbed him, punched him like a runaway truck, and thrown him . . . somewhere. He'd hit something in midair, felt a wrenching pull on his mind, then blacked out.

Now he stood in a huge vaulted space, devoid of any furnishings, still wearing his young memory body. The light was strangely hazy, making the distant concrete walls hard to distinguish. He couldn't make out the ceiling in the shadows above. It was like he'd fallen into an empty world. The air smelled stale and tasted like cement dust. When he started walking, his footsteps sounded distant and hollow.

He had no idea where he was, but he had to get out before Xiao caught up with him. He hated using the escape rune and abandoning the rest of the team. They were in terrible danger, but if he couldn't find them quickly, the best course might be to leave and advise Eirene to pull them out. Their planned surprise attack had been neatly turned against them.

Without warning, Xiao appeared directly in front of him and

punched him in the chest. The blow struck like a sledgehammer and blasted him off his feet. He rolled with the impact and came up ready to fight. He tried summoning a gun, but all he got was a worse headache.

Xiao approached with a little smile on her face. She wore a purple silk Chinese dress. Interesting that she chose a different color for this interview. If only he understood her enough to decipher any deeper meaning from the choice.

Melek shifted to his left. He couldn't outrun her, couldn't escape, and lacked the right weapons to beat her, but he refused to stand idle and wait for her to finish him.

Xiao's lips twitched with a hint of a smile. "Brave to the bitter end. You lie to yourself as much as you lie to your family."

"Words from a demon have no power over me," Melek said, trying to hide his fear. His best strategy lay in keeping her talking. He might learn something useful. Even if he didn't, every second he delayed her here increased the chances the rest of the team could escape the trap they'd walked into.

"But words of truth even you can respect," Xiao said.

"You speak no truth."

She shook her head, her expression sad. "You are deluded, Melek. You convince yourself you follow the cause of the just, yet you murder without remorse."

"I remove enemies of humanity, such as you."

"You don't know me."

"I know enough, demon."

Xiao shook her head slowly. "Labeling me does not define me. Have you bothered asking about my lives, about the good I've done, the peace I plan to instill upon this chaotic world?"

"We don't need your peace," Melek said, still circling. She was slowly closing the distance, but he dare not try running away. He wore a top battle suit, but she'd still tear him apart.

"Listen to yourself," Xiao said, clasping her hands behind her back in a thoughtful pose. "You sound like a foolish child telling a wise parent they don't need instruction, guidance, or discipline."

"Your mistake is assuming that you hold the role of wise parent," Melek responded.

"And yours is insisting on living in the past instead of recognizing truth."

"The world is free to choose its own course. I ensure it remains so."

She blurred across the distance between them, catching him by the throat. She pressed her face close to his and hissed, "You guarantee the world can never rise to greatness!"

"Ever have the wicked resorted to anger and intimidation when their arguments fail." Melek was proud his voice didn't crack.

Xiao released him. "And ever do the foolish go down to their graves ignorant to the damage they've done."

"You cannot convince me that bowing to you is wisdom. You kidnapped my son."

"Oh, no. I saved him from you. He is now part of the great work that will shape the future of the world and unify all mortals. From you, his family, he would find only death."

Melek refused to listen to her assume moral superiority over his own son. He would decide what was right for Alter, not her. He lashed out with his fist, despite the futility of the gesture.

Xiao swayed to the side, avoiding his fist by the barest margin, but made no other move.

Melek struck again, launching a rapid assault on this hated demon, pouring every ounce of enhanced strength and speed into the attack. Xiao dodged, but could not avoid all of his strikes and was forced to block his flying feet and hands. They sparred for a moment, Melek fighting with all his skill, his goal to land one solid blow on her face. On the fifth punch, he succeeded.

Her face felt like carved granite and he bruised his hand, but exulted in reaching her. She was not unbeatable, just very, very strong. If he could punch her, he could hurt her.

Xiao had remained on the defensive until that point, but his punch enraged her. She reversed course and struck with fists that moved so fast he couldn't see them coming. Xiao beat him off his feet and pounded him through the air, keeping him aloft with mighty blows that cracked even his enhanced ribs.

They crossed the gigantic room in a blur of pain until he struck the unyielding concrete wall so hard his vision clouded and pain nearly tore away his consciousness.

The beating stopped and he staggered, barely retaining his feet. It took several seconds of focused effort to stabilize and bring the four overlapping images of her into a single person.

His ears rang from striking the wall so hard. He tasted smoke, and every muscle ached. Breathing was agony. He'd never been so thoroughly beaten in his life.

"Thank you for proving my point," he mumbled through bruised lips, dribbling blood down his chin.

Xiao hissed, "You arrogant fool! You actually think you're suffering nobly?" She forced calm on herself with effort.

If he could rattle her this much, maybe he could get her to reveal more of her evil plans or the location of his son. "My nobility was built over a lifetime. Yours is an illusion, a cloak woven from the lives of all the souls you stole to prolong your evil existence."

Xiao raised a fist, anger in her eyes, but paused. "Who's wearing the cloak now, Melek?"

She made a brushing gesture with one hand, and a searing headache blossomed behind his eyes. Melek stumbled to one knee and his body shook as agony rippled from his head to his feet, like a sheet of lightning running through his torso.

He gasped and fell forward just as his hands changed into ones that he recognized from a lifetime of labor and training. He knelt up and stared in amazement at his own form. Somehow she had pulled him from the powerful young battle suit he'd been wearing, replacing it with his own familiar, broken form.

Melek stood, embracing the pain. He knew how to endure suffering in this form better than in any other. If she planned to kill him, he could think of no better way to face her than as himself.

Xiao gave him a disgusted look. "You're broken, Melek. Look at yourself. You pretend purity, but your own soul knows the truth you refuse to acknowledge."

"Your words are like gilded daggers, bringing death under a false coating of purity."

Xiao pressed one hand against his chest. "Will you shut up and listen to reason for once?" She actually seemed sincere. If this interview hadn't been so painful, he would have found it fascinating to gain this glimpse into her twisted mind. Could she actually believe the lies she spoke?

"What reason do you see?" Melek asked softly.

"You've lost your bond to your own personalized enhancements. Your body fails you and you cannot even see that it's your choices that cripple you," she said, her gaze surprisingly earnest.

"Life is complicated, but none of your business."

"It is my business. I've shown your son the truth and he has the wisdom to see it and to cast off the shackles of the past. Together we will forge a new dynasty, a world order of peace and unity. All will enjoy the same benefits, have the same opportunity."

He shouldn't be surprised she spoke like that. Only the grandest of lies could justify the countless atrocities she was planning. "Only one society ever reached such lofty goals. It was known as Zion, and it was built upon freedom and truth, not slavery and domination."

Xiao retreated a step. "I will grant you a boon, Melek, father of the hidden nation. I will preserve you alive to see the realization of my dreams. When you recognize the truth and come to me with broken heart and sorrowing repentance, I will forgive you and welcome you home."

The vile wretch was speaking as if she were a god. Melek snarled, "I refuse your offer. Come on! Fight me now."

He drew upon all his rounon, reaching for those elusive bonds to the great, shackled strength of his soul, but even now the bonds failed. Weak and slow, he still took a faltering step forward and grasped for her throat.

Xiao slapped his hands away and pushed him back to the wall. "Your lack of faith disappoints me."

Chains appeared on the wall beside him, capped with manacles that snapped around his wrists, then drew taught, pulling him against the wall, arms outstretched like a vertical sacrifice. Melek struggled against the unexpected restraints. Why humiliate him like this? She could kill him at any time. He wasn't a threat to her, was he?

Xiao leaned close and began tracing a finger across his forehead. "You will suffer for your belligerence, but first you will share the secrets only you possess."

"No!" Melek shook his head, trying to dislodge her finger, but she grabbed his face in a viselike grip, holding him fast, despite his struggles. He tried kicking her, but she ignored his feeble blows.

He could do nothing but scream as she completed the rune and began to rip knowledge from his mind.

62

SARAH GAPED as the massive head of an actual dragon lifted out of the waters of the nearby canal. Thick legs, capped with five-clawed feet pulled the sinuous, snake-like body of the dragon onto the middle bridge, crushing stone handrails like paper. With its upper torso on the bridge, its rear half was still concealed by the waters. It must be at least forty feet long.

Its head was ten feet wide, crested with a branching set of horns like a stag's. The long, fish-like scales along its back glittered golden in the sunlight, but those on its belly were azure blue.

Other colors rippled down its flanks when it moved, and symbols glowed on its torso above each leg. One looked like a three-legged crow, another a big, jade rabbit. Sarah couldn't see the symbols on the other side.

The dragon opened its huge jaws and roared, the sound so deep it set Sarah's teeth aching. With a heave, its lower half rippled up onto the bridge. Screaming tourists fled from the monster, and the movement drew its gaze.

With startling speed, it lunged off the bridge, shooting forward like a striking snake and snatching a fat American off his feet. It snapped off the man's head, then severed his torso in an explosion of blood and gore.

"But monsters aren't supposed to appear in real life," Sarah protested, as she struggled to believe what she was seeing.

"That rune messed things up good," Gregorios said, checking his shotgun that he'd brought from the memoryscape with him. "But a monster's a monster. I think bad things would happen if we left it in this time."

Spartacus stood, hefting his minigun with its large case of ammunition. "Let's see how it likes lead."

In that moment, more dragons boiled out of the canal. Smaller than the first dragon, they moved just as fast. They leaped onto the banks, oriented on Sarah and her companions, and charged in a horde of gaping jaws and shining scales.

Spartacus turned his minigun on them and opened fire. Its buzzing roar snapped Sarah out of her shocked stupor and she willed a gun into her hands. Nothing appeared, of course. This might be a nightmare, but it was no dream.

The dragons bled like living things, and Spartacus walked the explosive rounds across the head of the nearest dragon, shattering its skull in a wall of lead. Gregorios opened fire, and his shotgun fired normal slugs, not the specialty curtain call rounds. He took down a second dragon with well-placed shots into its glowing eyes.

Sarah was still holding her sword, so as the dragons closed on them, she vaulted ten feet into the air, soared over her companions, and shouted, "Watch your fire!"

Spartacus shifted left toward a smaller red dragon that was snorting actual flames from its long snout. When the explosive rounds met its fire-producing innards, the resulting explosion rocked the square, knocking three other dragons from their feet. The blast caught Sarah in mid-air and catapulted her all the way back to the southern gates.

She landed on a knot of tourists packed around the gate. The impact knocked a dozen of them to the ground.

"Sorry," she said as she jumped back to her feet.

An elderly Chinese woman grabbed her arm. Unlike most of the others, this woman wore an expression of exultant joy. "You must not hurt the nine sons of the dragon."

"The what?"

The old lady pointed toward Gregorios and Spartacus, who were retreating from the press of dragons. Gregorios had run out of ammo and used his weapon like a club, beating one dragon with glittering green scales on the snout before vaulting twenty feet away. Several tourists noticed the move and paused to turn their video cameras and phones toward the battle.

Not good. They didn't need this kind of press.

"They're trying to hurt us." Sarah started turning away, but paused. "What's the big dragon?"

"Imperial majesty," the woman gushed, even though the dragon was in the process of devouring a pair of blonde women who had tried to hide on one of the bridges. "The yellow and the azure dragons, manifested as one and marked by the yin and the yang. Heavenly favor is granted to the worthy."

Sarah said, "More like hell's unleashed on the world. Don't try petting it."

She couldn't get through the press, so she jumped the tight-packed tourists. That elicited more gasps of awe and, she was sure, many more photos. She was tempted to confiscate the cameras but needed to help deal with the monsters first. Gregorios and Spartacus had already killed five of the smaller dragons, but the others continued to attack with savage intensity.

One orange dragon whipped its tail around and caught Gregorios in mid-jump, swatting him through the wall of the building on the west side of the square. He crashed through wood and stone in a collision that must have broken bone, despite his armor.

Spartacus' minigun ran out of ammo just as two other dragons closed on him. He threw the gun at one of them, but the other snatched him into its jaws. Not large enough to snap him in half like the mother dragon could, it was still powerful enough to shear through his flesh and bit deep into his torso.

Spartacus screamed, a look of shock on his face. Apparently the damage that Hongwu had done to his protective runes in the memoryscape had carried back into the real world. Did that mean he'd lose that protection when he returned to his real body?

Weren't they in their real bodies?

The thought of maybe still lying asleep in the distant machine was uniquely disturbing. Would something weird and time-shattering happen when they returned and look down on themselves?

Sarah pushed those worries aside. They'd figure out reality later, if they survived. The most pressing truth at the moment was that she couldn't defeat these threats with a sword.

She dropped to one knee as a golden dragon spotted her and rushed in her direction, covering the eighty feet with terrifying speed. Sarah drew a softly glowing cipher onto the cobblestones, completing the marks and activating it just in time to conjure a protective barrier. The dragon rebounded off of it and stumbled, dazed by the blow.

Sarah swiped the cipher away, removing the barrier, and lunged, slashing the creature's exposed neck with her sword. The blow sank deep, half severing the monster's head. It flopped away from her, dripping indigo blood behind.

"No!" A soldier shouted from an open window of the building above the blocked gates. "Don't hurt the dragons."

Was he serious?"

Apparently. He raised his gun and aimed it at her.

"Of all the ridiculous . . ."

If the soldiers started interfering instead of helping, surviving this battle was going to require new tactics. Spartacus had escaped the jaws of the one dragon and wrapped his arms around its neck, trying to squeeze out its life. He was bleeding heavily and lacked the strength to crush the beast. All he managed was to hang on while it bucked and twisted and clawed at him. He'd lose his grip in seconds, then it would finish him.

Another dragon was disappearing into the building where Gregorios had crash-landed. She had no idea if he was in fighting form. A cipher appeared in her mind and she sucked in a hissing breath. It contained the power they needed, was terrifying and inspiring in its scope, but did she dare use it? She hadn't dared push the limits of how much power she could handle since she'd died, so she hesitated.

Then the mother dragon turned in her direction, fixing her in its amber-eyed gaze. Well, that answered that question. Certain death by dragon trumped possible death by cipher.

Sarah drew the new cipher onto her left bicep, her heart in her throat as she included at its heart the core of the master rune she'd just witnessed burning above Constantinople. She also included modifiers to limit the power to twenty percent.

The cipher blazed like a miniature sun when she activated it, encircling her in a pillar of golden light. Energy roared into her, filling her with strength almost as great as she'd felt in St. Peter's square while fighting Paul, the day she'd died. This master rune was so much more powerful than the others, it took her breath away. She felt a flash of renewed fear, but forced it down. She was managing the flow. She was all right.

The dragon was closing fast, but now its speed seemed unremarkable. Elated that she hadn't melted herself or anything, Sarah jumped eighty feet into the air, ripped away the front of her armor with fingers stronger than steel, and marked another cipher onto her right hip.

She knew this one all too well, but hadn't dared use it since the day she'd melted. Now, fueled by another master rune, she felt a renewed sense of confidence and dared attempt it again.

As she began her descent toward the waiting jaws of the mother dragon, lightning-like energy rippled through her and her flesh shifted to quicksilver, as it had in Rome.

Sarah's fingers became daggers and she twisted in the air as she fell into the dragon's snapping jaws. Its teeth sheared through her clothing and scraped deep into her flesh, but left no injury in her flowing, quicksilver form. Sarah drove her razor-sharp fingers into the dragon's lower jaw. It roared in pain and threw her across the square.

Sarah laughed as she soared through the air, unhurt. She loved being a real-life terminator!

She landed already running. With speed to match the dragons, she closed on the smaller beast still trying to dislodge Spartacus.

Sarah slashed its head from its neck with a single stroke of her bladed hands. She caught Spartacus and as she considered his injured form, a new cipher flashed into her mind.

It combined elements of the two ciphers she'd just activated on herself, drew from the Constantinople master rune as she had, but was wrapped in a different outer symbol, one that felt raw and reckless and indomitable, just like Spartacus.

She didn't have time to consider all the ramifications of what the new cipher meant, and wasn't really sure what it would do, but it felt right.

"I think I can help," she said as she drew the cipher across his shoulders, leaving glowing marks on his skin.

Spartacus coughed blood and tried to salute. "Lady of Steel, well met. I die smiling to see your glory."

"Don't be so melodramatic." Sarah completed the cipher.

This was either going to be amazing, or she was about to kill him a minute before he probably would have died anyway.

She bet on amazing and activated it.

Spartacus convulsed right out of her hands, his head arched back, and he screamed.

Not what she expected. Sarah reached for him, suddenly terrified she'd made a horrible mistake. But even as she grabbed him and prepared to mark the counter rune to block the cipher she'd just made, his body shuddered again and his wounds sealed as if she'd activated a super-strength healing cipher. His skin took on a golden, metallic hue, and he sagged in her grasp.

"Are you all right?" she asked, wondering if she should peel open his eyelid.

Spartacus' eyes snapped open, and his whites had turned golden. He laughed and leaped ten feet into the air. When he came down, fire flickered around his fingers.

He cried, "What sorcery is this?"

"No sorcery. Just a piece of history running through your veins." She hadn't killed him. She nearly cried with relief.

"I love you!" Spartacus grabbed her bladed hands in his burning ones. "You are the heroine of heroines, the warrior—"

It looked like he was planning to keep spouting new titles ad nauseum. Part of her wondered how long he could keep it up, but they didn't really have time for that.

So she said, "Tell me later. Slow down the queen mother while I find Gregorios."

Laughing, Spartacus raced away, fire dripping from his burning hands, heading for the mother dragon, which was gobbling up a praying Chinese man. He shouted, "Glory eternal!"

Sarah jumped a smaller dragon that was heading to the mother dragon's feast, and rushed into the broken building along the western wall where Gregorios and the other dragon had disappeared.

She found a badly battered Gregorios beating the dragon over the head with a brass sculpture. Sarah grabbed the wounded dragon by the tail and threw it back into the square.

Gregorios sagged to his knees. One arm was broken, his armor dented and bloody. He gave her shining, silvery skin an appraising glance. "That look didn't work so well for you last time."

Sarah peeled his armor away from his neck. "I'm not using the master runes that killed me."

"That's a relief," he said as she marked a cipher into his neck and shoulder. Again, a modified symbol snapped into her mind, as if she'd studied it for hours.

She wasn't sure why that was happening, but didn't have time to question it. Her new cipher had worked for Spartacus, so she was willing to take another chance.

"I'm using the new master rune." She added as she completed the cipher and activated it.

"Are you sure that's a good . . . Zeus, Mary, and Mohammed!" he bellowed as his body shook violently.

"You just swore in three different religions," Sarah chuckled, but she watched him closely to make sure the cipher really was working.

Gregorios grinned and leaped to his feet. He clapped her on the shoulder. "Whatever you did, I like it! I haven't felt this good since the day Eirene first said 'I do'."

A scraping in the doorway turned her around. The same stubborn dragon was back. Recovered from Gregorios' beating, it rushed into the shattered building, mouth agape.

Gregorios jumped straight up and hovered in the air as it passed below him, then swooped down onto its back. He drove it into the floor, and when it twisted back on him like a snake, he punched it between the eyes. Its eyes crossed and it sagged beneath him. Gregorios grabbed its head and twisted it right off with a single, mighty heave.

He tossed the bloody trophy away and considered his hands. "I like what you've done to my battle suit."

A series of explosions rocked the square. "I hope that means the cavalry has finally arrived to help," Gregorios said.

"Don't count on it." Sarah followed him to the broken door.

As she feared, a line of soldiers had taken up position just inside the southern gate and started firing RPGs at Spartacus, who was still fighting the mother dragon on the north end of the square.

"Even the Chinese can't be that bad at aiming," Gregorios said as he watched Spartacus run a zig-zag pattern across the square from east to west, dodging a series of rocket strikes. He caught one of them and threw it back at the soldiers. It blew a dozen feet in front of them and scattered them like sparrows.

Sarah shook her head. "No, they're actually shooting at Spartacus. They're trying to protect the dragon. One old lady told me they consider it sacred."

"When did you find time to talk to old ladies?" Gregorios demanded.

"Some of us are efficient."

Only two of the smaller dragons remained, and they were closing on the ranks of soldiers, who were beckoning the deadly beasts closer, as if offering sanctuary. The dragons tore into their ranks, ripping with claws and chomping off entire limbs with their deadly fangs. Screams echoed across the square, but still no one fired.

Gregorios said, "Idiots. At least dying will keep them busy long enough for us to deal with the big one. Come on."

"Wait, shouldn't we help the soldiers?"

"Why? They'll just try killing us for saving their lives and injuring a sacred symbol of China's glory." He leaped off the cracked steps and flew like a living incarnation of Superman across the square.

Sarah could jump far, especially with the quicksilver cipher powering her body, but she couldn't fly. So much energy pulsed through her, she could fight all day without tiring. The master rune she had tapped was powerful, but she could still manage the flow.

She jumped sixty feet, then got a running start and easily vaulted the canal. Gregorios didn't land until he reached the dragon, and he touched down more like a missile strike.

He drove into the dragon's side so hard the two of them tumbled up the stairs, through the gatehouse building on the north side of the square, and disappeared into yet another huge square on the far side.

Sarah raced after them, but Spartacus outpaced her, trailing fire in his wake. She wasn't sure how the ciphers did that. Then again, she wasn't sure how her own cipher transformed her into a quicksilver terminator. She'd seen herself on television enough times to recognize that however unexplainable it was, the cipher sequence worked.

She was playing with powers she barely grasped, and she hoped her luck held out a little longer. If they survived the day, she needed to study those ciphers and try to understand where and how her flashes of inspiration had come from, how those ciphers worked, and why the different placements affected the resultant superpowers so much. If she could harness those ciphers in the fight against Xiao, they might gain the advantage they'd been seeking.

First, kill the dragon.

Second, figure out if they were actually in the real world, or if she really had broken her mind.

Third, try to find Melek. Maybe with his help she could figure out the rest.

Sarah emerged in the next square and paused to stare. Beautiful buildings lined the huge open area, with the most magnificent of them directly across from her. Atop a three-tiered terrace, lined with more ornate handrails, she recognized the Chinese palace from movies like *Hero* and *Shanghai Noon*, two of her favorites. This was the emperor's palace, although she couldn't remember its formal name.

Gregorios and the dragon had landed in the middle of the square. He was now riding it, beating on its spine with one fist, the other buried in its scales. The beast roared and twisted, trying to unseat him. Then it started to roll.

Spartacus arrived and plunged his burning hands into the beast's open mouth, filling it with raging fire. It slammed its head forward in the world's biggest-ever head-butt, cracking him in the chest and sending him flying into a lesser palace in the east wall.

More tourists clustered in frightened groups along the walls, gaping at the battle or trying to flee. Far too many of them had cameras and phones out, recording everything. Sarah shot across the square and drove her bladed hands into the dragon's torso, right through the symbol of the three-legged crow. She slashed with all her strength, and the leg fell away in a gout of blood.

The dragon turned on her in a fury and engulfed her headfirst into its huge jaws, half swallowing her. It bit down on her torso with crushing force. It couldn't break her quicksilver skin, but it held her, preventing her from escaping.

Its hot breath smelled of recent kills. Its mouth was charred from Spartacus' fire, and it growled so deep as it chewed on her that her entire body quivered.

Sarah's head was wedged in the back of its mouth and she really didn't want to get swallowed. Her arms were pinned by its jaws, but she melted one of them free, reforming it into a long blade that she used to stab into the base of its jaw.

The dragon roared, a deafening sound like eighteen lions packed into a tiny room. It flung her away, tossing her through the many-columned entrance to the central palace.

Red-painted wooden columns snapped when she struck them like a cannonball, and she cartwheeled through the front wall and into the huge chamber beyond. She came to a halt at the base of a short flight of stairs leading up to the imperial throne. High above, a coiled dragon sculpture rested on the ceiling directly above the throne, the centerpiece of the intricately-designed ceiling.

Sarah turned back to the fight just as the entire front wall imploded. The dragon and Gregorios tumbled inside. He was clinging to its belly now, and had driven an arm to the shoulder into its torso. The dragon writhed with wild fury, smashing columns and antiques to splinters with its snapping teeth, while its claws tore through the floor. Gregorios held on, despite being thrown to and fro by the monster's crazed movements. He looked like he was thoroughly enjoying himself, and Sarah caught snatches of the Tenth's battle song.

Spartacus leaped through the broken front wall and tackled the dragon's head. Fire exploded out of his hands, engulfing its face. He too was laughing, and singing a song in Latin. Men. They thought they could get all the fun.

Swept up by a rush of battle fury, Sarah snatched a broken pillar and beat the monster on the snout, narrowly missing Spartacus.

The monster groaned, a terrible sound like a hundred large trucks grinding their clutches, and heaved into the air. It tumbled across the room, dislodging Gregorios, and crashed down over the imperial throne. With a final explosive breath that sent a flood of bloody gore cascading out its open mouth, the charred and broken dragon lay still.

Sarah and the others cautiously approached. Gregorios poked it in the face, then leaned close to listen. When he heard nothing for several seconds he grunted. "Tough old critter. I squeezed its heart to splinters twenty seconds ago."

Spartacus threw both hands into the air. "We are the new risen gods!"

Sarah said, "Forget it. Paul wanted to be a god. Didn't work out so well for him."

"Speaking of Paul," Gregorios said. "Where'd his freakshow mother run off to?"

Together they exited the broken palace and paused at the top of the steps. The square was full of soldiers, and two helicopters swept in from the south, loaded with heavy weapons.

"You'd think they'd be more grateful," Sarah said.

Gregorios said, "We did just kill the symbol of their national pride. People take that hard sometimes."

A voice boomed from a loudspeaker. "On your knees, or we will open fire."

Spartacus grinned. "Fire he says? I'll give him fire!"

He brought his hands up, and a wall of fire erupted from his palms, boiling thirty feet into the air and rolling out into the square. Sarah gaped, but Gregorios grabbed her by the waist and threw her into the air. She landed on the roof and the two men jumped up beside her.

Gregorios pushed her on. "Play tourist later. Time to go."

Together they jumped to the outer wall and down to the nearest street. The two helicopters swept over the wall after them, but Gregorios was ready.

He launched into the air and intercepted the lead helicopter, crashing right through the large cockpit window. Whatever he told the pilots was convincing, because the helicopters banked away, and he dropped out the side door.

When he landed, Gregorios spoke calmly, as if that stunt was an everyday occurrence. "I don't think they'll stay away for long. Let's go."

They raced away into the city, leaping congested traffic, running along rooftops, and riding on the back of a subway train for two stops. They finally slowed after half an hour of rapid progress and no sight of pursuit. They hid under an overpass, one of the few places they could find with no people pressing in on either side. There Sarah deactivated their ciphers.

"We should keep them," Spartacus insisted, looking with sadness on his non-burning hands.

"Too hard to hide like that," Gregorios said.

Sarah added, "Besides, although I didn't sense the master rune would ever run out of power, we were consuming a lot of juice. Let's save it for Xiao."

Gregorios nodded. "Good idea. Let's go see if we're still sleeping."

63

I am king of Akkad, commanding overseer of Ishtar, anointed priest of Anu, and great regent of Enlil. My ciphers declared my lordship over all thirty-four cities who defied me. Only Dagon himself knows runes I have yet to discover. If the dread god will confide in me, I will never die.

~THE LEGENDS OF SARGON, 24TH CENTURY B.C.

ALTER SAT in a hard-backed wooden chair ten feet from Xiao, his outward calm concealing his growing worry. His initial flush of victory after slipping the message out through Reuben had faded under a rising sense of fear.

Xiao had indeed entered the memoryscape, the machine powered by a beefy Chinaman Alter had never met before. The first indication that all was perhaps not as he'd been led to believe came when the enchanter Hongwu joined Xiao.

He took a second machine, powered by another facetaker Alter had never met, a slender Chinese woman whose pretty blue eyes looked misplaced in those features. Alter frowned at that. Hongwu was no facetaker. He couldn't walk into the memoryscape without a guide.

Looking closer, he noticed cables connecting the two machines in a new way. He longed to study the connection more closely. It appeared that Xiao was linking Hongwu to her memory journey, but powering his machine separately. That was a new twist, and anything new meant bad news for Sarah and the others.

With two facetakers powering their journey, they would have that much greater advantage over the team preparing the ambush. Alter silently ground his teeth in frustration. Sarah and the others already faced a daunting challenge, assuming they got the message he'd sent through Reuben. Alter still wasn't sure how Xiao could reach such ancient days. Had she really lived to see the great city fall? If not, what was she doing?

If Xiao could reach that moment and acquire the master rune, why did she need Hongwu along?

The second, more disturbing hint of brewing trouble was that Xiao had summoned Alter to witness the memory journey, but not participate. Alter suddenly worried what Xiao was intending.

If she wasn't including him in the memory journey, was she really looking for a master rune? She'd repeatedly told him that she wanted his sense of integrity and justice to help ensure all master runes reflected the best truths.

So if not for a master rune, why was she entering the memoryscape at a time that just happened to coincide with what he had hoped would prove a perfect opportunity for a surprise attack from his friends?

The two facetakers activated their nevra cores, sending Xiao and Hongwu into the memoryscape. Alter waited anxiously, hoping to see marks of injury appearing on the slumbering demon's body to indicate Sarah and the others had sprung their trap. He hated sitting so close to the helpless enemy but unable to destroy them. He wasn't worried about the four muscled charlatans flanking him. The fifth one seated across the room with a shotgun did give him pause.

He held no illusion that Xiao had told the man to use non-lethal force if he caused any problems. With his cui dashi powers, Alter instinctively knew how to release his host body, although he vowed never to do so. Still, if he caught a load of buckshot to the chest, he might not have any alternative.

If only he had a sword, or even a good hunting knife. He'd take the chance against the kashaph. All he'd need was a single solid swipe with a good blade to sever Xiao's head. It might take longer to really kill her, but he was a hunter and his prey was lying helpless before him.

He shifted in his seat and all of the kashaph noted the movement. He picked up hints of tension in their hands and faces. They were ready to intercept him. He'd have to fight through them all to get his chance. While he considered the best way to do that, an assistant hovering over the slumbering team suddenly exclaimed, "I've got blood!"

Indeed, wounds began appearing on Hongwu, but nothing on Xiao. Did that mean Sarah and her team had attacked? Was Xiao hurting them?

The assistant rang a little gong and the door burst open, allowing a flood of medical staff to rush in, loaded down with trauma gear. It looked like they'd been staged and ready. That confirmed Xiao had known she would be facing Sarah and the others.

Alter stood, but did not approach. The kashaph mirrored him, and the two farthest from him edged closer to hem him in. He ignored them, his eyes glued on Xiao's form. He still saw no blood on her, but the medical staff eased the slumbering enchanter onto his side and began working on his back. Alter caught sight of several gashes that looked more like blade cuts than bullet wounds.

What were they doing? They didn't have time to slice Hongwu apart. What were they doing against Xiao? No longer did he exult that the trap had been spring. Instead he worried Xiao had flipped the trap back on them, and silently urged Sarah to flee.

Wounds received in the memoryscape transferred to the waking body somehow, but there was a delay in the process. If one healed quickly enough in the dream world, they could prevent much of the damage from reaching their sleeping form. His fears started flashing images of Sarah lying bleeding and dying in a machine somewhere in the world.

One doctor looked up from where they were treating new cuts along Hongwu's arms and torso and called for an enchanter and more soulmasks. Two of the medical team rushed out to fetch more supplies. The kashaph shuffled uneasily and Alter watched them carefully. He might get his chance after all.

The female facetaker running Hongwu's machine suddenly sagged to the floor, barely holding on to the connection. The lights in the room flickered and Hongwu shook violently where he lay bleeding under the faceplate.

Then the entire room trembled, as if from an earthquake. The kashaph with the shotgun stumbled and moved to support the facetaker running the machine. The other kashaph were all distracted, exclaiming in fear at the sudden shaking. This was the moment he'd been waiting for.

Alter prepared to strike down the men closest to him, but the room stopped shaking with a suddenness that nearly knocked Alter from his feet. A calm blanketed the room, so deep it felt like the air had thickened.

The entire room twisted for a second, feeling like giant invisible hands had grasped it and wrenched it in opposite directions, like a photograph bent by a child. It felt wrong at such a fundamental level, Alter feared they were all about to die. Something had gone deeply wrong, in a way he'd never imagined possible, and fear froze him in his tracks.

Then a loud pop shattered the stillness, like a handgun firing close beside his head. A whooshing sound drew his gaze to where Hongwu had been lying, and he gaped. The enchanter was gone.

The man's body had simply disappeared. No trace of him remained. The woman who had been running the machine toppled to the floor, the purple fire of her nevron snuffed out, her sightless eyes staring at the ceiling. The medical staff descended upon her in a rush, focusing on reviving her with desperate energy. They probably appreciated having a tangible problem to worry about instead of dwelling on how their patient had been ripped out of the world from right under their hands.

"What happened?" the kashaph with the shotgun demanded, actually looking to Alter for guidance.

Alter approached Xiao's reclined form. She still slumbered, unaffected by the recent catastrophe. The beefy facetaker running her dream looked terrified. No one interfered as Alter stepped close beside Xiao. If he had a knife, he could have taken her head off right then. The thought barely registered.

What had happened to Hongwu? Had the same thing happened to Sarah? Were they sucked into the memoryscape somehow? Had a rune gone bad and trapped them in time? He had to know.

"They're in danger." He reached for the secondary helmet connected to Xiao's machine. "I'm going in to help."

No one had any idea what to do, so they couldn't decide whether to block his decision. He settled onto the nearest chair, slipped the helmet on, snapped the faceplate closed, and tried to settle his mind. The dreamworld sucked him in and he gave himself to it.

He awoke standing behind Xiao in a long, arched room. She was torturing his father, who was chained to a wall, with bloody runes marked onto his forehead and cheeks.

Alter didn't see Hongwu or Sarah or anyone else, and in that moment he forgot all about them. All he saw was his mighty father in pain, suffering at the hands of a demon.

Rage like he'd never known boiled through him and he lunged at Xiao with murder in his heart. A chainsaw appeared in his hands, already roaring, its aggressive chain spinning at full speed. The entire machine pulsed with the purple fire of his activated nevron.

Xiao spun at the sound, just in time for him to plunge the blade of the saw into her chest. He drove it through her steel-hard skin with every ounce of strength he possessed, magnified by the focused energy of his nevron.

The blade plunged into her torso, ripping out her back. She screamed in pain, a look of shock on her face. She probably hadn't felt so much agony in centuries.

"Get away from my father," Alter growled, heaving upward on the saw.

Instead of slicing up through her chest and severing her head as he had hoped, the saw jammed against her ribs and he ended up wrenching her off the ground and throwing her right over his head. She slipped off the blade and tumbled away, gushing blood and entrails.

Alter sheared the chains away from his father's arms and dropped the chainsaw to catch Melek, who wavered and nearly fell. He looked terrible, and Alter's fury burned even hotter. He'd cut Xiao to pieces for this.

"Alter?" Melek asked, blinking through blood. "Is it really you?"

"I'm here father," he promised.

"Alter!" Xiao screamed.

He glanced back and found her on her feet, the ghastly wounds closing, fury pouring off her in blistering waves. He should have killed her while he held the advantage.

"Avenge me, father," Alter said, marking the escape rune onto his father's stomach.

Melek faded from the memory just as Xiao grabbed Alter and smashed him into the wall so hard she split the stone and drove him out of the dream. He awoke spitting blood, knowing this nightmare was just beginning.

At least he'd saved his father from her atrocities. Whatever tortures she inflicted upon him in her fury, he would die smiling.

64

If I were not Alexander in this life, I would be Diogenes.

~ALEXANDER THE GREAT, 330, B.C.

"DO you have any idea what you almost did?" Melek exclaimed

Sarah didn't flinch away from the hunter's wrath. "Obviously not. That's why we're talking about it."

She'd been in the middle of explaining to the rest of the team what had happened to them in Constantinople before they were sucked out of the memoryscape and dropped into the Forbidden City with a bunch of dragons. She'd been relieved to find Melek awake when they had returned to the apartment. His face was swathed in bandages and he looked frail, sitting on the padded leather couch in the living room. Nabil hovered next to him, looking worried.

"I still can't believe real life dragons," Tomas said. He gripped her hand as the two of them sat on a love seat. He'd kept his arm around her shoulders ever since they'd reunited. He seemed to need the physical confirmation that she was really back and safe. She drew strength from him too.

"Don't get distracted." Gregorios gestured with his soft drink. "Sarah go on."

Sarah shrugged. "That's about it. I cut the rune and you all saw on TV what happened next."

The Chinese authorities had done a remarkable job trying to suppress the truth about the incident, but there had been too many foreign tourists with cell phones for them to block everything. International news channels had already begun airing footage. The video was shaky, but captured enough to force the Chinese authorities' hands.

"This is very bad," Melek muttered as he touched his bandaged face with one shaking hand.

"Tell me about it," Sarah said. At least one of the segments aired by the news had captured the rune-enabled super powers of her team. The return of the Sword of the Deliverer was big news, and it was getting picked up all over the world.

"You don't understand." Melek paused to cough, a wet, hacking sound that made Sarah cringe. He hadn't explained yet what had happened to him, but it had taken a severe toll on his already-injured body. "The combination of those runes is pure insanity. That enchanter, Hongwu, used the power of that master rune to link to the ascendant."

"And included a couple of those secret runes of yours," Sarah said. She wished she'd had more time to study the crazy rune sequence.

Melek wiped blood from his lips. "Those runes were never meant to combine. Such a construct would tie the flow of history to a specific moment and . . ." He paused, his brow furrowed in thought. "I'm not entirely sure what would have happened had he completed the rune."

Spartacus, who stood near the door, muscled arms folded, declared, "He failed to accomplish his designs most foul thanks to the intervention of our beloved Lady of Steel." He pounded his fist over his heart in salute.

Melek sighed. "That intervention was almost as bad as whatever Hongwu had planned. In that space, for those involved, you broke time."

Gregorios said, "Well it sounds worse when you say it like that. We came out safe on the other side."

When they had returned to the apartment, they'd learned that their bodies had simply disappeared from the chairs. The entire building had shaken as if from an earthquake, and the strain had nearly killed Eirene.

If not for Francesca backing her up and the remote charging rune linked to their nevron, she might not have survived. Francesca sat in a nearby chair, leaning on Quentin, looking utterly spent. Eirene was still resting in another room.

Melek rallied enough strength to glare at Gregorios. "This time, but what if they try it again and Sarah's not there to stop them?"

"You think they plan to break time?" Tomas asked, sounding incredulous.

"Not really. Breaking it would cast the world into chaos and destroy their plans. No, they wish to control time."

Anything sounded better than breaking time, but controlling it came in a pretty close second. Sarah struggled to wrap her thoughts around concepts that were so foreign to their normal world.

Would breaking time mean that time ceased to exist? Would history unravel? Would things change in the current moment or in the future based on something broken in the past?

Gregorios put down his drink. "It's clear they have the power to break things at an unprecedented level. No one's ever messed with time before."

"Not to this extent," Melek said.

Tomas squeezed Sarah tighter. "Life was so much easier when all we had to worry about was how to kill Xiao. This is getting crazy."

Francesca managed a weak laugh. "We left crazy back in Rome. Now we've got teleportation, breaking time, and dragons in China."

"Actually, we've got global war." Eirene entered the room, looking haggard.

Gregorios rushed across the room and gently embraced her, then led her back to his seat. He remained by her side, gripping her hand almost as insistently as Tomas still gripped Sarah's.

"You should be sleeping," Gregorios told her.

"Nonsense," Eirene said, but still leaned against him. "I just got off the phone with Harriett. She'll be here this afternoon. Besides, the general-secretary of the communist party of China is about to address the world. Greg, be a dear and turn on the television."

They found the station just as the stern-faced leader of China began his remarks.

"I can confirm an incident in the Forbidden City today. For the first time in recorded modern history, we witnessed a confirmed sighting of the sacred dragons. The sign of heavenly benediction of our great nation's current direction manifested at the Hall of Supreme Harmony. For millennia, this site has been the most sacred location in our country, the seat of imperial majesty."

After a pause to look gravely into the camera, he continued in a harsh tone. "Almost immediately, the sacred dragon was attacked by enhanced terrorists and butchered on the imperial seat. These west-erners have sent a message to the world, a message of scorn and insult. They have declared through this most heinous of acts their intention to see our empire fall."

Tomas muttered, "You've got to be kidding me. Of all the idiotic interpretations they could have taken."

The general secretary continued. "This insult cannot go unan-swered. It will not. I have issued orders to our military commanders to mobilize all forces. We will hunt down these terrorists, we will tear down any nation who supports them. We will respond to this act of war the only way our national honor will allow. Anyone and everyone involved in this attack will be punished."

He went on to deliver a stirring speech to whip his population into a frenzy, but Francesca turned down the volume.

"Good thing we've already started packing," Gregorios said.

Sarah couldn't believe how calmly he was taking the news. She exclaimed, "This is a disaster! We had to stop it or who knows how many people it would have killed."

Quentin said, "The body count might end up higher this way. You unwittingly handed to those elements within the Chinese government who support Xiao's agenda more than ample excuse to go to war."

"Everything we do just gets thrown back in our faces," she cried.

Gregorios said, "At least they don't crucify people any more. That was unpleasant."

The huge Maori enforcer Anaru entered the room and called Tomas over. After listening to the report, he changed the channel on the television. "You're going to want to hear this too."

Sarah instantly recognized Dr. Wang, the head archaeologist from the Egyptian dig that had found the fake artifacts Xiao had planted. She hadn't found time to examine the images from that stone covered in hieroglyphs that spoke of that Sutekh fellow. Now she wished she'd made time.

Dr. Wang looked excited. "Much is being said about the amazing events that took place today in China. As they should be. The rising of a fabled dragon and its death by the hands of enhanced terrorists was predicted in the prophetic writings my team unearthed."

"I quote: 'A day of infamy will dawn upon the world, a precursor to the great and dreadful day of the coming of the new king.' The text included a sign. Dark empires of the west would assault the honor of the supreme empire of the east and destroy their sovereign symbols in the very day they arise to declare to the world the day of change has come."

He paused to stare in open wonder at his own notes. "We just completed deciphering the text this morning when, to our amazement, we witnessed the fulfillment of our findings only minutes later. Ladies and gentlemen, brothers and sisters of the world, I cannot express how incredibly significant these findings are. I promise you we have redoubled our efforts to translate the text and share additional findings with the world as quickly as possible."

Gregorios glanced from the television to Sarah. "Why didn't we know about this first? He's capitalizing on this event brilliantly."

"We haven't deciphered the writings yet," Sarah said. "I can't believe we'll see that quote. Today's events were an accident."

"What if they fabricate it?" Tomas asked.

"Why would they do that?" Sarah asked.

Francesca studied Dr. Wang thoughtfully. He was responding to shouted questions and calls for proof from gathered reporters. "Perhaps he's not an innocent dupe like we've assumed. Perhaps he's part of the conspiracy Xiao has built to support her rising new empire."

Tomas nodded. "Either way, he's helping her. He only needs to stall everyone with these false claims for a little while. After that, it won't matter that he's a fraud."

Dr. Wang was indeed promising to make all of the materials available very soon. One of the reporters asked for updated scanned pages. In the past, he'd insisted they needed to get the information out as widely and as soon as possible, but in this new announcement, he deferred, suggesting everyone focus on the extensive images they had already released while his team worked to complete the newest finding.

Dr. Wang added, "Before we all get distracted by this amazing find, let me remind you that this prophetic text makes it clear that today's events are but a precursor to the great change, the coming of the one prophesied to sit in judgment upon the world."

The crowd erupted into shouting questions and accusations, and one vigorous fist fight.

Tomas shook his head slowly. "Check it out. They made sure to include Christians and Muslims in the crowd. They're all interpreting this with their own belief system and arguing already about whose Armageddon is on the way. This is going to spark all kinds of new conflicts, guaranteed."

Gregorios nodded. "You're right. We already have superpowers at each other's throats. The Chinese are mobilizing for war, and now we've got a religious aspect to the brewing conflict. This will suck in the rest of the world."

Quentin muttered a soft curse. "No doubt they have other steps planned to heighten the fervor. This is a world war in the making that will destroy everything."

Gregorios said, "Just what Xiao needs. Brilliant."

Francesca gave her father a sour look. "Don't sound too enthusiastic."

Exactly what Sarah was thinking.

He shrugged. "I admire the scope of her plans. We still have to kill her."

"I'm afraid that's going to be harder than ever," Melek said softly. He pulled off the bandages from his face. For the first time Sarah saw the bloody runes carved into his forehead and cheeks.

"We have a new problem."

65

What more could I have done? I edited all the historical texts in the great library as she commanded. Everyone believes every dynasty enjoyed the mandate of heaven. She promised my work would help ensure the dynasty continued its rule, but how is that possible when our armies are so thoroughly defeated? Still I would follow her counsel, but I hear the soldiers coming. I shall greet the final death early, but still cling to hope that she will restore the great dynasty in the end.

~LIU XIANG, 23 A.D.

XIAO RIPPED the helmet from Alter's head, cutting his jaw before the jagged faceplate came free. She stood over him, covered in blood, but through the rents in her blouse he could see she'd already almost entirely healed. Knowing he was as good as dead, Alter still lunged off the reclined chair. He would meet his fate on his feet.

Xiao threw him across the basement room before he could stand. He bounced off a stone pillar and fell to his hands and knees, groaning. Xiao lifted him off the floor and slammed him into the pillar repeatedly, hard enough to trigger shooting pains through his body, but not quite hard enough to break bones.

The beating left him dazed and helpless, unable to even try to fight her. His head cracked against the stone and he saw stars. He tasted blood and the smell of it permeated the air, although he wasn't sure if he was smelling his or hers.

Finally Xiao pressed his back to the stone hard enough to make it difficult to breathe. He blinked a few times to focus on her face and was surprised to see her wearing a little smile instead of a snarl of rage.

She shook her head slowly, her expression sad, like a mother disappointed that she must chastise a misbehaving toddler. "Alter, I had such high hopes for you, but your duplicity cannot go unpunished."

He wheezed through bloody lips. "My duplicity? You lied to me."

She released him and he nearly collapsed. Only by bracing himself against the stone pillar that was now streaked with his blood did he maintain his footing.

She faced him, frowning. "Who lied to who, Alter? You agreed to serve me, yet within seconds of that promise you were already plotting to betray me. You actually thought to betray me from within the machines I control while I was linked to your mind, and hoped I wouldn't know?"

Of course he'd hoped that. What else was he supposed to do?

"The wonderful irony of your actions is that you served me better than you could have imagined."

"What are you talking about?" he demanded, suddenly terrified for Sarah.

"Why do you think I told you about Constantinople? I allowed you to pass along just enough information to snare your foolish companions and draw your father to me."

"It was my father you wanted?" He had always assumed she wanted to destroy Sarah more than anyone.

"Of course. Only your father possessed the final secrets I needed to complete my goals. Thanks to you, I acquired them."

The words struck Alter like daggers. He'd led his father into the trap, given him to Xiao. He would have done better letting her kill him the first day she'd taken him.

She stroked his cheek. "You are my most profitable servant."

Alter lashed out, striking at her face and torso with his fists. She ignored the blows and it felt like he was punching living iron.

"I never said I'd help you hurt my family!" he cried, driving fingers toward her eyes.

Xiao slapped his hands away. "Your service has been profitable, so I will forgive you indiscretions. However I cannot allow further disloyalty."

"I'm through." Alter hoped she was lying. He'd arrived while she was still torturing information from his father. She wanted his help so she could set another trap. "I won't help you any more."

She raised an eyebrow. "You defy me?"

"I challenge you. A fair fight. Right now." It was a ridiculous move. His body ached from the recent beating and they both knew he stood no chance of hurting her.

She chuckled. "Youth can be so entertaining. No, dear Alter. Your time has not yet come. You are mine."

"I refuse."

He tried to push past her. If she was really going to let him walk from the room again, this time he'd find an exit, kill anyone who stood in his way, and make a break before she could stop him.

"That choice is no longer left to you." She pressed him back to the stone pillar and drew an ornate little knife covered with bright-colored Chinese runes. She raised it toward his head.

Alter fought with all his strength, every ounce of training he'd ever received, pounding on her with desperate blows, but to no avail. She held him against the pillar, her hand like an iron shackle. She ignored his futile blows that could have broken a mortal into a hundred pieces.

He screamed in her face. "No! I refuse."

She leaned close, her brow creasing a bit as she began inscribing a rune onto his forehead. Her eyes began to glow with the singular shade of her activated nevron. He tried shaking his head, but she grabbed his chin with an unbreakable grip, holding him like a child.

This couldn't be happening. He couldn't die like this, a helpless weakling. He reached for his nevra core and drew upon his soul powers. His hands began to burn as he fought to push her away, but she barely noticed.

Despite his struggles, she completed the rune in a matter of seconds. It activated like a branding iron on his skin and he howled with the pain that rippled through him like molten steel. The weight of it snuffed out his active nevron, preventing him from reaching for his powers.

Xiao retreated a step, allowing him to fall to the floor, twitching with agony.

"You are bound to me now, Alter. The pain will continue as long as you fight the effect, and will return if you ever attempt to disobey my will."

He'd rather die than serve Xiao, had thought he could trick her, but now everything was falling apart. The pain intensified as he fought the binding rune. It grew so terrible he pressed against the cool stone, screaming in pain. His thoughts scattered under the onslaught, and his struggles ceased.

As soon as he stopped, the pain evaporated, leaving him gasping.

Xiao knelt beside him and helped him sit up. She wiped blood from his face with the hem of her tattered skirt. Cupping his face with one hand, she kissed his forehead right where she'd bound him.

"Dear Alter, I hate to see you suffer. Your opposition is not your fault. You've been taught lies by those who should have prepared you for truth. In time you will understand and you will embrace your destiny."

It was hard to think. Her hand was so comforting, her words bored into his mind with exceptional weight and he found himself believing her. He tried not to, hated her for twisting his mind, but his reasons for fighting began to seem foolish.

"I don't . . . I can't." He tried to formulate words to deny her, but couldn't manage it.

Xiao sat on the stone floor beside him. "Alter, you are embarking upon the road of truth. I had hoped you would find it on your own, but my time is short so I must ease the start of your journey."

He wanted to scream that he was going to kill her, but ended up asking, "What truth?"

"The world is out of balance, Alter."

"That's why we have to kill . . ." Again his words failed. He couldn't quite say "you".

Xiao nodded agreement. "There are those who will have to be put down. Always there are some who refuse to see the truth and fight it with lies and terror."

He couldn't argue with that, could he?

"You know of master runes, but your father has never shared with you the deeper truths of the ascendant runes."

"The what?"

She explained to him about the ascendant runes, about how only the inner circle of hunters held the secret, how his father had shared it with Reuben and others but never with Alter. Her words tore down more of his stubborn resistance. How could his father have cared so little for him? He was one of the best runesmiths in the family, had proven himself worthy. Why keep secrets from him?

Xiao continued, her tone soothing, her expression tender. "He has withheld other truths. You fight kashaph but he never explained that the world is a wonderful, intricate melding of past and present, fueled by the souls of mortals and recorded by the ascendant runes through the nevra core they spawn. The rounon gifts that you and the kashaph share are a balancing power. The world has fallen out of balance, Alter, which is why more and more with rounon powers are being born. The world must be set right."

"Kashaph are evil," Alter said. That was true, wasn't it? "How could they balance the world?"

"No soul powers are evil or right in and of themselves. It is only in their application that we can interpret the morality of the souls using them."

"Kashaph choose evil," he declared with the last shreds of absolute conviction.

"At times. I've been teaching them a better way. The real problem is not the kashaph but the facetakers."

"Those demons aren't the ones trying to rule the world," he pointed out, but his words lacked his usual fervent zeal.

"Save the world," she corrected gently. "They've pushed the world out of balance, Alter. By congregating so many of their nevra core for so long in one region, they've skewed the balance of the ascendants, twisting those scrolls of history out of their natural course and tipping the world balance from neutral. That balance must be set right to prevent the rise of cataclysmic natural disasters, which are the world's coping mechanism if all else fails."

"That doesn't make sense."

She chided, "Think about it. It's a well-documented fact. Natural disasters have been on the rise all through the last century. The number of floods, hurricanes, earthquakes, and tornadoes has climbed every decade. What do you think has been triggering that rise?"

"Some claim it's climate change."

She laughed. "The climate is a living thing, Alter. Of course it changes all the time. It's the root cause of that change that mortals cannot grasp, but you can."

That sounded right, but he asked, "If what you say is true, why not just kill the demons and let the world return to normal? Why create war and chaos and take over?"

"Because I've seen dynasties fall," she said with surprising heat. "I've seen nations prey upon nations and millions suffer for too long. I can do something about it, Alter. I can change the world order and reset the balance at the same time. I can bring peace."

Something about her claim felt wrong, but peace would be nice.

Xiao rose and pulled him to his feet. "Get some rest, my chosen one. There is much to be done."

Alter headed for his room. Deep in his heart, a shackled core of his soul raged against every step he took in obedience to her, but it wasn't strong enough to slow his steps.

He smiled as he walked. Peace would be very nice.

66

You cannot be buried in obscurity: you are exposed upon a grand theater to the view of the world. If your actions are upright, your runes tuned to great truths, be assured they will augment your power and happiness.

~CYRUS THE GREAT

"THAT'S A BINDING RUNE." Sarah knelt beside the couch where Melek rested and lifted her fingers to the crimson rune.

The bleeding had stopped, but it looked ugly and raw. The marks were rough, deep, not the delicate artwork of a hunter. "I don't recognize the other ones."

The runes cut into his cheeks triggered a feeling of revulsion. They were ugly, somehow vulgar. She shivered and did not touch them.

Melek's voice was thin, pained. "Those are torture runes. Xiao used these to break into my mind and steal my deepest secrets."

"Oh no," Sarah breathed, horrified by the idea.

She squeezed his hand in silent comfort. She had suffered and nearly died several times at Xiao's and Paul's hands, but they'd never broken into her mind. The horror of such a violation left her trembling with rage.

Gregorios looked angry too. "That's why she left Hongwu and Vlad to keep us busy. She was after you all along."

"We were so stupid to walk into that trap," Sarah growled, hands clenching into fists. She wanted to punch something.

Melek closed his eyes, his expression anguished. "I was the worst fool. My arrogance blinded me to an obvious danger. I placed myself into Xiao's hands and compromised sacred knowledge she can use to further her designs to wrest control of time and the world."

Gregorios said, "They already had enough knowledge to break time. Don't you think you're exaggerating your own importance a bit?"

Melek opened his eyes and regarded Gregorios with a haunted gaze. "I wish that was all. There are secrets you don't know yet. She stole them all from me."

Eirene leaned forward in her chair, her expression disapproving. "Melek, what did we say about keeping secrets?"

"I know. You're right. I held back the deepest truths for fear that we might have a spy in our midst."

He weakly pounded his thigh with a fist. "I was the spy."

Gregorios grunted. "Well we're not going to shoot you yet, so stop whining and explain what happened."

"She was right, Gregorios. Xiao said I'm weak. I've been lying to myself, and my son is now paying a terrible price for my arrogance."

Gregorios shrugged. "I've been telling you that you're arrogant for ages."

"Stop it," Sarah snapped.

She wanted to slap Gregorios for his flippant remarks. This was serious. Couldn't he see Melek had been pushed to the breaking point? He needed encouragement, not harshness. "What do you mean about your son?"

"Alter somehow entered the memoryscape and interrupted Xiao. He fought her, hurt her." A proud smile tugged at his lips before his expression fell again. "I fear what she will do to punish him."

Sarah exulted to hear that Alter was still alive, still fighting Xiao, but she too feared what the angry cui dashi might do in retribution.

"I'm not worthy to lead my people," Melek said with a deep sigh.

Eirene said, "Oh, no. You aren't giving up now, Melek. The greatest dishonor would be quitting."

He looked up with an anguished expression. "I lack the strength to face her."

Eirene stood and looked down upon Melek, giving him a disapproving look. "Then do something about it. You're stronger than this, Melek. Gregorios has already offered the solution."

Sarah held her breath. The answer seemed so clear. Melek needed to take a different body, start a second life and leave this broken form behind. Only then could he do what needed to be done.

"I can't." He glanced at Nabil, who for the first time looked torn and didn't immediately denounce the evil of the devils and their body stealing ways.

"You can," Eirene insisted. Her tone softened as she dropped to one knee beside him and gripped his shoulder. "This is your moment, Melek, the moment you've prepared for all your life. You are a hunter, the only one who can lead your people against the greatest threat the world has ever faced, and we need you."

"We need you," Sarah echoed, taking his hand in hers. "Please."

Nabil paced away, then turned, his expression grim. "You are the father of our clan. There is no other who can take your place during this time of trial." He approached, his voice falling to a whisper. "We need you to be strong, father. Your son will understand."

Melek looked from Nabil to Sarah, then to Eirene. "I always thought you hated my family."

She shook her head, deep emotion in her eyes. "I've loved you for generations. Let it go, Melek. We can only do this together. Hunters and facetakers together. There is no other way."

She extended a hand. Melek slowly lifted one hand that shook as he extended it to hers. "Together then, may the fathers forgive me."

Sarah blinked back tears as she witnessed the long-awaited reunion. She felt so proud of Melek, she wanted to hug him.

Gregorios gave Melek an approving nod. "Good choice. Took you long enough."

Sarah punched Gregorios on the shoulder. "Oh, stop, you brute. You're just acting like that so no one sees you cry."

He winked at her. "Not even in your fondest dreams will you see me crying on Melek's shoulder. Tomas, go get the battle suit."

In moments they stood around two gurneys. Melek lay on one. The other held Reuben's empty body.

"You ready for this?" Gregorios asked.

Melek didn't hesitate now that he'd made his choice. "I am, but I want my grandmother to do it."

Sarah bit her lip to contain her emotion and wrapped her arm around Tomas' waist. He didn't seem as affected by Melek's words, but she really wanted to kiss the old hunter. He was making such a brave decision, stepping beyond centuries of hatred and distrust. It was a rare man who could do that.

Eirene seemed to be fighting her own emotions as she stepped to Melek's side. She kissed his forehead. "I've got you, dear one."

She placed her hands on his face in a gentle caress before wrapping her fingers around his jaw. She sighed once and her eyes began to glow with the purple light of her activated nevra core. Her fingers burned with purple fire and she drove them through the skin of Melek's jaw, reaching for the soul points that connected his soul to his body.

Eirene started to pull. The skin of Melek's face sloughed away as his glittering soulmask emerged. A crack appeared between the soulmask and the line of his jaw, widening slowly. Then the soulmask popped free with that terrible sucking sound.

Nabil, who stood at the foot of Melek's gurney, shuddered at the sound, his face anguished as he watched his leader submit to the cursed demons. Sarah moved to his side as Eirene lifted Melek's soulmask high, allowing streamers of flesh to fall free.

Skin flowed across the face of the vacated body, forming a smooth, mannequin mask, with only a slit where the nose should be. The translucent soulmask glittered with reflected light as it shrank until it looked like a party mask. Streamers of rainbow mist coiled below it.

Eirene stroked its cheek. "I'm proud of you."

"Please hurry," Melek's whisper-voice was deeper than most, but it held unmistakable fear.

Sarah gripped Nabil's arm. "He'll be all right."

Nabil gave her a resigned look. "No. He'll never be the same. His soul has been touched by a demon."

"You said he should do it," she reminded him.

Nabil met her gaze, his anguish clear. "I will follow him to the end of days, warrior. Fathers forgive me. What he does is necessary. That doesn't mean it's right."

She thought back to Gregorios' warning a few days before. The right choice was not always the traditional one. "I hope you realize some day that it is."

Eirene moved to Reuben's body and pressed Melek's soulmask to the empty face. The skin parted, allowing it to sink through and bond to the bone structure of the skull. The features of the head altered slightly to align with Melek's facial profile as skin flowed over the soulmask.

"Hold him," Eirene ordered as the light in her eyes flickered and extinguished.

Sarah and Tomas pressed the arms and legs down just as Melek began to shudder. Every muscle contracted and he rattled against the gurney.

Sarah had experienced that rush of sensation many times. When entering a new host, every muscle, every nerve connected with the soul, clamoring for attention. The experience could prove overwhelming, and grew more pronounced the longer a soul was dispossessed. Melek had only been away from his body for seconds, so it shouldn't be too bad for him.

Melek started to scream, his limbs thrashing harder.

Sarah exchanged a surprised look with Tomas and leaned her weight over Melek, straining to hold him down. Even Nabil threw himself into the effort of holding down Melek, and tears glittered in the young hunter's eyes.

Without her enhancement runes, Sarah never would have maintained her grip. Eirene stroked Melek's face, whispering soft words. After a moment he quieted, but continued to breathe fast, as if on the verge of panic.

"What have you done to him?" Nabil cried as he released his hold.

Eirene didn't look up from where she still stroked Melek's cheek. "It's all right. This is his first transfer, that's all."

After another minute, Eirene motioned Sarah and Tomas to release their holds, and she eased Melek into a sitting position. He raised his hands, examining them, eyes wide. Sarah couldn't tell if he looked amazed or horrified.

"I've forgotten what youth feels like," Melek whispered finally.

"It looks good on you. Welcome to your second life," Gregorios said, clapping Melek on the shoulder.

"To my everlasting shame, it feels good." Melek bowed his head and Sarah barely heard his whisper. "Oh my son, I am sorry."

Then he squared his shoulders and swung his legs off the gurney. "There is no going back. My course is set." He fixed Sarah with his gaze.

"Yours is about to be."

67

If any dare plunder the knowledge and secrets contained in this place, know that the gods who walk among us, enlivened by runes and purple fire will cast him down and erase his name, his seed in the land.

~INSCRIPTION ON CUNEIFORM TABLETS IN THE GREAT
LIBRARY AT NINEVAH, BUILT FOR ASHURBANIPAL,
ASSYRIAN RULER, 7TH CENTURY B.C.

BEFORE THEY RETIRED to the living room to talk, Melek paused over his recently abandoned body. He stared down at the scarred flesh of the head, the wounded corpse just barely alive.

"Do you want us to save it for you?" Gregorios asked.

"No. I can never return to it." Melek turned away.

Eirene hugged him. "We'll see it's disposed of properly."

He shook his head. "Send it to my home, please. We'll bury it with my fathers."

Sarah lingered behind the others with Tomas. They shared a tender kiss and a quiet moment together as she steeled herself for what was to come. Xiao had declared war on them and the world. They couldn't afford to fail again.

"You know, I've never attended my own funeral," Tomas said, glancing at Melek's old form. "I'm not sure it's the best idea for him to."

"How do you think his family will take it?" Sarah asked.

Tomas shrugged. "If you'd asked me that even a month ago, I'd have said with confidence that he'd be expelled, humiliated, and his name blotted from the clan's records. Now, I have no idea."

He touched her face and kissed her one more time. "I'm glad you're all right, Sarah."

"Let's keep it that way. For all of us," she said fiercely.

In reply, he wrapped her in his powerful arms. She held him tight, drawing strength from his solid presence. She hoped Melek's secrets proved powerful enough to finally turn the tide in their favor.

If not, they were facing at best a struggle that would see most of the world plunged into the worst war in history. She doubted she and Tomas and the people they most loved would survive once Xiao rose to power.

They reached the living room just as Harriett swept in. She looked fresh and energetic as always, despite her long trip, and exchanged exuberant hugs with her family. As she began extracting cookies and muffins from a satchel, Sarah rushed over to embrace her too.

"It's great to see you," Sarah said, accepting a triple-chocolate cookie that was somehow warm, as if Harriett had traveled with an oven.

"We're moving into the final course. I plan to help make sure Xiao pays the tab," Harriett said with a grin.

Gregorios motioned Harriett and Francesca both to sit on a couch between him and Eirene. While the rest of the group took seats, Melek paced.

Gregorios didn't give him much time before saying, "All right, Melek. Time is short and we've got a lot of catching up to do. Let's hear it."

Melek faced them, but for a moment did not speak.

Eirene gave him an encouraging smile. "We know it's hard, but you've got to trust us, Melek."

"And no more half-truths. We don't have time for any more hesitation," Gregorios added.

Melek glanced down at his powerful young hands and whispered, "I've already bonded to the runes on this body."

"That's one of the best battle suits I've ever worn. It'll serve you well," Gregorios told him.

Melek's expression turned pained. "Please. This is my son we're talking about."

Gregorios met his gaze and said simply, "Not any more. It's you. Get used to it and stop stalling. We have work to do."

Melek turned to Sarah. "Very well. It's time you understood your destiny, warrior."

"What destiny?" The intensity of his gaze was a bit unnerving. Sarah was having enough trouble managing her rune warrior powers. She didn't want some new destiny thrust upon her.

"The world is out of balance, and you alone possess the gift to restore that balance."

"I don't understand." By the looks on the others' faces, they agreed.

Melek gestured to each of the facetakers in the room. "I will try to explain. You already understand master runes, ascendant runes, and their connection to the active nevra core of the facetakers."

"A little." Understanding was definitely a strong word.

"Ascendant runes are the scrolls of time, recording between them every aspect of every moment of history the world has ever lived," Melek declared.

"How does that lead to the world being out of balance?" Sarah asked.

He pointed again to the facetakers. "It's their fault."

Gregorios rolled his eyes. "I thought we were beyond the whole evil demon monster finger pointing and name calling."

"I am not calling you names. I am explaining a truth that you have never seen. By congregating all of your nevra cores in Rome for so long, you twisted the ascendants out of balance, linking them too tightly to one place at the expense of other locations. This has slowly pulled the world out of balance."

Gregorios frowned as he considered that. Eirene asked, "Why didn't you explain any of this to us before?"

Harriett gestured with a muffin and said, "Right. Instead of just trying to kill us."

Melek shrugged. "Killing you was the easiest way to restore balance. It avoided approaching other dangerous truths."

"And it was more satisfying," Nabil added simply.

"You need to revisit your priorities," Gregorios said.

Melek shared a look with Nabil that seemed to say 'whatever'. "It is what it is. Maintaining balance was one of our tasks set since the antiquities. We can tell when the world is shifting out of balance by the increase in the number of people born kashaph."

"How do they fit in?" Sarah asked with a frown.

"The rounon gift is a counter-power to the ascendants. The more the world shifts out of balance, the more rounon-gifted are born.

There are other indicators, but this is the one we pay most attention to."

"So does that mean when the world is completely in balance we don't need the hunters either?" Tomas asked.

"No. There are always a minimum number of rounon on the world, just as there are always a set number of active nevra core."

That sparked Gregorios' interest. "How many? We could never tell if we had a full count."

Melek shrugged. "I don't know."

"So you say the world is out of balance," Sarah repeated to keep the conversation on track and make sure she was keeping up. "What's the danger and how does that tie in with what Xiao is doing?"

"The danger is that the world will reset itself if balance is not restored. It usually does that by catastrophic natural disasters."

"We usually try to avoid those," Tomas said.

Melek added, "It also ties to the current situation. The more out of balance the world becomes, the stronger the rounon gifts and, by extension, the stronger the cui dashi powers."

"So you're saying Xiao's army is growing in numbers and strength," Gregorios said.

"Exactly." Melek paced away before continuing. "That in itself is a danger, but coupled with the apparent plans Xiao has in motion to assault the structure of time and rise to rule the world, the instability of the ascendants poses a deeper threat."

"Are you saying she can corrupt the ascendants?" Eirene asked.

"In a manner, yes." Melek pointed at Sarah. "Rune warriors arise in times of juncture between ascendants. These are moments when ascendants are particularly vulnerable and must be protected."

"How do rune warriors do that?" Sarah asked. That sounded kind of cool, but not if it added another layer of arcane stuff she had to worry about not breaking when she needed to focus on killing Xiao.

"This is all very interesting," Gregorios interrupted before Melek could reply. "But we've known a handful of rune warriors and none of them brought balance to the universe."

Melek nodded agreement. "Joan of Arc was killed before she could fill her destiny."

"I thought you had her killed." Eirene said.

The old hunter shook his head. "We were trying to help her. I never learned who orchestrated her death, but they blocked our efforts with exceptional cunning. I'm starting to wonder if Xiao might have had a hand in it."

Eirene didn't look happy about that. "It's possible. We know she's been a player for a long time, but did she have the knowledge to recognize and remove rune warriors even back then?"

"I have no idea, but it's possible. Other rune warriors were never given these deepest truths because my ancestors removed what we thought were the threats of those days."

Gregorios said, "The trick with secrets is knowing when to share them."

Sarah wasn't sure what Melek was getting at, but didn't want to lose the main focus. "What exactly can Xiao do? And how do we stop her?"

Melek glanced at Nabil, who sat in a hard-backed chair at the edge of the group, hands clasped together, looking unhappy but determined. "This gets to the heart of the secrets Xiao stole from me, the deepest truths I failed to protect. Just as ascendant runes are a higher level rune than master runes, they in turn are subject to a higher order still."

She hadn't expected that. "How is that possible? Ascendants record history. I've glimpsed them. They go on forever."

Melek shook his head again. "Not forever. Only a very long time."

"I don't see the difference. What's higher order than that?" Sarah asked.

Melek held her gaze. "The difference is profound and of paramount import. The ascendants are part of the great whole, the eternal round of history sometimes referred to as the wheel of time."

"You're saying the wheel of time exists and it's like an eternal rune or something?" Sarah asked, not sure if she could believe that. If it was anyone but Melek speaking, she'd think they were making fun of her.

He nodded. "It is the greatest rune. It is known as the Daraka Kallpa, or more simply the Aeon."

"Now that's interesting," Gregorios said, leaning back in his chair, a far-off look in his eye.

"You're making connections too," Eirene stated, also looking thoughtful.

Gregorios nodded. "Everyone thinks they're different, but the more lives I live, the more I see everyone's more alike than they wished."

Quentin chuckled. "You're kind of annoying when you assume the wise old patriarch role. What connections are you seeing?"

"Almost every ancient religion and mythology deals with the concept of the wheel of time in one way or another," Eirene responded for her husband. "Aeon is a word that has connections to ancient Egyptian mythology through the serpentine god Chronos, who was the original Father Time."

Gregorios, looking fascinated by the ideas he was considering, added, "Aion, slightly different spelling, is also a Greek deity associated with time. Kind of useless most of the time, but what's important is that he was usually connected with the orb encompassing the universe and the zodiac."

Eirene smiled agreement. "Then there's the link between Aeon and the concept of kalpa. Both Buddhists and Hindus share that idea, which ties to the duration of the universe and cycles of time."

Melek nodded slowly. "The Greek notion of Aion is more closely aligned with truth than the Egyptian since the concept of time he represented was boundless and therefore more eternal in nature. Chronos was linked more closely to empirical time of the past, present, and future."

Eirene added, "I can see connections with Osiris too. There are links between Aeon and Osiris, Egyptian lord of the dead."

Sarah was struggling to keep up with the rapid-fire mythology lesson. "Hold on. You're saying all those old religions and myths were talking about the same thing and linking back to this Daraka-whatever rune?"

Melek nodded. "There is evidence that in the early epochs of recorded history, several societies understood these truths. It was only after the rise of an exceptionally powerful cui dashi in ancient Egypt that the dangers of this truth was manifest. Since that time, my family has worked to conceal these truths from the world to prevent the risk of another assault on time."

Sarah exchanged a surprised look with Tomas. She said, "It can't be coincidence."

"What?" Eirene asked as they all turned to Sarah.

"Those archaeologists and their phony prophecy. We've been assuming Xiao planted the evidence to add legitimacy to her attempt to take over the world, using Alter as her pawn. What if she lied about her plans for Alter, and it's a different king of the world she's prepping everyone to meet?"

Melek paled and whispered, "Abomination."

It actually comforted Sarah to hear him say that. He sounded like his old self again.

"What are you suggesting?" Gregorios asked.

Francesca sucked in a breath, snatched a cookie out of her sister's hand and pointed at Sarah with it. "Oh, that's good. We know Xiao's figured out how to go way back. We know she's tested altering the past. You all just proved that it's possible to suck someone from one time and place to another. It never made sense to me why she was messing with Egypt when she's Chinese. Melek, how dangerous was that cui dashi you were just talking about, the one from ancient Egypt?"

"He dates back to our earliest records, about 1400 B.C., the days of Moses and the Exodus. He was a powerful figure in Pharaoh's court and a bitter enemy of Moses. He launched an assault on time that very nearly succeeded. The patriarch of our line, Alter the Great, defeated him and defined the path our clan would follow ever since."

"Did that cui dashi do something Xiao hasn't been able to do?" Harriett asked as she produced another cookie to replace the one Francesca had stolen. "Even with the recent secrets she stole from you?"

Melek nodded, his expression grave. "He is the only person we know of who gained supremacy over an ascendant rune."

"And I bet his name was Sutekh," Tomas declared.

He was right. Sarah gasped as the magnitude of Xiao's plan boggled her mind. The combined power of three master runes had killed Sarah. The single master rune from Constantinople had been powerful enough to grant her, Gregorios and Spartacus super powers. Those were but tiny pieces of an ascendant rune. The thought of mastering an entire ascendant seemed impossible.

She asked, "How is such a thing possible? That much power would destroy even a cui dashi."

Melek spread his hands. "No one's sure. It's never been duplicated."

"What other information did Xiao steal from you?" Gregorios asked.

"Higher order runes, those required to strengthen her connection to her ascendant and facilitate access to her portion of history. She'll be able to move freely backward and forward along the scroll of time affiliated with her nevra core, but they don't grant her mastery of the full power of the ascendant."

Francesca polished off the last bite of her cookie and said, "That's it then. She's going after old Sutekh from ancient Egypt. He's got the last secret."

"Sutekh," Eirene repeated slowly, considering the name.

Melek added, "He was the high priest of Set."

"Set was the crocodile-headed guy that killed his brother, right?" Tomas asked.

Gregorios said, "It was more an aardvark. He was god of the desert, disorder, violence, and foreigners, among other things."

Melek said, "Many of the Egyptian temples actively sought kashaph for priests. They considered their soul powers divine manifestations of the will of the gods. Sutekh had amassed great knowledge and somehow learned secrets no one else had ever discovered. Many of the most secret runes we guard were first developed by him."

"Sounds like a dangerous guy," Tomas said.

Sarah agreed. It seemed unbelievable that for the first time they were considering a bad guy coming back from the dead. It didn't inspire the kind of hope that stories of Christ usually did.

Melek said, "He was defeated just prior to the final great plague, but our records indicate he did not die. He was banished to eternal purgatory."

"What does that mean?" Sarah asked, not sure she wanted to know.

Gregorios said, "Dispossession. Like what I did to Hitler, only longer. A soul that powerful could linger for thousands of years before finally dying."

"It's a miracle he never found another body to steal," Eirene said.

Gregorios said, "Not if he was hidden well enough. Maybe a sarcophagus or something."

Sarah shuddered to think of archaeologists uncovering a mummy wearing the soulmask of an ancient dispossessed cui dashi. It made the concept of the Egyptian curses far more terrifying.

Melek started pacing again. "Your idea has merit. Xiao now possesses the ability to return to those days and find Sutekh, but returning him to the present day would prove a challenge still. It is difficult to extract a soul from the scroll of time and move it to another position."

Eirene snapped her fingers. "Wait a minute. What if she didn't need to remove him so much as swap him for another soul?"

Melek considered the idea. "The soul would need to be a close match. The challenge would still seem insurmountable, but would be entire magnitudes easier to accomplish."

"It would have to be a cui dashi," Gregorios said, his expression grim.

Sarah met his gaze and the truth filled her with dread. She spoke in unison with Eirene and Melek.

"Alter."

68

My grand terracotta army stands ready to accompany me into the afterlife. The runes are applied to carry the souls whose faces they wear into my service for all time. Who needs a second life on this earth when they can enter the eternities with such an army?

~QIN SHI HUANG, FIRST EMPEROR OF CHINA, 210 B.C.

"THAT'S WHY SHE TOOK ALTER," Sarah exclaimed, clutching Tomas' hand so tight he winced. "She plans to sacrifice him!"

"The pieces are starting to fall into place. Melek, how do we use those secret runes of yours to stop her?" Gregorios asked with remarkable calm.

Melek's expression looked anguished. No doubt he was considering the terrible fate Xiao planned for his son. "We don't. Sarah does."

"Me? How?"

"It is your ultimate duty as rune warrior. You can use these runes as tools and ciphers beyond the ability of any of us. The runes I will share with you will grant you the ability to see the Daraka Kallpa as it really is and to return it to balance."

No way Sarah wanted to straddle time and try balancing it. She struggled to balance a checkbook.

"But it's time. How can we see it? It doesn't exist in our dimension." She'd glimpsed the ascendant runes, but only by passing her hand through that weird, invisible barrier and touching it in a place she couldn't actually see.

"No, it doesn't. Only a rune warrior can go there, travel the fourth dimension. There is a reason all rune warriors gain sword titles. Your ultimate duty is to become the Sword of History, the Aeon Champion."

That made Tomas smile. "Aeon Champion. I like the sound of that. You're Father Time's personal enforcer."

Sarah punched him in the shoulder. "This isn't funny. How am I supposed to do that?"

Melek gave her an apologetic grin, looking less sure of himself. "I cannot tell you. You alone possess the power to learn this. Inscribed within your unique rounon resides the instincts to wield it."

"My instincts already got me killed once," she reminded him.

"But you killed Paul too," Tomas said. He was trying to keep his tone light, but she read the worry in his eyes.

Spartacus leaped to his feet. "Lady of Steel, Sword of the Deliverer, Aeon Champion! I pledge my service to your cause and swear my sword to your honor." He banged his hand over his chest in salute.

Gregorios grinned. "I think he's nailed it. We're your team, Sarah. We've got your back. If you lead, we'll follow."

Eirene kissed her husband. "I love you." She then turned to Sarah. "Make us proud, dear."

Harriett gave her two thumbs up and added her oath. Quentin added his as he bowed formally over Sarah's hand. Tomas kissed her cheek and held her hand, his skin hot against hers.

The magnitude of what they were pledging stirred in Sarah a fierce desire to live up to their expectations. It helped fight down the growing terror at the weight of responsibility Melek was placing squarely in her lap.

They had to stop Xiao. They had to restore balance to the world, whatever that meant. She'd always felt driven to help fix wrongs, but had never imagined this ultimate extension of that instinct.

They had to prevent an ancient evil high priest from returning from the dead. They had to save Alter's life.

That thought took root at the core of everything, and she focused on it. She'd face Xiao again, wrestle with her for control over history itself if she must. She would attempt to become the tip of the spear in their final assault if she could save Alter and free him from this horrible fate.

So she took a deep, slow breath and said, "All right. What do we do?"

Melek smiled like a proud father. "We enter the memoryscape. There I will show you the runes and . . ." He shrugged. "Then you use them."

It took only a moment to return to the machines and get strapped in. Gregorios volunteered to power the machine, with Harriett again as backup. Sarah linked them to the Beijing remote charging rune, with the modifiers to allow them to tap all of it in ten percent increments, if needed.

As the first influx of power rushed into them, Gregorios' eyes shone with his nevron and he laughed. "That's quite a rush, girl."

Eirene grinned, with a twinkle in her eye. "Good. I like it when you're energetic."

Tomas helped Sarah with her helmet. "Be careful in there and don't run off again."

She kissed him fiercely. "Be back before you know it."

Only Melek joined Sarah and Eirene under the helmets. Spartacus and Tomas had argued that they should go too as protection in case Sarah ran into trouble, but Melek had waved them away.

"Xiao no longer needs to hunt us. We should be safe enough until Sarah learns the runes. After that, it's Xiao who should fear to enter the scroll of history."

Tomas didn't look convinced. "That's a lot of shoulds. They haven't worked out so well for us in the past."

"This time will be different," Melek promised.

"Why?"

Melek had fixed him with a hard stare. "Because we're done running."

He'd looked so determined that Tomas had let the matter drop. Melek might not be a match for Xiao, but he was no longer cowed. Ever since taking on Reuben's body, he'd carried himself with strength and determination that had been missing before.

Sarah liked the new Melek and sensed she was finally seeing the true soul of the greatest hunter. As her mind was drawn into Eirene's memories, she hoped he hadn't waited too long to embrace his path.

When the world formed around her, Sarah found herself sitting atop the square tower, close beside the gorgeous dome of the Florence cathedral. She took a deep, satisfied breath as she glanced across the expanse of the city. It looked vibrant, full of brightly-dressed people in medieval dress.

"This is a strange choice," Melek said.

"I love it." Sarah squeezed Eirene's hands.

"I know, dear. The Duomo holds a special place in both our hearts. What better place to come learn in peace?"

"Do you feel anyone tampering?" Sarah asked nervously.

"No."

Sarah hoped that didn't change. She applied the cipher marks to her central rune warrior mark to enhance her sensitivities. She too felt nothing amiss in the memoryscape. "I think we're clear."

Melek didn't look surprised. He wore Reuben's powerful young body in the memoryscape. "Good. If you'll excuse us, grandmother?"

"Of course." Eirene didn't seem offended that she was excluded from the secrets Melek was about to share.

She launched off the top of the tower and soared in a graceful arc over the length of the cathedral, landing on the cupola of the glittering dome. "Don't break anything, Sarah. I'll be visiting David."

Sarah reminded herself to visit here again with Eirene when they had a little more time. She loved this period of Florence and could happily play tourist in this memory for days.

A table appeared at the peak of the almost-flat roof of the tower and Melek led Sarah to it. With a quill that appeared in his hand, he began to draw the secret runes.

Unlike most of the other runes they used that were recognizable as Chinese or Egyptian symbols, these runes were different. The central form was that of a phoenix ringed in an orb of fire.

Melek explained. "The phoenix has always been a symbol of rebirth, of cycles of life. This symbol holds a power many cultures have sensed but never understood."

He went on to add other marks until the phoenix held the center of a complex maze-like pattern, ringed with almost-recognizable symbols. "These are precursors to symbols used in the ancient zodiac. You can find hints of them in the Dendera Zodiac, which is one of the oldest known zodiacs. It was discovered in the chapel of Osiris in the temple of Hathor in Dendera and is uniquely circular in shape for an Egyptian zodiac."

Sarah studied the composite symbol more closely and felt the power of it radiating off the table into the air like hot coals. Its force was more subtle than that of a master rune and felt more like that of the ascendants. Just looking at it gave her the same odd feeling like when she parted the curtain of air to reach into the dimension where the ascendants existed.

"It's magnificent," she breathed.

Melek said reverently, "It is our greatest treasure. With this, you can reach the aeon, travel its paths." He fixed her with a serious expression. "This is a tool that will allow you to bring balance or to destroy the fabric of history. Walk with caution."

"I will," she promised, but couldn't hide a grin that crept across her face. The more she looked at that rune, the more she wanted to use it. She could do this.

The memories of all the times Alter had cautioned her to be careful, that she was recklessly rushing into danger, flashed through her mind. She hesitated, unable to shake a creeping worry. What if she was overlooking something? What if Melek didn't know about dangers she was about to run into?

She felt like she'd learned her lesson, but still worried. This time if she failed, dying would be the simplest outcome. Worst case, she could destroy time and the world itself.

That was a heavy burden, and she wished she knew another way.

But she didn't. So she took a deep breath, whispered a prayer, and embraced her responsibility. She would find a way because she absolutely refused to accept the consequences of failing.

Sarah lifted the front of her shirt to expose her muscled abs and began tracing the rune on her skin with sure movements. She didn't need to glance back at the original for reference. The rune had already become part of her. Where Alter usually had problems with her choice of locations for her runes, Melek only nodded in approval.

When she completed the rune and willed it to life, light erupted through her, piercing her, but without pain. It filled her with glorious brilliance. She threw her head back and extended her arms, exulting in a feeling of joy so profound she couldn't describe it.

Sarah laughed and tendrils of white light bubbled out of her mouth like wisps of smoke. "This is amazing."

"Is it working?" Melek asked with a frown.

"You can't see this?" She gestured at the blazing rune that glowed like an intense light under her shirt.

"I see nothing."

"It's working. It's wondrous," she assured him.

"What do you see?" he asked eagerly.

Sarah turned a slow circle. The city below looked brighter than before, and she could see into the buildings. As she focused on that strange ability, it changed in a subtle way, and suddenly she could see through the memory, see the underlying construct of it. The entire memory sat upon the curve of Eirene's ascendant, linking the memory to that moment in time.

Sarah had never seen the ascendant so clearly. It stretched far beyond the city and arced into the air. As she followed its gentle curve, leaning back to look up, she noticed a second ascendant woven close around it, the two intertwined so closely she knew instinctively that the second ascendant was linked to Gregorios. The two had loved each other for so many lives, they'd twisted the weave of history around themselves.

It was the most awe-inspiring testament to their love she could imagine. Then she looked higher still and gaped. The entire heavens were filled with runes.

"I see it."

69

Whenever you can, act as a liberator. Freedom, dignity, wealth—these three together constitute the greatest happiness of humanity. If you bequeath all three to your people, their love for you will never die through all your lives.

~CYRUS THE GREAT

AS SARAH STARED at the glittering silver-gold runes that filled the sky, she felt the connection to them solidify like a tangible link, joined through the rune blazing on her stomach. That rune seemed to wrap around her waist and began lifting her off the tower into the air.

"What's going on?" Melek cried, grabbing her hand and arresting her ascent.

"Let go," Sarah said softly, not looking away from the incredible sight. If she stared long enough, she felt sure she could actually grasp its meaning. "I need to do this."

He released her and saluted. "May the fathers guide your steps, Champion."

Sarah floated into the sky, accelerating with every second until she rocketed upward like a reverse shooting star, slipping between gigantic looping arcs of the many ascendants. The air flowing around her felt far too gentle to be real. When she glanced down a moment later, she was startled to find she'd climbed so high the city looked like a tiny speck on the earth. That speck shrank faster until she could clearly see Italy spread below. Then all of Europe. Then the world.

She should be terrified as she rocketed into space above the earth, but she felt nothing but the limitless peace of that aeon dimension. She didn't feel cold, didn't have trouble breathing.

Although her body still slept in the chair in Beijing, she embraced this glorious vision. She rose above the arcs and whorls of the giant ascendants until she could look back on them and upon the world. Only then, when she could see the entire form of it, did her progression stop.

For a moment, Sarah thought she was standing in outer space, but then the vision shifted and the world shrank down into a sphere barely ten feet across. It hovered before her, a glittering, miniature image of the planet, covered by woven ascendants.

Everything else around her remained empty blackness. It felt like she stood in front of the world on an invisible floor. Weird.

Sarah paced around the ten-foot globe of the earth, studying the complex patterns of the ascendants. The pattern was slowly changing, and she realized that the ascendants were morphing into different forms as the seconds ticked by. They were somehow recording history. If only she understood how it worked.

When she stepped closer to the earth, she found that she could peer into it, as if it was a translucent cylinder. The ascendants plunged into its heart, their twisting spirals working back into history. Although she could walk around the globe, somehow when she peered into it, she sensed that its depth continued back to the creation of time.

The thought was mind-bending, and she couldn't quite understand. She tried tracing the curve of one ascendant, but its eye-twisting pattern defied her ability to follow as it rippled back deep into the shadowed heart of the past.

Each ascendant wrapping the globe was like a glittering cord of light, each a slightly different hue. Taken together, they formed an eternal rainbow that filled her with joy and defied the limits of her mortal comprehension.

When she touched one of them, its shape sharpened in her mind. Only then did she realize the ascendant was actually made up of thin disks, packed close together. With a start, she realized that each disk represented a single moment in time.

As she slid her fingers along the ascendant, she sensed vague images of the moments it recorded. A hint of a scent, the whisper of a storm, the distant echo of many voices. There had to be a way to bring the moment into focus. She needed to figure that out.

Sarah noticed tiny points of light glowing on the globe at the center of where each ascendant anchored to the planet. She touched one and sensed a nevra core. It was the soul that fueled that ascendant as it recorded a fraction of history. So awesome. So weird.

Marveling at the unique vision, Sarah drifted around the globe again, and noticed that the ascendants varied in density and thickness. She focused on one that glowed a vibrant, welcoming, golden color. When she touched it, she recognized it instantly.

Gregorios. This was his ascendant, the portion of history that fueled his nevron and captured history through him. It was perhaps the thickest of all the ascendants and thrummed with life.

Touching that ascendant linked Sarah to him somehow. She felt his determination, his eternal devotion to Eirene, and his love for a world he knew so well. Under his sometimes gruff exterior, he had the heart of a poet. That was fascinating.

As Sarah looked down the expanse of his ascendant, its shape sharpened under her eye. She sensed a pattern emerging, as if its long coils compressed into a three-dimensional spiral. The mundane moments drained away, leaving the critical moments, the master runes, and a grand spiral that defined it as a whole. When she focused on it, she caught a glimpse of it radiating up from the globe.

The power of that symbol rocked Sarah even in her tranquil vision state. This was the signature symbol of that entire ascendant. If she dared work it into a cipher, she could tie her soul to that ascendant. She wouldn't need to fear unlocking its power because she wouldn't have to try containing it. She would become one with it, able to draw upon its strength as her own.

Would such an act cost her soul?

She wasn't sure, but the magnitude of the fact that she could try it rattled her to the core. She could do it. She could activate that symbol upon her soul and become something the world had never seen. But what would that do to her? Would she still be Sarah, or would she cease to exist as an individual and be consumed by the ascendant?

She didn't dare explore the idea further. Sarah pulled her hand from Gregorios' ascendant and focused on the next nearest one. Its rope of history was almost as thick, and as she'd noticed before, it was tightly entwined with his. Now in her vision state, it glowed with a pure silver light. Sarah touched the spark that represented the nevra core anchoring it to the world, and smiled.

Eirene. Through that connection, Sarah sensed the fierce love for

Gregorios, the equally fierce determination to defend those she loved from harm. Eirene adored her children with a mother's intensity. That love extended beyond her long-beloved facetaker children to the multitudes of descendants spawned from her many lives spent with Gregorios. Sarah marveled at the depth of Eirene's love and commitment to family.

Sarah released Eirene's ascendant and continued pacing around the globe, soaking up knowledge that seemed to radiate off the incredible vision. Something caught her eye.

In a juncture between Eirene's and Gregorios' ascendants, a bright light blazed, as if a miniature sun had been caught in a fold of history. She drew closer to study it, and realized the light was encompassed by a cipher. Her cipher.

It was the remote charging rune she'd set up in Beijing. Wow. She hadn't expected to see anything she'd created show up in the aeon dimension. The cipher was drawing upon the power of souls, so it was similar to the arcane power fueling the ascendants and the aeon. Maybe that offered insights into how it worked.

She studied it, at first wondering if maybe she had inadvertently figured out a way to create a new master rune, one outside the bounds of the ascendants. She wasn't sure if that would be a good idea, but her theory proved false. Master runes were tied to specific moments in time, embedded within the ascendants, but the charging rune was tied to a specific location, spread over time.

As she examined the brightly blazing mass of power, she noticed that it was really a close-packed column of tiny slices of energy. Each slice linked to disks of the two ascendants, representing a specific second of time. Each second was therefore linked to the whole, but also self-contained. Each second contained the power drawn from souls in that specific moment. The older slices of time slowly bled away their power.

Since it wasn't anchored in a single moment, constructed by so many focused souls, the cipher lacked the durability of a master rune. Sarah had been tapping that remote charging cipher as a whole. Now she realized she could use modifiers to limit her access to specific moments instead. That was a fascinating idea, one she planned to explore further when she found more time.

So much to think about. She needed months to study the vision. Walking the aeon, she had plenty of time, but she didn't belong there. In the real world, time was ticking away. She needed to focus.

So Sarah again paced around the globe. She counted fifty-two ascendants and sensed the nevra cores of each of them. She touched Harriett's, savored the woman's passion for baking and her determination to succeed. She found Francesca's, basking in the woman's love of life and bubbling enthusiasm. She was surprised to learn Francesca was an accomplished musician and singer.

When she moved on, she noticed a brightly glowing, purple spark near the earth, but not anchored to it. That was unusual. There was another spark of active nevra core on the planet, but what was the second one? When she touched it, she gasped.

Bastien. How in the world?

Bastien had died, murdered by Paul in St. Peter's square. And yet, that spark contained him. All of him. Everything that had been Bastien had been absorbed into the ascendant at the moment of his death. She caught a glimpse of his long lives, his honor, his love of family, and his lingering regret that he'd failed at the end.

When Sarah touched the anchor point for that ascendant, she sensed a newborn girl in Africa. She was a new facetaker, a soul bound to the ascendant. Would the girl ever understand her powers? Would she live for thousands of years, or die after a single life spent in ignorance?

Troubled by that thought, Sarah continued her circuit. She noticed several ascendants all glowing with varying shades of red. She touched the thickest of the group, which glowed with a clear, crimson light, like an exquisite ruby.

Xiao.

Sarah sensed the woman's determination, her long-savored hatred for those who tore down and destroyed great things. She sensed Xiao's commitment to fashioning a new world that would remove such things, and that pure understanding rocked Sarah.

Xiao really did want to make things better. Sarah couldn't deny it, couldn't claim Xiao was lying. She felt the simple truth, and it tore away all of her justifications that she was fighting Xiao because Xiao was an evil monster.

Xiao's solution to the problem still seemed twisted, but now Sarah understood a little of what had motivated her choice. Xiao honestly believed she had earned the right to rule all things. She believed Gregorios, Eirene, Sarah, and their team were the warmongers, short-sighted fools who were preventing the world from finally achieving lasting peace.

From that point of view, it made perfect sense that they needed to be annihilated. Sarah recoiled from the ascendant and shuddered. She might understand Xiao better, but couldn't grasp how Xiao could think sacrificing millions of lives was a price worth paying.

It rankled that now Sarah understood a little of Xiao's reasoning. Her hatred for the crazed cui dashi faded, but the fresh knowledge only strengthened her resolve.

Sarah hated that Xiao's motivations resonated with her. She completely agreed with Xiao's desire to right some of the terrible wrongs in the world. If only she could find a way to reason with the woman, they could . . . What? Work together?

Unlikely. Xiao would never stop. She could never be reasoned with. She believed with a fixed resolve that she was right, and she would press forward with her plan through any and all opposition.

The only way to stop her was to kill her.

What a waste. How much could they accomplish together?

That was a silly dream, and thinking like that might weaken her at a critical moment. Still, she had to wonder if there might be a way.

As she considered the insights she'd gained about her adversary, Sarah slid her hand to the next ascendant.

She recoiled when she realized it was Paul's. Sarah didn't maintain the contact long enough to read anything from Paul's soul, or to investigate who his ascendant linked to now that Paul was gone. She already knew his mind was a cesspit of confusion and torture that she didn't want to look into.

A soft pink strand drew her attention. It too had a bright point near the end, another recently-deceased nevra-powered soul. She dared the briefest touch.

Mai Luan. In that brief contact, Sarah sensed Mai Luan's longing to be accepted, her fear of failure, and her drive to prove herself. Sarah recoiled, not wanting to sense anything more. When she touched the glowing point at the very end, she sensed the birth of a child in India.

There were a total of seven ascendants closely tied to Xiao's, all glowing with varying shades of red. They all held the souls of cui dashi. Xiao had created so many powerful children. The thought chilled Sarah, even there in her weird dream state.

Eager to leave the evil family cluster behind, she stepped around the globe to Europe and the next ascendant. It looked a sickly yellow color. When she touched it, she felt nothing special, but then noticed another glowing point of a nevra-powered soul that had died in the past. It was associated with that ascendant, but farther back along the spiral. Sarah reached into the shadowed depths of the globe and touched it, then shivered.

Vlad. Not the vampire himself, but the soul of the facetaker who died accidentally creating the deadliest vampire.

The man's horror radiated up Sarah's arm, and she clearly sensed the hundreds of years of torture he'd suffered as one of the many souls bound to the broken, twisted rune warrior vampire. Touching the spark of his life, his most vivid memory flowed up the connection before she could snatch her hand away.

Sarah watched in helpless, silent sorrow as the doomed facetaker positioned Vlad's soulmask over the corpse, already marked with the complex vampire runes. Those runes seared into her mind. They looked similar to the ones Melek had shown her, but she saw nothing of the ciphers Vlad used to twist the runes into something far darker and deadlier.

Then she realized, of course she wouldn't see those marks. The facetaker was not a rune warrior. He would not necessarily see everything Vlad could do. Alter had once mentioned that she could conceal her ciphers from others if she chose, although she hadn't bothered practicing.

Sarah recoiled from the gruesome memory before witnessing the man's nasty death at Vlad's hands. She whispered softly, "I will free you, somehow, and destroy the monster you brought to life."

She'd better, or she'd end up as the next victim, her soul a captive slave to the horrible creature.

Looking for a happier memory, Sarah paced around the globe until she found Alter's ascendant. His glowed a deep green, but was shot with flecks of red.

She touched the spark of his nevra core and savored Alter's honor, his love of family and of runesmithing. She was startled to feel the burning passion of his love for her.

It filled her with sorrow. He had fallen hard for her. The closeness of their interactions must have been a living torture for him. She loved him as a dear friend, and felt a fresh pang of regret at realizing that would never be enough for him.

Sarah did not retreat from the honesty of what she felt in his soul. It was such a refreshing change from Xiao's tainted soul. She concentrated on the very end of the ascendant, where it connected the earth in the present moment, and tried to peer through the hazy image of the moment Alter was currently living.

She caught only a glimpse, but it was enough.

Egypt. She couldn't tell the precise location, but it was Egypt for sure. She also noticed the rune marked onto his forehead and cringed. He was bound. Xiao was taking no chances of losing her sacrifice. They had to track him down soon, or they'd lose him forever.

"We'll find you, Alter," she promised.

Time to get to work.

Sarah returned to Xiao's ascendant, took a deep breath to focus her thoughts and calm her mind, then pressed her hand firmly against the very end of it. The hazy moment crept slowly out of the fog and she glimpsed a single image of Xiao speaking via teleconference with several men.

Despite the haze, Sarah recognized all of them. She gasped and recoiled from the sight. She stumbled back from the globe and stepped off the back of the platform holding her up in the darkness. With a shout of surprise, she tumbled away, the darkness splitting as she fell out of the aeon dimension.

With an abrupt jolt, Sarah returned to the roof of the tower next to Melek, who was practicing throwing knives at little wooden targets that appeared in the air all around him. Fifteen blocks floated around the tower, all with knives neatly piercing their centers.

The old hunter immediately rushed to her. "What did you learn?"

Sarah let him help her up, her mind still whirling from what she'd seen. "It's time to wake up."

70

"SHE'S GOT THEM ALL," Sarah exclaimed to the gathered group. "The US, England, and China. They were all there on the conference line."

Quentin frowned. "Why would the leaders of those nations speak with her? How did she coerce them to come to the table?"

Sarah scanned the group. The entire team had gathered, and their presence helped calm her racing heart. "You don't understand. It was the president, the prime minister, and the chairman, but it wasn't them. It was Xiao's children."

Gregorios slapped himself on the forehead. "Double stacks. Very clever, but very hard to maintain for long. I wouldn't have thought they could hold the facade long enough."

"Are you serious?" Sarah asked. The idea made sense, but at the same time it boggled the mind that Xiao had managed it.

Tomas grimaced. "Alter and I shared my body long enough to save you in Rome, but it was really hard to maintain, even in an emergency."

Eirene added, "Sharing one body, soulmasks stacked over each other, is one of the hardest tricks. The facetaker is in control, but the world sees only the outer mask."

Sarah frowned as she considered the depth of Xiao's treachery.

"But the other soulmask can fight, right? Someone has to have seen through the masks."

Gregorios shrugged, looking grim. "Usually I'd agree with you, but Xiao is ruthless and her children are likely just as bad. There are ways to weaken a soul, push it to the brink of cracking. If they tortured those world leaders in that way, they'd have no difficulty controlling them. It's still a constant drain to maintain a double stack for long, though."

Tomas frowned. "I could see them maybe infiltrating one, but all three? I don't know about China, but the US and England have very robust anti-rounon and anti-facetaker assets in their defensive protocols."

Gregorios considered that for a moment. "Xiao's been at this a long time. She's had time to work out the scheme. She could have gotten her children close by simply offering large campaign contributions to the US president."

Eirene said, "We know they've been in touch with the queen. In their attempts to take over that contract, they could have gained access to the prime minister."

Francesca and Tomas started discussing possible ways to circumvent those security protocols, but Gregorios waved away the discussion. "How they did it doesn't matter. What matters is that we understand now that no amount of truth is going to shake the world powers from the path of world war they're set on."

That was insane. There had to be a way to deal with the deceit, now that they understood.

Sarah protested, "We need to warn their nations somehow. Stop them."

Eirene chuckled. "Who's going to believe us? Xiao is holding all the cards. She's already chased us into hiding, branded us terrorists and demons, and twisted all of our efforts into reinforcement to her plan. She's been ahead at every turn."

"There has to be a way," Sarah insisted.

Spartacus stood and declared, "I will take a phalanx of warriors to Washington. I will storm the White House and remove the head of the impostor."

Gregorios looked like he liked that idea, but still shook his head. "You're not invincible any more. Besides, that wouldn't change the underlying issue. No, we need to stop Xiao first."

Spartacus looked crestfallen. Eirene patted his arm and said,

"You'll get a chance to fight, don't worry. If Xiao succeeds in bringing Sutekh into the world and gains his secrets, we're eternally defeated."

Sarah shivered to even consider that insane possibility. Even a week ago, she would have insisted such an idea was impossible. Sometimes it really sucked to know so much.

Eirene was right. They needed to focus on Xiao, but it offended her so deeply to think of those fake leaders driving their countries toward destruction.

She said, "We can't let her children stay in power."

Gregorios shrugged. "We could plan raids on each of those countries and remove those heads of state. It could be done, but it would take weeks of planning. We don't have that much time."

Sarah sighed. She hated to admit it, but he was right. "No we don't. My connection to that moment was very weak. It was like peering through a thick fog, but I got the sense they plan to start open fighting soon."

"They must be planning to coincide war with the arrival of Sutekh," Eirene said.

"There has to be more," Gregorios said.

"What do you mean? Isn't that enough?" Sarah demanded.

He admitted, "It's pretty bad. All the pieces are in place, but for Xiao's plan to work, she needs something else, a final push to launch the world into chaos and unrestrained global warfare."

Tomas said, "The president and prime minister could already trigger nuclear launches. That's pretty bad."

Gregorios shook his head. "I don't get the sense Xiao wants to rule a burned wasteland. Yes, they could trigger nuclear strikes, but the general populace isn't whipped into a frenzy yet. She needs that if she's going to succeed."

"Like after Pearl Harbor," Sarah said.

"Exactly. She's got to do something to get everyone so angry they'll rush headlong into war."

"What?" Sarah asked at the same time as Harriett.

He shrugged. "Maybe you should have stuck around to listen a bit longer."

"I should have, but I'm not sure how much more I could have understood. My connection was really weak. I wish I could see everything, then I could slide back through time and learn all her secrets."

Tomas said, "That would be amazing."

"And unnerving," Quentin said with a grimace. He added quickly,

"I trust you explicitly, my dear, but thinking of anyone having the power to scour history and see anything they wanted makes my skin crawl."

"I bet Xiao will figure out how to do it if we don't stop her," Eirene said. Then she gave Sarah a reassuring smile. "You accomplished much. We know what we have to do."

Sarah nodded, resolute despite her fear. "Both Xiao and Alter are in Egypt. If we're going to stop them, that's where we have to go."

Spartacus perked up. "I approve your bold declaration, Lady of Wisdom. Thus together united we will vanquish this enemy. We will take from them the cup of victory in the moment of their glory and dash it against their unworthy lips."

Gregorios said, "I like the way you're thinking, but we're going to need help. We're talking all-out war against Xiao and her forces."

Melek, who was pacing near Sarah's seat said, "Sarah will lead the assault in history, but we must destroy her in this reality too."

Tomas muttered, "That's always been the challenge. She's so fast and strong, it's going to be tough."

Gregorios said, "We've got a ringer. Sarah, do you think there's enough juice in that master rune to give each of us a temporary super power?"

"Usually I would protest the use of a master rune for personal enhancement," Melek said gravely. Then he gave Sarah a wry grin. "But under the circumstances I believe I'll need one too."

While Nabil sighed and shook his head, his expression long-suffering, Francesca laughed and gave him a wicked grin. "Oh, yeah. I've got the perfect idea for mine."

Most of the others quickly chimed in with ideas of what kind of super enhancement rune they'd like. Sarah appreciated their enthusiasm, and maybe with those unexpected new enhancements as their secret weapons, they could finally turn the tide against Xiao.

She said, "I'll see what I can do."

In her powerful, Amazon body, Eirene flashed a fierce grin. "That's the piece we've been missing. It'll give us the edge to finally stand against her as equals."

Melek's smile faded, his expression turning thoughtful. "That still leaves her supporters. Hongwu, Vlad, and all the kashaph she'll no doubt have on hand. She claims to have gained support of many."

Spartacus slapped a hand to the gladius he wore at his belt and declared, "The enchanter is mine."

Harriett pulled out her phone. "Her heka forces we can deal with. I'll mobilize Yurak."

Tomas added, "The Tenth will take care of Vlad. I've got a full team trained to deal with vamps. I've got a couple of rune ideas I'd like to discuss with you to take them to the next level, Sarah. And we'll call up every enforcer squad to support Yurak. My teams are eager for a chance at pay-back."

At the mention of Vlad, Sarah thought back to the many interactions with the creepy, powerful vampire. He was resourceful and devious, and if he managed to bite her again, she doubted her protective runes would save her. As she thought about him, she felt his presence prowling around her soul like an icy blast of winter wind.

Sarah loved Tomas, and did not doubt he and his men could destroy Vlad, if given a fair chance. Unfortunately, she also did not doubt that Vlad would never give them a fair chance. She had to figure out something to tip the scales in their favor.

As she considered the challenge, Quentin said with an eager glint in his eyes, "Tomas, have the Italian companies grab all my gear."

"I will call up my family to join the offensive, although Egypt is not a country we operate in easily," Melek offered.

Quentin said, "It's going to be tough for all of us to move the necessary hardware. The world is mobilizing, so moving so many troops is going to be tricky."

"I think I can get us in," Sarah said, getting a sudden idea.

"How?" Tomas asked.

She smiled. "I know the Pope."

71

The art of living well and the art of dying well in each life are one.

~EPICURUS

ON THE FLIGHT from Beijing to Cairo on a private jet that Eirene procured for the trip, Sarah settled into one of the luxurious chairs beside Gregorios. Most of the others were busy coordinating assets and personnel, drawing on their vast networks that spanned the globe.

Despite the damage Xiao's attacks and the world's negative opinion had caused, it looked like they'd still field quite an army to confront Xiao.

Sarah had already made her calls, activated a new vampire rune on Tomas' left shoulder blade, and designed modifiers with Melek that they would apply to Tomas' vampire hunting team when they met up. Feeling a little more confident they could dispose of the creepy Vlad, she nudged Gregorios, who was dozing in his seat.

"Are we there yet?" he asked even before opening his eyes.

"No. Gregorios, we need to talk."

He blinked open eyes and fixed her with a serious gaze. "I'm not giving Eirene my flying ability. Tell her to get her own super power."

"It's not that," Sarah said with a smile.

He and his wife had argued off-and-on all throughout the packing scramble, worldwide mobilization effort, and rush to the airport. Eirene was really struggling to decide on a super power. None of the others had spent nearly as long deliberating. They all assumed Sarah would succeed in figuring out the ciphers to make them work.

Eirene had exclaimed, "This is a once-in-a-lifetime opportunity. I don't want to squander it."

Now Sarah said softly, "I felt Bastien in the aeon."

"I wondered about that," he said calmly.

"You knew?"

"I suspected. You're the only one who could know for sure."

"How? You said you didn't know anything about ascendants and wheels of time and daraka kallpa and aeon and fourth dimensions and everything we've been dealing with," Sarah protested. Whenever she thought she understood Gregorios, he always managed to surprise her.

"I didn't, but that doesn't mean I'm totally blind. I've lived a long time, Sarah. I've seen things that even I don't understand, but unlike mortals, I've had many lifetimes to think about it."

He rubbed a hand across his face, his expression thoughtful. "I didn't know about ascendants and all those secrets Melek holds so tight, but I knew there had to be something more to our nevra cores and even to rounon powers. They all tie to the force of souls, linked to something greater, but those are not the only powers in the world."

"Cui dashi," Sarah suggested.

"No, they're related too. Even your rune warrior gift is only a different melding of those same soul gifts. With enough study, I suspect you'll figure out how it all connects. These things all make sense to me. I'm a part of it and I accept it. I'm referring to powers beyond the sphere of this world and the wheel of time that encompasses us all. I'm talking about religion. The power of faith."

"I don't understand. Are you saying you believe in God?"

"Don't you?" Gregorios asked, sounding completely sincere.

Sarah shrugged. "Right now I don't know what to believe."

The thought of god led her to thinking of religion, a topic she usually tried to ignore. Her parents' fanatical religious beliefs had made her life difficult. If religion made her parents treat her like dirt and always try to tear her down, she didn't want anything to do with it.

Gregorios patted her hand. "You'll work through it. I've met many religious figures over the years. I knew Muhammed early in his career. I've met apostles and I listened to a sermon by Jesus."

That blew her mind. "You're kidding! What was he like?" She'd wanted to ask Gregorios and Eirene about their interactions with religious figures. It seemed she'd always been too busy learning to defend herself or fight heka and cui dashi to find the time.

Gregorios considered that for a moment. "He was different. Different than regular mortals. The other well-known religious figures I've met over the years possessed a power alien to mine, alien to any of the soul-based rune powers we deal with."

"Wow." Sarah wasn't sure how to respond.

This was so cool. She wasn't sure which question to ask first, felt a thrill of excitement even thinking about what he knew. "You could tell everyone about it. You could remove centuries of doubt and confusion, tell everyone the way it is."

"It doesn't work that way," Gregorios said with a shake of his head.

"Why not? So many people could benefit if you just told them what you know."

"That's what's different. The power of religion is not in knowing. It's in faith."

"But faith has to be built on fact, doesn't it?"

"There's enough fact out there for the faithful to find."

"That doesn't make sense," Sarah protested. Why did religion always end up confusing her?

He fixed her with a serious gaze. "For a long time, that's what I thought. It took me lifetimes to understand what millions of mortals figure out in a single life. Faith is frail, but resilient. It takes nurture and a lifetime of aligning one's will to something greater. One does not access that power by hearing someone state facts. One must seek it. It's a personal, intimate journey."

Sarah didn't want to consider spending decades seeking a life like her crazy parents.

"How does this tie in with the fact that I felt Bastien's entire life embedded within his ascendant? If there's a god, why didn't Bastien go to heaven or hell or something?"

"Because he was a facetaker. Like I mentioned before, nevra core and religion don't mix. Melek explained the why of it already. We're bound to the ascendants, linked to them and to the fabric of history of this planet. Our souls are not free to move beyond the sphere of this world to whatever else may or may not be out there. It's foreign to us, but that doesn't mean it isn't real."

Sarah sighed, feeling the familiar frustration that always consumed her when she thought about religion. "But all the different religions interpret everything differently. How can Muhammed have real power when Islam and Christianity are constantly at war? How can Jesus be real and be what he said he was if other religions have power too?"

Gregorios shrugged. "They may interpret God differently. That doesn't mean God doesn't exist. Eventually the truth will come out. Every religion agrees on that point."

"The end of the world?"

He nodded and stated simply, "Armageddon. If we fail, that might be what the survivors get to experience."

Sarah shivered. "Does it bother you that there might be a god and that you're prevented from accessing the same eternity that mortals can?"

He shook his head, not looking concerned. "If I really wanted to find religion, I could. It is possible for a facetaker to reject their nevra core and turn from the ascendant that powers us. It would shift to another soul and bond to them, leaving us mortal like all the rest."

"How is that possible?"

"Like I said, the two powers are different, alien to each other. Bastien was a facetaker so when he died, his soul was absorbed into the great wheel of the aeon. It's comforting to know he's there and that much, at least, is real. Where mortals go after they die is a debate that's been ongoing since the dawn of time. No one knows until they step out of this life and move on to whatever comes next."

Sarah leaned back in her chair, considering his words. She still wanted to urge him to go public with what he knew if they survived the coming confrontation. He and Eirene held so much knowledge! They could correct the histories, perhaps resolve long-standing religious disputes.

Would anyone believe them? She didn't know. Once people decided to believe something, it could be impossible to get them to change their mind, no matter how much contrary evidence existed.

The home she'd grown up in had presented only one, greatly skewed, opinion on religion. There were others. Perhaps she'd been mistaken to ignore them all when she'd turned from the onerous path her parents had tried to force upon her?

Now that she had witnessed the aeon, what did she believe?

Gregorios rose and patted her shoulder before heading aft toward where Eirene was speaking with Francesca and Quentin. Sarah looked after him, lost in thought until Spartacus dropped into the recently-vacated chair beside her. The mighty Thracian gladiator looked strangely pensive.

"Are you all right?" she asked.

He nodded, but then actually sighed. "Indeed, Champion of History, I find my heart weighed down by unfamiliar worries."

Seeing Spartacus looking nervous rattled her more than she cared to admit. The indomitable gladiator had leaped into battle against live dragons with a laugh on his lips.

She teased, "I thought Hongwu didn't worry you."

Spartacus barked a laugh and slapped his thigh with his usual good humor, "Nay, Lady of Unmatched Battle Prowess, the enchanter represents no exceptional threat. Ever has the contest of arms challenged the best warriors of every age to manly contest. One will fall, and the other may survive. Thus it is, and I accept the outcome with contented heart."

He couldn't help grinning and adding, "And as always, I face the contest of arms confident of victory. My heart is pure, and always such creatures of deception give way before those walking a greater path."

Hearing him speak so confidently buoyed her spirits. "So what's bothering you?"

He sighed again, looking pensive. "Only this, Mighty Lady of Beauty and Wisdom. We will vanquish the dire threat that rises to challenge us for dominance, but my thoughts turn to the greater threat that lurks like the creeping shadow of dusk across an unsuspecting world."

That didn't sound good. Sarah did not need to hear about more problems. "Xiao doesn't have a freaky grandfather ten times more powerful than she is, does she?" she asked, although she really didn't want to hear the answer.

She'd thought Mai Luan had been deadly. Then she'd had to martyr herself to defeat Paul. Xiao terrified her more than she'd ever admit to anyone except maybe Tomas. She didn't think she could stomach hearing about anyone worse.

But Spartacus shook his head, "Nay, Champion Wielder of Souls. I know of no individual who poses a greater threat than Xiao, and that fact holds part of the weight of unfamiliar concern that weighs my heart."

"What do you mean?"

"I know how to challenge and defeat a tangible enemy, even a mighty foe such as Xiao and her minions. But once we defeat them, I find myself strangely unsure how to best defeat the greatest danger our world faces."

He sighed again and added, "Have you not recognized that the world languishes in complacency, selfishness, and lack of vision?"

The question caught her by surprise. Sarah managed to say, "Ah, sure. I mean, the world is full of imperfect people, right?"

"Indeed," Spartacus declared, slapping his thigh for emphasis. "In this, Xiao speaks with no guile. Although I disagree with her solution of order through slavery, I must confess I too feel called upon to stand against the tide of negative woe threatening to engulf the foolish masses of the world."

Sarah nodded, not sure what to say. She too agreed with that desire to help make things better, and that still made her uncomfortable. She felt driven to stop Xiao, but just as driven to find better solutions.

What if she eventually got impatient like Xiao and just decided to impose her will on people? Rune Warriors were destined to restore balance, right? What if that meant removing corrupted elements of the current world order? How would she be any different from Xiao then?

Spartacus continued, drawing her from her worries. "As I mentioned before, I wish to restore greatness, but in rare moments of quiet reflection, I begin to worry many will not choose to follow the path of wisdom when it is laid before them."

Sarah secretly sighed with relief. Spartacus was talking about the challenges of the mortal condition. "But Spartacus, problems like that have always faced the world."

"In some respects, you are correct, Great Lady of Battle Ciphers. And yet, I feel compelled to disagree. I have seen greatness, have witnessed entire societies rally behind a vision that elevates all to a better way."

"That would be nice," she agreed.

"Indeed. And yet, as I cast my gaze upon today's world, I see no one rising to inspire such greatness. Too many who should be leading do nothing but tear down others in the vain hope that the destruction of all else might somehow make their paltry lives look grander by comparison. Ever have the foolish striven for power while destroying the very greatness they could have gasped for."

Sarah felt fascinated by the insights she was gaining into Spartacus' character. He was so much more than a gung-ho, sword-wielding lunatic.

She gave him an encouraging smile. "That's why you need to gain honor and glory so they'll listen, right?"

He nodded, his confident grin snapping back into place. "Indeed, Lady of Steel. Thus I seek to offer my life as a fitting example of honor to perhaps inspire some few to rise above the uninspired existence they wallow within. I admit, I wonder if the task is perhaps greater than one even I can overcome alone."

Sarah appreciated his honest concerns, and she realized he had suggested the answer to her own worries. Realization eased the knot of tension in her stomach. She loved the idea of trying to inspire people to be better rather than imposing her own vision of a better life upon them.

So she said, "If we survive the final battle with Xiao, I promise to do what I can to help."

Spartacus grinned and saluted, banging his fist to his heart. "You renew my hope, great Sarah! The world already knows your beauty and might, and millions already feel inspired by your grandeur of soul. With your clarion voice sounding the trump of the advance, our banner will grow to fill the earth!"

Sarah chuckled. "I'd be happy with a quiet vacation, but we'll see what we can do."

Tomas interrupted the conversation at that point. "Sarah, Melek is ready to help you work on those ciphers for ammunition, and for increasing defense on our body armor."

"Perfect." Sarah rose, and Francesca hurried up the aisle to take the seat next to Spartacus.

The two leaned close together and immediately began an animated, if hushed, discussion. It looked like the continuation of a previous conversation.

Sarah didn't have time to listen, but followed Tomas to a table forward. Melek was already seated there, along with Nabil. Sarah was eager to get to work. With the hunters' help, she felt confident they could fine-tune her rune ideas and mark enough gear and ammunition when they landed to give their soldiers a better fighting chance.

This time, they were taking the war to Xiao.

72

My body is but wax and wick for a flame. When the candle burns out, the Light shines elsewhere.

~ANCIENT EGYPTIAN PROVERB

SARAH BARELY HAD time to register the heat and the dust of Cairo when she descended the private plane's stairs. Then she was engulfed in an enthusiastic hug by the burly Italian sergeant waiting eagerly at the base of the stairs.

"Carlo! It's so good to see you," she cried, hugging him in return.

Several other members of his team were stationed nearby, with more farther out, forming a protective perimeter. It was so good so see them again. She wished they were meeting under better circumstances, though.

"And you, signorina," Sergeant-major Carlo Salvatici laughed. "The angel of Rome come to Cairo. You are here to visit the symposium, no?"

"Unfortunately, no. I'm glad you were here for the conference, though. I need your help."

"For you, anything within my power," he assured her as he ushered her into a waiting SUV.

She was glad to get out of the sand-filled wind that smelled of grime and diesel fuel. The others piled in after, or moved to other waiting vehicles. Tomas waved to Carlo, but was busy overseeing the unloading of many crates of gear and the precious machines into waiting trucks.

When all was ready, Tomas' enforcers, along with a handful of Egyptian military and half of the Italian special forces team moved to military jeeps that led the convoy. The rest took up the chase position. Tomas joined Carlo and Sarah in the SUV. Quentin jumped in with them too.

The convoy sped through Cairo, which was a lot dirtier than Sarah had expected. She had expected to see lots of sand. This was Egypt, after all, but Cairo was filthy. It showed signs of neglect and lack of care that she'd never imagined from the photos she'd seen. She hoped the rest of the country was in better shape.

After a few minutes, the Italian said, "Will you explain why you are here, signorina? I received orders to meet you with my team and provide security, but nothing more."

"Did you hear from our agent in town?" Tomas asked.

"Si, signore. We are now en route to the facility your man told us about. It's on the edge of town. Very large."

"Good. We have friends coming."

"Friends with guns, no?" Carlo asked.

"Lots of guns," Tomas admitted with a grin.

Sarah was still amazed by the level of coordination achieved between the many teams involved in their planned assault against Xiao. In a single day Eirene, her daughters, Tomas, and Melek had coordinated a worldwide gathering.

Forces were flying from all over to marshaling points on Malta and Crete. Harriett had taken a different flight to Malta to take command of Yurak forces and prep them for the upcoming battle. Some enforcers were flying to Cairo on private jets, but most of the personnel and equipment were being loaded onto cargo ships and sailing for Egypt.

They'd arrive in the next twenty-four to thirty-six hours. It hardly seemed possible, even though they'd spent staggering amounts of money to pull it off. Sarah was happy they'd been able to move so fast. They didn't have much time.

Carlo sighed with mock hurt. "You came not only to see me again, no?"

Sarah smiled. "I wish that were all, but no. We're here on business."

He grinned. "Is what I expect. This is payback mission, yes?"

"Yes. We're going after Xiao."

"Xiao?"

"Paul's mother. We've learned a new name for her," Sarah explained.

He grunted. "Call her what you will, signorina. She is very dangerous."

Tomas added, "We've learned a few other things as well. This time we've got to finish her, or the entire world will pay the price."

Carlo nodded, his expression fierce. "I am glad you called, signorina. My men still owe vengeance for the assault on the Pope. We are happy to pay it forward to Xiao."

Sarah promised, "You'll get your chance. How are your enhancements?"

He grinned. "Miracoloso! My men, they are jealous."

"Today it's their turn."

"Si?" Carlo looked thrilled, but then hesitated. "I am not sure my captain will approve of so many enhancements."

Tomas said, "You no longer report to him. By the time we reach our base, you'll get the call. You report to Sarah until this is over."

Carlo seemed happy about that, but asked, "No offense, signorina, but signore, why not report to you?"

"Because the Pope likes me more," Sarah told him with a smile.

The Pope was such a dear, old man. He'd been thrilled to learn she had survived her martyrdom after all, and had been eager to assist their fight in any way possible.

Tomas asked Carlo, "What can you tell us of the archaeologists talking about this new king of the world prophecy?"

"I received this request too. What you want with crazy man they are now calling the prophet of Armageddon? He'll be excommunicated for sure." Carlo shook his head in disgust.

Sarah said, "I think he's beyond that. He's either been duped by Xiao, or he's another secret supporter."

"So maybe we kill him too?" Carlo asked, looking all too ready to remove the blasphemer from the world.

"We might not have a choice. What's he up to?" Sarah asked.

"His entire team, they move to Luxor. Kicked everyone out of the Karnak and the Luxor temples. Egyptian military cordoned everything off. They have lots of private security, men of many nations."

"Who do they work for?" Tomas asked.

Carlo shrugged. "They wear khaki uniforms with no insignia. They alone occupy the temple sites."

"Heka. At least we know where Xiao's army is," Tomas said.

Quentin spoke from the back seat. "We'll need numbers, placements, as much intel as we can get."

"I'll get an advance team in place by morning," Tomas promised.

Sarah felt a flutter of nerves to think they were really preparing to take the fight to Xiao, and in Egypt, no less. "They're really playing up the whole ancient Egypt god angle. Aren't those famous temples at Luxor?"

Carlo nodded. "Some of the most famous in the world. They are ruins, much like we have in Rome, but some parts still stand. Very impressive."

Tomas frowned. "It'll be a mess fighting in there. I visited the temples at the turn of the century. I doubt they've changed much. Lots of crumbling walls and statues. Fighting will be close and fierce."

Carlo looked confused. "Turn of century? You were baby in year two thousand, no?"

"Not that century," Tomas said simply.

Carlo laughed, but when no one else did, his expression fell. "Who are you, signore?"

"Try not to think about it. Focus on the mission. We're going to have to drive those forces out of those temples," Sarah advised.

Carlo swore in Italian. "Always with you is fight in historic place."

"At least it's not in your country this time," Tomas pointed out.

Carlo sighed.

Quentin said, "I've been on the phone with Gregorios in the other SUV. The Egyptian military is the unknown factor. Are they just being duped by the archaeologists, or are they in league with Xiao?"

Tomas said, "We'll have to plan for either case. We can implement contingencies in the next forty-eight hours once everyone arrives."

"You might not have that much time, signore," Carlo warned.

"Why not?"

"Those men, they claim their god will arrive tomorrow at noon."

73

The only true wisdom is in knowing you know nothing without a rune like mine.

~SOCRATES

THE HUGE COMPOUND near the Nile, at the outskirts of Cairo, was owned by Suntara. A high chain-link fence surrounded the paved expanse of mostly-empty parking lots surrounding half a dozen enormous warehouses. Sarah couldn't pick out any hints that it was anything but a quiet industrial area, baking under the brutal sun as the SUV drove right through the huge open doors of the third warehouse.

The doors closed immediately behind their convoy. The huge, vaulted space was full of military vehicles, piles of wooden crates, and a couple hundred men and women in uniforms of Suntara enforcers.

Eirene and Tomas led Melek and Francesca into a long trailer full of communications equipment to work on accelerating the arrival of their forces and to plan alternate battle scenarios. Sarah and Gregorios met with a dark-skinned Egyptian man who was the head of Suntara's operations in the Middle East.

His name was Abdallah and he was so ugly he had to be in his first life. Any other form he took would be an improvement, although his long, hooked nose might prove problematic no matter what suit he wore.

Abdallah spoke passable English, but he and Gregorios spent a few minutes conversing in Arabic. They then summarized for Sarah and explained that they were finalizing plans for hiring several river cruise ships. They were planning for additional support hardware like trucks and helicopters, as well as the proper bribes to get their forces through port inspections quickly.

Sarah wanted to check on the machines, but that had to wait until they boarded the river cruise ship in a few hours. In the meantime, Gregorios organized a team of enforcers to set up a work area for her.

On the plane, she'd fine-tuned her battle ciphers and she felt ready to take the fight to Xiao. There was plenty of other work to do, though. She started by arranging enhancements for Carlo's men through one of the resident channelers who worked for Suntara.

Then she set to work on ciphers to help the troops. She couldn't visit all the troops and mark ciphers onto their equipment, so on the plane they'd come up with the bright idea to use a velcro patch.

She would inscribe the protective ciphers on those patches and link them in advance to the remote charging cipher in Rome, which would power them. Sarah had checked the status of that remote cipher. It felt strong enough that she hoped it would both power the new individual defensive shields as well as reinforce the facetakers who would run the machines in their upcoming memory battle.

To activate the individual protective ciphers, Melek had suggested an elegant, two-step process. It was similar to how Alter had designed the escape runes for the memoryscape.

Sarah would link the protective ciphers on those patches to the remote power source, but the soldiers would need to make an individual mark prior to commencement of the battle. Although not rounon-gifted, that voluntary mark would link them to the protective cipher and activate it for their person.

Which mark they would use turned out to be trickier than Sarah had expected. They couldn't expect everyone to know an actual rune mark, and honestly that wasn't necessary.

For the Italian forces, she'd considered asking them to make the sign of the cross. They'd know that one, and would probably make it prior to battle anyway, but she'd decided against it. Using that symbol in that way was a bit sacrilegious, and it skirted the whole problem area of mixing soul powers and religion.

So they'd settled on the number seven. Although Gregorios' lucky number was nine, most people considered seven lucky, and such wide-spread belief in a symbol carried extra weight.

Once each soldier marked the number seven over their hearts, they'd link the cipher to them and activate it. Sarah felt proud of that clever cipher use. It allowed her to help spread the benefit of her ciphers to so many more people, all of whom were about to risk their lives supporting her in the upcoming fight.

Sarah settled into a folding metal chair beside a plastic camp table inside a large, square tent in one corner of the huge warehouse, with boxes of supplies already stacked and ready. She opened the first box, expecting to see rows of patches with the Tenth's bull mascot.

Instead, the patches showed an image of her in Rome, quicksilver body glittering, hands transformed into blades and raised to strike. Words around the edge of the image declared, "We fight for the Sword of the Deliverer!"

Shocked, Sarah pawed through the first three boxes. Every patch was identical. She couldn't believe it, hadn't expected anything like it. She glanced at Nabil, who sat across from her, his normally impassive face actually split by a smile.

She raised one of the patches and demanded, "Whose big idea was this?"

"Everyone's," he said simply.

"This is ridiculous," Sarah declared.

She'd accepted transition of Carlo's company to her command only because the pope had been so insistent. The entire team had sworn their support since she alone could challenge Xiao, but she hadn't expected them to take the idea to such an extreme level.

Nabil shook his head. "No, Champion. It must be. We all swore oaths to follow you into this battle. You alone can lead us, and you alone offer the path to unification."

"But . . ." Sarah protested softly, glancing from his honest expression back to the patch.

Nabil added, "There is no other way. My family would never wear the patch of the enforcers, and they would never accept the symbol of our clan. All will follow you."

Sarah felt deeply moved by his simple declaration. She blinked away tears as she glanced back down at that patch. That moment when she'd taken the power of those three master runes had been glorious, but fatal. Knowing that she'd matured in her power enough to tap them safely again bolstered her confidence, but that patch represented an awful responsibility.

In the past, the enforcers had followed Tomas, Yurak had

answered to Harriett, and Melek had led the hunters in their pure zeal. Now they all looked to her to lead them. United, they might just defeat Xiao, but every death they suffered would be her responsibility. She would bear the knowledge that she'd weighed those lives against the greater need and decided to accept the cost in blood that victory would require.

She didn't want to accept that, but she refused to walk away from this chance to give so many a better fighting chance. So she slapped the first patch onto the table, frowned at Nabil, and grumbled, "Fine. But I don't like it."

He flashed a rare smile. "That is why we will follow you, Champion."

Over the next two hours, they worked through hundreds of patches. Nabil was a master runesmith. Using a permanent marker, he drew the basic protective runes onto each patch. Sarah then added the modifiers to strengthen them, change them into battle ciphers, and tie them to the remote charging cipher.

Each cipher included modifiers to increase protection if required. A fraction of one percent of the available power should be enough to deflect a bullet, but more could be drawn to protect against explosions or more severe damage. She concentrated over each completed cipher patch, activating them, pending the final symbol each soldier would mark over their heart to tie the cipher to them.

It was a complex, elegant solution, but required deep concentration. The drain for each cipher was minimal, but hundreds began to add up. She didn't want to tap the remote charging rune in Beijing. It would be used heavily in the upcoming battle.

She could use one of the master runes. Her need was small, and in Beijing she'd proven that she could limit the amount of power she drew from a master rune.

Sarah took a blank patch and began marking a new cipher on it. Nabil glanced over at her, then dropped his marker and cried, "What are you doing?"

"Confirming a theory," she told him as she finished the symbol for the lesser master rune from the almost-death of Caesar. It was the least dangerous of the master runes she knew, and therefore represented the least threat if something went wrong.

Nabil drew in a long, slow breath, his expression disapproving. She said, "Oh, cut it out. When I walk the aeon, I can see thousands of master runes. Tapping a little energy to help us keep Xiao from gaining mastery over all that power is worth it."

He sighed, still not looking happy. "I swore to follow you, and I will, but have a care. Tampering with master runes killed you once."

"I know." She actually felt comforted hearing a hunter warn her of the dangers of following her instincts.

She could almost imagine Alter seated across from her, and she felt an intense yearning to see him again. She'd love to hug him, spar with him, and even deal with his clumsy attempts at flirting.

When they defeated Xiao, they'd free Alter. She knew the depth of his feelings for her. She wanted to be friends, wanted to spend time with him, but didn't want to torture him. She wasn't sure how to resolve that problem, but when they had some quiet time, they'd figure it out.

She activated the cipher, and a strong current of new energy flowed into her. It was nothing like the torrent that thundered through her when she drew upon the full might of a master rune, though.

She grinned at Nabil as she slipped the patch into her pocket. "It's working. I tapped just a tiny fraction of that power. Just enough to allow me to finish my work here."

"I don't want to know any more about it," Nabil said. He picked up his marker and resumed work.

That was probably the best she could hope for. Sarah returned to her work, her rounon well once more filled to overflowing from the power of that partially-tapped master rune. She was eager for a day without deadly cui dashi threats or heka assassins so she could consider new ways to tap the power of history to do good, like she had done for those dying children in Rome.

Once they completed all the patches, enforcers took the boxes away to begin distributing them to the soldiers already in Egypt. As additional forces arrived, they would each receive their patches. Sarah felt deeply satisfied. Those patches might save many lives.

She didn't have time to celebrate because that's when other soldiers began bringing different types of ammunition to mark with deadly, destructive ciphers. In the upcoming fight against Xiao, Vlad, and Hongwu, they were likely to face unprecedented enhancements and devilish rune webs.

So Sarah and Nabil worked for several more hours. Nabil again marked the basic runes, while Sarah added modifiers to change them into her unique ciphers. She linked those ciphers to the lesser master rune she had just tapped, granting each bullet, mortar, and grenade varying fractions of a percent of that available power.

She could never hope to enhance every bullet, but they marked enough that hopefully every soldier would get at least one enhanced magazine or grenade. That ammunition was perhaps the deadliest in the world.

It drew from the power of the master rune to strike deep and penetrate any defensive webs or runes the enemy might have activated. Once it penetrated, it would suck energy from the target and convert that energy to deadly, pure fire. The stronger the enemy, the more devastating the round.

Thinking about the agony her ciphers would cause in the looming battle made Sarah feel queasy. She only managed to complete the work by focusing on how many more of her own forces would die or suffer if she didn't enhance those bullets. She was now a general, and she had to weigh the lives of her people against the lives of the enemy, and weigh the cost of victory against the price of defeat. It was an ugly calculation, but necessary.

When she finally stopped to take a break, she again checked the strength of her remote charging cipher in Beijing. It had grown to a towering charge, nearly equal to a master rune. That much energy could turn the tide if things got desperate. It would also power the super enhancements she was crafting for her core team.

During the flight, she'd discussed those super-enhancements with Melek. He'd been impressed by her ciphers, but couldn't explain why they worked the way they did.

After they'd discussed them for nearly an hour, he'd sat back and rubbed his eyes, then said, "Some of what you do cannot be explained, Champion. We work with arcane powers of the soul that tap into history and the great aeon. As a rune warrior, you can do more than perhaps any of us realize. The most important aspect of your ciphers is that you believe they will work."

She did believe. She had to. They couldn't afford to fail. She would have preferred more concrete knowledge, but she'd take confident instincts, as long as they kept paying off.

Vlad had said something similar, but he'd pushed the limits too far and broken himself. If something went wrong in her battle against Xiao, she would prefer a clean death to transformation into a monster like him.

Nabil excused himself and took a break. Momentarily alone, Sarah leaned back in her uncomfortable chair and considered the question of Vlad. She needed to stop Xiao, and that meant she had to defeat Vlad once and for all.

No doubt he would be prowling around, ready to pounce and interfere. He'd proven multiple times that he was a devious, clever opponent. She had to be ready to take him out fast, before he sucked away her strength and took her soul. She needed a way to flip their next meeting against the devious vampire.

So she went looking for Quentin.

74

Success is dependent on effort to discover a better rune.

~SOPHOCLES

SARAH FOUND Quentin hurrying across the huge warehouse, heading for the communications trailer.

He paused to greet her with a smile and said, "My dear, I heard the patches are all marked, as well as many munitions. I appreciate how much you are doing to help safeguard our forces."

"It's the least I can do," she assured him.

"And what of you? Do you need anything?"

"Actually, I was wondering if you had any more of these crossbow bolts," she said, extracting from a thigh pocket the bolt he had given her in San Marino.

He smiled to see it, but shook his head. "I'm sorry, my dear. Those are not common outside of San Marino. I'll see if any can be found, but I am not hopeful."

Quentin then extracted from a pocket a grenade and offered it with a flourish. "May I suggest this as a fitting alternative? I've been making curtain call munitions, although not nearly as many as I would prefer."

Sarah grinned, but shook her head. "Gallant as always, Quentin, but I worry it might interfere with me at least as much as it does my target. I need something for up-close defense."

"You speak of Vlad," Quentin said gravely.

She nodded, not surprised that he figured out her worry. She'd already developed intricate warding ciphers that she activated whenever she slept to warn her if Vlad tried to strike while she was vulnerable. She planned to activate them if he appeared, but worried he might surprise her again.

"We will have a vampire-trained squad assigned as a protective detail at all times," Quentin assured her.

"Thanks. I feel like I need something more, though. A trump card in case things go wrong."

"I am a fervent supporter of every woman being prepared to defend herself."

Sarah extracted Eirene's silver piece of eight from her pants pocket. The little keepsake from Eirene's pirate days was a good luck charm, its mysticism reinforced by millions of people who watched the *Pirates* franchise. It was exactly what she needed to focus her ultimate defense through.

She held up the antique and asked, "Do you think you could get your hands on a chain so I could wear this like a necklace?"

Quentin grinned. "Excellent choice, my dear. And for you, nothing less than twenty-four carat gold, of course."

"You're always the gentleman," she told him with a grateful smile.

He winked. "Egyptian gold is excellent quality. I know a man who can get us exactly what you need."

"Thank you."

Quentin hurried away and Sarah paced the interior of the huge warehouse, weaving through the crowds of busy enforcers, around parked military vehicles and crates of weapons. She considered Vlad and reviewed in her mind the runes that had been used to twist the broken rune warrior into the world's worst vampire. If only she knew what marks Vlad had used to corrupt the vampire rune and make it worse.

As she paced, she extracted from her jacket pocket the vampire rune that Tomas had drawn for her. As she studied it, she eventually focused on the Ophiuchus symbol. It was a symbol she had never actually used in a cipher, but Sutekh's signature rune used it too.

That was a weird coincidence. Were there aspects to it that she hadn't considered yet? She thought about the last secrets that Melek had shared with her, and thought back to what she had seen of the aeon. In that moment, understanding clicked.

On the plane ride from Beijing, they'd studied Sutekh's signature rune and had looked up more information about the Ophiuchus symbol. It was a constellation, often depicted as a man grasping a serpent. Linking it to the other symbols in Sutekh's rune and the vampire rune, she realized it linked back to the aeon.

The Ophiuchus constellation had no opposite sign like other horoscope zodiac symbols. That made it difficult to counter, but that was exactly the key to beginning to unravel the powers that Vlad controlled.

As she paced, deep in thought, she realized the Ophiuchus symbol included a weakness. From late November to mid-December, it was usually obscured by the sun. Perhaps that was the real reason vampires could not survive direct sunlight. Might sunlight subvert the key symbol to their existence?

"Hey Sarah! You're hard to find."

She blinked and snapped out of her reverie as Tomas jogged up to her. She'd wandered to a remote corner of the warehouse, amid a maze of high-piled crates.

"Just thinking," she explained as she greeted him with a quick kiss.

"About what?"

"Vampires."

Tomas grimaced. "We'll get Vlad next time. I promise."

"I know. I plan to help. Tomas, is sunlight really a weakness for vampires?"

"Yes, although not for the reasons the movies say. A strong vampire like Vlad can walk in daylight, especially when cloaked by illusion. Direct, unprotected exposure to sunlight would still weaken him, though."

"Like melt his face?" Sarah asked hopefully."

"I wish, but probably not. We once chased a vampire into sunlight. The light definitely affected it and seemed to weaken its connection with its captured souls, but it didn't burst into fire. Why? Were you thinking of staking Vlad out in the desert to die slowly?"

"That would be fitting, but no. Just exploring ideas. Are there other weaknesses I should know about?" she asked as they started working back through the maze of crates toward the main central aisle of the warehouse.

"Not really. The best way to destroy a vampire is to get a facetaker to remove their soulmask. Otherwise, it's best to remove the head, crush it to dust, and incinerate it. I guess you could also spread it out in the sun and burn it with a really big magnifying glass."

"Thanks," she told him as they reached the long line of parked military vehicles.

"You've got that look in your eye. You're crafting a new cipher, aren't you?"

"Working on one."

"Good." He kissed her and drew her into an embrace. She loved the contact and held him for several long seconds, drawing comfort from him. He'd survived many intense conflicts for centuries. With his help, and with Gregorios and Eirene on their side, they'd defeat Xiao.

When she released him, he added, "Work fast. We've got another hour or so to wrap up our work, then we're heading for the river boat."

"I'll see you there," she promised, and headed back to her tent and work table.

Melek was waiting for her, a gold chain dangling in his grasp. He extended it to her and said, "A gift from Quentin."

"Thanks. He's amazing." She pulled out the piece of eight and threaded the chain through a hole near one end.

"May I ask what you plan to do with that?"

"I'm glad you're here. I'm trying to figure out ways to stop Vlad." She explained her thoughts regarding the Ophiuchus symbol, along with her discussion about vampire weaknesses with Tomas.

When she finished, he said, "I concur with what Tomas said, and as usual, your insights into the meanings of symbols is remarkable. You may be right about the Ophiuchus. The sun might subvert it enough to grant advantage over the vampire."

Sarah studied the piece of eight, puzzling over the symbols, seeking the right way to combine them to achieve the effect she was looking for. "I keep thinking about Tomas' remark about using a magnifying glass."

Melek chuckled. "I don't think there's a big enough one to fry a vampire, although it might prove very effective if it existed."

Sarah got an exciting new idea. "What if I designed a new cipher to absorb sunlight? We could use it like a laser to melt him."

Melek considered that for a moment, then dashed her hopes with a slow shake of his head. "I don't think it would work. All runes, even your ciphers, work with the power of souls. Sunlight is foreign to them, so I do not believe it would be possible to store solar power like you do soul power in your charging ciphers."

Sarah sighed. He was right, but the idea wouldn't leave her mind. "What if I didn't try storing solar power, though? What if I just set up a bunch of collection points to concentrate and funnel solar power into one single exit point?"

"Like cipher magnifying glasses?" Melek asked. He considered that, and smiled. "It's revolutionary."

"More evolutionary, I hope. I keep thinking there are better ways to use our powers, and this makes so much sense."

Melek smiled at her enthusiasm. "The sun is a very powerful symbol, but is not often used in runes because it is so often tied to religion."

That was a good point, but he went on to explain that in ancient days the sun was also associated with alchemy and the essence of spirit. That created a precedent to link sunlight to spiritual matters and the soul.

He concluded by saying, "If you keep those truths in mind as you mark your ciphers, you might well be able to manipulate sunlight as you propose."

Sarah grinned. "I love the idea of using sunlight against Vlad. It's powerful, but wouldn't drain souls like other ciphers."

Melek smiled in turn and said, "Then shall we get to work?"

With Melek's help, Sarah designed a dozen cipher blocks using ancient symbols for the sun. When placed in a circle, they would collect and magnify the sunlight streaming between them and release it through a distant exit point.

To test the evolutionary ciphers, Sarah asked Quentin to have people place three blocks around the roof of the warehouse, directly under the brutal Egyptian sun. Then she and Melek exited the warehouse and crossed the huge compound, traversing the blistering parking lots where shimmering heat waves danced.

They stopped in a secluded area, facing an empty cargo container. The steel container, painted dull gray, was like the ones used on trains and ships.

Melek gestured at it. "This should offer a fitting test."

Sarah agreed. Feeling excited and nervous, she marked on a small, round wooden block the exit point cipher they'd designed. Then she aimed it at the container, about a hundred feet away, and activated the cipher.

She felt it activate, felt it connect with the distant collection ciphers. The entire complex system snapped into place and an enormous shadow descended over the warehouse as the sunlight was sucked away through the collection ciphers.

A laserlike beam of pure, concentrated sunlight erupted from the cipher mark on her exit-point cipher. It struck the container in a blinding, golden flash.

Thunder pealed as the air cracked, so loud Sarah shrieked and nearly dropped the cipher block. The golden beam shook, splashing superheated sunlight across the container. Everywhere it touched, paint vaporized and thick steel bubbled.

Sarah quickly recovered and steadied the beam. The steel under the steady point of impact melted away. Within three seconds, she bored a hole through the metal and started working the stream of laser sunlight down the side of the container. It easily cut through with a hiss of boiling steel. Despite the distance, she caught a whiff of molten slag, and within seconds she cut the container vertically in half.

Sunlight kept pouring forth, and despite the awesome amount of damage she was doing to the container, the cipher drew only tiny amounts of power. She could keep that beam going until the sun set without taxing her rounon well.

Sarah terminated the ciphers, and the sunlight laser winked out, leaving the container walls smoking and dripping molten steel. She laughed and glanced at Melek, who was staring at the damage she'd done with open-mouthed amazement.

"That's what I call a vampire deterrent!"

Melek whistled softly, looking pleased that their experiment worked, but perhaps a bit nervous at the same time. "That is indeed a powerful cipher."

"I bet I could change it to create a wider area effect too," she said eagerly, considering the modifiers she would need. "I mean, the laser focus is super powerful, but with additional collection points, I could make a dozen laser strikes through the exit point, or meld them together into a wall of concentrated sunlight. Talk about instant sunburn!"

She laughed, but Melek's smile faded. She clapped him on the shoulder and said, "Come on, that's cool. Even you have to admit it."

He nodded and repeated, "Cool. But as always, I recommend caution."

Sarah laughed and kissed his cheek. In that moment he looked more like Alter than ever. "I'd be disappointed in you if you didn't."

Then she grabbed his arm and pulled him back toward the warehouse. "Come on. I'm going to set up collection points on all six of the warehouses, and see if I can tie in the energy-sucking cipher I marked on those bullets."

Melek paled as he considered the idea. "I am grateful you are on our side, Champion. I fear what might happen if you chose the side of evil."

Sarah grimaced. "If Vlad takes my soul, think of what he could do."

"It is one of my greatest fears," Melek admitted.

"Then stop being so cautious. I need these ciphers to make sure that can't happen."

"Just as Vlad needed his ciphers to protect his homeland from the Turks. I support your work, Sarah, but I hate that we must travel such unknown roads with such recklessness. I don't want to see you hurt."

Sarah felt moved by his worry. "I'll get hurt if I don't, so I'm willing to take the chance. Vlad didn't have your help. I do. We won't make the same mistakes he did."

Tomorrow they would know, one way or the other.

Melek drew her to a stop, his expression grave. "I believe we will vanquish Vlad. Your ciphers are new and unexpected, and we will have the support of both enforcers and hunters. However, I've been thinking that when you fight Xiao, you must be prepared for every eventuality."

"That's why we've been training to fight, and I've got all those ciphers ready to hit her."

Melek nodded, but didn't look satisfied. "Always in the past we have battled thus. Weapon against weapon, ciphers against her over-whelming strength. But there's a chance you might get drawn into a rune duel, and I fear you are not prepared."

"What's a rune duel?"

Sarah imagined facing Xiao in the middle of a dusty old western town in the memoryscape, but instead of pistols they wore runes on their belts.

"It is a battle of wits, and of runesmithing. It utilizes these runes, which can be used to link the souls of those involved in the duel to the outcome."

Melek drew a pad of paper out of his pocket and quickly sketched several unfamiliar runes. One was the Chinese kanji symbol for conflict, but it was wrapped in a greater symbol that gave the impression of a clenched fist. The Egyptian *ba*, with its extended arms, surrounded those. A couple of the other symbols she didn't recognize.

Melek said, "These are used nowhere else that I know of. I do not know their origin, but they are key marks to link the combatant souls into the outcome of the rune duel."

"So what runes do people use to fight a rune duel?" Sarah asked.

The concept chilled her. She'd used ciphers to attack Xiao, but this was a more intimate way to fight, one that she felt could be far more dangerous, especially against a brilliant runesmith like Xiao.

"It depends on the moment. Rune duels are rare, but one of Xiao's skill might feel confident luring you into one. No doubt she would hope you would not understand the stakes. In a rune duel, sometimes runes are used to strike the loser with crippling pain."

He sketched a couple of runes that could be used in that way. "Or to consume their souls to fuel an enhancement for the winner."

He sketched additional symbols. Sarah watched closely, filled with competing emotions. Part of her loved the idea of consuming Xiao's soul to fuel a special super enhancement, but the risk would be dire. Getting sacrificed to fuel Xiao's enhancements would be uniquely insulting.

Melek fixed her with a stern gaze. "Hunters try not to engage in rune duels with heka. We are honor bound not to fuel our enhancements with the lives of others, but heka do not understand those bounds. Or if they do, they might seek to make such an outcome a contingent of the duel so that even if they lose, they tarnish the soul of the hunter who defeated them."

"Have you ever participated in a rune duel?" Sarah asked.

Melek hesitated for a second, then nodded. "Once, when I was braver than I was wise. I defeated the heka enchanter, but vowed never to rune duel again."

"Why?"

Instead of answering, he said, "I consider rune duels a desperate choice, a route of last resort, but felt you should be prepared in case that treacherous creature tries to bind your soul to one."

"I appreciate it. I had no idea," Sarah said honestly. "I feel like I need to practice." When he frowned, she added quickly, "Not really duel anyone, but study the concepts. Just in case."

"I hope you'll never need this knowledge, but perhaps you are right. We should have time to study further while we're on the boat."

75

Mari has fallen! The great city of the Euphrates now bows to my rule and acknowledges the superiority of my runes. More than their great trade wealth, Mari is a prize that promises rune lore. I hear they have legends of one with strange powers and glowing eyes who holds the secret to life itself. I will know the truth.

~SARGON, KING OF AKKADIA, 24TH CENTURY B.C.

AS NIGHT BEGAN SETTLING over Egypt and the heat bled away, Tomas called Sarah to join him as the team boarded a three-story, luxury river cruise ship. Enforcer teams loaded trucks full of gear and weapons into the hold of a river barge anchored nearby. The cruise ship was beautifully appointed, with a huge chandelier in the entry salon, and expensive wood paneling and oriental rugs everywhere.

Sarah barely noticed the rest because Tomas led her into a long room on the third floor where Eirene and Francesca were already waiting. Many tables and chairs had been piled against the interior wall, suggesting it was usually used as a banquet room. In the cleared space, they'd set up the precious machines.

As the ship slipped into the slow-moving Nile to begin its race south toward Luxor, Sarah, Francesca, and Tomas strapped into the machine. Eirene offered to power their journey into memory. Sarah was glad Tomas would be with her until she stepped beyond the memoryscape into the aeon world.

The memoryscape formed around them, and Sarah stepped onto a beautiful white sand beach in a tropical location. It was warm and they were alone. The sun hung low on the western horizon, staining the sky with brilliant splashes of reds and oranges.

"This is lovely," Sarah breathed, spreading her arms and soaking in the stillness.

She wore a royal blue swimsuit, with a sarong wrapped around her waist. Tomas wore board shorts but no shirt, so she got to enjoy his excellent muscles. Francesca wore a skimpy yellow bikini

"This place doesn't really fit with the mission," Tomas said, but still gave Sarah an appreciative smile.

Francesca punched him in the shoulder. "Open your eyes, Tomas. Tomorrow we're all facing danger. I've found it's best to meet moments like that knowing I never missed a chance to kiss someone."

Sarah took Tomas' hand. "This one's mine. Sorry."

Francesca winked. "Girls don't mess with a sister's man. I made sure there's a bar behind those trees. The bartender's gorgeous. You two enjoy yourselves."

She walked away, leaving them alone.

Sarah sighed. "This is nice. We haven't found nearly enough time alone lately."

Hand in hand, they walked along the edge of the surf and Sarah tried to memorize every sense, every second. The wet sand slipping between her bare toes, the warm breeze that smelled like tropical flowers, the soft crashing of low waves breaking over the distant reefs.

After a moment they stopped and kissed. They took their time, enjoying the fact they didn't need to rush off to fight anyone. Tomas was more attentive than he'd been in days, and the worries that hounded Sarah faded away.

She ran a finger down his cheek. "I could get used to this."

"Me too," he said with a grin.

She kissed him again, passionately, and was thrilled to feel him respond. They spent a few minutes there, sharing their need for each other, drawing strength from the bond.

Finally Tomas pulled gently away, looking a bit flushed. "I need some air. That was amazing."

He took her hand and resumed walking. Sarah couldn't stop smiling. She realized she no longer considered her current form something foreign. She'd grown used to her second life and it felt like home. She had also accepted Tomas' current form.

She could love him in that body. In fact, she realized she would love him, no matter what he looked like. She loved him, his gallant soul, his honorable mind. She finally started understanding what the others had so often talked about. The physical shape mattered far less than she'd ever really recognized.

"Sarah, if Xiao's in there, don't challenge her," Tomas warned, his voice soft but urgent.

She sighed. Talk about breaking the mood. "Not tonight. We'll hit her tomorrow when everything's ready."

"It's going to be tough getting everything in place." Tomas stopped and gripped her shoulders. "Sarah, if things go badly tomorrow . . ."

"Don't." She refused to consider the worst case. Not yet.

He continued anyway. "We can't pretend they might not. Every time we've challenged her, we've lost."

"Not this time," Sarah promised. She wouldn't admit, not even to herself, that they might lose.

He smiled. "I think we have a good shot."

"I know you hate suicide charges," she teased.

"Sometimes they're necessary," he said with a grimace, quenching her attempt at humor. "If you have to choose tomorrow, remember the most important thing is stopping Xiao. Nothing else, no one else, matters more than that. If we don't destroy her, none of us will survive."

Sarah leaned against him and held him tight. "We'll stop her, Tomas."

Francesca stepped around a thick palm tree and gave them a disgusted look as she approached. "That's as far as you got? I figured I'd find a little cabana on the beach by now with silk curtains blowing in the wind and a happy couple inside."

Sarah grinned. She really liked that idea. "Tempting, but Tomas is old fashioned."

Francesca gave him a disgusted look, but ruined it with a wink. "I know, but I figured even Tomas would push the limits of his moral code tonight. You didn't even rip off any clothes, and Sarah's hair is barely mussed."

"He was a perfect gentleman," Sarah said.

"What a waste." Francesca chuckled.

"We had a very good time, thank you very much," Tomas said, his tone offended.

Francesca laughed. "For an old guy, you have so much to learn.

Party's over. Sarah, you'd better turn into super girl or whatever you do to commune with the aeon. Time's a wasting."

"I don't think I can really waste time in here," Sarah said, giving Tomas one slow final kiss.

Then she added the aeon rune to her stomach and it lifted her into the air again. She couldn't help but extend her arms and throw her head back as she savored the wonderful feeling that filled her and built upon the contented peace she'd enjoyed with Tomas.

Francesca's voice echoed up from below. "Told you, Tomas. Superwoman. You'd better nab her fast, lover boy, or you'll lose her."

"Working on it," Tomas said.

With a smile on her lips, Sarah slipped out of the world and into the realm of the aeon.

76

Why do the people fail to see the priests blind their minds with lesser runes? Only the priest of Aten can use the higher ciphers. If I must abandon all the other gods to gain the everlasting rewards he promises, how can I refuse?

~PHARAOH AKHENATEN TO HIS QUEEN, NEFERTITI, REGARDING HIS DECISION TO ABANDON TRADITIONAL EGYPTIAN MYTHOLOGY AND SUPPORT A SINGLE GOD

THE AEON SPACE WAS WEIRD, and marvelous, and breathtaking all at once. Sarah couldn't understand what she was seeing, so settled for accepting it and pretending it wasn't so weird.

Despite the importance of her mission, she paused to stare at the glorious spirals of the twined ascendant runes extending down in glittering whorls into the shadowed depths of the earth-globe. Again she stood before it in the absolute blackness of the aeon space.

She could easily spend days pacing around the globe. The miniature earth included exquisite details including glimpses of structures under the surface that no scientist had ever envisioned. She could spend additional weeks studying the ascendants and their ever-changing symbols.

She didn't have that kind of time. Sarah forced herself to focus on the ascendants where they touched the surface of the earth at various points around the globe, corresponding with the location of their linked nevra cores. This was where the present moment was being recorded, before the ascendants twined together to form the complete record of that moment in history.

Each ascendant extended over enormous sections of the earth, centered on their nevra core. In places like the cruise ship where multiple ascendants overlapped, they fractured into intertwining bands that spread outward over vast sections of the world to capture their section of the current moment. The global scope of the aeon, with its intertwined ascendants, dwarfed Sarah's understanding.

Unable to grasp the full aeon, Sarah stepped closer and touched Gregorios' ascendant, just under the surface of the globe, where it began to coil into the interior of the planet and twine with the others. There, at the formation of the great rope of history, Sarah slid her fingers along the outer edge of each ascendant, touching each coil momentarily.

She focused on Xiao's crimson strand, woven closely with the packed ascendants of her children. Sarah braced herself against the taint of Xiao's influence that colored everything her ascendant recorded. Then she grasped the ascendant just short of the end, where it recorded a recent past.

A foggy window opened into her mind, and Sarah slowly slid her hand along the ascendant until one moment sharpened into greater clarity. She pressed her face close and tried to pick out details.

As the view started sharpening, she felt the weight of time pressing upon her. The effort to connect to that moment and spy on Xiao drained her strength with astonishing speed.

Struggling to hold the connection, Sarah pressed against Xiao's ascendant. She wouldn't get much time before the connection exhausted her strength, but she needed something. So she gritted her teeth against the drain and focused all her senses.

A richly appointed suite slowly coalesced into greater detail. Xiao stood near a window, a phone to her ear, and Sarah glimpsed distant shapes in the gray fog that suggested military vehicles. This time, Xiao's voice reached her as if from a great distance.

"Luxor is secure. Make sure your forces are in position and ready to strike. As soon as the plague begins, order the advance."

Sarah dearly wished she knew how to step into that moment. She'd rush in and stab Xiao in the back. Then again, she wasn't walking the memoryscape. This was a recent snapshot of time, more like a movie.

Sarah could look but not interact. She sensed there had to be a way to step into that moment, but how much energy would such a move require? She doubted she had enough. Maybe if she tapped a master rune, but could one use a moment in time to break into another moment in time? She had no idea.

Hongwu entered the room as Xiao hung up the phone. He was dressed in traditional Chinese garb, as usual. "The webs are in place and ready to come on line."

"Good. How long can you maintain the plague dispersal across all the targets?"

"Two days at least. Capital cities of the fifty most powerful military nations in the world, plus the religious sites. Mortality rate will exceed ninety percent."

"Excellent. Activate the web in conjunction with Sutekh's arrival."

Sarah felt chilled with horror as she realized the full scope of their plan. Their calm discussion of such mass murder made her want to vomit. Her limbs started to shake under the strain of holding the connection, but the critical intelligence was worth the effort.

She managed to hold on for another moment, but learned nothing else useful. Finally she released the ascendant and stumbled to one knee, breathing hard, the earth-globe hanging in the air above her.

She felt an exhaustion so deep, she barely had the strength to roll off the edge of the invisible platform. Again the blackness parted and she fell through. She tumbled back onto the sands beside Tomas and Francesca.

Tomas lifted her into his powerful arms, his expression concerned. "That was fast. Are you all right?"

She rested her head against his shoulder, drawing reassurance from his solid presence, wanting only to sleep. "Not really. Get us out of here."

Francesca said loudly, "Mother, take us home."

It took only moments to remove the helmets and summon the rest of the team to hear Sarah's report. Her strength slowly returned as she sipped a Coke. Her hands still shook, but she focused on her anger at the thought of the cui dashi's cold acceptance of so many deaths.

Spartacus entered with a huge platter of hamburgers and sliced pears. Sarah felt impressed that he could find such a feast in Egypt, but she was so wrung out she wasn't even tempted to snag one of the burgers.

Gregorios entered last, along with Abdallah. Sarah said, "You were right. Xiao does have a final push planned. She's using plague."

Francesca cursed, "I hate the plague."

Gregorios only nodded. "The black plague wiped out a huge percentage of Europe. That was a heka construct too."

"Medicine's progressed a lot since then," Tomas protested.

"She's probably considered that," Eirene said, taking a seat, her expression thoughtful. "There are already medicine-resistant strains of bacteria and viruses out there."

Gregorios dropped to the seat beside his wife. "She could mutate strains of influenza into new plagues the world is not ready to tackle. She's no doubt got the souls for it."

Sarah nodded. "She does. Hongwu said they can keep dispersing it for two days. They're hitting the capital cities of the strongest military nations, plus important religious locations."

"Oh, that's brilliant," Gregorios said with a low whistle.

Sarah gave him a disgusted look and forced herself to sit up straight. "Do you mind? They're expecting a ninety-percent mortality rate."

Gregorios met her gaze calmly. "You have to admit, she's planned every aspect of this coup. She's got world armies on the brink of open conflict. Everyone's mobilized. She's got a prophecy in place to justify Sutekh's return. She's got the world hunting us instead of her, and now she's got a plague to cripple governments around the world and incite religious wars. There's nothing hotter than a fanatical religious war. It's brilliant."

Quentin flicked a bit of dust off his white shirt and said, "Well, that makes our job easier in a way." At Sarah's shocked look he added, "There's no going back now. No quarter asked, none given. No worry about surrender or negotiation. This fight is now boiled down to the simplest equation. Which of us can kill the other first?"

"Let's make sure we hold the answer to that one," Gregorios said. He regarded Sarah seriously and asked, "Can you gather any more intel for us from her history?"

"I doubt it. Not any time soon anyway." Sarah hated admitting to the limitation, but that last brief contact had exhausted her.

Melek offered, "I will review our deeper runes and see if I can glean additional meaning from any of them, given the new information you've shared about the aeon. Perhaps we can determine how to strengthen your connection to the ascendants to clarify your vision and lessen the drain of your strength."

"I would really appreciate that," Sarah told him with a tired smile.

Gregorios said, "Good. Keep me posted. That could prove invaluable. Abdallah, tell us about the temples."

Abdallah produced a laptop and projected images onto one white-painted wall. "Xiao's forces are still clustered around both main temple sites on the east bank at Luxor. The Luxor temple and the Karnak temple."

He showed them images of the ruins that were still partially intact. "Luxor seems to be the primary site, and is where the archaeologists plan to present their new-risen god tomorrow."

"That's where we'll hunt for Xiao," Eirene said.

Abdallah explained, "Luxor is the location of the ancient city of Thebes, also called Waset, the city of the scepter. This was the capital during much of Egypt's history, including the time of Thutmose II, the fourth pharaoh of the eighteenth dynasty, who is arguably the pharaoh mentioned in the Old Testament during the time of Moses."

Tomas interrupted. "Hold on. I thought that was Ramses."

"It was in the movies. There is some argument in academic circles still, but Thutmose II is considered by many to be the actual pharaoh."

"I hate it when movies get history wrong," Tomas muttered.

Sarah laughed. "How can they not get it wrong? It's been changed."

"Well, they should get what's left right," he insisted.

Abdallah continued. "Thebes was arguably the largest city in the world during those ancient days. These temples were built during those times. Today the ruins still declare their ancient glory."

"You'd make an excellent tour guide," Sarah said.

He grinned, flashing one gold tooth. "One of my sons has this job. I have heard the script many times."

Gregorios said, "We're not tourists. Show us how to get in."

Abdallah shared a series of photos taken by the advanced team of enforcer scouts, as well as photos and video clips from news agencies. The military cordon was extensive, including armored trucks with heavy machine guns, and a pair of tanks.

"Once the fighting begins, reinforcements will be called in," Abdallah warned.

Gregorios didn't look surprised. "We're working on that, but it's still a good idea to wrap things up quick."

"There is another challenge," Abdallah said, shifting to a photo of a crashed helicopter in a square. It was crumpled, but not burned. The logo of a prominent news agency was visible on the side. "This happened today, outside of the Luxor temple. This news helicopter flew closer than advised."

"They shot it down?" Tomas asked, looking surprised.

"No. It crashed on its own."

"Do we have video?" he asked.

"I'm working on it. Reports from the scene claim its engine went silent when it approached the temple site. It crashed, but did not explode despite plenty of fuel."

"What does that mean?" Sarah asked.

Abdallah shrugged. "I have no men inside that cordon, so I cannot say."

"Spartacus," Gregorios said, drawing the gladiator's attention from the plate of hamburgers he was devouring. The man pushed that gluttony rune of his to the limits.

"Remember that time in Rome we cornered one of your cells in the catacombs? They escaped because all of our torches went out and we couldn't get them started again."

Spartacus swallowed and laughed. "Indeed. 'Twas an ingenious rune devised by one you would call a channeler today. It sucked the life out of any fire in the vicinity of his web."

"How big could a web like that extend?" Eirene asked.

Spartacus shrugged. "With enough souls to power it, as far as one wished."

Gregorios grunted. "I hate being right sometimes. That may be what we're looking at. They may not have the power to create as extensive a protective web like the one they used in Rome, but maybe they don't need to."

Tomas had that slightly distracted look that meant he was considering all sorts of contingency plans. "So instead of protecting them from all physical damage, you think they've got a web in place to snuff out fire?"

"Easier, cheaper, but effective, especially with all the souls they'll need to hit the world with plague," Gregorios said.

Spartacus said, "We do not use torches today. I fail to see the point."

Gregorios said, "Guns. Engines. Those are the basis of today's armies. If there can be no fire, then no one can shoot within the temple. Even if a missile or bomb struck, it would cause no explosions, just the kinetic force of impact."

Tomas said, "We can actually do a lot with kinetic impact with some planning. Drop a big enough bomb on the complex and we could wipe out the entire thing."

Gregorios said, "I'm fine with blowing things up if we have to, but if we can avoid leveling the temples, I'd prefer that."

"You really think they'd set up a web just for snuffing fire?" Sarah asked. She felt like there had to be more, and feared they were missing something important.

Gregorios shrugged. "It's sound like the most plausible solution. If we're right, then inside that perimeter, no one can use guns."

"But those guys have guns," Sarah said, pointing at the heka visible in the scene. "And the army outside the perimeter have guns and tanks and helicopters."

"We'll have to disable the army," Gregorios admitted.

"Without killing too many, no doubt," Tomas added.

He actually looked more intrigued by the challenge than frustrated by the limitation. Sarah appreciated that. Tomas was a killer when he had to be, but she loved that he hadn't grown to like that option too much.

"Either the heka rifles are just for show, or they have blocking runes inscribed on them to protect them from the effects of the web," Gregorios said.

Tomas said, "If you're right, this is going to be a challenge. At least having the Karnak temple also secured by heka finally makes sense. That's probably the support site where they'll have the protective rune web set up."

"They'll probably set up the plague web there too," Gregorios agreed.

Made sense to Sarah too, but she had to wonder what else Xiao must be planning. The woman was so devious, going in on unproven assumptions was dangerous.

Eirene said, "We need more intel from the ground before we arrive in the morning."

"We'll get it," Tomas promised.

Gregorios turned to Sarah. "See if you and Melek can figure out the blocking runes to apply to our own weapons. We may need them."

Sarah nodded, grateful for a straight-forward task. "If it's possible for one of your scouts to snap some close-up photos of any of those weapons, I'd love a glimpse at what runes they're using. Might confirm what we're dealing with, and speed up the work."

Tomas said, "Good idea. I'll pass the word."

"We also need to determine what order to hit those two sites," Eirene said, looking up from her laptop where she'd been typing during the entire conversation.

Tomas said, "We'll dedicate the Tenth and Suntara enforcers to Karnak to take out the heka there and bring down those webs."

Spartacus declared, "I will join you in the assault. Hongwu must needs protect his web creations, and our duel is yet undecided."

Francesca winked at him. "Sounds like fun. I'll join you boys."

Tomas gripped Sarah's hand, his expression confident. "I like it. Xiao and her forces are gathered together, but dispersed enough that we can take advantage."

"They have a strong defensive position, and if they hold out long enough for Xiao to pull Sutekh from history and focus her attention on us, we're doomed," Sarah pointed out. She hated how they would need to disperse their own forces for the attack.

Tomas grinned. "Yes, but between now and then, the advantage is ours. We choose the time and manner of our assault. Xiao will be focused on the memoryscape, and you'll block her there."

"You bet," Sarah said, forcing confidence into her voice. Surely, with her newfound understanding of the aeon, she finally held an advantage, but the thought of facing Xiao alone still terrified her.

"You've got that old biddy," Francesca encouraged her.

Melek spoke up. "What of my clan? We're experienced disabling rune webs."

Eirene shook her head. "I need the hunters with me and Greg. Our job is to take Luxor and try to find Xiao, hopefully before she awakens from her machine. We'll free Alter and take her out."

That pleased Melek immensely.

Quentin said, "We'll have a full suite of mortar munitions ready to fire from one of the barges. Once you find her and save Alter, we can unleash enough destruction to kill even that woman. I'll manage additional enforcer reinforcements to deploy to either temple site, as needed."

Sarah said, "Vlad will probably be lurking around Xiao somewhere. Either that, or he'll target me directly."

Tomas squeezed her hand. "I've already assigned a squad of vampire-trained enforcers to your protective detail."

"My ciphers are ready to fight Xiao, and I've got plans for Vlad if he shows up." She told them about her new sunlight ciphers.

Francesca chuckled. "I'd say aim for his heart, but you'd probably get more effect laser-castrating him."

"My thoughts exactly," Sarah said as both Spartacus and Quentin winced at the thought.

Eirene said, "Vlad will definitely be there. He has to. He can't afford to miss Xiao's big moment. He'll want his reward, and probably a chance to harvest a few souls to add to his collection."

"I think I know just the thing to bring old Vladdy boy out of hiding. Should also help me slip inside ahead of time and act as our ringer. Think the pope's good for another favor, Sarah?" Gregorios asked.

"Don't tell me vampires are really vulnerable to holy water," Sarah asked. She hadn't even considered trying the movie remedies for her vampire problem.

Tomas chuckled. "We've never actually tried it, but I doubt it would work. Religion and runes don't actually mix very well."

Gregorios said, "Vlad's got a grandiose sense of his own importance. He loves fostering vampire legends, and he won't be able to resist taunting a good religious target."

"I am not putting the pope at risk again," Sarah said, folding her arms defiantly.

Gregorios chuckled. "Nothing so dramatic, my girl. Trust me."

Eirene rolled her eyes, smiling. "Uh, oh. Greg's getting creative again."

Sarah relaxed a little, intrigued to find out what Gregorios had in mind. "Sure. Let's give him a call."

Gregorios rose and said, "Good. The rest of you, we have till morning. Let's get everything in place."

As the others rose or split into groups to discuss strategies, Quentin approached Sarah. "My dear, will you do me the honor of joining me in my lab after your call?"

"Sure. What do you need?"

"With your help, I believe I can deal with the Egyptian military personnel without having to kill all the poor, ignorant fools."

Sarah kissed his cheek. "It would be my honor."

"As you Americans say, together we will rock their world."

77

Wisdom outweighs any wealth insufficient to purchase your next life.

~SOPHOCLES

THAT NIGHT as the river cruise ship powered south toward Luxor, Sarah settled into a comfortable chair at a long banquet table with the core team. She felt tired, but happy with the long day's work. She eagerly dug in to the sumptuous feast and forced herself to simply enjoy the quiet moment with Tomas at her side.

The others seemed to feel the same, and they spent a rare half hour simply laughing and enjoying each other's company. She hoped it wouldn't be the last happy dinner they would all enjoy together.

With that somber thought, it was time to get back to work. The others still needed their super enhancements. They would be facing the deadly triple threat of Xiao, Hongwu, and Vlad. No one had ever faced such a powerful enemy team and won.

As the team gathered in the main salon, Sarah sensed their eagerness. They fully expected her to make those super enhancements work. No pressure.

She had already started kicking around some ideas, jotting down different rune configurations that might work. Now it was time to make some decisions. Luckily Gregorios' and Spartacus' super enhancements were already done. Melek had pronounced them exceptional, and both men were happy to use them again.

Sarah started with Eirene, her biggest challenge. She already wore a powerful battle suit, her nevra core would protect her from vampires, and her many enhancements made her all but invincible against almost all heka. Eirene's greatest concern was that someone might need her help and it might take her too long to respond. That gave Sarah the idea for Eirene's special enhancement.

Speed. When she explained what she was thinking, the ancient facetaker grinned like a little girl at Christmas. As Sarah worked on the idea, Melek suggested a couple of runes that she had never used before, but which related to the concept of the aeon and time. One of them referenced the wheel of time, and another used part of the serpentlike symbol for Father Time.

With those at the heart of the new enhancement, Sarah realized they might end up affecting time around Eirene as much as improving her movement speed. The potential was astonishing, and a little unclear, but she liked it. It felt right, just like the ones she'd instinctively built for Gregorios and Spartacus.

So she trusted that instinct and marked the super enhancement with a permanent marker. She could never inscribe any of the super enhancements with a knife. They were fueled from parts of the Constantinople master rune. That power source was immense, but not inexhaustible.

When Sarah activated it, nothing visible happened, but Eirene's eyes widened and she gasped. "Amazing."

Then she moved.

She seemed to blur across the room, so fast that she was more a hint of movement, too fast to follow with the naked eye. She skidded on the smooth floor as she tried to stop, and crashed right through the doorway into the hall.

"Whoa! That's awesome," Sarah laughed. That was even better than she'd hoped.

She glanced at Melek, who nodded approval. Nabil scowled, looking displeased that he'd helped work abomination. It was comforting.

When Eirene rushed back in, laughing with joy, Gregorios said, "That's pretty impressive. What if we combined your super speed with my flying?"

Eirene seemed to teleport over to him and pressed her fingers to his lips. She shook her head, her eyes twinkling. "No way, Greg. I'm not letting you get your hands on my enhancements."

He wrapped his arms around her waist and said with a sly grin, "That's not what you said last night."

Tomas groaned, and actually looked like he was starting to blush. "You two are incorrigible."

Francesca laughed, "You're just jealous. You haven't figured out how to get your hands on Sarah's enhancements yet."

Sarah joined in the general laughter, and Tomas' blush deepened. He looked so adorable like that that Sarah couldn't help giving him a tender kiss.

She whispered into his ear, "You just tell me when you're ready."

He coughed a bit uneasily, and immediately changed the subject. "We've got a pretty solid assault plan against both temples, but they'd be stronger if I could get in close ahead of time and make sure there's no unexpected surprises."

Sarah asked, "You want some kind of illusion ability, like the vampires do?"

Melek scowled at that, and the Nabil exclaimed, "Abomination! I will not condone such a use of evil."

Sarah raised a hand to forestall his righteous indignation. "We would never do anything like that, but that doesn't mean we can't find a way to conceal Tomas better."

Hearing one of the hunters shout their favorite word helped her feel like Alter was close and still part of their assault plan. Knowing that he could do nothing to stop Xiao must infuriate him to no end.

Sarah couldn't wait until he returned to the team. It felt incomplete without him. She missed punching him in the face when they trained, and she even missed the smoldering intensity of his awkward attempts to flirt.

After discussing a few different ideas, Melek again provided the initial inspiration. He proposed a pair of runes that Sarah was not familiar with. Combined, they could affect light, sort of like a prism.

Sarah love that idea, and it sparked a flash of inspiration. She quickly added additional symbols, working in a frenzy of creativity to produce a beautiful composite rune she felt as excited about as she had been about Eirene's.

The only problem was that she needed to mark it across Tomas' face. Harriett chuckled as Sarah finished the work. "He looks like an angry raccoon."

Tomas had been the brunt of too much teasing that night, so Sarah quickly activated the new enhancement. Instantly, Tomas' face began to glow.

Francesca laughed, "We'll have to start calling you Saint Tomas now."

Eirene added, "We've never had a saint."

"What do you feel?" Sarah asked.

Tomas paced away, hands outstretched, a little smile playing across his very kissable lips. "I can see the light." He glanced at Harriett and cut her off before she could make a snide remark. "Not regular light. This light's different. Melek, I think your rune is working. The light is shifting around me like I'm the prism."

Nabil still did not look pleased that they were pushing the boundaries of traditionally approved uses personal runes, but Melek looked fascinated. Sarah appreciated the fact that once the man made a decision, he didn't waste time and energy with useless regrets or second-guessing.

Francesca folded her arms and said, "All right, prism boy, try bending the light, then."

It took Tomas a few minutes of experimentation. Sarah should have moved on to her next project, but was enthralled watching him practice.

Occasionally he blazed with multicolored light. Then his eyes suddenly took on different hues, or light suddenly bent across the room, creating shadows and bright spots. Making shadows and sneaking through them might be really effective.

All of a sudden Tomas disappeared.

"Whoa!" Sarah shouted while the others exclaimed in surprise.

Tomas' disembodied laughter rang across the room and he reappeared. "I didn't go anywhere. I figured it out. I can bend the light around both sides of me, forming a bubble."

Eirene spoke above a bunch of questions from the others. "Makes sense. If the light passes around you, then none of it bounces off. We see reflected light, but if you aren't reflecting any, there's nothing to see."

"It's weird, though. Since the light is reflecting around me, I don't get much of it either. So when I went invisible, all the color drained away. All I see is black and white, like an old movie."

"I like old movies. We should go sometime," Sarah said. She'd love to spend two quiet hours in a dark theater with Tomas.

While he continued practicing, Sarah turned toward the hunters, but Nabil quickly said, "I'm willing to follow Melek into battle, and I'm willing to accept that this must be, but I have never accepted an enhancement drawn by any hand but my own."

That was a little frustrating, but he was making far more concessions than any hunter ever had in the past.

Eirene said, "It's all right, dear. We'll need you to lead the rest of the hunters to hit the heka lines after we initiate our first strike. Your current enhancements, with the protective ciphers that Sarah has prepared for everyone, should be sufficient."

He looked like he wanted to argue against accepting those protective ciphers, but Melek shook his head slightly and Nabil sighed and held his tongue.

"Melek, are you still willing to participate?" Sarah asked him.

After an apologetic glance at Nabil, who kept his expression thankfully stoic, Melek nodded. "I've come this far, and I will do what it takes to save my son and stop this evil." His mighty rune covered battle hammer rested on the floor by his feet, and he fingered it as he spoke.

He had already given a great deal of thought to his personal super enhancement, and showed Sarah several runes that could be used as the heart of what he was looking for.

Sarah studied them. "What are you going for? I don't like how these symbols are connecting."

Melek explained that he did not want to be at Xiao's mercy again. She moved too fast, and he was looking for a way to keep her from overpowering him like she had the last time. That made sense, but the rune sequence didn't feel right.

Then she grinned. "I've got it! You need the advantage that I discovered in Berlin, fighting Mai Luan."

She quickly sketched out the enhancement. It had been her first accidental super enhancement, and it saved her life fighting the much more powerful cui dashi.

Nabil looked like he wanted to argue, but Melek nodded and gave her an approving smile. "I would be honored to go into battle wearing this enhancement, Champion."

He actually looked a little emotional, and Sarah remembered that that enhancement incorporated parts of Eirene's signature personal rune. Eirene looked very pleased by the idea too.

Happy that she had picked the right symbols, Sarah quickly marked the enhancement onto Melek's shoulder. Almost instantly, his body shimmered and faded, slipping into the ethereal state that Sarah had discovered by accident in Berlin. She grinned and tried to high-five him, but her hand passed right through his.

Grinning like a much younger man, he practiced by running through walls and leaping up through the ceiling. Sarah smiled, feeling a heady sense of contentment. It was working.

These enhancements would protect her closest loved ones and give them a critical advantage. They had failed every attempt to fight Xiao, and the thought of facing her again had terrified her. Now she allowed herself to feel a little hope.

After Melek, it took her only a few minutes to confer with Francesca about the super runes she wanted. It fit Francesca perfectly, sexy and naughty, and delightful.

Francesca asked her to keep it secret from the rest of the team. She wanted to surprise everyone. Sarah agreed because she was really curious to see how Francesca planned to bring that super rune to bear.

Harriett declined getting a super enhancement. She would probably not get involved in the direct fighting, but would be playing more of a support role.

While Tomas excused himself to check in on Carlo and his team and see how they were bonding to their new enhancements, Sarah returned to rune study. With Melek, she reviewed all of the forbidden runes, secret runes, and higher-level runes. She needed to know them as well as she knew her own enhancements. Fighting Xiao would certainly present unexpected challenges, and she would not have much time to react and craft new ciphers.

Some time later, she was surprised out of her deep study when Tomas returned and reported, "All of the Italians bonded their runes already. They're motivated and looking for payback. Nabil is even marking their blades with vampire fighting runes in case they get a chance to help us fight Vlad."

She loved hearing good news. Many times first runes did not bond for a day or two. That all of the Italians had bonded so quickly confirmed what she already knew about the integrity of their powerful souls.

She stole a quick kiss. "We're almost done here. I just want to review what I learned about the aeon and the ascendants."

Melek agreed, and they spent some time discussing in detail her experience in that strange aeon dimension. She wasn't sure she accu-rately conveyed everything, but Melek seemed excited by it. He produced a little leather notebook where he kept the most powerful runes, and flipped to a page near the back.

"Look. We have these runes from ancient history, the only glimpses of the truth about the aeon and the ascendants. Since none of us have ever experienced that dimension, it was impossible to know how to best apply the symbols."

Sarah eagerly studied them. They weren't Egyptian or Chinese or Norse, but felt ancient. They resonated with what she had felt in the aeon.

"From what you've explained, I think you can utilize these runes to help you connect more strongly with a particular ascendant, or point in time," Melek said excitedly.

As Sarah studied them, Melek explained, "Each ascendant should have a signature rune associated with it. If you can identify those symbols, you can closely link to that particular ascendant."

Sarah nodded. "I already sensed one of them."

It amazed her that Melek could guess such a thing. The man was really a genius. He was proposing remarkable new theories with nothing to draw upon but her brief experience with the aeon. She doubted even Xiao could have matched him in her first life.

"Good. Since I'm right about that, I believe you should also be able to scan across the ascendants at a particular point in history. The weaving of the ascendants should create similar signature symbols for each moment in time. By utilizing those symbols, you should be able to attach yourself to that moment in time and actually step into it."

Sarah let out a low whistle as she considered the idea and studied those runes. He might just be right. She had felt there must be a way to get a clearer view into the past. The next logical step was to actually step into that moment as a participant.

"Isn't that dangerous? I mean, all the sci-fi nerds I've ever heard talk about time travel warn about breaking and changing things in history. They talk about splitting off alternate realities, or having unexpected consequences, things like that, you know?"

Melek leaned back in his chair and spread his arms in a helpless gesture. "We cannot say for sure. I don't think anyone has ever succeeded in reaching the point that you and Xiao are approaching. I have no doubt that if she is allowed to run unchecked through history that she could indeed break the aeon. That would wreak destruction greater than the most terrible bombs. However, if you are careful, I believe that accessing history is worth the risk."

That wasn't entirely comforting. Sarah felt excited and nervous in equal measure as she considered becoming the world's first real time traveler. The potential for learning thrilled her, but that excitement was tempered by the fact that when pioneers made mistakes they were usually fatal.

She didn't want to screw anything up. At the same time, she vowed to undo anything Xiao planned. Focusing on that gave her the courage to seriously consider trying it.

She spent a few minutes memorizing those runes. Adding them to her arsenal might finally help turn the tide in the upcoming battle.

Or she might destroy them all. Tomorrow there would be no half measures either way.

Sarah leaned back in her chair finally, rubbing at her eyes. Even though she had been drawing additional power from her charging rune in Beijing, she had tapped her rounon well a lot. She felt deeply exhausted, and that was no way to go into battle against the most powerful evil creature in the world.

The door open and Tomas returned. He looked tired too as he approached the table and gestured for her to stand. "Sorry to interrupt the party, but it's time for bed."

Melek snorted an incredulous laugh. Sarah wrapped her arms around his neck and gave him a passionate, quick kiss. "I'm impressed. I hadn't expected you to take me up on that offer so soon."

Tomas stammered, blushing adorably again, so she kissed him deeply. When she finally released him, he looked a little breathless, but very happy. Part of her wished he really would take her up on that offer. They were facing the ultimate battle of their lives, and a little physical intimacy would sure feel good.

As much as she could tell he wanted her, she could also tell he wasn't ready to break his moral code, and she was willing to accept that. Tomas was a man of unflinching honor, and she couldn't ever see him compromising what he thought was right. She didn't really want him to, even if it meant delaying something she really wanted.

So she kissed him again and said, "Before anyone goes to bed, you need to take me up on deck and find a quiet corner and kiss me more thoroughly than you've ever kissed a woman."

He grinned and slipped an arm around her waist as they headed for the exit. "Show me the way."

78

No one really understands the true purpose of these images. Yes, they are useful for communication, and for recording the doings of the ancestors, but that is nothing! I now command more runes than anyone in the history of the world.

~FUXI, ONE OF THE THREE AUGUST ONES, CREDITED WITH CREATING THE FIRST CANGJIE WRITING, 2000 B.C.

BY TEN O'CLOCK the next morning, the Luxor temple site was packed. It might be autumn in other parts of the world, but already the sun felt hot. It would probably top a hundred degrees Fahrenheit again.

The Egyptian army maintained a security perimeter around the entire ancient structure to keep out the curious locals and the protesting religious fanatics. News crews from thirty top international news agencies were granted access to the interior of the temple, as were dignitaries from Egypt and several other countries who had chosen to attend.

Sarah wondered at that as she leaned over Eirene's shoulder and scanned the many news channels broadcasting on a dozen big screen TVs. They'd set up the bank of monitors in the communications hub on the cruise ship. Several staff members worked computers to either side, keeping the complex comms between the individual strike teams in place and coordinated.

Their views also included dozens of tiny cameras planted around the site by Tomas' advanced unit. The team had gathered an amazing amount of intel. It all reinforced their assumption that Xiao must be concealed somewhere within the Luxor temple complex. They still suspected the rune webs must be at Karnak. Although Karnak was a secondary site, it was protected by a couple hundred heka fighters and a strong cordon of Egyptian military.

Sarah studied the media circus, amazed that Xiao had pulled off her crazy plan. There was no way an announcement about the impending arrival of a new-risen god should be taken seriously, even when delivered by a famous archaeological dig. In the past, such an announcement would have been laughed off, but everyone was taking it as seriously as if the president of the United States had issued a formal declaration.

Eirene whistled softly as a convoy of black SUVs pulled up to the designated disembarkation location outside of the enormous Luxor pylon entrance. "We've got the US ambassador to Egypt, complete with security detail."

"That's very interesting," Gregorios responded over an open mic, his voice distorted by his current disguise.

Eirene responded. "Makes sense. Xiao wants the world to recognize this as a significant event. What better way to do that than get the US ambassador to show up?"

Gregorios said, "How about several ambassadors? I'm seeing two other convoys moving in before mine."

A moment later, Eirene picked them up on one of the video feeds. "Great Britain. Again, makes sense."

"And the third?" Sarah asked.

When the distant limousine door opened, Eirene whistled softly. "That's the Chinese Ambassador."

Gregorios said, "Xiao's stacking the deck."

Eirene's expression turned thoughtful. "I'm wondering if she's doing more than that. With these countries so close to open warfare, packing them all into that temple with what we know she has planned could lead to all sorts of interesting opportunities for violence."

"We'll keep an eye on it," Gregorios promised.

Eirene said, "Don't let it distract you from the mission. Are you all set?"

"Arriving for my grand entrance now."

Eirene altered one of the video feeds to a view of another convoy of vehicles rolled to a stop to disgorge its passengers. On the others, she watched feeds from team members in the nearby cars.

The limousine door opened and a full Catholic cardinal stepped out, followed by Carlo Salvatici. Cardinal Niccolo Alberti dressed in standard Catholic black cassock, with crimson piping. He was a tall man in his fifties, and seemed to be in better shape than many religious figures Sarah had seen.

She smiled to see him. She had originally worried the pope would hesitate to risk a full cardinal, but he hadn't hesitated to come to their aid. He really was a good man.

Other members of the Italian protective team poured out of the next two vehicles and formed up around the cardinal. The arrival of the cardinal triggered a wave of interest. News reporters scrambled to relocate from the Chinese ambassador to hurl questions at the arriving religious dignitary.

Cardinal Alberti waved and greeted everyone warmly. "I am here to investigate the veracity of claims of a significant religious event today. Even if the promised event is proven fraudulent, it's a beautiful day to visit this important historical location."

The ruins of Luxor made an impressive backdrop for the big event. The towering entrance pylon of Nubian sandstone stretched over two hundred feet across the front of the temple site. Made of two immense trapezoidal structures with walls sloping inward, the narrow gap between them formed the entrance passage.

Enormous colossi statues of Ramses II seated on thrones guarded the entrance, still rearing fifty-one feet despite heavy weathering. A solitary obelisk covered in bas-relief hieroglyphs towered over the statues at eight-two feet. Its base was encircled by ancient carved baboons.

Sarah couldn't remember what they represented. Its slightly shorter twin had long ago been relocated to the Place de la Concorde in Paris.

The cardinal's group followed the ambassadors toward the temple entrance, and Sarah imagined the glory of the site when it had been new. She felt a thrill of awe similar to how she felt around her favorite ruins of Rome.

Eirene monitored the team's progress and checked the hidden helmet cameras on each of the Italian soldiers. Sarah hoped they wouldn't have to break too much. Eirene pointed out the placement of armored vehicles and two tanks supporting the Egyptian military cordon. Those would be Eirene's responsibility once the main event began.

All of the Italians wore sidearms, as would be expected of a protective detail. Concealed under their jackets were additional pistols, some specialty grenades, and lots of spare magazines.

Unlike the men flanking the ambassadors, their weapons would work inside. Sarah had inscribed tiny ciphers on each of them to block the effects of the heka rune web.

One of the scout enforcers had snapped a pretty decent photo of a rune on one of the heka's weapons. It was a fairly standard blocking rune, with minor modifications. Sarah easily designed a custom cipher for their teams based on what she saw. When it came to a fight, they'd have the advantage.

"Carlo, let me know if you feel any physical effects from that web once you're inside," Eirene said after switching audio channels.

The team passed through the entrance gateway into the wide court of Ramses II. He'd been the last pharaoh to work on the Luxor temple, which was why the entrance and first court bore his name. The deeper one progressed down the center axis of the temple, the older the courts and chapels, since each pharaoh had built in front of the last.

The courtyard was surrounded on three sides by a double row of tall stone columns covered in ancient hieroglyphs. Statues in various states of decay stood between many of them. The symmetry of the court was broken on the left side by the wall of the mosque of Abu el Hagag.

Built in the nineteenth century by a clever sheik, who was now the area's prominent saint. He'd won the location by stratagem. At the time of building, the temple hadn't yet been excavated, so now the ground level of his mosque towered twenty feet above the current floor.

The central temple axis continued south, beyond the first court of Ramses, flanked by taller columns, but the area was blocked off by a pair of heka guards in khaki uniforms. It appeared the main event would be held right there in the first court.

While the cardinal spent a few minutes speaking with the dignitaries and news personnel, most of Carlo's team quietly spread throughout the court. No one paid them attention as all eyes were focused on the important visitors or up toward the patio of the mosque that towered above the court.

Carlo reported, "Signora Eirene. No physical effects of the web.

Also, it appears they mean to make their appearance from the mosque."

Eirene nodded. "Makes sense. Gives them the high ground, and that's the one place in that court they can conceal what they're really up to. All teams, mark the mosque as Primary One."

"Roger," came a string of soft replies.

Sarah listened as Eirene switched through the other channels and verified with each team their readiness. Sarah felt nervous excitement growing as they waited for the moment to begin.

She barely believed they hadn't run into any major problems yet. Had they really fooled Xiao and arrived in secret? It would be a nice first.

At every step, Xiao had outmaneuvered them, setting traps and making life increasingly difficult. They needed to turn the tables on her this time, and she felt like they had a good chance at succeeding. Their assault plans were straight-forward enough that they avoided unnecessary complications, and flexible enough that they should be able to respond quickly to the inevitable surprises.

On the cameras, Carlo's team had completed their initial sweep of the court and were in position. Just in time, too. The clock struck eleven, and Dr. Chang, the head of the archaeological team, stepped up to the railing of the mosque patio, high above the assembled crowd.

Sarah studied him. His previous scholarly enthusiasm had morphed into something more like religious zeal. Whether he was just fooled by Xiao, bound to her by rune, or a willing accomplice, it didn't matter. He was clearly playing a role she dictated.

He raised his hands for attention and the crowd fell silent. "Welcome to the day prophesied millennia ago. My team has completed our work deciphering the text of the ancient prophecy and I can reveal to you all the name of the One Who Comes, the one who will sit in judgment over the world, the one who will reign over a new era of peace."

Sarah muttered to herself, "Bunch of drivel."

She'd taken some time during the busy night to read the deciphered text of that stone supposedly discovered in the desert by Dr. Chang's team. It did include Sutekh's signature rune, which she'd memorized.

It had also included remarkable detail about the life of the high priest. If a fraction of his amazing goodness was true, he would have been more of a saint than any prophet she'd ever heard about. Xiao's team had laid it on pretty thick. Sarah did have to admit, they had found some creative ways to describe their future world from the point of view of a man from ancient Egypt.

One of the news reporters dropped his microphone and shouted, "False prophet! We will never bow to a false god!"

The man, who was supposedly from CNN, pulled a pistol from under his jacket, pointed it at the archaeologist, and pulled the trigger.

Of course it didn't fire. The fool didn't know anything about the protective rune web he'd walked into. The click of the weapon was drowned out by shouting security officers who tackled the hapless reporter.

In seconds he was cuffed, his screams muffled by a gag, and he was yanked back to his feet, flanked by a pair of burly guards. Heka security forces took him through a guarded door, then up to the mosque with Dr. Chang.

The reporter was pushed to the edge of the patio and pressed right against the rail. The heka thugs retreated from him, leaving him standing defiantly facing Dr Chang.

Dr. Chang pointed at the reporter. "This type of fanatical hatred will be done away once the new king of the world rises. There will be no more senseless violence, no more discrimination. All will be equal."

"Funny how they don't mention they're planning equality through chains and global murder," Eirene muttered.

A dark wind howled out of the interior of the mosque and encircled the patio. It moaned and wailed as it billowed over the area, obscuring everything in a thickening fog.

"We've got vampires," Eirene stated calmly.

"Impressive display for broad daylight. Vlad's pulling out all the stops," Gregorios commented.

The wailing vampire wind tugged at the reporter's clothing and hair. The man cowered in terror. Sarah watched in silent horror, shivering with a sudden chill as she heard Vlad's soft laughter ringing in her mind.

The vampire's hissing voice echoed out of his soul wind. "Starting today, the world will face a simple choice. Accept the new reality or be consumed by it."

Vlad stepped into view through the obscuring wind, right in front of the terrified reporter. Again he wore his crimson hat, with its band of pearls and huge, star-shaped, golden emblem above his forehead. He wore a black cape that billowed around him impressively, and a crimson waistcoat with golden buttons. His pinched face wore a smile, his goatee trimmed to a careful point.

The reporter sagged in helpless terror under the power of Vlad's gaze. The vampire pounced, yanked his head up, and sunk long fangs into the man's chin. He moved so fast, Sarah barely had time to gasp before the vampire savaged all the soul points along the man's jawline and turned his teeth to the man's throat. Bright arterial blood fountained into the air from the doomed reporter. The soul wind whipped around the vampire and his victim and absorbed the blood, its wailing cry intensifying into a heart-chilling lament.

Sarah wanted to scream as she watched Vlad consume the man's life and capture his soul. Part of her shuddered with terror, imagining what it would feel like to fall to his fangs like that poor fool.

Gregorios spoke with far too much calm. "He's confident of victory or he'd never risk such a public display."

"I'm glad we have so many enforcers with vampire runes," Eirene said.

Her expression was grave as she watched Vlad extend his jaws impossibly wide and bite both sides of the dying man's face. His fangs bit into the soul points again and with a savage yank, he ripped the man's soul right out of his body.

Sarah shuddered in revulsion. For a second, the poor man's soul-mask was visible as it tore free of his skull. Then its quicksilver glow faded to gray and it dissolved into mist that got sucked into Vlad's flaring nostrils.

He threw his bloody face back, a look of exultation on his demonic face. He clearly savored taking fresh souls to add to the host of his tormented minions. They would remain enslaved to him until someone killed him.

"He has to die today," Sarah growled.

In the court below, ambassadors were retreating and reporters were screaming. Some tried to flee, but heka fighters blocked the exits, military rifles held threateningly. At least a few cameramen kept their cameras rolling so the whole world got to watch a real-life vampire feeding. Several security officers from the American and British contingencies drew weapons and fired upon Vlad.

Nothing. Their weapons failed, and they suddenly began to realize just how dangerous situation was.

"Kill that mostro," Carlo cried as he raised his pistol.

The cardinal blocked his arm, and Gregorios said, "Easy, Carlo. You'll get your chance, but not yet."

"How can you say that? He just murdered that man," Carlo exclaimed.

"Killing him is harder than a bullet to the brain. We need to draw him in first. We'll get him, but on our terms."

Sarah spotted Carlo on a video feed from one of the other security member's concealed body cam. He didn't look pleased, but he was a professional, and he understood the need to follow a plan.

Sarah's heart went out to him. She felt the same deep-rooted revulsion. They'd both been bitten by that vampire in the bowels of Castel Odescalchi. No one who hadn't felt the deadly, cold touch of a vampire sucking their life through their soul points could really understand.

Up on the balcony, Vlad dropped the lifeless corpse and stepped to the railing. He looked down over the fearful crowd and smiled, his teeth red with blood. "Anyone else wish to protest?"

Most of those gathered shifted back. Many visibly paled under his powerful gaze. The US and UK ambassadors protested the senseless killing, but they both looked nervous. Their security couldn't actually defend them, even though the men were trying different magazines, vainly trying to figure out the problem.

The Chinese ambassador turned toward the other diplomats and said loudly, "All terrorists should be treated the same way. Without mercy."

Eirene muttered, "There's going to be blood between those groups before the day's out."

Cardinal Alberti alone stood his ground. He declared loudly, "As always, the church denounces the use of murder. We have seen more than enough petty tyrants attempt to rise to power through the use of murder and intimidation. Our own holy sites were recently desecrated by such a one. This unholy creature must be destroyed. If the man supposedly prophesied to arrive today employs such servants, tell him not to bother coming. The world does not need another murderer. It needs a peacemaker."

Eirene grinned at the camera. "Oh, that was a good speech. Let's hope it does the job."

"I'll draw him in," Gregorios promised. Sarah didn't even see the cardinal's lips move.

Eirene switched to another channel. "Tomas, Vlad's been drawn out. Begin your assault now."

Tomas responded instantly. "Roger. I'm going in."

On the balcony, Vlad laughed long and loud, then simply disappeared. His freaky soul wind howled across the temple court and faded.

"That can't be good," Sarah muttered.

"He'll return. Not even he likes standing in the spotlight for long. Watch your back, Gregorios," Eirene said.

Sarah silently wished Tomas luck and safety, and she hoped Gregorios was ready for whatever treachery Vlad had planned. She gripped Eirene's shoulder and said, "I'd better get into position too."

"Good luck, dear, and wear the right ciphers."

If she didn't, Xiao would rip out her soul.

79

TOMAS MOVED across the vast brick-paved square leading from the east bank of the Nile toward the Karnak temple compound. The Egyptian military's portable barriers cut across the middle of the square and ringed the entire Karnak site.

There must have been over a thousand troops dedicated to the task. Curious locals and a crowd of protesters milled around the square. Since no one knew what role this site would play in the coming of the prophesied new king, it had drawn far less attention than Luxor, two miles to the south.

Periodic chanting by protesters rose above the sounds of the city. It had startled Tomas to find how close the city sprawl approached the temple sites. The area smelled of dust and smoke, with the scent of camel dung underlying everything.

Tomas grinned despite the smell, the heat, and the heavy pack he carried. As he closed on the unsuspecting Egyptian lines, he marveled again at his new super-rune. Sarah had progressed from a newbie, knowing nothing about runes, into the world's most powerful-ever rune warrior in a remarkably short period of time.

Of course, she'd had unique motivations pushing her to the limits, but she really was a rune genius. If he hadn't had several lifetimes to build up his self-confidence, he might have felt a bit intimidated by this woman who had so thoroughly stolen his heart. Every day he learned something new about her to love. He wanted nothing more than to spend several more lifetimes getting to know her ever better.

For the first time in a very long time, he felt the urge to pray. If there was a god out there, now was the time for a little help. If they screwed up this mission, there would be no second chances. Tomas loved a good fight, but he hated suicide missions.

He'd spent most of the past couple days working with his teams to finalize their assault plans. Their careful planning would pay off, especially now that he had his new super rune.

Tomas slowed as he neared the Egyptian lines and extended one hand to admire the play of light around his fingertips. With the new super rune, light had become a tangible thing to him. He could feel it all around, and manipulating it was incredibly fun.

He still marveled at how quickly he'd picked up the trick to bending the light around himself to make himself invisible. In essence, he walked between the rays of light. If only he'd had that ability when he led the light brigade.

As Tomas slipped through the Egyptian lines and paused at each of seven trucks, four armored vehicles, and one heavy tank, he marveled at how easy his stealth mission had become. As long as he didn't make loud noise to draw attention to himself, he could move about at will.

The vehicles were idling, their drivers and gunners looking bored. If he had planned to kill these men, he'd have felt guilty to take such an unfair advantage. Hopefully most of them would survive the day.

After all of the specialty charges were set under each of the vehicles, Tomas crouched beside one of the ram-headed sphinxes that lined the main thoroughfare leading to the massive entrance to the Karnak temple complex.

Everything around him looked gray, like dense shadows on a dingy white background. It really wasn't that bad a thing here in Egypt. Instead of seeing the sand, rocks, and ruins in living dull browns and tans, they actually looked more exotic in his altered shadow-sight.

"Charges are set," he reported.

"No indication they know you're there, Captain," Anaru responded from inside the barge anchored nearby.

"It's been a cake-walk so far. Where's unit two?"

"You should have visual any second."

Tomas climbed atop the sphinx to see over the soldiers, and spotted a convoy of six large tanker trucks rumbling toward the temple site. They bore the emblem of a local septic company.

"I have visual. Excellent work on the paint job."

Quentin's voice came over the line. "Acquiring the trucks and filling them with sufficient quantities was far more challenging than painting them, my boy."

"Trucks will be in position in two minutes," Anaru said.

Tomas hopped down. "Roger. The entrance looks clear. Initiating infiltration of the temple. Proceed according to plan."

He jogged toward the main entrance, and even he felt impressed by the sight. The Karnak temple had existed since around two thousand B.C. and had stood at the heart of Egyptian theology for millennia.

It was like the Vatican of ancient Egypt and was perhaps the largest religious site in the world. The main sanctuary between the fourth and fifth pylons was so huge it could have fit the cathedrals of St Peter's, Milan, and Notre Dame all together within its walls.

The main entrance on the west side, facing the Nile and the sphinx-lined avenue, was known as the first pylon. The huge construct of sandstone blocks looked incomplete, with the right side rising higher than the left.

It still reared over a hundred feet, forming a massive gateway. Standing at the threshold of the temple, Tomas felt tiny, dwarfed by the sheer magnitude of the ancient construct. Unlike most ancient Egyptian temples, the Karnak site was so vast, it included a second main axis, although much of that one was reduced to little more than rubble.

A pair of heka sentries stood at attention in the entrance at the first pylon. They looked like locals, but wore the uniform of Xiao's personal army. The khaki color looked light gray to Tomas' altered vision, but he recognized the cut.

These two also wore soul packs strapped to their lower backs like fanny packs. Those no doubt held dispossessed souls to fuel enhancements or personal protective barriers. Even for Xiao, soulmasks represented a real cost. She'd spared no expense in outfitting her troops.

He slipped past the unsuspecting guards and ghosted into the first huge courtyard, happy that the ancient stone pavement was mostly swept clear of sand. He didn't leave telltale tracks.

A huge stone-paved court opened after the first pylon, with two rows of broken columns marching down the center. They were spaced far enough apart that they had probably once formed the boundary of an inner kiosk. Only one of the pillars remained intact. It lorded over the broken ruins of the others.

A hundred heka soldiers lounging in that central kiosk ruin. All of the soldiers carried automatic rifles, and racks of RPGs were set up near the broken pillars.

Tomas slipped around the left side of the open court. That's when he spotted several heavy machine guns mounted atop the outer walls and the top of the towering first pylon. The heka were well entrenched and ready for battle.

The left and right walls were lined with more columns and more sphinxes. There was a doorway in the distant right wall, leading into the small statue-lined chapel of Ramses III. A makeshift gate barred the chapel, guarded by burly heka soldiers. He'd have to investigate the chapel later when he returned from exploring the rest of the complex.

Despite the number of heka in the area, Tomas circled the court without issue. The men looked tough and most of them wore soul packs. That was unfortunate. When his team took out the rune web that prevented the use of weapons and machinery, it wouldn't affect the personal enhancements or protections fueled by those soul packs.

Tomas left the court behind and entered the most fascinating part of the entire temple. It was there where he expected to find the rune web. Known as the Great Hypostyle Hall, the vast area was filled with one hundred and thirty-four gigantic papyrus columns covered in hieroglyphs.

They flanked the central avenue and filled the hall in their regular rows. The twelve columns making up the rows to either side of the avenue were tallest at sixty-nine feet. The others might only be forty feet, but they were still awe-inspiring, like a forest of stone. Despite heavy weathering, the huge columns looked like they could stand for thousands of years.

A squad of eight shadowy heka marched into the far side of the avenue, so Tomas slipped into the rows of columns. He walked slowly down the aisle between the second and third rows, in part to reduce the chance of making a telltale noise, and in part to admire the colossal columns.

Fifty people could stand all together atop the largest of them.

Some of them still supported massive stone beams known as architraves that would have supported the roof of the ancient temple. The massive size of the construct dwarfed even many of the most impressive Roman monuments.

Tomas explored the columned expanse, but found no guards, no enchanters, no stacks of soulmasks linked into rune webs. He picked up the pace. The trucks would be in position in seconds and he'd hoped to have located the rune web by now. He reported his findings about the strength of the heka defenders to his assault team. He hoped to complete his mission before the main attack began so he could even the odds from the inside.

Anaru, Spartacus, and Francesca would lead the assault teams. They were concealed on the river barge docked nearby. As soon as the initial disabling ordnance was deployed against the Egyptian regulars to get them out of the way, the team would launch their assault.

Most of the enforcers had arrived, as had Melek's hunters. The hunters were dedicated to the assault on Luxor, supporting Gregorios' team. A third of the enforcers were staged as reinforcements for that primary target, so Tomas' strike teams would be a bit short-handed if it came to a pitched battle.

The troops from Yurak hadn't shown up yet, but they were steaming up the Nile fast with heavy weapons and equipment. Despite their best efforts, they were probably going to arrive an hour too late.

If this assault failed, they would launch a second strike and try to finish the job.

If it failed, they'd be back to a suicide mission.

80

Ten soldiers wisely led will beat a hundred without a head.

~EURIPIDES

THE EASTERN GATE beyond the Hypostyle Hall emptied into an expanse of broken walls and ruined statues. This had been an entire complex of temples and chapels but now was little more than a pile of rubble.

There was nothing of interest here. Tomas turned a slow circle in a wide stone field near a small, sacred lake. There could be no rune web concealed in this part of the temple. He'd missed something.

"Trucks in position," Anaru reported.

Tomas was out of time. He considered circling around to the south where the separate temple of Khonsu stood, but the Egyptian forces hadn't surrounded that building. That made it less likely to be the place. That left only one other option.

"I'll have the web located shortly. Initiate bombardment."

"Roger."

As Tomas ran back through the Hypostyle Hall, distant thunder rolled through the complex. The heavy stone walls diluted the sound, but it was unmistakable to him.

The large tanker trucks had all been set with special shaped charges. The trucks had spread around the Egyptian lines. No doubt, soldiers had already approached to order the drivers to move on. Terrorist attacks were all too common in this part of the world for them not to recognize the danger the huge trucks presented. The trucks weren't loaded with explosives, but with a far more complex ordinance.

Charges on trucks one, three, and five detonated first, rupturing their huge liquid tanks. Eleven thousand gallons of Quentin's custom hydrogen peroxide mixture burst out of each one. The liquid would flood the Egyptian positions, inundating their lines.

Concentrated hydrogen peroxide could burn the skin and bleach clothes, although the rest of the mix would help delay those effects. A little burn would be better for those soldiers than the alternative, though.

Tomas increased his pace, but half a dozen heka now massed in the far doorway leading back to the first court. As he drew closer, he noticed that the other heka, who had been lounging around the central row of pillars, had all grabbed up weapons

He didn't have time to wait for the group blocking the doorway to move, and couldn't afford to start a pitched fight yet. So he raced into the forest of columns to the high outer wall on the north side.

Another series of explosions shook the area as the other three tanker trucks blew. The charges on these had been set differently. Instead of simply rupturing the tankers and flooding the area, shaped charges burst the tanks to shower the Egyptian troops with a potassium iodide mixture. It would serve as the catalyst of a violent chemical reaction when it mixed with the hydrogen peroxide already pooling around their feet.

The reaction was similar to the popular elephant toothpaste chemistry experiment, on steroids, with some of Quentin's modifications mixed in. As shouting intensified outside of the temple, Tomas leaped ten feet into the air and kicked off a deep-carved hieroglyph.

That launched him another eight feet higher and threw him toward the nearest column, where he kicked off yet again. With each kick he gained another five to eight feet. Like a vertical pinball he ascended, bouncing between the wall and the column until with a final kick, he landed atop one of the enormous architrave beams.

The beams were laid across the tops of the pillars, but many were missing, and huge gaps yawed between them. Grinning from the exhilaration of the climb, Tomas vaulted across the gaps from one high architrave to another in an enhanced run. In seconds he reached the western edge of the hall, now overlooking that first court, facing the enormous entrance pylons on the far side. He stood high enough that he could scan the pandemonium that had transformed the well-ordered ranks of Egyptian soldiers around the temple.

The potassium iodide increased exponentially the rate of oxidation from the hydrogen peroxide. The escaping oxygen was captured by the dish soap included in the mixture, forming explosions of foam that erupted with spectacular speed all through the Egyptian lines packing the square outside the temple. Quentin had included dye packets that painted the foam in rainbow colors as it expanded to engulf the bewildered soldiers.

Tomas laughed, then clapped a hand over his mouth. Quentin had assured him the foam would work, had explained the concept of non-lethal dispersion of the Egyptian troops, but Tomas had failed to understand the mad genius of the plan. Soldiers struggled to escape the foam that clung to them in sticky gobs. It would foul their weapons and stick them to everything they touched. Tomas didn't envy them the job of cleaning up, but at least they'd survive the day.

The trucks and armored vehicles tried powering through the foam, gunners fighting to clear foam from their weapons as they searched for targets. The battle tank rumbled toward the broken tankers, its heavy gun rotating toward the fleeing enforcers who had driven the trucks into position.

Tomas extracted a detonator from a pocket and dialed in the proper sequence to signal the shaped charges he'd planted. Muffled booms echoed through the temple from outside, and vehicles lurched as their axles snapped. The tank ground to a halt as its heavy tracks slipped off the wheels. It was known as a mobility kill, and it would be enough.

"Can you see this mess?" Tomas asked.

"Roger. Bloody good show," Quentin laughed.

"Assault team is launching now," Anaru reported. "Thirty seconds to contact."

"Roger." Tomas needed to find the web before the rest of the team arrived. "Vehicles are disabled, but the tank's main gun looks like it's still operational."

Quentin said, "I'll take care of it. Good hunting."

"The heka will be ready, and some have personal soul packs," Tomas warned.

Already men were clustering in the gates, weapons at the ready. More of them rushed toward ladders positioned along the first pylon and outer wall. They all carried automatic rifles and many had snatched up RPG launchers.

Quentin sounded calm and professional, as always during a fight. "Prepping the Rainmaker for a volley. Get under cover."

"Roger."

Tomas dropped onto the second pylon that formed the inside boundary wall between the first court and the Hypostyle Hall. He scampered across the top of the wall before heka ascended to his position. He was tempted to kick the ladders over, but resisted the urge. Even though they couldn't see him, they might realize someone was up here. If they started strafing the pylon, they could still slow him.

When he reached the juncture with the wall forming the outside boundary of Ramses' temple, he jumped across to that one and circled it. Infiltrating roofless ruins had its advantages. There at the rear of the temple, nestled near the junction of the second pylon and the massive outer wall of the temple, a sand-covered tarp covered a twenty-foot square area.

Tomas shifted along the wall until he could see what the tarp was hiding. Suspended ten feet off the ground, the tarp concealed an enormous rune web.

Similar to the incredible rune web he'd found in the catacombs under Palatine Hill in Rome, this web was made of three levels. Not quite as large as that last one, it was still an impressive structure. It had to be consuming at least a hundred soulmasks, with more piled in bins nearby.

Four enchanters worked the web, scurrying along scaffolding that surrounded it like a steel skeleton, checking connections, replacing spent soulmasks, and inscribing new runes. The soulmasks still glittered like quicksilver even in his shadow-sight. The rest of the chapel looked strangely dim, as if steeped in deeper shadow than the rest of the temple complex.

"I've got eyes on target. Chapel on the right side of the first court. I'm going in," Tomas reported softly.

Anaru replied, "Roger. Trucks are free of the barge. Closing on the Egyptian lines."

Distant gunfire punctuated his words. Some of the Egyptian soldiers had escaped the foam.

"Taking fire," Anaru reported calmly.

"Snipers engaging," Quentin said.

Tomas didn't hear the snipers. They would be using suppressed guns as they fired on the Egyptian soldiers from a distance of six hundred yards. The drug delivery rounds weren't fatal, but they still packed a wallop. Mortals would succumb to the fast-acting drugs in less than three seconds. Gunfire faded away as the Egyptian soldiers fell to the enforcer barrage.

Heka were swarming up the first pylon and would begin firing on the trucks in moments. Tomas had to destroy the web now. He jumped off the wall, landing lightly on enhanced legs, already planning how to silently take out the enchanters and set his charges. With all the ruckus going on outside, no one would know anything was amiss until he blew this entire area.

His plans evaporated as excruciating pain lanced through his torso. His super-enhancement was still active, but suddenly colors snapped back to normal. He was no longer invisible.

Tomas gasped and staggered against the wall, his strength draining away as he was assaulted by an invisible force.

No, he realized too late. Not invisible. Some kind of defensive web. He'd actually seen it with his shadow-sight, but had failed to realize the truth of the strange darkness clinging to the temple.

He needed to escape, to regroup, but he dropped to one knee under the brutal onslaught, his thoughts slowing and becoming fuddled. He tried to call for help, but his voice wasn't working.

A shadow drew his gaze slowly upward.

Hongwu was striding toward him, a thick-bladed sword in his hand.

81

Time is like an enormous pot, into which all ugliness and beauty are thrown,
all happiness and grief, all life and all death.

~YO YO, GHOST TIDE

AS SARAH HEADED for the waiting machines, she reviewed the multiple layers of defensive ciphers she'd built around the room to protect against Vlad. She hoped the main events taking place in the nearby Luxor temple would keep him occupied, but couldn't ignore the possibility that he might try to take her soul again.

After the sight of him sucking out the soul of that poor, unfortunate reporter, she felt grateful she'd spent so much effort preparing her defenses around the machines. If Vlad tried to attack her while she lay helpless, mind stuck in the memoryscape, he was in for a very bad day.

A squad of enforcers with vampire runes and experience fighting them were on standby nearby. They could finish off the undead monster if he managed to escape the layered trap she had prepared for him. Everything was ready. She felt confident in the plan as she stopped for a quick bathroom break.

She hurried, eager to get into the memoryscape and get the dangerous mission over with. All she had to do was keep Xiao busy until Tomas or Gregorios could locate her sleeping body and incinerate it. She stepped to the sink to wash up, distracted by the many ciphers she planned to use in the upcoming fight.

A deep chill crept into her limbs and down her spine. She shivered, and recognized with a jolt of dread what that feeling meant.

She spun, a fraction of a second slow as she shifted gears from planning a fight to actually fighting. Invisible hands grabbed her ankles and hauled her feet out from under her.

She didn't have time to activate any of the ciphers she'd been planning, and barely managed a startled cry as her body was flung forward into the sink counter. She got one hand up to help break the fall, but still cracked her head solidly against the porcelain sink as she smashed through the counter with terrific force.

Momentarily stunned by the brutal attack, she offered no resistance as strong hands flipped her over. Vlad appeared next to her as his invisible illusion was flung aside. His pinched face looked smug as his paralyzing gaze sapped her strength. Clones appeared beside him as his howling soul-wind rushed around Sarah, flinging her hair in every direction and chilling her with the hopeless, agonized cries of the trapped souls.

Of all the rotten luck! She'd prepared so well to fight him in a room barely fifty feet away. She hadn't expected to have to fight for her life in a bathroom.

Sarah tried to lunge off the ground, but the clones seized her arms and slammed them back down so hard they cracked the tiled floor. Vlad leaned over her. At such close proximity, frozen by his evil gaze, her protective, anti-vampire runes began waning.

She struggled violently, but too many clones held her down. She lacked leverage against the slippery floor, and Vlad's influence was already draining her strength with terrifying speed. She felt icy cold slowing her muscles.

Vlad chuckled as he knelt over her, his expression hungry. He smelled like cheap cologne, but his yellowed teeth had not yet extended into fangs to rip into her jaw.

"Sarah, you untrained fool. How many times do I need to explain it to you? You belong to me." He reached out to stroke her cheek.

"Don't touch me!" Sarah screamed, fighting back her growing terror with anger.

She couldn't pull her arms out of the clones' grip, so she contorted her body and kicked the vile creature hard enough to catapult him right through both bathroom stalls. One of the toilets shattered and started spraying cold water into the room.

Before she could kick the clones off, two other clones appeared over her feet and dragged them down. Sarah struggled mightily, but they were immensely strong, and each felt like they weighed several hundred pounds, even though they looked like emaciated versions of Vlad.

The howling demon wind gusted over Sarah, rolling down her body with tangible weight, pressing her to the floor. The souls trapped in that wind changed their tune. It sounded mocking, taunting, and devoid of all hope.

Vlad returned in a flash and stood over her, looking amused by her attempt at defiance.

She said, "Don't you know it's rude to follow a girl into the bathroom?"

He chuckled and said, "Monster, remember? Kicking me in the ribs was plenty rude enough for a response. As I was saying, I own you, Sarah. I let you believe you were safe cowering behind that rune because it suited my purpose. I've tracked your movements and felt your preparations. All you've accomplished was to make it easier for me to harvest your soul now that the day of victory is at hand."

His words horrified her. Could he be telling the truth? Had he so completely manipulated her? She doubted it. He was a vile liar.

"If you're so tough, let me up and face me like a man instead of scuttling through the shadows like a cockroach."

His veneer of calm evaporated under a storm of rage. He seized her by the front of her shirt and hauled her off the floor, holding her several inches off the ground. He shouted right in her face, his voice magnified many times by the power of the hundreds of souls he'd consumed.

"I am more than a man! I am your master!"

"Master this, freak," Sarah spat back.

His angry move had freed her hands from the grip of the clones. Now she made a single mark with her finger, activating her personal, skin-tight protective shield. It formed around her, severing his grip and allowing her to drop to her feet. She immediately punched him center-mass with all her enhanced strength.

The blow should have knocked him through the wall. She hoped it would knock him through the next room and land him right in the middle of the waiting vampire-hunting enforcement squad.

It didn't.

Vlad simply vanished, his soul-wind laughing around her. He reappeared close to her left side and snatched her arms as she spun to face him. He was shockingly strong, and despite her enhancements, she couldn't break free.

"You can't try the same tricks twice, dear Sarah," he mocked as they shifted across the slippery, wet floor. He opened his jaws wide, and his fangs extended. She noticed with a shiver that they were marked with glowing runes.

"I thought you weren't a rune warrior any more," she exclaimed.

"I consume runes now. They no longer consume me. Hongwu marked this rune. Let me introduce you to it."

She couldn't quite make out the details of the rune, and he didn't give her time. He lunged, fangs aimed at her jawline again.

About time.

Sarah still recoiled uselessly, but he drove in for the kill anyway, his rune-covered teeth latching onto her protective shield right at her jawline. She felt terrified and relieved at the same time. She had needed him to do that, but couldn't let him know that's what she needed to spring her last-ditch defensive trap.

Hongwu's fang runes included a counter rune to cut through her shield, and Vlad's teeth sank into it as if it was a chunk of meat. He'd tear through in another second.

That was way too long.

As soon as his teeth made contact, they triggered the cipher on her silver piece of eight hanging by its golden chain around her neck.

The entire coin blasted off its chain, as if shot from a gun. The glittering coin drove up into Vlad's jaw so hard it speared right through the tissue at the bottom of his mouth and embedded into his skull at the top. The impact snapped his head back and somersaulted him off his feet.

Perfect shot. He glared up at Sarah as he rolled back to his knees, reaching for the coin driven up into his mouth.

That's when the fire started.

The second phase of the cipher activated, drawing from Vlad's own immense soul power and converting it into pure, fiery heat. White-hot flames ignited in his mouth, and he staggered back, shrieking and trying vainly to unseat the coin.

His undead skin melted under the fervent heat, and flames poured out his mouth and enveloped his head. The clones still gathered around Sarah faded away as he lost concentration.

Sarah grimaced in disgust, but still drew her pistol, pressed it to his temple, and said, "Own this, creep."

Then she pulled the trigger, firing a specialty round into his brain. That bullet contained another cipher, one she'd designed to strike at the heart of what made him a vampire.

It included the Egyptian symbol for Ra, the sun god, with supporting symbols from three other ancient civilizations that all reinforced the power of the sun. She hoped it would eclipse the Ophiuchus symbol, which formed the heart of the runes that created vampires.

Vlad convulsed and staggered back, but the bullet did not blast out the back of his head. Instead of spraying brain matter everywhere, three ghostly soul masks erupted from his eyes and zoomed away with faint, exultant cries before splatting greasily against the mirror.

Well, that was a start. If she could knock away captured souls with every round, she could eventually weaken him enough to do some real damage. So Sarah emptied the magazine. Holding onto his thrashing arm, she kept the pistol close to his head and pulled the trigger as fast as possible.

With every bullet, more captured souls erupted from the savaged vampire's eyes. His screeching intensified until it hurt her ears, and the howling of his soul-wind intensified like a tornado, tearing at the small room and ripping at Sarah.

She had to release him to reload, and in that second, his soul-wind snatched her off the floor and slammed her into the mirror. It shattered, and the shards whipped away, only to return a second later and break into dust as they speared into her. Without her shield, the glass would have torn her apart.

Sarah pushed away from the wall and tried to aim at Vlad's convulsing form. She'd fill him with so much lead, his head would explode from the sheer weight of the bullets.

Vlad disappeared.

One second he was staggering, hands grasping at his burning mouth, shrieking like a damned soul. Then he was gone. The silver piece of eight fell to the floor with a soft clang, and heavy silence settled over the bathroom, broken only by the steady splashing of the broken toilet pipe.

A second later, the bathroom door exploded off its hinges as heavily armed enforcers charged into the room, guns ready.

Had Vlad heard them, fled before they could finish what Sarah had started? Tomas had said Vlad was a master at running away. She was starting to understand his frustration.

Vlad's voice spoke softly into Sarah's mind. He sounded furious. *"You sealed your fate, Sarah. I'll torture you for endless days, but first I will take the soul my servant marked, one you care about, and his life will feed my healing."*

Sarah spun, gun up, ciphers at the ready, but Vlad did not reappear. Enforcers formed a defensive team around her, all facing out, seeking the vampire. Their leader, Dominic, asked repeatedly if she was okay, but Sarah waved away the question, turning slowly, gun ready, seeking the monster. She waited, breathing fast, expecting a new ambush any second, but none came. Vlad was really gone.

Dominic grabbed her arm and forced her to look at him. "Sarah, are you all right?"

She nodded, her tension evaporating, and she leaned against him, feeling exhausted. "I'm okay. I drove him off."

"Notify all teams the vampire made contact on the ship. Activate all defensive measures," Dominic ordered as he led her from the bathroom, their feet splashing through three inches of water from the gushing toilet.

Only when Sarah reached the hallway did she the vampire's final threat register. Who was he talking about? Had he marked someone else? Then it hit her and she gasped.

She wasn't wearing a throat mic yet, since she was supposed to be in the memoryscape so she turned to Dominic and said, "Quick. Warn Gregorios. Vlad is coming for Carlo!"

He relayed the message, listened for a moment, then said, "Gregorios acknowledges the threat. Says they've got a warm reception planned."

She sighed, feeling relieved by the response.

Dominic pointed down the hall toward the room with the waiting machines. "I'm glad you're okay. We'll escort you to your position."

She nodded and together they moved in that direction. She had work to do. She'd failed in every attempt to stop Xiao, and today she would face the dread cui dashi alone, but this time she had to win.

She wouldn't get another chance.

82

If only Grandfather knew what his rune would accomplish in the fertile ground of my young mind. To my knowledge, no one else has discovered his rune, and I lack the power to share it. So I will share the wonders of thought it opens to my mind. To honor him, I will continue to discover the secret truths of the world.

~ZHANG HENG, ASTRONOMER, MATHEMATICIAN, SCIENTIST, AND POET DURING THE HAN DYNASTY

EIRENE ROSE from her chair in the communications hub and handed her headset to Abdallah. Nearby, Quentin was coordinating the first strike with Tomas' team. It sounded like the assault would be as challenging as they'd feared, but they could pull it off.

She wanted to wait for Tomas to report on his assault of the web, but couldn't spare the time. She trusted him to get the job done.

"Abdallah, keep an eye on things. My turn." Eirene plugged in her tactical earpiece. "Assault team Luxor, I am commencing my run. Initiate storm cloud cover."

As voices chimed in with affirmatives she added, "Melek, begin your strike."

"Advancing on Egyptian positions now." His smile radiated through the connection.

"Remember the Egyptians are not the enemy today. Don't let your bias get ahead of you," Eirene reminded him.

"Roger. They're not the enemy today," Melek replied, sounding a bit disappointed.

"Good hunting," she added.

"And to you."

Nabil's voice came over the line in a muted grumble. "I can't believe we're wishing them good hunting now."

Eirene allowed a fierce grin on her Amazon features as she took the stairs down to the main deck three at a time. Dressed in battle gear, she only needed to don her wraparound sunglasses before calling to Sarah to activate her new, personal super-rune.

"Activating now. Good luck," Sarah told her.

Eirene sucked in a shuddering breath as raw energy rippled through her. She'd stayed up late practicing with the amazing new rune the night before, but still laughed with the thrill of it.

Everything around her seemed to slow. Even a nearby gull flapped its wings in slow motion. It wasn't an illusion. Sarah's mad cipher skills were truly exceptional. The new super rune slowed time for her, allowing her to slip between those lengthened seconds. To the outside world, she would be barely visible when standing still. And when she moved, that's when it got really fun.

With a burst of speed, Eirene shot down the gangplank toward the Egyptian lines. The soldiers looked alert. No doubt they'd heard about the assault just commencing against Karnak.

Unlike the Karnak complex to the north, the Luxor temple was situated very close to the Nile. They'd tied up the ship on the quay ridiculously close. She couldn't believe the entire area hadn't been blocked.

By the time she hit the street, Eirene was moving like the Flash or like Dash from *The Incredibles*. She loved that movie and loved that kid's attitude. Cars passing on the highway seemed only to creep along as she tore past and closed on the Egyptian lines at terminal velocity.

She circled the compound in what the world counted as three seconds. She could have moved faster, but was slowed by the need to pause at each truck, armored vehicle, and tank to slap onto their sides the magnetic disks that contained ciphers Sarah had prepared in advance.

Soldiers started when she rushed past. By the time they looked around to see what they'd glimpsed out of their peripheral vision, she'd already zipped away, leaving them wondering if they'd only imagined something. Eirene completed her circuit before the engine of the first truck coughed and fell silent. Each vehicle in turn followed suit.

The ciphers acted in a fashion similar to the rune web the heka had deployed within the temple grounds, snuffing out all fire. In addition, they triggered a powerful magnetic field that added another layer of trouble for those vehicles. Ammunition would stick to barrels and movable components would lock together, completely disabling the military hardware.

Eirene returned to the ship just as the first volley of specialty ammo was fired from the rainmaker aboard the support ship in the center of the Nile, four miles upriver. The projectiles arced high into the air before plummeting down over the unsuspecting troops stationed around the temple.

These rounds were set to explode at one hundred feet. Six shells delivered two types of payload. The first was standard tear gas, and the clouds of chemical mist scattered choking, coughing soldiers. Officers tried to retain order, shouting for their men to don gas masks.

Then the next round detonated. It was a custom bomb developed by Quentin, a special type of malodorant that dispersed clouds of stench across the target zone.

The orange fumes clung to anything it contacted and continued to emit a stench so foul, Quentin described it as a convention of toxic porcupines locked in a sewer filled with human feces, fermented in sulfur and brought to a boil. Eirene had caught a whiff of a less potent version of the chemical the day before and had nearly puked.

When the malodorant descended upon the already-disoriented troops, they scattered. The officers who had been trying to maintain order joined the mass exodus.

"Quentin, I owe you a kiss for that one. Brilliant," Eirene laughed, then added, "Assault team, roll out. Let's crash the party."

Bedlam enveloped the nearby Egyptian military lines and scattered spectators and protesters alike. A quarter mile away, the crews of two helicopters parked on a makeshift airstrip were scrambled to respond.

As the flight crews raced to their vehicles, Melek approached the pair of guards stationed at the outer perimeter barricade. He walked with purpose, but not in a threatening manner. His hands were thrust deep into his pockets, and he was looking at the ground.

He was whistling the theme song from *Ironman*, one of his all-time favorite movies. The guards didn't challenge him until he was twenty feet away. Still approaching, he looked up, his expression surprised.

"What?" he asked in Arabic, removing earbuds linked to an MP3 player clipped to his belt.

"Back away," the first guard shouted, his assault rifle pointing in Melek's general direction, but not yet in a firing position. "This is a restricted area."

"But my home is right over there." Melek pointed behind the guard.

The man actually turned to look at the nearby tenements on the far side of the next parking lot. His partner wasn't fooled, but unlike the first guard, he hadn't even unslung his rifle yet. His mouth opened to cry a warning, but by then it was already too late.

Melek crossed the distance to the first guard in two leaping strides, exulting in his youthful strength, magnified by his enhancement runes and special ciphers added by Sarah.

He'd never imagined he might accept runes applied by anyone but himself to his body. Sarah was the rune warrior, and he felt deeply honored to wear the special rune she'd designed for him. He might have strayed beyond the black and white lines he normally lived his life by, but the super rune he wore linked him to both Sarah and Eirene, and he felt no shame.

With a single right hook, he caught the gullible guard at the base of the chin, knocking him off his feet and into dreamland. The second guard was starting to pull his rifle around when Melek ripped the horizontal barrier pole from its flimsy mounts and clubbed him with it. The long wooden pole shattered, as did the guard's jaw.

Still whistling, Melek sprinted to the first helicopter, a deadly, American AH-64 Apache attack helicopter. In the air, it was one of the most feared aircraft.

On the ground, not so much.

The flight crew was in the process of climbing into the cockpit when Melek vaulted over them, landed on the roof, and ripped the main rotor off its mount with a single, mighty heave. He lifted the entire four-bladed rotor and drove one blade down through the windshield, the pilot's chair, and into the deck beneath.

He saluted the stunned pilots. "Don't think about it. Just take an early lunch break."

Melek jumped down from the disabled helicopter and turned

toward the second, an older model UH-60 Blackhawk. The door gunner had noticed him attacking the Apache and had reacted with remarkable speed for a simple, unenhanced mortal. The sound of the bolt racking back on the door-mounted M60 machine gun sounded loud over the distant screaming of soldiers caught in the clouds of tear gas.

Melek stopped whistling and charged, focusing on his new super rune and willing it to life. Sarah had set it to activate when he triggered Eirene's signature rune at its heart.

The door gunner opened fire and a barrage of lead ripped the air between them, punching through Melek's chest in twenty places.

He felt nothing. Could he really exult over the effects of a maybe-not-quite-all-pure enhancement?

Absolutely. Melek laughed as he sprinted through the torrent of lead, his body somehow dispersed in such a way that the bullets could pass through his flesh without tearing it. The bullets ripped into the side of the nearby Apache helicopter and the gunner reflexively released the trigger.

Melek couldn't tell if he was more surprised by the unplanned damage or by the specter of an enemy still advancing through such a barrage. Melek leaped into the cargo bay of the helicopter beside the shocked gunner and allowed his ethereal form to solidify. He was the only person beside Sarah herself who had ever used the ethereal form, and the experience was indescribably amazing.

He patted the man on the shoulder. "I know it's difficult. Just try to stay flexible."

Then he punched the man in the nose. No one was that flexible. The poor fellow's nose broke and he fell out of the door, moaning.

"Evacuate!" Melek shouted as he detached the heavy door gun from its mount and fired a warning shot into the cockpit above the pilots' heads.

When they obediently dove out of the helicopter, he hosed down the cockpit with machine gun fire, destroying every major component.

"I like this gun," Melek said to the groaning gunner when he dropped back to the pavement. "I think I'll keep it."

With the machine gun draped over one shoulder and the heavy case of shells in his other hand, Melek strode away, whistling again.

When he cleared the outer perimeter he called in. "Helicopter pad secure. I'm going to find my son."

'He just committed murder! We must denounce him.'

"Easy, Niccolo," Gregorios muttered.

'Easy? I agreed to help, agreed to submit to your devil ways upon the request of His Holiness! But this is madness. These men—'

"Just take it easy," Gregorios soothed.

Cardinal Niccolo Alberti was starting to struggle, to fight for control as all souls eventually did when sharing a form with another. The man's faith had helped him stay strong, and Gregorios had been impressed to discover the cardinal actually had a lot of faith to draw upon. It wasn't always a guarantee.

"Another few minutes and justice will be done."

He thought the words more than spoke them. With the cardinal's face layered over his own, Gregorios had entered the temple complex using the same trick Xiao's children were using to control the leaders of world super powers. It was difficult to maintain the stack without hurting the soul he was sharing the body with, but since this really was Niccolo's body, Gregorios tried to be a respectful guest.

Speaking through Niccolo's lips he shouted, "In the name of the holy church, I denounce the murder of that man and excommunicate you and the devil who killed him from communion."

'You can't do that,' Cardinal Alberti cried, his mind-voice shocked.

"It's all part of the act," Gregorios assured him. "I'm trying to get a response."

Dr. Chang looked surprised. Gregorios had no idea if the man practiced any religion, but a public excommunication clearly hadn't been part of his plans for the day.

He scowled and said, "Your authority is broken. Your day is past. The future has come!"

"That's not what I'm hearing," Gregorios said just as the first tear gas rounds exploded over the northern flanks of the Egyptian lines.

"What's going on out there?" Dr. Chang shouted as clouds of smoke billowed above the outer walls.

Gregorios could hear the soldiers scattering in confusion. He wished he could get a feed from Eirene to witness the chaos.

Heka fighters came running from where they'd been concealed deeper in the temple complex and massed in the main gate and near secondary openings into the ruin. These men carried heavier weapons, including RPGs and M60 machine guns.

The Chinese ambassador shouted, "Western terrorists! We will not submit to your atrocities again."

His security detail snapped firearms into shooting positions, pointing at the Americans and the Brits. Those ambassadors retreated behind their men, who drew their own firearms, even though none of the guns would work. No one fired yet, but the tension grew to palpable levels.

Dr. Chang made a dismissive gesture. "Put your guns away. They will not work here. This site is holy, purged of your corrupting technology."

"Is that why your men all carry assault rifles?" Gregorios asked.

"A precaution against interruption until the arrival of the new king of the world."

Heka fighters in the gateway gagged and retreated as the malodorant cloud billowed into the opening.

Gregorios waved toward the orange mist. "Smells like maybe your man's here."

A new wind punched through the gently billowing cloud. Dark and chill, it swept through the open court around the gathered officials and news personnel. Soft wails of torment teased their ears, and Gregorios recognized the chill of evil that attended Vlad.

He snapped, "Carlo. On me."

The big Italian drew close, his pistol in hand, eyes scanning for the threat he clearly recognized. He hissed, "The vampire comes, signore."

Vlad stepped out of the mist right in front of Carlo, expression furious, teeth already extended into fangs, clawed hands reaching for Carlo. The enforcer shouted in surprise and snapped his pistol toward Vlad, but the vampire batted it away and lunged for Carlo's face.

Perfect. His arrogance had moved him into exactly the position Gregorios needed.

Gregorios leaped forward, ejecting the cardinal's soulmask as he activated his nevra core. His eyes ignited with purple flame, and fire rimmed his fingers as he intercepted Vlad and grabbed the vampire by the jaw.

Vlad tried to recoil, his gloating anticipation for the kill snuffed out and replaced by terror, but Gregorios touched him and severed his ability to move. As Vlad collapsed, his soul wind howling uselessly around them, Gregorios straddled him and prepared to remove his soulmask.

"Checkmate, Vladdy boy," he grinned.

An ear-splitting shriek rang out right beside him. Before Gregorios realized what was going on, a heavy body slammed into him and knocked him away from Vlad. Surprised, he grappled with the thing as they rolled violently over each other. Through his active nevron, he immediately recognized his assailant.

Another vampire. It was far younger than Vlad, and although it raked at him with its claws, its ridiculous assault had served only to seal its fate. Gregorios grabbed its face, severed its soul points, and ripped away its soul mask in a single, mighty heave.

As the creature's corpse dissolved into gray sludge around him, Gregorios jumped to his feet, feeling rather annoyed. Vlad's day of judgment was long overdue.

Vlad was gone. Gregorios could feel his presence nearby as his dark soul-wind moaned around him. A soft, mocking laughter echoed around the square.

Carlo rushed up to him. "Are you all right, signore?"

"Fine, but keep your eyes peeled."

A wave of shrieking and hissing drew his gaze upward toward the high railing of the mosque. Twenty vampires rushed the rail and vaulted over.

"Heaven preserve us," Carlo breathed as most of the mortals, including the heka soldiers, screamed in fear. The tide of undead swept down toward the square in an impressive display of monster might.

83

"VERY CLEVER," Hongwu said, kicking Tomas onto his back.

Racked by pain, his strength sucked away by the infernal rune web he'd jumped into, he couldn't do anything but flop helplessly to the ground.

"I'm looking forward to removing your skin to study your concealment rune," Hongwu said calmly.

"How?" Tomas could barely form the words. His jaw ached, his entire body throbbed with pain that struck in constant waves. Blood pumped loud in his ears and he smelled sand and the acrid stench of melting soulmasks. He pawed clumsily for his sidearm.

Hongwu slashed with his sword, slicing Tomas' bicep to the bone. "None of that foolishness."

Tomas grunted. Pain wasn't dulled by the web trapping him, and sharp agony erupted in his arm. He very slowly clutched at the wound. Blood gushed out the severed brachial artery and a fresh wave of exhaustion dragged against his will.

He really should have grabbed one of the personal protection cipher disks that Sarah had made. They'd run short, so he'd decided to pass his on to one of his men. He had that super rune, so what could go wrong?

A lot, apparently.

Hongwu stepped back a pace, head cocked to one side, apparently willing to watch Tomas bleed out.

He needed to *move*, to fight, to escape.

All in good time. First he needed to trust his enhancements. Tomas closed his eyes, playing up the part of the terminally injured, although he hated to lose sight of Hongwu. Sometimes the best offense was guile.

The hot blood pumping around his hand had already slowed as his supercharged healing runes closed the wound. At least the strange web Hongwu had used to disable him wasn't interfering with that. He'd regret that oversight.

Tomas was captain of the legendary Tenth legion as much for the number of enhancements he could handle as for his tactical leadership abilities. Already his body was adjusting, his strength seeping back in. Tomas had learned long ago how to block pain when needed.

He blinked open his eyes and whispered, "How did you disable me?"

Immediately Anaru's voice spoke into his ear. "Roger that, Captain. Strike team is nearly at the foam perimeter. We're coming."

"Bring me the sun," Tomas whispered.

"Firing," Quentin spoke four seconds later.

Hongwu jabbed the tip of his sword into the stone in front of Tomas' face. "I expected interference, but since I knew not what form an assault might come, I prepared a general trap. I admit though, your creativity surprises me."

"I'll share another surprise with you," Tomas said, nodding upward.

Hongwu actually glanced into the sky.

Tomas clenched his eyes shut.

The searing light that exploded above the temple complex burned the backs of his eyelids. Hongwu cursed and clutched at his eyes. Other heka in the complex, particularly those atop the walls, cried out in surprise and fear.

Despite his lingering weakness, Tomas lunged to his feet and tackled the enchanter, grabbing for the sword. The starburst round Quentin had fired burned above the temple like a miniature sun and consumed all shadow.

Tomas and Hongwu struggled across the chapel. The only other nearby heka were enchanters working the web, but they were still reeling from the unexpected starburst attack. Tomas was about to knee Hongwu between the legs, but remembered he was a eunuch, so punched him in the throat instead. It felt like punching iron, and Hongwu gave no indication he felt any pain.

The Chinaman broke free and pushed Tomas back, slashing with his sword.

Tomas dove to the side and came up with his pistol at the ready. He emptied the magazine of hollow-point forty-fives, firing every round into Hongwu's face. Hongwu didn't even flinch, but lunged again, the sword flickering out to slash at Tomas' side. He deflected the blow with the barrel of his gun, scarring the metal.

Not the way to win a sword fight. Tomas threw a handful of sand at Hongwu's face, gaining half a second to leap up to the nearby scaffold catwalk. He dearly wanted to toss his charges onto the web of soul-masks glowing with the complex spell, but Hongwu was already pursuing.

Tomas vaulted across the small chapel to the top of the outer wall. As soon as he cleared the chapel, his strength returned in a rush, and color drained out of his vision. His invisibility protection had returned.

Hongwu sprinted to a row of rifles near the door and snatched one up. Tomas wasn't sure if he could somehow pierce the invisibility illusion, and didn't wait around to find out. He raced east along the wall.

In that moment, the heavy machine guns placed atop the first pylon opened fire, followed by a barrage of small arms. It sounded like they had M2 fifty calibers as well as the deadly gatling-style M134. If Anaru tried storming the temple in the face of that concentrated fire, he'd sacrifice a lot of good men, despite the protective barriers most of them had surely activated. He loved the fact that the heka weren't the only ones to enjoy personal protective shields.

"Taking fire," Anaru reported.

"Rain maker returning fire," Quentin replied. "Captain, I hope you're clear."

"Don't wait on me," Tomas shouted, breaking into an all-out sprint along the top of the chapel wall, silently counting down in his head.

The barge was moored in the middle of the shallow Nile, only a few kilometers away. The mortar would be set to a high trajectory since the 240 mm cannon could easily fire ten times as far. That still only gave him about three seconds to find cover.

Whistling sounded high above as Tomas reached the wall of the second pylon. It was higher than the inner wall he was running on so he threw himself into a leaping dive and cleared the lip of the wall by inches. Rolling into a forward tuck, he dropped inside the Hypostyle Hall.

Just in time. Several loud cracks sounded against the upper edge of the architrave directly above his head. He breathed a sigh of relief as he fell forty feet to the stone below, concealed in his world of shadowed gray.

The heka standing atop the walls and milling in the open court hadn't been so lucky. The barrage of armor-piercing projectiles that rained down over the temple complex like meteorites tore through their ranks, dropping many screaming to the ground.

Tomas rushed to the gateway leading back to the first court, expecting to find piles of mutilated corpses. He did spot a few, but many of the heka were still standing. Others were staggering back to their feet, ghastly wounds closing as their healing runes, powered by captive soulmasks in their soul packs kicked in. Others, who had exceeded the power of the soulmasks were in various states of injury, from scraped to critical.

The ancient ruin had fared worse. Several of the already-crumbling columns and statues lining the first court had shattered under the cluster bomb attack. The sight stoked his anger. Hongwu would pay for every bit of damage they were forced to inflict on this ancient holy site.

"Be advised," Tomas said as he jump-scaled another column to return to the better vantage atop the architraves above the Hall. "We still have at least eighty active heka in the temple compound. Soul packs protected many. Not sure how much damage they can take."

Anaru responded, "We're too close to risk another shredder round. Cutting the foam now."

"Can we use the horizontal slicer?" Tomas asked.

"Hold on," Quentin said as Tomas ran to the western edge of the Hypostyle Hall. There he peeked out a broken section of the outer wall and caught sight of the convoy of assault trucks heading for the first pylon.

They had split into three columns. The lead vehicles were the most heavily armored and sported specially coated, v-shaped snow plows. They powered through the dense foam barrier that had grown over ten feet deep in places and stretched a hundred yards of sticky no-man's-land. Many Egyptian soldiers had finally escaped the foam and fled, but more were stuck in it, calling for help, looking like flies that had landed in colored whipped cream.

The plows sent up geysers of foam that couldn't stick to their prepared surfaces, cutting paths for the others. The spray also helped conceal them from heka snipers, but once they broke through the foam, they'd have to run a deadly gauntlet before reaching the first pylon where they could close in battle.

"Negative," Quentin came back on, his voice sounding disgusted. "The horizontals are down in the hold. I've sent men to fetch them, but it'll be at least a minute."

"We don't have that much time." His men were going to get torn apart. "I'm on it. Anaru, slow down a bit."

Tomas clambered up the jagged gap in the wall, returning to the fragmented ceiling above the Hypostyle Hall. He crossed the huge architraves and jumped down onto the north wall, on the left side of the first main court. He sprinted its length, clobbering heka off the wall as he passed. The screaming men caught the attention of heka farther on the wall, and some of them started to shoot.

Tomas hit the deck, allowing the blind shots to pass over his head. "Be advised Hongwu's got a very powerful personal protective web. He wasn't wearing a soul pack, so it's got to be an external source. Stay out of the Ramses chapel. There's some kind of heka trap that nearly took me out of the game."

Spartacus said, "Leave Hongwu to me. His tricks will not avail him."

The blind firing over Tomas' head slowed so he leaped back to his feet and raced toward the nearest heka. They were peering down the wall, trying to find the elusive threat. Tomas knocked the first one off the wall and kicked the second one in the sweets.

This man had been bleeding from a cut to the face and he shrieked and clutched at his groin. By his agonized expression, his spare soulmask must have already burned out. Tomas spun him around, yanked his rifle up, and emptied the magazine along the wall. He killed three fighters and knocked two others over the edge before the bolt locked back.

Other heka positioned atop the first pylon returned fire, so Tomas crouched behind the hapless fellow, using him as a human shield. When the withering barrage trickled off, he tossed the corpse off the wall and resumed his charge. The wall was now clear all the way to the first pylon.

He leaped up the ladder, touching only three rungs before reaching the top of the first pylon. There he kicked the heka manning the nearby M134 gatling-style heavy machine gun off the wall. He then turned the weapon sideways, pouring an insane quantity of 7.62 bullets into other heka positions.

The M134, crew-served weapon was hard-point mounted on the wall and the sound of its multiple barrels firing sounded more like a crazy buzz saw than a gun. It shredded the air above the wall with a deadly sheet of lead. It tore through men, ripping them apart far faster than their healing runes could restore them, even powered by soulmasks.

A few had more extensive protective shields, but the storm of lead knocked them cursing from the wall.

"Get in here," he shouted as he blasted apart the next machine gun nest and turned the gun on another cluster of heka in the opposite direction. "I've got most of them distracted, but it won't last."

Anaru muttered, "First he says slow down. Now he says speed up." His powerful truck accelerated, spraying foam in an enormous sheet.

One heka fighter launched an RPG at Tomas' position, but it detonated as it tried to fly through the blizzard of lead. The explosion created a crater in the three thousand year old wall and tumbled more heka over the edge.

"He's invisible," Hongwu shouted to his men as he rushed into the square below. "But he's there. Kill him!"

Bullets and rocket grenades swarmed up from four dozen heka massing in the court. Tomas rolled off the outer edge of the pylon as bullets tore into the rock all around him. A second later a missile struck the M134 and blew it off the wall.

He whooped as he rolled down the sloping front edge of the pylon, the world spinning wildly around him. Despite the bruises and scraped skin he picked up on his fast descent, the distraction had worked. The first column of trucks from the assault convoy raced through the entry gateway.

Instead of the thumping of roof-mounted machine guns and screaming of heka caught by surprise, Tomas heard the most terrifying noise.

Silence.

84

"STRIKE TEAMS ARE ENGAGED," Harriett reported when Sarah entered the main salon on the first deck of the river cruise ship.

Sarah felt relieved to step inside the well protected room. Domenico and his enforcer team remained outside, on high alert for Vlad. Sarah activated the multiple layers of defensive ciphers she'd prepared to protect the room. Let Vlad try to attack her again.

Harriett had tuned a small speaker to the assault force's main frequency. She had only recently arrived by helicopter ahead of her fast-approaching Yurak forces. Harald, the big facetaker council member, had arrived with her. He would be powering their journey into the memoryscape.

Sarah cringed to hear the machine gun fire and explosions behind Tomas' voice. He sounded strong, excited even, but the danger had been all too clear. She hated that he had to take so many risks.

Harriett, who would be taking Sarah into the dreamworld, offered a cookie. "Need a hit before we go in?"

"No, I'm fine." Sarah's stomach was clenched so tight she couldn't eat anything.

She felt worried for Tomas and furious at Vlad. A nagging worry that they'd overlooked something gnawed at her.

"Well let's do this," Harriett said, settling into her half-reclined chair and pulling on the heavy helmet. "No time like the present."

Sarah placed the other helmet over her head and snapped the jagged faceplate into position. As the heat of Harald's nevron began to burn against her face, she heard Quentin's voice from the speaker.

"Strike team one, do you copy? The line's gone dead. We're only getting static."

"Wait!" Her worries blossomed to full-blown fear and she reached for her helmet. She had to know what had happened.

Harald's deep, calm voice filled the room. "Focus on the mission. You can't help them now."

The heat of his nevron flared and Sarah sagged against the chair as her mind was dragged into Harriett's memories. The two of them appeared together in a bakery with glass shelves covered with fantastic confections stretching away in every direction. A bank of five ovens filled a distant wall, and the mouth-watering smells assaulting her senses made it clear something delicious was baking. Sarah couldn't help taking a deep breath to savor the aroma.

Then she gripped Harriett's shoulder and said, "We have to go back. Something's gone wrong."

"Trust the team." Harriett patted Sarah's hand with flour-coated fingers. She wore a cherry-red apron coated with more flour, and her hair was covered by a cooking net. "They know what they're doing, and they've got Quentin and the reserve team backing them up."

"But . . ."

Harriett handed Sarah a hot cinnamon roll with glaze dripping along its sides. "Here. This is your favorite."

"How can you think about food at a time like this?"

"Food is my center. You need to find yours."

"Mine is Tomas," Sarah cried. She almost threw the roll, but couldn't quite make herself do it.

"He is a dear. I've known him a lot longer than you. He'll be all right," she assured Sarah.

When Sarah hesitated, Harriett pressed the roll to her mouth, forcing her to take a bite. It was delicious. She had to chew, and by the time she swallowed the hot, sugary bite she had her fear under control.

Harriett said, "You have to focus. As important as Tomas' mission is, it's just the side show." She tapped Sarah's forehead, no doubt leaving a floury mark. "Focus! You can't take on Xiao if you're distracted."

"I know." She hated admitting that truth. She took a vicious bite and chomped on the pastry.

The facetaker nodded in satisfaction. "You can do this. You're the only one who can."

"I can do this," Sarah repeated, trying to convince herself.

She was stronger than ever, armed with new ciphers, with connection to the ascendants and the aeon wheel of history. She was linked to the master rune from Constantinople, as were all the major players on their team.

Hopefully it would hold out long enough to fuel the mission. They were draining astonishing quantities of soul force to power their new personal super-enhancements. It was a chance they needed to take.

Sarah was also linked to the supercharged battery rune in Beijing. It was still growing, and had reached nearly the magnitude of the lesser master rune from Caesar's almost-assassination. It was her secret weapon, hopefully strong enough to make her the match for Xiao.

She had to be. Sarah breathed deep and took another bite. As she chewed more slowly, she thought back to everything Xiao had done to her, to Alter, to her other friends. She drew her anger around herself like a shield to fight off the debilitating fear that threatened her resolve whenever she considered facing Xiao alone. This time, one of them would not awaken.

Harriett watched her closely for another minute before nodding. "All right. I can see it in your eyes. You're ready." She kissed Sarah on both cheeks and gave her a hug. "Good luck."

"Let's hope this works," Sarah said as she inscribed the aeon symbol onto her stomach.

She included two of the additional runes she'd reviewed with Melek the night before. Hopefully it really would link her more tightly to Xiao's ascendant.

The modified aeon symbol activated and began to draw her into the air. Sarah felt a growing hope. It would work. There was no going back now.

The fabric of the memoryscape parted and she stepped into the aeon dimension where history existed as a tangible thing. Once more she stood upon the invisible platform in the pitch-black emptiness, facing the ten-foot glittering earth, covered with fifty-two ascendants. She spent a moment studying the awesome sight of those loops and spirals weaving in eye-twisting patterns back into the translucent center of the globe.

They stretched impossibly far, should have extended out the back side, but somehow instead continued back and back into the eternal heart of the globe.

Sarah pulled her gaze from the mesmerizing sight and shifted around the globe until she faced Egypt and the cluster of ascendants anchored there. She took a deep breath, then stepped forward and touched Xiao's ascendant close to the very end.

This time her hands sank partially into the ascendant, and a much clearer mental image formed in her mind. She smiled with victory. The additional modifiers were working.

A large, low-ceilinged room materialized around her, filled with stone columns. It looked like a shrine and matched photos she'd seen of the interior of the mosque at Luxor.

Xiao slept on a reclined chair, but oddly enough, she was not connected to a memory walking machine. That was odd. How was Xiao planning on traveling deep into the past to fetch Sutekh?

Alter lay chained on the floor nearby. He looked unconscious, a crimson binding rune cut into his forehead.

Sarah cringed. She hated those evil binding runes. They were like invisible chains that robbed the victim of the ability to fight back. Xiao was an evil coward, and the sight stoked Sarah's anger.

That was all she was going to get from that moment. She still couldn't actually step into that vision and attack the sleeping Xiao. So she pulled her hand back to rest on the surface of Xiao's ascendant.

Xiao had gone back into history. She wasn't using a machine, but Sarah felt sure of it. Not good. If Xiao had unlocked the ability to travel her own ascendant at will, they were even shorter on time than Sarah had feared. Sarah needed to understand how it worked.

So she grasped Xiao's ascendant and jumped.

As she plunged into the globe, sliding into the past along Xiao's ascendant, the globe expanded around her, stretching far beyond her sight. It was either growing, along with all the ascendants, or Sarah was shrinking. Either way, it was unnerving.

The sensation of sliding into the past, surrounded by the weaving, intertwining whorls of the ascendants was surreal. Sarah sped up, as if the pitch was steepening. The patterns of ascendants shifted so quickly she couldn't follow them.

She clung to Xiao's ascendant, her anchor to the journey into the past. It too had grown until Sarah could lie atop it, her whole body grabbing it like a giant, twisting fireman's pole.

The close contact gave her glimpses into Xiao's history as she slid down, ever accelerating into the past. She caught glimpses of Xiao's long life, of many atrocities, which she tried to avoid looking at too closely.

Then she saw something that caught her attention and despite the importance of her mission, she willed herself to slow so she could witness the moment. She wasn't sure how she controlled her speed, but the aeon symbol on her stomach grew warm, and the moment she was focusing on clarified into stark detail.

She recognized the Forbidden City, although it was far more extensive than in modern day. Soft paper lanterns cast colorful light across the emperor's inner city. It was springtime and the air smelled of lotus blossoms, roses, and lilacs.

Xiao stood over a young, very pregnant woman who wore fine silk robes. The pregnant woman looked terrified as she knelt on a narrow bridge spanning an ornamental stream, gasping in pain as Xiao brutally twisted her arm behind her back.

The victim cried, "You cannot do this."

"You have failed, Empress Xiao Gang Kuang." Xiao spoke the name with disgust. "The Yongli Emperor has brought disgrace upon this dynasty. Another bloodline has failed."

Sarah recognized the names. The Yongli Emperor had been the last emperor of the southern Ming Dynasty. That empress was one person they'd thought Xiao might have been. It looked like they might have been partially right.

"Who are you?" the empress pleaded.

"I am the one destined to rule again," Xiao said, releasing the pregnant woman's hand and gripping her face with fingers ringed with purple fire. "I am Empress Min."

"The suffering empress? But how? You died a thousand years ago."

"I am the ancestor of this nation, and I will not suffer another dynasty to fall."

The pregnant woman sobbed, "Ancestor. You bring the blessing of heaven upon us."

"That's right. I have a special blessing for you," Xiao said with a cruel smile.

She extracted the pregnant empress' soulmask with a single mighty heave, then dropped it to the planks of the bridge. In a moment, she extracted her own soulmask, took the empress' place, assuming her body and rising as the pregnant ruler of China.

Sarah witnessed the identity theft with horror. They'd been wrong about Xiao, had underestimated the length of her history. Whatever she had done as Xiao Gang Kuang had failed, but even back then she'd focused on returning to power and ruling China. Sarah wasn't sure who the suffering empress was, and wished she had time to find out.

Perhaps that failed attempt to rally the fading Ming dynasty had sowed the seeds of Xiao's eventual plans to create her own never-ending dynasty. It seemed staggering to think of how much time she'd spent plotting and preparing. Could Sarah really block her worldwide coup at the last second?

Only one way to find out.

The sight of Xiao casually shattering the real empress' soulmask and kicking her own old body into the stream for the fish to consume renewed Sarah's determination. No murdering psycho empress was going to destroy the world when Sarah could do something about it.

She resumed her journey, speeding down the spirals of history, clutching Xiao's ascendant, seeking the point deep in history where Xiao had traveled to. As she slid through the glittering, rainbow patterns of the eternal ascendants, she was tempted to take more time, explore more of Xiao's past.

If only she had the time. While linked to the aeon, she could explore history, but out in the modern day where her body slept, time was still ticking, and the strike teams were in danger.

She decided she had learned enough. Xiao had to die.

With that goal fixed firm in her mind, Sarah slid into the murky heart of the world. As she spun and swooped along the ascendant's eternal course like a unique, exhilarating roller coaster, she caught glimpses of moments she whisked past.

The sights passed so fast, she caught impressions more than details, but she saw enough to feel a growing sense of awe. She sensed the pivotal, world-altering moments of the master runes. But she also glimpsed bits and pieces of the lives of many of the billions of people who had lived, loved, and passed on.

The ascendants recorded it all, and she saw snapshots of every aspect of the human condition, from births, marriages, and heroism to murders, assaults, and terrible atrocities. The ascendants did not judge. They just recorded.

Sarah started to feel small. She was one person among uncountable masses, but she alone was privileged to witness these glimpses. Again she wished she had more time so she could slow her slide and soak in truth of what had really happened in the world.

As she slid farther and farther back into time, she became aware of a growing pressure around her. It was kind of like the increasing water pressure when diving, but she slid through history, not water. The weight of that history became nearly tangible, growing thicker as she plunged through it.

It was as if ancient history was set more firmly into the roots of the world. Could she travel back to the creation, or would her slide be stopped by history so dense it prevented even her passage?

She didn't get a chance to find out because Xiao's ascendant twisted awkwardly and intersected another ascendant and melded with it at a single moment in time. That was unusual. Although the ascendants wove around each other, they didn't quite touch. Well, Gregorios' and Eirene's twined so close most of the time, they might as well have.

That odd conjunction seemed wrong, so Sarah willed herself to slow to a stop. She recognized the hue of Alter's ascendant as she gripped that junction of vast ascendants and willed the moment to clarify.

Time locked on and the view opened to her mind as if she had pressed her face through a thin, obscuring sheet of water to see the other side. Xiao stood in an enormous room with walls built of enormous stone blocks and massive columns holding up the high ceiling.

Every surface was covered in bright-painted hieroglyphs. The alabaster floor was flat and smooth. Braziers set in the corners struggled to warm the vast space, and the air smelled of smoke, and faintly of incense.

An Egyptian woman stood nearby, and Sarah blinked a couple of times in surprise when she realized she could see Xiao standing inside the woman. Freaky.

Had she needed a host who had actually lived that moment to

connect her to it? She was like a ghost possessing the woman, and she'd clearly usurped control. Sarah's aeon sight penetrated the disguise, though.

The Egyptian woman that Xiao had invaded was dressed in a white robe, with a circlet of gold around her forehead that held her thick, straight black hair from her face. Did the fact that Xiao had to possess a historical person limit her powers in that moment? Sarah dearly hoped so.

Through the woman, Xiao was speaking with a burly figure of a man with a shaved head and ruthless features, who only wore one of those simple Egyptian linen kilts. His black brows were drawn into a scowl. The only other adornments he wore were one of those odd, curved Egyptian swords at his hip and a heavy gold medallion on a thick, gold chain around his neck. He had to be Sutekh. Sarah instantly disliked him.

Xiao was speaking, "The time of our union is at hand, beloved. The knowledge you imparted was the final piece I needed to unlock access to the secret of the ascendant."

"What lacked I yet?" Sutekh asked hungrily.

"I will teach you once we take our places as rulers of the world and time itself. Follow the script I shared with you in my last dream visit, and all will bow to us forever."

Sutekh nodded, looking satisfied. "And to think before your arrival, I had felt confident in my ignorance."

He gestured toward a bulky sarcophagus lying nearby on an ornately carved table. The open lid revealed a tightly-packed rune web made up of dozens of soulmasks. "You are the angel of victory and the mate of my eternal soul, for I had felt convinced I stood in the moment of victory over the hated Moses."

They were speaking ancient Egyptian, but somehow the words made sense to Sarah even though she lacked a facetaker's mind to translate through like they usually did in the memoryscape. Did the aeon rune help her understand what she saw? She didn't know, but she was grateful for it.

Xiao stepped closer and placed a hand on his muscled forearm. "Today will be a day of victory, but far greater than what you had intended."

"Very well. I accept your offer and your vision. Bring me to the future, and together we will impose our rule upon the weak world."

Xiao sounded exultant as she exclaimed, "An everlasting rule, a dynasty that shall never falter."

Sutekh caressed her face, as if he could see through the Egyptian woman's form and glimpse Xiao's true self lurking inside. "I know who I am, but to stand as equal partners and rule all, you must know yourself. I promised to help you find the symbols to create your true name. Were you successful in your search?"

Not good. The conversation going in all sorts of directions Sarah didn't want them to.

Xiao nodded, smiling victoriously. "I have, and you will be the first to learn my new name, beloved."

Really not good. Xiao pulled down the front of her robe and began marking a complex rune over her heart. She was working fast, so Sarah really needed to test Melek's theory.

She spotted a row of glowing runes running down Xiao's back, where she stood inside her host vessel. They looked familiar, similar to the runes she and Melek had studied.

In fact, she'd probably stolen them from Melek's mind. The ancient runes included the serpentine, three-headed Chronos, precursor to Father Time, as well as the signature rune for Sutekh's ascendant. A labyrinth wrapped those runes, and it emptied directly over the all-seeing eye of Ra.

The construct was intricate, beautiful, and compelling, and Sarah sensed that it was the key to Xiao's ability to access that moment in the past. The woman's grasp of runes and ascendants was impressive.

The resulting runes resonated with the complex ciphers Sarah had prepared with Melek's help, but Xiao was forcing herself into that moment in a different way. Xiao was a master runesmith, but still not a rune warrior.

Sarah alone could travel the full aeon, and that gave her the advantage. She risked pulling back from the moment and returning to the aeon space, kneeling atop Xiao's ascendant. She needed to find the signature rune created by that moment in time.

Xiao's ascendant stretched wide to either side of her, like a gigantic crimson conduit pipe. The world stretched away into the murky, heavy air. Other ascendants, fading into obscurity, crisscrossed the world in the gray distance. And yet, despite her close proximity to Xiao's ascendant, somehow she could feel the pattern of the other ascendants. When she focused on that wider pattern, it snapped into clarity in her mind. That was the anchor point she needed to complete her cipher.

Eagerly, Sarah drew the complicated cipher across the surface of the ascendant where she knelt. She focused on it, willing it to activate. For a moment, nothing happened, and all she felt was tremendous resistance, as if she was trying to punch a hole through the world's biggest rubber band. It stretched, but did not part.

Sarah touched the aeon symbol on her stomach, and the new cipher activated. The connection to that historical moment snapped into place. A hole tore into the outer shell of the ascendant, directly underneath her. Sarah plunged through and landed on her feet in the temple.

Time snapped into place around her with a crack that she felt in her soul rather than heard with her ears. She looked around in astonishment, awestruck that it had actually worked. She had stepped into the past. She felt solid, but sensed that her body was still lying prone on the ship. How did that work?

She didn't have time to figure it out. Neither Xiao nor Sutekh had noticed her sudden appearance. A complex new rune that flowed across Xiao's chest looked complete, but the softly bleeding lines were not glowing yet. She hadn't activated it, probably couldn't activate it in her ghost form while inhabiting the unsuspecting Egyptian woman. Sutekh was studying the rune, a look of awe on his face.

The angle was bad for Sarah, but she recognized the signature rune for Xiao's ascendant at her heart. The construct was complex and beautiful, and she sensed enormous power in it. Her eye was drawn to marks that she recognized from several of the master runes. Xiao had created a signature rune that linked her to many of the most important moments in history, and strengthened her bond to her ascendant.

"You are truly the Queen of Time," Sutekh said reverently.

He looked very pleased. Probably thought he was hooking up with the psycho woman from his wildest dreams. The name was a bit ostentatious, but if Sarah didn't find a way to stop her, it might just prove accurate.

Time to rain on their happy parade.

Sarah said loudly, "More like princess of broken minds."

They both jumped in surprise. Xiao's thunderstruck expression was beautiful, and it bolstered Sarah's hopes she could hurt the terrifying woman in her ghostly form. Sutekh looked confused as he stared at Sarah's modern tactical garb.

Sarah winked at Xiao. Even if she couldn't hurt the cui dashi in their current state, maybe she could mess with her mind. Then she faced Sutekh and marked a new cipher onto her thigh with a glowing finger.

"Honeymoon from hell planning is over. You don't get to kill millions. Today, it'll just be the two of you."

Her newest cipher activated, and Sarah's body transformed into living quicksilver. She lunged at Xiao.

Time to see if ghosts felt pain.

85

The greater the difficulty, the more the glory in surmounting it.

~EPICURUS

TOMAS RACED after the assault team's trucks, back through the main entrance, shouting, "Anaru! Report. What's your status?"

Only static answered.

The trucks had spread out as they entered the huge square, forming a fan pattern to take advantage of the widest field of fire and form a protective barrier for the enforcers who were boiling out the backs.

The square was empty.

"Where'd they go?" Tomas asked, but again heard only static.

The square had been teeming with heka only moments ago, but now it was empty. No way could they have escaped so quickly.

He jogged toward Anaru, who stood beside the hood of the lead truck, scanning the area through the sights of his rifle. Before he could reach his second, deeper shadows rose from the ground and filled the square.

Another web.

Hongwu was the worst kind of overachiever.

The weird, shadowy fog did not assault the team with debilitating pain like the web inside the chapel had. It boiled up off the ground and filled the entire square all the way up to the top of the only complete column.

From the blank looks of his men, they saw nothing. Only Tomas' super-enhancement gave him the sight to realize the spell was growing. In the blink of an eye the area lurched, everything blurring for a single heartbeat before taking shape again.

His team saw something now. Every one of them gaped. Instead of crumbling statues, sand-scoured stone, and ruined columns, they now looked upon the glory of the Karnak as it had appeared in ancient days. Even in Tomas' grayscale sight, it was awe-inspiring. In full color, it must be breathtaking. What a weird choice for a rune web.

"Now that's a sight you don't see every day," Francesca said with a low whistle. She'd exited one of the lead trucks and joined Anaru with Spartacus. Tomas jogged over to them.

"Tell me what you see," Tomas said.

Francesca yelped at his disembodied voice. Spartacus saluted in his direction. "Well met, Captain. You've gained much honor today."

"We'll divvy up the glory when this is over. It's a web, but unlike anything I've ever seen."

"It's like they've overlaid a memoryscape onto reality," Francesca said in an awed tone.

Tomas doubted Hongwu was trying to share something wonderful in hopes they could all be friends. "Tell me what you see. I don't get the whole effect."

Francesca explained that the ground was paved in polished stone. Columns sheathed in alabaster rose to a fully-enclosed ceiling. Hieroglyphs chiseled deep into the stone were painted bright, gem-like colors. Blues and reds shone against the white backdrop despite the cool dimness of the now-enclosed space.

As she spoke, faintly glowing shapes began to coalesce all around. Enforcers snapped weapons to the ready, but Tomas shouted, "Hold your fire."

The shapes solidified into the figures of men and women, dressed in ancient Egyptian garb. Kilts and skirts and those intricate head pieces favored by old Egypt seemed popular with the dream characters. They looked as real as any of the living. Peasants with little more than simple white cloths wrapped around their hips bowed to well-dressed nobles and priests dripping with gold. Within seconds, the court filled with fake people who passed around the enforcers and crowded the open spaces.

Anaru scowled. "This complicates things. What do we do now?"

"Shut it down." Tomas turned toward the chapel of Ramses.

The memoryscape overlaying the real world tried to conceal it with a solid stone wall, but he could see through the illusion. The Egyptians filling the court looked like living shadows to him.

Then one of them didn't.

Tomas squinted at one Egyptian who looked like a priest dressed in a white robe, with a golden head piece. Inside the false identity, Tomas caught sight of a shadowy figure dressed in a heka uniform, carrying a knife.

The concealed heka closed on Anaru, his hand raised to plunge the dagger into his back.

Tomas tackled the heka, driving him into the pickup. "Anaru, this one's real!"

Anaru spun at the sound of the impact behind him. When he heard Tomas' disembodied voice, he lashed out with a meaty fist that caught the concealed heka in the jaw. The impact snapped the man's head back, but his protective web held. He tried to bring the knife up again, but Tomas grabbed his hand.

Anaru seized the heka by the head and heaved. The man's feet whipped up and over in a complete somersault before Anaru slammed him brutally into the stone floor. Even protected as he was, the wild spin and bone-shattering impact left the heka dazed long enough for Anaru to zip-tie him.

Tomas scanned the court and picked out other disguised heka moving in for the kill. He shouted, "They're disguised inside some of the fake people. We've got hostiles closing from all sides!"

The enforcers opened fire, shooting anything that moved near them. Most of the shots drilled right through the holographic fake people, but some found their marks. Without Tomas' special sight that pierced the illusion, that could have gone badly.

Realizing their plan wasn't working, most of the heka retreated toward the Hypostyle Hall. There in the doorway, Tomas caught sight of several figures and the unmistakable sight of a heavy machine gun nest being hastily set up.

He vaulted into the back of the nearest truck, this one rigged with a Yurak foam gun. He turned the weapon on the heka group before they could open up with the machine gun.

The loud hissing of the foam cannon merged with the sharp echoes of the gunfire that bounced back and forth through the enclosed space. He hosed the entire doorway, filling it with clinging foam that hardened around the machine gun, completely fouling it.

Tomas called down, "The heka are retreating into the next hall. Anaru, you're on point. Flush them out."

As Anaru barked orders, Tomas dropped back to the ground and gripped Spartacus and Francesca on the shoulders. "You two on me. We're taking the web."

He pushed them in the correct direction and trotted toward the door to the chapel. He paused when Hongwu stepped right through the solid-looking stone, again hefting his thick-bladed sword.

"Hold, Captain," Spartacus commanded. He removed his shirt and drew a pair of gladius swords from his belt. "This duel is mine."

"We're kind of in a hurry," Tomas protested. In his invisible form, he could tackle Hongwu and hold him down until they disabled him.

"There is no greater honor than mortal combat," Spartacus said, saluting Hongwu with one gladius. "I will disable the web after I defeat this enemy most deserving."

Hongwu saluted in turn, holding his sword horizontal. "Today you die for the last time, Spartacus."

"This will be a duel to remember!" Spartacus turned to Francesca. "Peradventure, Lady of Souls, have you on hand a video recorder?"

"You want me to tape your fight?" Francesca laughed, fingering her carbine as she studied Hongwu.

"Indeed. The world entire will be honored to witness this moment of glory. Who better to record it for all posterity than one of the queens of the world?"

"Oh, you're good," Francesca said, flashing a smile. "If you win that boatload of glory, what are you going to give me for helping?"

"Anything you require," he declared without hesitation.

Her smile turned wicked. "I can work with that. Tomas, you have a problem with me helping Spartacus win some glory?"

"Just make it fast glory and get that web down."

"Done."

Anaru had already led the enforcer teams into the Hypostyle Hall, spreading out to either side of the central avenue, hunting through the forest of huge pillars. In that moment, gunfire erupted with dozens of shouts of "Contact!"

Something about the sounds seemed off. It sounded like they'd all stumbled upon clusters of the enemy at exactly the same time. After all the effort to conceal themselves, why drop the illusion?

Frowning, Tomas ran for the next hall after his men as screams and more gunfire echoed into the first court.

Behind him, Spartacus whooped and charged. "Glory and honor!"

"Honor and glory," Hongwu responded, rushing to meet him.

They came together with a crash of swords that rang through the court. Holographic figures of ancient Egypt turned to watch as the two champions battled through the living memoryscape. Francesca jumped to the roof of the nearest truck, holding a tiny video camera in her hands, focused on the duel as swords flashed silver through the air.

Tomas left them to it, entered the Hypostyle Hall, and slipped to the right. Enforcers were fighting in close combat all around. Shouts of "Contact" were intermingled with screams of pain and cries of, "Medic."

What Tomas didn't hear were screams from any heka.

He closed on a pair of men fighting with deadly intensity. With his shadow-sight, he could see that both wore concealing false identities, but both false identities looked like heka. He gasped as the truth struck him like a hammer-blow.

He'd sent his men into yet another trap. This was why Hongwu had needed so many soulmasks for his web. There were no heka in this hall. His men were caught in a deeper illusion.

They were going to kill each other.

One of the nearby fighters caught the other across the stomach with a knife. The brutal slash would have opened him up if he hadn't activated his personal shielding cipher patch. It still made him stumble, and the other enforcer lunged, whipping his knife up for a mortal slash at the other's throat.

Tomas caught the knife hand. "Stop! He's one of ours!"

Gripping both men, he recognized them.

"Captain?" they both asked in unison. Then they glanced at each other in surprise, recognizing each other's voices.

"What's going on?" one of them asked, knife still held at the ready, but looking confused.

"It's another trap." Tomas shouted. The radio still wasn't working, and the rest of his men were still trying their hardest to kill each other.

86

"YOU!" Xiao hissed. Using her fingernail, she began marking another rune onto her arm.

Not this time. Sarah punched her, connecting with Xiao's Egyptian host. The blow cracked the woman's sternum and sent her screaming and tumbling away.

Sutekh stepped in front of Sarah before she could pursue Xiao. He gaped at Sarah's quicksilver skin and made a little bow. "Indeed this is a day of conjunction of the stars when goddesses walk among men."

"Call me Ma'at," Sarah said, hoping she got the pronunciation right.

She lifted her left hand, shifting her first two fingers into the shape of a long feather. The Egyptian system of gods and goddesses was very complex. She doubted anyone living in modern day actually understood it fully, but she knew enough to play with his head. Ma'at was the goddess of truth, justice and balance. She kept chaos at bay and judged the dead with her feather.

Sutekh fell to one knee, making obeisance.

Good enough for now. Sarah rushed past him after the fallen Xiao.

Xiao was already rising. She'd completed her new rune, and as she rose, her ghostly form swelled inside the Egyptian host until she filled it, then consumed it. Her features shifted to the Chinese face Sarah knew. Her outfit became one of black leather, and a thick-bladed Chinese sword appeared in her hand.

"Zeus, Mary, and Mohammed," Sarah cursed, borrowing one of Gregorios' lines. They weren't in the memoryscape, so how could she summon a sword? Sarah didn't understand exactly how Xiao had reached that moment, so she wasn't sure what rules Xiao had to follow and which ones she could break.

That was super annoying. And potentially deadly.

"How did you get in here?" Xiao demanded. She looked annoyed, but not worried.

"You're not the only one with a brain," Sarah retorted as she shifted her hands into blades. She'd used her quicksilver form to remove the head of one cui dashi. She could do it again.

Xiao glanced past her and snorted at the sight of the kneeling Sutekh. "She is no goddess, you fool. She's an enemy trying to block our rise to power."

"What has Ma'at done to you?" Sutekh asked Xiao as he hesitantly rose to his feet.

Xiao said, "I have stepped into this moment, and now I control it."

"Not if I can help it," Sarah said.

Now that she was in the historical moment, she could feel the flow of history like water trickling past her ankles. Xiao wasn't part of that flow, but seemed to stand just outside of it. She was foreign and didn't belong there.

Sarah concentrated on the ascendant pattern that represented that moment and slashed one sword-arm, leaving a glowing mark, focusing on strengthening the moment against foreign invasion.

She felt her own connection with the moment waver, but she was secured to it too strongly to break away so easily. Xiao's form wavered and the Egyptian woman returned, with Xiao huddling inside of her.

Nice. If Sarah could drive Xiao from the moment, she could let Sutekh die the way he always had. That would wreck Xiao's announced king of the world arrival.

Xiao glared from inside her host. "What ascendant did you ride? I sense no other will fighting for control, yet you change things."

"I'm going to change a lot more than your face," Sarah promised.

Then the moment of wavering passed and Xiao snapped back into her Chinese form. The two lunged at each other, and Xiao moved with her customary blurring speed.

Fueled by her mighty enhancements, Sarah actually kept up, and the two of them closed with a flurry of blows. Slashing Xiao's neck felt like trying to cut living stone. Sarah's blade-hand left a faintly glowing scrape mark, but did not penetrate.

Xiao ignored the blow, striking with hands and feet like pistons, delivering enough force to shatter weaker bones. Even Sarah's quicksilver flesh vibrated from the impacts. She kept striking, slashing and stabbing with every ounce of power she could summon, using every trick Tomas and Alter had taught her.

Xiao kept up and showed no signs of feeling pain. Her blows seemed to only grown stronger, so Sarah shifted her arms, raising sharp spikes all down their length. Xiao punched her anyway, and the spikes barely dented her flesh. Xiao didn't even wince. So unfair.

Xiao snatched for Sarah's face with burning hands, but Sarah jumped back. Xiao caught her ankle and threw her across the room. She crashed into a stone pillar, shattering it, before flowing back to her feet. Sarah was breathing fast, more from fear and adrenaline than pain. In this form, she couldn't really feel pain, although if Xiao removed her soulmask, she wasn't sure what would happen.

She was doing it! She was actually holding her own against Xiao. Now she just needed to figure out how to kill the woman or drive her permanently from history.

Instead of chasing her, Xiao had knelt on the floor and began inscribing a complex series of runes with blazing-fast fingers. She scraped the marks into the stone with her fingernails.

Sarah recognized the secret runes Melek had shared with her, but they were mixed with runes she didn't know.

"Hurry," Xiao called to Sutekh, who had watched their duel with open-mouthed amazement. "The sacrifice is awaiting your coming. All you have to do is step through."

The air above Xiao's new rune began to glow, then to burn with fierce, black flames. The fire extended to form the rough shape of a door. A wind laden with the stench of freshly opened tombs howled into the huge room.

The construct filled Sarah with a dread that reached into her soul. This was wrong at a fundamental level. She understood the purpose of the rune, even though she had never seen some of its components before. Xiao had broken history, had punched a rift through time, connecting this point in history to the future.

The symbols that Xiao used finally helped Sarah understand.

Alter must share the same ascendant as Sutekh. That's how Xiao planned to pull Sutekh into the present. She wasn't so much breaking history as swapping two souls. She'd pull Sutekh's soul to the far end of the ascendant, but only because a similar soul mirrored the move. Sutekh's arrival would suck Alter back into the past, sacrificing him in ancient Egypt to allow Sutekh to walk in the future.

"No way," Sarah muttered. She charged.

Sutekh took one step toward the portal before Sarah caught him.

"Not so fast." With her blades morphed back into hands, she punched him twenty times in the face, smashing his nose and breaking one cheekbone.

The blows would have killed most mortals and even most heka, but although they knocked him senseless, he survived the barrage. The more she injured him, the more resistance she felt.

Sarah was standing in the past. Well, some part of her had taken physical form in the past, via her aeon dimension journey. Changing the past would mean actually changing one of the ascendants deep in the bowels of the earth. She sensed that the forces involved in making such changes dwarfed anything she'd ever tried to control.

She couldn't simply kill Sutekh.

So Sarah threw him across the room and left him in an unconscious heap while she rushed Xiao. She had to close that rift.

Xiao lunged to meet her in a flying tackle.

Perfect.

Sarah flowed into a ball and rolled under Xiao's flying form. She formed feet and kicked Xiao as she soared past, sending the cui dashi tumbling across the huge room. Sarah flowed back to her feet and shifted her right hand into a sharp-edged blade. She ran to the rift, slashing her blade through the construct.

"No!" Xiao shrieked, blurring across the room toward Sarah.

The rift didn't dissolve as Sarah had hoped. Instead it started to flicker, shifting from pure black to crimson, then rippling through all the colors of the rainbow.

The sight distracted Sarah for a second. That's all it took for Xiao to tackle her. The two fell to the floor and rolled, pummeling each other with fists and blades. Their writhing struggle rolled them right into the rift.

Everything stopped.

The flow of time ceased against Sarah's skin and silence gripped the world. The two of them hung suspended in blank, empty space. It wasn't black or white, but simply empty, colorless. Sarah felt no air against her skin, smelled nothing, heard nothing. Only she and Xiao existed there in the broken space between time.

She and Xiao exchanged fearful looks. Not good when that freak got scared by the mess she was making.

Then they were sucked backward so violently Sarah's body stretched. They returned to Sutekh's time with a concussion that rocked all Sarah's senses, threw both of them across the room in different directions, and shattered columns. Heavy stones rained down upon the polished floor. The rift was swaying violently as it gaped open wider. Sarah caught glimpses of the ruined, modern-day Luxor temple beyond.

A cacophony of howling, growling, and hissing filled the room as dozens of monstrous shapes rose from the floor and the walls. Monsters of every shape and size pulled themselves out of the stone on all sides. Some looked Chinese, others nightmares from Sarah's deepest fears, and yet others the strange hybrid shapes of Egyptian mythology, part man and part beast.

They howled and shrieked and writhed as every one of them were sucked into the rift and tossed out the other side.

Sarah gasped in horror. She and Xiao had broken something fundamental.

They'd cracked time, and nightmares were filling in the void as they always did when the integrity of memory moments were broken. But this time, those monsters were taking on tangible form like they had in China. Worse they were plunging through the portal and landing right in the middle of the unsuspecting crowd in Luxor.

It would be a massacre.

Sarah rose, intending to try to shut down the rift again. The view into Luxor began to flicker wildly, as if the rift were bouncing around the inner court. In one, she saw men fighting each other. In another, she witnessed men fighting monsters. Then she spotted Melek leaning over Alter's chained form in the mosque.

Xiao rose from the broken rubble of the wall she'd crashed into, her face livid. "Enough! Look what you've done, you witless worm."

"It's not as fun when someone stands up to you, is it?"

"I'm trying to make a better world," Xiao spat.

"From where I stand, it looks like you're trying to wreck it."

"My son thought to raise you to glory, but you lack vision."

"Come here and I'll show you vision," Sarah said, shifting her hands again into blades.

"So be it," Xiao said, assuming an imperial glare. "You think you're saving the future? Let's see how much you love a future when all those dear to you are already dead."

So much for trying to impose peace on the world. At every stage, Xiao only used intimidation and murder. Sarah was sick of it. As if she needed more reasons to deny Xiao the ability to master time and murder people in the past. Sarah really had to destroy the twisted freak.

"Your fight is with me," Sarah snapped as she charged.

She was mad, but Xiao had centuries more experience fighting. She met Sarah with such a fierce onslaught of fists that she tumbled away, momentarily dazed, despite her incredible enhancements and quicksilver form.

"Be ready, my lord husband," Xiao cried to Sutekh, who was sitting up, holding his bloody face. "I will return for you."

Sarah leaped at Xiao, but the cui dashi faded from the moment, leaving a terrified and confused Egyptian woman cowering on the stone floor.

Not good. Sarah couldn't let Xiao return to the present day to sacrifice Alter. With hands trembling with fear, Sarah inscribed another modifier to the aeon rune on her stomach. With a tremendous lurch, she was sucked out of the historical moment and crashed back into Harriett's memory. She tumbled through a glass display case and sent pastries flying.

"Are you all right?" Harriett asked, pulling Sarah to her feet with one hand. With the other, she was holding a pan of fresh-baked cookies.

"Not really. We need to go."

"Where's Xiao?"

"Should be waking up in Luxor. She's angry, and we need to stop her before she kills everyone."

87

He will win whose army is animated by the same spirit throughout all its ranks.

~SUN TZU

GREGORIOS GRUNTED as he scanned the tide of deadly vampires swarming down toward him. The square was mostly full of officials, reporters, and security forces whose weapons would not work.

Vlad was playing his hand early, which suggested they had rattled him and he felt threatened. That was all well and good, but it wouldn't help the dozens of people who were about to get massacred.

"Quentin, we have vampires," he said as he moved to intercept the lead monsters. "Carlo, no one faces these monsters alone. Pair up and concentrate fire on their faces."

Carlo was already barking orders, and his men were rushing to respond. They were experienced against humans, and although they had heard Carlo's tales about the vampire that had bitten him and Sarah, they were new to their enhancements. Things were about to get ugly.

Quentin responded. "Scout team, bring the sunshine now!"

The leading edge of the vampire horde bounded toward Gregorios, snarling, with fangs already extended, clawed feet scratching gouges in the stone floor in their excitement to feed.

He planned to give them severe indigestion. Gregorios ignored the screams of the civilians and the useless clicking of security firearms as he shook out hands already burning with his active nevron.

The vampires looked young, and they hadn't bothered with any illusions or soul wind. They were overconfident. Gregorios wouldn't have worried about taking on any two or three of them.

Nothing like a challenge to really feel alive. He'd lost sight of Vlad, but no doubt he'd show up when it was most inconvenient.

The closest vampires shrieked their soul hunger.

Gregorios charged.

Something blurred past him and slammed into the front ranks of the vampires, scattering them and breaking their momentum. Then the blur slowed, and Gregorios recognized Eirene as she ripped the soul mask off of one surprised vampire.

"You think you get to have all the fun?" She asked as she tossed the melting soulmask aside. Empty corpses dissolved into the stones. She blurred between three other vampires lunging toward her.

Gregorios grinned and leaped upon the nearest vampire, one of the ones she had knocked down. His nevron sealed to the monster's soul points, and he yanked the soulmask out in a single heave. "You've never taken more vampires than me. There's no way it'll happen today."

"You're on."

He launched into the air, his super rune activating, allowing him to soar over a couple of surprised vampires. Turning a deadly fight against undead monsters into a competition helped keep the fun alive.

He crashed down onto another vampire and took that soulmask in under two seconds. It was close to his record. Today, maybe he could beat it.

They'd distracted many of the vampires, but as fast as he and Eirene were, mortals were still in trouble. Then Carlo's team leaped into the fray, opening fire on the disorganized mess of vampires. That only served to draw the monsters' attention.

Eirene said, "You only got two because I distracted them."

"I never refuse a gift from a lovely lady," Gregorios said as he punched down a couple of vampires who were feeling a little too friendly. A heady feeling of battle lust swept through him, and he plunged into the thickest knot of vampires, shouting ancient Greek battle cries.

They were new enough creations that they didn't know how to deal with the debilitating effects of his active nevron. Most of them stumbled and shrank away from him, giving him a critical advantage. If enough of them swarmed him at the same time, they could give him a pretty bad day. He didn't plan to give them the chance to figure it out.

As he leaped back into the air again, he glanced across the square. Carlo's men were working with remarkable precision for mortals so new to the real world. They maintained a withering rate of fire into the vampires' faces, distracting their targets long enough so they could close with deadly blades.

Warned by Carlo's experience and some pointers from Nabil, and armed with rune-enhanced blades, they tore into the vampires with a vengeance. The Italians targeted the monsters' joints with deadly precision.

That meant they at least had a fighting chance. Even young and inexperienced vampires go down hard, and their feeding frenzy magnified their ferocity tenfold. Despite the Italians' fierce onslaught, the monsters slashed and bit, knocking soldiers aside and pouncing on them.

That fierce onslaught would overwhelm most of Carlo's team in seconds. Even Sarah's protective ciphers only slowed those deadly fangs as vampires seized struggling soldiers and bit savagely at their soul points.

Standing still like that, face turned at a perfect angle as they tried to bite through the protective ciphers made Gregorios' job so much easier. He'd never considered sending in soldiers as chew toys to distract vampires when he hunted them.

While Carlo's men fought with every bit of strength and skill, Gregorios changed tactics and swooped over the battle lines. He jumped from one almost-feeding vampire to the next, ripping out the soulmasks of the distracted monsters and tossing them aside.

He wished he could see Vlad's face. Well, he wished he could seize Vlad's face for about two seconds, but seeing the head vampire's rage would be fun too.

He might have planned to use his young vampires as a final defense to protect Xiao while she slept, but he'd unleashed them too soon. Worse, they were getting destroyed instead of subduing all the mortals in the square and spreading fear throughout the world through the media feeds.

Gregorios loved ruining Vlad's day. He'd never seen anyone create so many vampires. Vlad must have worked with that annoyingly competent Hongwu for months to accomplish the remarkable feat.

All that effort was about to melt into the stones.

Then a new chorus of howling, growling, and bloodlust shrieks echoed through the square, drawing his gaze to the column-lined path that led to the next square. At least thirty more vampires were rushing out of their hiding places and closing on them from a flanking position.

They were back to having a bad day. Gregorios swooped toward the new, onrushing horde, leaving his wife to deal with the initial swarm. "Quentin, we need that sun. Now."

In answer, five bright red flares launch over the temple complex from every side. Fired by the advanced scout team that had remained in position to offer special support, the flares reached their apex and deployed parachutes. As soon as they stabilized over the temple, the ciphers that Sarah had inscribed on them activated.

A shimmering pentagon of golden light snapped into place over the temple, and Gregorios shouted, "Eyes!"

He clenched his eyes shut just as the bright Egyptian sunlight streaming down on the temple poured through that cipher magnifying glass. Searing heat and light thundered down upon the temple. The unprotected mortals, many of whom had been looking up at the flares, screamed anew, clutching at blinded eyes.

It was worse for the vampires.

The intense sunlight drove into their ranks like a sledgehammer. Vampires shrieked in pain, so loud it temporarily shorted his specialty earplugs. The monsters collapsed to the ground, skin smoking, strength momentarily spent. The scent of rotting meat cooking wafted into the square.

Some of them tried to launch their protective soul wind, but the intense sunlight evaporated it. Dozens of captive souls escaped, wailing their newfound freedom before splattering against ancient columns and stone walls with greasy stains.

Perfect. Gregorios swooped down upon the disoriented mass of vampires like an avenging angel, ripping out soulmasks with both hands simultaneously.

He'd never done that before, and it felt really satisfying. Carlo's men dispatched their distracted vampires and rushed to help him. Once again, they'd flipped the battle back against Vlad.

As if on cue, Vlad appeared on the balcony of the mosque, shrieking with rage. His soul wind erupted from his open maw, split into five dense columns, and boiled into the air, aiming toward the flares supporting the deadly cipher.

Sometimes the crotchety old Wallachian was too clever for his own good. Gregorios focused on removing soulmasks as fast as possible, racing to defeat the vampires before Vlad could disable the cipher.

Unfortunately, that was the moment that over a hundred heka fighters charged into the central promenade from the next open court. They carried a variety of military rifles and started firing wildly as they charged.

Gregorios frowned as he yanked out another soulmask. They could finish off all the remaining vampires in a matter of seconds. They didn't have that much time.

Good thing Tomas and Eirene were such detailed planners. Time for plan B.

As lucky shots began ricocheting off the protective shields around Carlo and his men, Gregorios shouted, "Carlo, retreat and activate the shield."

Carlo and his men swiftly detached from the fight, rushed back to the main square, and spread out. Seven of them slapped some more of Sarah's clever cipher blocks onto ancient stone pillars scattered around the square.

The special adhesive stuck the little blocks to the stone stronger than superglue. As the heka fighters began pouring into the square, a shimmering silver dome snapped into place around the square, effectively sealing it off.

At the same time, Vlad's soul wind swarmed the parachute flares and consumed them. The magnifying glass effect winked out, leaving the square feeling shadowed and cold.

The fastest of the heka fighters had made it into the square before the shield went up. The rest of them pounded uselessly on the barrier and even tried shooting at it, which only caused ricochets to slam back into their group. With the debilitating sunlight gone, the angry vampires lunged back to their feet.

They were mad and hungry. They tore into the heka fighters like a fanged tornado. The men were protected by the rune web that Tomas still hadn't disabled, but the vampires seemed to be able to bite through it, if given enough time. The entire colonnade turned into a wild melee. It was a lovely sight.

"Quentin, please eradicate the pests in the colonnade," Gregorios said.

"Launching the rain maker. And deploying hunter teams to clean up," he replied instantly.

Good. The hunters would probably prefer getting to kill everything in the colonnade outside of the dome. First, Quentin would hit the mass of heka and vampires with a series of huge mortars, culminating in a thermobaric bomb that would shred any living flesh with its remarkable overpressure blast. The fact that it sucked out all oxygen in the blast radius meant it might even kill any heka whose shielding protected them from the initial blast. The hunters could mop up whoever remained.

Eirene intercepted the heka who made it into the square. Their indiscriminate fire had caught several unarmed civilians, but she blurred through their lines, knocking weapons out of their hands.

"Carlo, bind them," she ordered.

Carlo and his men swarmed them. Both groups were protected from most harm, but that didn't mean they couldn't get knocked down and tied up with steel-mesh zip ties. The Italians were far better fighters, but they were outnumbered.

So Gregorios flew over to the knot of nervous security forces ringing their ambassadors. "If you go help subdue those terrorists, I bet Sergeant Carlo will be willing to share some of their captured weapons."

The debate over whether it was better to stay close to their assigned officials with no way to actually protect them, or to abandon them to get some hardware took about half a second. The well-trained security personnel leaped into the fray with a will.

Gregorios left Carlo to deal with them. He turned back to the few remaining vampires in the square and dove back into the fight against them. He couldn't let Eirene have all the fun. She was absolutely destroying them.

Vlad shrieked with rage again. He was a deadly predator, but he was used to hunting helpless souls confused by his illusions and frozen with fear. He leaped off the balcony, taloned hands thrown wide.

Gregorios moved to intercept, eager to finally fight his ancient enemy. But instead of launching himself at him or Eirene, the mighty vampire swooped past Gregorios and landed in the square, right next to the cardinal's discarded soulmask.

Oops. Gregorios had forgotten all about it. Vlad snatched it up and held it aloft, his expression victorious. Mortals were easy prey for the ancient vampire. He could consume a dispossessed mortal even before Eirene could close the distance.

Vlad opened his mouth, no doubt to order them to back off before he destroyed the helpless cardinal. The soulmask burst into blazing, white light.

Vlad shrieked in pain and threw the soulmask aside, his expression incredulous. Gregorios felt just as surprised. There was real power in true faith, but he'd rarely seen it displayed so brilliantly.

Eirene continued to wreak havoc and destruction upon the vampires who had learned to fear her. Too late for them. Gregorios shot across the square, burning hands extended toward Vlad. The vampire exploded into a cloud of bats that swept past him and flew up toward the peak of their protective dome.

"Not this time, Vladdy boy," Gregorios vowed as he gave chase. This time he could keep up with Vlad's annoying tactics. Trapped together in that dome, there was nothing Vlad could do to escape.

That's when a shimmering doorway opened atop the mosque balcony with a thunderclap, and monsters started pouring into the square.

Of course.

88

What happened to all the books? Trajan's Forum is ransacked. Everything of worth is gone. I thought it wasn't targeted by looters. Stranger still, the looters never torched it like everywhere else. Someone simply carted everything away. Who would do that during a siege?

~GREGORIOS, 410 A.D., AFTER THE SACKING OF ROME

MELEK LEAPED down from the top of Luxor's towering first pylon to the rooftop of the mosque. Heka manning the entrance were distracted by the onrushing trucks of the enforcer reinforcements. It didn't look like anyone had realized two hundred hunters were swarming the sides of the temple.

They would in a moment. He could barely believe the opening assault had gone so well.

He stood high enough to look into the inner court. Carlo's men had performed as well as a squad of hunters. The square was looking almost secure, although the Chinese ambassador's men had somehow gotten their hands on working weapons. They looked about to start firing on the US and UK forces.

Gregorios and Eirene had defeated a host of undead, but from what he'd heard, Vlad was still at large. He hoped his hunters got to help take down the elusive vampire. Such a victory could do much to secure the fragile good will between his clan and the cursed facetakers.

But first, the difficult part of the mission.

Melek dropped from the roof of the mosque. A second later, the air nearby blurred into the shimmering outline of a doorway. For a second, he feared he'd triggered some kind of defensive measure, but then he blinked in surprise as monstrous nightmare creatures began pouring through.

Two heka gunmen rushed onto the patio and began firing down on Carlo's men. They didn't spot Melek. He didn't even bother shooting them with his M60, but instead struck them mighty blows with his hammer. The many runes worked into it blazed with power as the weapon punched through the invisible protective barrier of the rune web and crushed the heka's skulls.

Monsters poured over the railing, greeted by screams, cries of alarm, and gunfire. Melek hated turning his back on that fight, but he couldn't help them yet.

Instead, he strode into the mosque, activating his new super enhancement again. Four more heka lurked in the dim recesses of the mosque, and they instantly opened fire with three-round bursts from their AK47 rifles.

Melek walked through the hail of bullets and smashed each of them down with his hammer. The last one tried to run, forcing him to use the M60. The force of the onslaught drove the man across the mosque to the edge of the railing, where a hugely muscled monstrosity, covered in thick, black fir, snatched him into its maw.

Melek rushed on, his eyes drawn to the figure of his son lying bound in chains, a crimson rune marked on his forehead. Melek dropped his gun and pressed a tiny charge into the lock. Designed for this purpose, the blast broke the reinforced steel chains strong enough to hold enhanced battle suits like the one Alter wore.

Alter lay motionless under the influence of the binding rune, but his eyes watched Melek's every move. Melek leaned over his son and drew his heavy fighting knife as he deactivated his super enhancement.

"My son, I'm sorry I waited so long to do this."

He slashed down at Alter's face.

The blade sheared through the skin of Alter's forehead, severing the binding rune and peeling it away in a single, clean stroke. The wound bled freely, like all head wounds do, but Alter's healing rune would deal with it quickly.

Alter's entire body convulsed as the binding rune released its hold. He shouted with joy and lunged to his feet.

Melek caught him in a fierce hug. "Oh, Son, I've missed you."

"Thank you, Father." Tears shone in Alter's eyes as Melek pressed his sidearm into Alter's hand.

"Come, Son. Let's finish this together.

They turned to the deepest recesses of the room where Xiao slumbered in a padded chair, sleeping as if walking the memoryscape, even though she lacked one of the blocky helmets.

Not good. She had mastered her ascendant to a far greater degree than Melek had feared. Sarah was in grave danger.

As he and Alter rushed toward the cui dashi, Alter asked, "Where's Sarah?"

It did not surprise Melek that he chose that question. His heart felt heavy with sadness for his son because he could see Sarah would never be free to love him. Her heart was bound to Tomas. Would his poor son never find his place in the world?

"She fights the demon in history. Let's give her a hand."

He skidded to a stop beside the slumbering cui dashi and swung his mighty hammer with all his strength, all his hatred, all his pure zeal to destroy evil.

Her eyes popped open, and she caught the hammer.

Melek gaped. He wouldn't have believed even she could stop the might of that hammer.

Alter opened fire, emptying the pistol magazine into her face. The bullets were cipher-enhanced by Sarah, but they didn't penetrated her skin, so ricocheted away before the ciphers could activate.

Xiao ignored the bullets and flung Melek aside with a backhand blow that felt like he'd been hit by a truck. Alter grabbed at her face with burning hands, but she slapped him off his feet with terrifying ease.

She rose with inhuman grace and scowled. "You've annoyed me for the last time, hunter."

Both Melek and Alter rolled back to their feet. Alter's hands were still burning and he snarled, "I will kill you before you hurt anyone else, demon."

"Your path is chosen for you, fool," she said, giving him a dismissive look.

Melek hefted his hammer and said, "Today your evil dies."

She laughed and lunged with blurring speed toward him. Melek didn't even have time to raise his hammer. Instead he activated his super enhancement and prepared himself for what must come next.

This battle would decide all things.

89

"STAND DOWN!" Tomas shouted as he raced through the Hypostyle Hall, his voice echoing between the enormous pillars. "It's a heka illusion. You're fighting each other, not the enemy."

Some of the men stopped firing, but others either ignored him or were too caught up in the fight for his words to register. Still shouting, Tomas raced among them, knocking his own men down, separating them, beating sense into them if necessary. Everywhere he looked, he spotted bleeding enforcers.

They'd fought so hard, they'd found ways to injure each other, despite their protective shielding. Without Sarah's ciphers, he might have lost a lot of men to the infernal illusion.

"Use call signs. Secondary confirmation required," he shouted.

Anaru realized the danger quickly and his deep voice bellowed commands supporting Tomas. Between them they restored order in a few seconds and rounded the men into tight squads.

The deception enraged Tomas. Many of his men were injured, although they were healing quickly. That could have gone so much worse.

Anaru raged between two of the columns and shouted, "Where are you, cowards? Come out and fight!"

A grenade fell from above.

Tomas was the only one who noticed it. Somehow the illusion affecting his men concealed the grenade from them. He caught it and threw it away. It detonated on the far side of a nearby column.

"Danger from above!"

More grenades fell as his men opened fire, raking what looked to them like a solid ceiling. When Tomas focused, he could see through the illusion, but he lacked time to coordinate the enforcers' fire. He was too busy intercepting falling grenades. They were sitting ducks down there.

Heka fired down at the enforcers, bullets tearing into the trapped men from above. Their protective ciphers saved their lives, but if they didn't think of something fast, the entire team would still be destroyed.

Tomas spotted a section of the roof that really was mostly intact. He ordered Anaru to retreat to that area. At least they'd have a little protection from fire directly overhead. The enforcers were shooting blindly, but with enough lead flying upward, they could hold the heka at bay for a few seconds.

"Hold the line, Anaru. Keep firing. I'll call in backup."

"The com lines are dead," Anaru said.

"I'll be back."

Tomas rushed through the forest of columns, spotting heka above, and more creeping toward his men from the far side of the hall. He resisted the urge to close with the hated enemy. He had to focus on the more important mission.

So he raced back to the first court and found Spartacus and Hongwu still fighting, swords flashing, their duel raging across the court. Hongwu was protected, and Spartacus had activated his super enhancement. His skin glowed metallic, like living gold, and fire trailed his hands as he and Hongwu traded mighty blows. Francesca taped them from the top of a nearby truck, her video camera running.

Tomas shouted, "Stop messing around. I need that web down now!"

Spartacus saluted, but kept fighting. Francesca waved acknowledgment and jumped from the truck. Tomas left them to it, trusting they'd get it done. He raced up one of the heka ladders to the eastern wall. Atop the second pylon, he rose above the dense memoryscape overlay. As he had hoped, once he cleared the illusion, his radio worked.

"Quentin, do you copy?"

"About bloody time," Quentin responded immediately, worry clear in his voice. "What happened in there?"

Tomas' cry had alerted nearby heka. They couldn't see him, but they opened fire anyway. He ducked the wild bullets and rushed across the wall toward the southern end and the temple of Ramses.

"It was a trap," he explained more quietly. "All units are taking heavy fire. We cannot disengage. I need the slasher, and I need it now."

"Roger that. It's ready. Guide me in."

"Set it for seventy-four feet and deploy it directly over the main temple."

"Firing the slasher . . . Now. God speed."

Tomas jumped from the wall as whistling sounded in the air above. The whistling intensified as the specialty round fell toward the Hypostyle Hall. Then the sound changed to the whoosh of jets as the slasher round's reverse thrusters arrested its fall at exactly seventy-four feet. It stopped three feet above the top of the architraves where the heka were massed, shooting down at the trapped enforcer squads.

Tomas caught sight of some of them turning to stare at the munition hovering nearby, spinning like a top. Before they could try shooting it, and before most of them thought to duck, it exploded.

Thousands of sharp projectiles and tiny bomblets fired out horizontally in every direction, covering an area two hundred yards square, ripping through everything. The wave of death shredded the heka lines, killing many. Those whose protections saved their lives were still knocked off the architraves and into the Hypostyle Hall.

Anaru's voice was heavy with anticipation as he reported, "We have visual. Thanks, Captain. All teams, engage!"

A new barrage of rifle fire, followed by a wave of grenade explosions punctuated the order as the angry enforcers unleashed everything they had at the disoriented heka.

The battle was far from over, but Tomas had survived enough military engagements to recognize that critical moment when the tide turned. Sometimes it was a subtle shifting in the energies of battle lines, but always it was real. His men were on the offensive and they'd carry the day if the enemy didn't find new ways to turn the tide against them again.

Tomas turned toward the chapel of Ramses. He didn't plan to give Hongwu's forces time to try any more ploys. It was time to shut down the web for good.

"Francesca, I need you. Now."

"Be right there." Down in the square, she placed the recorder on a nearby broken column, pointing toward the dueling men, then jogged to intercept Hongwu. "Looks like old Spartacus needs my help after all."

"Make it fast," Tomas ordered.

"If I'm not there in twenty seconds, you can spank me."

90

Only the dead have seen the end of the war.

~PLATO

GREGORIOS HATED VAMPIRES. Each time a rogue facetaker had come up with the idea, they'd thought they were so clever. He'd grown tired of explaining to them the truth. Hunting down the vampires had always been gruesome, but those efforts had given rise to the legends of monster hunters.

Dealing with vampires created by the father of all vampires was even worse, but vampires weren't the freakiest thing living in the dark places of the world. Some of the nightmare monsters pouring through the strange rift gate beat them hands down.

He tried to decide which monster would win the title as he flew in a circle around a huge, nine-headed raptor. The annoying creature snapped and tore at him, moving so fast it was difficult to close with a blade. So he hovered just long enough to fire a slug from his shotgun into its torso.

It staggered. That was all the opening he needed. Gregorios swooped in, drawing a heavy-bladed kukri knife from his cardinal robes. In less than three seconds, he circled the beast two times and decapitated all its snapping heads.

Not bad, but plan B hadn't worked out so well. What plan were they on now? C for chaos, or N for nuts?

Eirene blurred past and drove her curved blade into a giant cobra, the living embodiment of Meretseger. Eirene gave the Egyptian goddess a taste of its own medicine by blinding the beast, then left it for a pair of Carlo's team to finish off.

Gregorios surveyed the chaos of the inner court. It smelled of blood and fear and the musky scent of a buffalo-headed monster bleeding out nearby. Most of the monsters looked Chinese or Egyptian, but there were a few weird oddities mixed in.

He couldn't imagine what Sarah and Xiao were doing, but they'd broken something important. A pessimist might start worrying.

More monsters kept tumbling into the court from the rift doorway. The annoying rift kept shifting positions away from its main anchor location above the mosque railing, making it impossible to organize a coherent fighting strategy.

Monsters plopped down into the court everywhere. The Chinese, American, and British security details that still lived had been forced to abandon their plans to murder each other and work together fighting monsters. They'd scavenged guns from fallen heka, but had suffered heavy casualties while they scrambled to respond to the unexpected attack.

Few people could handle the appearance of nightmares come to life. Those still living had reacted out of pure training instincts, but those who had hesitated had been ripped apart.

Most of Carlo's team was formed up in the center of the court, working in squads to kill the raging beasts. The Italians might have arrived late to the world of enhancements, but they were taking to it like long-time enforcers. Any of them who survived the day would no doubt get recruitment calls from Tomas.

If any of them survived. The day had plunged over the cliff. He doubted even Xiao had anticipated such a chaotic battle to celebrate the arrival of her false god. With all the distractions, he hadn't been able to plunge into the mosque to help Melek hunt for Alter.

Hopefully Melek had been successful in saving Alter and cutting Xiao's head off, but even saving Alter would be enough. If the hunters escaped, Quentin could unleash a devastating rain of napalm and destruction on that mosque. That might be enough to give Xiao a bad hair day and soften her up enough for their combined might to take her out.

"We need those reinforcements," he said as the rift flickered across the square and a lithe dragon slipped through.

It wrapped a Chinese security officer up like a python before opening its maw wide and rearing back to remove his head. Gregorios was tempted to let it. The Chinese had been so angry about the death of the dragons in the Forbidden City, let them honor the beasts with a little blood sacrifice.

With a sigh, he soared across to the monster. When it looked up, he blasted it in the snout with another slug from his stubby shotgun. Dragons might be holy in China, but they bled out like everything else.

"Reinforcements are fighting through heka resistance. Arrival in approximately one minute," Quentin reported.

Gregorios couldn't hear that additional firefight above the blasts of nearby weapons, screaming mortals, and howling monsters.

He circled the inner court, firing as fast as he could pump, helping keep monsters at bay from Carlo and his men. Eirene blurred around the outskirts of the square, covering the unarmed knots of mortals cowering in the corners. Between them all, they'd managed to stem the tide of nightmares so far.

Sarah needed to finish whatever she was doing in the memoryscape. Gregorios hoped she'd hurry up. If she didn't overwhelm Xiao quickly, the battle could easily turn against them.

Alter tumbled over the mosque railing, arms and legs windmilling, shouting curses. Gregorios swooped over and caught him.

"I take it you haven't slit Xiao's throat yet," he asked.

Alter swore in Hebrew. "Not hardly. She just woke up."

Not good. Gregorios dropped Alter near Carlo's men. "Where's your father?"

Up on the high balcony, Melek ran backward out of the mosque, firing a long burst from the hip with an M60. His rune-covered hammer was slung over his shoulder on a tactical sling, and he'd activated his super enhancement. Hints of the mosque showed through his shimmering body.

Xiao rushed out of the mosque, moving almost as fast as Eirene did. She dodged most of the bullets, but the ones that struck her ricocheted away as if her skin was reinforced concrete. She lunged, but flew right through Melek's ethereal form, a look of frustration on her face.

She landed in the square and surveyed the chaos with an angry scowl. Gregorios was happy to rain on her fake-god-rising parade, but if Sarah didn't show up to help them fight the super-villain, they faced a world of hurt.

He waved as he settled to the stone courtyard a hundred feet away.

Xiao glared at him, her eyes already glowing with the unique shade of purple of her supreme nevron. She didn't even give Gregorios time to make an insolent remark before launching herself at him.

Gregorios expected it, had experienced her raw speed before, and leaped into the air as he pulled the trigger, firing a modified splatter round point blank into her face.

Made of a custom mixture of powerful acids, Quentin had designed it to produce hyper-dissolution of organic tissue. Gregorios had witnessed the test round melt a cadaver's chest cavity to sludge in a matter of seconds.

Xiao passed below Gregorios, her grasping hand clipping his foot, but not quite grabbing hold. Despite her speed, her incredible strength, and her inhuman healing ability, the acid still eagerly ate into her face and eyes.

She stumbled to a stop, shrieking and pawing at her eyes. Almost immediately, the bubbling flesh started to heal. New flesh formed in its place, climbing back to cover the cheeks and replace the eye sockets.

The healing progressed rapidly, but the delay cost Xiao precious seconds. Eirene blurred past, curved blade slashing at Xiao's wrist. She clearly hoped to take the woman's hand off. A cui dashi without hands couldn't remove soulmasks.

It was a good idea, but despite the force of the blow, she barely scratched Xiao's toughened skin. They were going to need something far more powerful. Like maybe a missile strike from space.

"Anyone know where Sarah's napping?" he called.

Across the inner court, a raging minotaur that was bleeding heavily plowed into a column, squashing the UK security officer who had been shooting it. The monster also crushed one of the rune blocks forming the barrier around the inner court.

The barrier faded away.

Screaming civilians and most of the news media immediately fled, while a few still-living heka poured into the court from the inner colonnade. They hadn't come to attack, but their terrified expressions were focused behind them.

Gregorios glimpsed Nabil and the hunters swarming the remaining heka under. Those boys might be annoying sometimes, but when aimed property, they were very effective.

The surprised heka that escaped the hunters and made it into the square skidded to a halt as the rift appeared right in front of them. A huge hippopotamus thundered out of it and tore into their ranks. The huge male was the embodiment of Set and it was grumpy.

They probably wished they'd stayed to fight the hunters.

Finally, from the first pylon entryway, enforcer reinforcements arrived. Their vehicles skidded to a halt just inside the square, and they directed their roof-mounted machine guns and automatic grenade launchers into the monster ranks. The noise rose to a fever pitch, a wonderful din punctuated by staccato machine gun fire, and the explosive reports of grenades splattering nightmares come to life.

It was probably for the best they didn't attack Xiao. If they irritated her, she could murder them all in seconds, despite Sarah's protection ciphers.

As Xiao turned after Eirene, blinking her nearly-restored eyes, Gregorios wished he could summon new weapons. He needed more power.

Quentin responded to his earlier question. "Sarah's awake."

He was relieved to hear Sarah jump on the line. She sounded breathless. "I'm heading your way."

Gregorios racked another specialty round into the shotgun and fired the enhanced incendiary round at Xiao's back. The recoil nearly broke his wrist, despite his super strength. A wave of fire engulfed Xiao. She leaped thirty feet into the air and spun, her attention again riveted on him.

"Tag, you're it!"

"Tell her to hurry," Gregorios called as he soared across the inner court in the opening move of the most dangerous game of tag he'd ever played. "If she catches me, I'm out for good."

Xiao gave chase, ignoring Eirene's attempts to distract her, and running right through Melek's ethereal form when he lunged into her path.

Gregorios wasn't as fast, but he could hover longer than she could. He could also change directions while she had to continue straight in whatever line she launched herself. His greater maneuverability allowed him to just barely keep ahead of her.

He fired every last round at her, including all of the specialty ammo Quentin had worked up for him, but nothing slowed her down. He even tried the curtain call round, despite the danger of its area effect weakening some of his own men. It didn't even slow her down, curse her eyes.

Xiao chased him through the chaos of monsters and hunters, enforcers and heka, ignoring everything but him, murder in her eyes. It was just a matter of time before she caught him.

Gregorios grinned as he taunted and dodged. Every second he kept her distracted was one more second before she started murdering his people. He was so focused on the deadly game that he didn't see a phoenix-like bird launch into the air to intercept him.

He plowed into the creature and shoved his shotgun down its open beak before it could snap off his head. He was out of ammo, so he left the little gun there for a second while he slashed his huge kukri across its throat. Then he kicked the dying bird away and spun back to look for Xiao.

She'd taken advantage of his momentary distraction by leaping into the air, kicking off a heavy column, and soaring at him, arms outstretched with the promise of grisly death.

Gregorios twisted so hard he nearly left his legs behind. Xiao's grasping fingers scraped across his robes, half a centimeter from gaining a solid hold.

As she flew past, expression furious, so close that her long, black hair tickled his nose, she snarled, "Today you die, Gregorios!"

He made a Chinese obscene gesture he'd picked up from Sarah's research and called after her, "We've been tallying up the damage you and your kids have done around the world. Make sure you leave me the account you plan to use to pay the debt before I take your head off.

Xiao landed next to a squat, four-armed monster with a squashed-looking, rocklike head. Gregorios had no idea what it was, and Xiao didn't give him time to figure it out. Swearing in five different languages, she ripped the beast apart. Then she zipped across to the nearest row of columns, and started throwing the massive stones at him.

"You're such a cheater," Gregorios shouted as he swooped under a statue of Ramses.

"Get down here," Xiao shrieked. Her face was flushed with rage, her purple-glowing eyes blazing, and her voice so loud it nearly shorted out his ear protection. Gregorios grinned. He'd gotten her wonderfully frustrated.

"Xiao!" Melek interrupted. The hunter stood in the center of the inner court, with Alter at his side. Carlo's team had moved closer to the mosque, ceding the space to the hunters. Melek had shed his ethereal form and held his pistol to Alter's head.

That got Xiao's attention.

Melek looked deadly serious as he declared, "Surrender, or I will sacrifice my son to stop you."

Eirene skidded to a stop across the square, looking horrified.

Gregorios hovered, impressed. Melek was a man with legendary chutzpah. As much as Gregorios liked Alter, the boy played a critical role in Xiao's plot to bring Sutekh into the modern day. If they couldn't beat her, killing Alter really was their best shot at stopping her plan.

Unfortunately, Melek shouldn't have hesitated after making that demand. Xiao moved so fast she seemed to teleport to Melek.

She smashed into him, knocking him flying. He tumbled forty feet and slid across the stones, right under the legs of the Osiris Bull. It was in the process of goring a heka fighter while other heka, assisted by nearby hunters, all fired upon it.

Xiao gave chase and ripped the bull in half, spraying bloody gore over herself and everyone in a twenty foot radius. As mortals stumbled away from her wrath, she tossed the monster parts aside and stalked after Melek.

"Thank you for reminding me I'll harvest the nevra cores of the pesky facetakers soon enough," she said in a conversational tone as she wiped blood from her face. "But I can kill you now."

Eirene reached Melek's side as he painfully sat up and pulled his hammer to the ready position. She faced Xiao, her expression determined.

Melek pulled her back. "Nay, grandmother. This fight is mine."

"It's all of ours," Eirene countered as Xiao bore down on them with an implacable stride.

"Sarah's coming," Melek reminded her, his expression calm. "Allow me to play my part."

Eirene gave him a kiss on the forehead. "You were always a good one, Melek."

She retreated and circled to the right. Gregorios moved to flank Xiao on the opposite side. He snatched a rifle from a wounded heka. It helped him feel a little less helpless, but they lacked weapons to do her any serious harm. He hated seeing Melek step into harm's way, but as Melek shifted position slightly, Gregorios had to admit it was the right play.

He whispered into his throat mic as Xiao closed on Melek. "Sarah, hurry!"

91

SARAH RUSHED into the salon on the second floor of the command ship. The bank of huge windows provided a spectacular view of the nearby temple, complete with explosions and swarming soldiers.

"I have to get there," she cried.

Harriett was pulling on a flight helmet. "The chopper's warming up topside, but you need to make your statement."

"I don't have time."

Quentin turned from a complex array of communications gear and said, "Make time."

Nearby, four techs were finalizing setup of the cameras. "All forces are engaged and time is short, but if we lose today, we need the world to know what's really going on."

"You make the statement," Sarah said, terrified of what Xiao might be doing to the others without her help.

Quentin shook his head. "The world doesn't know me. Everyone needs to know you're alive."

"They'll listen to you," Harriett confirmed.

Sarah hated wasting any time, but had to admit they were right. "Are we ready to roll?"

"Ready," the first tech said. "We'll overlay your message onto eighteen news agency feeds. The others will pick it up once they see what you have to say."

Another tech switched stations on a nearby monitor, showing a live feed from one of the still-living reporters who was huddling in the center of Carlo's force in the inner court.

The sight of living monsters tearing into soldiers, of men fighting for their lives, looked unreal. Then she caught sight of Xiao closing on Melek. She needed to be there, or the plan would fail.

"Quick! Do it."

Sarah clipped on the microphone and stepped to the blank wall facing the camera. The tech gave her a thumb's up and she took a deep breath. This was it.

The world would know her, would know the truth. There would be no quiet second life now.

What choice did she have? Learning the truth was difficult. It had completely changed her life, and yet she would never go back to blind ignorance. Better to face evil, knowing what was really going on, and stand for truth.

This was the best way to help set things right, and she was the only one who could do it. So she stayed and faced the camera.

"Hello everyone," she started, flashing her signature smile. "My name is Sarah. Most of you know me as the Sword of the Deliverer."

She paused to allow that announcement to sink in as the cameraman zoomed in on her face. The closeup would help people ignore her different body, her change of hair color, and focus on her face. Her heart was pounding, but she forced control over herself. She's been in the spotlight before. She never liked it, but she could handle it.

"My body died in Rome, but I survived. The video shared at the UN committee was correct. My soul was removed from my dying body that day we defeated Paul."

"However," she added sternly, "most of the rest of what you've been told about the facetakers and current events in the world is a lie. The man who removed my soul was not a terrorist. What he did was not an act of evil, but an act of love."

The truth of her words resonated through her, filling her with confidence. Alter and Tomas together had saved her, and she loved them both dearly. She might not be able to return the same type of love that Alter wished, but she still cherished him as a dear friend. Thinking of Tomas filled her with determination and optimism.

Unfortunately, the world wouldn't understand that it was two men who had saved her together. So she said, "He saved my life. Now his life is in danger, as are the lives of the facetakers and their allies. They aren't the enemy. They're the only people in the world who can hope to stop Paul's mother, an evil woman named Xiao. She's the one who has orchestrated this conflict in an attempt to plunge our world into chaos so she can rise from the ashes as the global ruler."

"She's the one who orchestrated the lie of Sutekh. He lived in the time of Moses, and even back then he was an evil wannabe dictator. Gregorios and my team are here in Egypt fighting Xiao before she can bring Sutekh into our time and set themselves up as false kings. The archaeological discovery is a fraud. It's all part of the plan. The international conflict brewing between world powers has been set in motion by her followers."

She leaned forward, trying to convey the gravity of the conflict. "We don't have to let them destroy our nations, plunge the world into destruction, and kill millions of people. We can stand against them!"

"I call upon everyone willing to fight for their families, their countries, and their liberty, to rise and unite against this evil. It's more powerful than anything the world has ever seen, but even they can't defeat all of us."

"They've compromised the president of the United States, the prime minister of England, and the chairman of the Chinese central committee. Those men are slaves to Xiao's will, but the people of their great nations are not. You can stop them."

Harriett waved from behind the cameraman, gave Sarah a thumb's up and a smile, then a motion to wrap it up. On the monitor showing the live video feed, Xiao was standing over a bloody Melek, holding his rune-covered hammer in her hands. The situation was deteriorating. They were out of time.

Sarah marked her special rune and activated it, allowing her body to shift to quicksilver.

"I am Sarah, and I'm going now to fight to protect those I love. No matter what happens, don't surrender. Even if we don't win the day, that doesn't mean Xiao and Sutekh will succeed."

"I believe in you. I believe in the human spirit. I believe in freedom. Pray to whichever god you worship for help. Even if you're not religious, find something to believe in because we need to stand together."

She raised her fist. "For our families. For our lives. We can do this together!"

The cameraman clapped. "That's a wrap. Well done."

Sarah was already sprinting for the stairs, with Harriett close behind.

Quentin ran after them. "The Pope's office has already confirmed he'll make his public statement in twenty seconds. St. Peter's square is already full of people assembled for the convocation he called earlier. He'll support everything you said."

She shouted back, "Good. Let's hope the rest of the world listens."

The women jumped into the helicopter, its blades already spinning. Immediately the pilot lifted off the deck, and they rose vertically into the sky above the river. Sarah grabbed the outfit waiting for her on the seat and slid into it. Harriett helped her fasten the buckles.

By the time they reached two thousand feet and paused to hover, she was ready and moved to the door. The web still wasn't down, so they couldn't fly all the way into the temple, but that had never been the plan anyway.

"Good luck," Harriett said, giving Sarah a hug.

Sarah pulled on her helmet with its full face shield and integrated com system. She gave Harriett a fierce smile, took a deep, steadying breath, then jumped.

The rush of air was exhilarating and she grinned despite her fear that she might be too late. She focused on the distant temple and extended her arms and legs to catch the wind as Quentin had instructed her. The membranes of her wing suit snapped open, turning her free-fall into a targeted descent.

As she accelerated down her steep dive, she said, "I'm coming in. Get me a target."

"About time," Melek said, his voice heavy with pain. "I've almost got her in position."

No one gets it. Everything is fleeting. Everything is connected. It's so simple.

~REUBEN

FRANCESCA CIRCLED THE DUELING FIGHTERS, impressed by both of them. Spartacus' golden skin protected him from Hongwu's slashing sword as well as Hongwu's remote protective web, but it looked so much sexier.

She was very tempted to slide her hands down his rippling muscles and feel the living metal of his skin. Both men had taken several heavy blows, but neither looked injured. Neither had slowed. Spartacus' fiery hands hadn't done much against Hongwu, but they were still awesome.

The two men had fought back and forth across the breadth of the inner court. If left to their own devices, they looked like they could keep it up all day. As much as she'd love watching that, they were out of time. As always, when the men couldn't get it done, the women had to step in and finish things.

Behind the pair of fighters, an MK19 automatic grenade launcher slid out of the back of one of the pick-ups. Floating in the air, it headed for one of the ladders up to the eastern pylon.

Tomas must have finished his scouting of the Ramses chapel. By the look of the long belt of high explosive rounds floating away with the gun, he was starting his assault. He was about to grow impatient.

Hongwu delivered a mighty blow to Spartacus' chest, knocking him off his feet. In any other duel, that would have been a killing blow. Even though both men had delivered other should-be-fatal strikes, she decided this one was her chance.

Before Hongwu could lunge after Spartacus, who was already rolling back to his feet, Francesca stepped between them. Hongwu assumed a fighting stance, sword raised, ready to strike.

She had more imaginative plans, so sauntered closer, hands by her side, a playful smile on her lips. "Can't you think of anything better do with that thing?"

"I do not fear you, demon," he spat, pointing his blade at her chest.

"I wish you would," she said, sliding a finger along his bloody sword as she gently deflected it aside and stepped closer. "A little fear adds spark to a relationship."

He blinked, unable to hide his surprise. "Are you surrendering?"

She laughed. "What would be the fun in that?"

"What do you want?" He looked confused, exactly as planned.

She leaned closer. "Well, the fact that you're a eunuch makes that question a bit more complicated."

That rocked his calm. He stammered, "That—that life is long past."

"Good," she purred, stepping right up to him and touching his lips with a finger.

He was a fool to let anyone this close, but she had perfected the art of usurping control over men when she wanted something. "I've never met a man who could keep up with me. Think you've got what it takes?"

"I don't understand," he said, his sword slowly falling to his side as her smoldering stare held him riveted.

She'd worked on it for centuries, and she hadn't meet a man since William Wallace who could withstand the full weight of her attention.

"Let me be perfectly clear." She leaned close and pressed her lips to his. He smelled of sweat and cologne, and his obvious surprise was only matched by his stupidity in not recoiling immediately.

Francesca unleashed her super power.

Her lips glowed cherry red against his. Her skin grew hot as her new rune turned the kiss into the most deadly weapon she'd ever possessed.

Hongwu's skin grew brittle against hers as all the moisture was drained from his face. He tried pull away, but she grabbed his neck and kissed harder, her strength magnified by the force of all of his enhancements. Her super rune subverted and drained that strength away from him and into her.

Hongwu's face started to crack and his eyes bugged out in terror. He made pathetic whimpering sounds, but his lips remained stuck fast to hers as she drained every bit of his vitality. His skin blackened and began to smoke under the force of her rune.

All of his mighty enhancements faded away and he sagged under her touch. His sword dropped from limp fingers as she severed his connection from the remote protective rune that no longer bonded to his compromised soul.

Francesca broke the kiss with a flourish, savoring the rush of strength pounding through her. Hongwu fell to his knees, and she loved seeing him in that position.

Francesca wiped her lips, her grin wicked. "This is the best super-power ever."

"What did you do?" he gasped through broken lips, his voice a hoarse whisper.

She gave him a dazzling smile. "I call it the kiss of death."

Then she stepped to one side. Spartacus had stood unnoticed behind her, sword poised to strike. He plunged it into Hongwu's chest, sinking it to the hilt.

"I just call this death."

He ripped the sword out and Hongwu's lifeblood sprayed the inner court. Francesca seized Hongwu's soulmask, preventing him from falling. She activated her nevra core, snapping her nevron to all of his soul points. She now owned him.

"Tell me where the source of the plague is going to come from."

Hongwu tried to laugh, but only spat blood. "You broke my power, but you can never break my will."

"Oh, we'll see about that."

She dug burning fingers into the skin of his face, severed his soul points, and yanked on his soulmask. The shimmering mask began to slip free of the skin of his dying body, but she stopped pulling just before it popped free. Leaving it protruding halfway out of his skull, she withdrew her nevron, leaving him half-bonded.

Xiao's chief eunuch screamed, the sound echoing through the ruined temple. The pitch rose as torture beyond what a mortal soul should be able to withstand ripped at his sanity. She had left him the ability to scream, but nothing else.

Had he remained fully bonded to the body, that much pain would have snuffed his consciousness, protecting him from its full effect. In his half-dispossessed state, he couldn't escape. It was the worst torture any living soul could endure without cracking.

Francesca listened to the horrific screams, judging the pitch for twelve seconds, then reactivated her nevron, easing his torment. When his screams faded to panting breaths, she leaned close and whispered, "If I have to ask again, I'll leave you like this for a year."

Maybe a religious martyr might have possessed the determination to willingly embrace such a fate, but Hongwu was no martyr.

"The Hathor temple in Dendera," he sobbed, hatred and terror showing in equal measure in his expression. "Go, witch, and meet your death there."

"That wasn't so hard, was it?"

She knew of Dendera. It was one of the best-preserved temple complexes in Egypt. What was with Xiao and using temples to house her webs? Francesca pressed Hongwu's soulmask back into the skull and allowed him to fall to the ground and finish bleeding out.

Spartacus dropped to one knee before Francesca and saluted with his bloody sword. "You are indeed a goddess of combat."

"You're sweet," she said, finally getting a chance to touch his golden skin.

It was warm, and the contact thrilled her. She'd have to see if she could get Sarah to loan him this rune again some other time. "Good job, my gladiator."

"I'm not finished yet." He stepped past her and, with a single stroke, decapitated Hongwu. Then he stomped on the head until the skull cracked. He lifted the bloody mess into his hands and burned it with raging fire until it crumbled to ash.

Francesca retreated from the inferno and the stench of burning hair and skin. She hated how muscle always smelled so good when it burned, but the rest brought back too many ugly memories.

"I like your style," Francesca said when Spartacus dusted his hands of the last of Hongwu's charred remains. "Are you that thorough in everything you set your hand to?"

"Indeed." He turned his back on the fallen Hongwu and gave her an appraising look, a smile on his face. "You've proven your worth, Queen of Ages. I accept the challenge you cast at the feet of this unworthy adversary."

He clapped a hand over his chest. "I will be the man who can keep up with you, and I'll risk the kiss of death to prove my worth."

"You sure you want to take that chance?" she asked, sidling closer, enjoying the game.

"To win the greatest glory, one must take the greatest risk."

"If you survive," she said with a twinkle in her eye. "I guarantee the glory will be worth it."

He reached for her, clearly intending to take the risk right there, but she pushed him away. "We've got work to do. Glory later."

She pointed at one of the nearby trucks. "We've got a case of C-4 in that one. I'll set the detonators in the back."

"And I?"

She pointed at a heavy machine gun atop another truck. "You take that up the wall and help Tomas distract the heka in the chapel. Hurry. He gets grumpy when he's kept waiting."

While Spartacus unhooked the heavy gun, whistling a battle tune, she tapped her throat mic. "Harriett, the secondary web's in Dendera, the Hathor Temple. Be a love and destroy it."

"On it, Frannie."

Harriett, still in the chopper, turned away from the view of Sarah's dive toward Luxor. She'd been awaiting word of destruction of the web to order the helicopter in to join the fight. Its twin fifty-caliber door guns would be a huge help.

Now she faced north, up the Nile. After Xiao, the plague was one of the direst threats they faced. She had hoped that web would be bound in with the protective web in the Karnak, but it made sense to keep it in a secondary location. Only, now she knew where to find it.

As her pilot pushed the throttle to maximum speed and they zipped up the Nile, Harriett opened a laptop and activated the real-time feed to a Suntara satellite they'd tasked to orbit over Egypt. The link had been pre-staged by Quentin through the communications hub, so it came online in seconds.

Through that satellite feed, Harriett gazed down upon Egypt from space and zoomed the view down over the town of Dendera. She spotted the convoy of ships transporting her Yurak forces, churning full speed down the river toward the main conflict. They had only recently passed Dendera, which lay a little over an hour away from Luxor by car.

Beyond the community, she focused in on the Dendera temple

complex, a huge desert site, two and a half kilometers outside of town. It spanned forty thousand square meters and was surrounded by a mud brick wall.

No tourists flocked to the site today. The road was blocked by armored trucks, and over a hundred heka fighters manned the enclosure wall, protected by sandbag barriers. She spotted eight crew-served heavy gun positions. Storming the temple complex would cost many lives.

She studied the temple complex, noting the position of the temple and the many fighters as she formulated her plan. If she had more time, she could design an attack strategy that would overwhelm those defensive positions and storm the walls. She loved close combat against heka, loved the thrill of pitting herself against a deadly enemy.

Today they didn't have time.

Harriett switched to the Yurak tactical channel. "Turn those ships around. New target is Dendera. Prepare the rainmakers. We're going in under a full Apocalypse barrage."

Tomas waited until Spartacus set up his gun atop the huge architraves above the Hypostyle hall next to him. Then he fired the MK19 at the heka on the lower walls ringing the small Ramses chapel in the corner of the first courtyard.

The heavy chatter of the automatic grenade launcher was a beautiful sound. At this range, the explosive shells struck almost immediately, shattering the top of the perimeter walls of the chapel, catapulting the protected heka inside. Tomas continued the barrage, sending grenades tumbling into the open chapel.

From the top of the wall, Spartacus opened up with the M60. He sang a battle song as he fired through the smoke billowing out of the chapel from Tomas' barrage.

Spartacus shouted, "There is more glory found in personal combat, but the joy of wielding lightning akin to Zeus' own bolts enlivens the soul!"

They paused after a concentrated ten second burst. Anaru spoke into Tomas' earpiece.

"Captain, the enemy are routed. Teams are mopping up the last of the resistance. Can you get this illusion down soon?"

"Five seconds," Tomas promised.

Inside the inner court, Francesca gunned the engine of the explosives-laden truck, aiming at the entrance to the temple. Tomas would have preferred planting shaped charges around the web to bring it down without causing so much destruction, but the painful protective spell still filled the chapel. Even though he didn't have a choice, he still cringed to think what was coming.

Francesca bailed out of the truck twenty feet before it hit the entrance. She rolled smoothly back to her feet and sprinted in the other direction. The truck lost one of its mirrors as it tore through the opening and crashed into the chapel.

Tomas triggered the explosives.

The thunderous blast shattered the smaller chapel, cracking columns all through the temple that had stood unmoved for thousands of years. Dust billowed off the ground as the outer chapel walls blasted apart, and debris rained in every direction. It left a massive crater where the chapel had stood for so many centuries.

The blast knocked Tomas from his feet, but he managed to keep from falling off the wide architrave. He quickly stood and surveyed the damage. The illusion of the memoryscape faded away, leaving the temple again the ruined shadow of its former glory.

He muttered, "Xiao's going to pay for what she made us do here."

He tapped his mic and said, "Rune web disabled. Repeat, general web protection is down."

Then Tomas leaped off the high architrave, dropped to the ground fifty feet below, and ran for the nearest truck. "Anaru, finish securing this area. I'm heading to Luxor to help there."

Spartacus followed, and Francesca met them at the truck, looking a bit shaken. She'd still been too close to the explosion. The inner wall of the chapel hadn't broken, but it was badly cracked. It had spared her the worst of the blast, but she was covered in dust, and one arm was bleeding from debris. Spartacus helped her into the truck and Tomas slipped behind the wheel.

As they raced north out of the battle zone, past the still-dispersed Egyptian troops, he hoped they'd arrive in time to help.

So much rested on Sarah's shoulders. It was up to her now.

93

I do not create paradoxes. I only share the paradox visible all around us, for any with the vision to see. Most live only one life, but seek eternity. Some live many, but what more can they win than they have already achieved?

~GONGSUN LONG, CHINESE LOGICIAN

MELEK COUGHED, then gasped from the stabbing pains the movement triggered. Xiao's last punch had cracked ribs, and breathing was difficult.

He shuffled away from her on all fours. He hadn't even gotten in a single good strike with his hammer. She'd ripped the powerful heirloom from his grasp and now hefted it as she towered over him. A glance upward showed he was nearly in position.

Gregorios and Eirene continued shooting Xiao, trying to distract her, but she ignored most of their efforts as bullets ricocheted off her toughened skin. They had consumed all of their best ammunition and done little more than slow her.

The enforcers and his own family were still busy fighting the constant flow of deadly monsters. Hunters would have still swarmed to his defense, but he'd ordered them to stay back. Their deaths would not help.

As Gregorios swooped past, dangerously close, he shot Xiao right in the eye. The bullet did no noticeable damage, but she glanced up at him with an annoyed expression. "Don't you have anything better to do?"

"Not really," Gregorios said as he hovered twenty feet above them and shot her in her open mouth. He managed to chip a tooth that time.

Xiao glared. "Let's change that, shall we?"

She rushed away and snatched up one of the cameramen still brave enough to be transmitting a live feed. She leaped with the screaming fellow and his huge camera up to the mosque balcony, placed him down. She gestured for him to focus on her.

Gregorios swooped past, and Melek heard him say, "I can't believe it. She's launching into a prepared speech."

Melek sat up, extremely annoyed. No one seemed to be taking his imminent death very seriously. It seemed supremely insulting.

Up on the balcony, Xiao declared, "This world is wallowing under an unsupportable weight of corruption. Billions of you, my worthy subjects, are enslaved to tyranny and to unfair laws while a few elites enjoy endless wealth. Today that will change. The world order has failed and I am introducing a new government with my beloved, Sutekh, the greatest man who ever walked the earth."

"Are you getting this?" Eirene's voice through his earpiece was garbled by static. Melek couldn't see her. No doubt she was in the thick of things somewhere.

Even though Gregorios was shooting at her from high above the court, Xiao continued without interruption. "The corrupt governments of the world have failed. The major religions claim peaceful tenets, but they have spawned little more than hatred and violence. Today is a day of wrath and vengeance and judgment upon the world. Behold! Look to your capital cities. The plagues prophesied by every religion to punish the wicked are upon you!"

Melek said, "I'm thinking it might be time to destroy that camera."

"Too late if she's unleashing the plague," Gregorios responded.

He swooped down and grabbed the heavy Barrett sniper rifle from an enforcer perched atop one of the columns and fired a round at Xiao's left eye. It was a great shot, and that heavy bullet struck the vulnerable organ with enough power to penetrate half an inch.

Xiao barely flinched. She yanked the flattened piece of lead out, and her eye healed a second later. He did manage to interrupt the speech, though.

Gregorios handed the rifle back, then jumped off the pylon, flying across the inner court, drawing Xiao's angry gaze. "For one who claims the world is corrupt, your remedy doesn't make any sense. You plan to murder millions by plague because they're oppressed? That's like giving a drowning man a millstone to carry."

"I'll deal with you shortly," Xiao promised.

She leaped down to the lower court and scooped up an enforcer. Ignoring the bullets he pumped into her stomach, she threw him at Gregorios.

The hapless man screamed as he tumbled toward Gregorios, who snatched the rifle out of his hands. The enforcer struck a column on the far side of the inner court and bounced off. He thudded to the stone pavement, but immediately rolled back to his feet. Those protective ciphers had saved countless lives.

Gregorios shouted, "When the whole death queen of the world thing doesn't work out, I know a minor league baseball team that might sign you on."

"Shoot him!" Xiao shouted at several heka perched nearby on the mosque balcony. They turned rifles toward Gregorios, but then each of them collapsed, spraying blood from severed arteries.

"Perfect timing as always, love," Gregorios called. Melek hadn't seen Eirene, she'd moved that fast, but he recognized her handiwork.

"Keep him distracted," Eirene said as she rushed past.

"That's all I can do," Gregorios said, firing down at the raging Xiao.

"And pray for Sarah. I'm heading back to the boat to look for bigger guns and to check on efforts to counter that plague."

"Don't take too long," Gregorios said as he kept shooting uselessly at Xiao, who dropped back to the main square and turned again toward Melek. "There's not a whole lot I can do to stop her."

"Just be annoying, dear. No one can resist you when you do that."

Melek rose shakily to his feet and shouted, "I defy you, demon!"

That drew Xiao's attention. She rushed him, ignoring rounds fired from Gregorios and nearby hunters. They couldn't stop Xiao, but they didn't need to. She struck him off his feet, and although the impact shocked him with brutal pain, he felt grateful for his chance to lure her into their death trap.

"I wish we had more time to make your death meaningful," Xiao said, raising his precious hammer. "But time is short."

That she planned to kill him with that precious weapon was galling, but he held to the plan. He wouldn't shirk his duty, despite the personal cost.

He shuffled back another foot, drawing her into the perfect position.

Before she could bring the hammer down, Alter leaped upon her back and fired a forty-five caliber pistol into her ear, emptying the magazine in a single, concentrated barrage. The hollow point bullets might not be able to shatter her brain like they would any other living thing, but they must have stung because she cringed, then snatched Alter off her back.

He beat on her face with the empty pistol, but only succeeded in breaking the barrel. "Leave my father alone!"

"Your time is nearly come, dear Alter." Xiao caressed the struggling Alter's face, then punched him so hard in the stomach, he vomited over her shoulder.

Still carrying Alter, she jumped twenty feet to snatch a rune-canceling, steel-mesh web out of the air just as a hunter fired his weapon. She kicked the startled hunter over the nearby temple wall. Melek cringed at the sight of the brutal strike, and hoped the defensive cipher kept the hunter alive.

Xiao wrapped Alter in the web, then tossed him up to the mosque balcony. "Stay there till I return."

He immediately ripped the mesh apart, desperation fueling his strength. As he stood, the ever-shifting rift doorway appeared beside him and disgorged a huge, black monstrosity that Melek could not name.

It wrapped Alter in its many-tentacled arms. That was for the best. Things were about to get messy, and all the interruptions were starting to seriously annoy Melek.

"Activate number five," Melek spoke into his throat mic.

Sarah responded immediately. "Roger. Inbound. Six seconds out."

Good. The timing was working out after all. Xiao returned to stand over Melek, who had not moved.

He was glad Alter hadn't managed to keep her distracted any longer. Her speed and ability to shed virtually any damage their forces could inflict upon her were making her cocky. She could have killed him in the blink of an eye, then murdered everyone else within seconds. Instead she was enjoying the torture and her superiority.

Melek slid one of Sarah's rune disks out of a pocket as Xiao leaned over him and taunted, "You're weak, Melek. Die knowing I'm going to hunt down every member of your precious family and everyone they love and consume their souls."

"I am a hunter, demon," he replied, filled with pride for this opportunity to face down this most hated enemy.

He was surprised to realize he felt a sense of brotherhood with the facetakers as they all united in the greatest cause in the world. "Spending my life defeating you is the greatest honor."

"You haven't defeated me, fool," she snarled, leaning closer, eyes glowing with her active nevron as she reached for his face.

Melek smiled, savoring the victory as he dropped the rune disk Sarah had just remotely activated. It contacted stone, triggering its cipher.

As the shimmering glow of a mighty binding wrapped Xiao, slowing her movements to a crawl, he activated his super enhancement and shifted to ethereal.

Her burning fingers passed through him, grasping nothing. Sarah had warned that the binding wouldn't hold her for long, but they didn't need long. He spotted a spec in the sky growing in size as it rocketed down toward the temple.

He reared up until his ethereal face was inches from hers. "I am a hunter, and you've taken the bait."

Sarah struck like a missile, her quicksilver body growing dozens of spikes just before impact.

Melek enjoyed the perfect view as Sarah's metal body drove deep into Xiao, splattering blood and gore as she tore into Xiao's torso and skull. The impact cracked the paving stones and shook Melek even in his ethereal form. His vision blurred and it took a second to recover.

He realized a haze of bloody mist was clouding his vision. As it slowly settled to the dusty stones all around, he finally saw the gory mess that had been Xiao. His heart sang with joy. Sarah had done it! She'd destroyed the hated creature.

She wore Xiao all over her quicksilver body that had flattened and spread under the impact. Even as Sarah started to flow back to her normal shape, Xiao's broken skull began to glow with the unique shade of her nevra core.

Melek gaped. Impossible.

Xiao wasn't dead.

Sarah came to her senses slowly. Her body hurt all over. Her eyes focused as feeling returned and she realized she'd been squashed pretty badly by that crash landing. She took stock of her body and willed it to flow back to its normal shape.

That was when she realized she was lying in a gory mess that had been Xiao. Hitting the cui dashi had felt like striking an iron pillar. Any other flesh and blood shape would have exploded all over the temple from the force of the impact.

Xiao had been badly hurt, much of her inner fluids sprayed out under the incredible pressure, but her skeleton was still remarkably intact. Sarah had driven deep into her and they lay together, fused into a single form. Xiao's skull had cracked, her face mashed right up against Sarah's. She smelled of blood and stinking entrails. That was so gross. Sarah retracted her spiky protrusions and tried to pull her face away.

Xiao's eyes, pressed right against Sarah's, lit with her activated nevron.

Sarah gasped. No way Xiao should have survived that full-body missile strike.

She could feel Xiao dying, but she wasn't dead yet. Before Sarah could rip an arm free and sever Xiao's spine, the heat of Xiao's nevron grasped Sarah's soul. They were so tightly meshed that Sarah couldn't escape. Xiao's hands were shredded, but she didn't need hands to connect with Sarah's soulmask.

Sarah screamed as Xiao's nevron tore into her, seizing control. Xiao's voice spoke into her mind. *"You belong to me now, rune warrior. Take me back to my mate."*

Sarah tried to struggle, to throw off Xiao's control, but she was in too deep and could not stand against the force of Xiao's nevron. Xiao's soul force pulsed against her and she again sensed Xiao's linked ascendant rune.

Even though Xiao lacked the full access that Sarah could achieve, she could still slide back along her own ascendant. Now, propelled by Xiao's will, Sarah felt her consciousness sucked out of her body and carried back into the invisible reality of the ascendant as Xiao plunged down its length, back into history.

Sarah should be able to fight, to pull away. She was the rune warrior, after all, but she didn't know how to counter Xiao's control. As they accelerated back in time, sliding back down Xiao's ascendant, terror clouded her thoughts.

She couldn't break out of Xiao's nevron. It shackled her to the cui dashi's will. She'd nearly defeated Xiao, but in the moment of victory, she'd turned the tables on herself. Had she just given Xiao the power to complete her mission?

No way. If Xiao wanted to die in the past, then so be it.

As they plunged into the moment of history where Sutekh awaited their return, Sarah realized that a third soul had been caught in the vortex of Xiao's nevron.

Melek.

Quentin scanned the many news stations broadcasting views of some of the major cities of the world. From Washington D.C. to London, from Moscow to Paris, in every scene the same unexpected storm seemed to be raging. Dark clouds had gathered over the cities, unleashing howling winds and torrential rains.

Even cities that rarely saw rain, like Riyadh, Saudi Arabia, were being hit. Quentin's team had already logged reports of storms forming over the capitals of the fifty most powerful nations around the globe, as well as most of the largest population centers.

The magnitude of the event was mind-boggling. Panic had already seized most major metropolitan areas, fueled by Xiao's worldwide broadcast of impending doom.

He whistled softly. "What a bloody mess."

"Do you think they're delivering the plague through the rain?" Abdallah asked.

Quentin nodded, gravely. "They've got to have the biggest rune web the world has ever seen. It would be far simpler to corrupt an existing disease and allow it to spread naturally. If they're spreading it through those storms, then they're creating the viruses out of nothing and spreading them over millions of square miles."

"The scope of this evil is beyond understanding," Abdallah breathed.

"Brilliantly horrible. Makes my lab look like a child's toy. I was proud of the rainmaker, but that's nothing compared to this. They've figured out a way to infect tens of millions of people at one time. If this plague is as virulent as they claim, we'll be seeing entire cities wiped out in the next couple of days. There'll be no stopping it then."

"That's why we're stopping it now." Harriett's voice over the extended channel surprised him.

"What's your status? Some good news would be welcome."

"Moving assets into position. No resistance to the ships docking. The rainmaker will be ready in minutes."

"Hurry. The plague's already starting."

"Roger."

"This is interesting," Abdallah commented, drawing Quentin's attention to a screen showing Beijing. "No storms over China."

"Makes sense, I guess. Xiao seems to want to make China the seat of her new government. Even if she did nothing else, the Chinese are going to gain a critical advantage if they can fight with full military strength against countries crippled by plague."

"We've got storms over Jerusalem, Rome, and Mecca now too," Abdallah reported with a scowl.

"Not good." Attacking the religious centers was of questionable value. Xiao and Sutekh might be able to destroy those religious centers, but that was sure to make believers fight with religious furor.

His pondering about what Xiao might be thinking was interrupted by reports that the Chinese were already launching military air strikes against Thailand. They were also beginning a heavy missile bombardment of Japan.

Both of those countries had been on high alert already, and despite the threat of plague storms, were responding in kind. He felt a sinking queasiness in the pit of his stomach. This would drag other nations into the fight when the last thing they could afford was a war.

"How do we stop it now?" Abdallah whispered, his face ashen.

Quentin slowly shook his head. "I'm not sure."

94

SARAH FELL to the cold stone floor of the temple in ancient Egypt, panting, her heart racing. She tried to leap to her feet, but couldn't move. Xiao rose to stand beside her, looking fit and healthy.

She smiled down at Sarah. "Remain there, slave, until I decide your fate."

Sarah tried to stand again, but only managed to make her legs twitch. She tried to scream defiance at Xiao, but only managed a weak groan.

She'd imagined a lot of worst-case scenarios, but this trumped them all. Somehow Xiao's will was holding her prisoner like a choking, invisible hand.

As she struggled against it, searing agony tore at her innards, as if someone had plunged a burning knife into her guts. She gasped and her concentration scattered. As soon as she stopped struggling, the pain faded.

"You defeated her, and you returned in your true form," Sutekh laughed. He joined Xiao and bowed over her hand. "How?"

"Because I am now the master of all things. Time to complete the ritual and assume our places as the new gods of the future."

They really had returned to the time of Sutekh. Xiao no longer possessed the Egyptian serving girl, but looked like herself. Somehow through Sarah she had managed to step into that historical moment with much more of herself than before. Sarah too felt like herself, in her body, but her mind was trapped in Xiao's nevron and couldn't escape.

"False gods die young," Melek declared as he stepped around an alabaster pillar.

He really had somehow hitched a ride back with them. Sarah felt a dim ray of hope, even though he couldn't hope to stand against either of the cui dashi, let alone both of them. As long as someone remained to try, Sarah chose to hope.

Xiao studied Melek with a look of annoyance. "Your presence here is unexpected, and unnecessary." She turned her back on him.

Melek caught up a tall bronze lamp and charged, but his movements were no faster than a regular mortal. It was as if he'd lost his enhancements when they'd transported through history. Sutekh intercepted him, snatched the lamp away, and back-handed him, sending him tumbling.

The tough hunter rolled back to his feet, but Sutekh threw the lamp. It smashed him off his feet again. He lay on the stone, groaning and cradling a broken arm. Sarah expected to see him shake off the blow and rise again as he always did. She silently exulted when he rolled onto his side. He managed to stand, but only with great effort.

Sarah had to do something, had to help. She couldn't watch Melek get murdered. She was the rune warrior, she had to find an answer. She willed herself to move, to fight against Xiao's influence, but only managed to shift one foot about an inch. That triggered a wave of nausea that left her gagging.

She paused to allow the effects of her resistance to fade. That wasn't working. She'd kill herself before she could cover a single foot. She needed to fight smarter.

She took a long, steadying breath, but the incense that hung thick in the air was making her nauseous. The huge temple room they were in was strangely silent except for the soft echoes of Melek's shuffling footsteps as he made his painful way toward Sarah. If he could reach her maybe he could help her break free.

Before he could, Xiao intercepted Melek and with a negligent flick of her hand slapped him hard enough to send him tumbling across the huge room. He slammed into a stone pillar hard enough to crack ribs. He did not move.

Xiao moved to the unstable rift. There she dropped to her knees to mark additional symbols onto the complex rune that Sarah had broken. The changes stabilized the rift. Crap. Sarah didn't understand a fraction of what Xiao was doing, had destabilized the rift on pure instinct, but she'd done nothing more than delay Xiao's victory.

The rift doorway solidified, and through it Sarah could see Alter fighting a freakish, tentacled monster. He'd chopped most of its tentacles off with his long hunting knife, and was in the middle of plunging his blade into each of its four amber eyes. He was covered in its blood and the sticky, black sludge that coated it, but fought on, unaware that the rift had solidified right behind him.

Xiao gestured Sutekh toward the rift. "Now beloved, step through and take your place as the new-risen god of the future."

Sarah tried to scream her opposition, her intent to fight Xiao forever, but only managed a soft, "Nnnnnnn." Then she retched, her guts torn by the worst dry heaves she'd ever experienced.

Looking eager, but a bit apprehensive, Sutekh approached the rift. "My Queen, do not delay joining me. I will need your guidance to navigate the unknown world."

"I must complete the sacrifice, then I shall return to myself."

She glanced at Sarah, who was helpless to intervene. She couldn't even move a single finger to activate a cipher. "This cretin damaged me. Remove her corpse from me so that my body may heal. Call upon my servant Vlad to attend you until I return. He knows to act as your protector."

"Very well." Sutekh turned to face the rift.

Xiao caught his arm and swiftly marked a rune across his bicep. He studied it with a frown as it activated. "I am not familiar with this."

"It will translate the unfamiliar tongues to your understanding, and will project your words into English so all may understand your directives."

Sarah had never heard of such a thing. She lay at the wrong angle to see the rune, and craned her neck helplessly to see. That was a rune she'd love to know.

Her helplessness infuriated her, but making herself sick wasn't helping. So she forced herself to lay still and consider the runes she knew. She needed to craft a new cipher to break Xiao's control, but wasn't sure what would work.

She didn't know the forbidden rune that interfered with facetaker nevra cores, but that hadn't worked on cui dashi anyway. Xiao's words actually gave her the one tiny spark of hope she could cling to. Did Xiao understand that if Sutekh separated them, Sarah might be able to break free?

Or did Xiao plan to murder her mind before he completed that task? Sarah vowed to take advantage of the moment if she survived long enough. Maybe Gregorios would recognize the danger and free her first.

While she lay plotting and fuming, Sutekh pressed his hand against the rift. Glittering silver light burst out of it, surrounding him with shimmering glory. Sarah felt everything around her shudder, somehow felt the entire aeon quiver as that rift tore Sutekh out of history and cast his soul into the future.

A new rush of anger gave her the strength to flop over onto her stomach. The act of defiance triggered a new form of agony that felt like Paul was again driving his sword into her stomach. An acrid smell, like slag from a welding torch, floated into the room as the light crackled and snapped around Sutekh.

Wow, that hurt. Sarah sagged against the floor, panting, impotently furious. They'd tried so hard, but it hadn't mattered. She'd failed.

The light winked out and Sutekh staggered back from the rift. No, it wasn't Sutekh. It was Alter, wearing Sutekh's body.

That was why Xiao needed Alter, so he and Sutekh could swap places. It appeared not even she could pull a person out of history and leave a hole where they'd stood. Swapping souls was far more efficient, and ended in a net zero change as far as history was concerned.

Alter glanced around, his eyes wild, panicked. He didn't even seem to notice Xiao crouched next to the rift, but his gaze settled on Sarah. Ignoring everything else, he rushed to her side and dropped to his knees beside her.

"Sarah, are you all right?"

She exulted to see him alive and undamaged, but lacked the ability to even greet him. He glanced around, and noticed his father lying unmoving on the far side of the room. With a cry, he rose, but only then did he notice Xiao also rising to stand next to the rift.

Xiao laughed softly and said, "Of course she's not all right. Neither is your father."

Through the opening, Sarah could see the flow of monsters had stopped. Stabilizing the rift and sending Sutekh through had healed that breach. Sutekh stood at the balcony railing of the mosque wearing Alter's body, looking out over the bloody inner court, every eye fixed upon him. His clothing looked clean, his hair perfect. How had he managed that?

His voice echoed back through the rift as he raised his hands high. Words boomed out from him as if he was using an invisible loudspeaker. "I am Sutekh, king of the world. I have come as prophesied, and I command you all to lay down your weapons."

The rift faded to opaque, blocking the scene.

Alter rose to face Xiao. "What did you do to them?"

"That is the wrong question," Xiao said, approaching with a confident stride. An ornate little knife covered with bright Chinese runes appeared in her hand. It didn't look like much of a weapon, but Alter recoiled, fear in his eyes.

"The correct question," Xiao continued as she closed inexorably on the retreating Alter. "Is what is about to happen to you?"

95

GREGORIOS LOOKED from the figure of the man wearing Alter's body to the combined forms of Sarah and Xiao, who still lay together in the bloody impact crater. The glow of Xiao's nevron shone around Sarah's motionless head and had spread to encase the two women. He'd thought Sarah had done it, that she'd destroyed Xiao, but now he realized what idiots they'd been.

Sarah had been the only one who could stand against Xiao, but her greatest weakness had always been that Xiao might get her hands and her nevron onto her. She might be a rune warrior, but she was still a mortal. Even Gregorios couldn't withstand Xiao's nevron.

When the false king of the world had stepped into Alter's body, a brilliant silver light had burst across the inner court, vaporizing the monsters. Everyone had stopped to stare, and Sutekh had stepped right into that bubble of silence to capture everyone's attention.

Two news cameras still looked functional, and the cameramen were already zeroed in on the newcomer. One disheveled, wild-eyed reporter was clamoring about the man who had saved them from the monsters. The ridiculousness of that claim made Gregorios want to slap the idiot. Twice.

He muttered a few choice Greek curses then added, "I'd say we're not as close to victory as we had hoped."

Most of the civilians had taken shelter behind the enforcer vehicles and reinforcements. They formed a heavily-armed fighting line that extended out from the main entryway in a semi-circle into the main square. Carlo and his men had joined the enforcers. The ambassadors and their few remaining security personnel were moving to take shelter there too. Hunters clustered across the square in the entrance to the many-columned passage that led deeper into the temple complex.

Very few heka had survived the hunter charge and the monsters. Those few had retreated through the lower doorway into the mosque and were scrambling to form a fighting line to either side of the man who had swapped faces with Alter.

Somehow Sutekh had stepped into Alter's body from the past. Gregorios puzzled about that as he settled to the ground about ten yards in front of his men.

Eirene zipped around the massed enforcers, moving just a little slower than before since she was burdened by several heavy weapons. She skidded to a stop next to him and passed one bulky case to him. He grinned.

She said, "Don't you see? Somehow Xiao and Sarah have returned to history. Xiao is completing the ritual."

"Impossible. They don't have a machine."

"With all the runes they both know, perhaps the machines aren't needed."

Gregorios grunted. "That's annoying. I hate it when the rules change."

"You'd think you'd be used to that by now," Eirene said, trying a bit of humor.

"Let's see if he likes it when I change his face for a puddle of mush."

He dropped the case to the ground and threw back the lid to reveal the deadly piece of hardware. This was the gun he saved for desperate situations. He called it the Clincher.

Only then did he realize he had never summoned it in the memoryscape, even though it would have come in handy a couple of times. Well, that was dumb.

The clincher was a modified version of the Barrett XM109 25mm anti-material rifle. Designed to take out light-armored vehicles, this weapon weighed in at thirty-five pounds and fired both high explosive and armor piercing rounds.

Quentin had added some novel features to make the recoil manageable, but it still kicked at over fifty pounds, depending on the round. The custom, extended twenty-round magazine was already loaded, with the first heavy round in the chamber.

Gregorios lifted the weapon and exulted in the feel of its solid weight. This was the gun one needed to carry when facing a cui dashi.

Eirene gave him a hard look. "Don't you dare destroy that body, Greg. Not until there's no other hope for returning Alter."

"Don't worry. Sutekh can take a few hits."

The ancient cui dashi raised his hands and spoke, although the movement of his lips didn't match the booming voice that echoed across the square. "I am Sutekh, king of the world. I have come as prophesied, and I command you all to lay down your weapons."

At that moment, Tomas spoke over the tactical channel. "Web is down. Repeat, web is down. On my way with Francesca and Spartacus."

"Good man." Gregorios hefted the clincher and shot Sutekh in the forehead.

The armor piercing bullet drilled right through his skull, spraying brains and gore back across the balcony. Sutekh staggered, but did not fall. The ghastly wound healed almost instantly.

Cui dashi were more annoying than a plague of cockroaches. Still, that bullet might have simply bounced off Xiao. Gregorios doubted it would have made such a mess of her face. That meant Sutekh wasn't as powerful.

That shot burst the dam holding everyone immobile. Hunters and enforcers opened fire on the row of heka standing recklessly atop the mosque balcony. Bullets and grenades tore across the elevated exposed area. The heka, who were clearly still relying upon the remote protective web, abruptly learned that the web was down. Most of them died before they even realized the truth. The entire court stank of death and gunpowder and opened bodies.

Sutekh staggered back, blood spraying from dozens of injuries as he took heavy fire. With such concentrated firepower, they could take down the man before he could recover. All they had to do was sacrifice Alter.

Gregorios and Eirene shouted simultaneously over the general comm link. "Stand down! Cease fire!"

As their teams reluctantly complied, Gregorios glanced at Sarah's quicksilver form, still lying amid the gore of Xiao's broken corpse. They could attempt to destroy Xiao, but might kill Sarah too. That was annoying. Worse, he couldn't penetrate the cloud of Xiao's nevra core to reach Sarah. Maybe they could lasso Sarah and drag her out?

Before he could work out a plan, Sutekh shouted through broken teeth and bleeding lips, "Vlad! I call upon you to protect me."

All the lesser vampires were dead, but Vlad had remained concealed. Now, the ancient vampire appeared on the mosque balcony beside the wounded Sutekh. His maw gaped open impossibly wide, and the shrieking gale of his soul wind blasted forth.

Since the concentrated sunlight cipher had been destroyed, he could risk deploying his captured souls in the light of day without risking many of them. The moaning wind whipped around the square in a billowing, gray cloud that obscured vision and chilled souls. Most of the enforcers stopped firing, but scanned for a new target.

Eirene said, "Stay alert. Aim for the face if the vampire appears."

Gregorios started forward, enormous rifle at the ready, hoping for a shot at Vlad. Sutekh had lured the vampire out. Now Gregorios could kill him. He expected Sutekh to retreat until Xiao completed her devilry in history.

He was surprised to see him materialize through the gloom, rushing toward Xiao and Sarah. He raised the rifle, but Eirene pulled the barrel down.

She held a finger to her lips and whispered, "Wait. See what he's doing."

The air had changed from the intense heat of Egyptian sun to the blasted cold of Wallachia in the winter. Vlad was nearby. He would not be able to resist hunting. Gregorios wanted to activate his nevra core, but that would alert Sutekh to their presence if he hadn't noticed them already.

So all he did was direct a bit of nevron into the ring knife wedding band he wore. That bit of power would awaken the powerful runes marked into the little ring. It was a last resort weapon, but it seemed they were facing last resorts, so having it active comforted him.

Fifty feet away, Sutekh stepped into the glowing nimbus of Xiao's nevron. That simple act demonstrated his superiority over Gregorios and Eirene and any simple facetakers. He was a cui dashi, one of the world's most powerful monsters. Killing him would be so satisfying, if only they could find a way to free Alter.

As Sutekh leaned over Sarah, Gregorios tensed to fire. He wasn't sure what Sutekh could do to her in that quicksilver form, but he wasn't about to give the ancient cui dashi time to figure it out. Instead of attacking her, Sutekh simply grasped one of her metallic ankles and heaved. Sarah's body ripped free of Xiao's splattered, grotesque form and soared away.

"He freed her," Eirene whispered, echoing Gregorios' astonishment.

Immediately, Xiao began to heal. Sutekh looked satisfied as he turned to watch Sarah's unconscious form. Before she struck the hard stone ground, Vlad materialized and caught her.

With a look of ultimate satisfaction on his face, he turned her until her head fell back, exposing her throat. He opened his mouth wide, fangs extending, eyes glittering with anticipation. If he took Sarah's soul, they'd lose their best hope at defeating Xiao, and Vlad would become virtually indestructible.

So Gregorios and Eirene both shot Vlad at the same time. Gregorios fired a high explosive 25mm round that struck right through Vlad's open mouth and exploded against the back of his skull.

Eirene fired an MK19 40mm semi-automatic grenade launcher. In her Amazon body, with her many enhancements, she wielded the heavy weapon, usually vehicle-mounted, from the hip. The high explosive round caught Vlad in the chest.

The resulting explosions vaporized the vampire, releasing a dense cloud of freed spirits that moaned with glee as they sped away in every direction, splattering against walls and columns all around the square. The greasy marks of their passage from Vlad's service dripped slowly down the stone. Vlad's shriek of pain and fury echoed painfully around the square, threatening to overwhelm Gregorios' ear protection.

They hadn't killed Vlad, but it still felt good to hurt him and cost him so many captured souls. Any other vampire would have probably succumbed to the trauma.

Gregorios shared a grin with his wife. They'd upset Vlad, hurt him, hopefully driven him beyond his normal caution. In the past, he would have already fled, wisely choosing escape and survival over valor and death. Today, maybe he'd risk materializing again so they could finally destroy him.

"Quentin, we've got Vlad on the run. I'd love to hear some good news about that plague storm."

"Harriett is working on it. Her forces will be on site soon."

"I hope it's soon enough," Gregorios whispered.

Sutekh stared from the bloody mist that had been the vampire to Gregorios and Eirene. He stepped toward them, awe and confusion on his face.

"What is this devilry? Your strange weapons belch the flame of the gods and cast thunder and destruction, and yet you've allowed the temples to crumble to ruin."

"It's a matter of priorities, I guess," Gregorios said with a shrug as he turned his weapon toward Sutekh and shot him in the face. The explosive round turned his features into jelly, and the cui dashi fell to the stones.

"I told you to be careful with Alter's body." Eirene slapped him in the back of the head.

"I shot him in the face. It's the only part that's not Alter."

"The skull is."

"Then what do you want to do? We can't leave a cui dashi roaming around."

He was really interested in hearing what she intended. He didn't want to destroy Alter, and he honestly wasn't sure how to defeat Sutekh without Alter or Sarah to help, not if they wanted to preserve Alter's body. Before Eirene could answer, a cloud of bats churned down out of the gray, swirling soul wind that still filled the square.

The bats seized both Sutekh and Xiao's slumbering body and whisked them into the air, back toward the mosque. Xiao already looked nearly healed, despite her full-body splatter experience. How much regeneration remained to the woman before they wore her down?

After Xiao left the broken crater where she'd been lying, Melek's body materialized. It looked somehow faded and indistinct, and seemed to waver. That was weird. Had Xiao's nevron cloud affected his super enhancement?

Gregorios couldn't help the old hunter at the moment, so he trotted over to Sarah's prone form, her limbs splayed awkwardly where Vlad had dropped her. Eirene followed, watching his back in case Vlad tried to attack. Gregorios didn't feel the icy chill that always warned him that Vlad had taken corporal form and walked nearby.

Tomas rushed up through the billowing clouds and dropped to a knee beside Sarah. "What's wrong with her?"

"We think Xiao somehow took her back through time. Hopefully she's fighting Xiao in ancient Egypt," Eirene explained.

"Sutekh is here, up at the mosque by the rift. Either Sarah wins and wakes up, and Alter returns, or Xiao wakes up and we have to deal with her and Sutekh both," Gregorios explained.

"Vlad is near. I can feel him," Tomas said, glancing around eagerly.

"He wants Sarah. Nearly got her a minute ago," Eirene said.

"Ran off again, just when things got interesting," Gregorios added with a sour grunt. "Vlad the Annoyer, as always."

Tomas grinned. "That's new."

Gregorios shrugged. "Mayhem and chaos bring out the best in me, I guess. Now that you're here, you can watch over Sarah while we chase Sutekh." Gregorios activated his super enhancement and lifted off the ground.

Tomas looked furious at the thought of Vlad consuming Sarah's soul, but his voice remained calm. "Francesca and Spartacus paused to redeploy the reinforcements. When they catch up, I'll leave them here to watch Sarah. I'll join you."

Without warning, Gregorios' super enhancement fizzled, and he dropped back to the ground. Frowning, he tried to activate it again, but got nothing. "Hey, I can't fly any more."

Eirene tried running, but although she moved far faster than any unenhanced mortal, she no longer moved like the Flash. Tomas frowned and concentrated, but nothing happened, and his frown deepened. "I've lost my super enhancement too."

"I fear we've drawn too heavily on that master rune," Eirene said.

"Rotten luck," Gregorios grumbled.

Those super enhancements had broken all sorts of laws of physics, so they had to consume vast quantities of power. He'd banked on the master rune holding a bit more juice. He glanced over at Melek, who still lay slumbering, just like Sarah.

His super enhancement had faded too, and his body had solidified. Well, sort of. It still looked somehow shallow, as if some of it was missing. Had he gotten caught up in whatever duel Sarah and Xiao were still locked in? If so, could he escape?

Eirene noticed Melek too and rushed over to him. Gregorios followed as she knelt over her grandson and stroked his forehead.

Frowning, she said, "I've never seen anything like this. His soul is gone. It's worse than any memoryscape journey. It's like even the tangible parts of him are fading, being drawn somewhere else."

"Hopefully that gives him an advantage, wherever they are." Gregorios placed a comforting hand on her shoulder.

She looked up at him, not hiding her concern. "Without his super enhancement, can he come back?"

"I don't know."

They shared a grave look. Beyond their concern for Melek's safety, their super enhancements had been their trump card against Xiao. Without them, they were now at a distinct disadvantage, despite having a couple hundred heavily armed enforcers nearby and artillery strikes ready at their beck and call.

Francesca and Spartacus rushed through the billowing, chilly soul wind. Spartacus looked exultant, but also really annoyed. "I vanquished the foul Hongwu with the assistance of the Mistress of Seduction, but the burning glory of my victory has just winked out."

"All our super enhancements are down," Gregorios said as Eirene gave their daughter a quick embrace. "Vlad's prowling around. You and Francesca keep an eye on Sarah. We're going after Sutekh."

Spartacus saluted with fist to heart. He wore twin gladius swords strapped to his back, but hefted a fifty caliber machine gun at the ready.

"Let the villain show himself, and we will rip his black heart asunder. None shall assault the peaceful slumber of the Lady of Steel while we yet draw breath."

"We've got it," Francesca agreed with a smile at Spartacus. "Go finish this already."

Gregorios hefted his huge gun and led Eirene and Tomas toward the mosque. They'd do what they could, but really, success depended mostly upon whatever it was Sarah was doing.

96

Give me a lever long enough, a fulcrum on which to place it, and my rune of strength, and I shall move the world.

~ARCHIMEDES

SARAH FOCUSED all of her might on simply moving one finger. Xiao had commanded her to remain where she was, but she hadn't said Sarah couldn't move a finger. Concentrating on that exact interpretation of the command helped ease the debilitating pain a fraction.

With agonizing slowness, she began to trace a mark to activate a cipher she held fixed in her mind. It would link her back to the Beijing charging cipher. With that extra force, she might be able to break out of Xiao's control.

Xiao had almost caught up with Alter, who had retreated in a circle until he was approaching the huge sarcophagus with Sutekh's glittering rune web. Xiao wore a mocking smile on her lips, as if taunting him to break into a run.

Sarah wasn't sure what she intended with that little knife, but had no doubt it would seal Alter's fate. She redoubled her efforts to make a single, glowing mark. At the glacial rate her finger was moving, it would still take several seconds.

"Sarah, why can't I summon anything?" Alter called.

Xiao chuckled. "She can't help you. She's bound to me, just as you soon will be again, my beloved sacrifice. You cannot summon weapons because this is not a memory landscape for you. You are really here in ancient Egypt. You're the first man to have successfully time traveled."

Instead of celebrating, he'd get sacrificed. What a raw deal.

Xiao raised her knife, but before she could close the last two feet, Melek stepped out from behind a nearby pillar, carrying a six-barreled minigun. Its deadly barrels were already spinning.

Sarah blinked in surprise. She had forgotten about him, had figured he was out of the fight. By the momentary flash of surprise on Xiao's face, so had she. He looked strong again, as if he'd found a way to bond his enhancements.

"Alter might be standing firmly in this moment in time, but I'm straddling two moments," Melek said, and squeezed the trigger.

The gun buzzed like a hundred angry saws, and fired a torrent of explosive rounds. The racket as they blasted into Xiao boomed and echoed and shook the heavy stone room.

The destructive wave of modern fire catapulted Xiao off her feet. She screamed with rage as she rolled, driven by the savage barrage, her skin peeling away and blood spraying in every direction. Melek followed, walking the stream of devastation across her body toward her head.

Sarah silently urged him on. Seeing Xiao suffer bolstered her hope. They could figure out how to damage the deadly cui dashi.

Xiao suddenly planted her hands and performed a fantastic acrobatic flip, flinging herself straight up forty feet. The unexpected move threw off Melek's aim. He tried vainly to adjust, but her skin was already healing as she kicked off of a thick column and somersaulted back across the room.

"You're not the only one here straddling multiple times!" An RPG appeared in Xiao's hand as she soared close to the high ceiling. She fired it down at Melek.

He dove aside, dropping his minigun. The explosion sent him tumbling into one of the outer walls, but he rose to his feet again, looking unharmed. "I've found the secret to this memory, and I will stop you."

Alter picked up the smoking minigun. "Sounds like a plan, Dad."

Sarah frowned as she lay immobile, watching the unexpected turn of events. How could they summon modern weapons? They weren't in a memoryscape. Were they? Had the memoryscape they had traveled so many times touched the true record of history more closely than they'd ever known?

She'd always assumed they were walking inside the facetaker heads. Then again, she now understood that the facetakers served as anchor points for the ascendants. Had the machines accessed those ascendants through the facetaker memories and brought them back into that recorded history?

Now they stood in an actual historical moment, and they were changing it. She could feel the reverberations of their actions cracking the integrity of that piece of the ascendants. Could Xiao's and Alter's ascendants handle the stress, adjust to the new reality, or would they break? If they broke, would that unravel history or cast them into one of those alternate dimensions that fantasy authors, mad scientists, and quantum scientists sometimes talked about?

She didn't want to find out. Better to leave history unchanged. Dealing with fourth dimensional time travel was mind-twisting.

Xiao landed atop the huge sarcophagus, her face illuminated in a freakish way by the silvery light of the rune web. "Let's make this interesting then, shall we? Sarah, you stop Melek."

She had almost completed her cipher, could have already done so if she hadn't been distracted by Melek's charge and the unanswerable questions it sparked. Now Xiao's will swamped her mind and she stood, unable to finish the cipher.

As new purpose flooded her mind, her fear and horror faded to faint whispers. She focused on Melek and saw with remarkable clarity that he really did need to be stopped. Finally, something she could do.

Sarah rushed across the room at the hunter, whose expression turned horrified. He shouted her name, urged her to stop, but she punched him in the chest, sending him flying. Something about the feeling of hitting him felt wrong, but that didn't delay her from stalking after him.

Behind her, Xiao made a dismissive wave, and Alter's minigun disappeared. Her soft laughter echoed through the huge temple room. That too seemed wrong, but it was too hard to focus on those faint worries. Easier to fight. Sarah caught up with Melek as he rose, a pistol in his hand. She slapped it away. So easy. She caught him by the throat and lifted him off the floor, planning to crush out his life.

He stopped struggling.

Sarah frowned. She'd apparently stopped him, but wasn't she supposed to do something more? Fighting was easy, but thinking was too hard.

"Sarah," he whispered, barely able to breathe around her iron grip.

"You're the rune warrior. You're greater than this. You can fight her, Sarah. Stop Xiao or she's going to kill Alter."

Sarah glanced back at Xiao, who had beaten Alter to the ground and was dragging him toward the large sarcophagus by one leg.

"Sarah, help! Snap out of it," Alter cried.

She knew him, didn't she? She tried to think, but her mind was smothered by thick confusion.

"I can help," Melek said. He drew a tiny knife and raised it toward her arm.

Fight. She could do that. Sarah caught his hand and twisted the knife away. Growling, she dropped Melek and stomped on his legs, breaking bones. He screamed, but she left him there and jogged over to Xiao. She'd commanded Sarah to stop Melek. She'd done so. Now she had to ask the questions that formed in her mind like half-seen images in a fog.

"Take this one," Xiao said, tossing Alter to Sarah. She caught him and held him.

"Sarah, you can't do this." Alter looked close to tears. That tugged at something deep inside of Sarah, but she couldn't quite recognize it.

Xiao ripped off Alter's shirt, revealing Sutekh's well-muscled torso. An intricate rune was marked onto his stomach. It was dull, not bonded to Alter's soul yet. It looked somehow familiar, but Sarah couldn't quite focus on it as Xiao raised her knife to Alter's chest. "It's so much more satisfying to know you're the one helping me complete the ritual, Sarah."

Sarah smiled, filled with joy. Helping people was good, right? Then why did it bother her?

Xiao cut into the skin of Alter's chest, marking a complex rune with her ornate knife. Blood welled from the cuts and dripped down his skin. She wielded her knife with precision, but cut deeper than necessary. One more thing that didn't feel right. Sarah struggled to understand her growing unease, but couldn't quite grasp it.

Alter met her gaze, his expression earnest. He said simply, "Sarah, I love you."

Then he reached out to touch her face with a gentle hand. A memory grew in her mind, powered by that touch. Alter wasn't her enemy. He was special. He was . . .

Without warning, the compulsion Xiao held over Sarah's mind evaporated and she returned to herself with a start. Horror at what Xiao had done to her, what she was forcing Sarah to help her do to

Alter filled her with rage. Xiao had nearly completed the binding rune.

No way she'd get the chance.

With a cry of fury, Sarah released Alter, grabbed the blade, and wrenched it out of Xiao's hands. She drove it for the hated woman's throat, but Xiao deflected it. The sharp blade instead plunged into Xiao's shoulder.

Alter dropped to the floor between them and rolled away as Sarah twisted the blade in Xiao's shoulder. The cui dashi was tough. Cutting her felt like trying to cut stone, but Sarah wrenched at the knife with all her anger. Xiao shrieked, pain and surprise flickering across her smooth features.

"I'm going to cut out your heart," Sarah hissed.

With a heave, Xiao sent Sarah flying. She yanked the knife out of her shoulder, allowing the wound to close. "You've interrupted me for the last time, warrior. I swear a sacred vow that when I rule history, I will return to the time when you were a little girl and torture your parents and siblings to death in front of you. Then I'll find everyone you've ever loved and do the same. I will—"

Sarah still didn't understand how they could summon weapons in this moment, but no longer cared. They might crack or break or split history, but if she didn't fight with every possible weapon, Xiao would win.

So she focused on summoning her M4 rifle just as she did in the memoryscape. Remarkably, the weapon appeared in her hands. Sweet. She fired the shotgun-type round from the grenade launcher. Hundreds of little steel pellets blasted Xiao's face, tearing open her skin and driving into her open mouth.

"Shut up," Sarah growled as she opened the chamber to drop the spent round and load a high explosive round instead.

Alter, who had begun circling Xiao to attack from behind, suddenly threw his arms out wide and howled, his entire body shaking. The intricate rune carved on his stomach glowed with silver-white intensity. It was bonding to his soul and Sarah understood its purpose now as she gazed upon it without Xiao's compulsion clouding her mind.

That rune opened the power of his ascendant to him. Unlike trying to wield the entire force of multiple master runes, that rune united him to the ascendant. The rune made its power accessible to him, but did not try to channel it all through him. Somehow she recognized that he could wield that power, unleash it, without being consumed by it.

It was similar to the runes she'd noticed Xiao using when she possessed the Egyptian girl, but with a slightly different purpose. She recognized Sutekh's signature rune within the greater construct, and realized that complex rune was Sutekh's secret, the knowledge he alone had discovered.

He could access the power of his ascendant, but hadn't understood how to travel its twisting length. That was the secret Xiao had learned. Together they understood the full picture for unlocking their ascendants. Their combined knowledge threatened the world and time itself.

Alter shook, a silvery glow seeping out of his skin. His eyes became pools of periwinkle light, and fire of the same hue rippled along his hands and up his arms. "Whoa! That's amazing. I see everything."

Xiao looked worried for the first time, glancing from Sarah to Alter, then taking a slow step backward toward the sarcophagus and its rune web.

Sarah smiled. "Glad you're feeling better. Let's end this."

Xiao summoned a grenade launcher and fired, but Alter leaped and rolled away before the grenade struck. As Xiao tossed the spent tube aside, Alter smashed into her, tumbling her across the room.

Sarah had never seen him move so fast. Wearing Sutekh's rune was making him very nearly Xiao's equal. Sarah felt renewed hope finally creeping out of the icy hole in her heart where it had been hiding. She and Alter could defeat Xiao together.

Alter flashed Sarah a predatory grin, then chased Xiao. Sarah followed, pausing to fire an explosive round from her grenade launcher at a crocodile-headed statue that began to chase Alter. The round caught it in the throat and blew its head off.

Sarah frowned at the dead monster. One more clue that maybe the memoryscape was linked far more closely to actual historical events than she'd imagined. By traveling back along the ascendants, maybe they hadn't exactly traveled through time, but only reached the most realistic copy of what had happened in real life. But if that was the case, how could Sutekh have stepped out of that recording and taken physical form again?

No, they had to be standing in real history, but their connection to it was still not quite complete. They were travelers of the ascendants, somehow part of that moment, but also foreign to it. Thinking about the twisted weirdness of aeon space gave her a headache, and she didn't have time to puzzle out the truth. Maybe if they survived, she and Melek could work it out together.

Xiao stopped not far from the rift doorway and crouched on the floor to mark a barrier rune. It activated just before Alter caught up with her. Alter bounced off the barrier and pounded on it, cursing in frustration.

Sarah rushed over, super annoyed that Xiao was using her own tactics against her.

Alter cocked his head and gestured toward the distant outer door to the temple. "Hear that?"

For the first time, she noticed the sounds of fighting, clashing steel, and an occasional scream. How had she not heard that before? "More reinforcements for Sutekh?"

"Not hardly. I'm thinking that's Moses."

"Really?" She felt a thrill to think of meeting the iconic biblical figure.

"We're in history. This is the day Moses defeated Sutekh."

"Not any more," Xiao said, her voice slightly distorted by the protective barrier.

She was marking another, far more intricate rune on the floor. Its heart was similar to the rune she used to travel her ascendant. No, it was more like the one linking Alter to his ascendant.

Xiao had apparently also recognized the truth about that rune that Alter wore on his chest. That was the last piece she'd lacked to unlock the full force of her ascendant, and she was clearly planning to do so. If she completed her newest rune, she'd again turn the tide against them.

Sarah wanted to scream with frustration. They were so close! Every time they gained the upper hand, Xiao flipped things back on them.

Alter pounded on the barrier, but even with his enhanced strength, he couldn't penetrate it. Xiao was fueling her barrier from that nearby, unused rune web that Sutekh had prepared to battle Moses.

Sarah had spent so much time perfecting barrier ciphers. She should have also studied breaking them. Xiao's barrier looked very solid. Sarah doubted they'd break through in time.

She considered using the standard counter rune, but another glance at Xiao's barrier confirmed that the cui dashi had included marks to counter that approach. It was super annoying to face a master runesmith who also happened to be a super-powered, ultimate villain.

"Block her," Melek shouted from where he crawled desperately toward them. His badly broken legs had started to heal, but still wouldn't support his weight. Alter rushed over and scooped him up like a child, then carried him to Sarah.

"Block her," Melek repeated. "She cannot be allowed to link to her ascendant, or she can break the flow of history."

"I'm open to ideas," Sarah snapped, more sharply than she intended. Forgive a girl for getting a bit stressed in moments like that.

Xiao paused and looked up from her work. Instead of her normal haughty stare, she simply glared. Sarah had really ticked her off.

Great. Sarah winked at her.

Xiao's frown deepened and she said, "You wish to stop me, Sarah?"

"Of course. Take down this barrier, and fight me like a woman of honor." Xiao was big on honor, so Sarah hoped the appeal would prove effective.

Instead of dropping the barrier, Xiao said, "You alone challenge my mastery over time, so yes, I will grant your petition of challenge. We will duel."

"Like pistols at ten paces, or swords?" Sarah asked, but she had a sinking feeling she already knew what Xiao was talking about.

Xiao gave her a predatory smile. "You are uniquely gifted in those annoying ciphers of yours, but I've been a runesmith for centuries. Time to see whose runes will prevail, and who will die fueling the victory of the other."

Melek breathed, "Rune duel."

Alter set him down, blood draining from his face. He stepped to the barrier and pounded on it. "No. Duel me instead."

"Help her, if you like," Xiao offered with a grand gesture of invitation. Her eyes were cold, and her expression confident. "Melek can join you too. All of your souls will be consumed. Yours, dear Alter, will finalize Sutekh's transition to the future. Your father's will be spent augmenting his might, and Sarah's will be sacrificed to me, as is my right."

Sarah didn't like the sound of that. Xiao looked so confident, and she probably had every right to be. Sarah had never participated in a rune duel, although she'd fought with ciphers against Xiao enough times that she felt she'd proven her nimbleness of mind. Alter and

Melek were the best runesmiths in the hunter clan. Surely together they could defeat her.

She glanced at Melek, but he looked worried and said softly, "It is not wise to combine multiple participants on one side of the duel. It's just as likely we'll interfere with each other's work."

"I accept," Alter declared, his expression determined. He stepped back from the barrier and took Sarah's hand in his. "We can defeat her together."

"Together," Sarah repeated, drawing confidence from Alter's fiery gaze. She'd longed to reunite with him, to fight Xiao together. Now they had their chance.

Melek took a long breath and nodded, his expression hardening to one of absolute determination. "Together."

Xiao only laughed, then started marking runes with astonishing speed onto the stone floor. Sarah recognized the rune dueling marks that Melek had shown her. The duel was on.

Alter dropped to his knees beside his father, and the two of them began marking runes onto the stones with small knives. The blades cut the stone like it was made of soft clay, and they moved with speed, precision, and urgency. Sarah dropped to her knees beside them, frowning and feeling immediately out of her depth.

"How do you know what to mark?"

Melek said, "I will focus on defense. I am beginning with optimal counter symbols based on the initial symbols Xiao is using, and will build from there."

"And I'm working on offensive runes to bind her soul to the outcome and spend the vast energy she'll be controlling back against her." Alter gave Sarah a fierce grin. "She will be consumed by the fires of her own strength."

"Then what do I do?" Sarah asked as symbols began taking shape, weaving together in one of the most complex compound runes she'd ever seen. And they were doing it all off the cuff, at the spur of the moment.

It was impressive, and daunting. On the other side of the barrier, Xiao was working even faster than the two hunters combined. She never hesitated, barely glanced up from her work to check what they were doing. It was as if she had her entire rune already planned out in her mind.

Melek looked up for a second to give her an encouraging smile and gesture at their work. "We are covering the basic structure for you, but this duel will be decided by ascendants and the aeon. Your job is to counter her there, for your command of the aeon is your great advantage."

Sarah glanced over at Xiao's runes. The cui dashi was only five feet away, but separated by the protective barrier. She longed to pierce it somehow and beat on Xiao's face. That would be simpler, but she'd done that many times and it had never worked. Maybe a rune duel was their best bet for defeating her.

Xiao had added the signature rune for her own ascendant. She frowned and leaned closer to the barrier to study Xiao's work as the cui dashi added more symbols to that part of the rune. Understanding chilled Sarah with new fear.

"She's linking in her cui dashi children. She's joining the strength of their ascendants to hers."

Melek did not slow, but said, "Counter it. She lacks the final runes to control those other ascendants."

Alter looked worried. "She can still access a lot of their power through them. Sarah, how can we block that?"

It terrified her to realize she didn't know. She should be working frantically, marking symbols next to theirs, reinforcing their work, but her mind was blank as she considered the challenge. Even if Xiao ended up wielding only a fraction of the power of those multiple ascendants, it would overwhelm any master runes she could draw upon.

Xiao glanced up and noticed her sitting there, unmoving. She grinned, looking more confident than ever. She was going to destroy them. Sarah couldn't just kneel there, terrified, without even trying.

Focus, girl, she told herself.

Win or die, there were no second chances now. She needed more power, but where could she get it? She glanced back down at the runes Melek and Alter were still madly inscribing. The greater rune, combining their work, was beginning to take shape. Its power was so clear, so pure, but it was incomplete.

She realized with sudden despair that she could not stop Xiao. She lacked her own ascendant, and as such, was critically handicapped in this fight.

Melek glanced up again, and she read worry in his eye. "Sarah, how do we counter her?"

She couldn't. She lacked an ascendant. She opened her mouth to tell them they were doomed, but couldn't do it. There had to be a way.

There was.

Understanding struck like a thunderbolt, and Sarah cringed when she saw the truth. Could she really force another to pay such a terrible price? If she didn't, they would all die.

Sometimes being a hero really sucked.

"I'm on it," she told Melek as she made her choice.

Xiao glanced up again and mocked, "Are you really going to die without even trying to fight me? I own too many ascendants."

Sarah snapped, "You play with ascendants. I own the aeon."

"Foolish child." Xiao shifted to her left a little bit and marked a new series of symbols onto her intricate rune. That was the final piece, and the entire complex structure began to glow as it activated.

A stabbing pain shot up Sarah's legs, and her strength began to drain away. She gasped and nearly fell over. It was happening far faster than she'd expected.

Melek groaned, clutching at his stomach. "Sarah! We cannot complete our rune without your parts."

Alter leaned over the rune and marked a couple more symbols. Their runes began to glow, and Alter toppled over. He lay motionless, barely breathing. The pain subsided, and Sarah realized why. Alter had adjusted the rune so that he took the brunt of the drain. He was sacrificing his life to give her a little more time.

"Cheater," Sarah spat at Xiao, who was grinning at her.

She couldn't hesitate any longer. With glowing fingers, Sarah began adding her own symbols to their group battle rune. She included the rune warrior symbol to transform it into a battle cipher.

Then she wrapped it into the signature rune of Gregorios' ascendant.

"I'm sorry," Sarah breathed as she activated the cipher.

97

GREGORIOS COLLAPSED TO THE HARD, stone ground, clutching at his head and screaming so hard, it was a wonder he didn't spit up a lung. He'd never felt such overwhelming pain, but he couldn't sever the nerves like he'd always done in the past.

He was losing his nevra core.

The truth filled him with overwhelming terror. What was happening? How was Xiao attacking his very core? He screamed again as his nevra core flared, scouring his innards like white-hot irons. He couldn't control it as it raged through him. His connection to it wavered, then snapped.

Gregorios' nevra core disappeared, snuffed out like a candle plunged into icy water. His body shook, every muscle convulsing as his nevra core was yanked away, leaving him nauseous and weak.

Mortal.

Gregorios howled with pain and despair, clutching at his hair, trying to reach his core. It was such an integral part of him. He'd relied upon it for thousands of years, could scarce comprehend its loss.

Eirene's powerful Amazon arms encircled him, and her ever-loved face pressed close to his. "What's wrong, love? Where'd you get hit?"

"In the core," he muttered, shaking from the loss. He had never imagined being so utterly violated. The horror of dispossession was laughable compared to this.

"I don't understand." Eirene frowned, patting his chest, looking for a wound.

"My nevra core is gone," he whispered, shaking again as he voiced the horrible truth. "Someone just stole it."

"How is that possible?" Eirene gasped. She looked horrified, but she couldn't possibly understand. He never could have.

Tomas crouched close to them, his rifle at the ready. He glanced at Gregorios, expression concerned. "If Xiao can target your core, then Sarah's in trouble. I've got to see if I can help. I'm heading for the rift gateway."

Gregorios was in too much shock to respond, but Eirene nodded and Tomas rushed away, disappearing into the billowing dimness of Vlad's moaning soul wind.

Eirene turned back to Gregorios. "Are you absolutely sure? It's not some new level of illusion?"

He shook his head, trying to pull himself together. They'd never faced such a dire threat before, but if Xiao could target him, she could target Eirene. Knowing his beloved wife was in such danger helped center his mind.

"I'm sure. I don't know how it happened, love, but it's happened. I've got nothing. It's gone. Even my runes were snuffed out."

He felt weaker than he had since the early days of his first life. He was helpless, vulnerable.

Eirene glanced in the direction of the mosque where Tomas had headed and whispered, "What's happening?"

Gregorios forced himself to stand. He felt unsteady, but tried to mask his terror and weakness. Eirene needed him to be strong, and by the gods, he would be. Rising seemed to help, and his anger flared.

That was the lowest of low blows, and he'd flay Xiao's skin for daring attack him like that. "Whatever they're doing, Sarah had better have a good explanation for this."

He had work to do. The world seemed alien and fearful, Vlad's soul wind chilly and unnerving in a way he'd never felt before. He focused on the mission. He could cry later. "Let's go."

He'd dropped the clincher when he collapsed. He leaned down to scoop it up, but something slammed into him from behind. The brutal impact lifted him off the ground and wrenched his back and neck painfully. Without his enhancements, he couldn't handle a hit like that, and the breath whooshed out of him in a painful grunt.

Gregorios crashed into the stones hard enough to dislocate his left shoulder. He cried out in pain as he tumbled three times, pushed along by the invisible adversary. He came to stop on his back, feeling really annoyed.

Vlad leaned over him, grinning. His soul wind howled with chained mortals lamenting their fate. It circled them closely, black and ominous, and so cold it sucked at Gregorios' strength.

"Time for your last reckoning," Vlad gloated.

Most mortals would curl up and die when facing the ultimate vampire. Gregorios snarled and lashed out with his right hand, but the blow was slow and clumsy, and he only managed to bruise his hand against Vlad's iron-hard stomach.

Vlad's smile widened, his mouth extending beyond normal limits as his fangs extended. He crooned, "The great Gregorios is fallen, and your soul will feed my victory forever."

"You're so melodramatic," Gregorios growled. He drew his sidearm, a double-stacked forty-five and started pumping rounds into Vlad's chest.

The vampire hissed loud enough to make Gregorios cringe, and slapped the pistol aside so hard he broke Gregorios' wrist. Undiminished pain lanced up his arm, and he hissed too, just not as epic as Vlad.

An ancient Roman battle cry drew their attention. Eirene was charging with long, curved, kukri blades in both hands. In that Amazon body, she looked terrifying as she bore down on them, promise of death in her eyes.

"Been nice knowing you, Vladdy boy," Gregorios chuckled.

Vlad hissed, "No one can save you today!"

Suddenly, a dozen clones appeared around them, encircling Gregorios and Vlad. As one, they howled like wolves and leaped at Eirene.

She met them without slowing, her eyes burning with her active nevra core. Purple flames rimmed her body and her knives as she waded into the horde of clones. Knives flashed as clones bit and tore at her.

With every stroke, she drove a blade into the face of a clone, and it exploded into a gray cloud, releasing the enslaved soul powering it. The souls erupted away, moaning their last cry before disappearing.

The other clones didn't hesitate. They couldn't seem to hurt Eirene, protected as she was in her halo of active nevron, but they tried awful hard. For every clone that she dispatched, two more appeared and piled on.

They fought with undead savagery, trying to bring her down by sheer numbers. In her Amazon form, she was so enhanced she withstood their weight. She met their savagery with fierce determination, ripping through their ranks like a burning tornado. They would never stop her, and Vlad was losing many enslaved souls.

They did slow her, however.

Vlad turned back to Gregorios and pinned him to the stones with superhuman strength. "Your soul will give me the strength to destroy your cursed woman too."

"Not any more. You'll only get indigestion from me." Gregorios hated feeling weak, hated how Vlad's power now drained his strength and left him helpless. He needed to figure out how to—

Vlad lunged and bit deep along Gregorios' jaw, severing soul points. The excruciating pain tore at Gregorios, but somehow he lacked the ability to fight back, or even to scream. He raged helplessly at the insult. He'd hunted Vlad for centuries. He couldn't let the Annoyer defeat him now.

Vlad sucked deep, drawing strength and vitality from Gregorios as he sucked parts of his soul away. The pain was worse that Gregorios had imagined, and he wanted to scream and rip the vile creature's eyes out. He couldn't even clench a fist.

If Eirene didn't get to him in the next few seconds, Vlad would own his soul.

If she did manage to save him, she'd never let him live this one down.

Sarah gasped as the strength of Gregorios' ascendant thundered into her soul. She felt a fire blossom in the center of her being. Not painful, it was as if she'd swallowed a blazing sun and bound it to her heart.

She rose, but wasn't sure if she stood, or if she just floated upward, unable to stay crouched with so much strength pounding through her. Purple fire ignited along her hands. She looked at them with wonder, mixed with horror.

She'd taken far more than the strength of Gregorios' ascendant.

She'd stolen his nevra core, bonded her soul to the ascendant in his stead. She'd usurped his place and unlocked the full force of the ascendant.

Inside her protective barrier, Xiao cried out in pain and fell to the stones, her feet kicking against the ground as her body convulsed. Linked as they were through the dueling runes, she was now paying the price. Sarah's connection to the ascendant had tipped the balance against her, and Xiao's own torture attack had rebounded against her.

Even though they both had called upon the power of an ascendant, Sarah's had somehow trumped hers. Sarah looked from her cipher to Xiao's rune and realized the difference.

Xiao was master of her ascendant, but Sarah was rune warrior. By linking in the rune warrior symbol, Sarah was connected to the greater aeon, and that seemed to give her a higher level of connection to her ascendant, and therefore access to even more power.

Sarah was more than any single facetaker, or even any cui dashi.

She was a cui dashi warrior.

Sarah could feel the coiling, eternal lengths of her ascendant arcing away into the air, invisible to anyone else. She sensed that she could walk its length without having to step into the aeon space like she had in the past. And more than simply walking it, her connection to the ascendant and the aeon was deeper. She sensed she could move her ascendant, shift its course if she desired.

That was a terrifying possibility. What would that do to history? To the future?

Weeping with pain, Xiao rolled back to her rune and added more symbols with a shaking hand. She completed the marks she had begun, drawing upon the power of her children's ascendants, binding their souls to the outcome of the rune battle. She might not be able to unlock the full measure of each of the ascendants, but she was linking seven of them into her runes where Sarah only commanded one. The balance of power reached a point of equilibrium, then slowly shifted against Sarah.

Alter, who had coughed and sat up, now paled and clutched his head. He pleaded, "Sarah, stop her."

Melek had stopped drawing runes. He now moved to comfort his son. He glanced at Sarah and said, "Our work is complete. It's up to you now, warrior."

Nothing like a little pressure to motivate a girl. And death.

Sarah could feel the ascendants clustering around the room,

bound to this point in history, twisting out of their regular alignment. Ascendants were not meant to wrestle against each other, and as the titanic forces collided, the entire aeon began to destabilize. Sarah felt shudders rippling down her ascendant, felt similar shudders like echoes in the night from the others.

Then she felt a crack form in her ascendant. A rift cut through it, opening a gateway between sixteenth century England and modern day Kansas City. She felt souls bleeding out through the rift, shadows of those who had lived so long ago. Those shades of people long dead took physical form and began walking the streets of the modern world.

Not good. They'd had enough problems with monsters stepping through the cracks of the memoryscape, and into Luxor. If historical people started returning to life in the modern day, what would that do to their historical presence? Would it change things? She couldn't imagine all the ramifications.

She could easily imagine a firestorm of argument from the various religions. Would they claim the end times had arrived? Would they expect to see Jesus or some other religious figure coming to reign? If she failed, would Xiao and Sutekh succeed in convincing huge segments of the population that they were indeed the living embodiment of religious prophecies?

Other cracks began to form, like fault lines skipping along the ascendants. If the duel continued much longer, the integrity of the ascendant could become compromised and history broken. Sarah wasn't sure what that would mean, but even Gregorios would admit that would be very bad.

The shifting, colliding ascendants began creating a new pattern, like a distant ship creeping over the horizon. Sarah studied it as she drew upon the strength of her ascendant, focusing its power to ward off Xiao's renewed assault.

The first thing she noticed was Alter's ascendant. It wasn't controlled only by him, and its form was different than the others. It shone brightly in her aeon sight like the clear, green sea surrounding a tropical island. Unlike the others, it looped around itself, touching this moment in two distinct points, anchored by both Alter and Sutekh.

The transfer wasn't complete. They were both still tied to that moment. Both of them shared the same ascendant, and both of them were bonded to it. The rune duel would decide their fate along with the fate of history itself.

Their ascendant was positioned at the heart of the newly forming structure. As the symbols coalesced, Sarah felt its blazing power. This moment in time was becoming the focus of the entire aeon. Just as master runes focused pivotal moments in history, this moment was becoming a master ascendant, a signature rune for the aeon as it coalesced into a convergence of history.

It was beautiful, stretching away in every direction, built with the coiling loops of the ascendants and their weight of history, punctuated by the greatest of the master runes, all tied together into a higher symbol. The ascendants could split off from here into different directions, depending on how the moment played out. Sarah was standing astride a moment that would decide the fate of history.

Xiao completed her last symbol, linking in the last of her children's ascendant, and the weight of power tipped against Sarah. Alter passed out again, and Melek groaned and fell to the floor beside him. Sarah hadn't even noticed him add another modifier similar to the one Alter had used. He was using his soul as another sacrifice to protect her from Xiao's attack a little longer

They would die, unless Sarah figured out how to counter Xiao. She needed another ascendant.

Xiao leaped to her feat, her expression exultant as she laughed. "My moment of victory is here!"

"Not yet, psycho."

Sarah leaned over her cipher and drew another series of marks, her fingers moving with sure strokes, despite the anguish she felt as she stole the strength from another she loved.

With a trembling finger, she completed the new cipher and focused on it, willing it to activate. The cipher glowed silver-white, meshing with her already-active cipher and pouring additional strength into Sarah as she drew upon the power of Alter's ascendant.

That tipped the scale in her favor. Both Melek and Alter took long, shuddering breaths as the pain they'd been suffering evaporated. The entire aeon wheel of time creaked as the master ascendant signature rune solidified with an invisible thunderclap that rocked every ascendant.

The temple shook around them, great cracks forming in the floor and ceiling. Columns crumbled, sending tons of stone cascading down and filling the room with billowing clouds of dust.

One huge stone plunged down over the sarcophagus holding the rune web that powered the barrier rune. The soulmasks shattered, and the barrier rune winked out. Xiao didn't even notice. She had fallen to her knees, her expression shocked, mouthing words that Sarah couldn't hear over the din.

Sarah stood and caught a massive roof stone. It had to weigh several tons, but she barely noticed. Her mind was swept away in the vision of the aeon and the ascendants. She tossed it aside, her heart filled with exultant joy.

The new master ascendant, visible only to her, glowed pure white with transcendent beauty. She owned this moment, could dictate the future of the ascendants, could rewrite history as she saw fit.

All she had to do was reach out her hand and claim it.

The rune pulsed against her nevron, calling to her, so familiar it ached. This was Sarah's destiny. She could become the master of time.

She extended her fingers, and a crossbow bolt appeared in her hands, already glowing with the pure white light of the cipher Sarah had used to defeat Paul. Its length burned with the power of the three master runes that had melted Sarah's first life into the stones of St. Peter's Square.

Turning away from the master ascendant was as easy as shifting her weight, but choosing to turn her back on it was as hard as fighting Xiao's smothering will had been.

The feeling of loss brought tears to Sarah's eyes as she turned away from the master ascendant. She blew out a shuddering breath, trying to ignore the presence of the new rune that warmed her back like an afternoon sun. She leaped across the space between her and Xiao, who looked up with open disbelief in her wide, pain-filled eyes.

Sarah drove the crossbow bolt into her eye with all of her strength, and with the full force of her nevron. It punched into Xiao's eye, its explosive charge driven by the white-hot power of the three master runes.

98

He who knows other men is discerning; he who knows himself is intelligent.

~LAOZI

VLAD RELEASED HIS HOLD ON GREGORIOS' jawline and sat back. Blood dripped from his fangs, down his chin, but his exultant expression had turned confused. Gregorios dragged in a ragged breath as the overwhelming pain eased just a fraction.

"Ow," he grunted.

"What happened?" Vlad wondered.

He glanced to his left where Eirene was still savaging his horde of clones. "Your soul is potent, but I taste no nevra core. Where have you concealed your heart, Gregorios?"

Gregorios loved seeing Vlad thwarted in his moment of victory. He coughed, triggering a fresh wave of pain from his ripped jawline. He managed to mumble a few incoherent sounds, and gestured Vlad closer.

The king of all vampires actually leaned forward to hear. He sure let victory go to his head awful fast.

Gregorios weakly gripped Vlad's hair as the vampire leaned close and said again, "Tell me."

"My nevra core is gone," Gregorios admitted. Vlad gasped, and Gregorios added, "But I'm more than my nevra core."

And he slammed his left palm into Vlad's jawline.

The little ring knife, runes blazing, punched through the thin layer of skin and drove into Vlad's soul point with a burst of purple sparks.

Vlad shrieked and arced convulsively back. Gregorios held on with all his strength as the two of them tumbled over each other. The movement wrenched his dislocated shoulder painfully, but he gritted his teeth and held on.

Judgment day hurt sometimes, and he was okay with that.

As captured souls erupted from the breach, Gregorios slashed the little ring knife up Vlad's jaw, ripping through two more soul points. Vlad screamed again, clawed hands tearing at Gregorios' armor.

Dozens of captured souls exploded away from the vampire in a greasy, gray cloud. They poured over Gregorios' face, and he heard their moans of relief. The close contact triggered visions of their torment at Vlad's hands, and those glimpses renewed Gregorios' determination to end the monster.

Vlad's thrashing grew so severe that Gregorios couldn't sever any more soul points, but had to use all his strength just to hold on. They rolled and convulsed together, their faces inches apart. Vlad's expression had turned terrified, anguish and disbelief on his face.

The vampire panted, "No. I'm the mightiest of all undead. I cannot die."

Strong hands, glowing purple, seized the vampire and yanked him away from Gregorios. Eirene lifted the injured vampire high. Her Amazon form was scraped and battered, but her lovely eyes glowed with triumph as she slammed Vlad down to the stones so hard it sounded like a thunderclap. No doubt she'd just shattered most of the bones of his body. There was no sign of the clones.

"Are you okay?" she asked, glancing at him as she moved glowing hands toward Vlad's face.

"I'll live. Thanks, love."

Gregorios rolled painfully to his knees, grunting anew from the pain. Being mortal was a really raw deal after enjoying so many enhanced lives. He placed a restraining hand on her arm and said, "Allow me."

"But you have no nevra core," she protested.

Gregorios held up his glowing ring knife and winked. She laughed and kissed him soundly. "How can you still amaze me after all these lives?"

"Laughing keeps us young. So does killing monsters."

Vlad was trying to struggle, but Eirene's nevron kept him down, prevented him from transforming and escaping again. Plus, Gregorios had severed three soul points. Not even he could shed a wound like that very fast. The flow of escaping souls had slackened, but Gregorios could fix that.

He slammed the ring knife against the other side of Vlad's jaw and yanked it downward, slicing along the bone and severing soul points. More moaning souls erupted forth in a greasy, gray tide, released from servitude to the monster. Hundreds of souls boiled forth, and Vlad seemed to shrink and grow older as his stolen vitality fled.

Gregorios met Vlad's panicked eyes as he slashed the ring knife across the final soul points of Vlad's chin, releasing an even bigger storm of captured souls and severing the monster's connection to life.

"Rest in peace this time," Gregorios said as the light faded from Vlad's eyes.

Vlad's soul wind erupted away in a gale force explosion, full of howling, moaning souls. The chill darkness faded as Vlad's body melted into the stones. Bright Egyptian sunlight streamed into the square, revealing their forces still massed on the far side. Francesca and Spartacus stood guard over Sarah's slumbering form.

Up on the mosque balcony, Sutekh stood before the opaque rift doorway, holding Xiao's fully healed body in his arms.

Her face was burning.

"Well, that's finally a positive sign," Gregorios said as Eirene draped one mighty Amazon arm around his shoulders.

The angle wasn't great, but it looked like flames were shooting from Xiao's right eye, and the skin of her face was melting. She looked to be dying. About time.

Eirene urged in a tense whisper, "You can do it, Sarah."

Sutekh suddenly grasped Xiao's face and pulled her soulmask free of her burning skull. It glittering shape looked less brilliant than it should be. She was definitely hurting. Gregorios wanted to whoop for joy. He was feeling tired and sore, so watching Xiao melt would be a great chance to call for a lunch break.

Sarah was doing something right. The soulmask shrank upon itself, darkening as they watched. The rainbow smoke that normally coiled below it crumbled to dust.

On the mosque balcony, the rift shook and its outer edges blackened. A strong gust of wind blew out of it, smelling like a battleground, full of smoke and blood and the taste of ash. The shaking rift became transparent, showing a scene that confirmed Gregorios' hope.

Sarah knelt over Xiao, a rune-laden crossbow bolt driven into the cui dashi's eye. Xiao's entire head was burning.

"That's our girl!" Eirene cried, holding him tight enough that his ribs creaked. He loved having a strong woman.

"No!" Sutekh shouted, holding the soulmask aloft and gesturing with it toward the nearby rift doorway.

Tomas dropped from the mosque roof toward Xiao's soulmask with a heavy hammer in hand, poised to shatter it in her moment of weakness.

Sutekh noticed him and reacted with superhuman speed. He caught the hammer and spun Tomas around.

Tomas' boot struck the rift.

Silver light exploded out of the rift in a detonation so powerful it felt like Quentin had launched an Armageddon round directly over their heads. The blast shook the temple, toppling walls that had stood for nearly four thousand years.

Gregorios would have fallen if not for Eirene's aid as the ground bucked beneath them and the thunder of falling stone drowned out all thought. Clouds of dust choked them and filled the ruined inner court. Then the wind reversed direction and sucked back toward the rift, carrying with it a sandstorm of dust and debris.

When the dust cleared, all of the interior walls had collapsed, and even the enormous entry pylons had started to crumble. Their enforcer teams were retreating through the gap, drawing most of the civilians with them. The entire interior of the temple complex had collapsed. The roof of the mosque had fallen, leaving the building a pile of rubble. Somehow the balcony was still clear, but there was no sign of Tomas or Xiao's soulmask.

"Give me a view," Gregorios said urgently.

"Hold on." Eirene threw him.

Even though she sent him soaring nearly thirty feet straight up, she managed to make it feel somehow gentle instead of giving him whiplash. A woman who knew how to use her strength was so sexy.

At the apex of his ascent, Gregorios could clearly see Alter's body. It lay sprawled on the balcony, but the face was an empty shell. Sutekh's soulmask had been ripped free.

That's when Gregorios realized the rift doorway was gone too.

Eirene caught him gently and asked, "What did you see?"

He told her, then added, "I'm thinking that might have just made Sarah's job harder."

99

Good, then we shall have our battle in the shade.

~DIENEKES, SPARTAN WARRIOR, BATTLE OF
THERMOPYLAE, WHEN TOLD THE PERSIAN ARROWS
WOULD BLOCK OUT THE SUN, 480 B.C.

"ALL UNITS IN POSITION, awaiting your order."

"Roger," Harriett replied. "Any sign of police or military intervention?"

"Negative."

She allowed a tight smile. Her Yurak forces had moved with customary speed, their heavy vehicles rumbling off the transport ships at the Dendera docks and scattering the surprised dock officials. They'd exited the town without interference and raced southeast toward the Dendera temple complex. They would arrive in two minutes.

She doubted there would be any investigation by police or military with everyone so focused on events at Luxor. She rode in the helicopter, five thousand feet above the ships, using the Yurak satellite to scan the defensive measures around the temple complex.

"Is the rainmaker aimed and ready?" she asked.

"Coordinates are set. Awaiting your order," replied her artillery commander.

"Fire."

Billows of smoke puffed from the barge that served as their

artillery platform, floating at anchor in the center of the slow-moving Nile. All three rainmaker mortars fired at the same time, the echoing report reaching all the way up to her position.

"Ground troops, begin your assault," she ordered, then told the pilot to close on the temple complex with all speed. She scanned the southeast horizon and counted to four.

Even though she knew what to expect, the explosions were impressive. The Armageddon round was a sensor-fused cluster bomb, similar in form to the CBU-108 precision-guided weapon used by the U.S. military.

High above the temple, the rainmaker rounds burst, ejecting ten sub-munitions that each in turn carried several types of projectiles. Their sensors usually scanned for hard targets. These had been modified to scan for activated runes instead.

With so many soulmasks bound into the enormous plague-generating rune web, it must have shown up like a red-hot beacon to the bomb sensors. They locked on and fired their built-in rockets to accelerate to more than terminal velocity. The rain of destruction fell upon the temple complex in three waves.

First the armor-piercing rounds shattered the roof of the Hathor temple and leveled entire sections of the outer mud wall at each of the entrenched heka positions. Then the incendiary napalm and magnesium rounds struck, scouring the temple with purifying fire. Finally the HMX high-explosive rounds and shaped charges fell like the hammer of the gods, shattering everything that was left and spraying still-burning debris in every direction.

In a single strike, Harriett had called down Armageddon upon the ancient site. The attack leveled the Hathor temple and most of the surrounding structures, covering the entire complex in black clouds of destruction. She hated the fact that Xiao had forced them to obliterate such a priceless historical site, but the alternative was a pandemic of world-ending proportions.

The Yurak ground troops rolled into that devastated wasteland to mop up anything left alive. They didn't find much. Harriett left her commanders to it and ordered the pilot back toward Luxor.

She switched channels and reported, "Quentin, the web is down."

"Thank god. Storms are still raging around the world, but they already seem to be weakening without that web fueling them."

"Let's just hope the virus loses its potency fast and disperses before infecting too many."

They'd snuffed out the disaster before it had reached full intensity, but the number of people exposed to the mutated virus had to be already in the millions. If they'd caught that plague, the world still faced a deadly outbreak that would test the limits of medical facilities.

A lot of people were probably going to die.

100

Injustice exists in abundance, but evil can never succeed when we have better runes.

~*THE LIVING WISDOM OF ANCIENT EGYPT*
TRANSLATION

THE TEMPLE SHOOK. Worse than an earthquake, it vibrated like that entire moment in history was on the verge of splitting apart. The shaking tossed Sarah away from Xiao, and for a moment she feared the entire building would collapse and crush them.

The world wasn't the problem. The real danger were the ascendants shaking and cracking. Sarah could feel them shuddering. She reached a hand out, and it slipped through the invisible barrier separating mortal, three-dimensional space from the aeon space.

There she grasped the point where all the ascendants were colliding. At that collision point, they were cracking and splintering, as if on the verge of shattering.

She grasped the point and willed calm upon it. She wasn't sure how that would help, but through her connection to the aeon, she had already sensed she could exert great influence upon the entire structure of history. At her touch, the worst of the shaking eased, and she realized the problem.

Alter's ascendant had been twisted back upon itself like an overwound slinky, with both ends secured to the same point. She blinked through the billowing dust and saw that Melek still lay on the floor, but Alter had risen to his feet. He was staggering like a drunkard, hands clasped to his head.

His face was mostly obscured by a dense cloud of purple fire, and his skin seemed to be bubbling and rippling. It was almost as if he was trying to extract his own soulmask, but couldn't quite manage it.

The air smelled charged, electric, and her hair floated from her shoulders, filled with crackling power. Then with a thunderclap so sharp it struck like a hammer to her head, the shaking stopped. Everything froze as a deep silence settled over the entire scene.

The rift disappeared. In its place stood Tomas, looking dazed.

Sarah stood. "How is it possible?"

Melek surged to his feet and pointed, "Now's your chance to end this before time unravels!"

As Tomas took a faltering step to his right, shaking his head and blinking, Sarah saw what Melek was pointing at.

Xiao's soulmask. It hung two feet above the floor, but was settling slowly downward. It looked cracked and dull, and the shimmering tendrils of mist that should be cushioning it were crumbling to rainbow-colored dust.

Sarah glanced in surprise at Xiao. She was still lying on the floor, but her burning face was nothing but an empty mannequin mask, with the silver bolt sticking through the blank face.

"What the . . ."

"Quick! Before she touches solid ground," Melek shouted.

Sarah wasn't sure how Xiao had abandoned her host like that, how Tomas had appeared in history with them, or why Alter was ripping at his own face with hands glowing with different shades of purple nevron. She did understand the urgency in Melek's voice. For whatever reason, he didn't want Xiao's soulmask to touch down.

Finally, a simple problem.

Sarah rushed through the smoke and leaped piles of rubble. She willed Melek's rune-laden hammer into her hands, and it appeared instantly. With a shout of triumph, she raised the mighty weapon to smash Xiao's soulmask into a million pieces.

She was startled when Melek shouted, "No, wait!"

"Make up your mind," she told him.

Melek rushed to her, carrying a tiny sarcophagus. It looked like a stone version of the soul coffins used in modern day. He held it under Xiao's soulmask and allowed it to settle inside.

"We should kill her," Sarah insisted.

Melek shook his head. "I have a more fitting punishment planned for this monster."

Sarah didn't like the idea of leaving Xiao alive in any sense of the word, but she was willing to wait until she learned what Melek had in mind before going for hammer destruction again.

"Any problem with destroying her body?"

"Be my guest," Melek said, gesturing toward the empty host with its burning skull and crossbow bolt.

Before he could change his mind, Sarah leaped across the room and smashed the hammer on that burning skull. It shattered with a very satisfying splat, and sprayed blood and burning tissue across the stone floor.

Instantly, the rest of Xiao's body evaporated, and again Sarah felt the entire aeon shudder. This time in a good way. The pressure warping all the ascendants to that moment in history eased. Most of them snapped back to their previous shapes.

The entire room wavered and wobbled as reality seemed to ripple. The glorious master ascendant symbol she'd sensed in her mind began to fade as Xiao's ascendant, and those of her children, were released.

Xiao's influence over history was gone. Sarah sensed that the monster had lost her nevra core. She was no longer anything but a dispossessed mortal. She'd staked everything on that rune duel, and she'd lost.

Xiao's helium-high whisper voice screamed from inside the stone soul coffin. She raged and shrieked and howled her loss of power, and threatened eternal vengeance.

Melek placed a stone lid over the box and set it down. Sarah grinned and said, "I hate sore losers."

They shared a laugh, and Sarah's tension eased. She barely believed they'd defeated the cursed woman.

Only Alter's ascendant was still twisted unnaturally. Before she could try to figure out why, Tomas rushed to her and swept her off her feet in a crushing embrace. She exulted to see him safe, and was content to let the questions wait while she kissed him and simply enjoyed the fact that they were both alive, and seemed to have won.

"Alter, what's wrong?" Melek's words reminded her that they weren't out of danger yet.

She released Tomas and the two of them turned. Alter was still staggering, mouth open in a silent scream, burning hands gripping his own face. His features were shuddering violently, shifting between Alter's and Sutekh's.

Tomas grimaced. "That's bizarre."

"Worse than that. He's double-stacked," Sarah said with sudden understanding.

Alter's ascendant was the only one still out of position. Both ends were locked onto that moment, anchored in Alter's body, in the two mighty souls both striving to possess it.

She gripped Tomas' arm. "How did you get here? Did Sutekh come with you?"

"I'm not sure. I was attacking Xiao's soulmask. Sutekh had dispossessed her, and she looked vulnerable. But he intercepted me." Tomas frowned as he thought back. "I think I struck the rift. Then all I saw was flashing light, and now we're here."

He really was there. Sarah could sense that he had somehow been pulled body and soul back into history. He hadn't left his body behind like Alter. He was standing in that moment, but he didn't belong. He was foreign to it. She could sense that he wouldn't long remain there. Time would spit him out.

Where would he go? *When* would he go?

She glanced at Melek and sensed that somehow he was more real in that moment than he was back in the future. His soul had been pulled into the past with her, but he'd been in his ethereal state. It seemed far more of him had been sucked along for the ride, and he seemed to be solidifying more every second, as if that point in history was sucking the rest of him back there. But if he completed that journey, he too would be foreign, and would eventually be ejected.

Not good. Before she could figure out how to deal with their dilemma, she needed to figure out how to help Alter.

Tomas frowned at the struggling Alter. "If they're double stacked, then Alter should be able to eject Sutekh. He's got the base position. He was there first."

"But it's Sutekh's body, and he's the one who belongs in this time period," Melek said, worry clear on his face. "Alter is the interloper."

Sarah approached Alter and extended a hand. Through her active nevron, she could feel the battle of their wills. It formed an invisible cloud of power around them that thrummed against her skin. It didn't look like either had gained the upper hand yet.

They were both linked to the same ascendant, so she doubted either of them could draw more power from it than the other. That suggested their duel was more a battle of sheer determination and willpower than anything.

Good. Alter was one of the most stubborn people she knew. He'd been raised his entire life to not surrender his values. That trait was one of the things that she loved the most about him. And it was one of the things that sometimes made her most want to punch him in the face.

Alter was locked in a deadly battle, but she could help him. Through her connection to the aeon, and their link through the dueling rune, she could influence the fight. Together, she and Alter could defeat Sutekh.

She was tempted to simply grab their face and rip out Sutekh's soulmask, but they were so tightly locked together, she feared she might end up removing Alter instead. No, Alter needed to defeat Sutekh, but he didn't have to do it alone.

Sarah quickly marked a new cipher into the air with a glowing finger. Similar to the ones she'd used for all of the enforcers, she linked it to the Beijing charging cipher. She couldn't mark it on his body, because that would provide power to both Alter and Sutekh. She frowned as she considered how best to limit the influx to him, and glanced at Melek.

He seemed to have read her mind. "You need Alter's signature rune." He marked a symbol onto the stone floor with his knife. In included pieces of Alter's many personalized enhancements, built around a center made up of the Chinese symbol for integrity, the Egyptian balance scales that symbolized truth, and a Celtic ailm symbol that represented purity of soul.

"Thank you. It fits Alter perfectly," Sarah said as she added the symbols to her cipher and concentrated over the final construct.

It glowed as it activated, and Alter convulsed. His staggering and shaking ceased abruptly, and the skin of his face seemed to erupt outward in a ghastly, crimson explosion. For a second, Sarah feared she'd done something wrong, that she'd accidentally struck him instead of directed the cipher to help him.

But then Sutekh's soulmask erupted out the front of the bloody face. The soulmask glittered with nevron fire, and the mouth was open in a high-pitched, defiant wail.

Alter caught his defeated enemy even as the skin of his face rippled and settled back into his familiar, handsome features. He raised the soulmask high and shouted, "Victory!"

"Glad to have you back," Tomas grinned.

Sarah rushed to give Alter a hug, but Melek beat her. He embraced his son with enthusiastic strength and laughed with pride. "You did it!"

Laughing with joy, Alter turned to reply, but he spotted Sarah. Tossing Sutekh's soulmask aside, he quickly said, "Father, please."

Melek released him and Alter rushed to Sarah. He clearly wanted to sweep her into the same type of enthusiastic embrace that Tomas had, but restrained himself at the last second and extended an awkward hand. His eyes glowed with emotion that only a dead person wouldn't be able to read.

Sarah pulled him into a hug and said, "I'm so happy you're okay."

After a moment of startled hesitation, he eagerly returned the embrace. Sarah glanced over his shoulder at Tomas, who was trying to school his expression to neutral. He couldn't quite hide the fact that he wasn't happy with Alter hugging her so tight. She winked, and that seemed to mollify him a bit.

Melek picked up another stone sarcophagus soul coffin and deposited Sutekh's angrily cursing soulmask inside. Once he shut the lid, Sarah breathed deep, enjoying a moment of blessed peace.

That's when both Tomas and Melek started to melt.

101

Man is separated into Soul and Body, and only when the two sides of his senses are bonded together, does utterance of its thought conceived by mind take place.

~ANCIENT EGYPTIAN PROVERB

SARAH GASPED AS TOMAS STUMBLED, and Melek dropped to one knee. Tomas raised a dripping hand and gave it an incredulous look. "Hey, what's going on?"

"I thought we won," Melek said, his voice turning to an odd mumble as his lips began to sag.

"What's happening?" Alter cried. He grabbed his father's shoulder, but it melted under his touch and he recoiled with a cry of horror.

Sarah gaped, momentarily stunned. They'd defeated Sutekh and Xiao. They'd won! Had Xiao left a final, evil revenge rune in case she lost? It didn't seem likely, but what was going on?

Sarah activated her nevra core and reached out with burning hands, gripping both Tomas' and Melek's sagging shoulders. As soon as she touched them, she understood.

The rift was closed, the master ascendant released, the ascendants freed to return to their eternal course. This moment in time, which had stood frozen during their duel, was slipping back into the proper flow of history.

She was the cui dashi warrior, so she could slip in and out of time at will, but these men were stuck outside of time. They didn't belong here. They were foreign, and as she'd sensed earlier, they were being expunged from this moment as it returned to its natural course.

They no longer belonged in the future, had no bodies there. If they faded from this moment, she wasn't sure when or where they'd end up, or if they'd be lost to time forever.

That really sucked.

As soon as Sarah touched them, linked their bodies to her via the protective energy of her nevron, the men solidified, protected from the shifting flow of time by her power.

"What's happening?" Tomas asked, looking a bit wild.

"Time's starting to flow again. You don't belong here."

"So get us all home. We don't need to linger any more," Alter said.

When Sarah hesitated, Melek met her gaze. She could read in his eyes that he understood the truth. He said, "It's not that easy. We're here. There is nowhere, nowhen, for us to go."

Tomas gasped, and Alter protested, "But you opened a rift once. There's got to be a way."

"I know. There has to be." Sarah hated the sudden, renewed sense of panic that made her hands shake so annoyingly. She had thought she was done with being afraid.

The ascendant linking Alter and Sutekh was trying to return to its course like the other ascendants had. The rest of the aeon had stabilized, which increased the pressure on that last ascendant to snap back to its proper course again.

It still looped back upon itself though, linked to this moment in time by its connection to both Alter and Sutekh. The pressure began to mount. Sarah wasn't sure if it would eventually yank Alter's soul forcibly out of history and slam him back into his body in the future, or if it would rip free and leave him stranded in the past like the others. She could send him back, but didn't want to do anything until she figured out what to do for Tomas and Melek. She might need Alter's help.

As the pressure built, Sarah applied her will to holding the twisted ascendant in place, but the strain grew rapidly. She could only hold it another moment.

The men were looking at her expectantly. She tried to calm herself, to think. "Alter's ascendant might be the key. When I release it, you can ride it home to your body."

"What about the rest of us?" Tomas asked.

"That's the part I'm still trying to figure out," she admitted.

"You've got this," Tomas said with such confidence it melted her heart, and set it racing with new fear. She couldn't let him down. She had to find a solution, but what?

Even trying to swap Alter's and Sutekh's souls between their bodies while both of them were linked to the same ascendant had challenged everything Xiao had known about runes, and she was a far more accomplished runesmith than Sarah. Sarah did command the aeon, but her access to it didn't extend to Tomas.

The pressure to release Alter was growing fast, making it hard to think. If not for the strength of Gregorios' ascendant, she'd never hold Alter's any longer. Could she fashion a rune to allow Alter to bear Tomas and Melek back with him?

Maybe, but she didn't know it.

When she hesitated, Tomas suggested, "We could double-stack like what Gregorios did with the cardinal."

Sarah considered the idea, but shook her head. "No, the ascendant is bound to Alter's soul, and it works only on that link, not on Sutekh's body."

Despite her unique access to the aeon, she could not force the ascendant to remain out of its course much longer, not unless she identified a new master ascendant rune and activated it. That would give her far more control, but she feared she'd wreck time if she screwed up.

Besides, she didn't have time to figure out a new master ascendant. She'd lose Alter's connection in seconds, and the others would melt into the floor and die forever if she abandoned them to step into aeon space, even for a moment.

A headache formed and grew to a migraine. The forces at play were enormous and they'd tear her apart if she tried to hold on much longer. It was like a giant bungee cord extended to its uttermost end. Now it needed to snap back and she lacked the strength to prevent it from doing so.

The four of them huddled close together, and she read in their expressions that they understood the truth.

"Only Alter can go back," Tomas said softly.

"I could link any of you to the ascendant, but yes, it belongs to Alter, and it's a single ticket." Sarah hated herself for speaking the words.

"The others remain here," Alter said, tapping his Sutekh chest. "Trapped in history."

"One can take that body once you abandon it, but they would be trapped," Sarah confirmed.

Melek settled back on his heels and nodded slowly. He looked strangely peaceful. "I have no fear of this fate. The force of my soul is spent. I can feel myself fading. My super enhancement terminated while I've been trapped in history, and my body is gone."

"No, Father," Alter cried, but Sarah saw in his eyes that he understood Melek was right.

Melek shook his head with calm resignation. "Perhaps it is for the best. I've abandoned the creed of the clan and can never return. Besides, I've seen my enemy defeated. I am content."

Alter leaned close, and the two embraced. Tears shone in Alter's eyes and Sarah placed a comforting hand on his shoulder. They'd worked so hard to free Alter. It seemed the cruelest irony that in the act of doing so, he'd lose his father.

She felt deeply moved by Melek's calm acceptance of his ultimate sacrifice. He'd always said he was willing to give everything to save his son and to stop Xiao. He'd compromised his deepest-held beliefs, taken up the body of his own son, teamed up with facetaker demons and fought side-by-side with enforcers. So much sacrifice. It brought tears to her eyes.

Sarah couldn't bear to lose Alter again, not after fighting so hard to save him, but she couldn't lose Tomas either. How could she choose to consign one of them to a life thousands of years in the past?

She bowed her head, tears of anguish in her eyes as she struggled against the growing migraine, trying to think a way out of this. "I don't know what to do."

Tomas, sounding far more calm than he should said, "It's Alter's body. It's his choice."

Alter nodded, still gripping his father's hand. The only thing worse than having to choose between them was leaving that choice up to another. There was only one choice Alter could make and she couldn't think of any way to justify asking him to make a different one. Her heart broke as she considered leaving Tomas behind, to live out his final life alone, separated by so much time.

She shifted closer to Tomas and wrapped her arms around him, burying her face against his neck, trying to stifle her sobs. The pressure of the ascendant intensified until her vision blurred. She had to do this now, or Tomas and Alter would both be trapped.

"You have to choose, Alter," she said.

Tomas gripped Sarah so hard, it felt as if he was trying to memorize the feel of her in this last embrace. His whispered voice reached her as if from a great distance.

"It's all right, love. Sometimes suicide missions are necessary."

102

Love your wife with passion. You may not get another life with her.

~THE LIVING WISDOM OF ANCIENT EGYPT
TRANSLATION

ALTER GAZED upon Sarah as she held Tomas, tears shining against her cheeks, and as usual her beauty left him breathless. She was such an amazing woman and he yearned for her to hold him like that. He thought back to the first day they met. If only he'd found a way to capture her heart before she had committed to Tomas.

He thought back to the terrible day in St. Peter's square. He'd been forced to remove the soulmask of his own brother. Reuben had always been his hero, but he'd fallen to Paul's power. Then Sarah had chosen Tomas above Alter as the one she would bond her soul to for the final gambit against Paul. It was Alter who had saved her, using his unique power to salvage her soulmask from her melting body.

He'd saved her, not Tomas. He thought back to the countless hours he'd sparred with Sarah, her every touch a treasured memory. Even getting punched by her enhanced fists had been a joyous experience.

He thought of the many days and the long nights they'd spent huddled close together, bowed over runes, sharing the thrill of rune-smithing, of discovery, every breath flavored by her gentle scent. Those had been some of the best moments of his life.

He thought of the two times he'd kissed her, of the singing joy he'd felt touching his lips to hers. He longed for a life spent building more of such memories with her, of seeing the love she now directed at Tomas instead directed at him.

He was not going to get it.

Alter dropped his gaze from her perfect face. It was his right to insist he be returned to himself in the future. With that choice, Tomas would be lost to history, lost forever to Sarah. Would she then turn to Alter?

She'd made it clear she cared about him, that only her love for Tomas prevented her from choosing him. With Tomas out of the way, would she then make that choice and allow herself to love him?

If she did, this moment could grant to him his dearest desires.

She wouldn't, though. The truth made him want to howl. Tomas' ghost would haunt Sarah, as would the knowledge that Alter had made the choice that consigned Tomas to live thousands of years apart from her. No doubt she'd find ways to visit for brief moments through the aeon space. She'd never get a life with Tomas, but she'd never be free to choose Alter either. That was a barrier he could never hope to break.

If he took his body, he would return to life, hated by his family and resented by Sarah, lost, with no place in the world. He still faced that problem, one he hadn't figured the answer to yet. He despaired as he considered that empty, desolate life.

Alter gripped his father's hand. "I can't leave you."

"My fate is not yours to control, Son, but I have one final truth for you to consider, something I have only now come to understand."

"What truth?"

"A cryptic message left by our first forefather. He said, 'In the great day of our ultimate trial, the one bearing my name will rise. In him you must trust, for by knowing him, you will know me.'"

"What does that mean?"

Alter listened to the sounds of distant conflict. That was Moses and his assault force, including Alter the Great. He might get to meet his ultimate grandfather, and the thought helped ease some of his despair. He had expected to find Alter already here, helping them defeat Sutekh. It seemed wrong that they'd done all the work for him.

"It means, I know him because I know you."

"I don't understand," Sarah said through her tears, her face anguished from the invisible pain she was enduring as she held time in place until Alter made his choice. Every second he hesitated hurt her more.

Melek said nothing, only watched Alter, his expression strangely joyous.

Alter considered his words and understanding struck like a tidal wave. He gasped, nearly overwhelmed by the magnitude of the realization. "That's why we haven't seen him yet."

"Because he was already here," Melek confirmed.

"Will you two tell me what's going on?" Sarah snapped, rubbing her temples. "I can't think straight."

"I've made my choice," Alter said. He took one of Sarah's hands in his and said, "Send Tomas back."

"What?" they exclaimed together. The look of shock on Tomas' face was one Alter would treasure forever.

"You can't be serious," Sarah said between clenched teeth as she fought back a groan.

Alter said, "You're out of time. Do it."

"Alter, I . . ." What could she say? Her eyes spoke volumes as she held his gaze for a moment.

Then with trembling hands, she removed Tomas' soulmask. As soon as it popped free, Tomas' body melted. Sarah caressed Tomas' glittering soulmask as the rainbow tendrils of his soul drifted up around her hand. With a glowing finger, she marked a single line across his forehead. Alter wished he could see the symbols she used to bind Tomas to the future.

The cipher flared, and Tomas vanished.

Searing pain tore through Alter, and he collapsed to the floor. In an instant, his nevra core was snuffed out, extinguished, yanked from his soul. The abrupt sense of loss left him gasping.

When he blinked his eyes open a moment later, Sarah was seated on the floor, leaning over him, cradling his head in her lap as she stroked his face. "I'm so sorry, Alter. I had to link it to him."

He could have stayed like that forever, but she only gave him a moment, then helped him sit up.

"What do you mean?" he asked.

"Your ascendant, the source of your nevra core, belongs to Tomas now. It was the only way to send him home."

"I'm no longer cui dashi?" The idea stunned him. He'd never imagined it possible.

"I'm sorry," she said.

Alter leaped to his feet and caught her up into his arms in a joyous embrace. Laughing. "Are you kidding? I'm no longer tainted, no longer cursed."

"I thought you had accepted that the nevra core itself wasn't a curse."

"I prefer living without it," Alter said with a smile.

He might have sealed his fate, stuck himself in the past, destroyed any chance of ever sharing a life with Sarah, but he felt strangely content. He was free of the demon curse. It might not be the evil thing he'd first supposed, but he hated sharing the same power that Xiao and Paul and Mai Luan had borne, the same core the facetakers used to fuel their unnatural long life. Besides, instead of Tomas haunting his steps for the rest of his life, it was his sacrifice that would haunt Tomas. That was a satisfying thought.

Sarah sagged against Alter, wrapping her arms around his neck. She looked free of pain now that she'd released his ascendant, and he exulted to feel her embracing him as he held her close.

"Why? How could you do it?" she asked.

"I did it for you, Sarah," Alter said, savoring the feel of her standing willingly in his arms. "Not for Tomas. Why can't you see, I've done everything for you?"

For the first time, he saw true emotion shining in her eyes, directed at him, no longer masked, no longer hesitant. His heart sang.

Finally, she was seeing his worth. If only she could love him, he'd welcome as many lives as a nevra core could offer.

Alter gasped as a sudden, wild idea took root in his heart.

Sarah could hardly believe what Alter had done. She hugged him again, trying to share all of her thanks in the gesture. He'd just sacrificed everything so she could be happy, and his father had consented? She didn't understand.

"Alter, you're amazing. I do love you. I've just never been free to love you the way you wanted."

"Then do me one more favor," Alter said, an excited quiver in his voice. She couldn't imagine what might excite him. If she was trapped forever in ancient history, she'd be too busy moping.

"Give me Sutekh's ascendant."

"What?" She glanced at the soul coffin where Sutekh's soulmask was trapped. "I thought you loved being free of the curse."

"So did I, but I know my purpose. I cannot accomplish it without that nevra core."

"All right." Most men might have wished for a nevra core in order to wrest power in a corrupt world, but she knew Alter too well. He would never use that power for evil, and if possessing a nevra core helped ease his life stuck in ancient history, she'd gladly share it with him.

So Sarah formed the image of the cipher she would need to take the ascendant from Sutekh and transfer it to Alter. Then she slid one glowing finger down Alter's cheek and activated it. He started to smile at her touch, eyes closed, but then he shuddered and gripped her arms with convulsive strength. His eyes blinked open, and ignited with purple fire.

"Are you all right?" she asked.

He took a long, shuddering breath and nodded. The fires of his active nevron winked out and he grinned. "I never thought I would say this, but it feels remarkably good to get that back."

Now he and Tomas were both linked to the same ascendant, although separated by millennia. That fact seemed strangely right.

The outer door of the temple burst inward and a flood of armed men rushed into the temple, spreading through the ruined room. In the center of the group strode a tall, powerfully-built man with white hair and beard, carrying a thick wooden staff.

He must be old, but he walked like a young man. He approached with a confident stride, his piercing gaze settling over them with an invisible but undeniable weight. He lacked the purple glow of an active nevra core, but Sarah sensed he possessed a mighty power, something different than any soul power she knew.

She released Alter, prepared to fight, but he motioned her to wait as he faced the newcomers. "I am Alter."

"I am Moses," the powerful old man declared, his voice deep and commanding.

Alter bowed low. "It is a great honor. I offer my services to you and your cause."

"What?" Sarah exclaimed.

The humble greeting surprised her. Alter was almost never humble. She wished she was meeting the great Moses under better circumstances. At the moment, she was too distracted by worry about what would happen to Alter. "Shouldn't Alter the Elder be here?"

"I know no one by that name," Moses said.

"He's already here," Melek whispered, closing his eyes, a little smile on his lips. "My ultimate grandfather. My son."

The old hunter's breath rattled in his chest, then stilled. Sarah felt his soul drifting away, and his body melted into the floor. Alter looked stricken and Sarah wrapped her arms around him, crying with him. Melek was such a great man.

Then Melek's words registered and everything finally made sense. Sarah closed her eyes and reached for the looping ascendant that had belonged to Alter and Sutekh. The part that had been anchored to Alter's soul had left, rebounding back to the modern day, carrying Tomas away with it.

The other anchor point remained, but was now anchored in Alter's soul. She touched it and slid her thoughts along its length. What she found confirmed her recent understanding, but still left her amazed.

"Alter, it's you. You're Alter the Elder!"

He grinned, actually looking happy. "I know. I can hardly believe it. He was the greatest hunter who ever lived."

She squeezed his hand. "As are you. You're supposed to be here, Alter. I can see it now."

"So can I. This is where I'm meant to be." He looked amazingly content, considering what he had chosen to leave behind.

"Sarah, remember me," he said, his emotion written plain on his face.

She cupped his face with her hands, speaking past a lump in her throat. "Alter, you'll live forever in my heart."

"I guess that's the best I can hope for," he said with a wry smile.

Sarah drew his face forward and kissed him tenderly on the lips. She held it for a moment as he wrapped his arms around her. Alter was a great man, a special friend, a man she easily could have loved in a different life.

"I'll miss you," she said.

Moses interrupted, clearing his throat. "Where is the high priest of Set?"

Alter gestured at the small sarcophagi that held the soulmasks of Xiao and Sutekh. "I am a hunter, dedicated to destroying evil souls like those we've captured today."

Moses gripped his hand. "Welcome, Alter. We stormed the temple to stop him. Since you are united to our cause, I welcome you to unite with our people."

"It will be my honor. I'll oversee the disposal of Sutekh and his wife, who shares his same evil."

"Their acts were abomination," Moses said.

Alter grinned. "I couldn't have said it better myself."

He kissed Sarah again, a simple kiss, one of good-bye.

"I'll visit you sometimes," she promised.

Then she stepped through the invisible barrier between time and aeon space. A moment later, she blinked open her eyes and squinted against the bright Egyptian sunshine. She wasn't sure if her tears were of grief at parting, or of happiness at seeing Alter find his place.

Then a shadow leaned over her, blocking the sun. Spartacus' booming laughter echoed around the devastated square as he hauled her to her feet, slammed his fist to his heart in salute, and shouted, "Welcome back, triumphant Queen of Time and Glory!"

103

SARAH SUPPRESSED a shudder as she stared into the agonized, terrified face of a little girl dying from the plague. The girl, who couldn't be more than eight years old, was one of far too many victims Sarah had worked feverishly over the past frantic two weeks to save. The girl lay on a temporary hospital cot in a cramped corner room of the Army Central Hospital 108, near the center of Hanoi in northern Vietnam.

The room felt stuffy, and the stale air smelled of disinfectant and disease. The girl lay on the very last cot. The rest of the room was busy. Staffers transferred the dispossessed soulmasks of other patients Sarah had rescued before the disease claimed them to safe rooms. Counselors would help them deal with the trauma of their first dispossession.

Most of these patients had been too far gone for any hope their now-hibernating bodies would ever recover from the disease. So orderlies in full protective gear were wheeling the dying bodies to the incinerator.

Two doctors flanked Sarah, with several support staff hovering nearby, all garbed in similar, full protective gear to keep from getting infected.

Sarah wore her quicksilver body. It protected her from the disease, and she hated the stifling, restrictive protective clothing. Besides, she'd found that patients felt far more comfortable with the idea of getting dispossessed when they could see her in full quicksilver glory. She would have preferred not using the quicksilver cipher as often, but she didn't have time to waste, and it was the most efficient way to get the job done.

Sarah crouched beside the cot and placed a comforting hand on the little girl's head, speaking soothing words. She had no idea if the girl could understand English, or if she even realized anyone was standing over her. The girl was pretty far gone, with oozing, bleeding lesions across much of her dying body. Her face was swollen, her eyes covered in slimy puss, and she smelled like she'd already been lying in the grave for a week.

Too many victims, and not nearly enough time. Hanoi had suffered only a minor hit from the plague storm. It was the second-largest city in Vietnam, but not considered important enough to take the initial brunt of the storm.

Since it had been hit less severely, it had taken Sarah nearly two weeks of non-stop effort to work through the more heavily affected areas. She'd finally arrived there just in time to save the little girl's life.

She barely had to think about activating her nevra core before it ignited like a nuclear reactor in her heart. The nevra siphon from dispossessing mortal souls was small, but it added up over time.

She'd lost count of how many thousands of people she'd dispossessed in the past two weeks. She and the other facetakers had worked around the clock to save lives and stem the tide of disease that threatened to sweep the world in an unstoppable pandemic.

Without the tiny bits of strength she received from every patient she dispossessed, she would have collapsed days ago. With it she'd worked without sleep for eight days. She now had to remind herself to slow down and watch how hard she shook hands.

She was at least as fast as Xiao had ever been, her skin as strong as her quicksilver flesh. It was a little unnerving to know she would always be stronger than anyone around her. Then again, she'd survived four assassination attempts in the past week, so without her enhancements, she'd have died from fanatic heka or from governments nervous about the truths she could reveal.

With burning hands, Sarah gripped the little girl's face and drove her fingers into the skin to the soul points. The girl felt that, but before she could more than gasp, Sarah severed her connection to her dying young body and smoothly extracted the soulmask.

She'd perfected the art of removing soulmasks without that disgusting sucking sound that still made her skin crawl. Children's soulmasks slipped free easily. Like most of a child's anatomy, the soulmask binding points seemed a bit soft compared to adults, who had locked into their lives and lacked the same flexibility.

From what she'd heard, children tended to handle the bizarre experience of being dispossessed better than many adults too. She hated to think that some of the lives she'd saved might not fully recover from the ordeal. Well, if they spent time around her healing ciphers, that might help.

One nurse gently took the little girl's soulmask, and orderlies moved in to remove the body. The chief doctor bowed slightly to Sarah and spoke in cultured English, "That's the last of them. Thank you, Deliverer! You arrived just in time."

Sarah didn't remark on the use of the title so many people seemed anxious to pin on her. She was Sarah, but the world new her as its shiny, new heroine, the Sword of the Deliverer.

Other, more creative titles were already being thrown out there, and Sarah was glad none of them had stuck. Sword of the Deliverer was ostentatious enough.

"I'm glad the healing cipher slowed the disease long enough," she responded as they headed for the exit.

She was really looking forward to getting some fresh air. She'd breathed enough disease-laden hospital air for a lifetime. She wasn't sure how the doctors, nurses, and support staff did it.

They'd faced a daunting task over the past two weeks. The big, modern hospital had been one of a dozen locations transformed into plague treatment centers across the city. Normally equipped to handle roughly two thousand inpatients, the hospital had been quickly adapted to take in nearly ten thousand victims of the plague.

The professional, dedicated team had risen to the challenge, despite the risk of getting infected themselves. In the frantic recent weeks, she'd seen similar heroism repeated in more hospitals across more countries than she could count.

Their task would have been hopelessly tragic if not for the healing ciphers Sarah had created. She could feel the warm waves of healing power emanating from one of them situated nearby. It was powered by the souls of nearly twenty million Vietnamese people who lived in Hanoi.

They eagerly shared a fraction of their soul strength to help heal their families and friends. Nearly a hundred thousand people had caught the terrible disease in Hanoi, and more than ten percent of them had died before she'd gotten healing ciphers in place to slow, and in some cases, even reverse the disease.

One of the doctors broke protocol and hugged her. Sarah could see the woman's tear-streaked face through her protective faceplate, which was fogging up from her fast breathing. "Thank you! Your healing ciphers have saved so many lives. They will revolutionize healthcare."

"I hope so. I'm just glad we seem to be getting ahead of the plague finally," Sarah said, carefully patting the shorter woman on the back of her bulky suit.

Thinking about all the people they had dispossessed made her feel tired, but also a little awed. Had they really accomplished so much in so little time?

It would take time to fully defeat the last vestiges of that horrible plague that Xiao had unleashed. The vile woman had crafted a super plague as a variant of the deadly Ebola virus. Mortality rates of the rune-enhanced plague were over ninety percent for those who had contacted it in the early hours, when it was still driven by the Dendera rune web.

Highly contagious, the plague had spread rapidly, even though they'd destroyed the rune web so quickly. If they'd delayed even a few more hours before taking out that web, there might have been no stopping the pandemic. As it was, too many people had died.

With millions infected in dense population centers, the disease had threatened to burst out of all control. They could have faced casualties in the hundreds of millions.

They'd avoided that worst-case scenario, but Sarah still shuddered to think how close they'd come. She had appealed to the world governments to work together to fight the sickness. Tomas had led a team that had raided Xiao's Egypt headquarters and discovered detailed information about the plague that had helped the efforts to fight it.

A cure was being developed, but traditional channels would have taken too long. That's why Sarah had deployed special healing ciphers, powered by remote charging runes placed around each affected city. Each city in essence healed themselves by the strength of their own souls.

Few had objected to using her runes that way. Some religions were struggling with the reality of runes and the ethical questions of tapping the power of human souls, but people were motivated to not die. So, faced with the alternative of immediate, gruesome death, most of the faithful found ways to justify the use of a little soul power.

The remote charging runes had provided vast quantities of soul force to fuel the healing runes, which had also blocked the airborne virus from spreading. Without her efforts, Xiao's plague might still have crippled the world.

The next challenge would be dealing with replacement suits for all the dispossessed whose bodies were too sick to recover. More people had struggled with the idea of swapping bodies long-term, but Francesca was on it. Hopefully she had good news when they checked in next.

Moments later, Sarah completed the disinfecting spray down and reached the locker room. She gladly pulled out her clothing, released her quicksilver cipher, and returned to her normal self. As she dressed in casual cream colored linen pants and a blue cotton blouse, she sighed to feel the soft cloth against her skin.

She'd learned to morph the outer layer of her quicksilver skin to look like she was wearing form-fitting silver pants and shirt. That way she hadn't been walking around looking like a naked terminator. She also hadn't needed to worry about wearing unnecessary clothing that would only have to be disposed of after getting exposed to disease in the hospital wards. Overall, the solution had worked remarkably well, but it was nice to relax in her own current suit again.

Tomas was waiting for her in the hallway outside of the changing room. Alter's body looked good on him, but the busy past weeks were beginning to drain even his remarkable stamina. Dark circles had grown under his eyes, and he was starting to look haggard.

He was handling his newfound nevra core quite well, although Sarah hadn't found much time to train with him. Eirene and Francesca had helped him learn the basics, and Sarah looked forward to practicing with him, exploring together the full extent of their new powers.

Sarah stepped close and hugged him so tight he grunted. She kissed him, fast and hard, and grinned. "That was the last, unless you've heard of other hospitals we need to visit."

"Negative. Gregorios is wrapping things up in Bogota, and the cure is finally shipping worldwide starting tomorrow."

"Finally," she breathed

It had been an exhausting, terrifying couple of weeks as they tried to avert global meltdown. With the help of her ciphers, the world's best pharmaceutical companies had cranked out a cure in record time. They had even agreed to ship it around the world free of charge and take the financial hit themselves.

Of course, the fact that one of the most prominent pharma CEOs had turned out to be one of Xiao's undercover cui dashi children had helped motivate them. Footing a multi-billion dollar tab for helping inoculate the world from the terrible plague was a small price to pay for avoiding claims they had been colluding with Xiao in the first place.

As they headed for the downstairs lobby, everyone they met seemed eager to thank Sarah personally. Tomas tried hurrying them along, and even though no one looked threatening, he kept a wary eye out. He'd vowed that no one else would ever get the chance to try assassinating her again, and had already made good the threat twice.

While Sarah had been traveling the world with most of the other facetakers, dispossessing the plague-infected sick, Tomas had recruited Carlo and most of his team of Italian special forces. They'd established a new, elite paramilitary organization.

Known as the Aeon Corps, they were an international enhanced anti-terrorism and peace-bringing force, already four hundred strong, with thousands of applicants clamoring for a chance to join. They now served as Sarah's protective detail, with plans to work with Yurak International and military organizations worldwide to fight all types of terrorism.

"You look tired," she whispered to Tomas after stealing another kiss. "Are we still on for tonight?"

"Wouldn't miss it for the world."

"Liar."

They hadn't seen each other nearly enough in the weeks since the confrontation with Xiao. She couldn't wait for their upcoming date. It would be so nice just to relax and spend time together.

"Carlo received the latest update from San Marino," Tomas said as he guided her toward the escalators to the ground floor.

"I can't wait to visit." Sarah still hadn't been inside the big church in that lovely little town. She loved that they were building their company's headquarters there.

Tomas added, "Mirco is one of our captains now. He's still trying to convince everyone crossbows are the weapon of the future."

Sarah laughed. "Only when they're firing Quentin's bolts."

"Quentin's working on some new ones. He'll show them to you when he returns from the States."

Still trailed by a crowd of grateful and enthusiastic staff and government officials, Sarah finally made it to the exit and stepped out into the late afternoon sunshine. As usual, they implored her to stay longer. Although the plague had been curtailed, there was still a tremendous amount of work to do. She assured them that she would return as soon as possible, and promised to stay longer next time.

The air was still hot and humid, although not nearly so bad there, close to the river. She couldn't see the Red River, but she could smell it. The air smelled of recent rain, and that helped wash away some of the stench that always clung to big cities.

She tipped her head back and inhaled deeply. In recent days, she'd realized she was not only getting stronger, but her senses had improved. She liked getting the scent of a city, and had found that every city smelled a little different.

She hadn't had time to try taking the scent of Hanoi when she'd first arrived. They had helicoptered directly to the plague ward in the hospital from the airport.

While she stood there, motionless for a moment, she heard the whine of a heavy bullet just before it struck her cheekbone, just below her eye.

104

Painting is silent poetry, poetry is painting that speaks, and runes are the trumpets of a new life.

~PLUTARCH

THE BULLET RICOCHETED off Sarah's cheek, buzzing angrily as it tore into a nearby building. If she hadn't tipped up her head, it might have struck her in the eye.

"Sniper!" Tomas shouted, tackling her off her feet.

She went with him instead of holding her ground. She didn't want her boyfriend bruised, after all. Instead of scattering in panic like most crowds would, she was stunned to see many of the vulnerable people around her leap forward to stand between her and danger. They wanted to protect her with their bodies, but they were the ones who needed protection.

Sarah shoved Tomas off and leaped to her feet, trying vainly to get the people to move. They crowded close, shouting for her to duck.

It was such a display of bravery that she felt tears well in her eyes. Of course, that made them think she'd been wounded, and they screamed for medics, and tugged at her to come inside so they could treat her.

"I'm all right," she said, then turned to Tomas, who hovered close beside her, one hand pressed over his ear as he shouted for his team.

Sarah was taller than many of the locals, and she scanned for the threat. If the sniper shot any of those brave people, she'd personally rip off their arms and make them suffer before she even bothered asking for information.

"Keep your hand up," Tomas urged as he tried to pull her through the crowd toward the curb where their armored SUV was already racing in to pick them up.

That was good advice. She hated eye shots. Her eyes were still her most sensitive external organs. She'd been shot in the eye the week before, but it was a smaller caliber bullet, and she'd healed in seconds.

The shooter hadn't. Despite their many battles, she'd never seen Tomas so angry. There hadn't been enough left of the corpse to identify who he worked for.

She'd appreciated Tomas' intensity, hoped it would translate to their love life when she finally got him that far. Still, she felt obligated to encourage him to show restraint. At least until they found out who had ordered the hit.

Today's bullet had felt bigger. Probably a fifty cal. She liked that round, had shot Xiao many times with one, and knew just how frustrated the shooter must feel to realize his shot with that mighty bullet had not produced the desired effect.

The sniper fired again, but this time she was ready. She immediately oriented slightly to her right, her enhanced gaze tracking up to the fifth floor window of an office building several blocks down the street.

The shooter had used a suppressor, but her senses were so sharp, she caught the muzzle flash and picked up the muted report. The round tore through the air toward her, again aiming for her eye.

She caught it.

The impact smarted a little, but even though she no longer wore her quicksilver form, her skin was tougher than steel, so catching a rifle bullet, even a fifty caliber round, wasn't that big of a deal. The gathered crowd gaped at her as she held up the flattened bullet to Tomas and pointed up the street.

Tomas looked like he wanted to tackle her again, but seemed to realize there wasn't much point. So he shouted, "Aeon team, we have a fix on the shooter!" He relayed the location even as he pulled her through the crowd toward the curb.

Sarah waved, gripping hands and saying, "Thank you! I'll be all right. Please take cover." Over and over again.

The shooter might try again, and the ricochet might hurt someone. Or they might decide to use bigger ordinance, and she didn't want to see innocents die just for standing near her.

"I want them alive this time," she reminded Tomas.

"We're on it. With the new ammo, we should be able to capture them."

The armored SUV, driven by Carlo himself, skidded to the curb, and Tomas yanked open the back door for Sarah to jump inside. She waved a final time as Tomas piled in behind her and slammed the door. Carlo sped away, and two chase vehicles full of Aeon company's heavily-armed defensive squad fell in behind.

While they raced for the airport, they picked up a police escort to help them zip through the congested city. Tomas coordinated with his strike team, who were moving against the building where the shots were fired.

Government forces were closing in to assist, and Yurak fighters were prepping to launch from the airport. Sarah hoped they wouldn't be needed. Airstrikes would hurt too many. They were only dealing with a simple assassination attempt, after all.

It wasn't like Xiao had returned from the dead. That monster was dead, but the world was still far from a safe place.

Within three minutes, Tomas sat back with a relieved smile and said, "Well done. Notify me when they arrive at the interrogation facility."

"You have living prisoners this time?" Sarah asked. She felt relieved that none of their people had been hurt in the operation. The first couple of times people had tried assassinating her, she'd leaped into action herself, clobbering her attackers. She kept having to remind herself that she needed to let Tomas' team do their jobs, even though she was stronger and faster than any of them.

Tomas nodded, trying to look relaxed, but Sarah knew him too well. He would be raging inside, eager to interrogate the prisoners. He preferred when they took a while to talk. It gave him an excuse to beat them to a pulp for daring to attack her. His protective side was really endearing.

"The sniper team had fast-ascent ropes already hooked up for their escape. A Yurak helicopter intercepted a chopper inbound. Looks like they knew that round wouldn't do much, but hoped it would lure you into trying to take them out personally. Shaped charges and compressed napalm were planted throughout the building. They were going to try to melt you into a puddle."

By the time he finished, his nostrils were flaring, the only sign of his rage.

She patted his arm. "I'm glad they didn't detonate it when our team went in."

"Didn't get the chance. Those new bullets worked like a charm. If word gets out about these, Harriett will be begging you to make more for Yurak to sell."

"For now, they're our little secret."

She didn't want governments around the world getting their hands on her best ciphers. Those were for her people. She'd developed the new ciphers for some of the non-lethal ammo the Aeon protective detail used.

The rubber bullets deployed a cocoon-like barrier that immobilized targets, preventing them from speaking, fighting, or committing suicide. It even shorted out their comms. Their superiors would know they'd failed, but would not know the specifics. Let them sweat while Tomas' team interrogated the prisoners in a secure location.

Then Sarah would deal with the employers.

Within half an hour, Carlo pulled the SUV onto a special, private lot at the airport. The luxury Gulfstream jet Gregorios had assigned for her use was waiting nearby, and they hurried aboard, with the eight man protective detail watching the perimeter. All the security was overkill, since she doubted another attack would come there, but she did not protest.

While she settled into one of the plush leather seats at the fore end of the fancy jet, the team moved to the back and stowed their gear. Carlo went to speak with the pilots about their route to Washington D.C. Tomas sat beside her and opened a laptop connected via bluetooth to a huge television screen that folded down from a recess in the ceiling.

"We'll have Yurak fighter escorts all the way to Washington," he said.

"I'm surprised the U.S. is allowing Yurak planes over their soil."

He grinned. "They don't like it, but the president really wants to meet with you, and that was our condition. We'll have a sizable security force waiting for us when we land."

"You love making life difficult for them, don't you?" she teased.

"At the moment, yes. They screwed up royally letting Xiao infiltrate the White House."

"England didn't do much better," she pointed out.

"I know. Bloody embarrassing," he said, slipping into his British accent. She loved it, and kept pestering him to speak like that more often.

"Speaking of Xiao's children, what have they learned from them?"

"One of the things we need to ask when we land. They're keeping the intelligence pretty close, since they can't be sure who else is part of Xiao's network. One more reason to keep security tight."

When Xiao had lost the rune duel, her cui dashi children had also lost their ascendants. The ascendants had moved on, bonding with the pure, fresh souls of children around the world. That had helped restore the inner balance of the aeon, but had really screwed those undercover agents' lives.

Those cui dashi who had been impersonating world leaders had lost their nevra core and the ability to maintain their double-stacked disguise. Seeing their leaders' faces suddenly fall off their skulls, revealing the imposter's faces underneath had truly shocked those nations. The souls of those world leaders had been badly beaten, but Eirene had personally tended to them.

Those governments had been deeply embarrassed, so they were motivated to very publicly hunt down and arrest anyone with any kind of ties to Xiao. The U.S. Ambassador had been one of the first arrested. Sarah still needed to throw a big party to celebrate that man's downfall.

While they waited for the plane to depart, Tomas started a video call with Gregorios and Eirene, who were in Florence. The feed showed them sitting in a plush boardroom with spectacular views over the famous Florence duomo. The two facetakers looked tired, but happy. Eirene still wore her striking Amazon suit.

Gregorios waved. "Welcome to the new headquarters of the Aequitas League."

Sarah flashed a happy smile. "How did you get that location?"

"I have my ways," he said with a grin.

Gregorios was acting CEO of Sarah's new international organization for equity and truth. He'd tried to convince her to call it the Justice League, especially if she created another super power rune for him.

He hadn't argued too much when she refused, and only once had he reminded her that her stewardship of history had come only because she'd stolen his ascendant. The least she could do was give him a super power once in a while. She hadn't made any promises.

She still felt terrible about stealing his ascendant, and Tomas felt horribly guilty about having a nevra core when Gregorios didn't.

Sure enough, Tomas offered, "Gregorios, now that the plague is mostly contained, I'm sure Sarah can transfer my nevra core to you."

Gregorios shook his head. "That one won't do, sorry. From what Sarah said, mine is intertwined so closely with Eirene's, it's the only one I could ever take back."

Eirene rolled her eyes, but gave him a quick kiss. "Still as romantic as always."

He winked. "With you wearing that Amazon, I'd be insane to tick you off, although I do like a hint of danger in my romance."

Sarah smiled to see them so relaxed. She had worried she'd fundamentally damaged Gregorios when she stole his ascendant, but he was taking it remarkably well. She said, "I'm happy to return yours."

"Keep it for now. I'm going to enjoy this life for a while. Maybe find religion for once."

That was an idea that might prove remarkably interesting, given what he'd seen through his long lives. It might also shake whatever religion he chose to its roots.

Eirene added, "Besides, we've already tested and confirmed I can still share some of mine with him."

"Even though he doesn't have a nevra core?" Tomas asked. They really needed to study that.

Gregorios shrugged. "We're connected so deep, it's a wonder our cores haven't merged already."

As her CEO, Gregorios was proving a talented administrator. With his resources, his long leadership experience, and his intimate knowledge of the inner workings of so many countries, he was perfect. He loved the idea of making world leaders squirm too.

Sarah wasn't above making threats, if she had to. She'd established Aequitas as a way to formalize her voice. Spartacus had been right. The world seemed desperate for a strong voice, and many had turned to her.

She had become a world hero. Many fanatics tried worshiping her as a goddess, but she refused to accept that label. Others proclaimed her the Sword of the Deliverer. One hunter had made the mistake of mentioning she was really the Aeon Champion, and that label had spread like the plague around the world.

She had decided that if the world would always know her name, she'd make sure she defined what they knew her for. She'd discussed her ideas with Gregorios, Eirene, and Tomas. They had worked in the shadows for so long, they took some convincing before agreeing that working in the limelight might work even better.

Gregorios and Eirene had secretly helped many world relief organizations for decades. Sarah decided to take it a step farther. With her connection with the aeon, she could slip back and forth through history and around the world. There was literally nothing she couldn't learn when she put her mind to it.

She could cut through the lies and double-talk that so many political leaders relied upon, and she'd already started calling them on it, forcing them to deal more honestly. She wasn't foolish enough to think she'd completely change the system, but she might make it a little less corrupt. That would be a pretty good start.

She had a lot of leverage. The U.S., U.K., and Chinese governments were all among her loudest backers as they tried to recover from Xiao's infiltration. Eirene had leveraged the situation to secure huge donations to Sarah's fledgling organization.

With the world knowing the truth about how they'd been duped into war by Xiao, those major world powers had all withdrawn their armies. Most were making admirable efforts to restore international relations. The rest of the world followed suit, cowed by the plague and world opinion that all the wars were due to Xiao's manipulations.

No one wanted to be seen as supporting Xiao's world genocide insanity. A few smaller countries had launched strikes against each other, hoping to capitalize on the chaotic situation in the world, but Sarah had promised to deal with them personally if they didn't back down.

They all had.

Eirene picked up a phone on her end and said, "Francesca and Spartacus want to join the call."

"Link them in," Sarah said eagerly. She'd been planning on checking in with them soon anyway.

105

I am sorry to report we arrived too late to reach the villa before Vesuvius erupted. You were right, the mountain destroyed Pompeii entirely, and the villa is buried under a mountain of ash. I'm afraid the scrolls must be destroyed.

~YEHUDI, HUNTER TEAM LEADER, OUTSIDE OF
HERCULANEUM, 79 A.D.

SARAH GRINNED to see Francesca and Spartacus when they appeared on the screen. Spartacus wore a tight-fitting t-shirt that read, "Ask Spartacus".

Figured. Ask Spartacus had already become the number one downloaded app around the world.

"I see you've moved into merchandising," Gregorios said with a chuckle.

"Indeed, King of Intrigue," Spartacus boomed with his normal cheer. "Mortals around the world have access to my advice twenty-four seven."

"The world will never be the same," Gregorios muttered.

Sarah decided to believe Spartacus' growing influence would be a good thing. He still seemed intent on driving the world toward honor and integrity, and those were ideas she fully supported.

Francesca was wearing a sarong, with a crimson bikini top, sipping a glass of wine. She looked relaxed, which was remarkable given the insane hours they were all working.

She winked at Sarah and waved. "Hey, Queen of the Plague."

Sarah shuddered. "That's not even a little funny."

"Sure it is," Francesca said, turning serious. "You saved so many lives, it's a wonder every world religion hasn't already sainted you."

"They're trying," Tomas said.

"We're stalling, though," Gregorios added. "Getting them all scheduled for different months is tricky, but I think we can arrange it so we celebrate at least one holiday dedicated to Sarah every month of the year."

"Look what you started," Sarah said to Francesca, not having to pretend to be annoyed by the idea. "Satisfied?"

"For now, but I'll let you know when I get a better idea."

"Did you find new lives for everyone?" Sarah changed the subject. At the last count, there had still been nearly two hundred thousand dispossessed awaiting transfer.

Francesca smoothly transitioned to business. "Working on it. We've never faced transitions of this scale before, but we've got the world body bank set up in most countries. Anyone who slips into a coma and loses all brain function, but whose body is still sound can opt for dispossession and donate the body for someone in need."

"And people are going for that?" Tomas asked, sounding incredulous.

"Better than you'd think. The plague has a way of helping people re-think their priorities. There are still some who can't think outside of a single life, but they can easily opt out."

"What about the convict program?" Gregorios asked.

Francesca nodded. "That too. Death-row inmates in quite a few countries are soon going to be able to choose dispossession as an alternative punishment."

"Fools. It's not a pleasant fate," Gregorios muttered.

Eirene patted his arm. "Better than dying. For them, anyway. No dark, scary soul coffins for murderers and rapists."

Francesca nodded agreement. "We're pushing the idea with a plan to have them placed on their own international wailing wall, tended by other inmates on a work-release program. It's all going to be over-seen by faithful members of the Order of the Deliverer."

Sarah rolled her eyes and groaned. "Really? That group of fanatics again? Did you have to give them credibility?"

Francesca shrugged. "Don't knock down people who love you.

They're true believers. I say, give them a job. The faithful work harder."

Spartacus lifted an enormous hamburger into view from the table next to their computer and gestured with it for emphasis. "This woman is a goddess, I tell you! How she has time to do so much and still visit me is a miracle."

Francesca patted his hand, giving him a genuine smile. "I have to make time for you, big guy. You're the first man I've ever met who's able to keep up. I wouldn't want you to wander off with some other woman."

"Impossible. You are a queen of the world. All other women are like cattle in comparison."

"And he wonders why I keep him around," Francesca asked with a grin.

"Is your video still ranking?" Sarah asked, pleased to see how happy they made each other, but still feeling a bit weird about the whole situation.

She had grown to genuinely like Spartacus, but he was still wearing Tomas' old body. Sarah was wearing one of Francesca's old bodies, and Tomas was now wearing Alter's. Reality for them had gotten really bizarre.

Spartacus boomed, "Forty-five billion hits. Imagine that! So many eager to witness my moment of glory."

"Our moment of glory," Francesca corrected. "It was a duel of the ages, for sure, but I think they mostly want to see the kiss."

Spartacus laughed, "They'll all see it. Filming for our movie begins next week."

"*Kiss of Death* is scheduled for worldwide release next February," Francesca confirmed. "It's going to be huge."

The thought of the two of them starring in a feature film still boggled the mind. The world would never be the same.

Gregorios interrupted. "I'm linking in Harriett from Yurak, Harald from Suntara, and Nabil from the hunter clan."

"Wow, everyone's online at the same time. That hasn't happened since, well, ever," Eirene said.

Soon three more video feeds joined the call. Sarah was glad they had a big screen to see everyone. It almost felt like they were all seated together in the same room. She was looking forward to the day when they could actually do that.

After they exchanged greetings, Sarah asked Harald, "What about history?"

"Being rewritten as we speak," he said with a smile.

His office in Suntara had been re-tasked to head a global effort to carefully straighten out the many lies propagated through the ages. Since they'd been the ones to insert most of those lies, they were best qualified to set the record straight. "The reawakened are proving to be a brilliant marketing stroke."

"I'm glad we found use for them," she said sincerely.

They'd managed to salvage two hundred and seventy-eight soul-masks from the thousands that Xiao had dispossessed as fodder for her rune webs. Those poor victims had become known as the Reawakened, a term coined by a clever journalist, and had instantly become famous in a world seeking heroes after the crazy events in Egypt. Working with Harald's history rewriting group was a great PR idea.

"And the internship program?" Sarah asked.

"We're working the machines seven days a week," Harald reported. "As many hours as we have facetakers free to work them, but we can't keep up. We had seventy-six million applicants looking for chances to memory walk. It's already the most sought-after research program of all time."

"Good," Sarah said, earning a grumpy look from the tired facetaker. "We want the world to embrace this. It helps secure our credibility."

"Fewer torch-wielding mobs. Don't really miss those," Gregorios agreed.

Harald sighed, then said, "People are responding far better than I ever would have imagined. I had worried mortals would feel only anger at knowing history is not what they thought it was."

Sarah felt pleased that her faith in humanity had paid off. "Most people know history's tweaked. It's just the extent of the damage that startles everyone. But since you're providing not only true accounts, but unprecedented access to the past, what's not to get excited about?"

Harriett saluted with a cookie. "Harald, you're a rock star. It's official. You've got your own fan club. I think you're the only man ever featured in People magazine and National Geographic in the same month. I saw the proofs. Both issues ship in two weeks."

The big facetaker seemed pleased by his newfound fame. "I had my doubts about this new approach, but you were right, Sarah. People do want to know the truth."

"Of course she's right," Tomas said with a laugh. "No one's going to mess with her."

"Not with your team backing me up," Sarah said, giving him a warm smile.

Harriett added, "And Yurak too. Half the world has contracts with us for tech and enhancements. They'd never jeopardize that."

"And Suntara," Eirene added softly. She hadn't spoken much, but looked very content just listening.

"And me!" Spartacus cried, standing and raising his hamburger high. "I will challenge anyone who impugns your honor, Lady of Steel!"

"Get in line," Tomas said, looking a bit surly that Spartacus would assume the role of protector.

Sarah turned to Nabil, the last member of the meeting, who looked more subdued than the others. He no longer looked like he was itching to assassinate them all, but still looked a bit uneasy, even though they weren't actually in the same room. "And how are our dear friends in Jerusalem?"

"We're actively hunting down remnants of Xiao's forces, with the help of Anaru and the Tenth," He admitted a bit reluctantly.

"I'm glad the partnership is going so well."

He cringed at the word partnership, but didn't correct her. Anaru had been promoted again to captain of the Tenth when Tomas moved on to the Aeon Corps. The arrangement seemed to suit everyone extremely well.

"I'm sorry I missed Melek's funeral," Sarah said.

Nabil nodded his thanks. "It is understood. You were busy saving lives. He would have approved."

Melek's funeral had been a grand celebration, attended by dignitaries of many countries. Although far too many funerals were happening, mostly for cremated remains, the world had unified to celebrate Melek.

The hunters preferred to live and work in secret, but Sarah had shared with the world Melek's contributions to defeating Xiao and Sutekh. He was a considered a world hero in most countries.

"What word of Alter?" Nabil asked.

Sarah smiled to think of dear Alter. "He's doing well. I visited him in the wilderness the day before yesterday. Skipped a few years. His family's grown to twelve children."

"Twelve! Where does he find the time?" Tomas exclaimed.

Sarah shrugged. "Well, they are wandering for forty years. What else do you want him to do? He tossed the sarcophagus with Sutekh and Xiao into the Red Sea during the crossing."

Gregorios looked pleased to hear that. "Serves them right. May they rot till the end of days."

Lingering in a soul coffin under the cold, dark sea was a terrible fate, but in their case, it was fitting. Sarah felt no pity. And since she'd stripped their nevra cores, she felt no fear they could somehow pull off some fantastic escape, like bonding to a fish, or something.

They were both extremely powerful souls, even without their nevra cores, so no doubt they would languish for centuries, slowly going insane. Well, more insane, before they finally expired.

Eirene added, "Since we're sharing reports, I'm happy to state that Suntara assets are restored, and the organization is preparing to expand."

That was good to hear. Suntara had thrived for centuries in the shadows, but now it was becoming a major world power, right out in the open for all to see.

"How are the children?"

Sarah had identified all of the children around the world who had inherited connections to the ascendants freed from Xiao and her children. Someday, those kids would learn to activate their nevra core. She'd also identified the remaining facetakers who had not yet been found by Suntara. They were being approached and recruited.

Eirene reported, "We're sponsoring their education, setting up facilities in each country where they live to help maintain the balance. Once they reach sixteen and begin to activate their nevra cores, we'll start their training."

"Good." With proper nurture, Sarah hoped none of them would turn rogue or hurt people with their marvelous gifts.

Sarah glanced across the feeds of her dear friends and felt a surge of love for them all. "Things are going to be all right."

Gregorios saluted with his glass of wine. "You've got great things in store, my dear. We're moving into uncharted territory, but I'm optimistic."

"You're optimistic because we're leaving on our honeymoon tomorrow," Eirene said, giving him a kiss on the cheek.

"Rightly so," Gregorios said with a smile. "I'm the luckiest man alive."

"When will you return?" Sarah asked. They still had a lot of work to do.

Gregorios said without hesitation, "Six months. After the honeymoon, we're going to visit the children."

"The girls will help out while we're away," Eirene assured Sarah.

Francesca nodded. "Perfect chance to hit the machines again. I want a rematch. That last memoryscape race was rigged."

"You're just a sore loser, Franny," Harriett said with a grin.

Sarah could use some simple play time in the memoryscape, but said, "You're on. As soon as we get back from D.C."

After they terminated the call, Sarah sat back and allowed herself to relax as the plane prepared to depart. Her thoughts returned to Alter and her last visit.

While his twelve children had played outside his spacious tent, he'd talked about the formation of the hunter clan and his plans for preparing them for their mission. He'd aged well, had matured into a very competent leader and father. His wife and clan were very lucky to have him.

Then he'd surprised her by requesting she not visit him ever again. The request had surprised her. She felt a growing suspicion that he planned to do something rash. He had requested she give him Sutekh's ascendant, after all.

He still felt cursed. He'd assured her he planned nothing of the sort, but that he had determined his purpose and that he needed to walk his path alone, undisturbed.

Now, as Sarah leaned back in her comfortable, leather chair, she considered his words. What had he meant? What had he planned to do with his life? She'd learned enough from Nabil about the legend of the great Alter that she knew there was some confusion about his death.

So where had Alter gone after that first life? What had he done? As a cui dashi, he could have lived a long time. In fact, he might have . . .

Sarah sat up abruptly and gasped as she made the connections.

"What?" Tomas asked, immediately on alert.

"Nothing. It's all right. But can we head west instead of east and make a side trip to Rome before D.C.? I need to drop in on Quentin."

"Of course. Why?"

"I need to follow up on a hunch."

"That's cryptic," Tomas pointed out.

"Sorry. I can't say more yet. I'll only need a day, then we can head to Washington."

"No worries. I wanted to get back to Italy anyway. Let's extend the stay another day. The world can give you that long."

"Why?" she asked, intrigued. He had that look in his eye like he was planning something devious. She liked it when he looked like that.

"My turn to be cryptic," he teased.

"Touché." She kissed him, then settled back into her seat as Tomas called forward to alter course.

106

To speak the name of the dead is to make him live again.

~ANCIENT EGYPTIAN PROVERB

SARAH SLOWED her rental car at a pull-out just north of the picturesque Liechtenstein town of Balzers and stepped out to enjoy the breathtaking view. The Rhine River flowed past to her right, while majestic mountains erupted out of the ground on the opposite side of the small valley, with the town nestled in the center.

The ancient Gutenberg castle lorded over the town from the top of a hill near the center of town. Definitely a site Sarah planned to visit before she left.

They'd landed in Rome the day before and spent a wonderful, relaxing afternoon with Quentin in his mansion. He was busy working in Suntara, but had dropped everything to play host with his usual style.

Tomas had eventually gotten swept into enforcer business when Anaru and a few other enforcers dropped in to see them. Sarah had slipped away to visit the female doctor on Quentin's medical staff who had helped them so much. Within minutes of that visit, Sarah had confirmed her suspicions and extracted the location she needed.

Liechtenstein had been a surprise, but she couldn't stop now. She'd taken the jet to Zurich. The hardest part of the journey had been convincing Tomas and the Aeon corps to let her travel alone.

Tomas had surprised her by agreeing to stay in Rome. He had

some work to do, but he'd insisted Carlo take a full team with her to Zurich. Once they landed, she'd had to threaten to bind them with ciphers if they didn't let her finish the journey alone.

It was only a two hour drive from Zurich to Balzers, and she'd enjoyed the excellent scenery and rare privacy. She couldn't guarantee Carlo wasn't calling in for air support to shadow her, but as long as they kept their distance, she wouldn't complain.

A few minutes later, she pulled into the driveway of a beautiful old house on a lovely, green property, surrounded by high, well-groomed hedges. The house was a tall, three-story structure that looked like it dated back several hundred years.

The slate roof was steeply pitched, the exterior painted white, with dark-stained wooden trim. A long garage and several other outbuildings flanked the main house, but Sarah saw no one as she pulled up to the barred iron gate.

Suddenly feeling a bit nervous, Sarah pushed the call button. Several seconds later, a male voice spoke in German. It was clearly a question, probably asking who she was.

"My name is Sarah. I don't have an appointment, but I need to speak with the owner of the house. He'll know me."

She waited a long, breathless moment before the iron gate silently swung open. Eagerly, she pulled forward and stopped on the gravel driveway near the main entrance. The aged wooden door with wrought iron hinges swung open before she could knock, and she instantly recognized the figure standing in the entrance, despite his age.

"Alter, is that really you?" she breathed. She'd been so sure she'd read the clues right, but seeing him standing there still rocked her to the core.

"Hello, Sarah," Alter said with a friendly smile as he stepped closer and extended his hands.

Sarah threw her arms around his neck, hugging him tight and laughing with joy. He returned the embrace with equal enthusiasm.

He wore a solid, middle-aged body, and his face was lined from sun and long years, but his black eyes glittered with the same energy she remembered. He looked so much like Melek.

"I knew you'd figure it out, but wondered how long it would take." He ushered her through the beautiful entryway and into an airy salon.

Tall, arched windows offered excellent views of the lush gardens behind the house. The walls were painted white, with rose patterns around the windows. The high ceiling was decorated with a golden house crest on light blue background.

He gestured her to take a seat on a soft blue couch and settled on the cushions beside her. She laughed again and said, "I still can hardly believe it. You've lived over four millennia since I last saw you! How did you survive the soul fragmentation from so many lives?"

"By pacing myself, and by building a machine during the height of the Roman Empire."

Sarah blinked, and couldn't hide her amazement.

He chuckled. "Don't look so surprised. I knew those machines better than anyone. The trick was figuring out how to power it. I had to develop the technology nearly two thousand years early. But I had a lot of time to figure it out, and I knew how to find the best minds in the world to help me."

"Of course. With a machine, you could keep your soul intact. Plus, you're cui dashi, so you're more resilient anyway."

Alter grimaced. "I try not to activate my nevra core except when absolutely necessary. The nevra siphon has been key in keeping me alive, but that doesn't mean I like it."

"I know what you mean. I've had to dispossess tens of thousands of people in the past weeks. It has an effect."

"One that I am sure you will manage far better than I. Have you been in the memoryscape lately?"

"Not much. I usually travel the aeon directly now, but I plan to visit it again soon with Francesca and Harriett."

"I've seen Reuben and spoken with him many times. Keep your eye out for him."

"I will. I still don't understand how he moves through the memoryscape like he does. He's not a rune warrior, or a facetaker. He's not anchored to an ascendant."

Reuben's soulmask hung in a place of honor among the hunters, but no one had dared restore him to a body. Paul's sinister runes had twisted his mind, and he couldn't be trusted not to slip into another murderous rage.

Sometimes when she ran into him as she slid through history he shouted profanities. Other times he stalked away after making face. He never made sense.

"I'm not entirely sure either, although I plan to study his condition when I have more leisure. The last time I spoke with him, he sounded almost sane, but I fear it's just a new symptom of his broken mind. He didn't seem to realize we defeated Xiao, even though he acted like I was an idiot for reminding him. Then he kept spouting about time running out, and a sinister threat we were ignoring."

Sarah placed a comforting hand on his arm. "I'm sorry about Reuben. I wish we'd defeated Paul sooner."

Alter sighed. "Me too. That is still one of my great regrets."

Sarah could perhaps understand that guilt a bit. She hadn't been forced to dispossess her own brother before he could embark upon a murder spree. Instead, she'd been forced to abandon a dear friend to what had seemed a terrible, lonely fate. At least she could celebrate Alter's remarkable survival. Would poor Reuben ever recover?

"When we have time, I'll help you," she promised.

"Thank you. I would appreciate it, but the future is yet unclear. It's the past that I excel in."

"Tell me about it," she urged, settling back on the couch, eager to hear the story.

Alter leaned back against the cushions. He looked relaxed and confident in a way he had never managed as the young, hot-headed Alter she knew. The difference reminded her that he really wasn't the same man she'd left just weeks ago. Four millennia ago.

He gestured with his left hand, showing a simple, worn, gold ring. "I'm married. You met my wife, Sofia."

"She's how I found you, although I hadn't realized you two were married. Once I put the pieces together, I realized those clues she gave us couldn't have been from you in your first life."

Alter grinned. "I thought I'd overcome the temptation to interfere long ago, but watching you all struggle was far more difficult than I had expected. I very nearly revealed myself to you."

"You should have," Sarah said, but immediately realized that might have been a bad idea.

He shook his head. "Appearing in your midst would have skewed events, perhaps disastrously. I could not risk it. It was extremely risky the times I dared venture anywhere near my younger self. I could feel history warping around us, and worried I was breaking things without even intending it."

"When? Why didn't we notice?"

If he'd taken a young body, would she really have realized it wasn't young Alter? His face would have been the same. Who would ever imagine a friend might be the long-lost historical reincarnation of a future that hadn't happened yet?

Even thinking about Alter's unique situation challenged her understanding of how history worked, even though she walked the aeon nearly every day.

Alter chuckled. "Again, Sofia provided an invaluable service. We double-stacked."

"Really? I'm impressed that Eirene and Gregorios didn't sense it."

Simply amazing. He really had learned a lot. The Alter she knew never could have restrained himself like that, especially double-stacked and moving in a woman's body.

"Actually, Eirene sensed something once. I was worried we would be discovered that first day you came to visit Tomas after he was wounded, when you first arrived at Quentin's."

"I didn't even notice," she admitted.

"You had a lot on your mind." Alter sighed, looking content. "Sofia is truly my great love. We met in fifteen twenty-seven when I saved her from the sacking of Rome."

"Whoa," was all Sarah could think to say as she absorbed that remarkable declaration.

"Her father was Pietro Borghese. He died in Rome, but I was there salvaging some artifacts I wanted for my collection." He smiled as he thought back on the memory. "Even then, in her first life, Sofia was a remarkable woman, with a love of life and a powerful soul that reminded me so much of you, I had to intervene."

Sarah felt flattered. "I'm looking forward to getting to know her."

"She's eager for that too. We've shared many lives together, and we keep no secrets."

She never would have survived so many soul transfers without the aid of Alter's machine. Sarah leaned back, feeling a bit overwhelmed as she considered his accomplishment. Alter had figured out the intricate melding of runes and technology before technology even existed. "Do you still have that machine?"

"I've kept all my prototypes. You could say I have an extensive collection." He laughed, as if that was particularly funny.

Before she could ask him about it, he added, "With Sofia, I thoroughly enjoyed the renaissance. We learned to sculpt, to paint, and studied every branch of science. She has a quick mind and an effervescent soul that has made every life a gem."

"I'm so glad to hear it, and that you've found good use for your lives."

"The past century has been a bit more challenging. There's so much to learn, but we hold more degrees than I can count, and speak virtually every language ever known."

"I imagine you've got quite a family," Sarah asked. She loved hearing about Alter's history, and that he had found such a remarkable woman to share so much of it with.

"We've fostered tens of thousands of children through the years, mostly rescued from various wars, but we've kept our direct lineage strictly limited."

"Why?" Sarah thought of Gregorios and Eirene and their very prolific offspring.

"Because my goal was not to change history. Fathering a vast nation would have made that goal impossible. Plus, I'm cui dashi, remember? My offspring tend to have higher-level rounon powers, although I've never fathered a facetaker. We had children, and we've guarded our family carefully from becoming noticed by either the hunters or the facetakers. They would have interfered and perhaps forced my hand."

That made sense, but seemed like a tremendous sacrifice. Alter had exercised remarkable restraint. He was a man out of time, hidden from his own clan and from the facetakers. She was glad he'd found his place.

"Wow, living so long, knowing what you know, it must have been hard to resist the urge to change things."

Sarah had seen enough of history to know the aeon scroll was full of much good, too much bad, and a heartbreaking amount of very ugly. She wasn't sure she could have lived through some of those dark times without stepping in to stop some of those atrocities. She was happy to hear Alter had focused on helping children.

"It became easier when I realized my place was not to alter history, but to preserve it."

"What do you mean?"

"Come. I'll show you." He extended a hand, a little smile playing across his lips.

He led her through the house and out to the large barn. The inside was cleaner than most garages. Alter led her to a small storage area in the back that was empty but for a short, three-legged stool and an iron ring set into a stainless-steel wall. It looked like a milking station, but she hadn't noticed any cows.

Alter pulled the ring out from the wall, revealing a recessed button, which he pressed. The floor began sinking. He winked at her surprise.

She said, "A secret elevator? I'm liking this."

The elevator descended at least a hundred feet, lit by LED lights along the smooth, steel shaft. It emptied into a large room with stone walls, empty but for a small rail car with four plush seats, sitting on a narrow gauge rail line that ran into the darkness.

"You're not going to tell me anything till we get there, are you?" Sarah asked as Alter gestured her aboard.

"What would be the fun in that?" he asked with a twinkle in his eye. She settled into one of the front seats, eager to see the final destination.

Alter sat beside her and pressed a button on the dash. The rail car accelerated into the dark tunnel on silent electric power. The bright headlight illuminated the rounded tunnel, empty but for occasional lights along the ceiling. They did little to dispel the pitch black gloom.

The railcar moved fast, and Sarah estimated they covered more than half a mile in a perfectly straight course before the car began to slow and approach the first curve. If she hadn't gotten turned around, she figured they'd traveled due east. That meant they were deep under one of the towering mountains that flanked the town. Sarah loved secrets, and Alter's secret must be impressive.

The railcar slowed to a crawl as it navigated a ninety-degree turn to the right and stopped in an empty room identical to the starting point. Alter jumped out and extended a hand to Sarah. She accepted the gentlemanly gesture and eagerly followed him to a huge steel door that reminded her of the vault beneath Alterego. The memory made her shiver, but she couldn't make herself believe Alter would bring her to a secret stash of captured soulmasks.

Alter typed in a long code on the keypad beside the door, and it slowly swung open on massive hinges, gliding smoothly and silently. Darkness so deep that not even Sarah's heightened vision could penetrate it greeted them on the far side.

Alter stepped through with the confidence of a man who knew he owned that space. As soon as they passed the threshold, lights blazed on, and Sarah gasped.

"Oh, Alter," she breathed as she stared in wonder at the enormous cavern stretching nearly a quarter of a mile into the mountain.

They stood on an observation platform at least two stories above the smooth cavern floor, with excellent views across the entire expanse. The cavern was full, and Sarah couldn't figure out which of the historical treasures to look at first.

Sarah spotted furniture, pottery, clothing, and weapons from every culture, but Alter had not limited himself to normal museum pieces. Dozens of boats hung along the walls in custom slings. Some were tiny canoes, while others were full-sized ships. She even spotted an authentic Viking longboat, complete with furled sail, and oars ready to deploy.

Alter chuckled as he surveyed his unique treasure trove. "So much more was happening in the world than anyone suspects. It was really a remarkable journey."

"How did you get all this in here? Especially those ships?" Sarah asked.

"There's another, larger entrance on the southeast corner of the cavern. It connects to a narrow ravine with a stream that empties into the Rhine. I chose this spot because it's remote, but still has river access out to the North Sea, and from there to the rest of the world."

"How did you find it?" she asked, not bothering to look at him as she drank in the sights. She'd need weeks to survey everything.

"I spent one entire life searching for the right spot. Come, I want you to see this."

He led her to a set of stairs and descended to the ground floor. The massive treasure collection was split by regular pathways. He followed one to the right, then turned right again and stepped through a door set in the wall. It had been invisible from above, and she eagerly followed him.

The door was made of thick glass, and the seal made a whooshing sound when it opened. An identical, inner door blocked the way ten feet inside. Alter waited for the outer door to close, and for air to pressurize around them before opening the inner door. Again, lights snapped on when they stepped through. Sarah hadn't expected anything could surprise her again, but she was wrong.

They had entered a climate-controlled vault about a hundred feet deep that stretched to the left and right for at least a hundred yards. It was packed from the floor to the twenty foot ceiling with row after row of scrolls, papyrus, and ancient, leather tomes.

Alter grinned with pride and said grandly, "My greatest treasures. This is the most extensive library of historical documents in the world. I've preserved well over a million documents from every culture I could reach, including many from more than a dozen of the most famous libraries of all time."

He gestured to the right. "Down there is an entire section from the House of Wisdom from ancient Baghdad, and to the left I've got entire rows from the legendary library of Alexandria."

"You're kidding," Sarah breathed.

His smiled widened. He was clearly enjoying her amazement. "Legends claim there were at least half a million papyrus scrolls stored in Alexandria alone. I think there were more. I managed to salvage over a hundred thousand works of literature, along with texts on history, law, mathematics and science. I even saved many of the academics from the blaze in 48 B.C. I salvaged more from the destructive reign of Roman Emperor Aurelian. Some of their ancestors helped me set up the original library here. We've done some upgrades since."

"This is amazing," Sarah said as she approached the nearest stack of documents.

She felt immensely tempted to pick up one ancient leather tome that seemed to hold history on its cover like a thin layer of invisible dust. With an effort, she restrained the urge. She didn't want to wreck anything.

They exited the library, but spent an hour exploring the vast historical treasure trove. Alter explained that he had carved out the cavern with the help of one of Caesar's legions. The Romans were among the best architects in the world.

He'd dedicated himself to preserving accurate histories and detailed records from every major, and most minor, civilizations around the globe. He'd traveled all around the world while most people still thought it flat. The more he spoke, the more awed Sarah felt.

When they finally returned to the observation platform, she placed a hand on his arm and whispered, "Alter, this is incredible. I thought I was privileged to walk the aeon, but you lived the history that I can only visit. This will change the world."

"That's the plan. Now's the perfect time to begin revealing all this information. Coupled with what you're doing, we're going to usher in the greatest age of discovery the world has ever known."

He looked excited by the idea, and Sarah shared his enthusiasm. In fact, she could barely contain her excitement. That was exactly what the world needed.

Too many were still so steeped in hatred and conflict. Her efforts to refocus world attention on truth was helping, but too few could see what she could. Only those who won the coveted spots in the machines could walk history, while the rest of the world only heard about their stories. Harald was trying to figure out a way to record some of the sessions.

That would help. This, though. This was physical, tangible proof that people could touch, read, and videotape. She threw her arms around Alter and laughed.

"Deal. I like the idea of changing the world for the better, and I'm so glad you're back."

"I love seeing you again," he admitted with a grin.

"Hey, you're married," she teased. She felt so relieved that he seemed so happy, that they could enjoy being close friends without all the tension and drama of his first-life crush.

He gave her that annoyed look he used to use on her so often, making her grin. "Don't get your hopes up, Sarah. I love my wife more than I could ever express. I would never dishonor her or you with improper actions. You are dear to me, Sarah, and always will be, but I have learned to accept what I cannot change about each life."

"Just teasing," she assured him. "I'm so thrilled you're back, and I can't wait to tell everyone."

"Everyone?" he asked with a raised eyebrow.

"Of course." Tomas might not be thrilled to hear Alter was back, at least until he learned Alter was long married. "Hey, Tomas is still wearing your first body. We'll arrange to return it."

Alter smiled. "That would feel really good. I've missed it."

"I'll make it happen." She sighed then and added, "I'm so happy I found you. I wish I could spend days here, catching up and hearing your stories and exploring your treasure trove, but I can't stay. Not yet. We'll have to come back for another visit, and I'm sure the rest of the team will be eager to see you."

Alter said, "I've been waiting so long for the chance to tell Gregorios he's not the oldest man in the world after all."

Sarah chuckled as they headed back to the rail car to return to the elevator. Alter said, "I understand. I've been watching your exploits on the news. You're taking over the world more thoroughly than Xiao ever could have."

"I am not. I'm just helping," Sarah insisted, although he did sort of have a point.

She'd been forced to take a very prominent position, and she wouldn't back down from this chance to help make the world a better place while people were willing to listen.

"Well, keep helping," Alter chuckled.

"I doubt Xiao really understood how much work it would take to run the world. It's overwhelming just doing the little I'm trying to do."

"You're accomplishing more than you know, and the world loves you for it," Alter assured her in a tone that hinted at wisdom gained through millennia of lives.

He really had grown so much. She couldn't wait to understand the new Alter. The man who had returned was much more than the man who had left.

It was good that she'd discovered him when she did. Sarah had definite plans for Tomas, and it would have been awkward for all of them if Alter had shown up and wanted his body back after she set her plan in motion.

107

SARAH LEANED BACK in her chair, savoring the cool of early evening in Florence. She and Tomas sat in a private room on the second floor of her favorite ristorante, overlooking the Ponte Vecchio.

It wasn't far from her new global headquarters, and she looked forward to many more meals there. The crowds had thinned and the lights of the city bathed the scene in soft light and shadow. She breathed deep, enjoying the hint of steak still hanging in the air.

"How was your dinner?" Tomas asked. He looked a bit nervous, even though his new body fit perfectly.

Alter had chosen to return to Rome with her. He'd wanted to visit Sofia again anyway. His appearance had created quite a stir, and Sarah smiled to think how big that stir was going to become.

Zuri and her team in Suntara were working on orchestrating the earth-shattering news of Alter's historical treasure trove. That should elevate their efforts to focus the world's attention on truth and historical discovery to whole new levels.

Tomas had accepted Alter's return with far better grace than Sarah had feared. Of course, the fact that he looked old enough to be Sarah's father, and he was married, seemed to help a lot.

Sofia had been thrilled with his change into his young, first-life body. She'd given Alter a wicked smile and teased that it was time for another honeymoon since they had to break in that virgin suit of his.

He might be over four thousand years old, but Alter had blushed just as deeply as Sarah had ever seen.

The Suntara body bank was much depleted as the world need for replacement suits was so high. Eirene had felt obliged to offer some of their existing stock to help get some affected world leaders back on their feet. Some had lost bodies to the plague, while others might eventually heal. Still, she had held back some of the best suits for their needs.

Altruism was good, but the world was far from a safe place and they couldn't afford to have an important team member go down without a replacement suit handy.

So Tomas had managed to score a gorgeous suit. Eirene had found one that Sarah immediately approved of. It was nearly a twin to Tomas' original battle suit that she'd fallen in love with. After adding her custom healing rune, marking her new toy as Francesca liked to tease, she'd accepted the change wholeheartedly.

She hoped Tomas wouldn't have to change again for a while. She had learned not to focus so much on the external physical form, but still didn't want him swapping more often than absolutely necessary.

Now she scanned him up and down, then met his gaze, and gave him an approving smile. "Looking good tonight, Tomas."

He leaned over the table and she met him halfway in a passionate kiss. He'd indicated several times that he was past his previous hesitation about moving their relationship to the next level, and she welcomed the change. This rare, quiet date was just the chance she'd been looking for.

When Tomas sat back, he scanned out the window out of habit. Sarah had done the same thing every few minutes. They were enjoying a peaceful date, but they weren't stupid. Dangerous people still opposed them, although if an assassin tried to wreck their date, Sarah didn't think the fool would live long enough to reach an interrogation chamber.

She had still insisted that Tomas turn off his earpiece. An Aeon Corps protective detail was prepped and ready in their nearby headquarters, although she'd told them they would not be needed. She and Tomas could handle themselves, but the team knew how to make contact if they needed to. She'd made it clear that they had better not need to.

Tomas sighed and gave her a wide smile. He looked happy, although a bit nervous. "I think we needed a break."

She took his hand in hers and massaged it. She knew how much he liked that. "I agree. I had a wonderful time. It's been too long since we got to enjoy a simple meal together."

Tomorrow they had to return to Rome and fly to Washington. The president had accepted their delay, but she could tell he was growing impatient.

He could wait. They needed the quiet time.

"But it won't be the last," Tomas added. He cleared his throat a couple of times, looking more nervous than ever. He abruptly stood, and Sarah looked around, but saw nothing alarming.

Then Tomas dropped to one knee and took a glittering ring out of his shirt pocket.

Time seemed to slow, although she hadn't activated any of her aeon ciphers.

"Sarah," he said, his voice hoarse, his expression turning determined, as if he was planning a suicide charge. "I love you. Will you marry me?"

Sarah resisted the urge to fling herself upon him and shout "Yes! It's about time."

He'd made her wait way too long, so he could suffer for five seconds. Well, three.

Unable to wait longer, she cupped his face in her hand and grinned. "Of course I will. I love your soul, my Tomas."

He slipped the ring onto her finger with trembling hands. She laughed and drew him to his feet, then leaped into his strong arms and really kissed him.

She held nothing back, and lost herself in that kiss for a long time. She exulted to feel him respond, to no longer resist. He held her tight and didn't seem to want to ever let her go.

The only problem was that they both kept breaking into laughter and foolish grins. At least that gave them a chance to break for air before they launched into another round of fierce kissing.

She felt happier than she'd ever imagined possible. Tomas was finally committed, finally willing to join with her for what would hopefully become a multi-generational love affair to rival even Gregorios and Eirene.

Sarah liked a challenge, and she hoped to give them a run for their money.

Some indeterminate time later, they finally took a break. Sarah maintained her grip around his waist. Tomas looked a bit shaken, but his eyes glowed with pure, unabashed love. She hoped he could see the depth of her emotion too. She planned to show him every single day.

Tomas blew out a breath and laughed again. She loved the play of his muscles across his chest as he shifted his grip around her shoulders. After another passionate kiss, he breathed, "Wow."

"Wow yourself." He was a really good kisser. She was looking forward to finding out what else he could do. She gave him a wicked grin and said, "You'd better not be thinking of a long, drawn-out engagement."

"Well, there are certain norms—" he began.

Sarah interrupted by pulling his head down for another long kiss. When she release him, she pressed her lips close to his ear and said in a soft, but fierce whisper. "Fine. We hold a huge reception, with ten thousand people if you insist. But only if you elope with me right now. This afternoon."

"Sarah, that's . . ."

She pressed a finger to his lips and shook her head. "No, Tomas. I have very definite plans for you tonight. You're a proper fellow, and I respect that. This way we both get what we want. Your propriety is honored, all our friends get a big reception. We can even exchange vows again at whatever alter you prefer. But tonight is for us, and I'm afraid I'm going to insist we find someone to marry us within the hour."

Instead of stammering excuses with that remarkably innocent blush of his, he surprised her by nodding. She read undisguised longing in his eyes as he kissed her yet again.

Then he said, "Make it half an hour."

PLEASE, MAY I HAVE SOME MORE?

Of course! It's hard to end such an epic series, so to make parting a little less painful, we've got one final piece of exclusive content.

THE MYSTERY OF THE MARY CELESTE

An unsolved maritime mystery . . .

A ghost ship, abandoned but seaworthy. No trace of the crew.

Is the search for answers about the *Mary Celeste* just another research trip into the memoryscape?

Or a treasure hunt?

Or something far more important?

Join Sarah and Eirene for this adventure on the high seas as they sail into uncharted waters.

Because reality is always stranger than fiction!

Get your free copy here: https://BookHip.com/GBRLJF

And if you still haven't read the other exclusive content yet, last chance:

Face Lift: https://BookHip.com/GWHZMS

Ciphers of Gold: https://BookHip.com/GFPWGJ

Rock, Paper, Scissors: https://BookHip.com/LKZKLF

THUMBS UP? OR THUMBS DOWN?

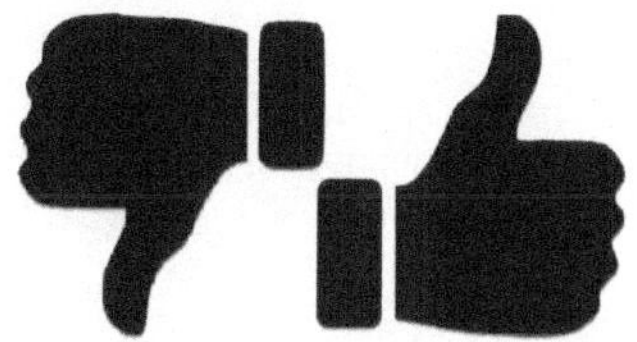

Reviews are still the best way to support your favorite authors (other than buying 5000 copies of all of their books to share with everyone you know for Christmas).

So are you willing to take 5 seconds and share your thoughts with the world? Now, while it's still fresh?

You love this book and this series, so don't hold back. Tell the world!

Post a review of *Aeon Champion* here: https://smarturl.it/ed2cci

Thank you!

Frank

AUTHOR'S NOTE

Wow! To think the Facetakers series is finished! I'm super thrilled you've gotten to read it all, and so happy to see the story fully realized.

As I've mentioned before, the Facetakers started as a dream where a character who became Gregorios was searching for his wife, using a cool ability to remove souls in the process. Such a freaky awesome dream, I had to develop it.

And the rest is history. I hope you enjoyed the journey as much as I have.

Thank you for sticking with me all the way to the end! You rock!

Now that you feel lost, without another Facetaker book to read, feel free to check out my other books, or reach out to me through my Facebook fan page to discuss upcoming projects.

ABOUT THE AUTHOR

Frank Morin is a storyteller, an outdoor enthusiast, and an eager traveler. He is the author of fast-paced grab-you-by-the-eyeballs-and-don't-let-go adventures, including *The Petralist*, his epic teen fantasy series, full of explosive magic, huge adventure, and brilliant humor. Frank also writes *The Facetakers* fast-action historical fantasy thrillers you've been enjoying.

When not writing or trying to keep up with his active family, he's often found hiking, camping, Scuba diving, or traveling to research new books. Find out more about his novels and his shorter fiction, or join his readers group here.